Step by Step! 圖解 狄克生片語

一本學會470個關鍵日常英文片語

作者 Matt Coler　譯者 李盈瑩　審訂 Judy Majewski

片語必學內容一起背
可調整語速／播放／複誦模式訓練聽力

- 字義／同義反義／例句／延伸說明，一次學會
- 標示高中字彙、全民英檢、多益字級，快速掌握單字難度
- 睡眠學習，複習片語幫助記憶

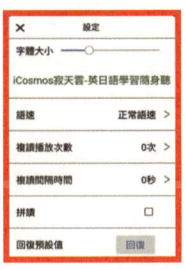

- 全文／片語中譯模式切換
- 設定自動／手動／單詞循環播放，訓練聽力超有感
- 7段語速調整，設定複誦間距／次數，扎實訓練聽力口說

自訂單字簿集中背誦

將要複習片語加入單字簿，自訂單字分組，集中背誦想要加強的片語

三種測驗驗收學習成果

語音辨識比對　強力口說練習
拼寫練習幫助記憶片語

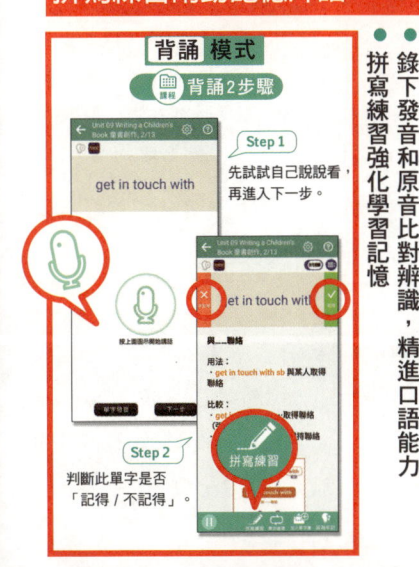

錄下發音和原音比對辨識，拼寫練習強化學習記憶，精進口語能力

快速查詢字義 (iOS)

- 可查詢中英文字義，理解例句生字，或搜尋網頁，查詢延伸學習內容
- 可搜尋片語學習

自動擬定學習計畫

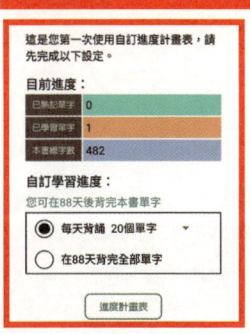

設定學習目標，APP會擬定每天背誦／複習片語，學習有目標更有效

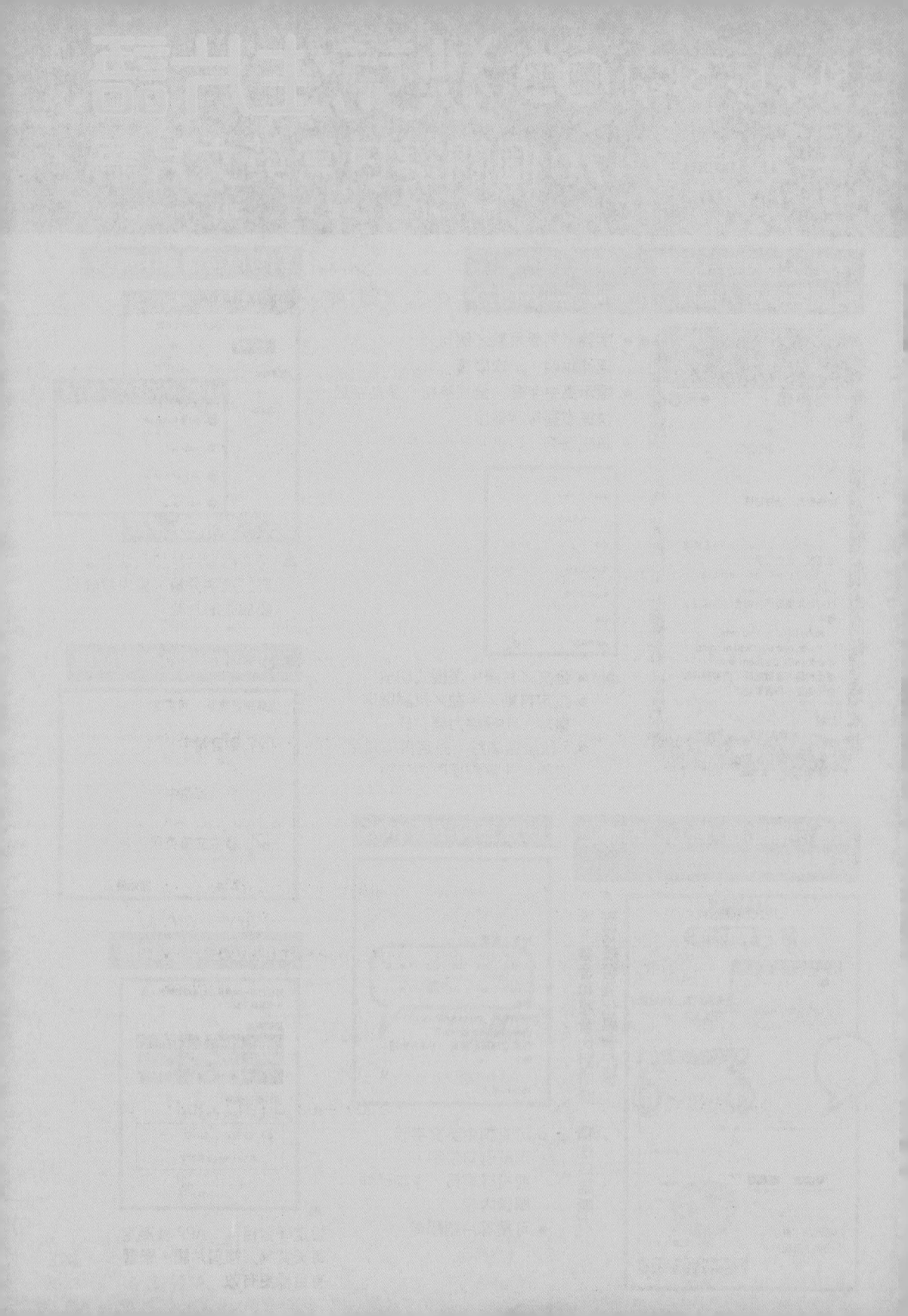

Step by Step! 圖解
狄克生片語

一本學會 470 個關鍵日常英文片語

作者 Matt Coler　譯者 李盈瑩　審訂 Judy Majewski

如何聆聽 MP3 音檔

❶ 寂天雲 APP 聆聽
① 先掃描書上 QR Code 下載 寂天雲 APP。
② 加入會員，進入 MP3 書櫃首頁，點下方內建掃描器
③ 再次掃描 QR Code 下載音檔，即可使用 APP 聆聽。

❷ 在電腦或其他播放器聆聽
① 請上「寂天閱讀網」（www.icosmos.com.tw），註冊會員並登入。
② 搜尋本書，進入本書頁面，點選 🔊 MP3 下載 下載音檔，存於電腦等其他播放器聆聽。

Introduction 片語動詞

本書分成 39 單元，整理共 470 個狄克生片語，並逐一拆解結構，全方位講解片語的詞性、特性、用法、同反義語、例句等。本書收錄的片語中，有許多為「片語動詞」（Phrasal Verb）。片語動詞由「**動詞＋介副詞**」所組成，英文母語人士在日常生活中也經常使用片語動詞，例如同樣要表達「考慮」，口語上會使用片語動詞 think over，consider 則更常用在書面上。

○ 片語動詞的動詞與介副詞

片語動詞裡的**動詞**多為**意義簡單的詞語**，常見的有 take、get、break、bring 等；**介副詞**則多能表示**方向**與**意象**，如 on、in、up、down、over 等。兩者加在一起時，**介副詞**會賦予片語動詞**核心意義**。

舉例來說，介副詞 over 有「跨過」、「越過」的意象，含有 over 的片語動詞就會隱含 over 本身的涵義：

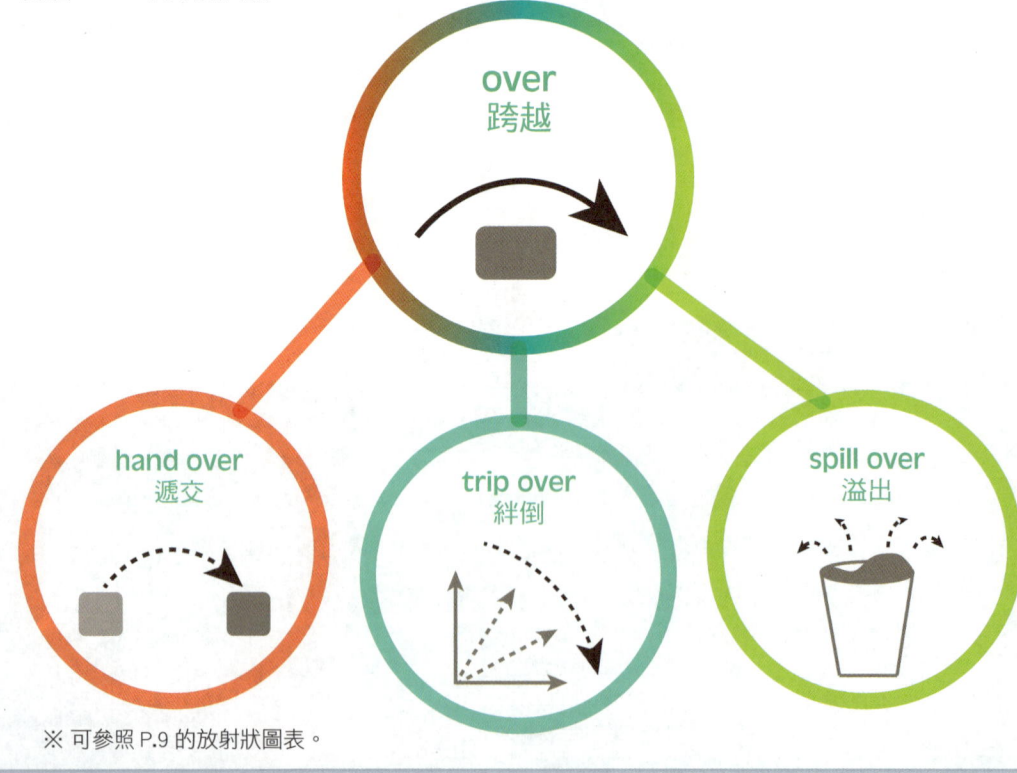

over 跨越

hand over 遞交

trip over 絆倒

spill over 溢出

※ 可參照 P.9 的放射狀圖表。

片語動詞的特性

1 多種涵義：

一個片語動詞，可以有多達五種以上的意思，因此片語動詞真正的涵義得由句中的上下文來判斷，如：

pick up	
❶ 拾起	❶ John **picked up** the kitten and took it to its mother.
❷ 購買	❷ We can **pick up** some food on the way to the library.
❸ 汽車接送某人	❸ I have to **pick up** my sister from soccer practice.

2 分成「及物」或「不及物」：

及物的片語動詞後面要接受詞；不及物的片語動詞後面則不可接受詞。如：

- Derek **made up** the story. 德瑞克瞎掰了這件事。
  ↳ make up 及物，後面要接受詞
- Jessica didn't **show up**. 潔西卡並未現身。
  ↳ show up 不及物，後面不可直接加受詞

3 分成「要分開」、「不可分開」或「分不分開都可以」：

❶ 要分開與不可分開

	要分開的片語動詞	不可分開的片語動詞
規則	受詞置於動詞和介副詞之間	受詞置於介副詞之後
例句	I **talked** my father **into** letting me buy the computer. 我說服我爸讓我買電腦。	They are **looking into** the problem. 他們正在研究那個問題。

❷ 分不分開都可以

有些片語動詞兼具兩種特性，既可以分開使用，讓受詞夾在動詞與介副詞之間，也可以合在一起，受詞放在介副詞後面。唯獨當受詞為代名詞（如 he、she、it 等）時，一定要分開使用，如：

- Gary **tore** the letter **up**. 蓋瑞把信撕了。
- Gary **tore up** the letter. 蓋瑞撕了信。
- Gary **tore** it **up**. 蓋瑞把它給撕了。
  ↳ tear up 的意思是「撕毀」，可以分開，也可以不分開；
  但受詞若為代名詞，則代名詞一定要放在 tear 和 up 的中間。

Study Guide 使用導覽

1. 情境對話

Unit 01　The School Test 學校考試

Sandra and Nick talk about their history test.
珊卓拉和尼克在談論歷史考試。

Sandra: Hey Nick, where have you been? I've been trying to **call** you **up**¹ for a few hours, but you never answered your phone! Did you just **get up**²?

嘿，尼克，你到哪去了？我**打電話**找你找了好幾個小時，你都沒接電話！你才剛**起**

> 生動的雙人對話融入單元教學片語，實際示範片語的日常應用，並以中英對照顯示。

2. 片語教學

> 片語詞性與特性：
> 分為片語動詞（又分可否分開、代名詞是否要放中間等特性）、副詞片語、名詞片語、形容詞片語、慣用片語。

10

throw （拋） ＋ away （離開）
→ **throw away**

❶ 扔掉　❷ 浪費（才能或機會）及

| 片語動詞 | 可分開 | 受詞為代名詞時定要分開 |

用法比較
- **throw sth away** 扔掉某事物
- **throw in** 插入
- **throw one's money around** 亂花錢
- **throw over** 拋棄；斷絕關係
- **throw off** 扔掉；擺脫

同 ❶ desert　❷ waste

> 片語解釋編號，對應例句中的片語意義。

> 片語用法說明與比較：
> **sb** = somebody（某人）
> **sth** = something（某事物）
> **sw** = somewhere（某地）

> 標示同反義字，舉一反三。

💡 **throw away** 有「因愚蠢而丟失；浪費」的意思。

❶ Those old shirts really smell terrible; maybe you should just **throw** them **away**.
那些舊襯衫的味道真的很難聞，也許你該把它們**丟**了。

❷ You've spent four hours studying—don't **throw** it all **away**.
你已經唸了四小時了，千萬不要**白白浪費**了。

> 豐富例句一目了然，提昇應用能力。

iv

3. 學習檢驗

Ⓐ 選擇題

1. When the pie is done, please _____ the oven so the crust doesn't burn.
   Ⓐ turn off　Ⓑ pick up　Ⓒ get in　Ⓓ put on

Ⓑ 閱讀文章，從字表中選擇詞彙填入，並依人稱時態等做適當的變化

get up	at first	get off	turn on
take off	pick up	turn off	get on
sooner or later	call up		

　　When Dave ❶_____ the plane, he was very excited. It would be his first time in Italy, and he couldn't wait to get to Milan. The first thing he did when he entered the plane was ❷_____ his winter coat and hat

Ⓒ 引導式翻譯，並依人稱時態等做適當的變化

1. 應徵人數在四月分時會**增加**。
   The number of applicants will _____ _____ in April.

> 單元後設計三種題型的訓練題組，方便檢驗學習成效。

4. 片語索引

> 整合全書片語，含用法、比較、同義、反義等，方便查找翻閱。

Index

A

a bargain（划算）　271
a few（不多）　80
A goes with B（A與B相配）　87
a good few（相當多）　80
a good many（相當多）　80
a great many（相當多）　80
a great number（相當多）　80
A is named after B（A是由B的名字來命名）　179
a large number（相當多）　80
a small number（不多）　80
a steal（買到便宜貨）　271
above all things（尤其是）　147
above all（特別；尤其）　147
accidentally on purpose（假裝不小心但其實故意地）　25
according to（根據；據……所記載）　153
act for（代表）　189
adhere to（堅持）　220
again and again（一再）　67
agree to（同意；接受）　86, 145

as for sth（關於某事）　105
as for（關於）　105
As it turns out . . .（結果原來是……）　114
as regards（關於）　105
as respects（關於）　105
as soon as possible（儘快）　76
as soon as（立即；一……就……）　76
as to（關於）　105
as usual（一如往常；照常）　15
ask for it（自找麻煩）　315
ask for sb（要求某人）　315
ask for sth（要求某事物）　315
ask for trouble（自找麻煩）　315
ask for（應得；要求）　115, 315
at all（絲毫；根本）　31
at any rate（至少）　31
at first（起初；原來；剛開始）　8
at hand（在附近）　271
at heart（實際上；內心是）　155
at its heart（本質上）　155
at large（一般而言）　163
at last（最後；終於）　8
at least（至少）　31
at most（至多）　31
at no time（從不；絕不）　77
at once（馬上；立即）　6, 77

be certain to（一定會）　153
be cut out for sth（適合某事）　243
be cut out for（勝任；適合）　243
be cut out to be sth（有成為某事的能力）　243
be cut out to do sth（有做某事的能力）　243
be cheated（被欺騙）　243
be even with（報復）　252
be fed up with（忍無可忍）　276
be fooled（被騙）　243
be had（被騙）　327
be in (someone's) place（站在某人的立場）　325
be in (someone's) shoes（站在某人的立場）　325
be in (the/one's) way（阻礙；造成不便）　163
be in a better situation（情況變好）　179
be in charge of（管理……；負責）　76
be in love with（愛上）　71
be in the charge of（由……管理）　76
be in touch with（與……聯絡）　181
be in（在家；在公司；流行）　323

v

Contents

Unit

01	The School Test 學校考試	2
02	Shopping 逛街購物	12
03	Going to a Party 參加派對	20
04	The School Play 學校戲劇表演	28
05	Schoolwork 學校作業	38
06	Getting Sick and Stressed 生病與壓力	46
07	Hunting for a New Job 找新工作	56
08	Planning for the Weekend 週末計畫	64
09	Writing a Children's Book 童書創作	74
10	Choosing a Pet 挑選寵物	84

Unit

11	Waiting for a Friend 等朋友	94
12	The New Mobile Phone 新手機	102
13	Walking Along the Beach 海邊散步	112
14	Babysitting 照顧小孩	120
15	School Life 學校生活	128
16	The New Neighbor 新鄰居	136
17	The Surprise Party 驚喜派對	144
18	Finding a Lost Dog 尋狗啟示	152
19	Applying to a University 申請大學	160
20	Finding a Lost Cat 尋貓啟示	168

Unit

21	**Handing in a Paper** 交報告	176
22	**The New Teacher** 新老師	184
23	**The Weekend Party** 週末派對	194
24	**Schoolwork Problems** 課業問題	202
25	**Cheating on a Test** 考試作弊	210
26	**The New Coworker** 新同事	218
27	**Falling Behind in Class** 課業落後	226
28	**Breaking Up** 分手	234
29	**Being a Designer** 成為設計師	242
30	**The Ruined Cake** 毀掉的蛋糕	250

Unit

31	**Moving Away From Home** 離家	258
32	**Being Kicked Out of School** 被退學	266
33	**Kicking the Habit** 戒掉惡習	274
34	**Getting Married** 結婚	282
35	**The Missing Phone** 失竊的手機	290
36	**Checking In** 辦理住宿登記	298
37	**Showing Off** 炫燿賣弄	306
38	**The First Week at College** 大學生活的第一個星期	314
39	**Getting Home Late** 晚回家	322
	Index 索引	330
	Answer Key 解答	342

Unit 01

🔊 001

The School Test
學校考試

Sandra and Nick talk about their history test.
珊卓拉和尼克在談論歷史考試。

Sandra: Hey Nick, where have you been? I've been trying to **call** you **up**[1] for a few hours, but you never answered your phone! Did you just **get up**[2]?

嘿，尼克，你到哪去了？我**打電話**找你找了好幾個小時，你都沒接電話！你才剛**起床**嗎？

Nick: No, I've been awake for a few hours now. I think I forgot to **turn on**[3] my cell phone this morning. Come in and **take off**[4] your jacket. Make yourself comfortable.

不，我醒來好幾個小時了。我想我早上忘記**開機**了。進來**脫下**夾克，別拘束。

Sandra: We don't have time to chat here. **Put on**[5] your jacket and let's go!

我們沒時間在這裡聊天了。把夾克**穿上**，我們快走吧！

Nick: Why?

為什麼？

Sandra: We have that big history test to study for.

我們要準備歷史大考了。

Nick: I'll study for it **sooner or later**[6]. What's the rush?

我**遲早**會準備的，急什麼呢？

Sandra: The test is in three hours!

考試再過三個小時就要開始了！

Nick: Yikes! I forgot! We'd better get started **right away**[7]. Let me call my mom to **pick** us **up**[8] and take us to the library.

天啊！我都忘了！我們最好**馬上**出門。我要叫我媽來**接**我們，送我們到圖書館。

Unit 01 The School Test 學校考試

1

🔊 002

call（打電話）＋ **up**（口語，無意義）
→ **call up** 打電話給某人 [及]

片語動詞 / 可分開 / 受詞為代名詞時定要分開

用法
- ◆ **call up sb** 打電話給某人
- ◆ **call up sb** 徵召某人入伍
- ◆ **call up sth** 回想起某事

同
1. give sb a call
2. give sb a ring
3. ring up（英式用法）

💡 **call up** 是可分開的片語動詞，**up** 常省略，屬及物動詞。受詞可以接在 **call up** 之後，或放置在兩者之間，但受詞若為代名詞時，則一定要放在 **call** 和 **up** 之間。

- I was bored Friday night, so I **called up** some old friends and organized a party.
  → call up sb：受詞可放在片語動詞的後面
  星期五晚上我很無聊，就**打電話**給幾個老朋友，籌劃開一個派對。

- Derek told the pretty girl she could **call** him **up** sometime, but she never did.
  → call sb up：受詞為代名詞時，動詞片語一定要分開，而將受詞放在中間
  德瑞克告訴那個漂亮女孩改天可以**打電話**給他，但她從未打過。

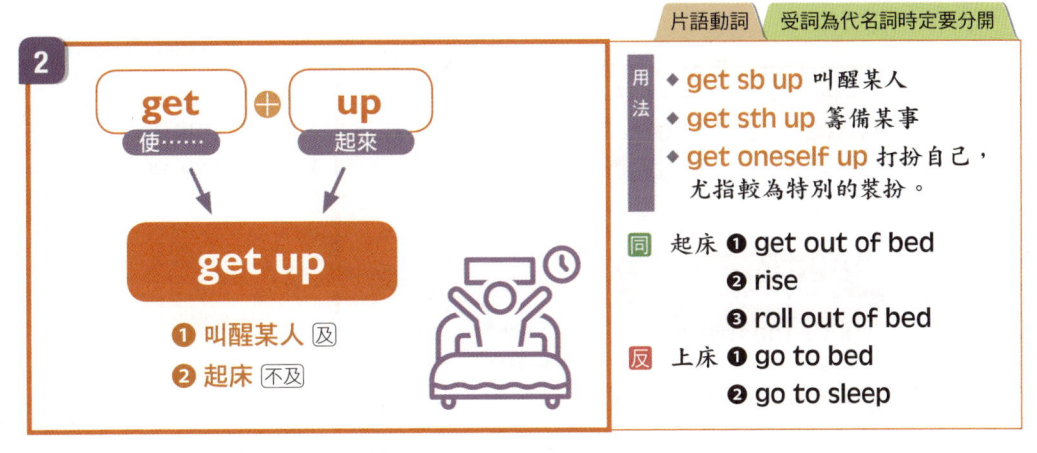

2

片語動詞 / 受詞為代名詞時定要分開

get（使……）＋ **up**（起來）
→ **get up**
1. 叫醒某人 [及]
2. 起床 [不及]

用法
- ◆ **get sb up** 叫醒某人
- ◆ **get sth up** 籌備某事
- ◆ **get oneself up** 打扮自己，尤指較為特別的裝扮。

同 起床
1. get out of bed
2. rise
3. roll out of bed

反 上床
1. go to bed
2. go to sleep

💡 **get up** 可當及物動詞或不及物動詞，不使用被動語態。

1. My mom **gets** me **up** every day before school. 我媽媽每天上學前會叫我起床。
   → get sb up：受詞為代名詞時，動詞片語一定要分開，而將受詞放在中間

2. I brush my teeth twice a day: when I **get up** and before I go to bed.
   我每天刷兩次牙：**起床**後和上床前。

3

turn （轉動） ＋ **on** （運轉中）
→ **turn on**

❶ 打開（電器或設備）及 可分
❷ 突然攻擊某人 及 不可分

片語動詞 ｜ 受詞為代名詞時定要分開

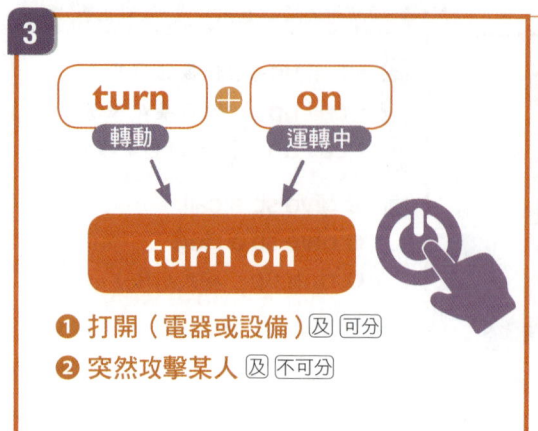

用法
- **turn sth on / turn on sth**
  打開電器或設備
- **turn sb on (to sth) / turn sb on (to sb)** 使某人對某事或人感興趣
- **turn on sb / turn upon sb**
  突然攻擊／抨擊某人

同 打開 ❶ switch on ❷ put on
反 關掉 ❶ turn off ❷ switch off
　　　　　❸ shut off

💡 **turn on** 除了有「打開電器或設備」的意思之外，也有「突然攻擊某人」或「嚴厲抨擊某人」之意，做後者之意時，為不可分開的及物片語動詞。

❶ Hey, **turn** the TV **on**, or we'll miss the game!
嘿，**打開**電視，否則我們就要錯過比賽了！

❶ Frank couldn't figure out why his dinner was still cold until he saw that he had forgotten to **turn on** the oven.
法蘭克想不透為何晚餐還是冷的，直到他發現忘了把烤箱**打開**。

❷ I tried to help her stand up, but she **turned on** me, shouting, "Get off!"
我想扶她站好，但她**突然吼**我說：「滾開！」

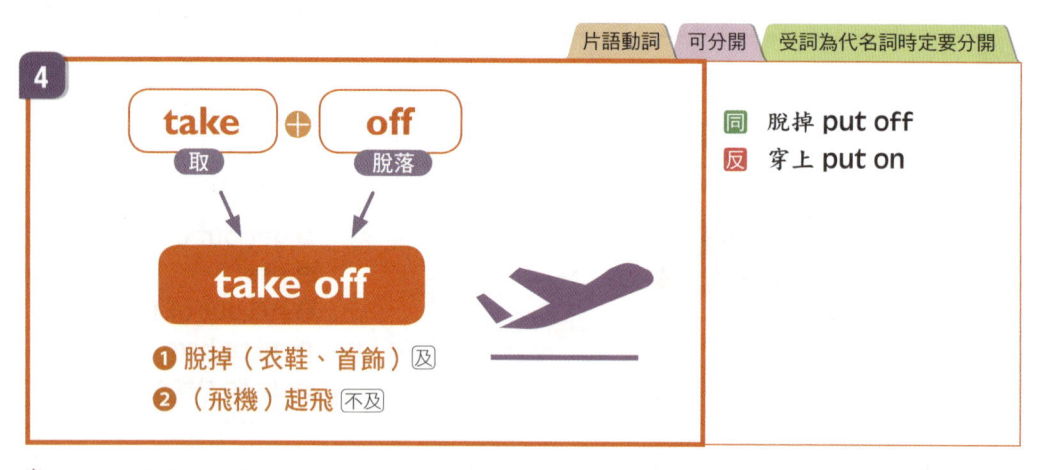

4

take （取） ＋ **off** （脫落）
→ **take off**

❶ 脫掉（衣鞋、首飾）及
❷ （飛機）起飛 不及

片語動詞 ｜ 可分開 ｜ 受詞為代名詞時定要分開

同 脫掉 put off
反 穿上 put on

💡 **take off** 指飛機「起飛」時，為不及物動詞，後面不可接受詞。其名詞為 **takeoff**。

❶ When entering an official building in America, a male should **take off** his hat.
在美國，進入講究門面的大樓時，男士一定要**脫帽**。

❶ It was cloudy out, so Jen **took** her sunglasses **off** and put them in her pocket.
外面天空陰陰的，所以珍**摘下**太陽眼鏡放在口袋。

4

5

put（放置） + **on**（在……上） → **put on**

❶ 穿戴（衣服或配件）❷ 塗抹
❸ 增加體重 ❹ 愚弄 及

> 片語動詞 / 可分開 / 受詞為代名詞時定要分開

用法
- **put on makeup** 上妝 ＝wear makeup
- **put on lipstick** 抹口紅 ＝wear lipstick
- **put on perfume** 搽香水 ＝wear perfume
- **put on weight** 體重增加
（反義字：lose weight 減重）

💡 put on 指「穿的動作」，wear 則指「穿的狀態」；兩者亦皆有「塗抹」、「搽抹」的意思，如搽化妝品、噴上香水。

❶ I **put on** my watch every morning before work.
我每天早上上班前會戴上手錶。

❶ Tim **put** his winter hat **on** before he went out to play in the snow.
提姆在出去玩雪前，把冬帽戴上。

❷ Is there a mirror somewhere? I need to **put** my makeup **on**.
這裡有鏡子嗎？我得補個妝。

❸ He's **put on** a lot of **weight** since he gave up smoking. 他戒菸後胖了好多。

❹ You didn't believe him, did you? He was just **putting** you **on**.
你沒有把他當真對吧？他只是在耍你耶。

6

sooner（早些）+ **or** + **later**（晚些）→ **sooner or later**
遲早；總有一天

> 副詞片語

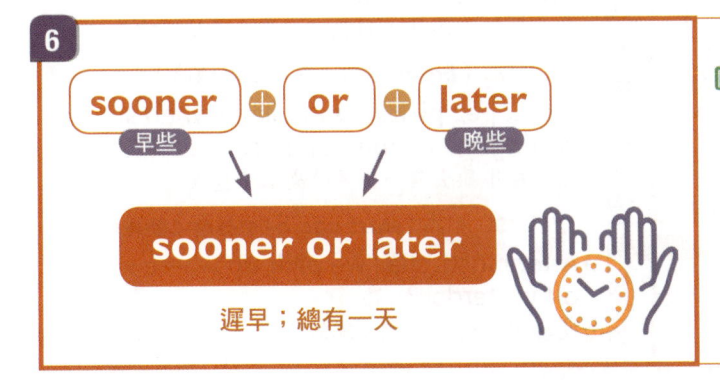

同 ❶ some day or other
❷ sometime

💡 「副詞片語」是指具有副詞功能的片語，用來修飾動詞、形容詞、副詞等。

- Jay isn't sure when he'll finish his paper, but he's convinced he'll complete it **sooner or later**. 傑不確定何時會完成論文，但他相信他遲早會完成的。

- Life may be difficult for you now, but **sooner or later** it has to get better.
現在生活對你來說也許很困難，但情況總有一天會好轉。

7

right (作強調用) + **away** (即刻) → **right away** 馬上；立刻

同
1. right now
2. at once
3. in no time

💡 right away 當時間副詞片語使用，是非正式用法。

- I have to leave **right away**; otherwise, I will be late. 我必須**馬上**離開，否則會遲到。

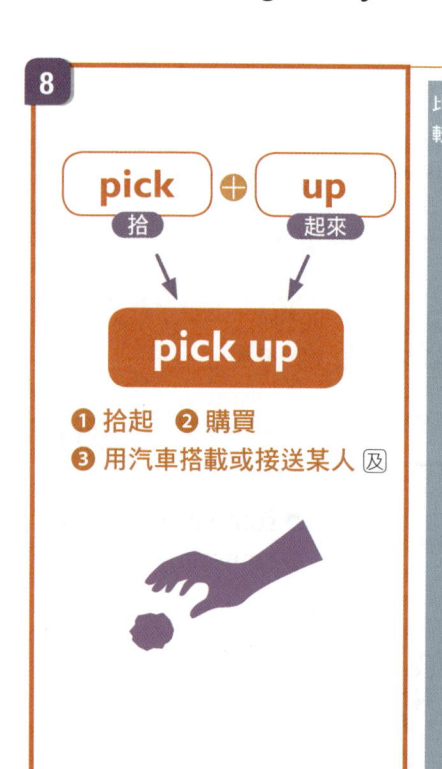

8

片語動詞 / 可分開 / 受詞為代名詞時定要分開

pick (拾) + **up** (起來) → **pick up**
1. 拾起
2. 購買
3. 用汽車搭載或接送某人 [及]

比較

- **pick sth up**（*buy*：用便宜的價錢買到某物）
→ I **picked up** some real bargains at the sale.
我在大拍賣上買到了幾個便宜貨。

- **pick up**（*increase*：增加；起色）
→ Sales **picked up** a bit during the Christmas period. 聖誕節時買氣**上升**了一點。

- **pick sth up**（*learn*：自學或藉由練習而學會某種技術或語言）
→ When you live in a country, you quickly **pick up** the language.
你要是待在國外，很快就會**學會**當地語言了。

- **pick up**（*become ill*：感染上某種病）
→ Ms. Lopez **picked up** malaria when she was visiting the country on business.
羅培茲小姐去國外出差時**染上**了瘧疾。

- **pick (sth) up**（*start again*：被打斷之後再繼續）
→ After lunch, shall we **pick up** where we left off yesterday?
吃過中飯後，我們要**繼續**昨天未完成的嗎？

1. Jake **picked up** the kitten and took it to its mother.
傑克**撿起**了小貓，把牠帶到媽媽的身邊。

2. We can **pick up** some coffee and food on the way to the library.
我們可以在去圖書館的路上**買**些咖啡和食物。

3. I have to **pick up** my sister from soccer practice and drive her home.
妹妹練完足球後我必須去**接**她，然後載她回家。

9

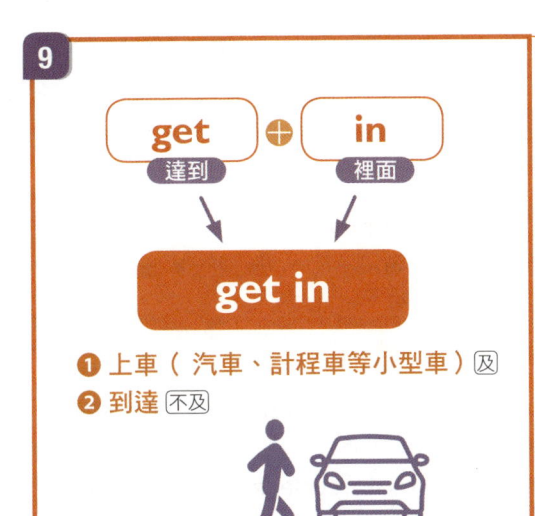

get（達到）+ **in**（裡面）→ **get in**

❶ 上車（汽車、計程車等小型車）及
❷ 到達 不及

用法
- **get in** + 交通工具
  上某種小型而密閉的交通工具
- **get sth in / get in sth** 購買生活用品
→ I must **get** some extra milk **in** for the weekend.
  我週末得去多買一些牛奶。

反 下（車）**get out of**
- Linda **got out of** her car to fix the flat tire. 琳達下車修理爆胎。

💡 **get in** 指搭上「上小型密閉的交通工具」，因一上車就直接進到車裡，不需要踩著階梯或踏板上車或登機，所以用 in。

❶ **Get in** the car, and I'll give you a ride! 上車吧，我載你去！
❷ Do you know what time Mark's plane **gets in**?
   你知道馬克的飛機幾點到嗎？

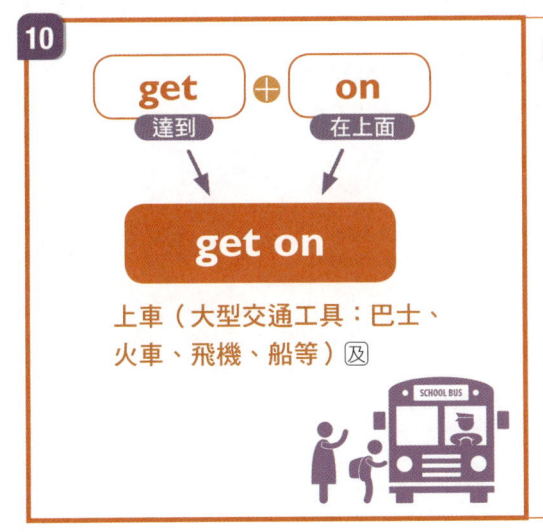

10

get（達到）+ **on**（在上面）→ **get on**

上車（大型交通工具：巴士、火車、飛機、船等）及

反 下（大型的車）**get off**
- We need to **get off** the bus at the next stop.
  我們要在下一站下巴士。
- After the long flight, it was a relief to **get off** the plane and stretch my legs.
  在長途飛行後，下飛機舒展一下雙腿很舒服。

💡 **get on** 指上大型的交通工具，例如巴士、火車、飛機、船等等。

- If you don't have a ticket, you can't **get on** the train.
  如果你沒有車票，就不能上火車。
- The plane was almost full by the time I **got on**.
  我上飛機時，機上幾乎已經都坐滿人了。

11 at first

at 在 + **first** 最初

→ **at first** 起初；原來；剛開始 [及]

| 比較 | ◆ **at first**
通常指一系列見解的**第一個**，或各個階段或步驟中的第一個。
◆ **at the beginning**
常指某一階段、某一週、某一本書或某一件事情的**開始**。|

反 最後；終於 at last

- Joel has graduated from high school **at last**! 喬終於高中畢業了！
- **At last** my motorcycle is fixed—I've been waiting for weeks.
  我的機車**終於**修好了，我已經等好幾個星期了。

- Although English was hard **at first**, after I had studied it for a few months, it became easier.
  雖然英語**剛開始**很難，但我學了幾個月後，就變得比較容易了。
- When Joan met Lou, she didn't like him **at first**; however, ten months later, they were married.
  珍和陸相遇時，她**起初**並不喜歡他，但是10個月後，他們結婚了。
- If **at first** you don't succeed, try and try again. 一試不成功，就再試一次。

○ 片語動詞：介副詞帶來的意義轉變

如同前言所說，片語動詞是由動詞與介副詞合成，且**介副詞會賦予片語動詞核心意義**，使整個片語動詞的意思，與動詞本身不同。
請見以下例子：

- break 破壞；打破
- in 進入 → break in 闖入 不及
- through 越過 → break through 突破
- up 徹底 → break up 打碎；分手
- into 向內 → break into 闖進 及
- off 休止 → break off 中斷；斷絕
- out of 出去 → break out of 逃出
- down 向下 → break down 瓦解；崩潰
- away 遠離 → break away 擺脫；逃跑

Unit 01 The School Test 學校考試

Unit 01 Test Yourself!

Ⓐ 選擇題

1. When the pie is done, please _____ the oven so the crust doesn't burn.
   Ⓐ turn off   Ⓑ pick up   Ⓒ get in   Ⓓ put on

2. Before entering a house, many Taiwanese people _____ their shoes.
   Ⓐ pick up   Ⓑ turn on   Ⓒ get in   Ⓓ take off

3. Abe promised to _____ his mother as soon as he arrived in America.
   Ⓐ get in   Ⓑ take off   Ⓒ call up   Ⓓ turn off

4. I was late for work because I didn't _____ on time.
   Ⓐ pick up   Ⓑ get up   Ⓒ call up   Ⓓ turn off

5. Please _____ the baby and put him in his bed.
   Ⓐ take off   Ⓑ pick up   Ⓒ get in   Ⓓ put on

6. When he saw Beth, he gave her the birthday present _____; he didn't want to wait.
   Ⓐ sooner or later   Ⓑ right away   Ⓒ at first   Ⓓ just now

7. As soon as Ariel _____ Derek's car, she regretted it because he is a terrible driver.
   Ⓐ got in   Ⓑ got off   Ⓒ took off   Ⓓ turned on

8. _____ the TV; I want to watch the news.
   Ⓐ Take off   Ⓑ Call up   Ⓒ Turn on   Ⓓ Get in

9. I'll finish this painting _____; there's no rush.
   Ⓐ at first   Ⓑ right away   Ⓒ just now   Ⓓ sooner or later

10. _____ Carol liked living in Taipei, but after a few months, she began to miss the countryside.
    Ⓐ At last   Ⓑ Sooner or later   Ⓒ At first   Ⓓ Later on

B 閱讀文章，從字表中選擇詞彙填入，並依人稱時態等做適當的變化

get up	at first	get off	turn on
take off	pick up	turn off	get on
sooner or later	call up		

When Dave ❶_____ the plane, he was very excited. It would be his first time in Italy, and he couldn't wait to get to Milan. The first thing he did when he entered the plane was ❷_____ his winter coat and hat because it was warm inside. Once the plane was in the air, he ❸_____ his iPod® so he could listen to his music, and he quickly fell asleep. When he ❹_____ hours later, he was amazed to see that he was already in Italy. The plane had landed! He ❺_____ the music and ❻_____ the plane.

The first thing Dave did when he got to the city was look for a hotel. ❼_____ he didn't know where to look, but then he had an idea. He remembered that his old friend Paul lived in Italy. So he began searching for a pay phone so he could ❽_____ Paul. When he found a phone, he realized that he had only dollars; he didn't have a single euro. Dave is lucky, though, and he saw some change on the ground; it wasn't much, but it was enough to make a call. Dave ❾_____ the money and called Paul. Of course, Paul was surprised to hear from Dave, but Dave reminded him that he had always said that he would visit Milan ❿_____.

C 引導式翻譯，並依人稱時態等做適當的變化

1. 應徵人數在四月分時會**增加**。
   The number of applicants will _____ _____ in April.

2. **下**巴士後，我過了一條街便到家。
   After I _____ _____ the bus, I walked a block to my house.

3. 你**遲早**是要面對事實的呀。
   _____ _____ _____, you will have to face the facts.

4. 我**起初**以為她在開玩笑，但我後來才發現她是認真的。
   _____ _____, I thought she was joking, but then I realized she meant it.

5. 她突然轉而**抨擊**我，指責我暗算她。
   Suddenly, she just _____ _____ me and accused me of undermining her.

Unit 02

🔊 006

Shopping
逛街購物

Dylan and Natalie are talking as they walk down the city sidewalk after a long day of shopping.
在街上逛了一整天後，狄倫和娜塔莉在市區的人行道上邊走邊聊天。

Dylan: Did I tell you that we were invited to a party at my office next month? It'll be formal, so we'll have to **dress up**[1].

我有提過我們受邀參加公司下個月的派對嗎？派對很正式，我們必須**盛裝打扮**。

Natalie: How exciting! I guess I'd better **look for**[2] some new clothes. Hey, let's go now to my favorite shop—it's not far from here. We can **look at**[3] that dress I told you about yesterday. However, I think it's pretty expensive.

真令人興奮！我想我最好**找**些新衣服。嘿，我們現在就去我最喜歡的那家店，就離這裡不遠。我們可以去**看**我昨天跟你提過的那件洋裝。不過我覺得它很貴。

Dylan: **Never mind**[4] the price. We can pay for it in installments, **little by little**[5]. It's important that we look great and impress my boss.

別管價格，我們可以**慢慢**用分期付款的。重要的是我們要看起來很體面，讓老闆印象深刻。

Natalie: Maybe I can **find out**[6] when they're having a sale. Then we could save some money.

也許我能夠**查一下**何時會有折扣，這樣我們就可以省點錢了。

Dylan: That's a good idea. After we check out that shop, let's go home. We've been walking around a lot, and, **as usual**[7], all this shopping has really **tired** me **out**[8].

好主意。我們看完那家店就回家吧。我們已經走了好久，**就像往常一樣**，逛街真把我**累壞**了。

1

dress（穿戴） + **up**（徹底） → **dress up**

❶ 特殊打扮 及
❷ 為正式場合盛裝打扮 不及

用法：
◆ dress sth up 裝飾；粉刷
→ You could **dress** this house **up** with some bright colors.
你可以用一些亮一點的顏色來粉刷房子。

反：
❶ dress down 非正式打扮；著便裝
❷ dress-down Fridays
便服日；上班時不用穿制服的日子

💡 形容詞做 dressed up（穿上盛裝的）；名詞 dress-up，則是指小孩子的化妝遊戲（playing dress-up）；另外，名詞 dressing-down，是指「斥責」、「打」的意思。

❶ He **dressed up** as a cowboy for the party. 他**打扮**成牛仔來參加派對。
❷ If you go to a wedding, it is important to **dress up**. **盛裝**參加婚禮很重要。
❷ Because Lucas didn't **dress up** for his job interview, he looked unprofessional.
盧卡斯參加工作面試時沒有**穿著正式服裝**，所以看起來很不專業。

---

2 片語動詞 不可分開

look（看） + **for**（為了） → **look for**

尋找 及

同：
❶ search for ❷ search after
❸ seek out   ❹ seek after

→ search for/after 的用法較正式，通常表示「尋找失蹤的人或物」，或表示「希望得到想要的東西」，但 look for 可以接表示抽象意義的名詞來當受詞。

💡 look for 指「尋找」，強調尋找的過程，可用進行式；find 指「發現」或「找到」，強調找的結果，不可用進行式。

● Pablo spent the entire morning **looking for** his car keys.
帕布羅花了整個早上的時間**尋找**車鑰匙。
● The children walked all over the neighborhood **looking for** their lost dog.
孩子們走遍整個街坊**尋找**走丟的小狗。
● He spent his life **looking for** the truth. 他窮極一生都在**追尋**真理。
  ↳ look for 可接抽象名詞當受詞

13

3 片語動詞　不可分開

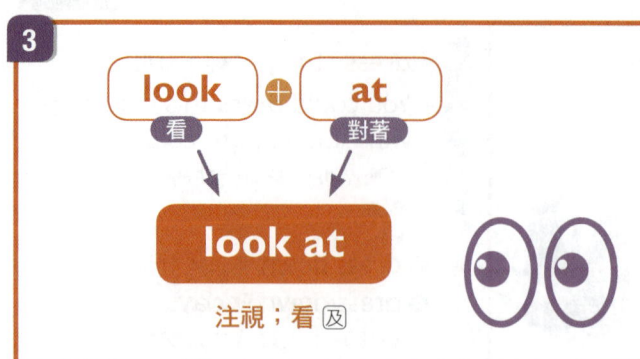

look（看）＋ **at**（對著）→ **look at** 注視；看 及

同 have a look at

💡
❶ **look at** 表示特別把目光轉向某個目標「看著」它。
❷ **watch** 表示看著某人或某物移動、改變、發展或進行某種動作（例如 **watch TV**）。
❸ **read** 表示「閱讀」、「讀出」（例如 **read a/the newspaper**）。
❹ **see** 表示用眼睛「注意到」、「觀察到」或「目擊到」，而如果要表示「已經看過」一部電影或一場比賽，多用 **see** 這個字，而不用 **watch**。

- Before his big date, Carl **looked at** himself carefully in the mirror.
  在赴重要約會前，卡羅仔細地注視著鏡中的自己。

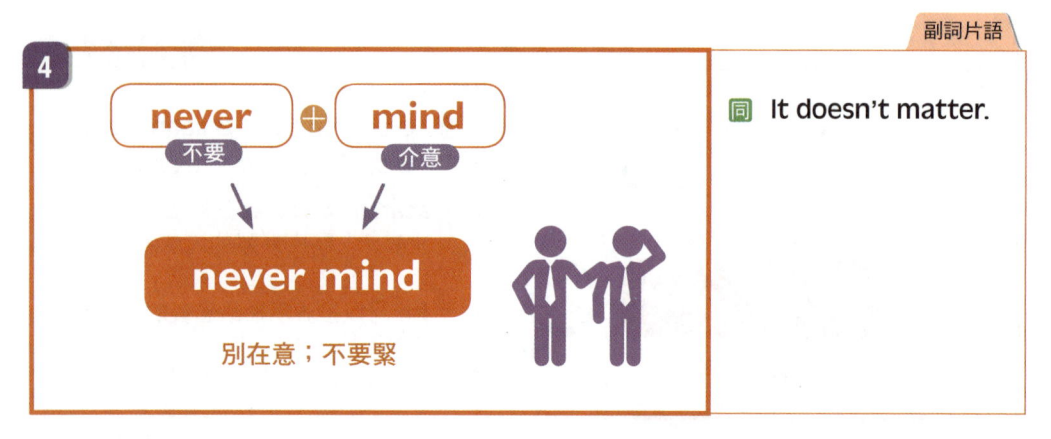

4 副詞片語

never（不要）＋ **mind**（介意）→ **never mind** 別在意；不要緊

同 It doesn't matter.

💡「Never mind.」最常用來回應別人的道歉，表示「沒關係」、「別擔心」的意思。

- **Never mind** your coming late; no one even noticed you weren't here.
  遲到沒關係，反正沒人注意到你不在這裡。

- My suggestion that you stay awake all night was a bad idea, so **never mind**.
  我提議整晚不睡是個爛主意，所以你別放在心上。

5

little (一點點) + **by** (接著) + **little** (一點點)

→ **little by little** 逐漸地

副詞片語

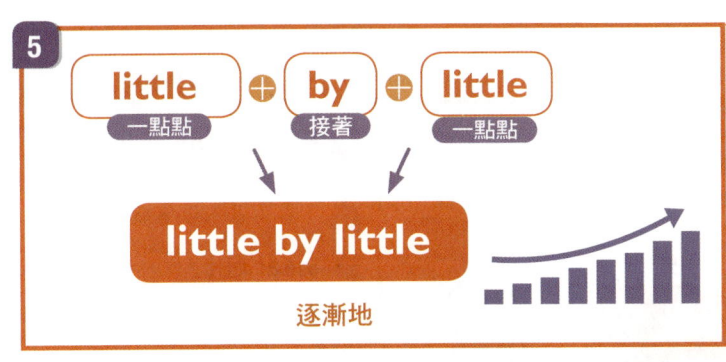

同
❶ bit by bit
❷ step-by-step
❸ stage by stage

- **Little by little**, the kitten came to love and trust her new owner.
  小貓漸漸開始喜歡和依賴新主人了。
- At first I didn't like my math class, but **little by little**, I began to really enjoy it.
  我剛開始不喜歡數學課，但我逐漸得到其中真正的樂趣。

6

find (找) + **out** (出來)

→ **find out** 發現；找出 及

片語動詞 ｜ 可分開 ｜ 受詞為代名詞時定要分開

用法
◆ **find sb out** 發現某人做了壞事
◆ **find out who** + 名詞子句 發現某人做了壞事
◆ **find sth out** 發現某事
◆ **find out that** + 名詞子句 發現某事

- Last Monday, Jake **found out** that he was getting a promotion.
  傑克上星期一發現他升官了。
- I hope no one **finds out** about my embarrassing mistake!
  我希望沒人發現這個令人難堪的錯誤！

7

as (一如) + **usual** (平常)

→ **as usual** 一如往常；照常

副詞片語

同
❶ as a rule
❷ as always

💡 **as usual** 表示狀況和平常一樣；**as a rule** 則用於泛指一般的情況。

- Harry came to the meeting late, **as usual**. 哈利照例開會遲到。
- **As usual**, Mom had prepared a delicious dinner for the family.
  我媽媽就像平常一樣為全家人準備美味的晚餐。

8

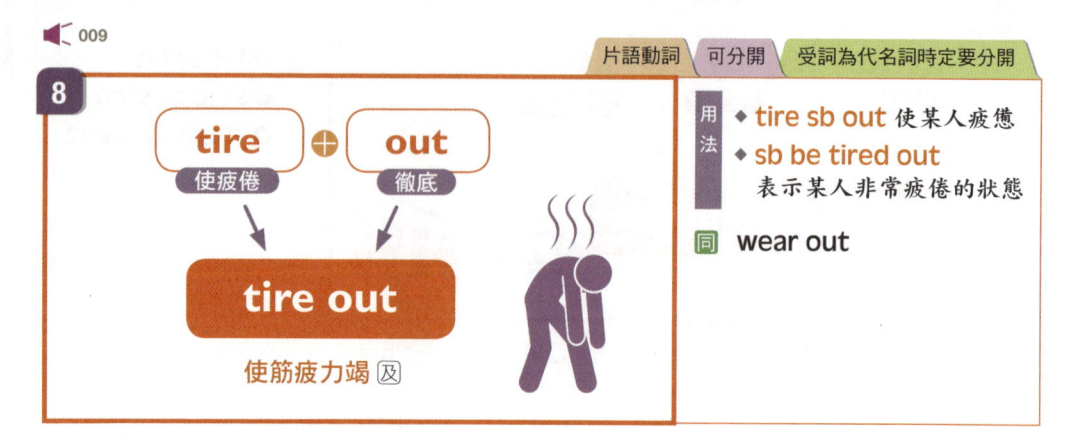

片語動詞 | 可分開 | 受詞為代名詞時定要分開

tire（使疲倦）+ **out**（徹底）→ **tire out**
使筋疲力竭 及

用法
- **tire sb out** 使某人疲憊
- **sb be tired out** 表示某人非常疲倦的狀態

同 **wear out**

- Gabe really **tired** himself **out** by walking around New York City all day.
  在紐約走了一天，蓋比**筋疲力竭**。
- We **tired out** the dogs by playing with them in the park for a few hours.
  我們和狗狗在公園裡玩了好幾個小時，把狗狗給累壞了。

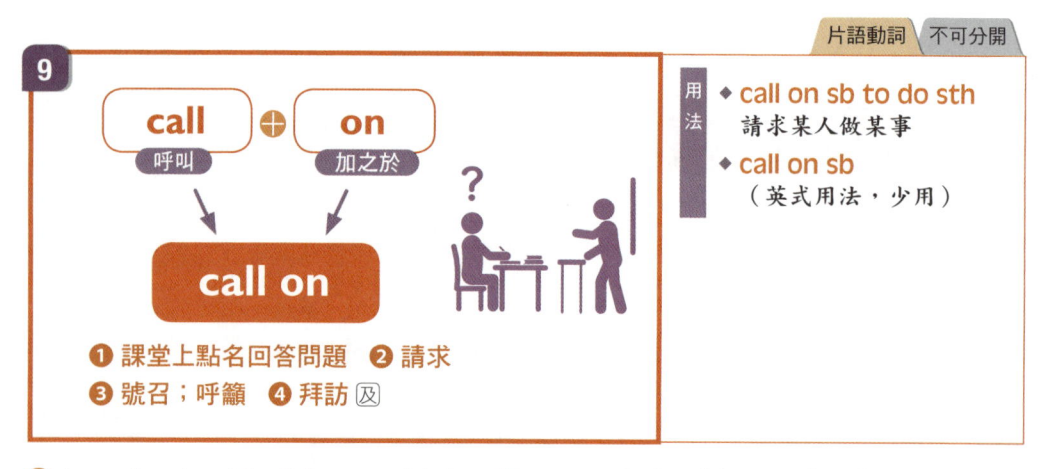

9

片語動詞 | 不可分開

call（呼叫）+ **on**（加之於）→ **call on**

❶ 課堂上點名回答問題　❷ 請求　❸ 號召；呼籲　❹ 拜訪 及

用法
- **call on sb to do sth** 請求某人做某事
- **call on sb**（英式用法，少用）

❶ I was hoping Ms. Baker wouldn't **call on** me during history class because I didn't know the answer.
希望貝克女士不要在歷史課**指名**我**回答問題**，因為我不知道答案。

❷ I now **call on** everyone to raise a glass to the happy couple.
我現在**請**每一個人都舉起杯子，向這對幸福的新人致意。

❸ The university official **called on** the professors to help raise the school's reputation. 學校高層**號召**教授幫忙提升學校的聲望。

❸ Scientists **have called on / will call on** the government to end political interference in science.
科學家**呼籲**政府應該不要再對科學界做政治上的干涉。

❹ I will **call on** a friend this weekend. 我這個週末會去**拜訪**一位朋友。

形容詞片語　副詞片語　感嘆語

Unit 02 Shopping 逛街購物

10

all（所有一切）＋ right（恰當的） → **all right**

❶ 沒問題　❷ 好吧；好的　❸ 可以嗎　❹ 好啊　❺ 還好嗎 [及]

💡 ❶ **all right** 可做形容詞片語，表示「安好的」、「好的」。
　❷ **all right** 可做副詞片語，表示「可以」、「好吧」。放句尾時，表示詢問「可嗎？」
　❸ **all right** 還可以當感嘆語使用。

❶ This book is **all right**, but it isn't anything special. 這本書不錯，只是沒什麼特別之處。
　　　　　　　　↳ 做形容詞片語的用法

❷ **All right**, so I made a mistake. 好吧，是我的錯。
　　↳ 做副詞片語，表示「好吧」

❸ Tell me if you start to feel sick, **all right**? 如果你開始覺得不舒服，就跟我說好嗎？
　　　　　　　　　　　　　　　　　　　↳ 做副詞片語，用於詢問「可以嗎」

❹ **All right**! They scored! 好耶！得分！
　　↳ 做感嘆語

❺ "**All right**, Mike?" "Not bad, thanks, and you?" 「麥克你好嗎？」「還不錯，謝了。妳呢？」
　　↳ 做感嘆語，在此做問候語

副詞片語

11

all（全部）＋ along（沿著） → **all along**
從一開始就；自始至終；一直

比較　◆ **all along the line**
到處；在每一個階段、環節或時刻
→ The project has been plagued with financial problems **all along the line**. 這個計畫的每個環節都有財務上的問題。

同　❶ all the time　❷ all the while
　　❸ right along

● We were shocked that Gloria had known about the late phone bill **all along** but hadn't told anyone.
葛洛莉亞從一開始就知道電話帳單過期了，卻沒告訴任何人，令我們非常震驚。

● It was supposed to be a surprise party for Rudy, but actually he knew about it **all along**.　原本是要給魯迪的驚喜派對，但他事實上打從一開始就知道了。

● Do you think he's been cheating us **all along**? 你想他是不是從一開始就在騙我們了？

17

Unit 02 Test Yourself!

A 選擇題

1. After a long night of studying, Erica really _____ herself _____.
   Ⓐ tired . . . out   Ⓑ dressed . . . up   Ⓒ called . . . on   Ⓓ found . . . out

2. It took Steve a long time to _____ for the graduation ceremony because he had to iron his clothes and put on a tie.
   Ⓐ look at   Ⓑ dress up   Ⓒ call on   Ⓓ find out

3. After a long wait, my friends came _____.
   Ⓐ all right   Ⓑ called on   Ⓒ at once   Ⓓ at last

4. By putting aside a few dollars each week, _____, Amanda saved up enough money to go on vacation to Hawaii.
   Ⓐ never mind   Ⓑ at once   Ⓒ little by little   Ⓓ all right

5. I failed the test because I only _____ about it the day before, and I didn't have enough time to study.
   Ⓐ found out   Ⓑ called on   Ⓒ looked for   Ⓓ tired out

6. Ed spent a few weeks _____ his passport, but he couldn't find it anywhere.
   Ⓐ finding out   Ⓑ tiring out   Ⓒ dressing up   Ⓓ looking for

7. Although this laptop isn't the newest model, it is fast enough and seems to work _____.
   Ⓐ all right   Ⓑ little by little   Ⓒ never mind   Ⓓ at last

8. I _____ the photo for a long time, but I didn't recognize anyone in it.
   Ⓐ looked at   Ⓑ found out   Ⓒ called on   Ⓓ dressed up

9. Isaac is the smartest boy in class, so it wasn't a surprise when he got an A⁺ on the test, _____.
   Ⓐ at last   Ⓑ never mind   Ⓒ all along   Ⓓ as usual

10. I thought I had forgotten my MP3 player, but I was surprised to see that it had been in my pocket _____.
    Ⓐ little by little   Ⓑ never mind   Ⓒ all along   Ⓓ at last

B 閱讀文章，從字表中選擇詞彙填入，並依人稱時態等做適當的變化

| look at | all right | all along | little by little |
| tire out | as usual | dress up | look for | find out |

❶_____, Rachel got home from school around 4:00, just as she did every day. However, what happened next was not expected at all. Indeed, Rachel was shocked to ❷_____ that her brother Ben had just asked his girlfriend to marry him. Although everyone in the family was surprised, Ben told them that he had planned it ❸_____. Although Rachel didn't like Ben's girlfriend when they first met last year, ❹_____ they became good friends, so Rachel was very happy with her brother's decision.

　　Rachel knew she would have to ❺_____ for the wedding, but she had no idea what to wear. She ❻_____ every dress in her closet, but nothing was perfect. She was going to need a new dress, which would be expensive, but it was worth it. After all, this was her brother's wedding! Moreover, she would have to find them a suitable present. She decided to ❼_____ the ideal gift downtown. Although many shops had some gifts that would be ❽_____, nothing was perfect. After a few hours of shopping, she was ❾_____, though she still hadn't bought anything. In the end, Rachel decided to buy the new couple a gift certificate to Ben's favorite restaurant.

C 引導式翻譯，並依人稱時態等做適當的變化

1. 他以為他耍了我，其實我從**一開始**就知道真相。
   He thought he had me fooled, but I knew what he was doing _____ _____.

2. 他們**號召**所有滿 17 歲的男子都來從軍。
   They're _____ _____ all males over the age of 17 to join the army.

3. 我喜歡為派對做**打扮**。
   I love to _____ _____ for a party.

4. **別在意**我說什麼，那不重要。
   _____ _____ what I said; it wasn't important.

5. 你看一下那本書就可以**找到**安迪的電話號碼了。
   You can _____ _____ Andy's phone number by looking in the book.

6. 哥倫布在**尋找**前往印度的捷徑航線時，發現了美洲大陸。
   Columbus was _____ _____ a shorter route to India when he discovered America.

Unit 03

Going to a Party
參加派對

🔊 010

Ron and Donna chat about a party this weekend.
朗和唐娜在聊有關這週末的派對。

Ron:	Hey there, Donna! How are you doing?	嗨,唐娜!妳好嗎?
Donna:	Well, not so well. Actually, I **talked over**[1] my plan to go to your party this weekend with my parents, and they don't like the idea.	嗯,不怎麼好。事實上,我和我的父母**討論**過去參加你的週末派對的計畫,但他們不喜歡這個主意。
Ron:	Really? I'm in no rush, so **take your time**[2] and tell me what the problem is.	真的嗎?我不趕時間,所以**慢慢來**,告訴我問題在哪裡。
Donna:	Well, they are concerned that the party will be unsupervised. They also don't want me to stay out **all night long**[3].	嗳,他們認為派對裡沒大人看著,而且他們也不希望我**徹夜**未歸。
Ron:	But we won't be there **by ourselves**[4]; my parents will be there. Maybe if my dad called your mom to tell her this, it would **make a difference**[5] to her.	但又不是只有我們**獨處**而已,我的父母也會在。假如我爸打電話給妳媽,告訴她這點,對她或許**有所差別**。
Donna:	Yeah, maybe you're right. After all, our parents **get along with**[6] each other.	是啊,也許你說的對。畢竟我們的父母很**處得來**。
Ron:	Exactly! Plus, the party won't go so late. You can be home before 11.	沒錯!還有,派對不會到那麼晚,妳可以在 11 點前回到家。
Donna:	That will make my mom feel better.	我媽會覺得那樣比較好。
Ron:	Great! So why are you still **sitting down**[7]? **Stand up**[8], go home, and tell your mom that my dad will call later.	太好了!所以妳為何還**坐在**這裡?快**站起來**,回家告訴妳媽,我爸晚點會打電話過去。
Donna:	Okay, cool. See you soon!	對,好極了。改天見!

1

talk (談話) + **over** (關於) → **talk over** 商量；討論 及

片語動詞 | 可分開 | 受詞為代名詞時定要分開

用法
- **talk sth over** 詳細討論某事
- **talk over with sb** 和某人磋商某事

- There's no need to make a decision now; we can **talk** it **over** tomorrow.
  不用現在就做決定；我們可以明天**再討論**。
- Kerry **talked over** her request for a raise with her boss.
  凱莉和老闆**商量**要求加薪。

2

take (取得) + **one's** (某人的) + **time** (時間) → **take one's time** 慢慢來；別急

慣用片語 | 不可分開

用法
- **take one's time over sth** 不慌不忙地做某事
- **take time** 需要花比較久的時間（主詞通常用物）
- **take the time** 力圖
- **take time out** 暫時停止某種活動

比較
- **in a hurry** 匆忙；緊急
- Sorry! I'd love to chat with you—but I'm **in a hurry**!
  不好意思，我很樂意和你聊天，但是我在**趕時間**！

- **Take your time**; I'm in no rush. **別急**，我不趕時間。
- Bob didn't care that he was late; he continued to **take his time** eating his lunch.
  鮑伯不在乎遲到，他繼續**慢慢**吃午餐。

3

all(整個) + **night**(晚上) + **long**(始終)
→ **all night long** 一整晚

副詞片語　時間副詞

比較
- all week long 一整個星期
- all month long 一整個月
- all year long 一整年
- all day long 一整天

同
① the whole night
② all night

- Lou stayed up **all night long** studying. 盧整個晚上都在熬夜唸書。

4

by(靠) + **oneself**(某人自己)
→ **by oneself** 獨自；某人自己；單獨地

副詞片語

同
① all by oneself
② on one's own

- Jenny's younger sister doesn't like to be left **by herself** for very long.
  珍妮的妹妹不喜歡長時間一個人獨處。
- The first day we left the puppy at home **by himself**, he made a big mess.
  我們第一次把小狗獨自留在家裡時，他把房子搞得一團糟。

5

make(造成) + **a** + **difference**(不同)
→ **make a difference** 造成差別；對……產生影響

慣用片語

用法
- make a difference to sth/sb 對某事或某人造成差別
- make a big difference 造成很大的差別
- make all the difference 讓一切變得很不同
- make a world of difference 造成很大的改善
- for all the difference sth makes 即使那樣做也沒有差別；知其不可為而為

反
① make no difference
② not make any difference
③ not make the slightest difference

💡 通常以**物**做主詞，後面加 **to**，指針對某事或某人。

- Jill saw that cleaning her dorm **made a big difference** in how it looked.
潔兒發現大掃除讓宿舍看起來**截然不同**。
- A healthy diet **makes a difference** in the way you feel.
健康的飲食會對身體**產生影響**。
- Sleeping an extra ten minutes a night **makes no difference** in how I feel the next morning. 每晚多睡 10 分鐘，對我隔天早上的感覺**不會有太大的影響**。

片語動詞 | **不可分開**

6

get （處於） + **along** （一起） + **with** （與）
→ **get along (with)**
和睦相處；進展

用法
- **get along with sb**
  與某人相處融洽
- **get along with sth**
  某事有所進展

💡 **get along with** 後面若無受詞，則省略 **with**。

- Although Harry is a nice guy, for some reason Beth never **got along with** him.
雖然哈利是個好人，但是基於某些原因，貝絲就是和他**處不來**。
- I wonder how Alex is **getting along** in his new job.
不知亞力克斯的新工作**做得**如何

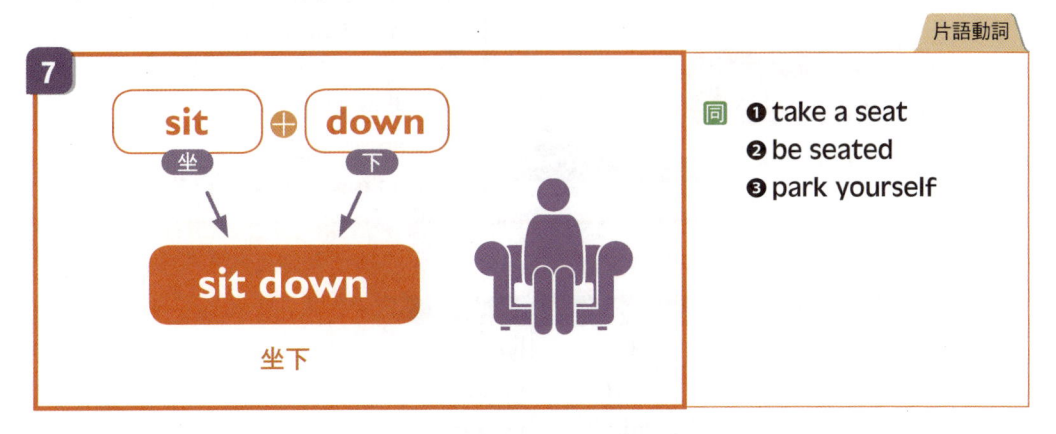

片語動詞

7

sit （坐） + **down** （下）
→ **sit down**
坐下

同
❶ take a seat
❷ be seated
❸ park yourself

- As soon as the teacher entered the classroom, all the students **sat down** and stopped talking. 老師一走進教室，所有學生都**坐下來**停止說話。

8

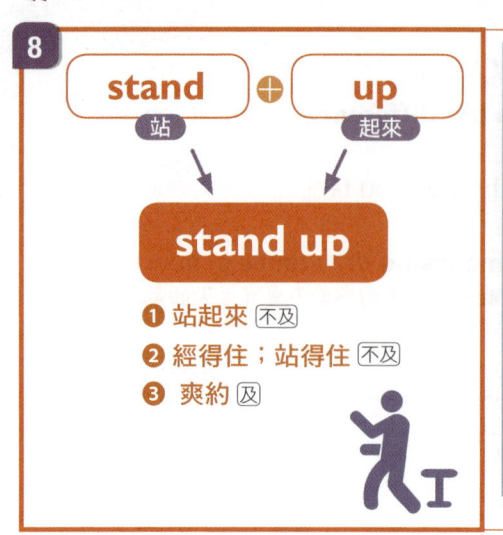

stand (站) + **up** (起來) → **stand up**

❶ 站起來 [不及]
❷ 經得住；站得住 [不及]
❸ 爽約 [及]

比較
- **stand up to sth** 經得住某物
  （例如能耐高溫 stand up to high temperature）
  → These cars can **stand up to** being driven over rough terrain.
  這些車子能夠在顛簸的路面上行駛。
- **stand up for sth** 捍衛或堅持某事
  （例如捍衛真理 stand up for truth）
  → Don't be bullied; learn to **stand up for** yourself and what you believe in. 別被嚇到了，學著去捍衛自己和自己的信仰吧。

❶ After spending the entire day sitting in class, Paula said it felt good to **stand up** and walk around.
寶拉覺得上課坐了一整天後，**站起來**走一走的感覺很舒服。

❷ Their evidence will never **stand up** in court.
他們的證據在法庭上根本**站不住腳**。

❸ Xavier and I had a date for dinner, but he **stood** me **up**.
傑維爾和我約好了要一起吃晚餐，結果他**放我鴿子**。

9

lie (躺) + **down** (下) → **lie down**

躺下 [不及]

比較
- **lie down on the job** 工作偷懶打混
  → The new police chief fired two officers after accusing them of **lying down on the job**.
  新任警長以**工作摸魚打混**的理由將兩名警察炒魷魚。
- **lie up** 藏匿
- **lie low** 不出聲；隱藏

💡 注意以下三個動詞的各個形態：

釋義	原形	過去式	過去分詞	現在分詞
躺；擺放	lie	lay	lain	lying
說謊	lie	lied	lied	lying
下蛋；鋪設	lay	laid	laid	laying

- Garth **lay down** on his bed and tried to sleep, but he couldn't.
  加爾斯**躺**在床上試圖入睡，但他睡不著。
- As soon as I **lay down**, I fell asleep. 我一**躺下來**就睡著了。

Unit 03 Going to a Party 參加派對

10 pick + out

pick 挑選 + out 出來 → **pick out**

❶ 挑選　❷ 辨認出 及

❶ When Terry arrived at the store, his father told him he could **pick out** any shirt he wanted. 泰瑞到店裡時，父親要他**挑選**任何他想要的襯衫。

❷ Kim searched the audience for her friends but had trouble **picking** them **out** of the crowd. 金在觀眾群中找尋朋友的蹤影，卻無法在人群中**找到**他們。

11 on + purpose

on 在……上 + purpose 目的 → **on purpose**

刻意；有目的地

比較
◆ accidentally on purpose 假裝不小心但其實故意地
◆ serve a purpose 有用處

- I came late **on purpose**; it wasn't a mistake. 我**故意**遲到，並不是誤會。
- Franz lost the card game **on purpose** because he wanted to go home. 法蘭斯玩牌時**故意**輸掉，因為他想回家了。

12 take + out

take 找 + out 出來 → **take out**

❶ 拿出來　❷ 和某人約會 及

用法
◆ take out sth 把某樣東西拿出來
◆ take out sb 殺死某人
◆ take sb out 找某人出去約會
◆ take sth out on sb 拿某人出氣
◆ take sb out of themselves 改變某人的心情，讓他們不要一直陷在憂鬱的情緒中

❶ Mom asked me to **take out** the trash before I left. 媽媽要我出門前把垃圾**拿出去**。
❶ The dentist **took** Jack's tooth **out**. 牙醫**拔掉**傑克的牙齒。
❷ Warren **took** Lidia **out** for the first time last Friday. 華倫和莉蒂亞上星期五第一次**約會**。

25

Unit 03 Test Yourself!

A 選擇題

1. After eating a big dinner, Wanda _____ in bed and fell asleep.
   Ⓐ took out   Ⓑ stood up   Ⓒ lay down   Ⓓ picked out

2. Although I told my sister it was an accident, I let the bird out of its cage _____ because it looked so sad.
   Ⓐ all along   Ⓑ as usual   Ⓒ by herself   Ⓓ on purpose

3. Before the party, Glenn spent a long time _____ something to wear.
   Ⓐ picking out   Ⓑ sitting down   Ⓒ talking over   Ⓓ taking out

4. My teacher and I _____ some universities I might want to apply to.
   Ⓐ stood up   Ⓑ talked over   Ⓒ took out   Ⓓ lay down

5. When the jazz band stopped playing, everyone _____ and clapped loudly because the music was so good.
   Ⓐ took out   Ⓑ lay down   Ⓒ picked out   Ⓓ stood up

6. We ran for several miles and then _____ on the park bench to rest.
   Ⓐ sat down   Ⓑ talked over   Ⓒ picked out   Ⓓ took out

7. When it got cold, Vince _____ his winter clothes _____ of the boxes in his closet so he could wear them.
   Ⓐ talked . . . over   Ⓑ took . . . out   Ⓒ sat . . . down   Ⓓ stood . . . up

8. Although Rob was very late, he _____ getting ready.
   Ⓐ picked out   Ⓑ stood up   Ⓒ talked over   Ⓓ took his time

9. Wally volunteers at the hospital because he wants to _____ in the lives of others.
   Ⓐ get along with   Ⓑ stand up   Ⓒ make a difference   Ⓓ pick out

10. Sometimes I want to be alone so I can think quietly _____.
    Ⓐ on purpose   Ⓑ all along   Ⓒ by myself   Ⓓ all right

11. Because it was Stefanie's first time in Hawaii, she was on the beach _____ enjoying the sun.
    Ⓐ picking out   Ⓑ all day long   Ⓒ on purpose   Ⓓ reading up

12. Alan is very friendly, so it is no surprise that everyone _____ him.
    Ⓐ picks out   Ⓑ stands up to   Ⓒ makes a difference to   Ⓓ gets along with

B 閱讀文章，從字表中選擇詞彙填入，並依人稱時態等做適當的變化

make a difference	take one's time	pick out	talk over
by oneself	lie down	on purpose	get along with
take out	all day long		

At first, Kim wasn't sure she had ❶ _____ the right university to attend. Although she ❷ _____ and thought about it a lot, it was still a hard choice. She also met with her high school teachers so they could ❸ _____ it _____ after class, but she still felt unsure. At night, when she ❹ _____ on her bed, she couldn't sleep; instead, she stayed up late, thinking over her decision. In the end, she applied only to the university that was closest to her home. She did that ❺ _____ – so she could visit her family on the weekends. Just knowing she could visit her mom and dad often ❻ _____ and helped her feel calmer.

The day before she had planned to leave her home and move into the dorm, she ❼ _____ all her clothes from the closet and packed them in a suitcase along with some of her other things. After a week at her new school, she knew she had made the right choice. Although she was busy ❽ _____, she had a lot of friends in her classes. Also, she ❾ _____ her professors. So even though she was living ❿ _____ for the first time in her life, she wasn't scared or nervous.

C 引導式翻譯，並依人稱時態等做適當的變化

1. 一點點的同情心，對被飽受欺凌的人就**有**極大的**不同**。
   A little sympathy _____ _____ world of _____ to someone who's been badly treated.

2. 他們努力想在人群中**認出**母親。
   They managed to _____ _____ their mother from the crowd.

3. 我不知道她是**爽約**還只是會晚到，我會再等個半個鐘頭。
   I don't know if I've been _____ _____ or if she's just late. I'll wait another half hour.

4. 我養了多年的貓剛開始和新來的小貓**處不來**。
   At first my old cat did not _____ _____ _____ the new kitten.

5. 你**一個人**就把整個都吃掉嗎？
   You ate the whole thing _____ _____ ?

6. 他們開除了馬克斯，因為他老是在**摸魚**。
   They fired Max because he was always _____ _____ on the job.

27

Unit 04

The School Play
學校戲劇表演

Mark and Cheryl have a conversation about the school play.
馬克和雪若正在談論學校的戲劇表演。

Mark:	Did you hear about this year's school play?	妳聽說今年學校的戲劇表演了嗎？
Cheryl:	No, tell me about it.	沒有，說來聽聽。
Mark:	Well, it **takes place**[1] in London. If you're interested in learning more about it, you can **look** it **up**[2] online.	嗯，它會在倫敦**舉行**。如果妳有興趣想知道更多訊息，可以上網**查詢**。
Cheryl:	OK, it sounds cool. Are you **taking part in**[3] it?	好，聽起來不錯。你會**參加**嗎？
Mark:	Of course! In one scene, I work in a restaurant and **wait on**[4] the play's hero.	當然！我在一個餐廳的場景中，負責**接待**劇中的男主角。
Cheryl:	Wow! I'd like to be in the play, too—but I'm not a good actress **at all**[5].	哇！我也想參與演出，但是我的演技一**點也**不好。
Mark:	Well, we are looking for **at least**[6] three more actors, so you should really consider it.	喔，我們還在找**最少**三位演員，妳真的應該考慮看看。
Cheryl:	All right. I'll **think** it **over**[7].	嗯，我會**仔細考慮**的。
Mark:	OK, but don't think too much! Anyway, I'd better go and **try on**[8] my costume.	好，但別想太多！總之，我最好去**試穿**我的戲服了。
Cheryl:	See you, and good luck!	再見，祝你好運！

🔊 015

Unit 04 The School Play 學校戲劇表演

1 慣用片語

```
take (佔有) + place (場地)
      ↓
   take place
   ❶ 舉行  ❷ 發生
```

用法
- take place + 時間/地點 舉行

比較
- take the place of sb/sth 代替某人或某物
→ Nowadays, plastics have **taken the place of** many conventional materials. 如今塑膠已**取代**了許多傳統材料。

💡 take place 的意思同 happen 和 occur，但用法上比較正式；這些字全部都只能使用**主動語態**。

❶ The party will **take place** in two weeks. 派對會在兩個星期後**舉行**。
❷ When does the class **take place**? 那堂課何時開始？
❷ Not all engineering failures **take place** suddenly and dramatically.
工程問題的**發生**，不一定都是很突然很劇烈的。

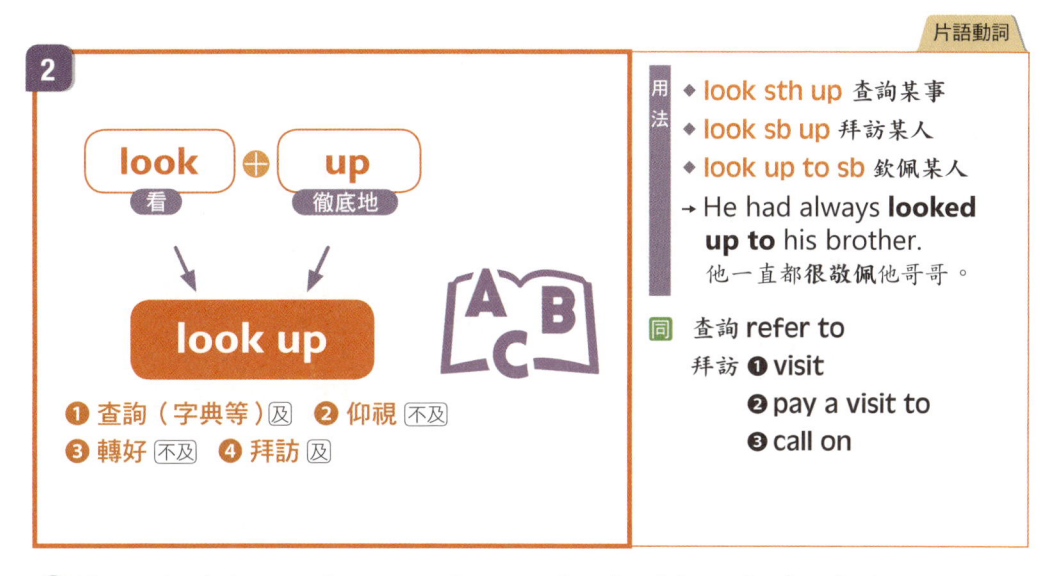

2 片語動詞

```
look (看) + up (徹底地)
      ↓
   look up
   ❶ 查詢（字典等）及  ❷ 仰視 不及
   ❸ 轉好 不及  ❹ 拜訪 及
```

用法
- look sth up 查詢某事
- look sb up 拜訪某人
- look up to sb 欽佩某人
→ He had always **looked up to** his brother. 他一直都很**敬佩**他哥哥。

同
查詢 refer to
拜訪 ❶ visit
　　 ❷ pay a visit to
　　 ❸ call on

❶ If you don't know what a word means, just **look** it **up** in the dictionary.
如果不知道某個生字的意思，就**查**字典。
❷ She **looked up** from her book as I entered the room.
我進屋時，她停下看書**抬眼看**了一下。
❸ I hope things start to **look up** in the new year. 希望新的一年情況會開始**好轉**。
❹ **Look** me **up** next time you're in Paris. 下次來巴黎時要來**找**我喔。

29

🔊 016

慣用片語

3

take（取得）＋ part（部分）＋ in（於……）
→ **take part in**
參加；參與

同 ❶ participate in
❷ join in

💡 take part in 後面如果不接受詞，可省略 in。在表示參加某活動時，take part in、participate in、join in 可以通用，take part in 和 participate in 尤著重指參加且投入某活動。

- Will you **take part in** the school musical this year?
  你會**參加**學校今年的歌舞劇嗎？
- The teacher told us that it would help our grades if we **took part in** class discussions.
  老師說我們如果**參與**課堂討論，對分數會很有幫助。

片語動詞

4

wait（服侍）＋ on（對……）
→ **wait on**
（服務生或店員的）服務；接待 及

用法
◆ wait on table(s)
　上菜（美式）
◆ wait at table(s)
　上菜（英式）

- Although the food wasn't very good, the young woman who **waited on** us at the restaurant was very nice.
  雖然這家餐廳的食物不是很好吃，但是**接待**我們的女服務生很親切。
- We sat for twenty minutes before we were **waited on**.
  我們坐了 20 分鐘才有服務生來點餐。

30

5

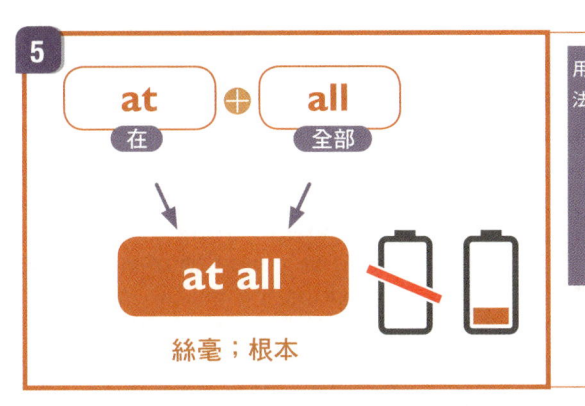

at (在) ➕ **all** (全部) → **at all** 絲毫；根本

用法
- ◆ not at all 不客氣；一點也不
- → "Thanks for helping."
  「感謝幫忙。」
  "Not at all." 「不客氣。」
- → I'm **not at all** happy about it.
  對此我一點也不高興。

💡 **at all** 用於加強語氣，主要用於否定句，也用於疑問句或條件子句。用於否定句時，通常與 **no**、**not**、**hardly** 連用，表示「完全不……」。

- There's nothing left in the house **at all**; everything has been moved out.
  房子裡**什麼**也沒有，所有東西都被搬光了。
- The police asked Marty why he ran away from them, but he had nothing **at all** to say.
  警察詢問馬堤為何逃跑，但他**絲毫**無話可說。

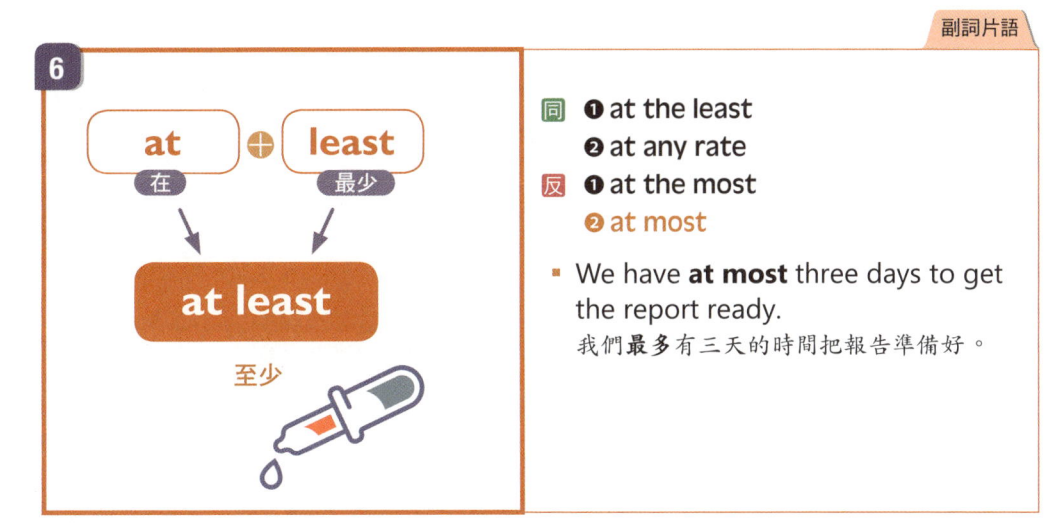

6

at (在) ➕ **least** (最少) → **at least** 至少

同
❶ at the least
❷ at any rate

反
❶ at the most
❷ at most

- We have **at most** three days to get the report ready.
  我們**最多**有三天的時間把報告準備好。

- When you are at the store, please pick up **at least** three pounds of onions.
  請你到商店買**至少**三磅的洋蔥。
- When I have a family, I want **at least** two children.
  等有了家庭後，我**最少**想要兩個小孩。

Unit 04 The School Play 學校戲劇表演

🔊 017

7

think （想） + over （從頭到尾）
↓
think over

仔細考慮；深思熟慮 及

片語動詞 | 可分開 | 受詞為代名詞時定要分開

用法比較

- **think sth over** 仔細考慮某事

- **think sth through**
  仔細考慮清楚某事直至得出結論
  → I need some time to **think** it **through**—I don't want to make any sudden decisions.
  我需要一些時間把它**想清楚**，我不想倉皇地做出決定。

- **think sth up** 想出新的點子
  → I don't want to go tonight, but I can't **think up** a good excuse.
  我今晚不想去，但是我還沒**想到**有什麼好藉口。

- **think sth out** 考慮很周詳
  → The scheme was well **thought out**.
  這個計畫經過周詳的**考慮**。

- Jan wasn't sure if it was a good idea to buy the car, so she **thought** it **over** for a few days.
  珍不確定買車是否是個好主意，所以她**仔細考慮**了好幾天。

- After **thinking over** the assignment, Marion got started with her research.
  瑪莉安在**認真思索**過這份工作後便開始進行研究。

8

try (試試) + **on** (穿上) → **try on** 試穿 ⓥ

| 片語動詞 | 可分開 | 受詞為代名詞時定要分開 |

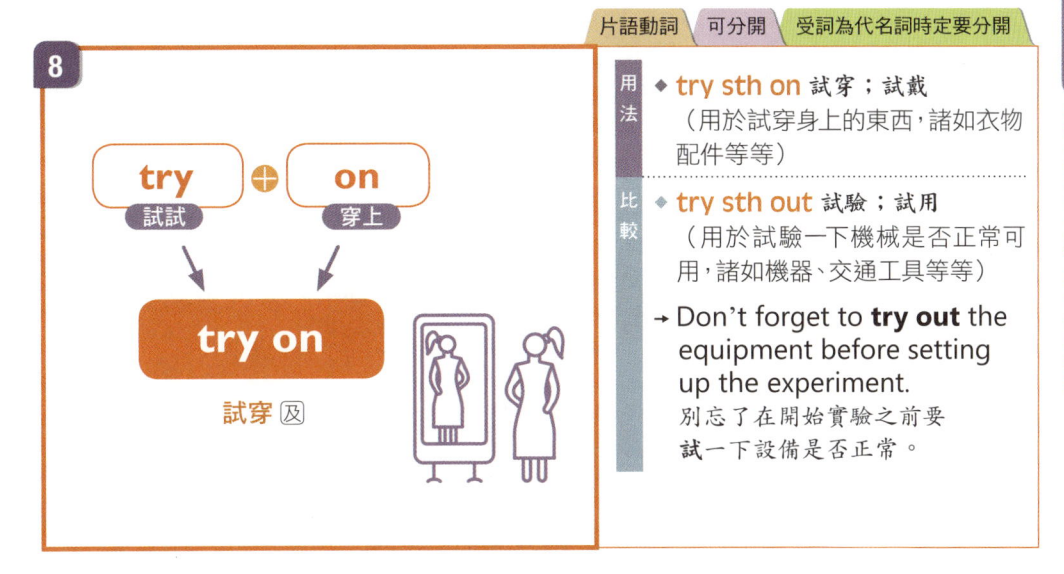

用法
- **try sth on** 試穿；試戴
  （用於試穿身上的東西，諸如衣物配件等等）

比較
- **try sth out** 試驗；試用
  （用於試驗一下機械是否正常可用，諸如機器、交通工具等等）

→ Don't forget to **try out** the equipment before setting up the experiment.
別忘了在開始實驗之前要**試**一下設備是否正常。

- Before you buy those jeans, **try** them **on** to make sure they fit.
  買牛仔褲前，記得要**試穿**以便確定是否合身。
- If you don't have any nice shoes to wear with your suit, you can **try on** mine; if they fit, you can borrow them.
  你若是沒有好看的鞋能搭套裝，可以**試穿**我的，如果合腳你可以借去穿。

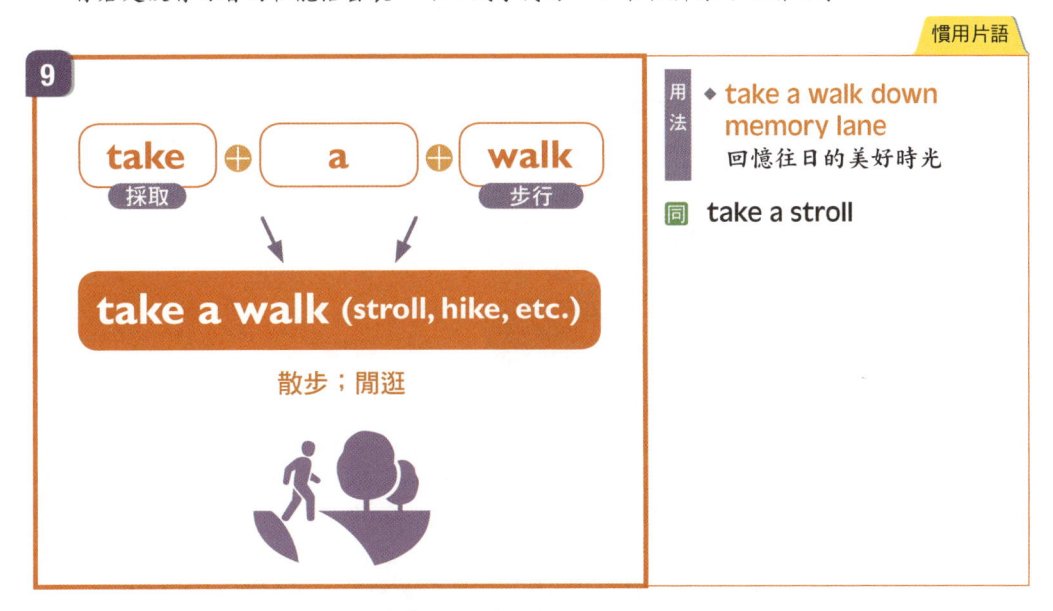

9

take (採取) + **a** + **walk** (步行) → **take a walk** (stroll, hike, etc.) 散步；閒逛

| 慣用片語 |

用法
- **take a walk down memory lane**
  回憶往日的美好時光

同 **take a stroll**

- After a large dinner, Tracy likes to **take a stroll** around the park.
  崔西喜歡在用過豐盛的晚餐後到公園裡**散步**。
- Last weekend, Franz and his family went on a picnic and then **took a hike** in the nearby hills. 法蘭斯上星期和家人去野餐，然後在附近的山區**健行**。

33

10

take 採取 ＋ **a** ＋ **trip** 旅行

→ **take a trip** 遠行；旅行

慣用片語

用法
- take a trip down memory lane
  回憶往日的美好時光

- Reg won't come in to work next week because he's **taking a trip** to Chicago for a business meeting. 雷哲下星期不會來上班，因為他要**到**芝加哥出差開會。
- This summer, Barbara plans to **take a trip** to Mexico.
  芭芭拉計劃這個夏天到墨西哥**旅行**。

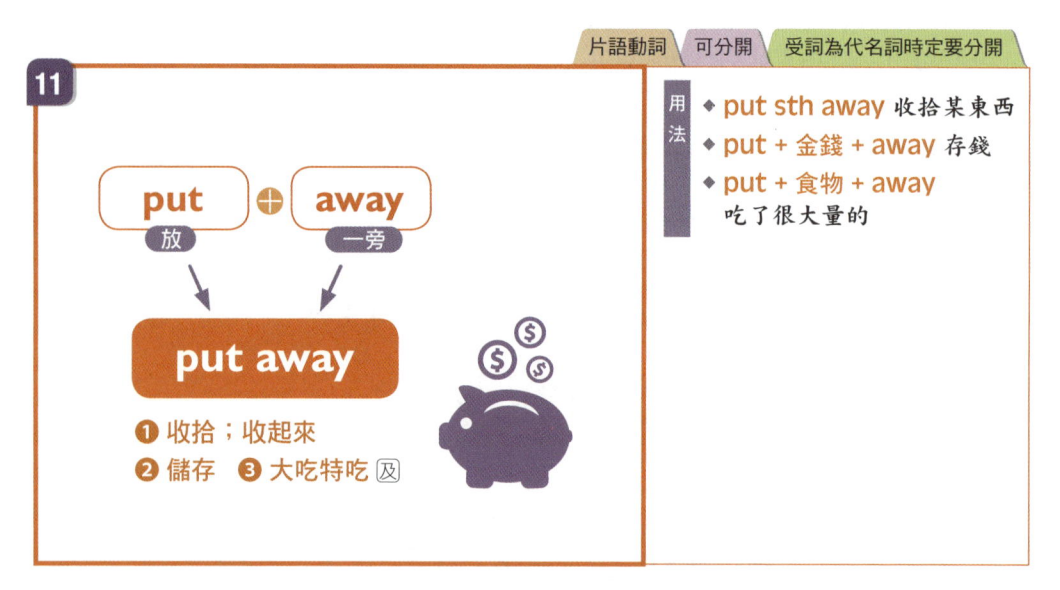

11

片語動詞 ｜ 可分開 ｜ 受詞為代名詞時定要分開

put 放 ＋ **away** 一旁

→ **put away**
❶ 收拾；收起來
❷ 儲存 ❸ 大吃特吃 及

用法
- put sth away 收拾某東西
- put + 金錢 + away 存錢
- put + 食物 + away
  吃了很大量的

❶ James told his little sister to **put away** all her toys before their parents got home.
詹姆斯叫妹妹在父母回來前把玩具**收拾好**。

❶ The teacher told me to **put** my cell phone **away** because I was using it during class. 我上課時在用手機，老師要我把它**收起來**。

❷ I decided to **put away** a few dollars each week. 我決定每個星期都要**存下**一點錢。

❸ He **put away** a whole box of chocolates in one evening.
他一個晚上就**吃掉**了整盒巧克力。

12

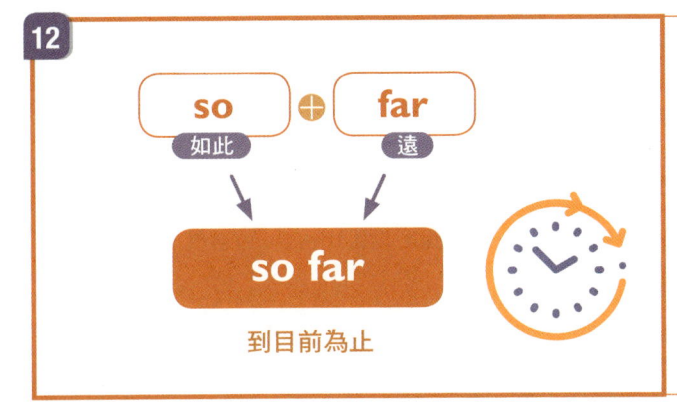

so (如此) + **far** (遠) → **so far** 到目前為止

[同]
1. thus far
2. up to now
3. till now

> so far 通常與**現在完成式**或**簡單現在式**連用，可放在句首、句中或句尾。亦可表示「到此處之範圍」（作地方副詞），或是表示「到此一定之程度」（作程度副詞）。

- My first semester at college is going well **so far**—though we haven't had any tests yet. 我在大學的第一個學期**到目前為止**都很順利，儘管我們還沒考過試。

- **So far** during this car ride, we've passed three gas stations without stopping. **到目前為止**，我們已經開車經過了三間加油站，但都沒有停下來。

Unit 04 Test Yourself!

A 選擇題

1. _____, I haven't gotten any calls from my cousin in Boston.
   Ⓐ So far   Ⓑ At all   Ⓒ Up to   Ⓓ Just in

2. We looked everywhere in the shop for a pen, but there weren't any _____.
   Ⓐ up to   Ⓑ at all   Ⓒ just in   Ⓓ so far

3. If you aren't sure which university to apply to, you should _____ it _____ for as long as necessary.
   Ⓐ look . . . up   Ⓑ try . . . on   Ⓒ think . . . over   Ⓓ put . . . away

4. If Andy gets a new job, he needs to earn _____ $12 per hour.
   Ⓐ at all   Ⓑ until now   Ⓒ so far   Ⓓ at least

5. The test will _____ on the last Wednesday of the semester.
   Ⓐ take place   Ⓑ flip a switch   Ⓒ wait on   Ⓓ call up

6. The best part about staying at a hotel near the sea was _____ down the beach each night.
   Ⓐ flipping a switch   Ⓑ taking a walk
   Ⓒ jumping through hoops   Ⓓ taking a trip

7. Pam wasn't sure where Mogadishu is, so she _____ it _____ in the atlas.
   Ⓐ looked . . . up   Ⓑ thought . . . over   Ⓒ put . . . away   Ⓓ tried . . . on

8. You should have _____ that jacket _____ before you bought it—it is much too big for you!
   Ⓐ put . . . away   Ⓑ tried . . . on   Ⓒ looked . . . up   Ⓓ thought . . . over

9. Before the test began, the professor told the students to _____ their notes _____.
   Ⓐ look . . . up   Ⓑ put . . . away   Ⓒ think . . . over   Ⓓ try . . . on

10. Every few years, I try to _____ to Tokyo because the food there is delicious.
    Ⓐ take part   Ⓑ jump through hoops   Ⓒ flip a switch   Ⓓ take a trip

B 閱讀文章，從字表中選擇詞彙填入，並依人稱時態等做適當的變化

try on	at all	take a walk	look up
take a trip	at least	wait on	take place
think over	so far	put away	

　　Last winter, Luke and Betty ❶ _____ to visit New York City. Betty had never been there, so before they left, she ❷ _____ all the best stores, restaurants, and sights in a guidebook. That way, she could be sure to visit them. As soon as they arrived in the city, Betty wanted to ❸ _____ down Broadway. They went to many shops and Betty ❹ _____ a lot of clothes. However, she didn't buy anything ❺ _____. She wanted to ❻ _____ it _____ before spending all her vacation money. They stopped at a restaurant, and Luke asked the man who was ❼ _____ them to take their picture.

　　After some time, Luke and Betty went to their hotel. The front desk clerk told them that a holiday party would ❽ _____ in the lobby that night. The first thing they did after getting to their room was to ❾ _____ their clothes in the closet and dresser. They were both very tired, but that wasn't surprising; ❿ _____ _____, they had seen a lot of the city, but they had also walked ⓫ _____ five miles. They decided to rest a bit before the party, so they took a nap.

C 引導式翻譯，並依人稱時態等做適當的變化

1. 如果沒有下雨，畢業典禮會在室外**舉行**。
   The commencement exercises will _____ _____ outdoors unless it rains.
2. 馬克慢跑後**大啖**了一頓豐盛的晚餐。
   Mark _____ _____ a hearty supper after jogging.
3. 我們的財務狀況終於**好轉**了。
   Our financial situation is _____ _____ at last.
4. 我爸和我哥都**試開**過了那輛新車。
   Both my father and brother _____ _____ the new car.

Unit 05

Schoolwork
學校作業

Joe and Erin talk about schoolwork.
喬和愛琳在談論學校功課。

Joe:	Have you finished writing your history paper yet?	妳的歷史報告寫完了嗎？
Erin:	No, I've been **putting** it **off**[1] until I **get over**[2] this illness.	還沒，我一直**拖**到**病好了**才開始趕作業。
Joe:	What's wrong? Did you **catch a cold**[3]?	怎麼回事？妳**感冒**了嗎？
Erin:	Yeah. I spent a weekend taking care of my sick aunt, by the time I **got back**[4] I was already feeling bad.	沒錯，我上週末照顧生病的阿姨，在**回家**路上就已經覺得不舒服了。
Joe:	Well, I hope you get better soon.	嗯，希望妳早日康復。
Erin:	Thanks. I'm taking it easy **for the time being**[5]; however, I am thinking about going to the movies tonight with my boyfriend.	謝謝，我**現在**感覺還可以，不過我今晚想和男朋友去看場電影。
Joe:	I see. You know, I think you should **change your mind**[6]—otherwise, you'll never write that history paper!	我知道了。我跟妳說，我覺得妳最好**改變主意**，否則妳永遠別想寫歷史報告了！
Erin:	You may be right, but it's too late. I've already **made up my mind**[7] to go out. There's no way I'm going to **call off**[8] my date!	也許你是對的，不過太遲了，我已經**決定**要出去了，絕對不可能**取消**約會！
Joe:	Well, what can I say? Good luck!	嗯，那我能說什麼呢？祝妳好運！

38

Unit 05 Schoolwork 學校作業

1

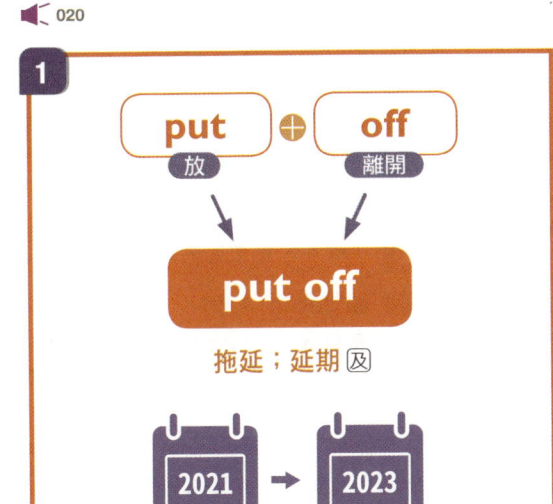

put(放) + **off**(離開) → **put off** 拖延；延期 及

2021 → 2023

片語動詞 | 可分開 | 受詞為代名詞時定要分開

用法
- **put sth off** 拖延某事
- **put sb off** 推遲與某人的約會
  → He keeps asking me out, and I keep **putting** him **off**.
  他不斷約我出去，而我不斷**推辭**。
- **(sth/sb) put sb off**
  某物或人令人反感（英式）
  → The smell of hospitals always **puts** me **off**.
  我一直都很**討厭**醫院的味道。

同 ❶ hold off ❷ set back ❸ drag on

- Never **put off** till tomorrow what you can do today. 今日事今日畢。〔俗諺〕
- If you **put off** writing this essay until the weekend, I'm sure you'll regret it.
  如果你拖到週末才寫報告，你一定會後悔的。
- Rudy didn't want to go to the doctor; however, when he woke up with a terrible headache, he realized he couldn't **put** it **off** any longer.
  魯迪不想去看醫生，但當他頭疼欲裂地醒來時，他知道看醫生一事無法再拖下去了。

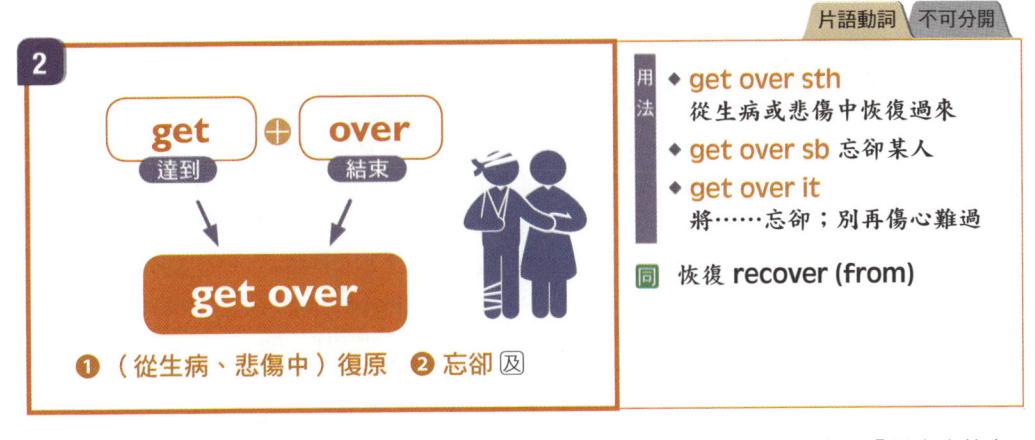

2

片語動詞 | 不可分開

get(達到) + **over**(結束) → **get over** ❶（從生病、悲傷中）復原 ❷ 忘卻 及

用法
- **get over sth** 從生病或悲傷中恢復過來
- **get over sb** 忘卻某人
- **get over it** 將……忘卻；別再傷心難過

同 恢復 recover (from)

💡 **get over** 通常作為及物動詞，不可分開使用，後需接名詞或代名詞，表示「從疾病等中痊癒」、「克服心裡創傷」或「忘卻某人或某事」。

❶ It took Martin a few days to **get over** failing the final exam.
馬汀花了好幾天才**走出**期末考不及格的**陰影**。

❶ The day Wendy **got over** the infection, she returned to work.
溫蒂在病情**好轉**的那天回到工作崗位。

❷ It took him months to **get over** Nicole after she ended the relationship.
在妮可提出分手之後，他花了好幾個月的時間才把她給**忘了**。

🔊 021

慣用片語

3

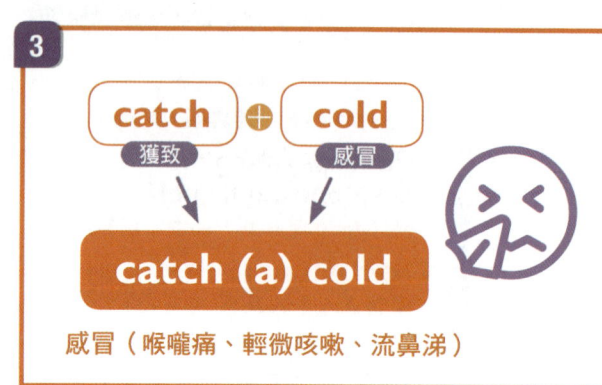

catch（獲致）＋ **cold**（感冒）
→ **catch (a) cold**
感冒（喉嚨痛、輕微咳嗽、流鼻涕）

用法
- catch a bad/nasty/severe cold 重感冒
- catch a slight cold 輕微感冒
- catch sth from sb 被某人傳染某疾病

同
1. get (a) cold
2. have (a) cold

💡 **catch** 可接傳染性疾病，如 **catch the flu**（患流行感冒）、**catch chicken pox**（長水痘）。

- Miranda missed class because she **caught a cold**. 米蘭達因感冒而未去上課。
- Every winter, Vince **catches** at least one **cold**. 文斯每年冬天至少會感冒一次。

4

片語動詞　可分開　受詞為代名詞時定要分開

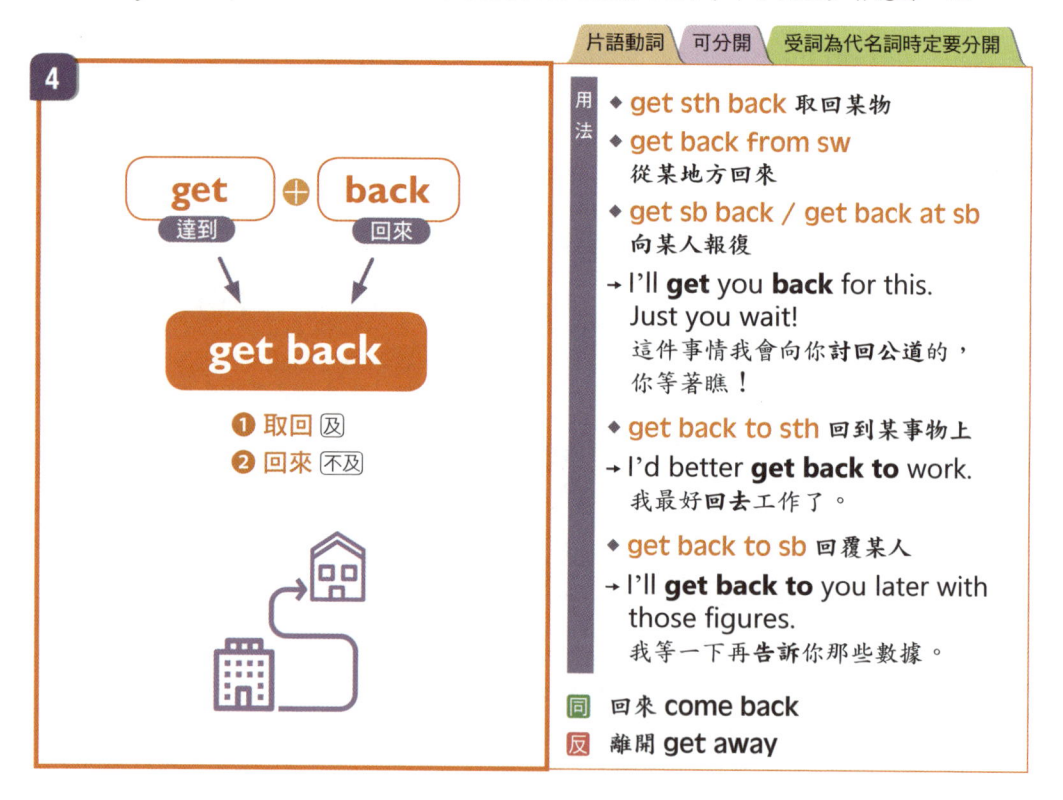

get（達到）＋ **back**（回來）
→ **get back**
1. 取回 及
2. 回來 不及

用法
- get sth back 取回某物
- get back from sw 從某地方回來
- get sb back / get back at sb 向某人報復
  → I'll **get** you **back** for this. Just you wait!
  這件事情我會向你討回公道的，你等著瞧！
- get back to sth 回到某事物上
  → I'd better **get back to** work.
  我最好回去工作了。
- get back to sb 回覆某人
  → I'll **get back to** you later with those figures.
  我等一下再告訴你那些數據。

同 回來 come back
反 離開 get away

💡 表示「取回」時，**get back** 可分開使用，但接代名詞時，代名詞需放中間。

1. Can you please **get** my MP3 player **back** from Janet?
   你可以幫我向珍娜拿回我的 MP3 播放器嗎？
2. Mandy **gets back** from work around 3 o'clock or so. 曼蒂約三點下班回到家。

5

for (在) + **the time** (時間) + **being** (現在的)

→ **for the time being**
現在；目前

同
❶ for the moment
❷ for now
❸ at the present time
❹ at present

反 永遠 for good

副詞片語　時間副詞

💡 **for the time being** 通常置於句首或句尾，常與現在簡單式或進行式搭配使用，表示「目前的情況只是暫時的，並不會持續下去」。**being** 在片語中作為形容詞，表示「現在的」。

- **For the time being**, the students don't have any questions, but they may feel differently tomorrow. 學生**現在**沒有任何問題，但明天可能就不一樣了。
- I'm not hungry **for the time being**, but by noon I'll be starving.
  我**現在**不餓，不過中午前就會餓了。

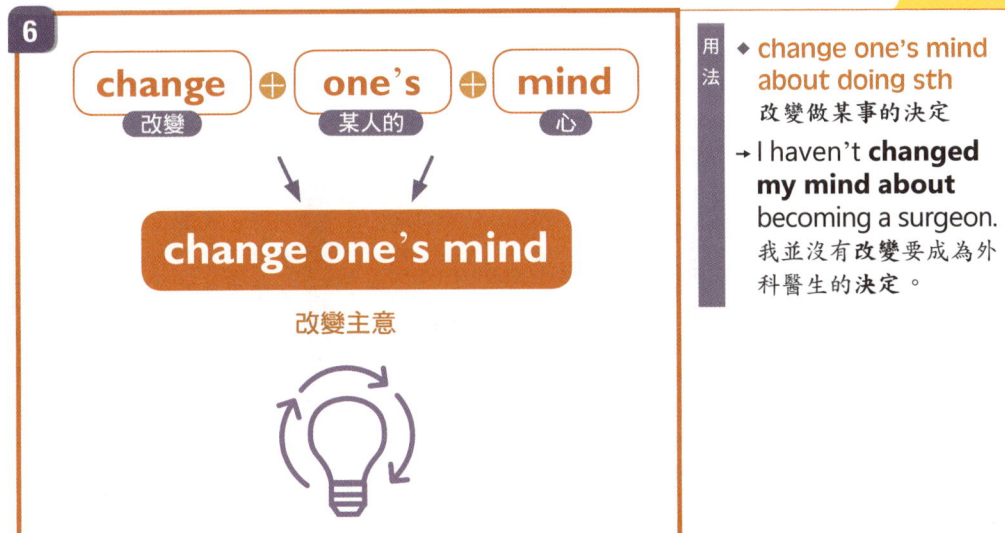

6

change (改變) + **one's** (某人的) + **mind** (心)

→ **change one's mind**
改變主意

慣用片語

用法 ◆ **change one's mind about doing sth**
改變做某事的決定

→ I haven't **changed my mind about** becoming a surgeon.
我並沒有改變要成為外科醫生的決定。

💡 **one's** 為所有格，如 **my**、**our**、**your**、**his**、**her**、**its**、**their**。

- My girlfriend always **changes her mind** a few times before making a big decision. 在下重大決定前，我的女朋友總會三番兩次地**改變心意**。
- You'd better be sure this is the car you want because once you agree to buy it, you can't **change your mind**.
  你最好確定這台車就是你想要的，因為一旦你同意買下它，就無法**改變主意**了。
- When I first met him, I didn't like him; however, since then I've **changed my mind**. 第一次和他見面的時侯，我並不喜歡他，但後來**我的看法改變了**。

7

make (做) + **up** (完成) + **one's** (某人的) + **mind** (心)

→ **make up one's mind**
下定決心；決定

用法
- make up one's mind / make one's mind up
  使某人下定決心

同
1. decide
2. determine
3. resolve

💡 **make up one's mind** 表示「下定決心」或「認清事實」，**up** 不可省略。

- There are so many flavors of ice cream here that it is hard to **make up my mind** and choose one. 這裡有好多種口味的冰淇淋，我很難**決定**要選哪一種。
- Ralph couldn't **make up his mind** about going to the park or not.
  瑞夫無法**決定**是否要去公園。
- Gwen can't **make up her mind** about whether to visit L.A. or Miami this summer.
  關無法**決定**今年夏天要去洛杉磯還是邁阿密。

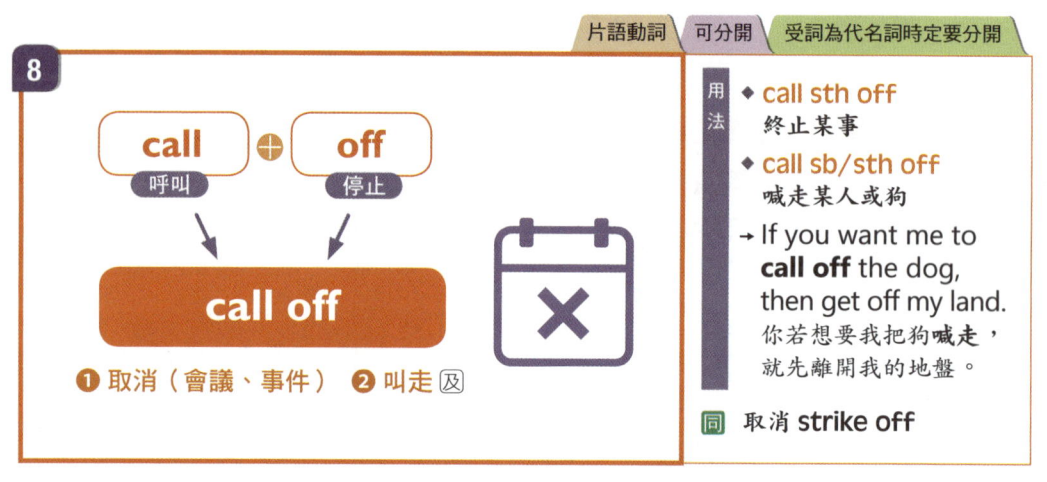

8

片語動詞 | 可分開 | 受詞為代名詞時定要分開

call (呼叫) + **off** (停止)

→ **call off**
1. 取消（會議、事件） 2. 叫走（及）

用法
- call sth off
  終止某事
- call sb/sth off
  喊走某人或狗
→ If you want me to **call off** the dog, then get off my land.
你若想要我把狗**喊走**，就先離開我的地盤。

同 取消 strike off

💡 **call off** 為及物動詞，可用於被動語態，亦可分開使用，但接**代名詞**時，代名詞需**放中間**，如 **call it off**。

1. Because it was raining, Diane **called off** the outdoor volleyball competition.
   下雨了，黛安**取消**了戶外排球比賽。
1. The CEO **called off** the meeting and told his employees to go home early.
   執行長**取消**了會議，要員工早點回家。
1. Tomorrow's match has been **called off** because of the weather.
   由於天氣寒冷的緣故，明天的比賽已經**取消**了。

9

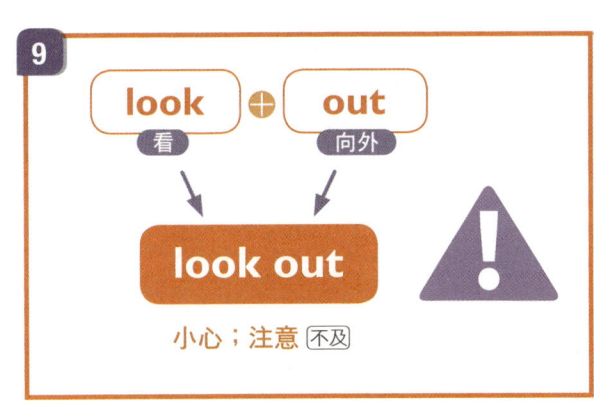

look (看) + **out** (向外) → **look out** 小心；注意 [不及]

> **look out** 常用來「提醒他人要小心」，雖然也有「向外看、眺望」的意思，但通常會加上介系詞 **at** 或 **of**，如 **look out at**（眺望）；**look out of**（由……朝外看）。

用法 ◆ **look out for sth/sb**
留意某事／人

同 **watch out**

- **Look out**! The teacher is coming, and he'll see that you are skipping class.
  小心點！老師快要來了，他會發現你翹課。
- If you travel alone at night, be sure to **look out** for robbers.
  晚上單獨出門，要留意搶匪。

10 慣用片語

shake (搖) + **hands** (手) → **shake hands** 握手

用法 ◆ **shake hands with sb**
與某人握手

→ On the way out, the president stopped to **shake hands with** many people in the audience.
總統離開時停下來和群眾握手。

◆ **shake sb's hand** 與某人握手

同 **join hands**

- In America, it is important to **shake hands** firmly or people will think you have a weak personality. 在美國，握手時把手握緊很重要，否則別人會認為你的個性軟弱。

11 副詞片語

for (為得) + **good** (利益) → **for good** 永遠地；永久地

同 ❶ **forever**
❷ **forever and ever**
❸ **once and for all**

> 同「**for good and all**」（英式），原指獲致全部利益，有一勞永逸之意，後引申為「永久地」。

- After the graduation ceremony, Lou knew that he was done with high school **for good**. 畢業典禮過後，盧知道他的高中生活永遠結束了。

43

Unit 05 Test Yourself!

A 選擇題

1. Chuck is a stubborn guy; he will not _____ his _____ once he has made it up.
   Ⓐ make up . . . mind　　Ⓑ go on . . . way
   Ⓒ shake . . . hand　　Ⓓ change . . . mind

2. After Stella and Mel were introduced, they _____ and traded business cards.
   Ⓐ called off　Ⓑ made up their minds　Ⓒ shook hands　Ⓓ looked out

3. Because Felix disliked geography, he _____ studying for the exam until it was too late.
   Ⓐ looked out　Ⓑ got over　Ⓒ put off　Ⓓ got back

4. James had a hard time _____ Tina after they broke up.
   Ⓐ getting over　Ⓑ putting off　Ⓒ calling off　Ⓓ catching a cold with

5. Hurry up and _____—I don't have much time!
   Ⓐ catch a cold　Ⓑ make up your mind　Ⓒ put off　Ⓓ shake your hand

6. Norman _____ his date with Lydia because his car broke down.
   Ⓐ turned off　Ⓑ got over　Ⓒ called off　Ⓓ looked out

7. Wash your hands often with warm soap and water, or else you'll _____.
   Ⓐ call it off　Ⓑ catch a cold　Ⓒ make up your mind　Ⓓ put it off

8. By the time we _____ to the hotel, Joe had already left.
   Ⓐ got back　Ⓑ called off　Ⓒ looked out　Ⓓ put off

9. _____, Rob doesn't need to use the phone—but he will need to make a call later.
   Ⓐ For good　Ⓑ Never again　Ⓒ In a hurry　Ⓓ For the time being

10. Darryl said he wouldn't _____ till very late.
    Ⓐ put off　Ⓑ get back　Ⓒ look out　Ⓓ call off

11. After Adam broke his leg a second time, he knew he was done with skiing _____.
    Ⓐ for good　Ⓑ in a hurry　Ⓒ never again　Ⓓ through and through

B 閱讀文章，從字表中選擇詞彙填入，並依人稱時態等做適當的變化

change one's mind	call off	shake hands
make up one's mind	for the time being	get back
catch a cold	put off	for good

After Rick lost his job, he started looking for a new one. One day, he saw a job advertised in the newspaper and decided to apply. He wasn't sure if it was the best job for him, but he ❶ _____ to go to the interview. However, two days before the interview, Rick started coughing and realized he had ❷ _____. He thought about ❸ _____ the interview for a couple of days, but he was worried that the company would give someone else the job and ❹ _____ his interview ❺ _____.

Fortunately, Rick started feeling better the day before the interview. When he arrived at the office, he introduced himself and ❻ _____ with the boss who had just ❼ _____ from a business trip to Boston. Because the boss was in a hurry, the interview was very short. She told Rick that he was the best applicant she had met so far and that the job was his ❽ _____. So, unless the boss suddenly ❾ _____, Rick begins his new job next week.

C 引導式翻譯，並依人稱時態等做適當的變化

1. 你在市區的時候，要小心街上奸詐的攤販。
   While you're in the city center, _____ _____ for the dishonest street vendors.
2. 雖然珍妮喜歡住在巴黎，但她並不會長久住在那裡。
   Although Jenny likes living in Paris, she doesn't plan to stay there _____ _____.
3. 警察一個小時前停止了搜尋失蹤男孩的行動。
   The police _____ _____ the search for the missing boy one hour ago.
4. 他花了好幾年的時間才從母親過世的打擊中走出來。
   It took him years to _____ _____ the shock of his mother's death.
5. 我的牙齒很痛，看牙醫的事無法再拖了。
   My tooth hurts so much, I can't _____ _____ going to the dentist any longer.

Unit 06

Getting Sick and Stressed 生病與壓力

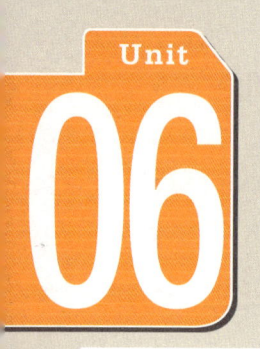

🔊 023

Didi tells her friend Jay why she is feeling sick and a bit stressed.
蒂蒂把感覺不舒服和緊張的原因告訴朋友傑。

Jay:	What's wrong? You look a bit **under the weather**[1].	怎麼了？妳看起來有點像是**生病**了。
Didi:	As a matter of fact, I'm not feeling so good. I just started classes in a new school, and it isn't easy **making friends**[2].	事實上，我覺得不太舒服。我剛到新學校上課，**交朋友**不太容易。
Jay:	Don't worry about that! It takes time to meet people. You need to focus on feeling better.	別擔心！那是需要時間的。妳需要集中注意力在保持好心情。
Didi:	Well, the other thing that is stressing me out is that someone keeps calling my cell, and when I answer, the person **hangs up**[3] without saying a word. I just don't know what's **going on**[4].	嗯，還有一件讓我很緊張的事情，就是有人一直打我的手機。當我接起來時，對方不說話就**把電話掛掉**，我不知道**發生**了什麼事情。
Jay:	Oh, man! I'm sure that really **gets to**[5] you; but you know what I think? I bet somebody has a crush on you and is too scared to talk.	噢，我敢肯定妳一定很**困擾**，妳知道我的看法嗎？我打賭一定是有人愛上妳了，而且還不敢開口。
Didi:	Really? I never thought about that before. **All of a sudden**[6], I feel a bit better. I can always **count on**[7] you to make me feel more positive.	真的嗎？我從來沒想過這些。我**突然**覺得好多了，都是**靠**你幫忙，我才能往好的方面去想。
Jay:	No problem. Good people like you are **few and far between**[8]. You deserve to be happy and calm.	沒什麼，像妳這麼好的人已經**很少**了，妳本來就應該要快樂平靜。

46

Unit 06 Getting Sick and Stressed 生病與壓力

1

under (受影響) + **the weather** (天氣)
→ **under the weather** 身體不舒服；生病

形容詞片語

用法
- **be under the weather** 生病
- **feel under the weather** 感覺不舒服

同
❶ **in a bad way** 狀況不佳
→ We were **in a bad way** until Adam joined the team; after that, we began winning some games. 我們的**表現一直不太好**，直到亞當加入球隊，之後我們才開始贏一些比賽。

❷ **out of sorts** 身體不適
→ They have had a busy day and are tired and **out of sorts**. 他們今天很忙碌，所有人都累壞了。

💡 原本用來指「天氣對人類身體的影響」，後來引申表示「生病」，但病情通常不太嚴重。常置於 be 動詞後面，作為主詞補語，在口語中相當常見。

- Walt canceled the discussion group because he was feeling a bit **under the weather**. 華特因為**身體不舒服**，取消了團體討論。
- After a long day of walking in the cold rain, Roberta felt a little **under the weather**. 羅伯特在寒冷的雨中走了一天，感覺**身體有點不舒服**。

2

make (成為) + **friends** (朋友)
→ **make friends** 交朋友

慣用片語

用法
- **make friends with sb** 與某人交朋友
→ Richard is an outgoing boy and easily **makes friends with** other children. 理查是個外向的男孩，並且很容易和其他孩童**交朋友**。

💡 **make friends** 可後接 with，再接名詞，表示與某人結交為朋友。

- Because Pam was new at the school, it took her a couple of weeks to **make friends**. 潘是新生，所以她花了好幾個星期才**交到朋友**。
- Mark is a great guy, so he **makes** new **friends** easily. 馬克是一個很棒的人，所以很容易**交到新朋友**。
- I've **made** a lot of **friends** at this job. 這份工作讓我**結交到許多朋友**。

47

3 片語動詞 | 可分開 | 受詞為代名詞時定要分開

hang (懸掛) + **up** (上去) → **hang up**

❶ 懸掛（衣服）及
❷ 掛斷電話 不及

用法
- **hang sth up** 懸掛某物
- **hang up** 掛斷電話
- **hang up on sb** 掛某人電話
→ She started shouting, so I **hung up** on her.
  她開始嚷嚷，所以我掛了她的電話。

同 掛斷電話 **ring off**（英式用法）
反 不掛電話 ❶ **hold on**
　　　　　❷ **hang on**

💡 **hang up** 作為**及**物動詞時，表示「**拖延、擱置**」，可使用被動語態；作**不及**物動詞時，指「**掛斷電話**」，主詞通常為人。

❶ Ray **hung up** all his clean shirts in the closet.
雷把所有乾淨的襯衫**掛**在衣櫥裡。

❷ Joel was so mad at his cousin that he **hung up** without saying goodbye.
喬爾很氣他的表弟沒說再見就**掛掉電話**。

---

4 片語動詞

go (進行) + **on** (繼續) → **go on**

❶ 發生　❷ 繼續下去 不及

用法
- **go on with sth** 繼續做某事情
→ Please **go on with** what you're doing.
  請**繼續**做你手邊的事情。

- **go on to do sth**
  完成某事後，繼續做另一件事情
→ Tom admitted his company's responsibility for the disaster and **went on to** explain how the victims would receive compensation.
  在湯姆承認公司要為這次的災害負起責任後，他**繼續**解釋受難者要如何獲得理賠。

- **go on doing sth** 繼續做某件正在做的事情
→ We really can't **go on** living like this. We'll have to find a bigger house.
  我們不能**繼續**住在這種房子了，我們必須找一間大一點的房子。

同 繼續 ❶ **keep on**　❷ **continue**
　　　　 ❸ **carry on**　❹ **proceed with**

💡 **go on** 指「**繼續做某事**」時，後面可接**動名詞**或**不定詞**。

❶ Do you know what's **going on** with your son in L.A.?
你知道你的兒子在洛杉磯**發生**了什麼事情嗎？

❷ By the time Frank arrived at the meeting, it had already been **going on** for a few minutes. 法蘭克到達時，會議已經**進行**了好幾分鐘。

片語動詞

5

```
  get    +    to
  得到         目的
          ↓
        get to
    ❶ 可以做（某事）
    ❷ 到達
    ❸ 感到困擾 及
```

用法
- **get to sb** 影響某人
  → The heat was beginning to **get to** me, so I went indoors.
  我開始受到外頭的高溫**影響**，所以我進屋內去了。

- **get to sb** 使某人惱怒
  → I know he's annoying, but you shouldn't let him **get to** you.
  我知道他很討厭，但別被他惹惱了。

同 到達 arrive in/at
（**in** 後接大地點，如國家；**at** 後接小地方，如飯店）

💡 ❶ **get to** 後接**名詞**時，表示「動作的最後結果、到達（某一地方或年齡）、開始或著手」。
❷ 後接**動名詞**或**原形動詞**則表示「動作的開始」，常見於口語中。
❸ 表示「**到達某地**」時，若地點為 **here**、**there**、**home** 等地方副詞時，則需省略 **to**，如 **get home**。

❶ If Beth gets an "A" on her history test, her mom said she'll **get to** have a party.
如果貝絲歷史考試得到「A」，媽媽說她**就可以**舉辦派對。

❷ When do you think we'll **get to** the city center?
你覺得我們什麼時候會**到達市中心**？

❸ The barking dog was really **getting to** me, so I called my neighbor and asked her to do something about it.
我覺得那隻狂吠的狗很**煩**，所以我打電話給鄰居要她處理一下。

6 副詞片語

all（加強語氣）+ **of**（在……之前）+ **a sudden**（無預警的情況下）
→ **all of a sudden** 突然；毫無預警

同 ❶ all at once
❷ suddenly

💡 **all of a sudden** 為**副詞**，通常置於**句首**或**句尾**。

- **All of a sudden**, it started raining and we got wet.
  天空**突然**開始下起雨，我們淋濕了。
- Lucy was shocked when Evan asked her **all of a sudden** to marry him.
  艾文**突然**向露西求婚，令她非常震驚。

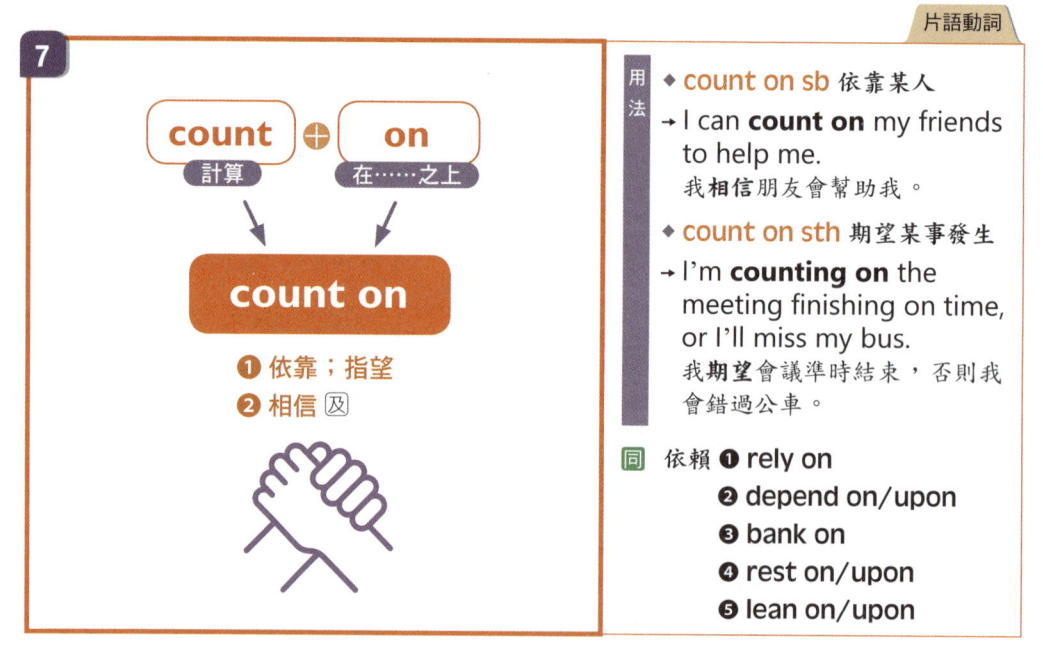

7 片語動詞

count（計算）+ **on**（在……之上）
→ **count on**
❶ 依靠；指望
❷ 相信 及

用法
◆ **count on sb** 依靠某人
→ I can **count on** my friends to help me.
　我**相信**朋友會幫助我。

◆ **count on sth** 期望某事發生
→ I'm **counting on** the meeting finishing on time, or I'll miss my bus.
　我**期望**會議準時結束，否則我會錯過公車。

同 依賴 ❶ rely on
　　　❷ depend on/upon
　　　❸ bank on
　　　❹ rest on/upon
　　　❺ lean on/upon

💡 **count on** 後可接名詞或動名詞，後接人時，可再接不定詞，表示「指望某人做某事」。亦可寫成 **count upon**。

❶ If you ever need help, remember that you can **count on** me.
　如果你需要幫忙，要記得你可以**依靠**我。
❷ Ryan knows that he can **count on** his uncle to meet him at the airport.
　雷恩**相信**叔叔會在機場和他見面。

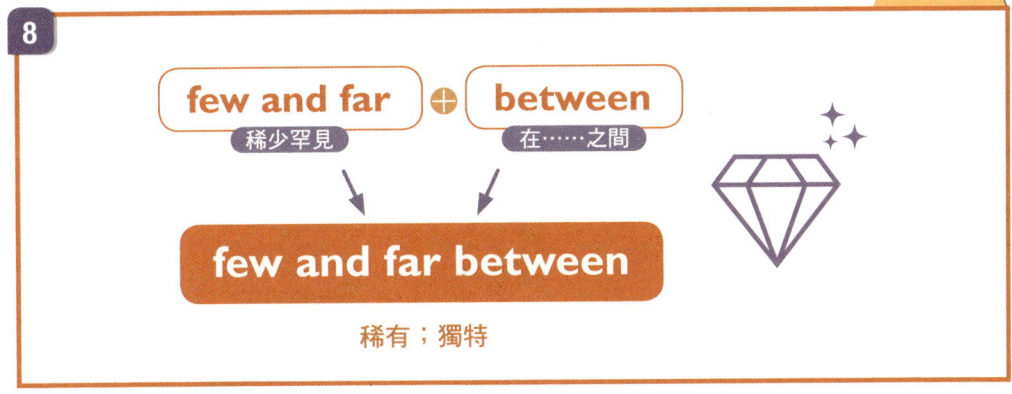

形容詞片語

8

few and far（稀少罕見） + between（在……之間）
→ **few and far between**
稀有；獨特

💡 **few and far between** 通常作為主詞補語。

- Good Indian restaurants are **few and far between** in Austin.
  奧斯汀好吃的印度餐廳**很少**。
- Apartments that are both comfortable and reasonably priced are **few and far between**. 既舒適、價錢又合理的公寓並**不多**。

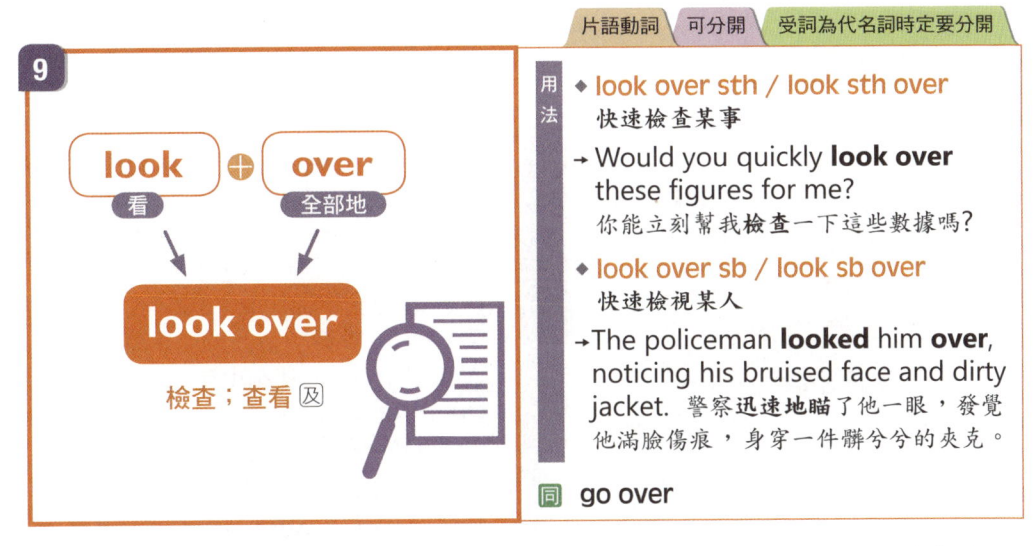

Unit 06 Getting Sick and Stressed 生病與壓力

片語動詞　可分開　受詞為代名詞時定要分開

9

look（看） + over（全部地）
→ **look over**
檢查；查看 及

用法
◆ **look over sth / look sth over**
快速檢查某事
→ Would you quickly **look over** these figures for me?
你能立刻幫我**檢查**一下這些數據嗎?

◆ **look over sb / look sb over**
快速檢視某人
→ The policeman **looked** him **over**, noticing his bruised face and dirty jacket. 警察**迅速地瞄**了他一眼，發覺他滿臉傷痕，身穿一件髒兮兮的夾克。

同 **go over**

💡 **look over** 為及物動詞，可分開來使用，後接名詞，表示「快速地檢視、掃描或查看」。

- Before buying a used car, **look** it **over** very carefully to be sure it doesn't have any problems.
  買二手車前，記得要仔細**檢查**，才能確定車子沒有任何問題。
- Ms. Perry **looked over** the students' papers before grading them.
  派瑞女士在打分數前，**仔細檢查**學生的報告。

51

🔊 027

形容詞片語

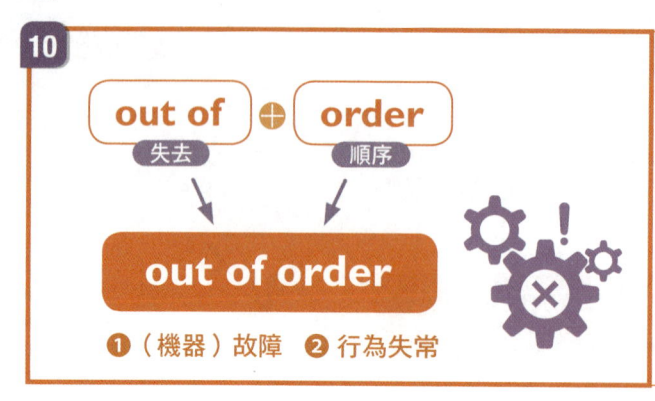

10

out of (失去) ＋ order (順序)
→ **out of order**
❶（機器）故障　❷ 行為失常

同 故障 out of commission
反 正常運作 in order

💡 **out of order** 通常置於 be 動詞後面，作為主詞補語，可表示「雜亂無章」或「機器故障」。**out of order** 解釋為「故障」時，通常是指公用物品，私人物品故障會使用 broken，如車子故障會寫成：「**The car broke down.**」。

❶ The snack machine at the office was **out of order**, so we went to a restaurant for lunch. 辦公室裡的點心販賣機**故障**了，所以我們到餐廳吃午餐。

❶ The sign on the pay phone informed Tina that it was **out of order**.
緹娜由公共電話上的標示得知電話**故障**了。

❷ The remark Harry made in the workshop yesterday was totally **out of order**.
哈利昨天在研討會所做的評論完全**錯誤**。

片語動詞　可分開　受詞為代名詞時定要分開

11

put (使朝向) ＋ out (消失)
→ **put out**
❶ 拿出去　❷ 關閉　❸ 熄滅
❹ 打擾　❺ 推出 及

用法
◆ **put out sb / put sb out**
對某人帶來不便
→ Would it **put** you **out** if we came Thursday? 假如我們星期四過去，是否會**造成**你的**不便**呢？

◆ **put out sth / put sth out**
使某物停止燃燒
→ Would you mind **putting** your cigarette **out**, please?
你介意**把菸熄掉**嗎？

◆ **put out sth / put sth out** 推出；生產
→ The company **puts out** millions of pairs of shoes a year.
該公司每年**生產**了好幾百萬雙鞋子。

💡 **out** 的解釋通常為「向外」，但在此指「消失」，類似 **blow out**（吹熄）、**run out**（用盡）。**put out** 後接 fire、lights 等名詞時，表示「撲滅、熄滅」，可用於被動語態。

❶ Dad asked me to **put out** the trash. 爸爸要我把垃圾**拿出去**。

❷ Please **put** the lights **out** before you leave the house. 出門前請把燈**關掉**。

❸ The campers poured water on the fire to **put** it **out**. 露營的人用水把火**澆熄**。

12

take 取得 ＋ time 時間 ＋ off 離開

→ **take (time) off**

（一段時間）不工作；休假 及

用法比較
- ◆ take sth off ……休假
- ◆ give sb time off 准某人休假

同 have (time) off

- time 通常為實際休假的時間，如 **take the afternoon off**（下午請假）。
- My wife's birthday is next Monday, so if possible, I'd like to **take** that day **off** of work. 下星期一是我老婆的生日，可以的話，那天我想要休假。
- The companies let the workers **take off** two weeks every year for vacation and holidays. 這家公司的員工每年都有兩個星期可以休假。

Unit 06 Test Yourself!

A 選擇題

1. Before leaving for his first date, Brandon _____ himself _____ in the mirror to make sure everything fit right.
   Ⓐ counted . . . on   Ⓑ looked . . . over   Ⓒ hung . . . up   Ⓓ got . . . on

2. I don't feel sick enough to see a doctor; I just feel _____.
   Ⓐ out of order   Ⓑ under the weather   Ⓒ counted on   Ⓓ hung up

3. My roommates _____ very easily, but I am shy and spend a lot of time alone.
   Ⓐ count on him   Ⓑ hang up   Ⓒ make friends   Ⓓ take off

4. What was _____ last weekend?
   Ⓐ going on   Ⓑ hanging up   Ⓒ taking off   Ⓓ counting on

5. It was totally quiet until a dog started barking loudly _____.
   Ⓐ under the weather   Ⓑ all of a sudden
   Ⓒ out of order   Ⓓ making friends

6. If you want your room to look neat, you should _____ your jacket and hat so they are not on the floor.
   Ⓐ hang up   Ⓑ make friends   Ⓒ count on   Ⓓ get to

7. Debbie's boss let her _____ a month after she had the baby.
   Ⓐ count on   Ⓑ hang up   Ⓒ take off   Ⓓ get to

8. Help us save electricity by _____ the lights in the room when you leave.
   Ⓐ hanging up   Ⓑ putting out   Ⓒ counting on   Ⓓ taking off

9. I was unable to get any money from the ATM because the sign said it was _____.
   Ⓐ under the weather   Ⓑ counted on   Ⓒ out of order   Ⓓ hung up

10. Jess is a nice person, but you can't ever _____ him to be on time.
    Ⓐ count on   Ⓑ hang up   Ⓒ get to   Ⓓ take off

11. Sometimes my little brother's bad behavior really _____ me.
    Ⓐ hangs up   Ⓑ makes friends with   Ⓒ gets to   Ⓓ takes off

B 閱讀文章，從字表中選擇詞彙填入，並依人稱時態等做適當的變化

all of a sudden	have . . . off	out of order
few and far between	make friends	look . . . over
hang up	count on	under the weather

It was a long day at work, and Miranda was feeling ❶ _____. Her new job as a stewardess was going well, but she was having a hard time ❷ _____ with her colleagues. There was, however, one exception: Damon. Damon was the kind of guy you could really ❸ _____ when you were in trouble, and friends like him are ❹ _____. Miranda was taking a break when, ❺ _____, the phone rang. It was Damon! He said that he ❻ _____ the weekend _____ and asked if she wanted to see a movie. Suddenly, she didn't feel sick anymore. Miranda ❼ _____ herself _____ in the mirror. She looked good, but she wanted to wash her new blouse, which was ❽ _____ in her closet. Unfortunately, her washing machine was ❾ _____. Oh well! She'd find something else to wear.

C 引導式翻譯，並依人稱時態等做適當的變化

1. 你有**關掉**樓下的燈嗎？
   Did you _____ the lights _____ downstairs?

2. 在你**掛電話**前，我想和喬治說句話。
   Let me speak to George before you _____ _____.

3. 詹姆斯停下來點了一根香菸，然後**繼續**描述意外發生的經過。
   James paused to light another cigarette and then _____ _____ with his account of the accident.

4. 這份工作**搞得我很煩**，我不知道我還能夠撐多久。
   This job's really _____ _____ me. I don't know how much longer I'll last.

5. 提姆**突然**覺得又熱又累。
   _____ _____ _____ _____, Tim felt very hot and tired.

Unit 07

Hunting for a New Job 找新工作

028

Steve tells Caroline why he wants a new job.
史帝夫告訴卡洛琳想要新工作的原因。

Caroline:	You've been quiet all weekend. I can't **figure out**[1] what's bothering you.	你整個週末都好安靜，我**想**不透你在煩惱什麼。
Steve:	I'm just thinking about my job. I don't like it so much. For one thing, I need to **be up**[2] at 5 a.m. if I want to get to the office **on time**[3]. And work **is**n't **over**[4] until 7 p.m.	我只是在想我的工作。我不是很喜歡我的工作。首先，我若想要**準時**上班，必須早上五點**起床**，然後一直工作到晚上七點才**結束**。
Caroline:	Oh! That sounds tough. What happens if you **get sick**[5]?	噢！聽起來真難熬。**生病**的話怎麼辦？
Steve:	My boss always makes me come in, no matter how sick I am.	無論我的病情有多嚴重，老闆總是要我去上班。
Caroline:	Now I see why you're **thinking of**[6] looking for another job.	我知道你為何**想**找別的工作了。
Steve:	Sometimes I **would rather**[7] not work at all, but then my sister **points out**[8] that I shouldn't leave this job before I find another one.	我有時候**寧願**完全不工作，但我姐姐**提醒**我，在找到其他工作前，我不應該辭掉這份工作。
Caroline:	I think she's right.	我想她說的對。

Unit 07 Hunting for a New Job 找新工作

1

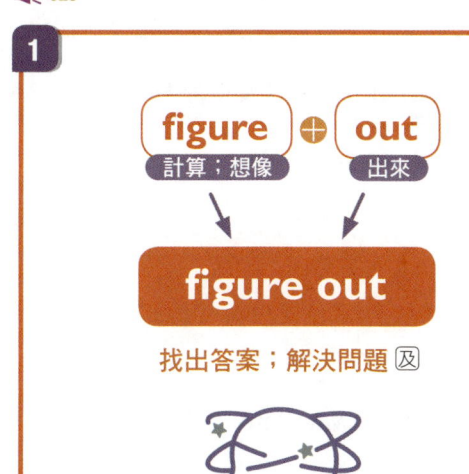

片語動詞 | 可分開 | 受詞為代名詞時定要分開

figure（計算；想像）+ **out**（出來）
→ **figure out** 找出答案；解決問題 及

用法
- **figure sb out / figure out sb** 理解某人
  → I find Susan really odd—I can't **figure** her **out** at all.
  我認為蘇珊是個怪人，我完全無法理解她的行為。

- **figure sth out / figure out sth** 理解某事
  → He spent an hour trying to install the software, but Rita finally **figured** it **out**.
  他花了一個小時試圖安裝軟體，但最後是靠芮塔找出問題。

同 **work out**

💡 **figure out** 後接表數量的名詞或名詞子句時，表示「計算出」；有時後接名詞或名詞子句則表示「想出、斷定」。

- No one could **figure out** how Darryl lost his keys. 沒人知道戴倫是如何弄丟鑰匙的。
- Every student looked at the puzzles, but no one could **figure** them **out**.
  每位學生都看著文字填空的題目，但沒人找得出答案。
- Laura couldn't **figure out** how she spent all her money.
  蘿拉想不透她是如何花光所有的錢。

2

慣用片語

be（是；表狀態）+ **up**（起來）
→ **be up** ❶ 醒來 ❷（時間）到了

同 起床 **get up**
反 就寢 **go to bed**

❶ Janet can't stay out too late tonight because she has to **be up** at 5 in the morning. 珍娜今晚不能在外面待到太晚，因為她必須早上五點起床。

❶ Although Gwen pretended to be asleep, she **was** really **up**.
雖然關假裝睡著了，但她其實是醒著的。

❷ The teacher told us when the time for the test **was up** and we had to put our pencils down. 老師說考試結束時，我們必須把鉛筆放下。

57

3

on 在……之上 + **time** 某時間 → **on time** 準時；依照時間

副詞片語

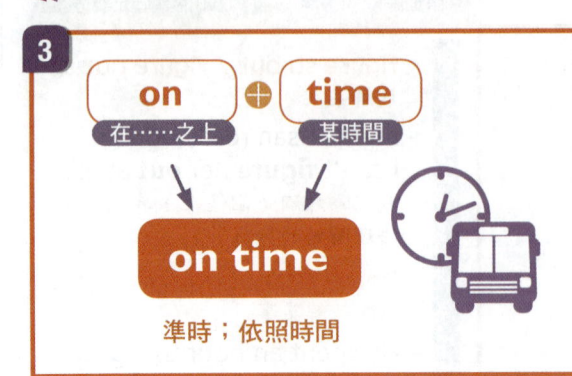

比較 ◆ in time 及時（參考第60頁）
同 on schedule

- Marianne never arrives anywhere **on time**; she's always late.
  瑪莉安從來沒有準時抵達過，她老是遲到。
- This bus is always **on time**, so you can rely on it.
  這班公車總是很準時，非常靠得住。

4

be 是；表狀態 + **over** 結束 → **be over** 結束

慣用片語

同
❶ finished
❷ ended
❸ alone

💡 表示「放學」可以寫成「School is over.」；表示「下課」可寫成「Class is over.」。

- What time **is** this show **over**? 這場表演何時會結束？
- French class **is over** before lunch. 法文課會在午餐前結束。

5

get 變得 + **sick** 生病 → **get sick** 生病

慣用片語

比較
◆ get well 好了　　◆ get wet 濕了
◆ get busy 忙碌　　◆ get tired 累了

→ After watching 10 minutes of the boring movie, Mitt **got tired**.
這部無聊的電影，米特才看10分鐘就累了。

◆ get mad 生氣
→ If you come home late, mom will **get mad**.
如果你太晚回家，媽媽會生氣。

同 feel sick

- **get** 也可換成 **be** 動詞，如 **be sick**。但在英式英文中，**be sick** 表示「想吐；反胃」，因此表示「反胃」時，使用 **be sick to one's stomach** 會更為明確。表示生病時，亦可使用「**get +** 疾病名稱」，如 **get food poisoning**（食物中毒）。

- The old man **got sick** while he was away and had to come home.
  那位老先生在外面的時候**生病了**，所以必須回家。

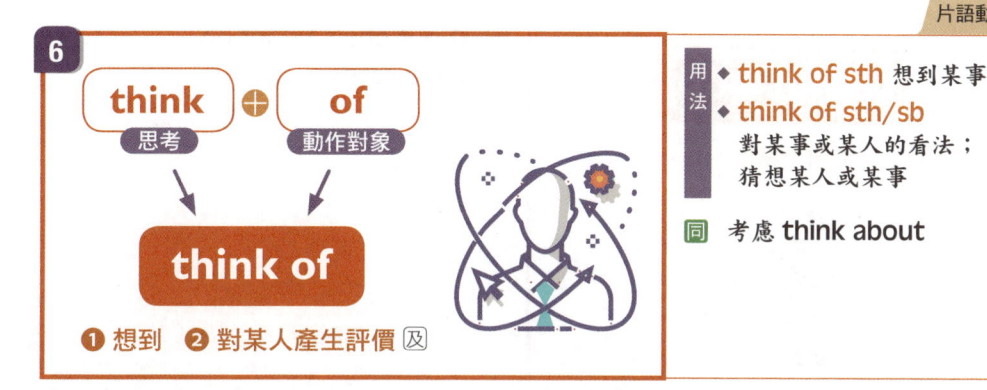

6　片語動詞

think（思考） + **of**（動作對象） → **think of**

❶ 想到　❷ 對某人產生評價（及）

用法
- **think of sth** 想到某事
- **think of sth/sb** 對某事或某人的看法；猜想某人或某事

同　考慮 **think about**

- **think of** 後接人、事、物時表示「想起」；後接動名詞時表示「打算做某事情」。

❶ Suddenly, Jon **thought of** a great idea for his new book and got to work.
強突然**想到**一個關於新書很棒的主意，並且開始進行。

❶ What do you **think of** the new mayor?　你覺得新上任的市長如何？

❷ Meredith was new in our class, so no one knew what to **think of** her.
瑪芮迪絲是我們班上的新生，所以沒有人對她**作出評論**。

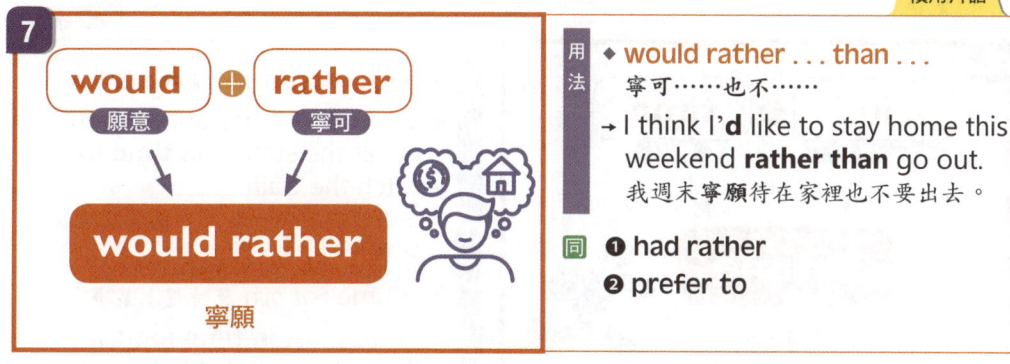

7　慣用片語

would（願意） + **rather**（寧可） → **would rather**
寧願

用法
- **would rather . . . than . . .**
  寧可……也不……
→ I think I'**d** like to stay home this weekend **rather than** go out.
  我週末**寧願**待在家裡也不要出去。

同　❶ had rather
　　❷ prefer to

- 常縮寫為「'**d rather**」，否定型式為 **would rather not**。後接不帶 **to** 的不定詞時，表示「現在或將來寧願」；後接 **that** 子句時，表示「某人寧願另一人做某事」。**would rather** 的意思和 **had rather** 相同，皆用於假設語氣，但 **would rather** 的語氣較為強烈，常與 **than** 搭配使用，表示「寧可……也不……」。

- Instead of going shopping today, I'**d** much **rather** stay home and watch TV.
  與其要我今天去逛街，我**寧願**待在家裡看電視。

- **Would** you **rather** live in Florida or Georgia?
  你**比較**想住在佛羅里達州還是喬治亞州？

8

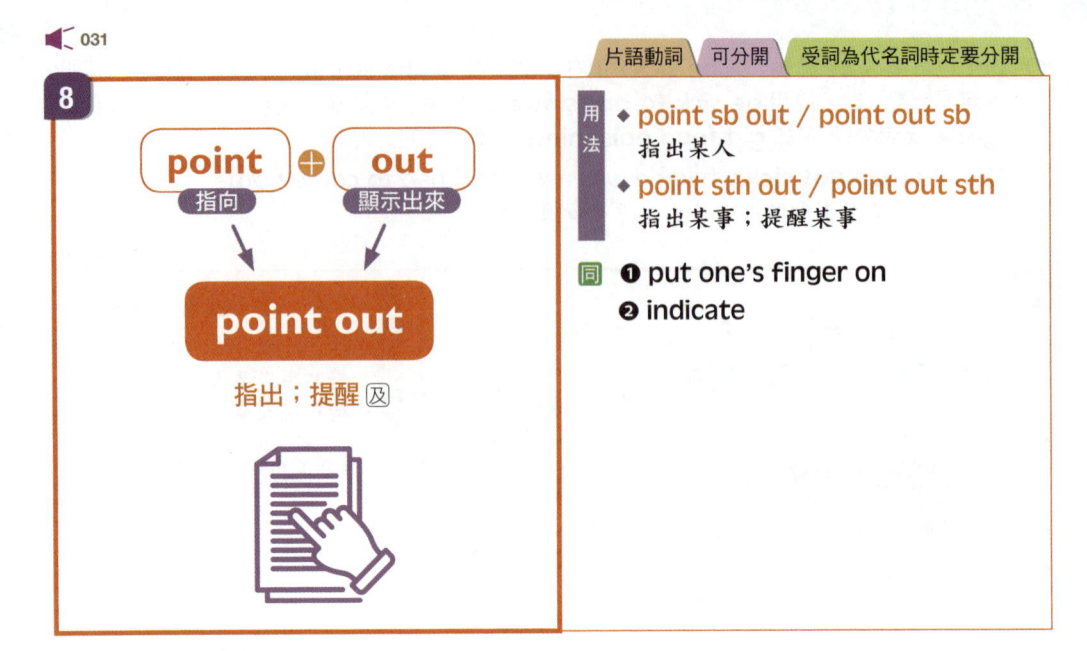

point (指向) + **out** (顯示出來) → **point out** 指出；提醒 及

片語動詞 | 可分開 | 受詞為代名詞時定要分開

用法
- **point sb out / point out sb**
  指出某人
- **point sth out / point out sth**
  指出某事；提醒某事

同
1. put one's finger on
2. indicate

💡 **point out** 表示「指出」，可分開使用，後可接具體的人、事、物，亦可接抽象的名詞或子句。

- Tory **pointed out** her sister to us. 托莉把她的姐姐**指**給我們看。
- Before his mom **pointed out** that today is Friday, Wayne thought he had to go to school tomorrow. 在偉恩的媽媽**指出**今天是星期五前，他一直以為隔天還要上課。
- I thought that my English was perfect, but my teacher **pointed** my mistakes **out**. 我以為我的英文很通順，但老師**指出**了我的錯誤。

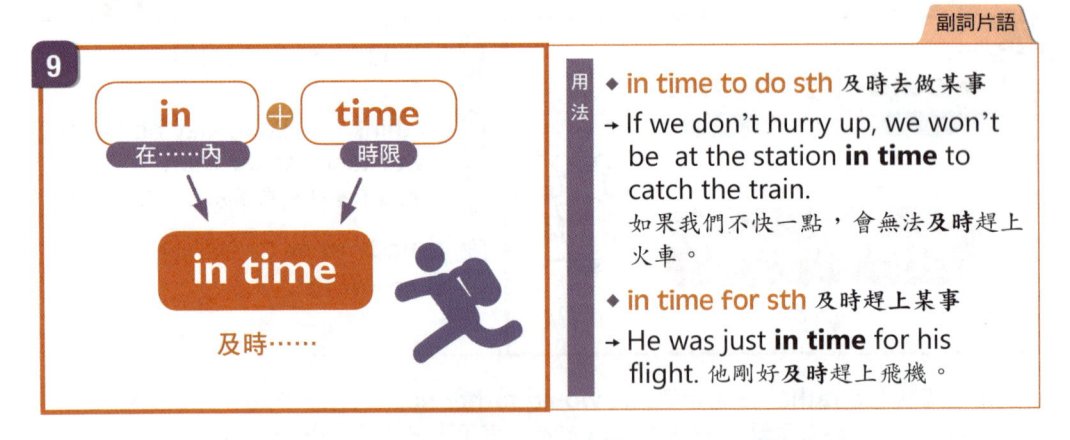

9

in (在……內) + **time** (時限) → **in time** 及時……

副詞片語

用法
- **in time to do sth** 及時去做某事
  → If we don't hurry up, we won't be at the station **in time** to catch the train.
  如果我們不快一點，會無法**及時**趕上火車。

- **in time for sth** 及時趕上某事
  → He was just **in time** for his flight. 他剛好**及時**趕上飛機。

💡 **in time** 是「及時、來得及」的意思，**time** 在這裡是指時限 (**time limit**)。

- If we don't leave now, you won't get to the airport **in time** to catch your flight.
  我們若不現在離開，你就無法**及時**趕到機場登機。
- Sean needs to be home **in time** to meet his sister.
  西恩必須**及時**趕回家，才能和他的姐姐碰面。

60

10

call（召喚）＋ **it**（它）＋ **a day**（一天）
→ **call it a day** 結束當天的工作；到此為止

慣用片語

用法
- ◆ **call it a night** 結束當晚的工作
- → The men **called it a night** after spending most of the evening going over the architectural blueprints.
  那些男人在看了幾乎整晚的建築物藍圖後，**結束了當晚的工作**。

💡 **call it a day** 表示「結束當天的工作、下班」，這種用法常出現在工作場合中。

- After spending the entire morning and afternoon working on her report, Liana decided to **call it a day**. 黎安娜整個早上和下午都在忙報告，她決定今天就**到此為止**。

11

get（變得）＋ **better**（更好）
→ **get better** 情況好轉

慣用片語

- 同 become better
- 反 惡化 get worse

💡 **get** 表示「變得……」，意思和 **become** 相同，後可接形容詞原級或比較級，例如 **sick**、**well**、**tired**、**busy**、**wet**、**nervous** 和 **excited** 等。

- Despite practicing every day, George never really **got better** at the piano.
  儘管喬治每天練習，但他的鋼琴技巧卻不見**進步**。

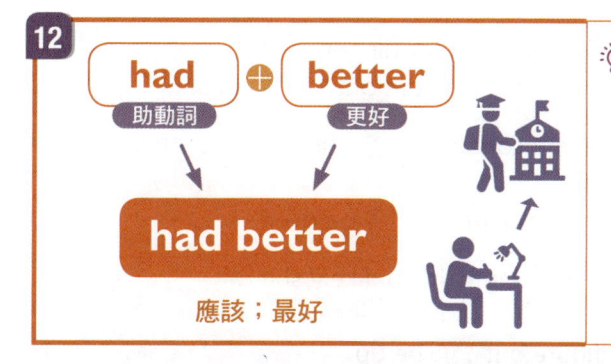

12

had（助動詞）＋ **better**（更好）
→ **had better** 應該；最好

慣用片語

💡 **had better** 只有一種型式，常縮寫為「**'d better**」，後接原形動詞，表示「應該……最好」，常用於提出建議或間接命令時。**better** 在此並無比較的意思。口語中常省略 **had**。

- If you want to go to Yale, you**'d better** study more.
  如果你想進入耶魯，**最好**多讀點書。
- Sam **had better** practice the flute every day if he wants to play in an orchestra.
  如果山姆想要進入管絃樂隊，**最好**每天練習吹長笛。

Unit 07 Test Yourself!

A 選擇題

1. Too bad you didn't come _____ to say goodbye.
   Ⓐ in time   Ⓑ point out   Ⓒ figure out   Ⓓ call it a day

2. Although we tried our best to stay dry in the rainstorm, it wasn't long before we all _____.
   Ⓐ figured it out   Ⓑ were over   Ⓒ got wet   Ⓓ pointed out

3. When will this semester _____?
   Ⓐ figure out   Ⓑ point out   Ⓒ call it a day   Ⓓ be over

4. Cynthia was surprised that she didn't get an "A" in math, but her teacher _____ that she didn't do all the homework.
   Ⓐ pointed out   Ⓑ was over   Ⓒ would rather   Ⓓ called it a day

5. My boss says I must always _____ for work.
   Ⓐ be on time   Ⓑ be up   Ⓒ be over   Ⓓ be through

6. Raul spent a few hours researching the report, but he just couldn't _____ what to write next.
   Ⓐ think of   Ⓑ be over   Ⓒ call it a day   Ⓓ run about

7. The doctor told Faith that she _____ get more sleep if she wants to get over the flu.
   Ⓐ would rather   Ⓑ had better   Ⓒ was over   Ⓓ thought of

8. Amelia _____ the more she argued with her boyfriend.
   Ⓐ was over   Ⓑ figured out   Ⓒ got angrier   Ⓓ was on time

9. I _____ get Indian food than Chinese food for dinner.
   Ⓐ think one might   Ⓑ would rather   Ⓒ figure out to   Ⓓ might

10. The members of the football team couldn't _____ how they lost the game; it was too hard to understand.
    Ⓐ figure out   Ⓑ think up   Ⓒ get better at   Ⓓ be over

11. Rosita was playing video games all night; it's unlikely she will _____ in time for school.
    Ⓐ be over   Ⓑ get wet   Ⓒ figure out   Ⓓ be up

12. I'm so tired! Let's _____ and order some pizza.
    Ⓐ get worse   Ⓑ call it a day   Ⓒ think of it   Ⓓ get sick

B 閱讀文章，從字表中選擇詞彙填入，並依人稱時態等做適當的變化

be up	get better	be over	on time
would rather	point out	figure out	think of
in time	had better		

　　Randy tried his best to be ❶ _____, but he was always late. His family and friends ❷ _____ this _____ to him many times, but somehow Randy never ❸ _____ at being on time. People knew that if Randy said he would come at 7, they ❹ _____ arrive at 8 or else they'd be waiting for him for an hour.

　　On the day of his sister's wedding, Randy promised that things would be different. He ❺ _____ early and ❻ _____ the best way to get to the church by looking at a map. He even ❼ _____ a nice speech to give when the ceremony ❽ _____. Although he ❾ _____ have been in bed or watching TV, he made it to the church ❿ _____ to see his sister get married. Everyone in the family was very surprised.

C 引導式翻譯，並依人稱時態等做適當的變化

1. 你覺得我的新鞋如何？
   What do you _____ _____ my new shoes?

2. 我覺得有點累了，是否該結束今天的工作了呢？
   I'm getting a bit tired now. Shall we _____ _____ _____ _____?

3. 我想不透他為何要這麼做。
   I can't _____ _____ why he did it.

4. 週末的火車幾乎從不準時。
   The train is almost never _____ _____ on the weekends.

Unit 08

Planning for the Weekend 週末計畫

Douglas and Mary consider how to spend their weekend.
道格拉斯和瑪麗在考慮如何度過這個週末。

Mary:	Let's go to the opera this weekend! It's from Italy, and it'll be a good chance for me to **brush up on**[1] my Italian.	我們這週末去看歌劇吧！那是一齣義大利歌劇，對我來說，這會是一個**複習**義大利文的好機會。
Douglas:	I know we said that we would **take turns**[2] deciding what to do on the weekends, and even though it's your turn, I was hoping we could **go out**[3] and see a baseball game.	我知道我們說好要**輪流**決定週末要做些什麼，不過就算這星期是輪到妳決定，我還是希望我們可以**出去**看籃球比賽。
Mary:	Well, you need to **pay attention to**[4] the weather; it's supposed to rain, so going to see the game is totally **out of the question**[5].	噢，你必須多**注意**天氣。那天可能會下雨，所以絕對**不可能**去看比賽的。
Douglas:	Who cares about a little rain?	下毛毛雨有什麼關係？
Mary:	I've told you **over and over again**[6] that I hate getting cold and wet.	我**一再**告訴你，我討厭變冷和被淋濕。
Douglas:	Well, I **was about to**[7] buy the tickets online—but if you're sure you don't want to go, I guess the opera won't be so bad. However, I don't think there are hot dogs at the opera.	噯，我**正要**上網買票。但妳如果真的不想去，我想歌劇也不是個太差的主意。不過，我認為歌劇院裡不會有賣熱狗。

64

🔊 033

片語動詞 | **不可分開**

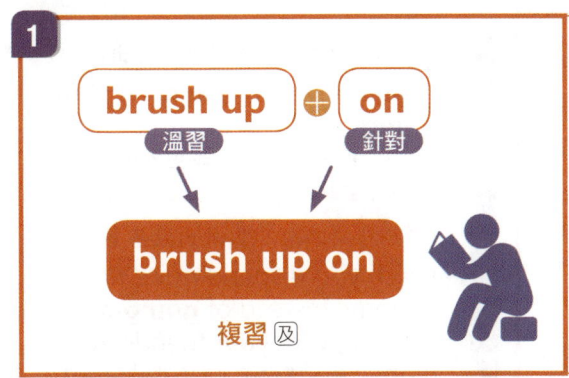

1

brush up (溫習) + **on** (針對) → **brush up on** 複習 ㊥

用法: **brush up on sth** 複習某事物

同: brush up

- I really need to **brush up on** my Japanese before visiting Tokyo next month.
我真的需要在下個月去東京前，**複習**一下我的日文。
- Ivan **brushed up on** Greek history before the test. 艾文在考試前**複習**希臘歷史。
- **Brushing up on** computer skills is important for anyone who is thinking about getting a new job. **複習**電腦技能對想換新工作的人來說很重要。

慣用片語

2

take (採取) + **turns** (輪流) → **take turns** 輪流

用法:
- **take turns doing sth** 輪流做某事
→ The students **took turns** reading the story aloud in class.
學生**輪流**在課堂上把故事大聲唸出來。

- **take turns to do sth** 輪流做某事
→ We **take turns** answering the phone.
我們**輪流**接聽電話。

比較:
- **by turns** 交替；輪流
- **in turn** 按順序
→ Each of us collects the mail **in turn**.
我們每個人**按照順序**領取信件。

同:
❶ take one's turn
❷ alternate
❸ take it in turns（英式用法）

💡 take turns 後常接動名詞，表示「輪流做某事情」。英式英文中，亦可後接不定詞。

- When the kids play on the swings, we try to make sure they **take turns**.
他們在盪鞦韆的時候，我們試著讓每個孩子**輪流**玩。
- Ariel and Mac **took turns** using the laptop.
艾芮兒和麥可輪流使用筆記型電腦。

Unit 08　Planning for the Weekend　週末計畫

3

go (去) + **out** (外面) → **go out**

❶ 離開（家、學校、辦公室）外出
❷ 熄滅 [不及]

用法

- go out for sth 為某事而外出
  → It's terribly smoky in here—I'm **going out for** a breath of fresh air. 這裡煙霧瀰漫，我要**出去**呼吸一下新鮮空氣。

- go out doing sth 外出做某事
  → I wish you'd spend more time at home instead of **going out** drinking with your friends every night. 我希望你能多花一些時間待在家裡，不要每晚都和朋友**出去**喝酒。

- go out with sb 與某人約會、交往
  → How long have you been **going out with** Jason? 你和傑森**交往**多久了呢？

❶ We usually **go out** on the weekends and have dinner or see a movie.
我們週末通常都會**出去**吃晚餐或看電影。

❶ Do you want to **go out** after work today? 你今天下班後想要**出去**嗎？

❷ When the fire **went out**, it started to get cold. 火熄滅後就開始變冷了。

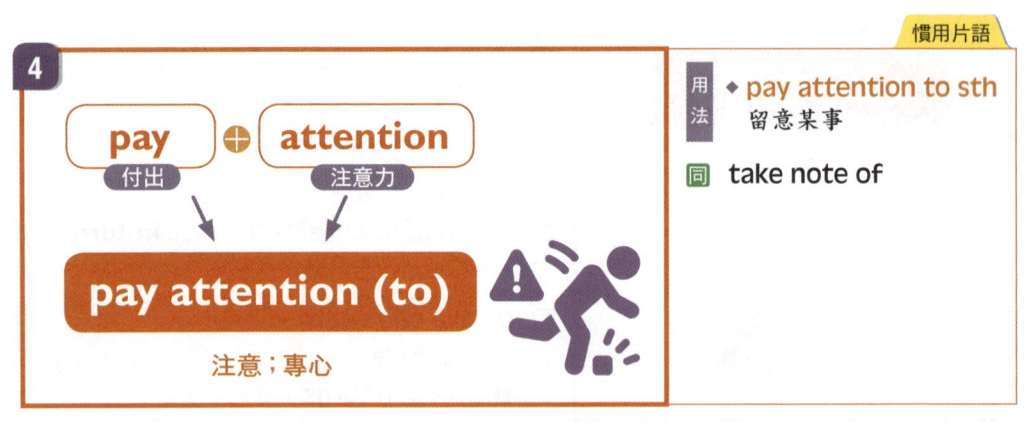

4 慣用片語

pay (付出) + **attention** (注意力) → **pay attention (to)**

注意；專心

用法

- pay attention to sth 留意某事
- 同 take note of

💡 to 為介系詞，後需接**名詞**或**動名詞**。

- It's no wonder you didn't pass the test; you never **pay attention** to what the professor is saying. 難怪你沒通過考試，你從不**注意**教授說的話。

- Don't **pay** any **attention** to what that woman says; she's crazy.
別去**注意**那女人說的話，她瘋了。

形容詞片語

5

out of (在……之外) + the question (某個問題)

↓

out of the question

不可能發生

用法
- **be out of the question**
  某事不可能發生
- **be no question of (doing) sth**
  不可能做某事情
→ There's **no question of** agreeing to the demands.
  我們**不可能**同意這項要求。

同 impossible
反 possible

💡 out of the question 通常只可以作為**主詞補語**，表示「不可能的；不值得考慮的」。

- Unless I pay for the trip myself, going to Boston is **out of the question**.
  除非我自己出錢，否則波士頓之旅是**不可能**成行的。
- Buying that huge TV is totally **out of the question** unless I win the lottery.
  除非我中樂透，否則絕對**不可能**買那台大電視。

副詞片語

6

over (一次) + and (又) + over (一次)

↓

over and over (again)

一再；再三

同
❶ again and again
❷ time and again
❸ once again

💡 over and over (again) 為副詞片語。通常置於句尾，作修飾語。指「一再；重複」。

- I hate to do the same work **over and over**. 我討厭**反覆**做同樣的工作。
- The little boy kept asking **over and over** if I'd buy him some candy.
  那個小男孩**一再**問我是否會買一些糖果給他。
- Ed read the article **over and over again** until he finally understood the main idea. 艾德把文章讀了**一遍又一遍**，直到他終於了解重點。
- I read the article **over and over** till it made sense.
  我把文章看過**一遍又一遍**，直到看懂為止。

67

7

be about (打算) + **to** (要)

→ **be about to**

正要去做；準備去做

用法
- be about to do sth 正要做某事

同
1. be just going to
2. be on the point of

- We **were on the point of** giving up hope when the letter arrived.
  就當我們正要放棄希望時，信就送到了。

反 just now

💡 **be about to** 後接**原形動詞**，表示以**客觀的角度**描述「即將發生的事情；正要……」。
要記住，**be about to** 不能搭配表**未來**的時間副詞使用。

- I **was** just **about to** leave the house when the phone rang.
  當我正要出門時，電話響了。
- What **were** you **about to** do when the Martins arrived?
  馬汀一家來的時候你原本要做什麼？

8

have (有) + **to do with** (與……有關)

→ **have to do with**

1. 與……有關
2. 在不同的情況（困境）中生存

用法
- have to do with sth 與某事有關
- have to do with sb 與某人有關
- have much to do with
  與……有很大關係
- have something to do with
  與……有些關係
- have nothing to do with
  與……沒有關係

同 與……有關 be to do with

❶ This conversation doesn't **have to do with** you, so please go away.
這段談話**與你無關**，所以請你走開。

❷ The restaurant didn't have any cake, so Joe **had to do with** the fruit salad.
這家餐廳沒有蛋糕，所以喬只好吃水果沙拉。

❷ When Esther lost her job, she **had to** learn to **do with** less.
當愛絲特丟了工作，她必須學會在**困境中生存**。

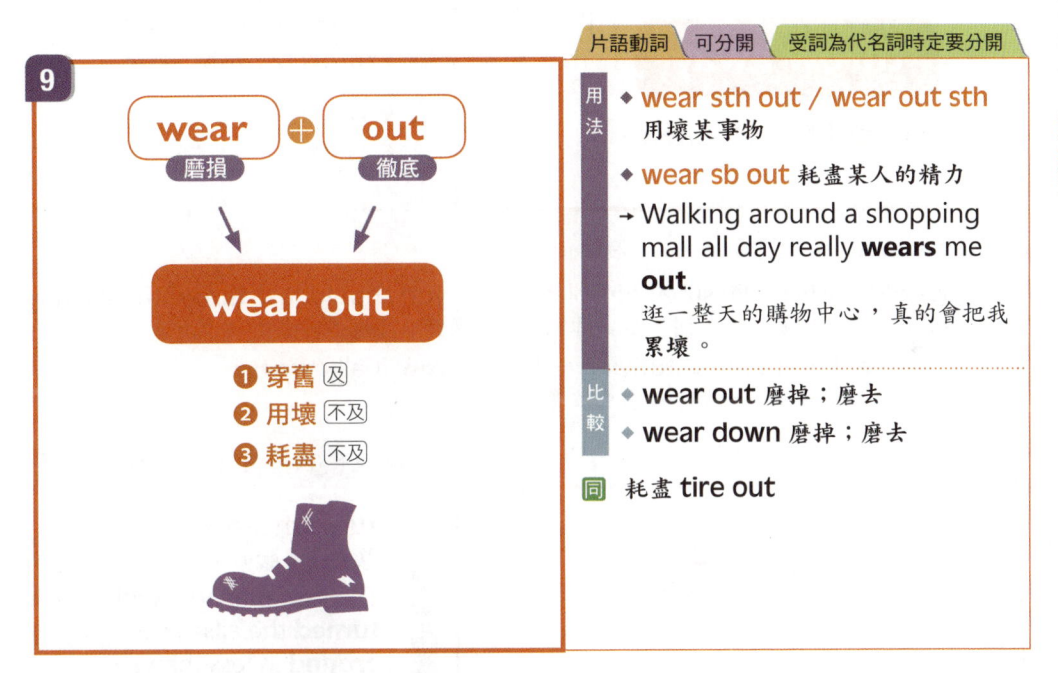

9

wear 磨損 ＋ out 徹底
↓
wear out

❶ 穿舊 及
❷ 用壞 不及
❸ 耗盡 不及

| 片語動詞 | 可分開 | 受詞為代名詞時定要分開 |

用法
◆ **wear sth out / wear out sth**
用壞某事物
◆ **wear sb out** 耗盡某人的精力
→ Walking around a shopping mall all day really **wears** me **out**.
逛一整天的購物中心，真的會把我累壞。

比較
◆ **wear out** 磨掉；磨去
◆ **wear down** 磨掉；磨去

同 耗盡 **tire out**

💡 ❶ **wear out** 表示「**穿舊**」時，作及物動詞，可分開使用，主詞為人；表示「**用壞**」時，作不及物動詞，主詞為壞掉的東西。

❷ **wear out** 亦表示「疲乏；耗盡」，主詞為**人**時，使用**被動語態**；主詞為**抽象名詞**時，則使用**主動語態**。

❸ **wear away**、**wear down** 和 **wear off** 皆有「**磨損**」的意思，但較接近「磨掉；磨去」，而 **wear out** 則較接近「磨破；用壞」。

❶ I love these jeans so much, but it's only a matter of time before they **wear out**.
我很喜歡這件牛仔褲，但它遲早會被**穿舊**。

❸ If you don't turn the digital camera off when you're not using it, you'll **wear out** the batteries quickly. 不使用數位相機時若沒有關閉，電池很快會**耗盡**。

10

throw(拋) + **away**(離開) → **throw away**

❶ 扔掉　❷ 浪費（才能或機會）及

| 片語動詞 | 可分開 | 受詞為代名詞時定要分開 |

用法
- throw sth away 扔掉某事物

比較
- throw in 插入
- throw one's money around 亂花錢
- throw over 拋棄；斷絕關係
- throw off 扔掉；擺脫

同
❶ desert
❷ waste

💡 **throw away** 有「因愚蠢而丟失；浪費」的意思。

❶ Those old shirts really smell terrible; maybe you should just **throw** them **away**.
那些舊襯衫的味道真的很難聞，也許你該把它們丟了。

❷ You've spent four hours studying—don't **throw** it all **away**.
你已經唸了四小時了，千萬不要白白浪費了。

11

turn(轉向) + **around**(往相反方向) → **turn around**

❶ 轉向 及 不及
❷ 使情勢徹底改觀 不及

| 片語動詞 | 可分開 | 受詞為代名詞時定要分開 |

用法
- turn sth around 改善某事物的情況
  → The new management team **turned** the ailing company **around** in less than six months.
  新的管理團隊不到六個月的時間就改善了公司的營運狀況。

💡 **turn around** 原指「轉身；轉向」，亦可用來表示「情況好轉」或「改變先前的想法」。名詞為 **turnaround**。

❶ When Ike **turned around**, he saw that the puppy was following him home.
艾克轉身發現那隻小狗在跟他回家。

❶ As soon as Rachel realized that she had forgotten her camera, she **turned** the car **around** and went back home. 芮秋一發現忘了帶相機，就將車掉頭回家。

❷ When the weather got better, the entire weekend **turned around,** and we finally had a good time at the beach.
整個週末隨著天空放晴而改變，我們於是在海邊度過了一段愉快的時光。

12

fall 墜入 + **in love** 愛

→ **fall in love**

墜入情網

用法	◆ **fall in love with sb** 愛上某人
	◆ **fall in love with sb at first sight** 與某人一見鍾情
比較	◆ **fall for sb** 愛上某人
	→ Yvonne always **falls for** unsuitable men. 伊芳總是愛錯人。
同	❶ be stuck on　❷ be in love with
反	吵架 fall out

慣用片語

- Four weeks after **falling in love** with Maria, Jack asked her to marry him.
  傑克和瑪麗亞墜入愛河四星期後，他便向她求婚了。
- As soon as Verona saw Sid, she **fell in love**.
  薇諾娜一見到希德便愛上他了。

Unit 08 Test Yourself!

A 選擇題

1. Mom told the children that if they couldn't play with the toy together, they would have to _____ playing with it.
   Ⓐ go out   Ⓑ take turns   Ⓒ turn around   Ⓓ brush up

2. Those winter boots look cheap; I'm sure they will _____ fast.
   Ⓐ wear out   Ⓑ take turns   Ⓒ brush up   Ⓓ turn around

3. The class was interesting to Lulu because it _____ her favorite topic: French history.
   Ⓐ brushed up on   Ⓑ had to do with   Ⓒ fell in love with   Ⓓ turned around

4. We _____ order dinner when Isadora suddenly felt sick.
   Ⓐ turned around to   Ⓑ were about to
   Ⓒ took turns to   Ⓓ paid attention to

5. It seems as if Amanda really has _____ with your older brother; she talks about him all day.
   Ⓐ fallen in love   Ⓑ turned around   Ⓒ taken turns   Ⓓ brushed up

6. Wendy is a good daughter and always _____ what her parents tell her.
   Ⓐ falls in love with   Ⓑ pays attention to   Ⓒ takes turns with   Ⓓ goes out

7. This is Tabitha's favorite movie; she has watched it _____.
   Ⓐ turned around   Ⓑ over and over again   Ⓒ brushing up   Ⓓ taken turns

8. I heard someone calling my name, so I _____ to see who it was.
   Ⓐ took turns   Ⓑ brushed up   Ⓒ fell in love   Ⓓ turned around

9. Mira _____ the uneaten food because there was not enough room in the fridge.
   Ⓐ paid attention to   Ⓑ threw out   Ⓒ turned around   Ⓓ fell in love with

10. Gina _____ the piano music before the big concert because she hadn't practiced in a long time.
    Ⓐ turned around   Ⓑ brushed up on
    Ⓒ fell in love with   Ⓓ paid attention to

11. On her first night in Miami, Daphne decided to _____ and explore the city.
    Ⓐ brush up   Ⓑ go out   Ⓒ fall in love   Ⓓ turn around

12. I know it is a nice day, but going to the beach is _____ because I don't have time.
    Ⓐ about to   Ⓑ turned around   Ⓒ out of the question   Ⓓ falling in love

B 閱讀文章，從字表中選擇詞彙填入，並依人稱時態等做適當的變化

be about to	over and over again	pay attention to
wear out	fall in love	turn around
go out	brush up on	out of the question

Nathan tried calling Kristen, but she didn't pick up her phone. He kept trying ❶ _____ until finally she answered. Kristen told him that her cell phone's battery had ❷ _____, but she had recharged it, so they could talk now.

The reason Nathan called Kristen was to ask her to ❸ _____ with him. Kristen agreed, and they decided to meet at the mall. Just as Kristen ❹ _____ enter the mall, she remembered that she was supposed to ❺ _____ her English for the big test on Monday. So she ❻ _____ and went back home.

On the way home, she called Nathan on his cell phone to tell him that meeting him was ❼ _____ because she was too busy. At times, she thought she was ❽ _____ with him, but she knew that this was a bad idea because she needed to ❾ _____ her schoolwork, and focus on getting into a good university.

C 引導式翻譯，並依人稱時態等做適當的變化

1. 我的初戀在 18 歲。
   I was 18 when I first _____ _____ _____.

2. 這趟旅途**把**傑克給**累壞了**，所以他一到飯店便倒頭大睡。
   The journey _____ Jack _____, and he went straight to bed as soon as he got to the hotel.

3. 我的其中一位同事**將要**生第二胎了。
   One of my friends at work _____ _____ _____ have her second baby.

4. 你不應該**扔掉**這些報紙的，它們可以回收。
   You shouldn't _____ those newspapers _____ ; they are recyclable.

Unit 09

🔊 037

Writing a Children's Book
童書創作

Grace tells John about her ideas for an upcoming children's book. 葛芮絲把有關新童書的想法告訴約翰。

Grace:	Good morning, John! Why are you so sleepy?	早安，約翰！為什麼你這麼沒精神？
John:	Well, when you **got in touch with**[1] me this morning to invite me out for coffee, you **woke** me **up**[2].	唔，妳今天早上和我**聯絡**、約我出去喝咖啡時，把我**吵醒**了。
Grace:	I'm sorry about that! Actually, I wanted to see you right away because I'd like you to help me write a children's book. I know you're a great artist, so I want you to **be in charge of**[3] the drawings in the book. Can you do that?	真是抱歉！事實上，我當時急著找你，是因為我希望你能幫我寫一本童書。我知道你是一個很棒的畫家，所以想要請你**負責**書中的插畫。可以嗎？
John:	Sure. I'll have a lot of time **as soon as**[4] I finish classes next week. This sounds like a fun project. I bet I'll **have a good time**[5] working with you.	當然。只要**一**結束下星期的課，我**就**會有許多時間。這聽起來是一個很有趣的案子。我相信和妳合作會**很愉快的**。
Grace:	I think you will. Together, we'll have the entire book finished **in no time**[6]. Have you ever done anything like this before?	沒錯。我們**很快**就會一起完成整本書。你曾經做過類似的工作嗎？
John:	Well, I **used to**[7] draw cartoons for a comic book, so it shouldn't be hard to **get used to**[8] this kind of project.	嗯，我**以前畫過**卡通漫畫，所以要**適應**這件案子並不難。
Grace:	Perfect!	太棒了！

Unit 09 Writing a Children's Book 童書創作

慣用片語

1

get 取得 + **in touch** 接觸 + **with** 與

↓ ↓

get in touch with

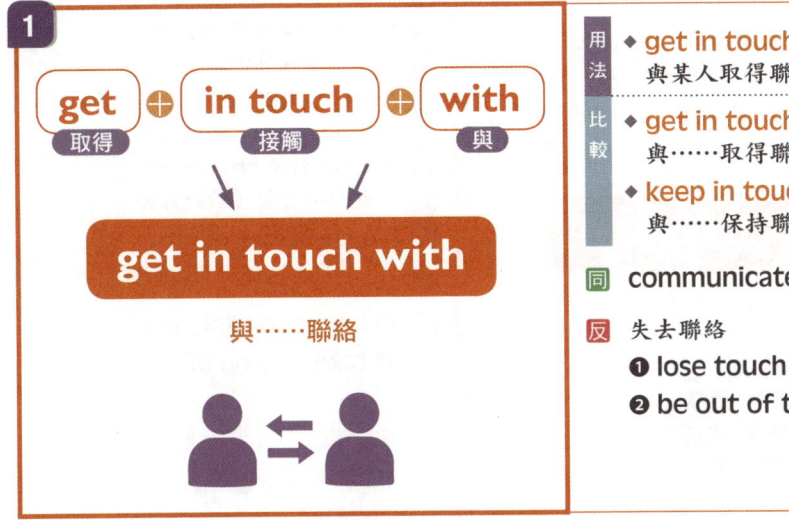

與……聯絡

用法 ◆ **get in touch with sb**
與某人取得聯絡

比較 ◆ **get in touch**
與……取得聯絡（強調動作）

◆ **keep in touch**
與……保持聯絡（強調狀態）

同 **communicate with**

反 失去聯絡
① **lose touch with**
② **be out of touch**

- Verona will **get in touch with** you as soon as she hears some news.
  薇諾娜一有消息就會和你聯絡。
- It's been years since he **got in touch with** my cousin.
  他已經和我表哥聯絡了好幾年。

2

片語動詞 可分開 受詞為代名詞時定要分開

wake 醒著 + **up** 起來

↓ ↓

wake up

① 醒來 不及　② 叫醒 及　③ 使警覺 不及

用法 ◆ **wake sb up**
叫醒某人；使某人覺醒

→ I set the alarm clock to **wake** me **up** at 6 a.m.
我設了早上六點的鬧鐘叫我起床。

◆ **wake up to sth** 開始警覺到某事

→ Governments are finally **waking up to** the fact that the environment should be cleaned up.
政府終於警覺到生態環境需要整頓了。

① What time did you **wake up** this morning? 你今天早上幾點起床？
② Companies need to **wake up** and take notice of the public's increasing concerns about the environment.
公司必須有所警覺，注意民眾有越來越關心環境問題的趨勢。

75

3

be in (在……中) + **charge** (掌控) + **of** (行為對象)

→ **be in charge of**
負責；管理

慣用片語

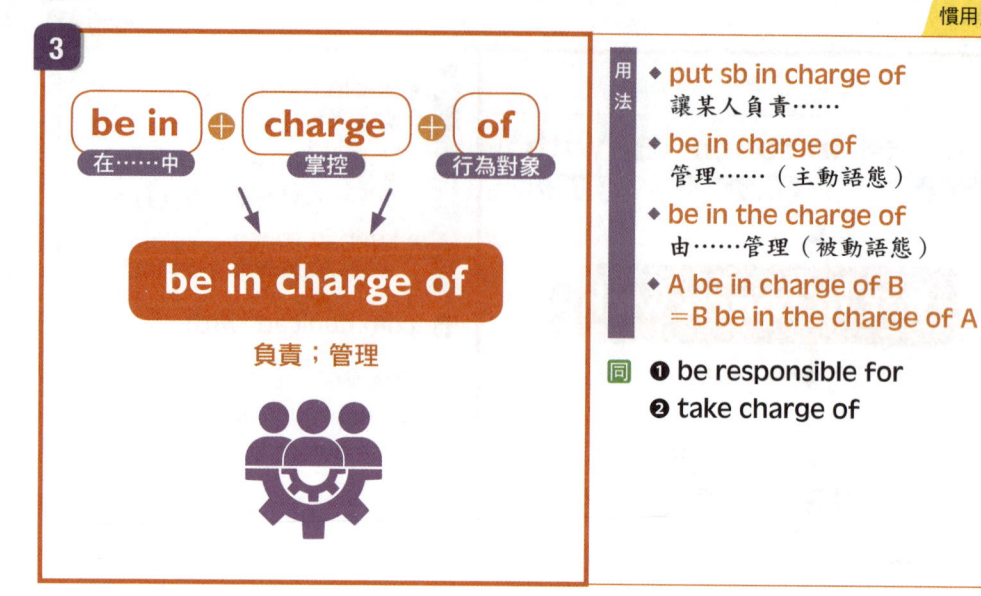

用法:
- put sb in charge of
  讓某人負責……
- be in charge of
  管理……（主動語態）
- be in the charge of
  由……管理（被動語態）
- A be in charge of B
  ＝B be in the charge of A

同:
❶ be responsible for
❷ take charge of

💡 **in charge of** 表示「負責管理……」，為主動語態，可用來修飾或作主詞補語，作主詞補語時，主詞通常為人。

- Emily **is in charge of** the class pet this week.
  艾蜜莉這星期要**負責**照顧班上的寵物。
- Jeremy is the football team's coach, so he**'s in charge of** making sure the players perform well.
  傑諾米是足球隊的教練，所以他**負責**確保球員都能有好的表現。

4

as (像) + **soon** (迅速地) + **as** (與……一樣)

→ **as soon as**
❶ 立即 ❷ 一……就……

副詞片語

用法:
- as soon as possible 儘快
  → We need the repairs done **as soon as** possible.
  我們必須**儘快**修好。

同: 一……就……
the moment (that)

💡 **as soon as** 為連接詞，可用來引導時間副詞子句，第一個 **as** 為副詞，第二個 **as** 為連接詞。
as fast as 指「速度和……一樣快」，但 **as soon as** 表示「一……就……」。

❶ I'll call you **as soon as** I can. 我會**儘快**打電話給你。
❷ **As soon as** I opened the door, I knew there was a problem.
  我一開門，**就**知道有問題。

5

have 擁有 + **a good time** 一段美好時光
↓ ↓
have a good time
玩得愉快

慣用片語

同
❶ have fun
❷ have a lot of fun

反 過得不愉快
❶ have a bad time
❷ have a hard time

- Did you **have a good time** at the concert last weekend?
  你在上週末的演唱會中**玩得愉快**嗎？
- My older sister **had a good time** at the park because the weather was perfect.
  天氣很好，我姐姐在公園**玩得很愉快**。

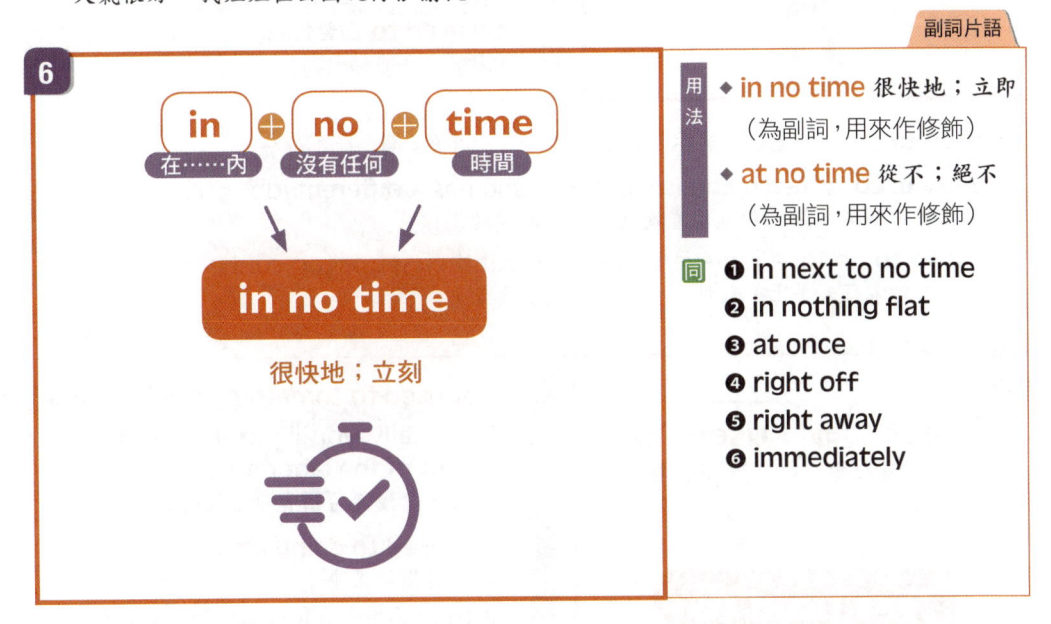

6

副詞片語

in 在……內 + **no** 沒有任何 + **time** 時間
↓ ↓
in no time
很快地；立刻

用法
◆ **in no time** 很快地；立即
（為副詞，用來作修飾）
◆ **at no time** 從不；絕不
（為副詞，用來作修飾）

同
❶ in next to no time
❷ in nothing flat
❸ at once
❹ right off
❺ right away
❻ immediately

- The book was so interesting that the students finished it **in no time**.
  這本書非常有趣，學生**很快**就看完了。
- Dylan had been thinking about his Greek history report for several days, so when he started working, he finished it **in no time**.
  狄倫過去幾天一直在思索希臘歷史報告，所以他開始不久後，**很快**便完成了。
- I pulled my blanket around me, and **in no time**, I was fast asleep.
  我蓋上毯子後**很快地**便進入夢鄉。

🔊 040

7

慣用片語

used (過去習慣) ＋ **to** (不定詞)
↓   ↓
used to
過去經常；過去習慣

用法
- ◆ **used to do something**
  過去經常做某事；過去習慣做某事
- → I **used to** visit my parents at Christmas every year.
  以前每年聖誕節我都會回去探望父母。
- → Ruby **used to** love cats; however, one attacked her, and she doesn't like them anymore.
  盧比曾經很喜歡貓咪，但被貓攻擊後，她便不再喜歡牠們了。

比較
- ◆ **used to** 過去經常；過去習慣
  （後接原形動詞）
- ◆ **get used to**
  逐漸適應；過去不習慣的變成習慣
  （後接名詞或動名詞）
- ◆ **become used to** 逐漸適應；習慣於
  （後接名詞或動名詞）
- ◆ **be used to** 已習慣於
  （後接名詞或動名詞）

💡 **used to** 後接**原形動詞**，表示「過去習慣……」，而該習慣現已不存在。

- Betty **used to** teach English, but now she has a different job.
  貝蒂曾是英文老師，但她現在找到了一份不同的工作。
- I **used to** go for a jog every morning, but then it got too cold outside.
  我以前時常每天早上去散步，但後來天氣變冷了。

8

慣用片語

get (達到……狀態) ＋ **used to** (習慣於)
↓   ↓
get used to
逐漸適應；習慣於

用法
- ◆ **get used to something** 逐漸習慣於某事
- → Eventually, you'll **get used to** the smells of the laboratory.
  你最後會慢慢**習慣**實驗室裡的味道。
- ◆ **get used to doing something**
  逐漸習慣做某事
- → It took Frank a few weeks to **get used to** living so far from home.
  法蘭克花了好幾個星期才**習慣**遠離家鄉的生活。

同 **get accustomed to**

78

💡 **get used to** 後接名詞或動名詞，表示「逐漸習慣於……」。

- At first, Natalie didn't like sushi; but after living in Tokyo for a few weeks, she **got used to** it. 娜塔莉一開始不喜歡壽司，但她在東京住了幾個星期後便**習慣**了。

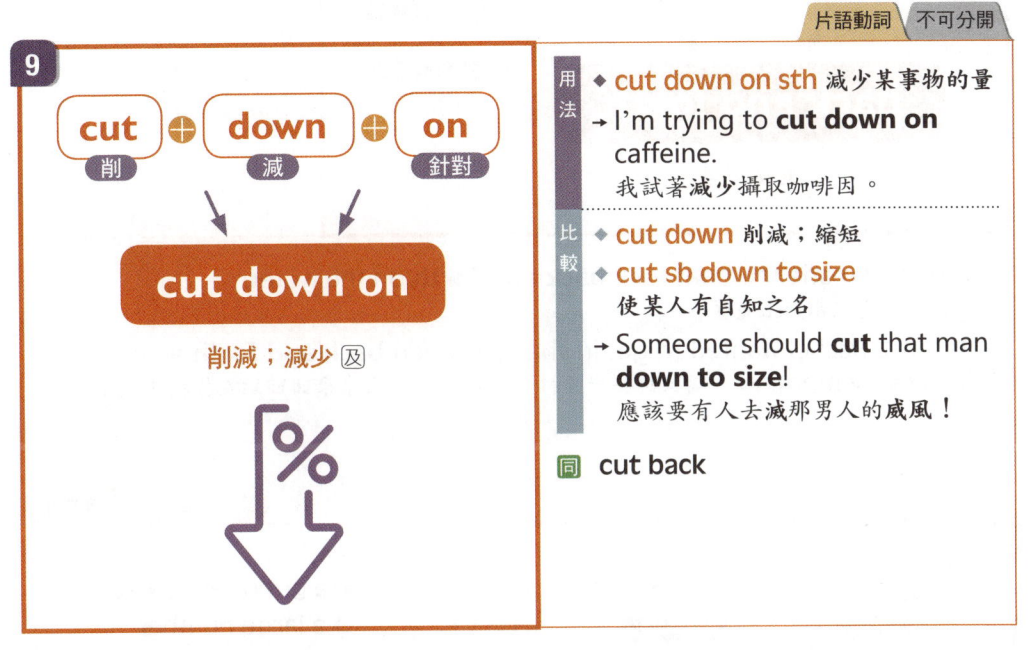

9

片語動詞 | 不可分開

cut 削 ＋ **down** 減 ＋ **on** 針對

↓

cut down on

削減；減少 及

用法
- **cut down on sth** 減少某事物的量
→ I'm trying to **cut down on** caffeine.
我試著減少攝取咖啡因。

比較
- **cut down** 削減；縮短
- **cut sb down to size** 使某人有自知之名
→ Someone should **cut** that man **down to size**!
應該要有人去滅那男人的威風！

同 **cut back**

💡 **cut down on** 表示「減少；削減」，使用時需明確指出事物或對象。

- Because Dean was trying to lose weight, he **cut down on** the number of snacks he ate.
狄恩想要減重，所以他**減少吃零食**。
- If you want to **cut down on** the amount of money you spend at the supermarket, never shop when you're hungry.
如果想要在超市少花點錢，就別在肚子餓的時候去買東西。

10

back(向後) + **and**(又) + **forth**(向前)

→ **back and forth** 來來回回

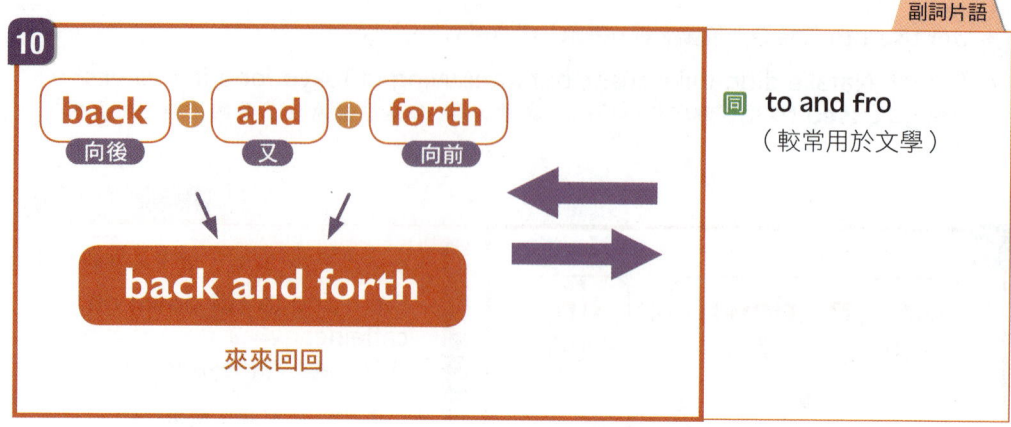

同 to and fro（較常用於文學）

- The wind made the boat rock **back and forth** on the water.
  風把船吹得在水面上晃盪。
- Because Rachel wanted to get in shape, she ran **back and forth** across the field every morning. 瑞秋想要好身材，所以每天早上來來回回地在操場上跑步。

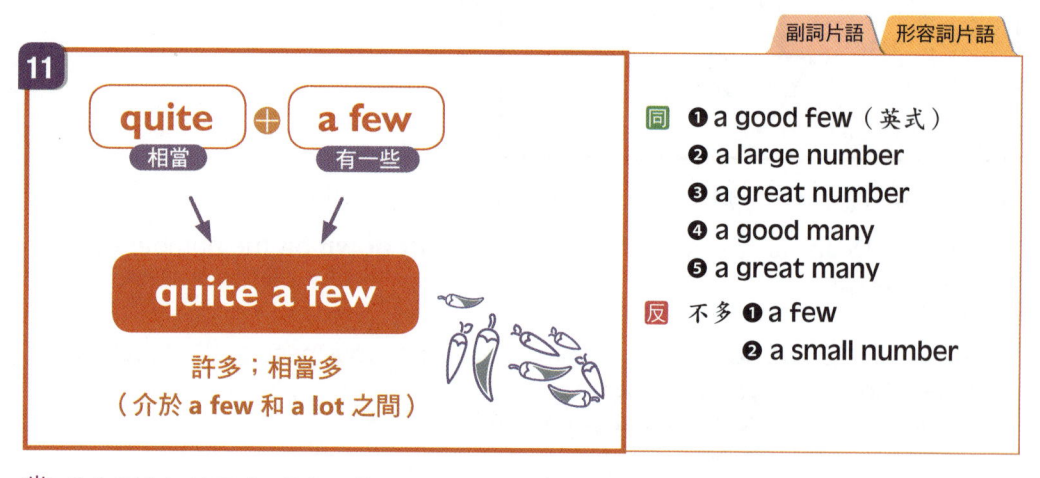

11

quite(相當) + **a few**(有一些)

→ **quite a few** 許多；相當多（介於 a few 和 a lot 之間）

同
1. a good few（英式）
2. a large number
3. a great number
4. a good many
5. a great many

反 不多
1. a few
2. a small number

💡 作為形容詞使用時，修飾可數名詞，後接複數動詞；作副詞使用時，可置於 less、more 等前作修飾，例如 quite a few more。

- Casey wanted to make his own apple juice, applesauce, and apple pie, so he bought **quite a few** pounds of apples at the market.
  凱西想要自己做蘋果汁、蘋果醬和蘋果派，所以他到市場買了**好幾磅**的蘋果。
- There was a big sale at the bookstore, so Floyd bought **quite a few** books.
  書店在大減價，所以佛洛伊德買了**許多**書。

12

be (是) ➕ **used to** (習慣於)
⬇
be used to

已經習慣於……；熟悉

用法
- ◆ **be used to sth** 已經習慣某事
  → I **am used to** cleaning up other people's messes.
  我習慣替別人處理麻煩事。

- ◆ **be used to sb** 與某人熟悉
  → We'**re used to** tourists here—we get thousands every year.
  我們已經習慣了到這裡來的觀光客，這裡每年都有上千名觀光客到訪。

同 be accustomed to
反 不習慣 be unaccustomed to

- Joan **is used to** horses, so she wasn't scared of riding one.
  瓊已經習慣了馬兒，所以她不害怕騎馬。
- I **am used to** cooking my own dinner. 我已經習慣自己準備晚餐了。

Unit 09 Test Yourself!

A 選擇題

1. When mom asked if I _____ at the mall, I told her that I didn't.
   Ⓐ had a good time   Ⓑ woke up   Ⓒ got in touch   Ⓓ cut down

2. Jim _____ read a book every week, but lately he's been too busy.
   Ⓐ got in touch with   Ⓑ used to   Ⓒ was in charge of   Ⓓ cut down

3. Tim wanted to quit smoking, so he started _____ the number of cigarettes he smoked each day.
   Ⓐ cutting down on   Ⓑ being used to
   Ⓒ getting in touch with Ⓓ being in charge of

4. Glenn must _____ every day at 7 a.m. to get to school on time.
   Ⓐ get in touch   Ⓑ cut down   Ⓒ wake up   Ⓓ be in charge

5. I still haven't _____ using a digital camera—I guess it will take more practice.
   Ⓐ cut down on   Ⓑ gotten used to
   Ⓒ been in charge of Ⓓ gotten in touch with

6. I _____ doing a lot of exercise, so taking a walk is no problem.
   Ⓐ am used to   Ⓑ cut down on   Ⓒ am in charge of   Ⓓ get in touch with

7. _____ I smelled smoke, I knew there was a fire.
   Ⓐ In no time   Ⓑ Back and forth   Ⓒ Having a good time   Ⓓ As soon as

8. Feel free to _____ me whenever you have some free time!
   Ⓐ get in touch with   Ⓑ be in charge of   Ⓒ get used to   Ⓓ cut down on

9. After the CEO quit his job, everyone was wondering who would _____ the company.
   Ⓐ wake up   Ⓑ get used to   Ⓒ be in charge of   Ⓓ cut down

10. Arnold promised that he'd be home _____, but it actually took several hours because of the heavy traffic.
    Ⓐ as soon as   Ⓑ having a good time   Ⓒ in no time   Ⓓ back and forth

11. I don't know how many pairs of shoes Agatha has, but she definitely has _____.
    Ⓐ quite a few   Ⓑ been in charge of it   Ⓒ cut down   Ⓓ had a good time

B 閱讀文章，從字表中選擇詞彙填入，並依人稱時態等做適當的變化

get in touch with	as soon as	back and forth
be in charge of	quite a few	used to
have a good time	wake up	be used to

On Monday, Jamie ❶ _____ early in the morning. She started working ❷ _____ she could because it was a very important day. Every year, Jamie's town has a festival, and the children of the town always compete in a race. This year, Jamie ❸ _____ that race, and she had a lot to do. First, she had to ❹ _____ the mayor in order to organize the prize for the winner. There were other things to do, too. For example, in previous years, the children ❺ _____ run along the road. However, this year there would be more cars, and that probably wasn't safe. Instead, Jamie chose a path that went ❻ _____ through the park. First, she had to check the park to make sure that it was a good place for the race and that everyone would ❼ _____ there.

❽ _____ children showed up for the race, but there was only one winner: a little girl named Lucy. She was a fast runner, and because she ❾ _____ running in the park, she knew the path well. Everything went well during the race, and the mayor thanked Jamie for her help.

C 引導式翻譯，並依人稱時態等做適當的變化

1. 對於在溫熱環境下長大的人來說，**適應寒冷的天氣**是一件很不容易的事情。
   It's not easy _____ _____ _____ cold weather if you were brought up in a hot climate.

2. 娜塔莉的衣著和舉止都顯現出她**已經習慣**當模特兒了。
   Natalie's clothes and manners show she _____ _____ _____ being a top fashion model.

3. 大衛離職後，這個部門會是誰**負責**呢？
   Who will _____ _____ _____ _____ the department when David leaves?

4. 孩子們很快地把晚餐**吃完**。
   The children ate their dinner _____ _____ _____.

5. 她隨著音樂慢慢地**前後搖擺**。
   She swayed gently _____ _____ _____ to the music.

83

Unit 10

Choosing a Pet
挑選寵物

042

Ava and Ethan are choosing a pet in a pet store.
愛娃和伊森正在寵物店挑選寵物。

Ethan: OK, Ava. We have to **make sure**[1] that we get a pet we'll be happy with and won't ever want to **get rid of**[2].

好了,愛娃,記得**確定**要選一隻我們滿意的寵物,而且永遠不要**丟棄**他。

Ava: That's true! A pet is not something we can take care of **now and then**[3]; it's a big commitment.

沒錯!養寵物並不是**偶爾**照顧一下而已,而是一項承諾。

Ethan: How about that white rat? His white fur will **go with**[4] your white jacket.

這隻白老鼠如何?他身上的白毛和你的白色夾克很**配**。

Ava: No way! Oh, look at those kittens playing together. Look at that one there; he's really cute.

不要!噢,看那些玩在一起的小貓。你看那邊那隻,好可愛噢。

Ethan: I agree. Let's buy him! But before we take him home, we should **see about**[5] getting some cat food and some toys for him before the stores close.

我也這麼認為。我們就買他吧!但是帶他回家之前,我們應該**考慮**在商店打烊前去買一些貓食和玩具給他。

Ava: Okay, but let's go now. If we **make good time**[6], we can get back to the pet store quickly. I don't want anyone else to take our kitten!

好,不過我們現在就走吧。我們如果**走快**一點,就能夠趕快回到寵物店。我不希望有人買走我們的小貓!

Unit 10 Choosing a Pet 挑選寵物

慣用片語

1

make (使……) + **sure** (確定)
↓
make sure
確定；確認 [不及]

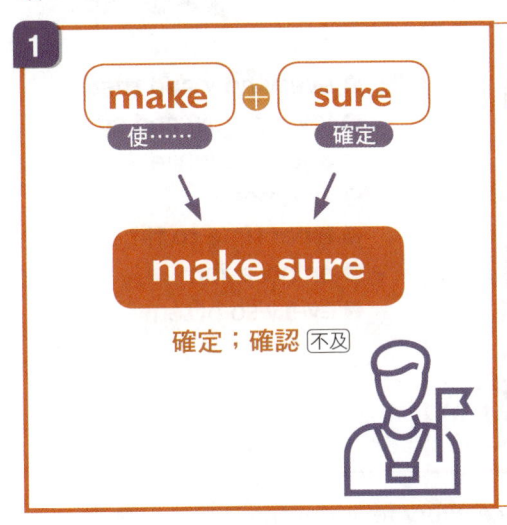

用法
- **make sure of sth** 確認某事
  → You must **make sure of** the time and place. 你一定要確認地點和時間。
- **make sure to do sth** 確定要去做某事
  → **Make sure to** lock the bike after parking it. 停好腳踏車後要確認上鎖了。
- **make sure that** 確定……
  → **Make sure that** we have enough drinks for the party.
    要確定我們的派對有足夠的飲料。

同 make certain

💡 **make sure** 可作為不及物動詞，**make sure** 的語氣比 **make certain** 還要重。

- Before you leave the house, **make sure** that you turn all the lights off.
  出門前，要確認所有的燈都關了。
- I need to **make sure** that I call my parents if I'm going to be late.
  若是要晚歸，我一定要確定先打電話給爸媽。

慣用片語

2

get (使) + **rid** (去除) + **of** (行為對象)
↓
get rid of
去除；丟棄

用法
- **get rid of sth** 丟棄某物；脫手某事物
  → Have you managed to **get rid of** your old Lamborghini yet?
    你那台舊的藍寶堅尼脫手了嗎？
- **get rid of sb** 擺脫某人
  → We **got rid of** our unwelcome guests by saying we had to go to bed. 我們為了擺脫討厭的客人，向他們表示我們要休息了。

同 ❶ get shot of（英式）
　 ❷ escape from
　 ❸ do away with　❹ be rid of

💡 過去分詞 **rid** 在此作為形容詞使用，後接具體名詞表示「除去；丟棄」；後接抽象名詞則表示「擺脫；打消」。

- How do I **get rid of** all these ants in my house? 我該如何消除屋內所有的螞蟻？
- Drinking herbal tea will help you **get rid of** your sore throat.
  飲用花草茶能幫助你消除喉嚨痛。

85

3

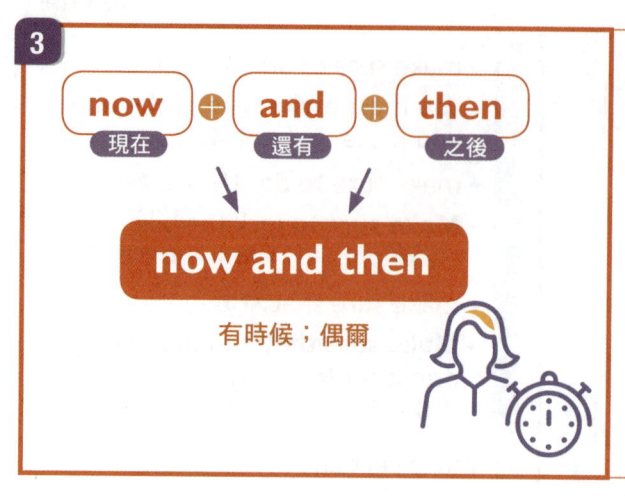

now 現在 ＋ **and** 還有 ＋ **then** 之後
→ **now and then** 有時候；偶爾

副詞片語 | 時間副詞

同
① every now and then
② (every) now and again
③ once in a while
④ at times
⑤ from time to time
⑥ on occasion
⑦ every so often

- We meet up **now and then**, maybe once every few months.
  我們**偶爾**會見面，大概幾個月見一次面。
- Call your parents **now and then** and let them know you care.
  偶爾打電話給你的父母，讓他們知道你很關心他們。
- Every **now and then** I'll take the kids to the playground.
  我**有時候**會帶孩子們去遊樂場玩。

4

go 相配 ＋ **with** 與
→ **go with**
① 與……搭配（通常指衣服、食物）
② 與……交往
③ 與……看法相同 及

片語動詞 | 不可分開

用法
- **A goes with B** A與B相配
  → I'm not sure that this necklace really **goes with** that dress.
  我不確定這條項鍊是否和這件洋裝很**配**。
- **go with sth** 與某事物看法相同
  → I think we can **go with** the advertising agency's suggestions, don't you? 我想我們可以**按照**廣告商的建議去做，對吧？
- **go with sb** 與某人交往
  → Did she **go with** anyone else while they were living together?
  他們同居的時候，她有沒有同時和其他人交往呢？
- **go well with** 與……很相配

同　與……在一起 keep company with
　　同意 agree to

❶ That orange tie definitely does not **go with** that pink shirt!
那條橘色領帶顯然和粉紅色襯衫不太**相配**！

❶ Do you think red or white wine **goes with** this lasagna?
你覺得這道千層麵要**配**紅酒或白酒呢？

片語動詞 ／ 不可分開

5

see（查看） + about（關於）
↓
see about
❶ 留意；關照
❷ 安排；考慮 及

用法
◆ **see about sth** 留意某事物；考慮某事
→ I'll **see about** movie times and call you back.
我會**留意**一下電影場次，然後回電給你。

◆ **see about sb** 注意某人
→ I know Lucy isn't interested in basketball, but let's **see about** Ron.
我知道露西對籃球沒有興趣，我們**問看看**朗吧。

同 照料 ❶ see to ❷ take care of
　 再三考慮 think twice

💡 後接名詞或動名詞，表示「留意；關照」；後接事物，表示「考慮」。

❷ I'm not sure if Carla is coming to the party; I'd better **see about** sending her an invitation.
我不確定卡拉是否會來參加派對，我**打算**寄邀請卡給她。

❷ My dad said he was going to **see about** buying me a motorcycle.
我老爸說他**打算**買一台摩托車給我。

6

make 達到 + **good** 好的 + **time** 時間

→ **make good time**
❶ 旅程順利（較快到）　❷ 做事快速

> make good time 主詞通常為**人**。good time 在這裡表示「**短時間**」,而非「美好時光」。

❶ We **made good time** driving to Taipei because the traffic was light.
由於路況順暢,我們**很快**就開車到達台北。

❷ Although we left later than planned, we **made good time** and arrived before the show started.
雖然我們比計畫中還要晚離開,但我們**速度很快**,所以到達時並不會太晚。

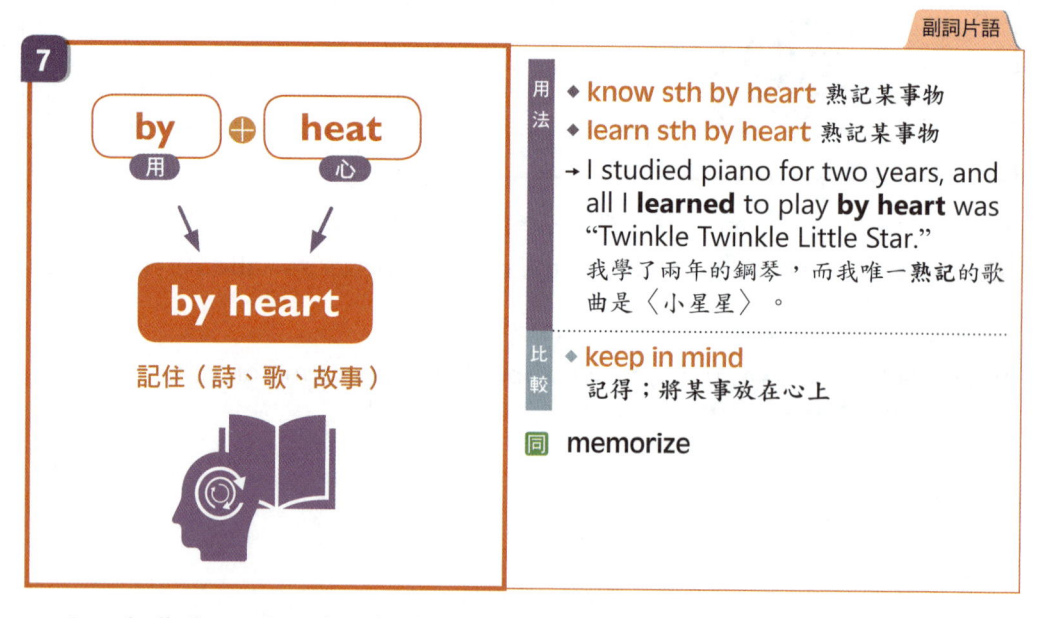

---

7 副詞片語

by 用 + **heart** 心

→ **by heart**
記住（詩、歌、故事）

用法
- know sth by heart 熟記某事物
- learn sth by heart 熟記某事物
→ I studied piano for two years, and all I **learned** to play **by heart** was "Twinkle Twinkle Little Star."
我學了兩年的鋼琴,而我唯一**熟記**的歌曲是〈小星星〉。

比較
- keep in mind
記得;將某事放在心上

同 memorize

- Annabelle loves *Hamlet*; she knows most of the famous lines **by heart**.
安娜貝爾最愛《哈姆雷特》,她**記住**了大部分有名的詩詞。

- Jack studied his lines in the play until he was sure he knew them **by heart**.
傑克一直在背他在劇中的臺詞,直到他確定都**記住**了。

8

come（來）＋ **from**（出自）
→ **come from**

❶ 出生於；來自
❷ 從……取得結論
❸ 由……引起 及

片語動詞 | **不可分開**

用法
- **come from sw** 來自某地
→ Some of the best wines **come from** France. 許多好酒都是**來自**於法國。

- **come from sth** 來自於某事物
→ Does that quote **come from** Shakespeare? 那句引文是**來自**於莎士比亞嗎？

- **come from sth** 由……引起
→ "I feel awful." "That **comes from** eating too much."「我感覺糟透了。」「那是**因**為吃太多的關係。」

同　來自 ❶ come of
　　　　 ❷ originate from
　　　　 ❸ derive from

💡 使用現在簡單式時，come from 表示「出生地或籍貫」；使用過去式時，則是詢問對方剛從哪裡過來，如「**Where did you come from?**」。

❶ My best friend Bill **comes from** Chicago. 我最好的朋友比爾**來自**芝加哥。
❶ Where did all these hats **come from**? 這些帽子是哪裡來的？
❶ If you ask me, the best cherries **come from** Washington.
　如果你問我，我會說最好吃的櫻桃**來自**華盛頓。

9

形容詞片語

every（每）＋ **other**（另一個；其他的）
→ **every other (one)**
每隔……

用法
- **every other sth** 每隔……
→ I have English class **every other** Monday. 我隔週的週一都有英文課。

- **every other sth** 所有其他的
→ Our team defeated **every other** team. 我們球隊打敗了**所有其他的**隊伍。

💡 **every other** 表示「每兩個中之一」或「所有其他的」，應解讀為何者，需視前後文而定。

- Terrance visits his uncle and aunt **every other** week.
　泰倫斯**每隔**週都會去拜訪叔叔和阿姨。

Unit 10 Choosing a Pet 挑選寵物

89

10

mix（混合）＋ **up**（完全地）→ **mix up**

❶ 使混亂
❷ 搞混 及

片語動詞　可分開　受詞為代名詞時定要分開

用法

◆ **mix sth up / mix up sth** 弄亂某事物
→ If you **mix up** the photos in these envelopes, I'll never find them.
如果你把這些信封裡的相片**弄亂**，我會找不到。

◆ **mix sb up / mix up sb** 把某人搞混
→ I think you're **mixing** me **up** with my brother.
我想你把我和我弟**搞混**了。

◆ **mix sth up / mix up sth** 把某事搞混
→ I **mixed** the appointments **up** and went for a haircut on the wrong day. 我**搞錯**了約定的日子，在沒預約的日子跑去剪頭髮。

◆ **be/get mixed up** 被弄亂；被搞糊塗

◆ **be/get mixed up in sth**
被捲入、牽扯某事物

◆ **be/get mixed up with sb** 與某人廝混

❷ It's easy to **mix up** Richie and Lou because they're twins.
瑞奇和盧是雙胞胎，所以很容易把他們**搞混**。
❷ I always **mix** your birthday **up** with Seth's.
我老是把你和塞斯的生日**搞混**。

11

make（使） ✚ **out**（顯露）
　　↓　　　　　↓
make out

① 辨別出 [及][可分]
② 理解 [及][可分]
③ 填寫 [及][可分]
④ 試圖證明 [及][不可分]
⑤ 成功辦到 [不及]

用法

◆ **make sth out** 理解某事
→ I can't **make out** what the teacher is writing on the blackboard.
我看不出老師在黑板上寫些什麼。

◆ **make sb out** 理解某人
→ She's a strange person—I can't **make** her **out** at all.
她是個怪咖，我完全不了解她。

◆ **make sth out** 填寫；寫出
→ I **made** a check **out** for $3,000 to Mr. Whiteman.
我開了一張3,000元的支票給懷德曼先生。

◆ **make out sth** 試圖證明
→ She **made out** like she had been living in Paris all year.
她聲稱她整年都住在巴黎。

◆ **make out** 成功辦到
→ How is Tina **making out** in her new job?
緹娜是如何在新工作有如此成功的表現？

同 理解 make sense of
　　辨別 identify

反 不理解 make nothing of

片語動詞　受詞為代名詞時定要分開

Unit 10 Choosing a Pet 挑選寵物

💡 ❶ make out 後接 plan、idea 等抽象名詞或 what 子句，表示「**理解**」。
　❷ 後接 document、check 等文件名詞，表示「**填寫；寫出**」。
　❸ 後接 that 子句，表示「**試圖證明；假裝**」。

❶ The TV volume was so low that it was hard to **make out** what the actors were saying.
電視的音量很小，實在很難**聽出**演員在說什麼。

91

Unit 10 Test Yourself!

Ⓐ 選擇題

1. I don't want to bring my little sister on my date with Andy; how can I _____ her for a few hours?
   Ⓐ come from Ⓑ get rid of Ⓒ go with Ⓓ see about

2. Sorry, but those sneakers definitely don't _____ that formal suit.
   Ⓐ get rid of Ⓑ make out Ⓒ go with Ⓓ come from

3. This is my girlfriend's favorite song—she knows all the words _____.
   Ⓐ now and then Ⓑ by heart Ⓒ mixed up Ⓓ every other

4. Dale doesn't go out to eat much, just _____ weekend or so.
   Ⓐ every other Ⓑ now and then Ⓒ mixed up Ⓓ see about

5. It was a long drive, but Paulette is a great driver and we _____.
   Ⓐ made sure Ⓑ came from her Ⓒ made good time Ⓓ mixed up

6. Please _____ that you brought your passport before we get to the airport.
   Ⓐ mix up Ⓑ make good time Ⓒ make sure Ⓓ go with

7. Abe enjoys going to the movies _____.
   Ⓐ every other Ⓑ mixed up Ⓒ now and then Ⓓ by heart

8. I couldn't _____ what he said, but he seemed to be quoting from something.
   Ⓐ get rid of Ⓑ mix up Ⓒ make good time Ⓓ make out

9. I'm getting hungry; maybe we should better _____ getting something to eat.
   Ⓐ see about Ⓑ mix up Ⓒ come from Ⓓ make out

10. Arnold is American, but his wife _____ Europe.
    Ⓐ mixes up Ⓑ sees about Ⓒ makes out Ⓓ comes from

11. Sometimes people _____ Tyrone _____ with his father over the phone because their voices are so similar.
    Ⓐ make . . . out Ⓑ see . . . about Ⓒ mix . . . up Ⓓ make . . . sure

92

B 閱讀文章，從字表中選擇詞彙填入，並依人稱時態等做適當的變化

get rid of	see about	make sure
by heart	now and then	mix up
come from	go with	make out

Mrs. Deerfield is a high school music teacher. ❶ _____, she likes to do something special for the students, and when she does, it is her job to ❷ _____ that everyone learns something new. One day, she had a surprise; she had invited musicians from around the world to come to the school and play their native music ❸ _____. There were so many musicians that she ❹ _____ many of their names; it was also hard to ❺ _____ their names because the room was noisy and Mrs. Deerfield had trouble hearing them.

When the students arrived, Mrs. Deerfield asked the first musician, Ivan, to start playing. His music was beautiful. Some students even wanted to ❻ _____ the other musicians so Ivan could play the whole time. Then, the other musicians started playing their instruments together with Ivan. Their music ❼ _____ Ivan's perfectly, and other teachers and students looked into the classroom to see where all the great music was ❽ _____. Some students started dancing! In the end, everyone agreed that this was a first-rate class. When the students left, the first thing Mrs. Deerfield did was to ❾ _____ doing it again next year.

C 引導式翻譯，並依人稱時態等做適當的變化

1. 這項方案的資金要**從何處**取得呢？
   Where will the money for the project _____ _____?

2. 別**弄亂**這些瓶子，如果你這麼做的話，就得重做一次實驗了。
   Don't _____ _____ the bottles—you'll have to repeat the experiment if you do.

3. 雖然我很喜歡你的建議，但我還是會**按照我原本的想法去做**。
   Although I liked your suggestion, I'll _____ _____ my original idea.

4. 你應該**考慮**去修頭髮了。
   You should _____ _____ getting your hair cut.

5. 噢，你上電視節目了？你是怎麼**辦到**的？
   Oh, you were on a TV game show? How did you _____ _____?

Unit 11

🔊 047

Waiting for a Friend
等朋友

Jaime is waiting for Marc under an apple tree.
Finally, he arrives—15 minutes late.
潔咪在蘋果樹下等馬克,終於,他出現了,在遲到了 15 分鐘後。

Jaime: Hey, Marc! Why are you late? What have you **been up to**[1]? | 嘿,馬克,你為什麼遲到?你**都在做**什麼呢?

Marc: Sorry! I had a hard day at school. Can we talk about it for a minute? This morning, my professor seemed to **find fault with**[2] everything I said during class. He wanted me to totally **do** my report **over**[3]. Really, he seemed to **be carried away**[4] with new ideas, and his thoughts were hard to **keep track of**[5]. | 對不起,我今天在學校過得很不愉快。我們可以聊一下嗎?今天早上教授對我在課堂上的發言好像很**有意見**,他要我**重寫**報告。真的,他似乎**被**新的思想**影響**,很難**猜測**他在想什麼。

Jaime: Don't worry! You'll **get through**[6] it; it's only a paper! | 別擔心!你**寫得完**的,不過是報告而已!

Marc: I guess you're right. But **from now on**[7], I think I'd better try being a better student. Hey, did you bring any food in that bag? I'm hungry. | 妳說得對,但是我想我**今後**最好試著當個好學生。嘿,那個袋子裡頭有吃的嗎?我餓昏了。

Jaime: **Keep away from**[8] my bag! There's a surprise in there for you—but you have to wait. I don't want you to see it yet. | **別靠近**我的袋子!裡面是要給你的驚喜,但是你必須等等,我還不想給你看。

1

be（是） + **up to**（忙於） → **be up to**

❶ 預計在某時段做某事　❷ 由……決定
❸ 做壞事（違法的事情）

慣用片語

用法
- be up to sb
- be up to sth

同　計劃 plan

❶ What **are** you **up to** this weekend? 你這週末**要做什麼**？
❷ I don't know if we'll play video games tonight; it's **up to** you.
　我不知道今晚是否要打電動，**由你決定**。
❸ I'm sure Walt **is up to** something; he's been acting so strangely lately.
　我確定華特一定**在做什麼見不得人的事情**，他最近的行為很奇怪。

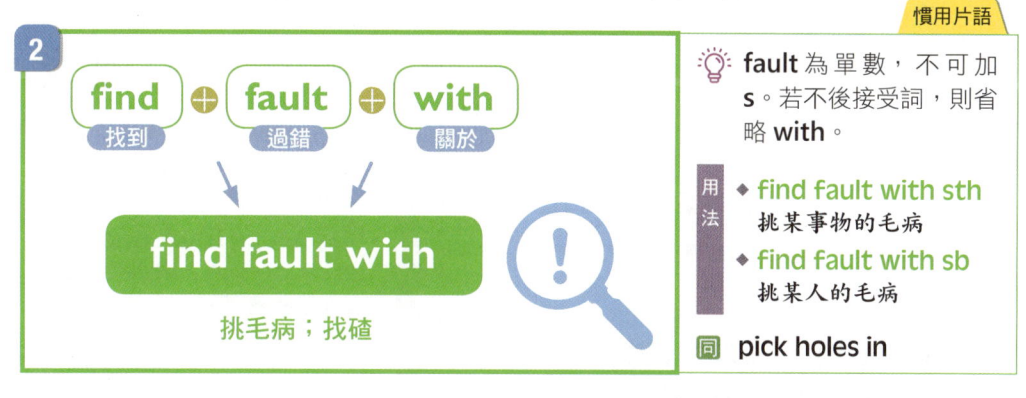

2

find（找到） + **fault**（過錯） + **with**（關於） → **find fault with**

挑毛病；找碴

慣用片語

💡 fault 為單數，不可加 s。若不後接受詞，則省略 with。

用法
- find fault with sth
  挑某事物的毛病
- find fault with sb
  挑某人的毛病

同　pick holes in

• George is so critical; no matter how good things are, he always **finds fault with** something. 喬治很吹毛求疵；就算東西再好，他也能夠**挑出毛病**。

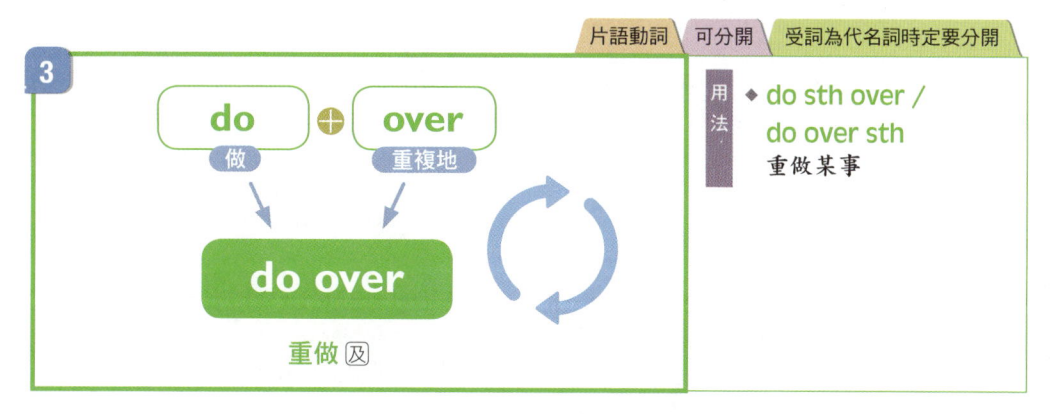

3

do（做） + **over**（重複地） → **do over**

重做 及

片語動詞　可分開　受詞為代名詞時定要分開

用法
- do sth over / do over sth
  重做某事

• My math teacher said I could **do** the last quiz **over** because I did so poorly on it. 因為我考得很差，所以數學老師說我可以**重考上次的小考**。

🔊 049

慣用片語

4 be（被）＋ carried（帶）＋ away（走、離開）

be carried away
開心到忘我的境界

同 get carried away

- Tina likes baking so much that she **was carried away** and made hundreds of cookies.　堤娜熱愛烘焙**到忘我的境界**，她不小心做了一堆餅乾。
- Harry **was** so **carried away** by the good news that he couldn't calm down.
哈利**沉醉**在好消息中，無法冷靜下來。
- People in the crowd **were carried away** by Clinton's passionate speech.
觀眾因柯林頓滿腔熱血的演講而**興奮不已**。

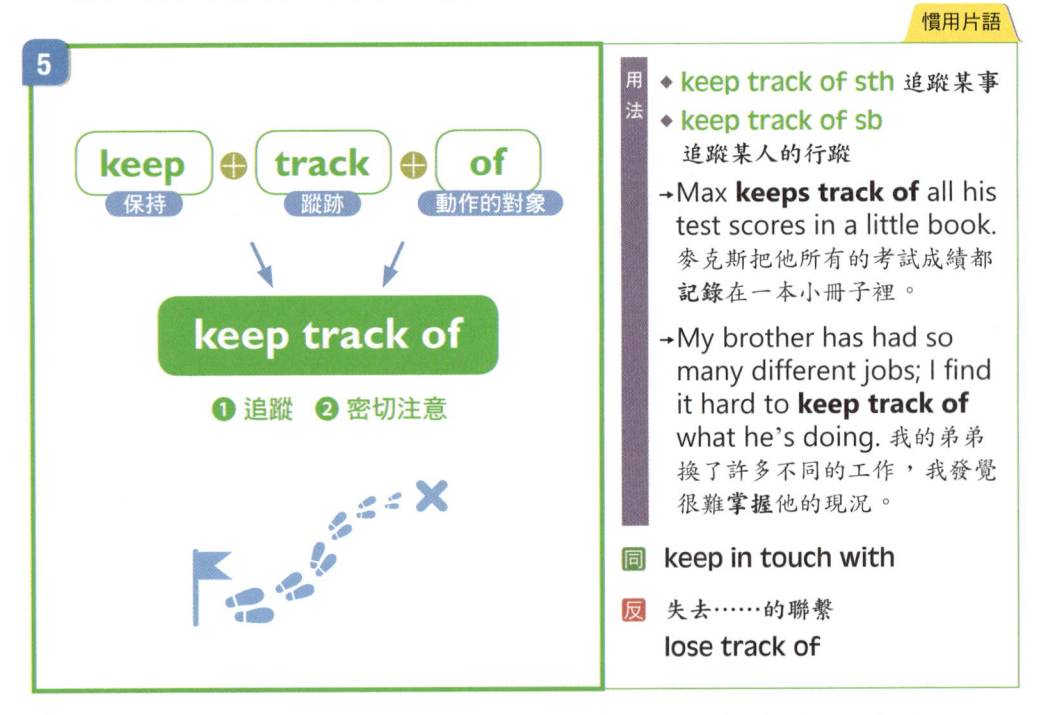

慣用片語

5 keep（保持）＋ track（蹤跡）＋ of（動作的對象）

keep track of
❶ 追蹤　❷ 密切注意

用法
◆ **keep track of sth** 追蹤某事
◆ **keep track of sb** 追蹤某人的行蹤

→ Max **keeps track of** all his test scores in a little book.
麥克斯把他所有的考試成績都**記錄**在一本小冊子裡。

→ My brother has had so many different jobs; I find it hard to **keep track of** what he's doing. 我的弟弟換了許多不同的工作，我發覺很難**掌握**他的現況。

同 keep in touch with

反 失去……的聯繫
lose track of

❶ Agatha is always traveling, and I can never **keep track of** where she is.
雅嘉薩老是在旅行，所以我永遠無法掌握她的**行蹤**。

❷ The babysitter is supposed to **keep track of** my little sister.
保姆應該要**隨時注意**我的妹妹。

Unit 11 Waiting for a Friend 等朋友

片語動詞　不可分開

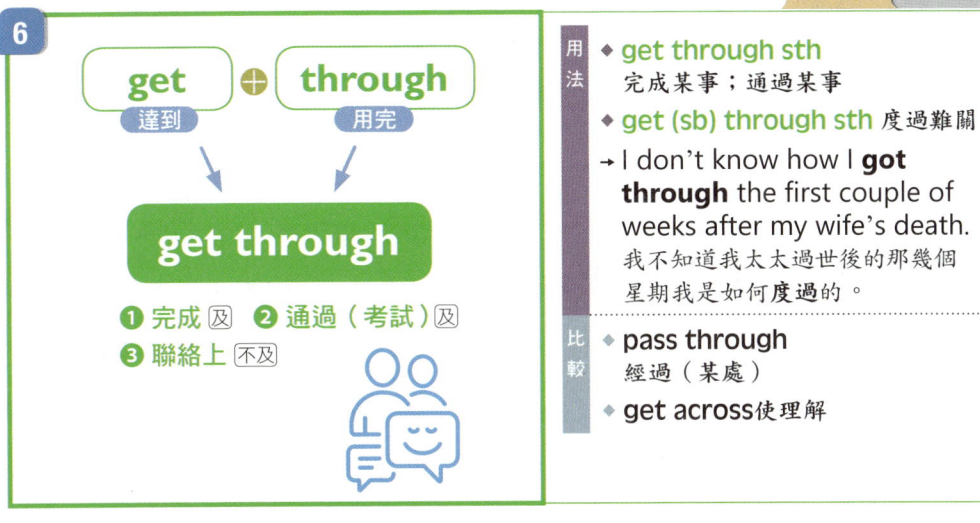

6

get (達到) + through (用完) → **get through**
❶ 完成 及　❷ 通過（考試）及
❸ 聯絡上 不及

用法
- **get through sth** 完成某事；通過某事
- **get (sb) through sth** 度過難關
  → I don't know how I **got through** the first couple of weeks after my wife's death.
  我不知道我太太過世後的那幾個星期我是如何度過的。

比較
- **pass through** 經過（某處）
- **get across** 使理解

❶ Please leave Jimmy alone; he won't **get through** his work if you keep chatting with him. 請不要煩吉米，你一直和他聊天，他無法完成工作。

❷ Jimmy **got through** his exams without too much trouble.
吉米輕輕鬆鬆地通過了考試。

❸ I tried to phone her, but I couldn't **get through**.
我試著打電話給她，但是聯絡不上。

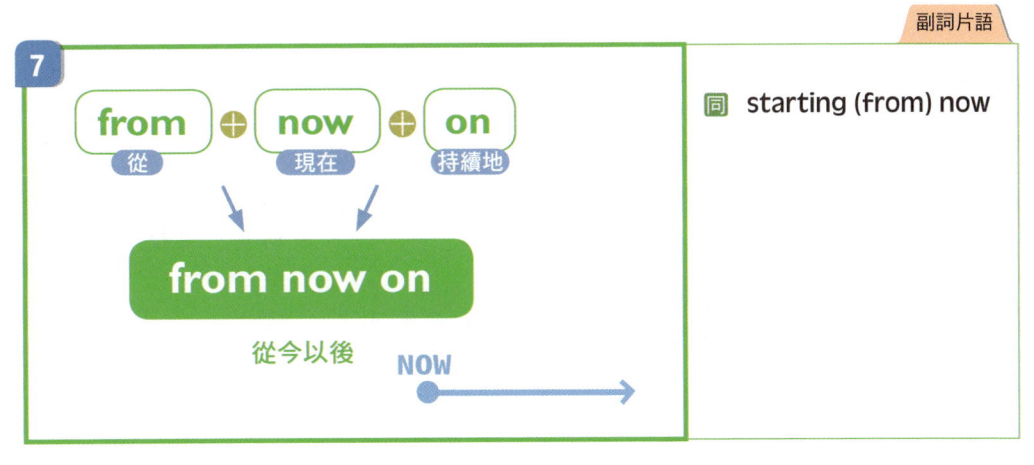

副詞片語

7

from (從) + now (現在) + on (持續地) → **from now on** 從今以後

同 starting (from) now

💡 now 可換成某個特定的時間點，如 **from then on**（從那時起）、**from that moment on**（從那一刻起）。

- **From now on**, you must be home before midnight.
  從今以後，你必須在午夜前回家。

- Because I overslept again, I have to work the late shift **from now on**.
  由於我又睡過頭，從現在開始我必須上晚班。

- **From now on**, the gates will be locked at midnight.
  從現在開始，大門半夜都會上鎖。

8 keep + away

keep 保持 ＋ **away** 離開

keep away (from)

遠離；不許靠近 及

用法
- keep sth away 不接近某事
- keep sb away 不讓某人接近
- keep away from sb 遠離某人
- keep away from sth 遠離某事物
- keep sb away from sth 使某人遠離某事

同 ❶ keep out ❷ keep off

- There was a notice saying "**Keep off** the grass."
  那裡有個「請勿踐踏草皮」的標誌。

- Danielle is just a child, so be sure to **keep** her **away from** the road.
  丹妮葉拉還是個小孩，所以千萬**別讓她靠近**馬路。

- I suggest you **keep away from** Jane; she has a cold.
  我建議你**別靠近**珍，她感冒了。

- **Keep away from** the edge of the cliff. 別太靠近懸崖。

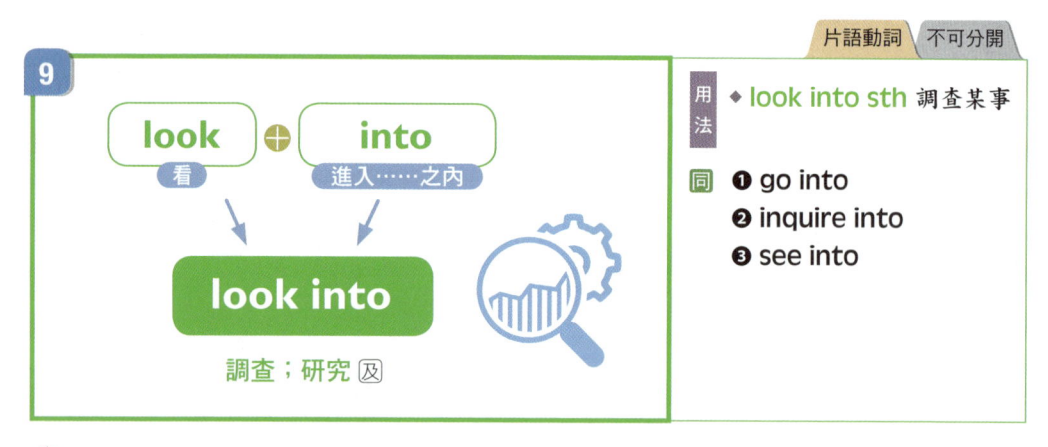

9 look + into

look 看 ＋ **into** 進入……之內

look into

調查；研究 及

用法
- look into sth 調查某事

同 ❶ go into
   ❷ inquire into
   ❸ see into

💡 look into 通常後接 matter、background 等名詞，表示「調查」。

- Vince was **looking into** the possibility of working in Canada.
  文斯正在**研究**到加拿大工作的可能性。

- I'm not sure if that's a good price for that car; let me **look into** it.
  我不確定那是那台車最好的價錢，讓我**研究**一下。

- They're **looking into** the possibility of merging the two departments.
  他們正在**研究**合併兩個部門的可能性。

10

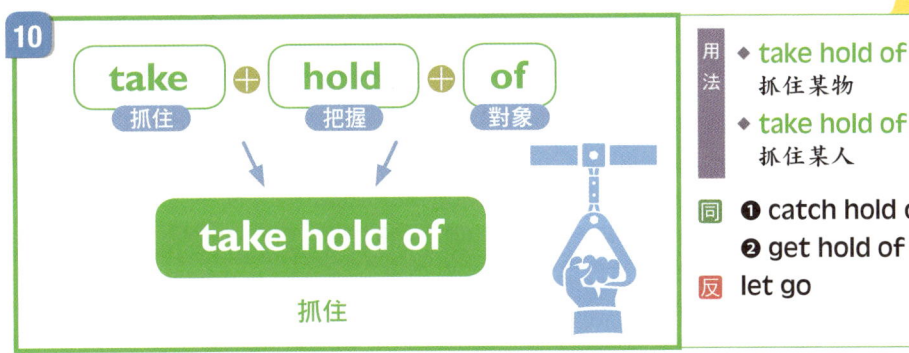

take (抓住) + **hold** (把握) + **of** (對象) → **take hold of** 抓住

慣用片語

用法:
- **take hold of sth** 抓住某物
- **take hold of sb** 抓住某人

同:
1. catch hold of
2. get hold of

反: let go

- The boy **took hold of** his mother's hand before they crossed the street.
  男孩在過馬路前**抓住**媽媽的手。
- When they got to the city center, Patty **took hold of** her camera and didn't let go because she was afraid it would get stolen.
  他們進入市中心後，派蒂怕相機被偷，所以**緊抓著不放**。

11

ill (不健康的) + **at ease** (安心) → **ill at ease** 緊張；不安

形容詞片語

同: uneasy

- As he was waiting for the test results, Carl felt **ill at ease**.
  卡爾在等待考試成績時感到**緊張**。

12

片語動詞　可分開　受詞為代名詞時定要分開

keep (保持) + **out** (在外面) → **keep out**
1. 不許進入 [及]
2. 避免捲入某種情況 [不及]

用法:
- **keep sb out** 禁止某人進入
- **keep sth out** 禁止某事物進入
- **keep sb out of sth** 避免某人捲入某事
- **keep sth out of sth** 避免某事扯上某事

同: get in

💡 keep out 為不及物動詞時，有時會後接「of + 受詞」，表示「不介入……」；作及物動詞時，受詞通常置於**中間**，表示「不讓……進入」。

1. I want some privacy now, so please **keep out** of my room.
   我現在想要有一點隱私，所以請**不要進入**我的房間。
2. If you see two people arguing, it's best to **keep out** of it.
   如果你看到兩個人在爭吵，最好**別被牽扯進去**。

Unit 11 Waiting for a Friend 等朋友

Unit 11 Test Yourself!

A 選擇題

1. My grandmother told me that _____ I must call her every weekend.
   Ⓐ finding fault with her   Ⓑ from now on
   Ⓒ over and over   Ⓓ to get carried away

2. I _____ by the good news and hugged everyone in the room, including my boss!
   Ⓐ got through   Ⓑ was carried away   Ⓒ did it over   Ⓓ was keeping out

3. Hey, _____ the stove; it's hot!
   Ⓐ keep away from   Ⓑ find fault with   Ⓒ be up to   Ⓓ take hold of

4. Irma needs to _____ this book before class tomorrow or her teacher will be unhappy.
   Ⓐ take hold of   Ⓑ do over   Ⓒ get through   Ⓓ keep track of

5. My boss is _____ the option of hiring my brother!
   Ⓐ taking hold of   Ⓑ getting through   Ⓒ doing over   Ⓓ looking into

6. The policemen talked to the man who was standing in front of the bank—they wondered if he _____ something.
   Ⓐ got through   Ⓑ was up to   Ⓒ did it over   Ⓓ looked into

7. You look _____; is something wrong?
   Ⓐ keeping out   Ⓑ ill at ease   Ⓒ doing it over   Ⓓ getting through it

8. Drake tried to convince Michelle that she should call her friend and apologize, but Wanda told him to _____ of the situation.
   Ⓐ get through   Ⓑ keep out   Ⓒ do over   Ⓓ look into

9. Mrs. Williams asked Don to _____ how much fruit the store sells over the weekend.
   Ⓐ keep track of   Ⓑ get through   Ⓒ do over   Ⓓ take hold of

10. I think I did pretty badly on the test; do you think Prof. Burns will let me _____?
    Ⓐ look into it   Ⓑ take hold of it   Ⓒ do it over   Ⓓ get through it

11. I'm sure Prof. Stevens will _____ my essay because it isn't very detailed.
    Ⓐ find fault with   Ⓑ take hold of   Ⓒ do over   Ⓓ keep track of

B 閱讀文章，從字表中選擇詞彙填入，並依人稱時態等做適當的變化

look into	from now on	find fault with
be carried away	ill at ease	do over
take hold of	be up to	keep away

As Sam walked to the restaurant, he worried about how dinner would go with his girlfriend, Sandy. He arrived at the restaurant and found Sandy waiting, just as he had hoped. The two sat down at the private table he had reserved by the fireplace. As he was about to order, Sandy noticed how ❶_____ he seemed. She was about to ask why when Sam began to ❷_____ everything the waiter suggested. Nothing was right, and Sam was wondering if he would ❸_____ the challenge—he was about to ask a question that could totally change his life. This meal had to be perfect; it was not something he could take back or ❹_____.

Before leaving home, Sam had even gone online to ❺_____ ways to make the evening unique. He hoped that Sandy would ❻_____ by all the romance. Sam asked the waiter to ❼_____ and give them some time alone. Finally, he dropped to one knee, ❽_____ Sandy's hand, and asked her to marry him. When she smiled and said yes, he told her that ❾_____ his heart belonged only to her.

C 引導式翻譯，並依人稱時態等做適當的變化

1. 理查看起來**很不安**，不像平常的他。
   Richard seemed _____ _____ _____ and not his usual self.
2. 珍娜的文章寫得不夠好，所以她看過後便決定**重寫**。
   After Jenna read her essay, she decided to _____ the whole thing _____ because it wasn't good enough.
3. 你最近都在**做什麼**呢？
   What have you _____ _____ _____ lately?
4. 我的老闆總是在工作上**找我麻煩**。
   My boss is always _____ _____ _____ my work.
5. 我可以獨自**完成**更多的工作。
   I can _____ _____ a lot more work when I'm on my own.

Unit 12
The New Mobile Phone
新手機

Josh tells Abby about his new mobile phone. 喬許把新手機的事情告訴艾比。

Abby: Wow! Is that your new cell phone?

哇,那是你的新手機嗎?

Josh: You bet. Cool, isn't it? My old one was really **out-of-date**[1].

沒錯,很棒吧?我的舊手機真的**過時**了。

Abby: Well, this one sure is **up-to-date**[2]. But I thought your old phone worked fine.

嗯,這支確實**很新**。但我以為你的舊手機還可以用。

Josh: Actually, I really needed this one. Last weekend, the old charger **caught fire**[3] when I plugged it in. Good thing it happened when I was around; otherwise, I might have **burned down**[4] the apartment building!

事實上,我真的需要換支新的了。我上週末使用舊的充電器時,竟然**著火**了。好險我當時就在旁邊,否則整棟公寓可能會**燒掉**!

Abby: Okay, so it **stands to reason**[5] that you needed a new phone—but what made you choose this model?

嗯,那你**理所當然**需要新手機。但你為何會選擇這個款式呢?

Josh: I think it looks cool! **As for**[6] the old phone, I gave it to my friend.

我覺得它很好看!**至於**舊手機,我送給朋友了。

Unit 12 The New Mobile Phone 新手機

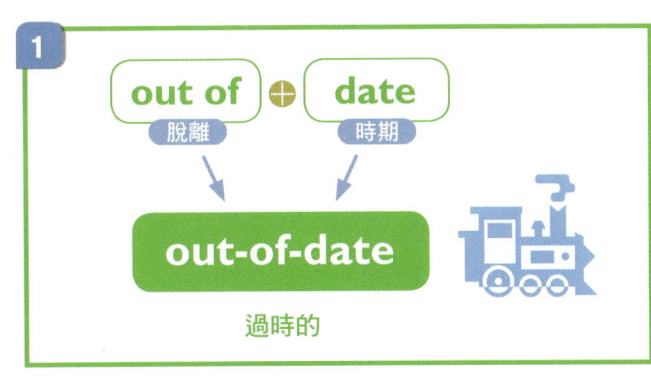

🔊 052

1 形容詞片語 | 副詞片語

out of (脫離) + **date** (時期) → **out-of-date** 過時的

同 out of fashion
反 流行的 ❶ up-to-date
　　　　 ❷ in fashion
　　　　 ❸ in style

💡 **out-of-date** 為副詞時，作修飾語；也可作為形容詞，作主詞補語或修飾語。

- This computer is so **out-of-date** that it can't even connect to the Internet.
  這台電腦很**老舊**了，就連網路也無法連接。

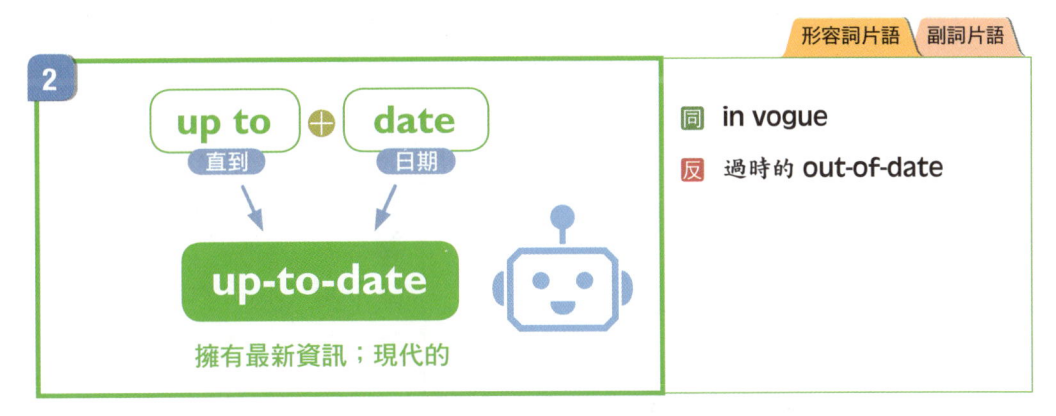

2 形容詞片語 | 副詞片語

up to (直到) + **date** (日期) → **up-to-date** 擁有最新資訊；現代的

同 in vogue
反 過時的 out-of-date

💡 **up-to-date** 為時間副詞時，與**現在簡單式**或**現在完成式**連用，表示「現在；直到現在」；也可作為形容詞，作主詞補語或修飾語，表示「最新的；現代的」，後需接名詞。

- If you want to work as a reporter, you really must keep yourself **up-to-date** on current events. 如果你想成為記者，就必須隨時掌握**最新**消息。
- A good fashion designer stays **up-to-date** on the newest styles and trends.
  優秀的服裝設計師總是能夠掌握**最新**的流行款式和趨勢。
- This new laptop player is really **up-to-date**—it's a new model.
  這台新的筆記型電腦確實是**最新的**，它是全新的機種。
- Keep your boss **up-to-date** on your progress.
  隨時向你的老闆報告**最新**進度。

103

3

catch (燃燒起來) + **fire** (火) → **catch fire** 著火

同 take fire

💡 **catch fire** 需用於主動語態，被動語態需使用 **set fire**。

- Despite being wet, the wood that they put on the stove finally **caught fire**.
  儘管他們放在火爐上的木頭是濕的，最後還是**燃燒**了起來。
- If you don't move that candle away from the curtains, they may **catch fire**.
  如果你不把蠟燭從窗簾移走，窗簾可能會**著火**。

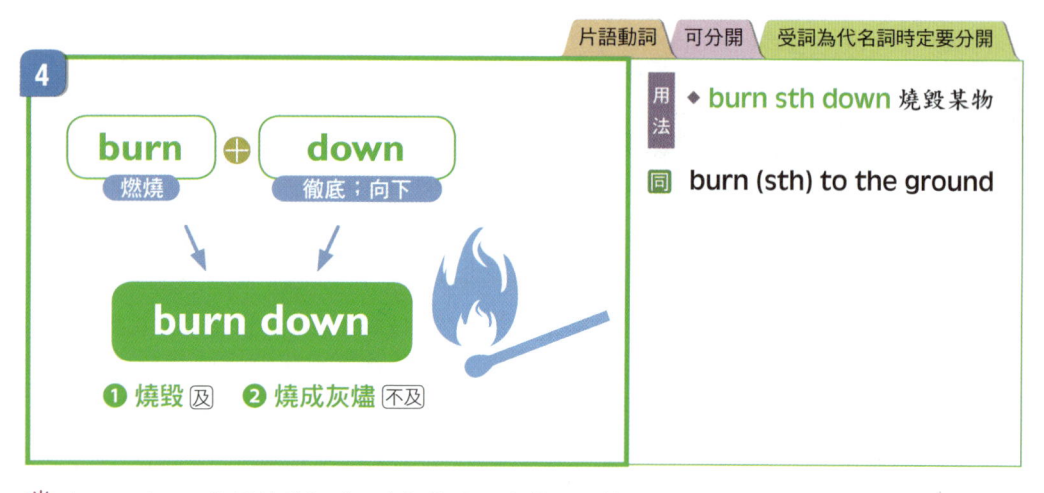

4

片語動詞 | 可分開 | 受詞為代名詞時定要分開

burn (燃燒) + **down** (徹底；向下) → **burn down**
❶ 燒毀 [及]　❷ 燒成灰燼 [不及]

用法 ◆ **burn sth down** 燒毀某物

同 **burn (sth) to the ground**

💡 **burn down** 為及物動詞時，主詞為人、火等，可使用主動或被動語態；為**不及物動詞**時，主詞通常是**物**。

❶ Don't ever light matches in my house. I'm afraid you'll accidentally **burn it down**.　不要在我家點火柴，我很怕你不小心會把房子**燒掉**。

❷ Fortunately, the Stern family had fire insurance, so when their house **burned down**, they were able to buy a new one.
幸好史坦一家有火災保險，所以他們的房子**燒掉**後，他們能買新房子。

5 慣用片語

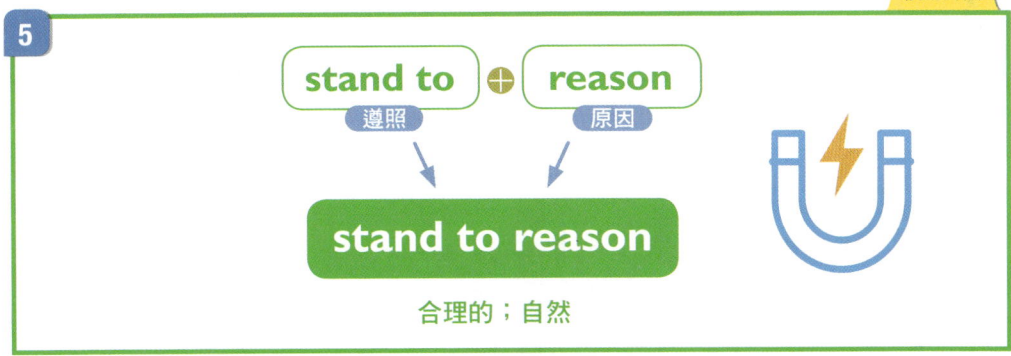

stand to (遵照) ＋ **reason** (原因)
→ **stand to reason**
合理的；自然

- If you never brush your teeth, it **stands to reason** that you'll spend a lot of money at the dentist's office. 如果你從不刷牙，花很多錢看牙醫是很**合理**的。
- It **stands to reason** that students who study the hardest get the best grades. 用功的學生成績較好，這是**理所當然**的。

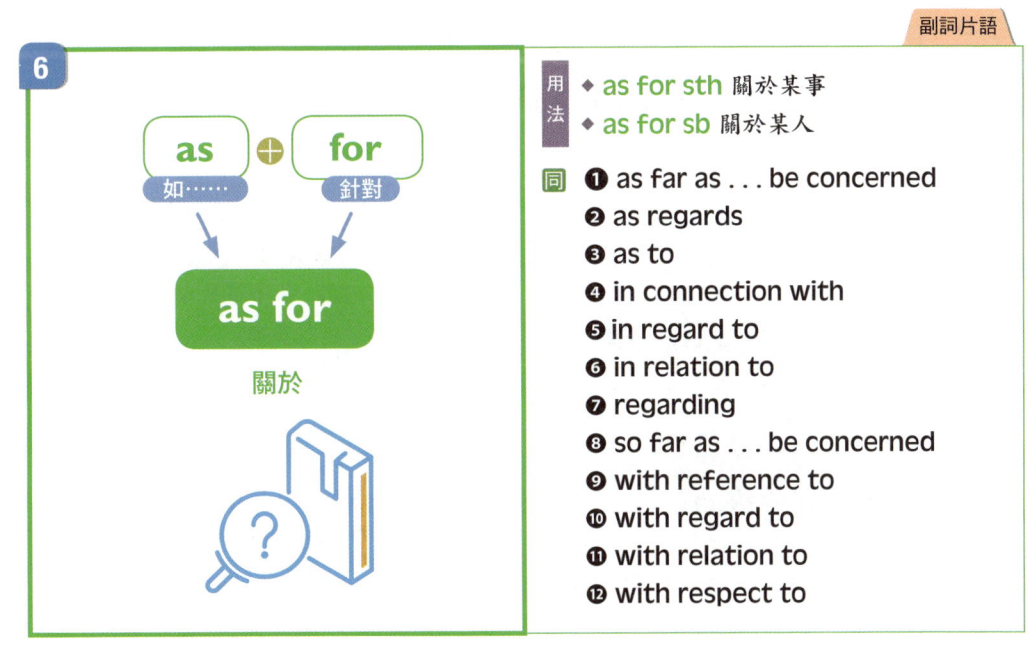

---

6 副詞片語

as (如……) ＋ **for** (針對)
→ **as for**
關於

用法
- as for sth 關於某事
- as for sb 關於某人

同
1. as far as . . . be concerned
2. as regards
3. as to
4. in connection with
5. in regard to
6. in relation to
7. regarding
8. so far as . . . be concerned
9. with reference to
10. with regard to
11. with relation to
12. with respect to

💡 **as for** 通常至於句首，用來表示「再次提到剛才已談過的事情」。

- **As for** Bill, he ended up writing a book and becoming famous. 至於比爾，他最後因寫了一本書而變得很有名。
- Today is a beautiful day; **as for** tomorrow, however, we can expect rain. 今天天氣晴朗。**至於**明天，可能會下雨。

Unit 12 The New Mobile Phone 新手機

105

7

burn (燃燒) + **up** (完全) → **burn up**

① 燒光 及/不及　② 使發怒 及

| 片語動詞 | 可分開 | 受詞為代名詞時定要分開 |

用法
- ◆ burn up sth / burn sth up 燒光某事物
- ◆ burn sb up 使某人發怒
- ◆ burn up 發燒
  → "You're **burning up**!" he said, touching her forehead.
  他摸了她的額頭後說：「你在**發燒**！」
- ◆ burn up with sth 因某事而發怒
  → She was **burnt up with** jealousy and suspicion. 她因忌妒和猜忌而發怒。

同 燒掉 burn off

💡 **burn up** 表示「燒光」時，可作及物或不及物動詞。

❶ The photographs in Ray's bedroom were **burned up** in the fire.
雷房間的那場大火，**燒光**了他的照片。

❷ The bad news really **burned** him **up**. 那個壞消息真的令他很**生氣**。

8

burn (燃燒) + **out** (疲倦；失去知覺) → **burn out**

① 使筋疲力盡　② （機器）燒壞；燒盡 及/不及

| 片語動詞 | 可分開 | 受詞為代名詞時定要分開 |

用法
- ◆ sth burn out 某物壞掉
- ◆ sth burn sb out 某事讓某人累壞
- ◆ sb burn out 某人累壞
- ◆ sb burn oneself out 某人把自己累壞
- ◆ sb burn sth out 某人把某物燒掉

比較
- ◆ burn down 燒毀
  → The police are hoping to find the people who **burned down** the apartment.
  警方希望能找到**燒毀**這棟公寓的縱火犯。
- ◆ burn up 燒光
  → The apartment was **burned up** in the big fire. 那棟公寓被大火**燒光**。
- ◆ burn out 燒壞
  → It looks like the starter motor on the car has **burnt out**.
  看來是車子的啟動馬達**燒壞**了。

💡 **burn out** 可作及物或不及物動詞使用，表示「燒壞；燒盡」，也可使用被動語態，表示「使某人筋疲力盡」。

❶ In his last year of high school, Louis **burned out** and got terrible grades.
路易在高中的最後一年**累壞了**，所以成績很糟糕。

❶ The writer **burned** himself **out** as he finished his first book.
作者完成了第一本書後便**累壞了**。

❷ After she used the old laptop for six hours straight, it **burned out** and wouldn't turn on anymore.
那台舊筆記型電腦在她使用了整整六個鐘頭後便**燒壞**，再也無法開機了。

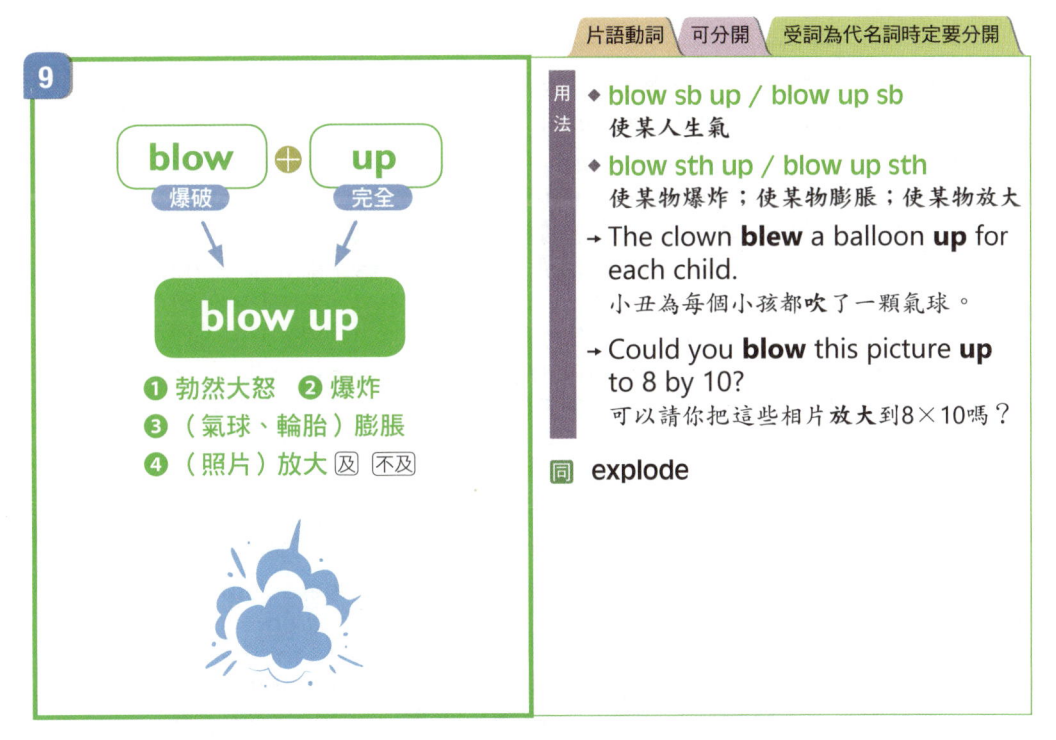

9

片語動詞 | 可分開 | 受詞為代名詞時定要分開

blow（爆破）+ **up**（完全）→ **blow up**

❶ 勃然大怒　❷ 爆炸
❸（氣球、輪胎）膨脹
❹（照片）放大　及　不及

用法
◆ blow sb up / blow up sb
  使某人生氣
◆ blow sth up / blow up sth
  使某物爆炸；使某物膨脹；使某物放大
→ The clown **blew** a balloon **up** for each child.
  小丑為每個小孩都**吹**了一顆氣球。
→ Could you **blow** this picture **up** to 8 by 10?
  可以請你把這些相片**放大**到8×10嗎？

同 explode

❶ My dad **blew up** when he saw the phone bill.
我爸爸看到電話帳單後**氣炸了**。

❷ The best part of the action movie was when the gas tank **blew up** and started a huge fire.
這部動作片最精采的部分，就是油箱**爆炸**而引發大火了。

107

10 break + out

break 破裂 + **out** 向外 → **break out**

❶ 突然發生（爭執、戰爭）
❷ 爆發（傳染病）
❸ 逃跑 不及

片語動詞 / 不可分開

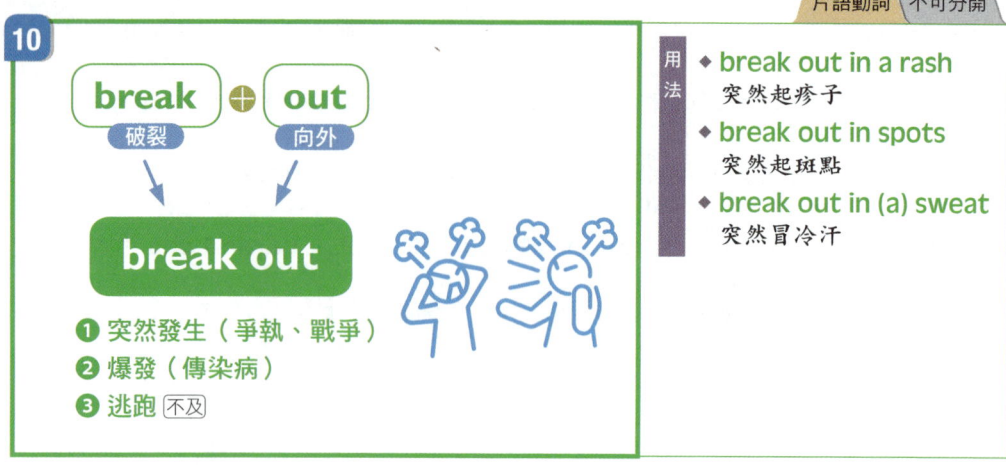

用法
- ◆ break out in a rash
  突然起疹子
- ◆ break out in spots
  突然起斑點
- ◆ break out in (a) sweat
  突然冒冷汗

💡 **break out** 常用來表示「突然爆發戰爭、暴動、疾病或火災」等。
名詞為 **outbreak**，通常會寫成 **outbreak of sth**。

❶ Irma and Gina got more and more angry with each other, and it wasn't long before an argument **broke out** between them.
由於娥瑪和吉娜越來越生對方的氣，於是他們之間的爭吵**爆發**了。

❷ When Damian returned from school, his mother saw that he had **broken out** with chicken pox.
當戴明恩從學校返家後，媽媽發現他突然長了水痘。

❸ In the news today I saw that three thieves **broke out** of jail!
我在今天的新聞上看到有三位小偷**逃獄**了！

---

11 feel + sorry + for

慣用片語

feel 感覺 + **sorry** 遺憾 + **for** 為了…… → **feel sorry for** 深表同情

用法
- ◆ feel sorry for sb
  對某人深表同情
- → I **feel** so **sorry for** the children—it must be really hard for them.
  我很**同情**那些孩子，這對他們來說一定很難接受。

同
❶ be sorry for
❷ have pity on
❸ take pity on

- I **felt sorry for** Matilda when I heard she was kicked out of her apartment.
  當我聽到瑪蒂蓮達被趕出公寓時，我對她**深表同情**。

- Seeing that poor bird in the little cage really made me **feel sorry for** it.
  我很**同情**那隻被關在小籠子裡可憐的鳥兒。

12

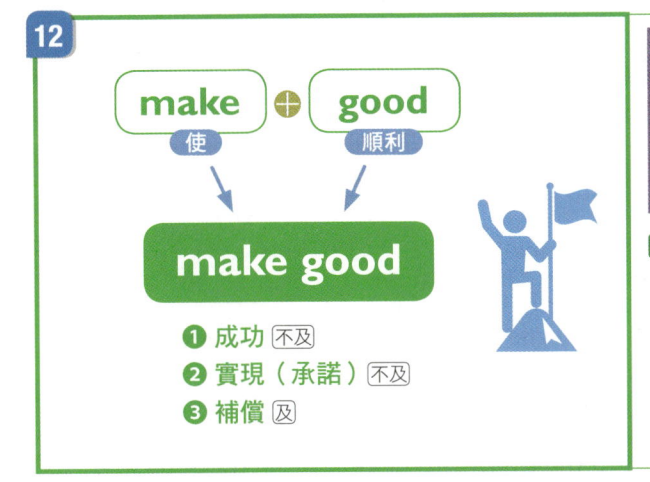

make （使） + good （順利）

→ **make good**

❶ 成功 [不及]
❷ 實現（承諾）[不及]
❸ 補償 [及]

用法
- **make good sb's sth**
  成功地完成某件難事
  → Michael **made good** his escape from the hospital.
  麥可**成功地**逃出了醫院。

同 make it

💡 ❶ **make good** 表示「成功」時，為不及物動詞，主詞通常為人。
　 ❷ 表示「實現承諾」時，為不及物動詞，後接 **promise** 等名詞。
　 ❸ 表示「補償」時，為及物動詞，後接 **damage** 等名詞，亦可使用被動語態。

❶ She was described as the local girl who **made** it **good** in Hollywood.
她代表了在好萊塢**大放光彩**的鄉村女孩。

❷ Brad **made good** on his promise to study more and get better grades.
布萊德**實踐**了他會更用功以取得好成績**的承諾**。

❷ Linda **made good** on her decision to study economics.
琳達**實現**了決定讀經濟學**的承諾**。

慣用片語

Unit 12 The New Mobile Phone 新手機

Unit 12 Test Yourself!

Ⓐ 選擇題

1. To keep herself _____, Julia reads the paper every morning and watches the news at night.
   Ⓐ burned out Ⓑ blown up Ⓒ up-to-date Ⓓ broken out

2. After lightning struck his house, it _____.
   Ⓐ caught fire Ⓑ stood to reason Ⓒ broke out Ⓓ burned out

3. If you ask me, it _____ that she wants to go to Harvard because all of her brothers and sisters did.
   Ⓐ breaks out Ⓑ stands to reason Ⓒ burns out Ⓓ catches fire

4. Although the police officer put the robber in the police car, he somehow _____ and ran away when no one was looking.
   Ⓐ caught fire Ⓑ burned up Ⓒ made good Ⓓ broke out

5. The news that his daughter had gotten married without telling him really _____ him _____.
   Ⓐ caught . . . fire Ⓑ burned . . . up Ⓒ made . . . good Ⓓ stood . . . to reason

6. My mom's cell phone is enormous, ugly, and very _____, but she doesn't care.
   Ⓐ burned out Ⓑ blown up Ⓒ out-of-date Ⓓ burned up

7. Don't work too hard or you'll _____, and then you won't want to do anything.
   Ⓐ burn out Ⓑ make good Ⓒ catch fire Ⓓ stand to reason

8. _____ the topic of your salary, we will discuss it after lunch.
   Ⓐ Making good Ⓑ In and of Ⓒ Feeling sorry for Ⓓ As for

9. I _____ on my promise to enter med school and become a chief surgeon.
   Ⓐ burned up Ⓑ made good Ⓒ blew up Ⓓ caught fire

10. How much will it cost to take this photo and _____ it _____ to twice its current size?
    Ⓐ blow . . . up Ⓑ burn . . . down Ⓒ break . . . out Ⓓ burn . . . out

11. I _____ Jane's cousin who was in a motorcycle accident last weekend.
    Ⓐ blew up Ⓑ caught fire Ⓒ felt sorry for Ⓓ broke out

12. The school _____ because someone lit a fire in the trash can.
    Ⓐ broke out Ⓑ burned out Ⓒ made good Ⓓ burned down

B 閱讀文章，從字表中選擇詞彙填入，並依人稱時態等做適當的變化

out-of-date	burn up	feel sorry for	up-to-date
blow up	as for	make good	burn down
catch fire	stand to reason		

There was a disaster at the office yesterday. Someone accidentally put some metal into the old microwave, which is very ① _____, and after a few minutes it ② _____; flames were everywhere! A few seconds later, there was a loud explosion as the microwave ③ _____! The fire continued to grow, and we worried that the entire kitchen was ④ _____.

⑤ _____ the firemen, they ⑥ _____ on their promise to put out the fire. It ⑦ _____ that we'll need a new kitchen in the office, but at least no one was hurt and the building didn't ⑧ _____.

However, I ⑨ _____ my boss because it turned out she was the one who put the metal in the microwave. I imagine the next microwave we buy will be more ⑩ _____!

C 引導式翻譯，並依人稱時態等做適當的變化

1. 那棟建築物昨天深夜**失火**了，真正的起火原因尚無法得知。
   For reasons that are not yet clear, the building _____ _____ late yesterday evening.

2. 你可以幫我**吹**這些氣球嗎？
   Would you help me _____ _____ these balloons?

3. 我們晚出發就會晚到，這是很**合理**的。
   It _____ _____ _____ that if we leave late, we will arrive late.

4. 他會**成功**的，你等著看吧。他很努力，也知道該追求什麼。
   He'll _____ _____, you'll see. He works hard and knows what he's doing.

Unit 13

Walking Along the Beach
海邊散步

056

Jolene and Charlie are talking while taking a walk along the beach.
裘琳和查理在海邊一邊聊天一邊散步。

Charlie: You know, it's **once in a blue moon**[1] that we have this kind of weather in the spring. It's perfect for taking a walk on the beach! It's something we shouldn't **take for granted**[2].

唉，我們**很少**能在春天有這樣的天氣，到海邊散步正好！我們不應該**認為這是稀鬆平常的**。

Jolene: You're right, Charlie, especially if we **take into account**[3] that usually it's raining this time of year. Things really **turned out**[4] well.

你說的沒錯，查理。尤其是**考慮到**現在已經是春天了，每年這個時節通常都在下雨，天氣能**變成**這樣真好。

Charlie: Hmm, maybe it'll rain after all. Let's go back. Taking a walk on the beach this time of year really **calls for**[5] umbrellas.

嗯，可能快要下雨了。我們回去吧。每年此時到海邊散步真**需要**帶把傘。

Jolene: You **give up**[6] too easily! A little rain never hurt anyone.

你太容易**放棄**了！這種毛毛雨不會有影響的。

112

1

once (一次) + **in** (在……的時候) + **a blue moon** (藍色月亮)

→ **once in a blue moon**
很少；不常

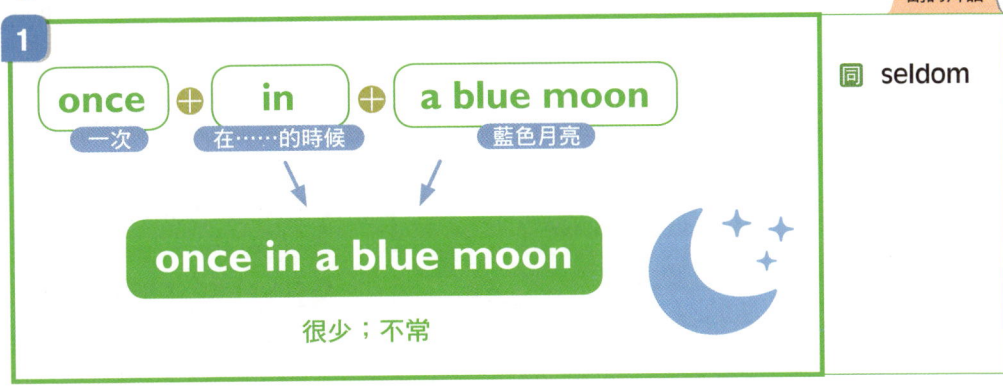

同 seldom

> 💡 **once in a blue moon** 常用來表示「非常罕見的事情」。在天文學中，藍月（**blue moon**）是指在同一個月中的第二次月圓，然而藍月並非如古人所說的很罕見，在天候許可的情況下，有時也可以看到真正的藍色月亮。

- Amy's brother is always traveling, so they see each other only **once in a blue moon**.
  艾咪的哥哥一直都在旅行，所以他們**很少**見面。
- **Once in a blue moon,** a woman gives birth to triplets.
  很少有女人能生出三胞胎。
- My cousin lives in Philadelphia, so I get to see him only **once in a blue moon**.
  我的表弟住在費城，所以我**不常**和他見面。

2

take for (把……當作) + **granted** (被承認的)

→ **take for granted**
將……視為理所當然

慣用片語

用法
- **take sth for granted**
  把某事視為理所當然
- **take sb for granted** 不重視某人
- **take it for granted that ...**
  想當然……
  → We **take it for granted that** our children will be better off than we were.
  我們**都認為**孩子會青出於藍更甚於藍。

- Sheila helps her brother a lot, but sometimes she feels **taken for granted**.
  席拉幫了她哥哥很多忙，但她有時感覺**不被重視**。
- Only after her computer broke did she realize how much she **took** having a laptop **for granted**.　她在電腦壞掉後，才知道她忽視了電腦的重要性。
- Many people **take** it **for granted** that the future will be better.
  許多人都認為未來理所當然會更美好。
- So many of us **take** clean water **for granted**.
  許多人都把乾淨的水視為理所當然。

3

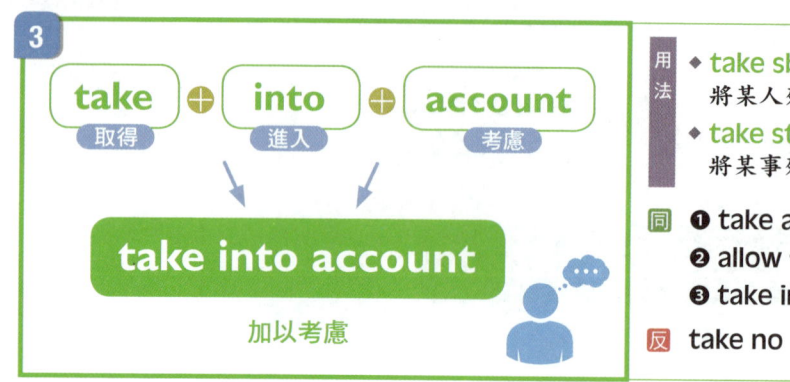

take(取得) + **into**(進入) + **account**(考慮)
→ **take into account** 加以考慮

用法
- take sb into account 將某人列入考慮
- take sth into account 將某事列入考慮

同
1. take account of
2. allow for
3. take into consideration

反 take no account of

- Even if you don't do well on this test, the teacher is sure to **take** your good attitude and hard work **into account** when she gives you your final grade.
  就算你這次考不好，老師在打總成績前，會把你良好的學習態度和努力**列入考慮**的。
- Beth had planned to write her research paper over the weekend, but she forgot to **take into account** the fact that the library would be closed then.
  貝絲計劃在週末寫研究報告，但她沒有**考慮**到週末圖書館不開放。

片語動詞　可分開　受詞為代名詞時定要分開

4

turn(轉變) + **out**(出現；外面)
→ **turn out**

1. 結果是 不及
2. 出席 不及
3. 生產（產品）及
4. 關掉 及

用法
- As it turns out... 結果原來是……
- It turns out that... 結果證明是……
- turn out to be... 結果是……

同 關掉
1. switch off
2. shut off
3. turn off

結果 fall out

反 打開 turn on

💡 turn on/off/out 和 switch on/off 皆可用來表示用旋鈕開關電器等；put on/out 則表示打開或關上電器。

1. As things **turned out**, it was a good idea to go on vacation last month.
   事情**證明**了上個月去度假是一個好主意。
2. When the president gave a speech in Central Park, thousands of people **turned out**. 總統在中央公園發表演說，有上千名民眾前往**參加**。
3. They **turn out** thousands of shoes every week.
   他們每個星期**生產**好幾千雙鞋子。

5

call (召喚) + **for** (為了) → **call for**

❶ 需要　❷ 要求　❸ 接某人 及

片語動詞 / 不可分開

用法
- ◆ call for sb 接某人
- → I'll **call for** you at eight.
  我八點會**去接**你。
- ◆ call for sth 需要某事物
- → It's the sort of work that **calls for** a high level of concentration.
  這是一份需要集中注意力的工作。

同　要求 ask for

❶ Wow, a toothache like that definitely **calls for** a dentist.
哇，牙齒痛成那樣絕對**需要**看牙醫。

❷ When Tommy couldn't finish the project on his own, he **called for** help.
當湯米無法自己完成這項企畫，他**要求**支援。

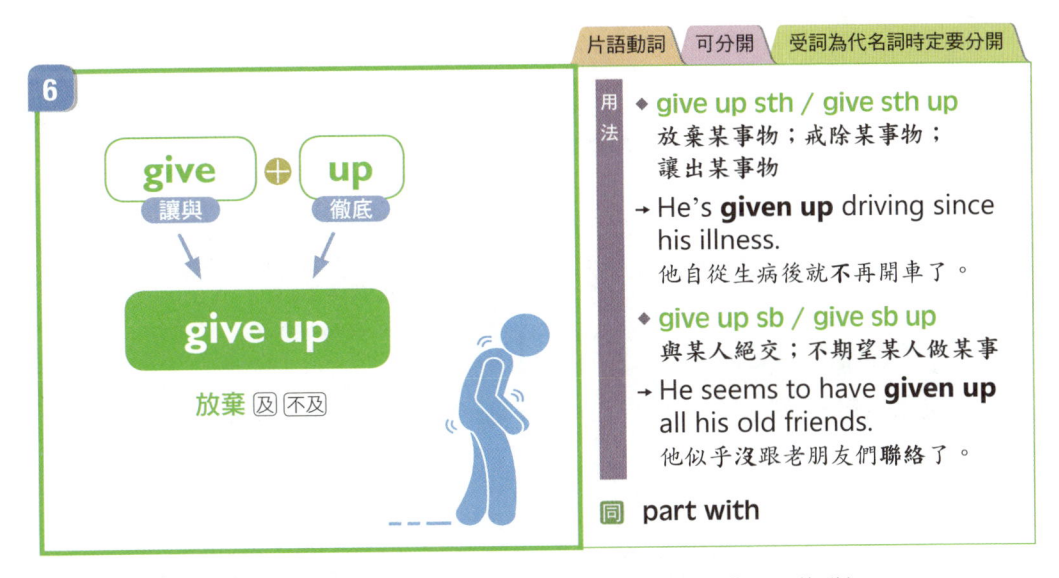

6

give (讓與) + **up** (徹底) → **give up**

放棄 及 不及

片語動詞 / 可分開 / 受詞為代名詞時定要分開

用法
- ◆ give up sth / give sth up
  放棄某事物；戒除某事物；讓出某事物
- → He's **given up** driving since his illness.
  他自從生病後就**不再**開車了。
- ◆ give up sb / give sb up
  與某人絕交；不期望某人做某事
- → He seems to have **given up** all his old friends.
  他似乎沒跟老朋友們**聯絡**了。

同　part with

💡 表示「放棄；停止」，可作及物動詞，後接名詞或動名詞，亦可作不及物動詞。

- Don't ever **give up**; just keep trying. 永遠不要**放棄**，要不斷嘗試。
- I know things look difficult now, but don't **give up** on your dreams; if you work hard enough, things may get better.
  我知道事情現在看起來很難，但別**放棄**你的夢想。只要你夠努力，情況就會好轉。
- Starting next week, Felix plans to **give up** smoking.
  菲力斯計劃從下星期開始**戒菸**。

Unit 13　Walking Along the Beach 海邊散步

115

7

make 使 + **clear** 清楚 → **make clear** 使清楚明白

用法	◆ make clear sth / make sth clear 使某事清楚明白 ◆ make it clear that . . . 將某事解釋清楚
同	make heads or tails of

💡 **make clear** 表示「使某人明白某事」，**make** 和 **clear** 中間有時會插入需使人明白的事情。

- Ronald really didn't **make clear** what time we were supposed to show up.
  羅納多並沒有**清楚說明**我們應該何時出席。
- Dr. McCormack **made** it perfectly **clear** that you were supposed to come to work early today. 麥科馬克醫師**清楚交代過**，你今天應該要提早來上班。

片語動詞　不可分開

8

come 到達……狀態 + **to** 到 → **come to**

❶ 恢復意識 [不及]
❷ 合計 [及]

用法	◆ come to sth 合計 ◆ come to sb 突然想起 → I can't remember her name— it'll **come to** me in a minute. 我不記得她的名字，我等一下會想起來的。
同	醒過來 ❶ come to life ❷ come to oneself ❸ come to one's senses

- I wondered how long it would take you to **come to your senses**.
  我在想要多久你才能**醒悟過來**。

💡 作不及物動詞時，表示「恢復知覺」，主詞為人或動物，後面亦可加上 **oneself**。

❶ It took Amy a few hours to **come to** after the operation.
艾咪在手術過後幾個小時才**恢復意識**。

❶ Has she **come to** yet? 她**恢復意識**了嗎？

❷ With tax, your bill **comes to** $450.24. 加上稅金後，您的帳單**總共是** 450.24 元。

9

break(毀壞) + **down**(徹底) → **break down**

❶（機器）故障 [不及]
❷ 崩潰 ❸ 衰退 ❹ 腐敗 [及]

> 片語動詞 / 可分開 / 受詞為代名詞時定要分開

用法
- **break down sth** 使某事物衰退、腐敗
→ One sniff of that chocolate was enough to **break down** my determination not to eat sweets. 只要一聞到那個牌子的巧克力，我不吃甜食的決心就會動搖。

比較
- **break down** 故障（指當時的動作）
- **out of order** 故障（指之後的狀態）

- Just as we were driving away from the house, our car **broke down**.
我們正要開車離家時，車子壞了。

10

have(持有) + **on**(在……之上) → **have on**

穿戴（衣服、首飾、鞋子）[及]

> 片語動詞 / 可分開 / 受詞為代名詞時定要分開

用法
- **have sth on** 穿戴某事物

同 wear

- Gary's wife was angry with him when she saw that he didn't **have** his wedding ring **on**. 蓋瑞的太太發現蓋瑞沒戴婚戒時，她很生氣。
- Carol didn't want to answer the door because she **had on** only a bathrobe.
卡蘿不想開門，因為她身上只穿著浴袍。

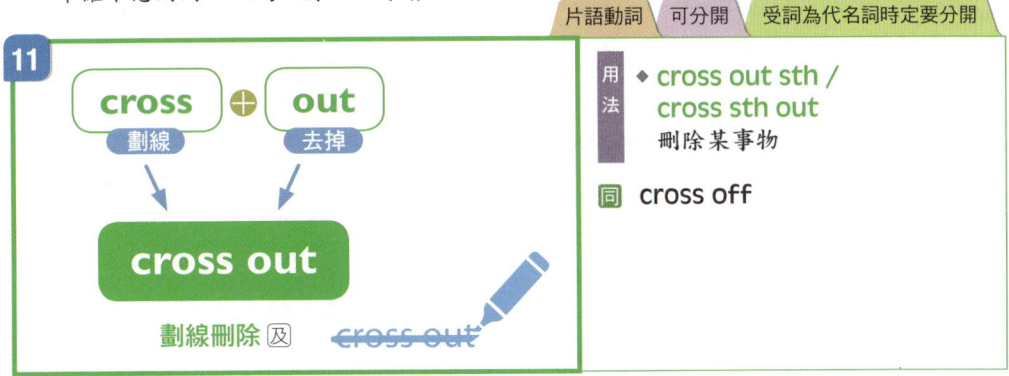

11

cross(劃線) + **out**(去掉) → **cross out**

劃線刪除 [及]

> 片語動詞 / 可分開 / 受詞為代名詞時定要分開

用法
- **cross out sth / cross sth out** 刪除某事物

同 cross off

- The teacher **crossed out** a lot of my text and told me to write those parts over.
老師把許多我寫的字劃掉了，還要我把那些部分重寫。
- It was hard to see who the letter was from because someone had **crossed out** the return address. 有人把回信地址劃掉了，所以很難看出信是誰寄的。

Unit 13 Test Yourself!

Ⓐ 選擇題

1. My pencil didn't have an eraser, so I _____ the parts I didn't like.
   Ⓐ took for granted   Ⓑ crossed out   Ⓒ turned out   Ⓓ broke down

2. Kevin was knocked out when he fell off the ladder; however, after a few minutes he _____.
   Ⓐ cleared out   Ⓑ came to   Ⓒ broke down   Ⓓ turned out

3. If your truck _____, you should ask my neighbor to take a look at it—he's a mechanic.
   Ⓐ turns out   Ⓑ gives up   Ⓒ crosses out   Ⓓ breaks down

4. Before you travel to Brazil, be sure to _____ the fact that they speak Portuguese there. You may want to learn a few words first.
   Ⓐ cross out   Ⓑ take into account   Ⓒ make clear   Ⓓ give up

5. The reason Jared never became a successful cellist is that he _____ too easily.
   Ⓐ crossed out   Ⓑ gave up   Ⓒ broke down   Ⓓ turned out

6. Although Ely lent his car to Pauline for the weekend, she didn't even thank him, and he feels _____.
   Ⓐ taken for granted   Ⓑ crossed out   Ⓒ called for   Ⓓ broken down

7. The doctor said that Joel's heart condition _____ a specialist.
   Ⓐ comes to   Ⓑ breaks down   Ⓒ clears out   Ⓓ calls for

8. Because Nelly doesn't make a lot of money, she goes out to eat only _____.
   Ⓐ once in a blue moon   Ⓑ day-to-day
   Ⓒ month in, month out   Ⓓ once daily

9. Lauren _____ it _____ that we were not supposed to even touch her laptop, much less use it.
   Ⓐ crossed . . . out   Ⓑ made . . . clear   Ⓒ cleared . . . out   Ⓓ broke . . . down

10. Ralph tried making a cake, but it didn't _____ good.
    Ⓐ turn out   Ⓑ break down   Ⓒ give up   Ⓓ cross out

11. I hope they'll _____ her age _____ when they're judging her work.
    Ⓐ take . . . for granted   Ⓑ take . . . into account
    Ⓒ cross . . . out   Ⓓ make . . . clear out

B 閱讀文章，從字表中選擇詞彙填入，並依人稱時態等做適當的變化

take into account	turn out	break down
call for	once in a blue moon	make clear
come to	give up	

When a dog is about to have puppies, it sometimes ❶ _____ the help of an animal doctor. Even if the animal doctor cannot come to your house, you can call him and he can ❷ _____ what must be done. He will know what sort of things must be ❸ _____. Note that after the puppies are born, it may take a few minutes for them to ❹ _____. Don't worry, though; in most cases, everything ❺ _____ fine.

When my dog was having puppies, we called the animal doctor; however, his car ❻ _____ on the way to our house. We didn't ❼ _____, though, and we did everything we could to help the mother. In the end, she had very special puppies—they were born with stripes! That sort of puppy is born only ❽ _____. And our dog had three striped puppies, which is even more rare!

C 引導式翻譯，並依人稱時態等做適當的變化

1. 好的建築師會將建築物的周遭環境**列入考慮**。
   A good architect _____ _____ _____ the building's surroundings.

2. 雖然辦公室的影印機昨天很正常，但今天稍早卻**故障**了。
   Although it was working fine yesterday, the office photocopier _____ _____ early this morning.

3. 蘇珊娜試著修理電視，但是結果**出來**卻不如她所預期。
   Suzanna tried to fix the TV, but things didn't _____ _____ as she had hoped.

4. 我喜歡你昨天晚上**穿**的那件洋裝。
   I loved that dress you _____ _____ last night.

5. 這個好消息**需要**喝香檳慶祝！
   This good news _____ _____ champagne!

6. 緹娜不太會打網球，但是她不想**放棄**。
   Tina wasn't good at tennis, but she didn't want to _____ it _____.

119

Unit 14

🔊 060

Babysitting
照顧小孩

Sam and Nancy have a chat.
山姆和南西在聊天。

Sam:	What are you doing tonight?	妳今晚要做什麼呢？
Nancy:	I have to **look after**[1] my little cousin Billy while his parents are **eating out**[2].	我必須**照顧**我的表弟比利，他的父母今晚要**在外面吃飯**。
Sam:	You have a cousin named Billy? I've never **heard of**[3] him.	妳有個表弟叫做比利？我怎麼從來沒**聽說**過他。
Nancy:	That's because his family lives in Ontario, Canada. They're visiting my mom for a few weeks.	因為他們家住在加拿大安大略省。他們這幾個禮拜是來探望我媽媽。
Sam:	Are you **looking forward to**[4] spending time with your cousin?	妳**期待**和你的表弟一起玩嗎？
Nancy:	**As a matter of fact**[5], it won't be fun at all. Billy always **has his way**[6], so he is really poorly behaved.	**其實**，那一點也不好玩。比利總是**為所欲為**，他是一個不聽話的孩子。
Sam:	Oh, sorry to hear that. Do you have to do this? Maybe your uncle and aunt can find someone else to take care of him.	噢，真遺憾。妳一定要照顧他嗎？也許你的叔叔和阿姨可以找其他人幫忙照顧他？
Nancy:	I have no choice; it's **cut-and-dried**[7]. But I'll **hear from**[8] my aunt as soon as they're on their way home. If you **feel like**[9] it, we can see a movie afterward.	我別無選擇，這是**事先安排**好的事情。但在他們回來的路上，我阿姨會**通知**我。如果你**想要**的話，我們之後可以去看場電影。
Sam:	Good idea!	好主意！

Unit 14 Babysitting 照顧小孩

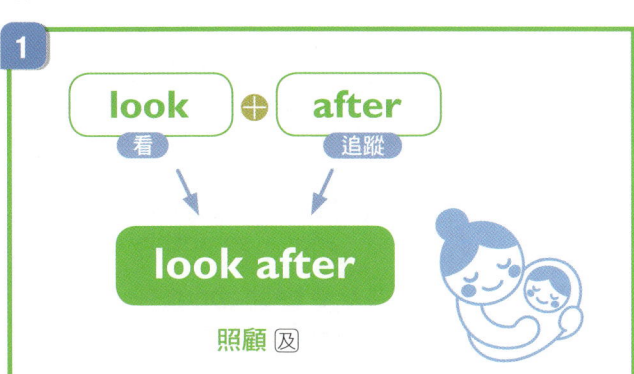

片語動詞　不可分開

1

look（看） + after（追蹤）

→ **look after**

照顧（及）

用法
- **look after sb** 照顧某人
- **look after sth** 照顧某事

同
1. watch over
2. take care of
3. care for
4. attend to

💡 **look after** 為及物動詞，後接人或物，可表示「照顧；目送」；後接抽象名詞時，表示「追求」，亦可使用被動語態。

- When my folks are at work, I **look after** my little sister.
  父母去上班時，我要照顧我妹妹。
- Who **looks after** your dog when you are in class?
  你去上課的時候，誰來照顧你的狗？
- I **look after** the neighbors' cat while they're away.
  鄰居不在的時候，我替他們照顧貓咪。

片語動詞

2

eat（吃） + out（在外面）

→ **eat out**

在餐廳用餐（不及）

同
1. dine out
2. go out to eat
3. eat at a restaurant

反 在家用餐 **eat in**

- To save money, Andy **ate in** instead of going to a restaurant.
  安迪為了省錢而不去餐廳用餐，他都在家裡吃飯。

💡 **out** 在這裡作為副詞，不需加受詞，表示「用餐的方式」。**eat out** 的意思雖然和 **dine out** 相同，皆表示「在餐廳吃飯」，但 **dine out** 的用法較為正式。另外，若是在親友家吃飯時要使用 **dine out**，不可使用 **eat out**。

- There's nothing good to eat at home, so let's **eat out** for dinner.
  家裡沒有什麼好吃的東西，所以我們到外面吃飯。
- When I lived in Seattle, I used to **eat out** all the time.
  我住在西雅圖的時候，都在外面吃飯。

🔊 062

片語動詞 不可分開

3

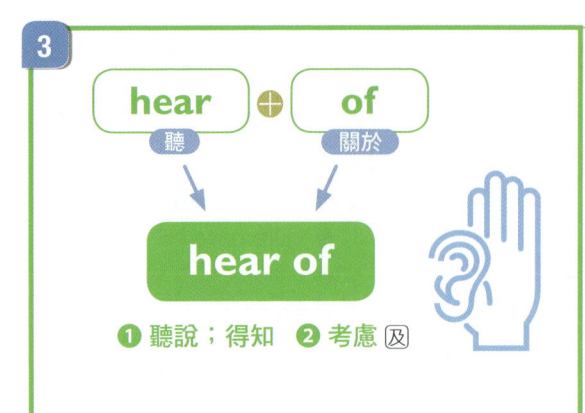

```
hear  +  of
 聽       關於
    ↓   ↓
  hear of
❶ 聽說；得知  ❷ 考慮 及
```

用法	◆ hear of sth 聽說某事
	◆ hear of sb 聽說過某人
比較	◆ hear from sb 從某人那聽到（from 後常接人）
	◆ hear about 聽到（hear 和 about 中間可加入 a lot、something 等字）
同	得知 ❶ hear about
	聽從 ❶ listen to

💡 **hear of** 常用於否定句和疑問句。

❶ Before my trip to Africa, I had never **heard of** Madagascar.
到非洲旅遊前，我從沒**聽說**過馬達加斯加島。

❶ There are many classical musicians whom I've never **heard of**.
有許多古典音樂家我都沒有**聽**過。

❷ Damien wanted to go out with his friends Wednesday night, but his mother wouldn't **hear of** it because he had school the next day.
戴明恩星期三晚上想要和朋友出去，但他媽媽因為隔天要上課所以不同意。

片語動詞

4

```
look  +  forward  +  to
 看       往前        向
    ↓      ↓       ↓
    look forward to
       期待；盼望 及
```

用法	◆ look forward to sth 期待某事發生
	→ I'm really **looking forward to** the holiday. 我真的很**期待**假期的來臨。
	◆ not look forward to
	→ I'm **not looking forward to** Christmas this year. 我不太**期待**今年的聖誕節。
反	指望 ❶ count on ❷ expect ❸ anticipate
	回顧 look back

💡 其中的 **to** 為介系詞，而非不定詞，需後接**名詞**或**動名詞**。

• I always **look forward to** three-day weekends because I am able to do some traveling. 我總是**盼望**著一連三天的週末到來，那樣我就可以出外旅遊。

• My little brother is **looking forward to** his birthday party.
我的小弟**期待**著生日派對的到來。

122

5 副詞片語

as（如同） + **a matter of**（和……有關） + **fact**（事實）

→ **as a matter of fact** 事實上

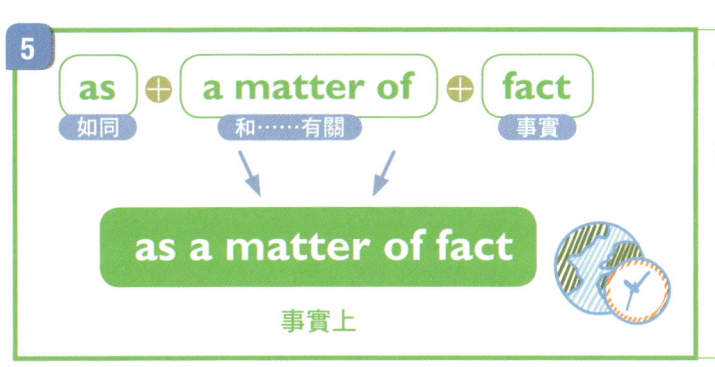

💡 通常置於句首或句中，作轉折語。

同 ❶ in fact
　❷ in effect
　❸ in reality
　❹ in truth

- **As a matter of fact**, Martin recently graduated from college.
  事實上，馬汀最近大學畢業了。
- Cindy just got a new TV, **as a matter of fact**.
  事實上，辛蒂才剛買了一台新的電視。

6 慣用片語

have（如同） + **one's**（和……有關） + **way**（事實）

→ **have one's way** 照某人的意思去做；為所欲為

同 get one's way

💡 亦可寫成 **have one's own way**，own 通常可以省略。**have one's way** 可表示「照某人的意思去做」，也有負面的意思，表示「不顧別人的反對而執意去做」。

- Sometimes it feels like I never **have my way**. 我有時覺得天不從人願。
- Because Carol is the youngest child, she always **has her way**.
  卡蘿是家中的么女，所以她好像老是為所欲為。

7 形容詞片語

cut（切好的） + **and**（且） + **dried**（乾燥的）

→ **cut-and-dried** 可預期的；明確的

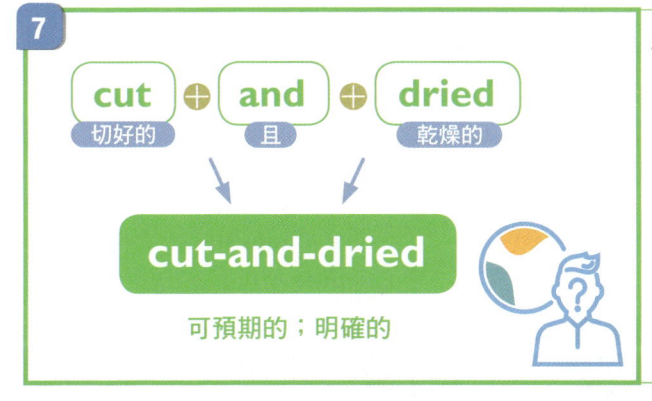

💡 **cut and dried** 的含義實際上跟 cut 和 dry 都沒有什麼關係。**cut and dried** 的意思是：老套的，是人們所預料的，或是根據以往的老做法來行事。任何事情要是被說成 **cut and dried**，那就很可能是沒有什麼吸引人的地方，因為缺乏新鮮內容。（出自《美國之音》）

- After the discussion, the CEO reached a **cut-and-dried** decision.
  討論結束後，執行長得到了一個**預料中**的結論。
- The choices we make in life are rarely as **cut-and-dried** as we would like.
  我們在人生中所做的選擇，通常是無法**預期的**。

123

8. hear + from

hear 聽到 + **from** 從…… → **hear from** 接到某人的消息 及

片語動詞 / 不可分開

用法 ◆ **hear from sb** 從某人那聽到

> **hear from** 可表示「得到某人的消息」或「聽某人談論某事」。

- I hope Ray is okay. I haven't **heard from** him since he arrived in the United Kingdom. 我希望雷沒事。自從他去了英國，我就沒聽到他的消息。
- Teresa expects to **hear from** Samuel next week. 泰瑞莎盼望下星期能接到山姆爾的消息。

9. feel + like

feel 覺得 + **like** 像；想要 → **feel like** 想要做某事

慣用片語

用法 ◆ **feel like (doing) sth** 想要（做）某事
→ I **feel like** (going for) a swim. 我想要（去）游泳。

> **like** 在這裡作介系詞。**feel like** 表示「摸起來像、感覺像」時，需以 **it** 或物作主詞；在疑問句和否定句中，**feel like** 也可用來表示「想要（做某事）」，主詞為人，後接名詞或動名詞。

- Do you **feel like** going to the movies tonight? 你今晚想要看電影嗎？
- I don't **feel like** going out for Chinese food; my stomach hurts. 我今晚不想出去吃中國菜，我胃痛。

10. once + and + for all

once 一次 + **and** 而且 + **for all** 永遠 → **once and for all** 一勞永逸地

副詞片語

> **once and for all** 表示「僅此一次，沒有下次」，此片語是由 **one time and for all time** 所衍生而來的。

用法 ◆ **not . . . once and for all** 永遠不再

- As soon as Jared stapled the pages of his report together, he knew he was done with it **once and for all**.
  傑瑞德把報告裝訂好後，便了解到他終於把它完成了。

11

make (使成為) + **fun** (玩笑) + **of** (動作對象)
↓
make fun of
嘲笑

慣用片語

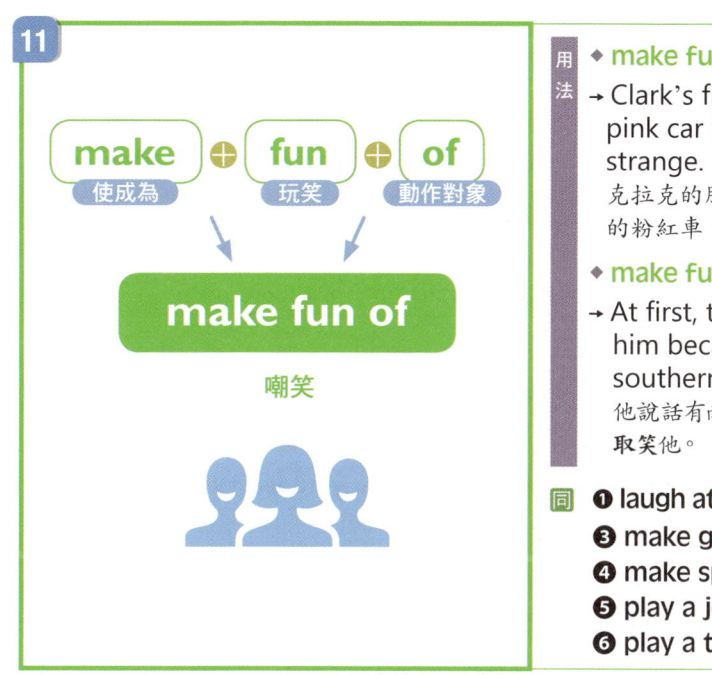

用法
- ◆ **make fun of sth** 取笑某事物
- → Clark's friends **made fun of** his pink car because it looked so strange.
  克拉克的朋友**取笑**他那台看起來很怪的粉紅車。

- ◆ **make fun of sb** 取笑某人
- → At first, the kids **made fun of** him because he spoke with a southern accent.
  他說話有南部的口音，孩子們剛開始常**取笑**他。

同
❶ laugh at　❷ poke fun at
❸ make game of
❹ make sport of
❺ play a joke on
❻ play a trick on

- Diane's new suit was so unusual that it was hard not to **make fun of** her.
  黛安新買的套裝很奇怪，令人很難不去**取笑**她。

12

come (成為) + **true** (真實的)
↓
come true
實現；成真

慣用片語

💡 come 為連綴動詞，沒有被動語態。

同 ❶ carry out　❷ realize
反 落空 fall through

- We found a buyer for our house, but then the sale **fell through**.
  我們找到了房子的買主，但這場交易後來**落空**了。

- Although Warren always dreamed of buying a Ferrari, he never thought the dream would **come true**. 雖然華倫常常幻想能買一輛法拉利，但他從沒想過會**實現**。
- The party was everything I had hoped for; it was as if all my wishes **had come true**. 這個派對就是我想要的，假如我的願望都能**成真**的話。
- The good things we've been hoping for are actually **coming true**.
  我們一直期望的好事真的**實現**了。

Unit 14 Test Yourself!

A 選擇題

1. Marianne is _____ her first day at the university; she has even picked out what she's going to wear.
   Ⓐ eating out   Ⓑ looking forward to   Ⓒ looking after   Ⓓ making fun of

2. Ralph learned a lot of new things in his history class; he even read about some people he had never _____ before.
   Ⓐ felt like   Ⓑ heard of   Ⓒ looked forward to   Ⓓ looked after

3. _____, you may be surprised to learn that Harold got married last weekend.
   Ⓐ Day in and day out   Ⓑ As a matter of fact
   Ⓒ Once and for all   Ⓓ Better late than never

4. Some people believe that if you wish upon a star, your wish will _____.
   Ⓐ look after   Ⓑ eat out   Ⓒ come true   Ⓓ feel like

5. What do you _____ doing this weekend?
   Ⓐ make fun   Ⓑ look after   Ⓒ hear of   Ⓓ feel like

6. Let's _____ at that new Japanese place!
   Ⓐ jump on   Ⓑ eat out   Ⓒ look forward   Ⓓ charge on

7. It's not good to always let your son _____ his _____; he'll quickly become spoiled.
   Ⓐ get . . . desserts   Ⓑ run . . . mouth   Ⓒ have . . . way   Ⓓ speak . . . mind

8. I'd like to come with you to the festival, but I have to stay home and _____ my cousin because he can't be left alone.
   Ⓐ look forward   Ⓑ hear of   Ⓒ eat in   Ⓓ look after

9. It's been a while since I _____ my sister. Maybe I'll give her a call.
   Ⓐ felt like   Ⓑ heard from   Ⓒ came true to   Ⓓ looked forward to

10. The teacher told the children not to _____ others because that was mean.
    Ⓐ make fun of   Ⓑ look forward to   Ⓒ hear of   Ⓓ come true to

B 閱讀文章，從字表中選擇詞彙填入，並依人稱時態等做適當的變化

hear from	come true	as a matter of fact
have one's way	look forward to	hear of
eat out	once and for all	look after

Yesterday, my dream ①_____: I won the lottery! After I got the news, I ②_____ many old friends who suddenly wanted to visit; I even got some calls and letters from people I had never ③_____! That's okay, though. I'm just happy that my life will change. I'll be able to ④_____ at expensive restaurants whenever I want, for example. I'm ⑤_____ getting everything I want once I receive the money; it'll be nice to finally ⑥_____ all the time. The first thing I'll do is hire an accountant to help me ⑦_____ the money.

Also, lots of people think I'll quit my job; ⑧_____, I'll probably keep working, at least for a few months. Finally all my financial problems will be solved ⑨_____.

C 引導式翻譯，並依人稱時態等做適當的變化

1. 我們不在的時候，有一位朋友會替我們**照顧**狗狗。
   A friend will _____ _____ the dogs while we're away.

2. 我一直幻想能擁有自己的房子，但我從來沒想過會**成真**。
   I had always dreamt of owning my own house, but I never thought the dream would _____ _____.

3. 我們必須在這個星期內得到一個**明確**的結論。
   We need a _____ decision by the end of the week.

4. 其他孩子以前老是**取笑**瑪莉，因為她既胖又戴著眼鏡。
   The other children were always _____ _____ _____ Mary because she was fat and wore glasses.

5. 在讀過這位作家的最新作品前，我從沒**聽說**過她。
   I had never _____ _____ this author before reading her latest book.

6. 我正**期待**著我的倫敦之旅。
   I'm _____ _____ _____ my trip to London.

Unit 15

🔊 064

School Life
學校生活

Raul and Emily gossip about school life.
勞爾和艾蜜莉在討論學校生活的八卦。

Emily: Did you hear what happened with the teacher who is **filling in**[1] for Ms. Santos today?

你聽說今天**代替**山托斯女士的那位老師所發生的事情了嗎？

Raul: No. What happened?

沒有，怎麼了？

Emily: She arrived for her first day of teaching with her shirt **inside out**[2]!

她第一天代課就把襯衫**穿反**了！

Raul: Ha, ha, ha! That's funny! Is she a good teacher at least?

哈哈哈！真好笑！至少她是個好老師吧？

Emily: Yeah, she's ok. First she made us **fill out**[3] some forms, and while we were doing that, she left for a few minutes. Some people started making jokes and talking. When she came back, she was mad.

是啊，她還不錯。她一開始要我們**填寫**一些表格，我們在填的時候，她離開了一下子。有些人便開始講話和開玩笑，所以她回來後就生氣了。

Raul: What did she say?

那她說了些什麼？

Emily: She said that she is **in touch**[4] with Ms. Santos, and if we don't behave, she'll **take** this problem **up with**[5] her personally.

她說如果我們表現不好，她會**和**山托斯女士**聯絡**，然後當面**和**她**商量**。

Raul: It may be tempting for the students to **take advantage of**[6] the situation now, but **in the long run**[7], it isn't a good idea. Ms. Santos isn't a forgiving person!

現在這種情形其實**對**學生很**有利**，但這**終究**不是一個好主意。山托斯女士並不是一個性情溫和的人！

128

🔊 065

1

片語動詞 | **可分開** | **受詞為代名詞時定要分開**

fill (填) + **in** (在……中) → **fill in**
❶ 填寫 〔及〕
❷ 代替 〔不及〕

用法
- ◆ **fill sb in** 告訴某人額外資訊
  → I **filled** Ryan **in** on the latest gossip.
  我把最新的八卦**告訴**了萊恩。
- ◆ **fill sth in / fill in sth** 填寫某事物
  → **Fill in** the entire form, and then click "Submit." 把整份表格**填完**後,點選「送出」。

同 填寫 fill out

💡 亦可使用被動語態。

❶ The directions on the test were to **fill in** the spaces with the correct answers.
作答方式為在試卷上的空格**填入**正確答案。

❷ I'm not his regular secretary—I'm just **filling in**.
我並不是他固定的秘書,我只是來**代班**的。

2

副詞片語

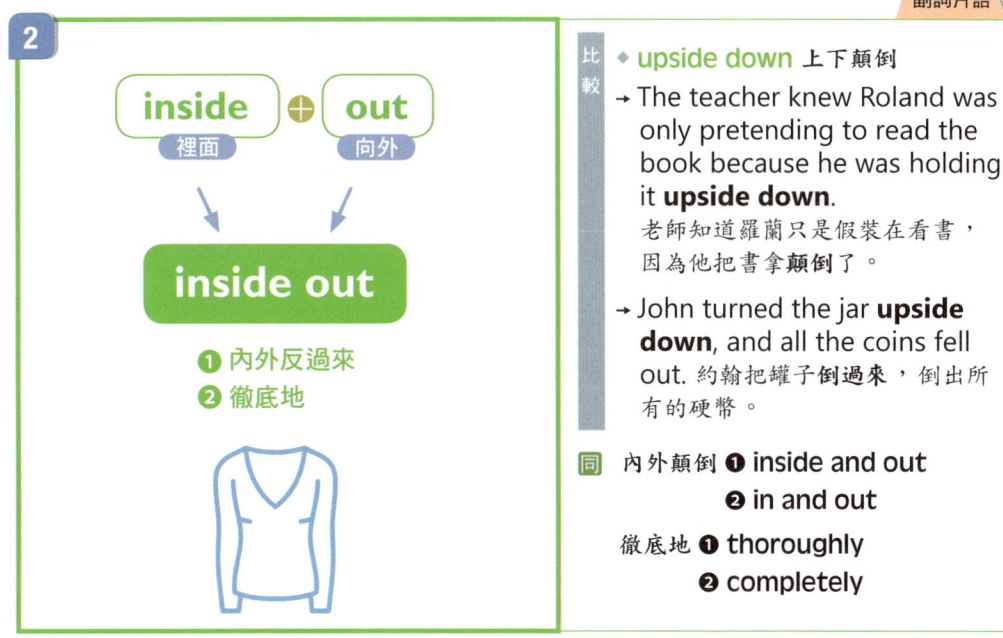

inside (裡面) + **out** (向外) → **inside out**
❶ 內外反過來
❷ 徹底地

比較
- ◆ **upside down** 上下顛倒
  → The teacher knew Roland was only pretending to read the book because he was holding it **upside down**.
  老師知道羅蘭只是假裝在看書,因為他把書拿**顛倒**了。
  → John turned the jar **upside down**, and all the coins fell out. 約翰把罐子**倒過來**,倒出所有的硬幣。

同 內外顛倒 ❶ inside and out
　　　　　　❷ in and out
　　 徹底地 ❶ thoroughly
　　　　　　❷ completely

❶ How embarrassing it was to arrive at school with my pants **inside out**.
我到學校才發現把褲子穿**反**了,真糗。

❶ She had her sweater on **inside out**. 她把毛衣穿**反**了。

片語動詞 可分開 受詞為代名詞時定要分開

3

fill 填 + out 出 → **fill out**

❶ 填寫 及　❷ 增胖 不及

用法
- fill out sth / fill sth out
  填寫某事物

同 填寫 fill in
　　 增重 gain weight

反 減重 lose weight

❶ If you want to apply for a passport, you have to **fill out** many forms.
如果你想申請護照，必須要**填寫許多表格**。

❶ All students must **fill** this document **out** before taking the SAT.
所有參加 SAT 考試的學生都必須先**填寫**這份文件。

❷ Her figure began to **fill out** once she started college.
她上大學後便開始**增胖**了。

副詞片語

4

in 在……狀態 + touch 接觸 → **in touch**

（透過電話、信件、電子郵件或其他方式）和某人聯絡

用法
- in touch with sb 和某人有聯繫
- in touch with sth 知道某事
  → My father is not really **in touch with** what young people are interested in.
  我的父親不太**知道**現在的年輕人喜歡些什麼。

同 in contact

反 失去聯絡；對事情毫無概念
  out of touch

- After graduation, Peter fell **out of touch** with many of his old friends.
  彼得畢業後和許多老朋友**失去聯絡**。

- My grandparents are nice people, but they're definitely a bit **out of touch**. They don't even know what a DVD is!
  我的祖父母人很好，但是他們對許多事情都**毫無概念**，他們連DVD是什麼都不知道！

💡 **in touch** 前面通常搭配 **be** 動詞或 **keep** 使用，作為主詞補語。

- Katherine and I have been **in touch** since high school.
  我和凱瑟琳從高中到現在一直都有**聯絡**。
- I want to keep **in touch** with you even after I move away.
  我就算搬家也想和你**聯絡**。

5

片語動詞 | 可分開 | 受詞為代名詞時定要分開

take (拿) + **up** (起來) + **with** (和……一起)

→ **take up with**
與某人商量某事 及

用法
- **take sth up with sb**
  對某人提出某事

比較
- **take up** 開始（某興趣）；占據
  → Over the summer, Bill **took up** bird-watching.
    比爾整個夏天都在賞鳥。
  → The new sofa sure does **take up** a lot of room!
    這張新沙發的確很占空間！
- **take up with sb** 和某人交往
  → My sister has **taken up with** a former high school sweetheart.
    我妹妹和以前高中時期的男朋友在交往。

- I think it's time to **take up** the issue of a raise **with** my boss.
  我想我該和老闆**商量**加薪的事情了。
- If you don't like the policy, **take** it **up with** the manager.
  如果你不喜歡這項政策，就和經理**商量**。

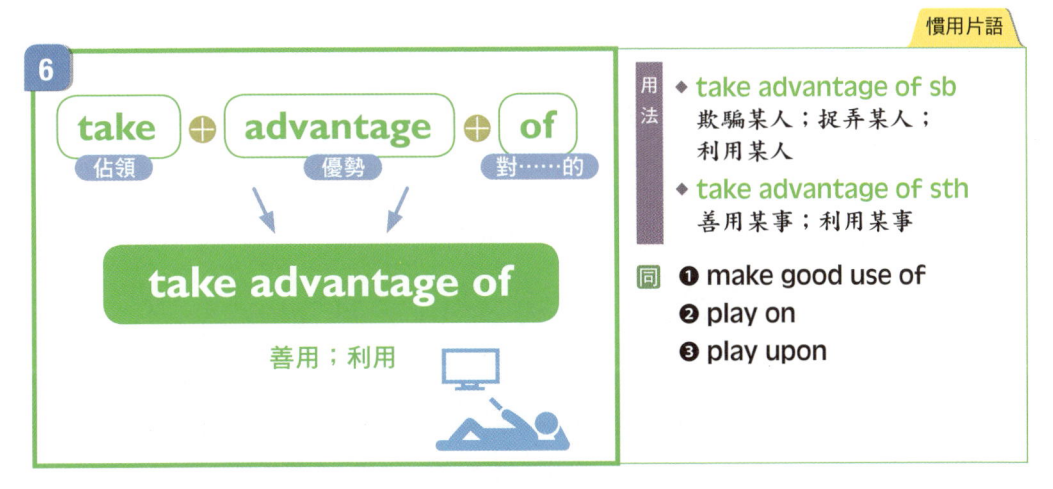

6

慣用片語

take (佔領) + **advantage** (優勢) + **of** (對……的)

→ **take advantage of**
善用；利用

用法
- **take advantage of sb**
  欺騙某人；捉弄某人；利用某人
- **take advantage of sth**
  善用某事；利用某事

同
1. make good use of
2. play on
3. play upon

💡 此片語不一定都是表示負面的「利用」，有時也有正面的意思，如「善加利用」。

131

- Suzanna **took advantage of** the gym on campus and worked out every day.
  蘇珊娜**善用**學校的健身房，她每天都去健身。
- I think he **takes advantage of** her good nature. 我覺得他在**利用**她善良的本性。
- I thought Francesca was nice until I saw how she **took advantage of** Dale and made him do all her work.
  在我發現法蘭西絲卡**利用**戴爾替她完成所有的工作前，我一直以為她是個好人。

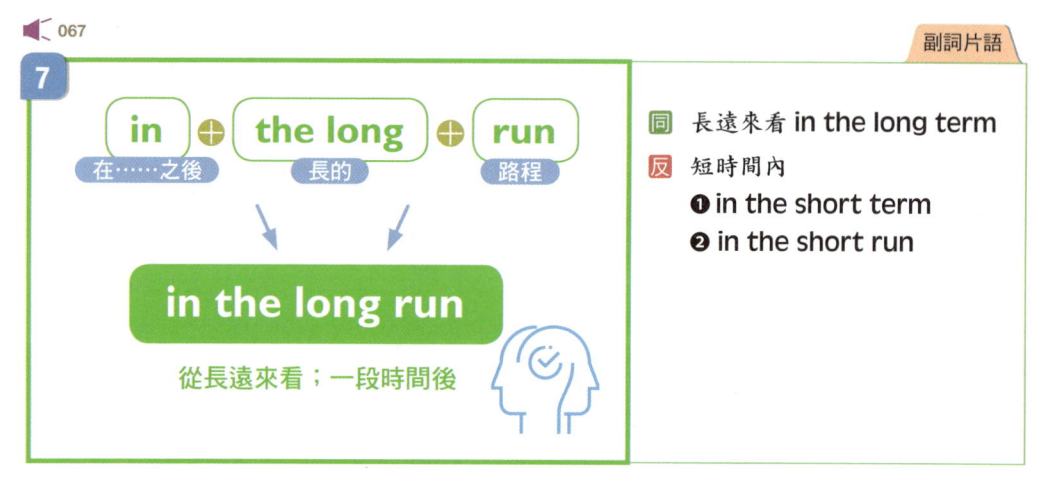

7

067

副詞片語

in（在……之後）+ **the long**（長的）+ **run**（路程）

→ **in the long run**
從長遠來看；一段時間後

同 長遠來看 in the long term
反 短時間內
❶ in the short term
❷ in the short run

💡 此片語原本用來表示「賽跑者一路跑到最後」，後來引申為「從長遠來看；最後」。

- You may not like the idea of getting braces, but **in the long run**, it is the right thing to do. 你也許不喜歡戴矯正器，但**久了以後**你會發現這麼做是正確的。
- Buying these baby kittens may seem like a good idea now, but **in the long run**, it may be a mistake.
  買小貓現在看來是一個好主意，但**一段時間後**你可能會覺得這是個錯誤。

8

片語動詞　不可分開

take（取得）+ **after**（模仿）

→ **take after**
長得很像（通常指親戚）及

用法 ◆ **take after sb**
和某人長得像

同 resemble

💡 通常後接人，表示「長相、行為、舉止與某人相似」或「以某人為榜樣」。

132

- Everyone tells me I **take after** my father because we are both tall and have red hair. 每個人都說我和父親**長得很像**，因為我們都很高，也都有一頭紅髮。
- Francine really **takes after** her older brother; they have such similar interests. 法蘭欣和她哥哥真的**長得很像**，他們的興趣也很相近。
- Most of my children **take after** my wife, both in appearance and character. 我孩子的外貌和個性都和我太太**很像**。
- Tina **takes after** her mother's side of the family. 緹娜和她媽媽那邊的親戚**長得很像**。

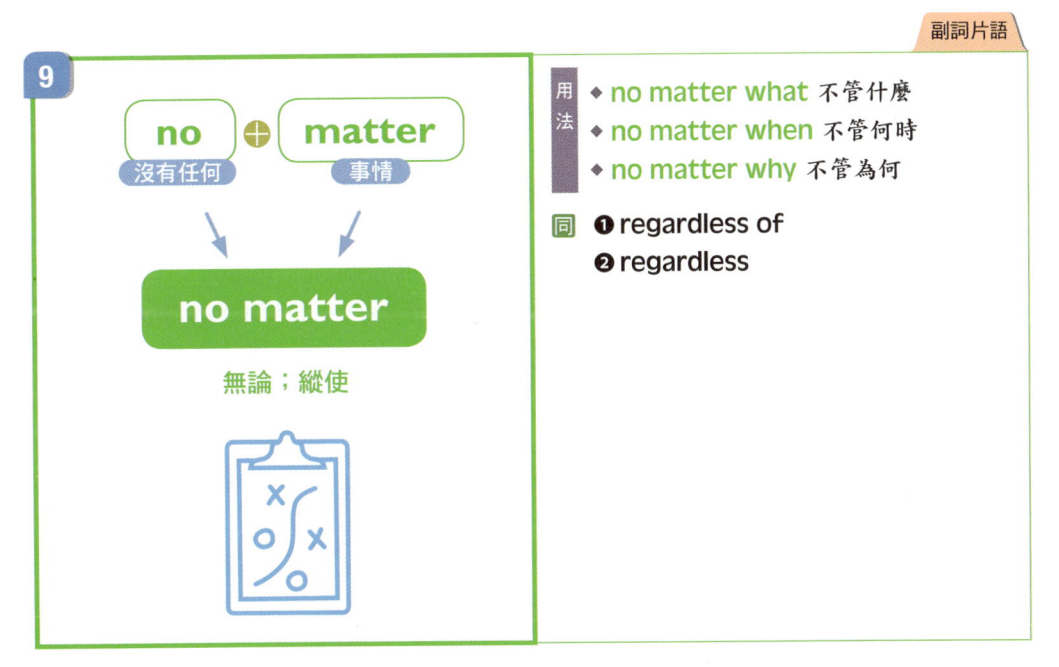

9

no （沒有任何） + matter （事情）
↓
no matter
無論；縱使

副詞片語

用法
- no matter what 不管什麼
- no matter when 不管何時
- no matter why 不管為何

同
❶ regardless of
❷ regardless

💡 **no matter** 後需接以 **how**、**what**、**when**、**where**、**whether**、**which**、**who** 等字作開頭的副詞子句，有時亦可置於句尾。

- I don't want to take any calls, **no matter** who it is. 我不想接任何電話，**不管**誰打來都一樣。
- We'll definitely play basketball this weekend, **no matter** what the weather; we'll play even if it is raining! **無論**天氣如何，我們這週末一定會去打籃球，就算下雨也會去打球！

Unit 15 Test Yourself!

A 選擇題

1. Evelyn and I stay _____ with LINE chat.
   Ⓐ in touch   Ⓑ upside down   Ⓒ filled out   Ⓓ inside out

2. Without realizing it, Vanessa arrived at school with her dress _____.
   Ⓐ filled in   Ⓑ inside out   Ⓒ taken after   Ⓓ out of touch

3. If you refuse to do your job, I'll _____ this issue _____ your boss.
   Ⓐ take . . . up with   Ⓑ fill . . . in
   Ⓒ put . . . in touch with   Ⓓ fill . . . out

4. Before seeing the doctor, Luke had to _____ a detailed form.
   Ⓐ put up   Ⓑ take up   Ⓒ fill out   Ⓓ take after

5. Sometimes we must do things that are difficult now but good _____.
   Ⓐ in the long run   Ⓑ over and over   Ⓒ no matter   Ⓓ time and time again

6. Years after my disagreement with Louis, we still do not talk to each other and remain totally _____.
   Ⓐ inside out   Ⓑ taken after   Ⓒ out of touch   Ⓓ filled in

7. Whom do you _____ more, your mother or your father?
   Ⓐ fill out   Ⓑ take after   Ⓒ take up   Ⓓ take up with

8. You spend so much time playing video games; maybe it's time to _____ a new hobby.
   Ⓐ take up   Ⓑ fill in   Ⓒ take after   Ⓓ fill out

9. Don't let anyone into the meeting room, _____ who it is.
   Ⓐ the long run   Ⓑ over and over   Ⓒ no matter   Ⓓ taking up

10. Because Iain couldn't work at the restaurant, Wilma _____ for him.
    Ⓐ took up   Ⓑ filled out   Ⓒ took after   Ⓓ filled in

B 閱讀文章，從字表中選擇詞彙填入，並依人稱時態等做適當的變化

inside out	in touch	no matter
in the long run	take advantage of	take up
take up with	take after	fill out

134

It was a tough day for poor Harriet. Although she wanted to ❶ _____ the weekend by ❷ _____ painting and getting ❸ _____ with some old friends, she had to work on her college applications. She didn't want to spend her free time applying to universities, but she knew it was important ❹ _____. Just as she finished ❺ _____ some application forms, her boss called.

He wanted her to come into the office over the weekend and do some important paperwork, ❻ _____ what else she had planned. He had forgotten to do it earlier, and now he didn't have time. The truth was, Harriet was a bit mad—not only because she would be working on the weekend, but also because she didn't like it when her boss called her during her time off.

Harriet decided to ❼ _____ this issue _____ her boss as soon as possible. Then, just when it looked like things couldn't get any worse, she got to work and realized her pants were ❽ _____. Clearly, Harriet is a bit disorganized; in this way, she ❾ _____ her father, who is one of the most disorganized people in the world. The funny thing is, Harriet's father is her boss, and if he was more organized, she wouldn't have to be working on the weekend.

C 引導式翻譯，並依人稱時態等做適當的變化

1. 我不想**占用**你太多時間。
   I don't want to _____ _____ too much of your time.

2. 丹妮絲**趁著**好天氣到海邊去。
   Denise _____ _____ _____ the nice weather and went to the beach.

3. 艾森曼女士並不是我們平常的老師，她只是來**代課**。
   Ms. Eisenman isn't our usual teacher, she's just _____ _____.

4. 我要如何和你母親**聯絡**呢？
   How can I get _____ _____ with your mother?

5. **從長遠來看**，良好的經營技巧能為員工帶來更進步的環境。
   Good management in the short term brought improved conditions for workers _____ _____ _____ _____.

6. 這些數據已和現實**脫離**了，無法作為憑據。
   These statistics are _____ _____ _____ with reality and cannot be used.

135

Unit 16

The New Neighbor
新鄰居

🔊 068

Tommy and Adrian talk about a new neighbor.
湯米和雅德恩娜在討論新鄰居。

Tommy: How are you getting along with your new neighbor, Mr. Dasey, these days?

妳這幾天和妳的新鄰居戴西先生相處得如何？

Adrian: Well, to be honest, things aren't as bad as before. Although we don't always **see eye to eye**[1], we've been **making the best of**[2] things.

嗯，老實告訴你，比以前好多了。雖然我們的**看法**常常不**相同**，不過我們都**盡力**了。

Tommy: That's good. **For once**[3], there doesn't seem to be any serious problem between you two.

那很好啊。**至少這次**你們兩個之間沒什麼嚴重的問題。

Adrian: I **keep in mind**[4] that Mr. Dasey is an old man and that he's **hard of hearing**[5], so sometimes he doesn't understand everything I say. The only problem now is that he keeps the TV on very loud because of his hearing problems.

我會**記住**戴西先生是一個老人家，而且有**重聽**，所以有時會聽不懂我說的話。現在唯一的問題就是，由於他聽力很差，他老是把電視開得很大聲。

Tommy: I bet you'd like it if his TV suddenly **went off**[6] and never came back on.

我相信妳一定想要他的電視會突然**壞掉**，而且修不好。

Adrian: I'm not that mean!

我沒那麼壞心！

see eye to eye 看法相同

hard of hearing 重聽

Unit 16　The New Neighbor 新鄰居

1　慣用片語

see (看見) + **eye to eye** (眼睛對眼睛) → **see eye to eye** 看法一致

用法：
- **see eye to eye on sth** 對某事看法一致
- **see eye to eye with sb** 和某人看法一致

同：agree with
反：反對 object to

💡 **see eye to eye** 原本用來表示「彼此對望」，後來引申為「看法一致」。此片語常用於**否定句**。後接**人**時，需使用介系詞 **with** 作連接。

- Although Beth and I don't get along, we definitely **see eye to eye** on a lot of political issues. 雖然我和貝絲處不來，但我們的政治理念許多都是**一致的**。

2　慣用片語

make (做) + **the best** (最佳) + **of** (動作對象) → **make the best of** 充分利用

用法：
- **make the best of sth** 充分利用某事物

同：make the most of

💡 **make the best of** 表示「在不利的情況下充分利用」，通常後接名詞，或由 **what** 所引導的名詞子句。

- Although it rained the entire time, we decided to **make the best of** our camping trip and went fishing and hiking. 這次露營雖然一直在下雨，我們還是決定**把握機會**去釣魚和健行。

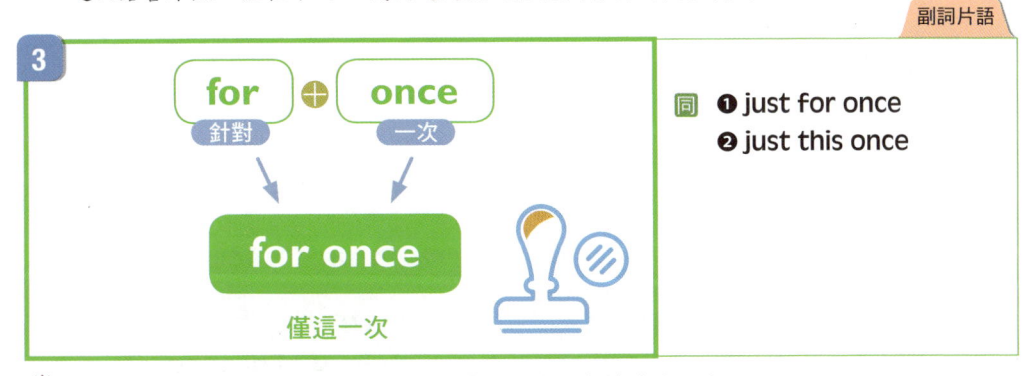

3　副詞片語

for (針對) + **once** (一次) → **for once** 僅這一次

同：
① just for once
② just this once

💡 **for once** 常用來表示**負面**的語氣，指「某事的發生就這麼一次」。

- **For once**, Darren arrived to class on time. 戴倫就**這麼一次**準時到學校上課。

🔊 070　　　　　　　　　　　　　　　　　　　　　　　　慣用片語

4

keep (保存) + in mind (在心裡) → **keep in mind** 記住

用法比較	◆ keep sth in mind 記住某事

◆ have in mind 想到；打算
→ What do you **have in mind** for this vacation? 你想到放假要做什麼了嗎？
→ I am not sure exactly what to buy my dad for Father's Day, but I **have** a few things **in mind**. 我還不確定要買什麼父親節禮物給老爸，但我有想到幾樣東西。

🟰 bear in mind

- **Bearing in mind** how young she is, I thought she did really well. 記住她的年紀還很輕，我認為她的表現真的很不錯。

💡 keep in mind 常用於簡單式。此片語在祈使句中通常不使用主詞；若使用主詞，則會加上 **must** 或 **should** 來加強語氣。

- Before you go out to the party this weekend, **keep in mind** that there is an exam on Monday. 在你週末去參加派對前，記住星期一要考試。
- When you are making dinner, you must **keep in mind** that Anne's brother doesn't eat meat. 你在準備晚餐時，要記住安的哥哥不吃肉。

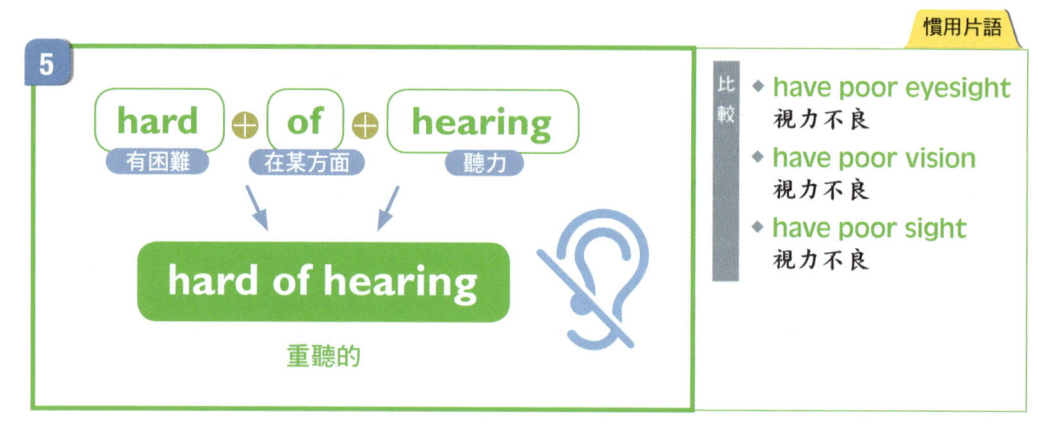

慣用片語

5

hard (有困難) + of (在某方面) + hearing (聽力) → **hard of hearing** 重聽的

比較	◆ have poor eyesight 視力不良

◆ have poor vision 視力不良
◆ have poor sight 視力不良

- When Erin's grandmother watches TV, she has to turn the volume way up because she is **hard of hearing**. 因為艾琳的奶奶重聽，所以她看電視時必須把音量轉很大聲。
- My father is quite old now, and he's increasingly **hard of hearing**. 我的父親年紀大了，重聽也越來越嚴重了。

6

go (運轉) + **off** (停止) → **go off**

1. 機器停止 2. 離開 3. 警報響起
4. 爆炸 5. 發生 6. 變糟 7. 食物壞掉 [不及]

比較
- **set sth off / set off sth**
  爆炸；燃放
  → Apparently the bomb was placed in a locker, and someone **set** it **off** with a cell phone.
  顯然有人把炸彈放在置物櫃裡，然後透過手機來**引爆**它。

💡 **go off** 通常用於主動語態。

1. During the thunderstorm, all the lights in the house suddenly **went off**.
   暴風雨來臨時，屋內所有的照明突然都**斷**電了。

2. I think Janet **went off** to the market a few minutes ago.
   我想珍娜幾分鐘前才剛**離開**到市場去了。

3. The alarm on Dean's wristwatch **goes off** every day at lunch.
   狄恩手錶上的鬧鐘每天午餐時間都會**響**。

4. The bomb **went off** at midnight. 炸彈在半夜的時候**爆炸**。

5. The protest march **went off** peacefully with only two arrests.
   示威遊行在和平中**進行**，只有兩個人被逮捕。

6. That paper has really **gone off** since they got that new editor.
   那家報社自從聘請了那位新編輯後，品質就**變得很糟糕**。

7

cut (切) + **off** (除去) → **cut off**

1. 切斷；剪短
2. 中斷（電話、有線電視、網路）[及]

片語動詞 | 可分開 | 受詞為代名詞時定要分開

用法
- **cut sth off / cut off sth**
  切斷某事物；隔離某事物
- **cut sb off / cut off sb**
  打斷某人；中斷某人的通訊；孤立某人
  → The telephone operator **cut** us **off**.
  接線生**切斷**了我們的**線路**。

1. Nina **cut off** the top of the carrots before cooking them.
   妮娜在煮紅蘿蔔前先**去頭**。

2. When Todd stopped paying his bills, the company **cut off** his Internet connection so he couldn't go online anymore.
   陶德停付帳單後，電信公司便**中斷**了他的網路，所以他再也不能上網了。

071

片語動詞 | 可分開 | 受詞為代名詞時定要分開

8

cut（切）+ **out**（去掉）

→ **cut out**

❶ 剪下　❷ 停止　❸ 排除 [及]

用法

- **cut it out** 停止
→ Would you please **cut it out**? I'm trying to get some work done here.
可以請你**停止**嗎？我正試著要完成手邊的一些工作。

- **cut sth out / cut out sth** 剪下某事物
→ James **cut out** the beautiful scenic picture from the magazine.
詹姆斯從雜誌上**剪下**漂亮的風景圖片。

- **cut sth out / cut out sth** 戒除某事物
→ You should **cut out** eating ice cream and get more exercise.
你應該**戒掉**冰淇淋，並且多運動。

- **cut sb out / cut out sb** 排除某人
→ They **cut** me **out** of the conversation.
他們**不讓我加入**談話。

同 刪掉 leave out

💡 後接名詞或動名詞，表示剪下、切下、戒掉。

❶ Nelly **cut** her ex-boyfriend **out** of all the photos she had of them.
奈莉把所有前男友的照片都**剪掉**。

❷ Phillip, will you **cut** that **out**! I can't study if you're making noise.
菲力普，你能**停止**嗎！你這麼吵我沒辦法唸書。

片語動詞

9

get（達到某狀態）+ **along**（一起）

→ **get along**

❶ 有進展　❷ 相處　❸ 生存 [不及]

用法

- **get along with sth** 某事有所進展
→ How are you **getting along with** your new courses? 你的新課程**進展**得如何？

- **get along with sb** 與某人相處
→ My kids really **get along with** their cousins. 我的孩子和表兄弟姊妹很**合得來**。

同 相處融洽 get on

💡 **get along** 為不及物動詞，表示「度過；過活」。後接 **with** 時，則表示「某事的進展」，亦指「相處」。

❸ It's hard **getting along** in a new city. 在陌生的城市中很難**生存**。

140

片語動詞　不可分開

10

grow (長大) + **out of** (脫離)

→ **grow out of**

❶ 因長大而不適合（衣服、鞋子）
❷ 因長大而戒除　❸ 產生於 及

用法
- **grow out of sth** 長大而戒某事
  → Jason did a lot of stupid stuff in high school, but I always thought he'd **grow out of** it.
  傑森高中時期做了一些蠢事，但我一直以為他長大便會改掉。

- **grow out of sth** 產生於某事
  → The idea for the story **grew out of** a strange experience I had last year.
  這個故事的想法是來自於我去年經歷過的一件怪事。

比較
- **grow into sth** 長大而穿得下某衣物
- **grow into sb** 長大成為某人

💡 ❶ 表示「因長大而不適合」時，後接 clothes、shoes 等名詞，主詞通常為人。
　 ❷ 表示「產生於」時，後接名詞，通常不使用被動語態。
　 ❸ 表示「因長大而戒除」，後可接名詞、動名詞或代名詞。

❶ The new mother didn't want to spend too much money on shoes for her baby because she knew he'd **grow out of** them quickly.
新手媽媽不想要花太多錢買寶寶的鞋子，因為她知道他長大後很快就會穿不下。

慣用片語

11

on (以……立著) + **one's toes** (某人的腳趾)

→ **on one's toes**

保持警覺的

比較
- **step on sb's toes** 冒犯某人
  → It's hard to make changes in the department without **stepping on** a lot of **toes**.
  處理人事調動時，很難能夠不得罪人。

- **tread on one's toes** 冒犯某人
  → I'd like to make some changes to the working procedures, but I don't want to **tread on anyone's toes**.
  我想把工作流程做一些修改，但我不想要冒犯到任何人。

💡 原表示「賽跑時，選手踮起腳尖準備起跑」，後引申為「準備好的；提高警覺的」。

● Having twins really keeps my mom **on her toes**.
有雙胞胎小孩真的讓我媽變得非常小心。

Unit 16　The New Neighbor 新鄰居

Unit 16 Test Yourself!

A 選擇題

1. If you want to enjoy life, you must learn to _____ every experience, even the bad ones.
   Ⓐ cut out   Ⓑ go off   Ⓒ make the best of   Ⓓ grow out of

2. My boss is a really observant guy; he keeps me _____ my _____.
   Ⓐ on . . . toes   Ⓑ at . . . home   Ⓒ up . . . alley   Ⓓ in . . . head

3. When I _____ an item of clothing, my mom gives it to my younger brother.
   Ⓐ cut out   Ⓑ go off   Ⓒ keep in mind   Ⓓ grow out of

4. _____ that you have to water the plants twice a week.
   Ⓐ Keep in mind   Ⓑ For once   Ⓒ Move ahead   Ⓓ Having in mind

5. Mary-Anne needed shorts, so she _____ the legs _____ a pair of jeans.
   Ⓐ cut . . . out   Ⓑ grew . . . out of   Ⓒ cut . . . off   Ⓓ had . . . in mind

6. _____ it did not rain, and we had a nice weekend.
   Ⓐ Keeping in mind   Ⓑ For once   Ⓒ Having in mind   Ⓓ Moving ahead

7. Paul _____ all the photos he could find of his favorite bands and pinned them on his wall.
   Ⓐ grew out of   Ⓑ cut out   Ⓒ went off   Ⓓ got along

8. If you listen to loud music when you are young, you'll probably be _____ later in life.
   Ⓐ hard of hearing   Ⓑ going off
   Ⓒ seeing eye to eye   Ⓓ growing out of it

9. I'm not sure what to do today; what do you _____?
   Ⓐ go off   Ⓑ move ahead   Ⓒ have in mind   Ⓓ see eye to eye

10. Nora's TV is broken; when she wants it to _____, she has to unplug it.
    Ⓐ go off   Ⓑ move ahead   Ⓒ keep it in mind   Ⓓ grow out of it

B 閱讀文章，從字表中選擇詞彙填入，並依人稱時態等做適當的變化

grow out of	make the best of	cut off
get along	for once	keep in mind
go off	see eye to eye	on one's toes

Living in a large family really keeps me ❶ _____. Although I don't always ❷ _____ with all my brothers and sisters, we usually find a way to ❸ _____ in our small apartment. One thing that I don't like is that when my brother ❹ _____ his clothes, my mom gives them to me. If I need shorts, my dad just ❺ _____ the legs of an old pair of his pants. ❻ _____, I'd like new clothes. However, it's important to ❼ _____ that there is a good side to having a big family. For example, when the lights ❽ _____ during last week's storm, my sister ❾ _____ it and told us ghost stories. We had a really good time that night.

C 引導式翻譯，並依人稱時態等做適當的變化

1. 公車**就這麼一次**準時到達。
   _____ _____, the bus came on time.

2. 我的年紀比同事年長一倍，所以我必須隨時保持**警覺**。
   I work with people who are half my age, so that keeps me _____ _____ _____.

3. 這三明治聞起來有點怪，你覺得是不是**壞掉**了呢？
   This sandwich smells a bit funny—do you think it has _____ _____?

4. 假如你三天內沒有把帳單繳清，瓦斯就會被**切斷**。
   If this bill is not paid within three days, your gas supply will be _____ _____.

5. 我和我弟弟的女朋友真的**處不來**。
   I don't really _____ _____ _____ my brother's girlfriend.

6. 我和我的姊妹對於這件事情的安排**意見不一致**。
   My sisters don't _____ _____ _____ _____ with me about the arrangements.

Unit 17

The Surprise Party
驚喜派對

🔊 072

Rob and Gale discuss a surprise party.
羅伯和格兒在討論一場驚喜派對。

Gale:	It's funny to think that just two days ago, I was convinced that celebrating my birthday was a **lost cause**[1].	現在回想起來很好笑，但兩天前，我還覺得要好好慶祝我的生日是**不可能的**事情呢。
Rob:	What do you mean?	什麼意思？
Gale:	Well, I had invited my friends over, but they all **turned** me **down**[2].	唔，我那時邀請我的朋友，但他們全都**拒絕**了我。
Rob:	That's terrible!	真糟糕！
Gale:	It was! Then, as my dad and I were **shutting up**[3] his shop last night, I heard some strange noises.	本來很糟！然而，昨晚我和我老爸在**關**店時，我聽到一些奇怪的聲音。
Rob:	Oh! Was someone **breaking in**[4]?	噢！有人**闖進去**了嗎？
Gale:	No, it was a surprise party! My dad and my friends were there with a cake, so I made a wish and **blew out**[5] the candles.	不，是個驚喜派對！我爸和我朋友都在那裡，還有一個蛋糕，所以我許了願望，然後把蠟燭**吹熄**。
Rob:	That sounds like a big shock; **above all**[6], it sounds like you had a great time!	聽起來像是個超級大驚喜。**最重要的是**，妳似乎度過了一段很愉快的時光！

144

073

Unit 17 The Surprise Party 驚喜派對

名詞片語

1

lost（輸的）＋ cause（訴訟）
→ **lost cause**
敗局已定；毫無希望

💡 **lost cause** 原指打輸的官司，但可引申為「某事敗局已定；毫無希望」。

- I tutored Jane every day for a few months, but when I realized it was a **lost cause**, I gave up. 我每天教珍功課已經好幾個月了，但當我發現毫無幫助時便放棄了。
- Arnold practiced the trumpet every day for three months, but finally he decided it was a **lost cause** and sold it. 阿諾三個月來每天練習吹喇叭，但最後他認為沒有希望便把它賣掉了。
- Gina has already made up her mind, and it's a **lost cause** to try to change it. 吉娜已經下定決心了，想要使她改變心意是不可能的。

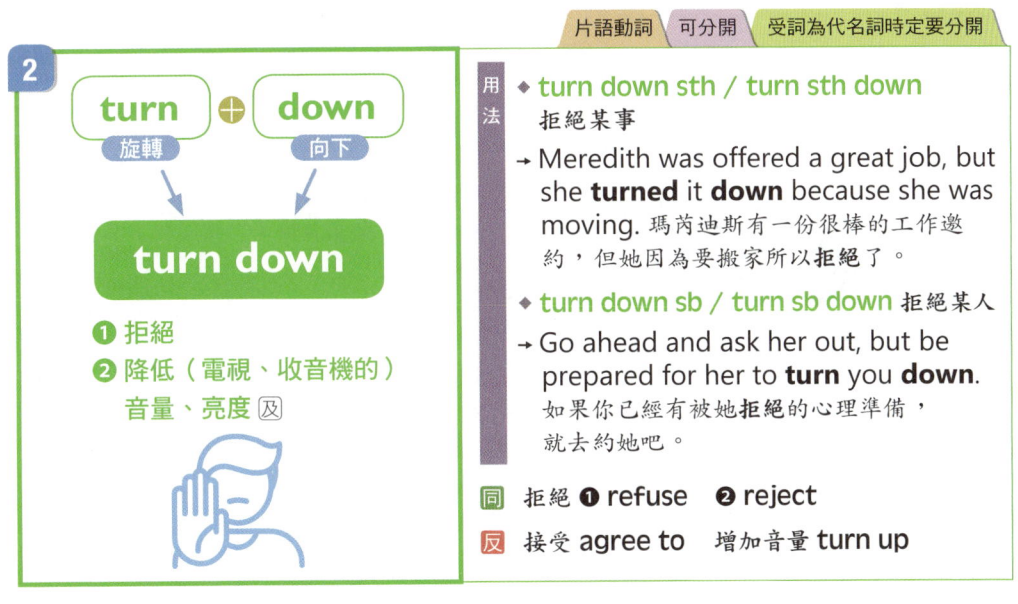

2

片語動詞　可分開　受詞為代名詞時定要分開

turn（旋轉）＋ down（向下）
→ **turn down**
❶ 拒絕
❷ 降低（電視、收音機的）音量、亮度 及

用法
◆ **turn down sth / turn sth down**
拒絕某事
→ Meredith was offered a great job, but she **turned** it **down** because she was moving. 瑪芮迪斯有一份很棒的工作邀約，但她因為要搬家所以拒絕了。

◆ **turn down sb / turn sb down** 拒絕某人
→ Go ahead and ask her out, but be prepared for her to **turn** you **down**. 如果你已經有被她拒絕的心理準備，就去約她吧。

同 拒絕 ❶ refuse　❷ reject
反 接受 agree to　增加音量 turn up

💡 **turn down**；表示「降低、轉小（音量）」時，後需接受詞。

❶ When Mike asked Barbra to the dance, she **turned** him **down**. 當麥可邀請芭芭拉跳舞時，她拒絕了他。

❶ Ryan **turned down** the job because it involved too much traveling. 萊恩因為這份工作需要常出差，所以拒絕了。

❷ Please **turn down** the volume on the computer; I can't concentrate when you are playing video games. 請把電腦的音量轉小，你打電動會讓我無法專心。

3

shut（關閉） + **up**（徹底地） → **shut up**

❶ 關閉（英式用法）及
❷ 閉嘴（不禮貌的用法）不及

片語動詞 | 可分開

用法
- shut (sb) up 使（某人）安靜
- shut (sth) up 使（某物）關閉
- shut sb/sth up
  把某人或動物關起來

同 關閉 ❶ shut down ❷ close
保持沉默 hold one's peace

反 放開 let go
開口說話 find one's tongue

💡 **shut up** 表示「要求某人閉嘴」，在口語中相當常見。表示「關閉」時，後需接 **house**、**shop** 等名詞。

❶ Before leaving for the night, the manager **shut up** the shop.
經理晚上離開前把店門關上。（英式用法）

❷ Please **shut up**! I'm trying to study. 請閉嘴！我在試著唸書呢。

4

break（破壞） + **in**（進入） → **break in**

❶ 闖入 不及
❷ 打斷談話 不及
❸ 使用後逐漸適合 及

片語動詞 | 可分開 | 受詞為代名詞時定要分開

用法
- break sth in / break in sth
  使用後逐漸適合某物
  → These shoes will be more comfortable after I have **broken** them **in**.
  等我穿習慣了，這雙鞋子就會變得比較舒適。

同 闖入 break into

- Somebody **broke into** her house and stole her jewelry.
  有人闖入了她的房子，並且偷走了她的珠寶。

💡 **break in** 表示「強行進入或打斷談話」時為不及物動詞。

❶ Ralph was shocked to find that someone had **broken in** and stolen his laptop. 瑞夫發現有人闖入，並且偷走他的筆記型電腦時，他很震驚。

❷ Fran **broke in** on the conversation and asked my name.
法蘭打斷了談話並問了我的名字。

5

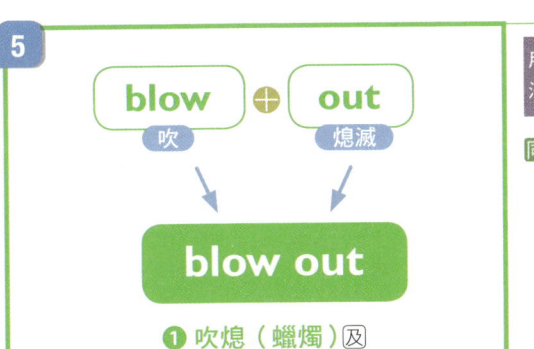

blow (吹) + **out** (熄滅)

blow out

❶ 吹熄（蠟燭）及
❷ （輪胎）爆裂 不及

> 片語動詞 / 可分開 / 受詞為代名詞時定要分開

用法 ◆ blow sth out / blow out sth
吹熄某事物

同 熄滅 put out

❶ Steve took a deep breath and **blew out** all the candles on his birthday cake.
史帝夫做了一個深呼吸，然後把生日蛋糕上所有的蠟燭都**吹熄**了。

❶ Richie lit a cigarette and quickly **blew** the match **out**.
瑞奇點燃香菸後，立刻把火柴**吹熄**。

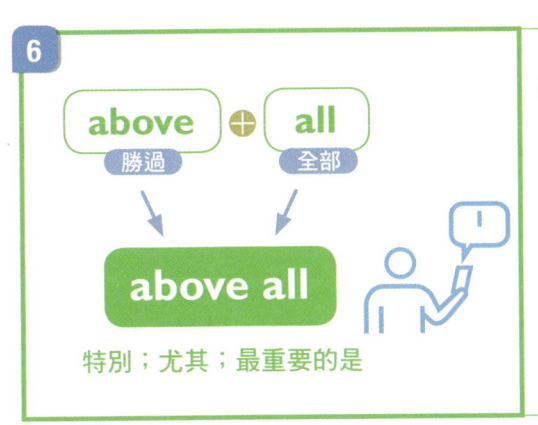

6

above (勝過) + **all** (全部)

above all

特別；尤其；最重要的是

> 副詞片語

同 尤其是 above all things

- I value my family **above all things**.
我重視我的家人勝過其他**事物**。

💡 通常置於句首或句中作插入語，以強調。

- Mindy is a nice girl—she's hard-working, clever, and **above all**, honest.
敏蒂是個好女孩，她做事認真、聰明，**最重要的是**，她很誠實。

- She loved swimming and jogging; but **above all**, she loved her family.
她熱愛游泳和慢跑，但**最重要的是**，她愛她的家人。

Unit 17 The Surprise Party 驚喜派對

147

7 片語動詞 不可分開

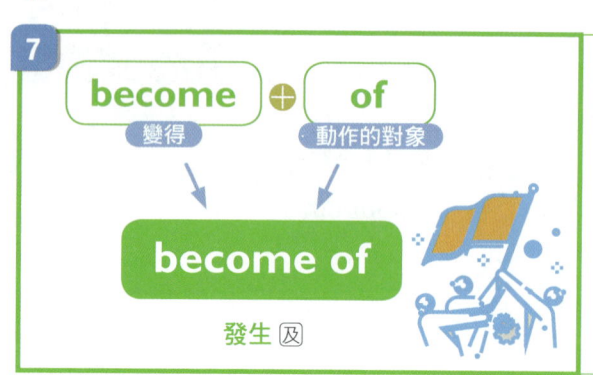

become (變得) + **of** (動作的對象)
→ **become of** 發生 [及]

用法
- become of sb 某人發生何事
- become of sth 某事結果如何

💡 **become of** 表「……的結果如何」，通常是指「不幸的事情」，主詞需為 **what** 或 **whatever**。

- After she moved to Egypt, Aunt Sarah stopped sending letters, and no one knew what **became of** her.
  莎拉阿姨自從搬到埃及後便不再來信，所以沒人知道她**發生**了什麼事。
- I'm not sure that we'll ever know what **became of** my cat after it ran away.
  我的貓不見後，我不確定我們是否能知道牠**發生**了什麼事。

8 慣用片語

have (擁有) + **got** (得到)
→ **have got** 擁有；持有

用法
- have got sth 擁有某事物

- I **have gotten** a new bicycle, and I am riding it every day.
  我**得到**一台新腳踏車，而且我每天都會騎它。
- What **have** you **got** in your bag? 你的包包裡**有**什麼？

9 慣用片語

have + **got** (做強調用) + **to**
→ **have got to** 必須

148

💡 **have got to** 表示「必須」，其中的 **got** 可用來強調 **have to**。

- I **have got to** get to class now, or I'll be in trouble.
  我現在**必須**去上課，不然會有麻煩。
- Frank **has got to** leave the party before 8, or he'll miss his bus home.
  法蘭克**必須**在八點前離開派對，否則他會錯過回家的公車。

片語動詞

10

keep (保持) + **up** (徹底) + **with** (與……一起)
↓
keep up with
不落後於；跟上 及

用法
- **keep up with sb** 趕上某人
- **keep up with sth** 跟上某事

比較
- **catch up with** 迎頭趕上
  → I ran after Kelly and managed to **catch up with** her.
  我跑在凱莉後面，想盡辦法**趕上**她。
- **come up with** 提出辦法
  → He's **come up with** an amazing scheme to double his income.
  他**提出**一些能夠增加一倍收入的驚人方法。

同 **keep/hold pace with**

💡 **keep up with** 後接**時間**則表示「跟上時代」。

- Terrance walks so fast, it's hard to **keep up with** him sometimes.
  泰倫斯走路很快，有時候要**跟上**他的腳步很難。

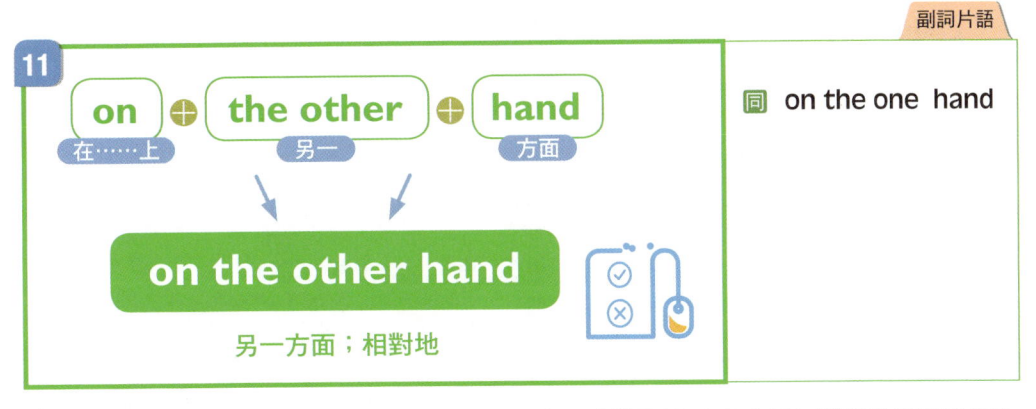

副詞片語

11

on (在……上) + **the other** (另一) + **hand** (方面)
↓
on the other hand
另一方面；相對地

同 **on the one hand**

💡 **on the other hand** 前面常與 **on the one hand** 搭配使用，可用來引導與前述相反的事實或觀點，表示「一方面……另一方面……」。

- That car looks so cool, but **on the other hand**, it is very expensive.
  那台車看起來真酷，但**另一方面**，它也很貴。
- I was happy we bought a new flat screen TV, but **on the other hand**, it was so big I didn't know where we would put it.
  我很高興我們買了一台平面電視，但**另一方面**，因為它很大台，所以我不知道要把它擺在哪裡。

149

Unit 17 Test Yourself!

A 選擇題

1. Because Amy works for a music magazine, she has to _____ new musicians and music trends.
   Ⓐ blow out   Ⓑ become of   Ⓒ keep up with   Ⓓ turn down

2. The new apartment was big, comfortable, and _____, cozy.
   Ⓐ above all   Ⓑ a lost cause   Ⓒ fifty-fifty   Ⓓ on the other hand

3. Frank discovered that he had lost the key to his brother's house, so he had to _____ through the kitchen window.
   Ⓐ turn down   Ⓑ blow out   Ⓒ break in   Ⓓ become of

4. As she was talking, he suddenly _____, saying, "That's a lie."
   Ⓐ broke in   Ⓑ turned down   Ⓒ blew out   Ⓓ moved in

5. Before you go to sleep, be sure to _____ the candle.
   Ⓐ turn down   Ⓑ blow out   Ⓒ become of   Ⓓ have got

6. I hate rainy days because they are inconvenient, though _____, the water is good for the garden.
   Ⓐ a lost cause   Ⓑ on the other hand   Ⓒ turning down   Ⓓ fifty-fifty

7. After three months of dieting, Ariel decided that her plan to lose weight was _____.
   Ⓐ on the other hand   Ⓑ fifty-fifty   Ⓒ a lost cause   Ⓓ above all

8. I have a list of things that I _____ to do today.
   Ⓐ have got   Ⓑ blow out   Ⓒ turn down   Ⓓ break in

9. When Alice asked her boss for a raise, he _____ her _____.
   Ⓐ broke . . . in   Ⓑ turned . . . down   Ⓒ blew . . . out   Ⓓ moved . . . in

10. When Kenneth stopped calling his girlfriend, she wondered what _____ him.
    Ⓐ blew out   Ⓑ turned down   Ⓒ kept up with   Ⓓ became of

11. The little boy tried very hard to _____ his older brother's accomplishments.
    Ⓐ keep up with   Ⓑ break in   Ⓒ turn down   Ⓓ blow out

B 閱讀文章，從字表中選擇詞彙填入，並依人稱時態等做適當的變化

above all	turn down	become of
break in	have got to	a lost cause
shut up	keep up with	

When Clarence got to his shop and saw that someone had **1** _____ and stolen a few TVs after he had **2** _____ it _____ for the night, we were all worried. It was terrible news. **3** _____, we wondered what would **4** _____ his store. Clarence was very sad; he said there was nothing we could do to help him feel safe again. He thought that having any kind of business was **5** _____. In the end, a friend suggested that we buy Clarence a security system and split the cost fifty-fifty.

When I first told Clarence about this, he **6** _____ our offer; but when we pointed out that he **7** _____ do something, he agreed. I think that if he **8** _____ the latest security technology, his store will be safe.

C 引導式翻譯，並依人稱時態等做適當的變化

1. 艾利克斯在接到州立大學入學通知前曾被四所學校**拒絕**過。
   Alex was _____ _____ by four schools before finally being accepted at the state university.

2. 這個輪胎就快要**爆胎**了。
   This tire is about to _____ _____.

3. 你**必須**做完哪些工作才能下班呢？
   What _____ you _____ _____ do before you can leave work?

4. 我不在的時候，有人**闖了進來**，並且偷走了所有的東西。
   While I was out, somebody _____ _____ and stole everything I had.

5. 米蘭達的冰箱裡**有**什麼，怎麼那麼臭？
   What _____ Miranda _____ in her refrigerator that smells so bad?

6. 等我**穿習慣**了新的登山靴，一定會很舒適。
   My new hiking boots will be great once I've _____ them _____.

Unit 18

🔊 076

Finding a Lost Dog
尋狗啟示

Sally and Mohammed talk about a lost dog.
莎莉和穆罕默德在談論走丟的狗狗。

LOST DOG

SUBSTANTIAL REWARD

Sally: Have you seen my dog, Rex? I've been looking for him all day.

你有看到我的狗狗雷克斯嗎？我已經找他找了一整天了。

Mohammed: No, but **according to**[1] my neighbor, there was a dog digging in our garden earlier.

沒有，但**根據**鄰居的說法，之前有隻狗在我家院子裡挖洞。

Sally: That **is bound to**[2] be Rex!

那**肯定**是雷克斯！

Mohammed: How did he get away, anyway?

話說他是怎麼不見的？

Sally: Well, when we **ran out of**[3] dog food, my mom sent me to the store to buy some more. I opened the door and **was about to**[4] go out when Rex just ran away.

就是我們家的狗飼料**沒**了，我媽要我去商店買。我**正好**打開門要出去，雷克斯就跑了出去。

Mohammed: Oh man! Let's go to my house and see if he's around there.

噢，天啊！那我們去我家那看他是否還在那裡吧。

Sally: I hope so. It'll feel nice to **tear up**[5] all these "Lost Dog" signs once I get Rex back.

希望他還在。只要找到了雷克斯，就可以開開心心地把這些尋狗啟示給**撕掉**了。

1 副詞片語

according（根據） + **to**（針對）
→ **according to** 根據；據……所記載

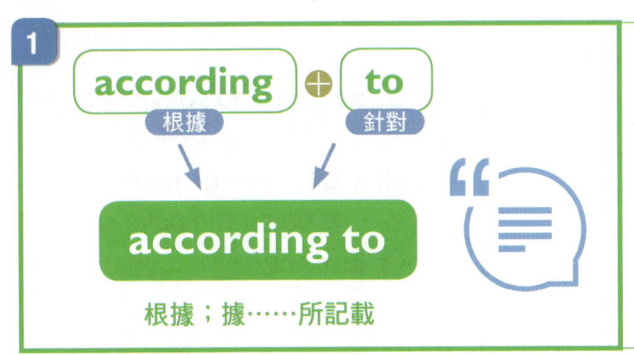

> **according to** 常後接所根據的消息、資訊或規則等。表示「根據某人的看法」時，需使用「in (one's) opinion」或「(one's) opinion is that . . .」等來表示。

同 **in accordance with**

- **According to** many scientists, it will be possible to live on Mars one day.
  根據多位科學家的說法，人類也許有一天能夠居住在火星上。
- You've spelled the word incorrectly **according to** the dictionary.
  根據字典上所寫，你拼錯字了。

2 慣用片語

be bound（必然的） + **to**（不定詞）
→ **be bound to** 可能（肯定）會發生

> **bound** 為 **bind**（綑綁）的過去分詞，**be bound to** 原指「負有……的義務」，後來引申為「肯定會」。

用法 ◆ **be bound to do sth** 肯定會發生某事

同 ❶ **be certain to**
　❷ **be sure to**

- With all the traffic tonight, Craig **is bound to** arrive late.
  今晚大塞車，克雷格鐵定會遲到。

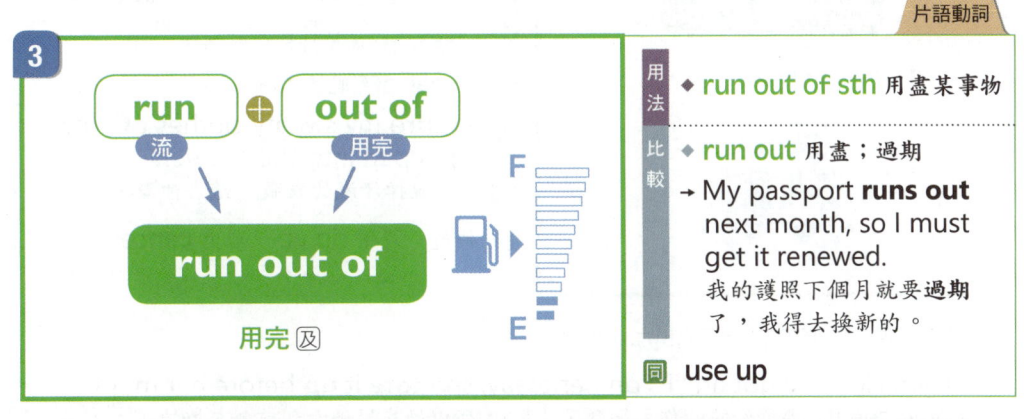

3 片語動詞

run（流） + **out of**（用完）
→ **run out of** 用完 及

用法 ◆ **run out of sth** 用盡某事物

比較 ◆ **run out** 用盡；過期
→ My passport **runs out** next month, so I must get it renewed.
我的護照下個月就要過期了，我得去換新的。

同 **use up**

- So many people came to our restaurant yesterday that we **ran out of** eggs.
  昨晚餐廳的生意很好，所以我們的雞蛋都用完了。
- When Gina's grandpa **ran out of** coffee, he sent her to the store to buy more.
  吉娜的爺爺喝完咖啡後，便要吉娜到商店再多買一些。

153

🔊 078　　　　　　　　　　　　　　　　　　　　　　　慣用片語

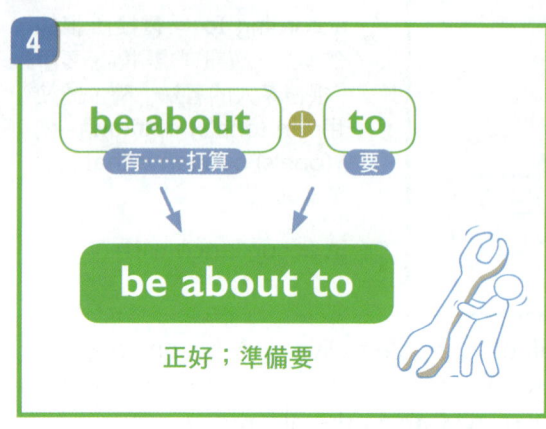

4

be about （有……打算） ＋ **to** （要）　→　**be about to** 正好；準備要

用法 ◆ be about to do sth 打算做某事

同 即將要 ❶ be just going to
　　　　　 ❷ be on the point of

反 剛才 just now

💡 **be about to** 表示用客觀的角度來描述「正要做某事」或「即將發生某事」，**about** 為形容詞，不可搭配表未來的時間副詞使用。

- I **was about to** call my girlfriend when she knocked on my door.
  我女朋友敲我的房門時，我**正好要**打電話給她。
- Diane **is about to** have her first baby. 黛安**就快要**生第一胎了。

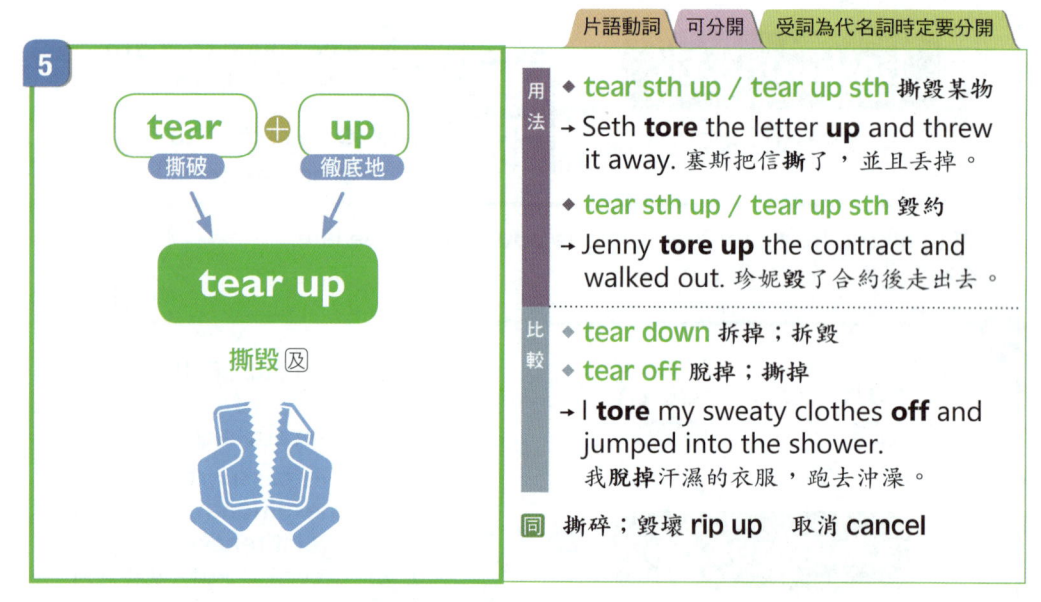

片語動詞｜可分開｜受詞為代名詞時定要分開

5

tear （撕破） ＋ **up** （徹底地）　→　**tear up** 撕毀 及

用法 ◆ tear sth up / tear up sth 撕毀某物
→ Seth **tore** the letter **up** and threw it away. 塞斯把信**撕了**，並且丟掉。

◆ tear sth up / tear up sth 毀約
→ Jenny **tore up** the contract and walked out. 珍妮**毀了**合約後走出去。

比較 ◆ tear down 拆掉；拆毀
◆ tear off 脫掉；撕掉
→ I **tore** my sweaty clothes **off** and jumped into the shower.
我**脫掉**汗濕的衣服，跑去沖澡。

同 撕碎；毀壞 rip up　　取消 cancel

💡 表示「把某物撕毀」，也可引申為「毀約」。

- When Florence got an "F" on her essay, she **tore** it **up** before her mom could see it. 佛羅倫絲的作文得到了「F」，所以她在媽媽看到前就先**撕掉**了。
- After Eric broke up with his girlfriend, he **tore up** all the love letters she had sent him. 艾瑞克和女朋友分手後，他把所有她寄的情書都**撕掉**了。

6

tear (撕破) + **down** (徹底；向下) → **tear down** 拆除 及

| 片語動詞 | 可分開 | 受詞為代名詞時定要分開 |

用法 ◆ tear sth down / tear down sth 拆除某物
同 pull down
反 建造 ❶ set up ❷ put up

💡 **tear down** 通常用來表示「拆除房屋或建築物」。

- The family **tore down** some of the old walls before adding a new room to the house. 這戶人家在蓋新房間前，把一些舊的牆**拆掉**。
- Because the tree house seemed unsafe for the children, Mr. Grey **tore** it **down**. 對孩子來說，樹屋好像很不安全，所以蓋瑞先生把它**拆掉**了。

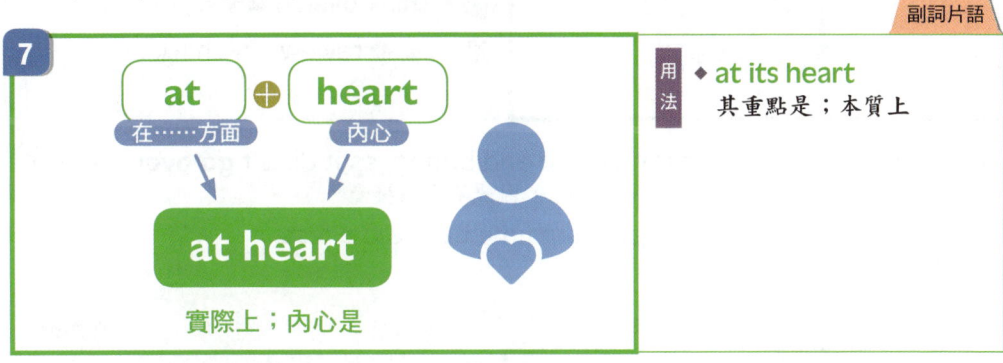

7

at (在……方面) + **heart** (內心) → **at heart** 實際上；內心是

| 副詞片語 |

用法 ◆ at its heart 其重點是；本質上

- Although Mr. Williams may act grumpy, he's a good guy **at heart**. 雖然威廉斯先生性情乖戾，然而他**實際上**是個好人。
- No matter how much bad news I read, I still believe that most people are good **at heart**. 無論看了多少不好的新聞，我還是相信人其實**內心**都是善良的。

8

for (針對) + **sure** (確信的) → **for sure** 肯定；確定地

| 副詞片語 | 形容詞片語 |

同 for certain

- Jessica will win the race **for sure**; she's a fast runner. 潔西卡**肯定**會贏得比賽，她跑得很快。
- We're coming to visit you **for sure** this weekend. 我們這星期**肯定**會去拜訪你的。

9

go (進行) + **over** (徹底地；從頭到尾) → **go over**

❶ 被接納 [不及]
❷ 仔細檢視 [及]
❸ 複習 [及]

用法
- go over sth 複習某事物；解釋某事物
  → Could you **go over** the main points of your argument again, Professor?
  教授，您可以再**解釋**一次您的論點嗎？

- go over sth 仔細檢視某事物
  → I've **gone over** the problem several times, but I can't think of a solution.
  我已經把問題**仔細檢視**了好幾次，但還是找不到解決之道。

比較
- read over 全部讀過
- think over 仔細考慮

同 檢查 ❶ review ❷ check up

❶ Mr. Belvedere's first class was long and boring, so it didn't **go over** very well.
貝維德雷先生的第一堂課既漫長又無趣，因此不太**被接受**。

❸ Let's **go over** the article one more time before the test.
我們在考試前再把文章**複習**一遍吧。

10

take (接受) + **for** (代替) → **take for**

誤以為 [及]

用法
- take A for B 把 A 誤認為 B

同
❶ look on . . . as
❷ mistake for

- I often **mistake** him **for** his father on the phone.
  我在電話中常把他**誤認為**他父親。

- After Roxanne made a big mistake, some teachers **took** her **for** a fool; however, she's very clever.
  在羅姍妮犯下大錯後，有些老師把她當傻瓜，但其實她非常聰明。

- Do you **take** me **for** a fool? 你以為我是傻瓜嗎？

- I **took** her **for** Mrs. White. 我把她**誤認為**懷特太太。

Unit 18 Finding a Lost Dog 尋狗啟示

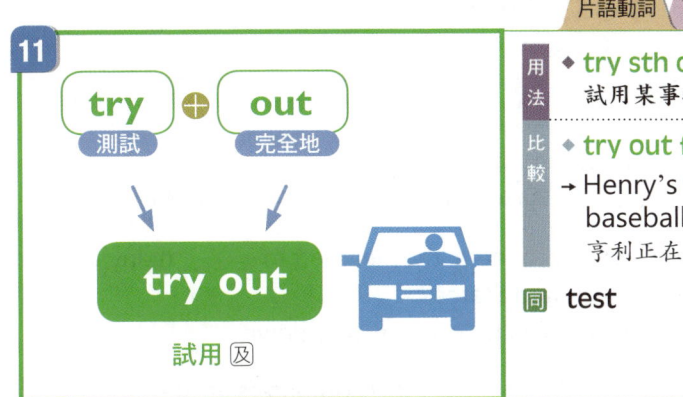

片語動詞 | 可分開 | 受詞為代名詞時定要分開

11

try 測試 ＋ out 完全地
→ try out 試用 及

用法 ◆ **try sth out / try out sth**
試用某事物

比較 ◆ **try out for sth** 參加選拔
→ Henry's **trying out for** the college baseball team.
亨利正在**參加**棒球校隊的球員**選拔**。

同 test

💡 通常用來表示「試用機器、車子」或「測試某想法或實驗」。

- Before you buy a new scooter, you should **try** it **out** to make sure you like it.
買新摩托車前最好要先**試騎**，以便確定你是真的喜歡。
- Do you want to **try out** my new digital camera?
你想要**試用**看看我新買的數位相機嗎？
- Don't forget to **try out** the equipment before setting up the experiment.
開始實驗前別忘了先**測試**一下儀器。

片語動詞

12

do 做 ＋ without 在沒有的情況下
→ do without
❶ 沒有……而將就 及
❷ 過著沒有……的日子 不及

用法 ◆ **do without (sth)** 沒有某事物也可以
→ There's no cheese left, so you'll just have to **do without**.
沒有起司了，所以你得**將就**一下了。

◆ **can/could not do without sth**
某事物造成困擾

同 沒有……也可以 **manage without**

💡 do without 前面若使用否定詞 cannot、can't 則表示「沒有……不行」，without 後可接受詞，也可不接。

❶ When Brenda lost her job, the family had to learn to **do without** many luxuries.
布蘭達丟了工作後，她的家人必須要學會**放棄**許多奢侈品。
❷ While spending the summer in China, Bill had to **do without** some of his favorite foods. 比爾在中國度過夏天時，必須要**放棄**他最愛的食物。

157

Unit 18 Test Yourself!

B 選擇題

1. Zelda _____ go to sleep when the phone rang.
   Ⓐ went over to   Ⓑ ran out to   Ⓒ was about to   Ⓓ was bound to

2. When the Smiths moved abroad to India, they learned to _____ many of the meals they usually ate in the United States.
   Ⓐ be bound to   Ⓑ do without   Ⓒ try out   Ⓓ tear down

3. Before choosing a new laptop, Dan _____ a few computers at the store.
   Ⓐ tried out   Ⓑ tore up   Ⓒ did without   Ⓓ tore down

4. Although the class was interesting, we had to stop the discussion because we _____ time.
   Ⓐ tore out   Ⓑ ran out of   Ⓒ tried out   Ⓓ did without

5. Wendy _____ the play many times before the performance.
   Ⓐ tore down   Ⓑ went over   Ⓒ tore up   Ⓓ ran out of

6. I'll be there tomorrow _____; you can count on me.
   Ⓐ for sure   Ⓑ about to   Ⓒ at heart   Ⓓ without hope

7. _____ my professor, we must know history if we want to understand current politics.
   Ⓐ About to   Ⓑ According to   Ⓒ For sure   Ⓓ At heart

8. Jenny felt that she _____ win the swimming competition because she had practiced so much and was very fast.
   Ⓐ tore up   Ⓑ was bound to   Ⓒ tore down   Ⓓ tried out to

9. Aaron was so angry after reading the letter that he _____ it _____.
   Ⓐ tried . . . out   Ⓑ tore . . . down   Ⓒ tore . . . up   Ⓓ went . . . over

10. Instead of fixing the old office building, the company just _____ the place and built a new office.
    Ⓐ ran out   Ⓑ tore up   Ⓒ was bound to   Ⓓ tore down

B 閱讀文章，從字表中選擇詞彙填入，並依人稱時態等做適當的變化

be about to	run out of	do without
according to	tear up	for sure
go over	be bound to	

As soon as Roberta learned that she had failed her math test, she knew she ❶ _____ be in trouble with her parents. There was no question that they'd be very mad. ❷ _____ her mom, if she failed a test, she could not go out on the weekends with her friends.

"But that's not fair!" Roberta thought. After all, she had ❸ _____ the chapter before the test. Roberta ❹ _____ destroy the test by ❺ _____ it _____, but she knew if her parents found out the truth, she'd be in even more trouble ❻ _____ .

In the end, Roberta ❼ _____ ideas and decided to be honest. Although it might be boring, she'd just have to ❽ _____ her friends for the next
few weekends.

C 引導式翻譯，並依人稱時態等做適當的變化

1. 他們將會**拆除**舊的警察局，然後蓋一棟新的。
   They're going to _____ _____ the old police station and build a new one.
2. 她**內心**其實是個保守的女性。
   She was a conservative woman _____ _____.
3. 我想我必須學會如何過著**沒有**你幫忙的日子。
   I guess I'll just have to learn how to _____ _____ your help.
4. 你**肯定**為了明天的面試而緊張不已。
   You _____ _____ _____ feel nervous about your interview tomorrow.
5. 我**正好要**離開的時候，喬治來了。
   I _____ _____ _____ leave when George arrived.
6. 黛安**沒時間了**，沒能完成最後一道問題。
   Diane _____ _____ _____ time and didn't finish the last question.
7. 我**確定**我沒辦法去參加派對了。
   I know _____ _____ that I won't be going to the party.

Unit 19

Applying to a University
申請大學

Leo and Catherine talk about applying to a university.
里歐和凱瑟琳在討論申請大學的事情。

Leo: So, did you get any university acceptance letters yet?

妳接到任何一所大學的入學許可了嗎？

Catherine: No, I didn't. I'm afraid **putting up with**[1] all the boring applications that the guidance counselor **passed out**[2] and comparing all the different programs was **in vain**[3].

沒有。我**受不了**指導老師**發**的無聊申請書，還有**白費力氣**比較所有不同的課程。

Leo: You haven't received any replies yet? Oh man! I bet that is all you think about **day in and day out**[4].

妳還沒收到回覆嗎？噢，老天！我敢肯定妳**每天**都在想這件事情吧。

Catherine: You better believe it! I've applied to so many colleges, I can't **tell** their names **apart**[5].

沒錯！我申請了好幾間大學，但**分**不**清楚**它們的名字。

Leo: Maybe you should have focused on just two or three schools and put more effort into the applications.

也許妳應該專心申請兩、三家學校就好，然後多做點努力。

Catherine: I suppose so. **All in all**[6], I should have thought about this more carefully.

我想也是。**總之**，我應該再仔細想一想。

1

put up (撐住) + with (與) → put up with
忍耐 及

片語動詞　不可分開

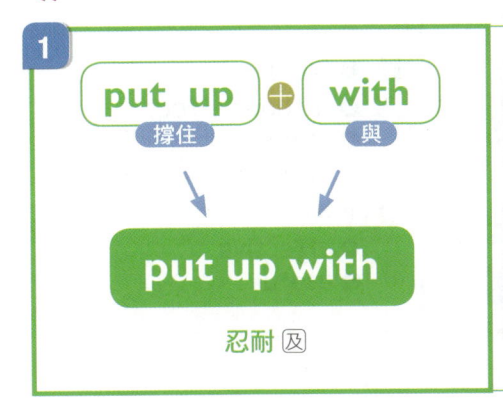

用法
- **put up with sth** 忍受某事
  → We had to **put up with** the inconvenience.
  我們必須忍受著不便。
- **put up with sb** 忍受某人
  → She's so moody—I don't know why he **puts up with** her.
  她的喜怒無常，我不知道他是如何忍受得了她。

💡 **put up with** 表示「忍耐某人、事、物，而沒有怨言」。

- When Rich moved near the highway, he had a hard time **putting up with** the noise. 瑞奇搬到公路附近後，他無法忍受噪音。
- After a long, tough day at school, it is sometimes hard to **put up with** my little sister. 在學校度過了既漫長又艱難的一天後，我有時會無法忍受我妹妹。

2

片語動詞　可分開　受詞為代名詞時定要分開

pass (轉移) + out (失去知覺) → pass out
❶ 分配 及　❷ 昏厥 不及

用法
- **pass sth out / pass out sth**
  分配某事物

比較
- **knock out** 擊倒
  → Sam hit his head on the ceiling and **knocked** himself **out**.
  山姆的頭撞到了天花板，昏了過去。
- **pass away** 去世
  → Sherry's terribly upset because her father **passed away** last week.
  雪莉的父親上週剛過世，所以她的情緒低落。

同　分配 ❶ give out　❷ hand out
　　　昏倒 ❶ faint　❷ pass out cold

💡 **pass out** 表示「分配」時，後接實物；表示「昏厥」時，主詞通常為人。

❶ Please **pass out** these forms to everyone who comes to the meeting.
請把這些表格發給所有出席這次會議的人。

❶ The professor asked Mindy to **pass out** a test to each student.
教授要敏蒂把考卷發給每一位學生。

❷ When a baseball hit Martha in the head during the game, she **passed out** for a few minutes. 馬莎在比賽中被棒球打到，昏過去好幾分鐘了。

3

in (在……中) + **vain** (徒然的) → **in vain** 白費

副詞片語

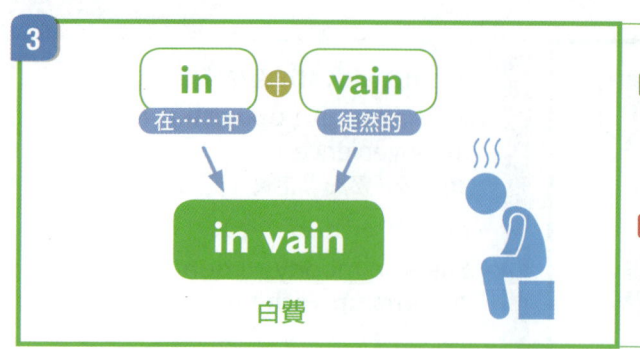

同 ① fruitlessly
② without effect
③ vainly
④ of no use

反 有效的
① effective
② useful

💡 **in vain** 作副詞，表示「徒然；毫無結果地」，亦可作主詞補語，表示「白費的」。

- Two weeks of constant studying were **in vain** as Mabel got a "D" on her chemistry exam. 美貝的化學考試得到「D」，她連續唸了兩個禮拜的書都**白費**了。
- Francis tried **in vain** to arrive on time to her first class of the semester. 法蘭西絲為準時上這學期第一堂課所做的努力都**白費**了。

4

day in (一天) + **and** (又) + **day out** (一天) → **day in and day out** 每天

副詞片語

同 ① from day to day
② day after day

- The same problems keep coming up **day after day**. 每天都會發生同樣的問題。

- The traffic to New York City is terrible **day in and day out**. 往紐約市區的交通**每天**都很亂。

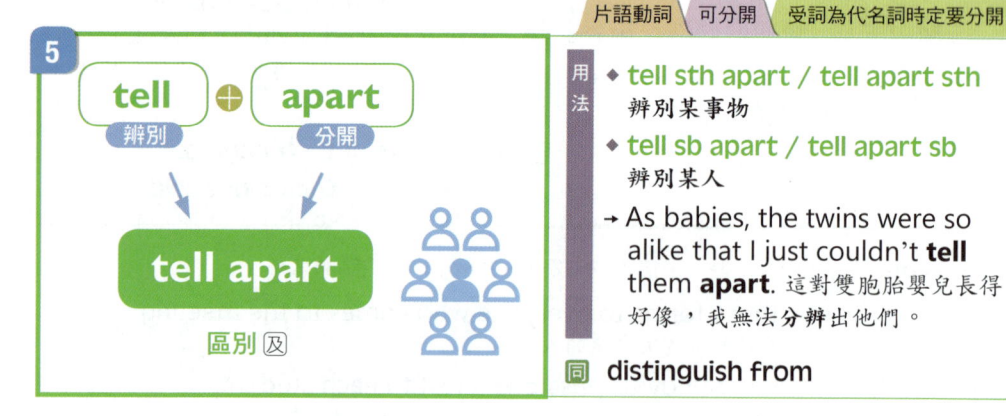

5

片語動詞　可分開　受詞為代名詞時定要分開

tell (辨別) + **apart** (分開) → **tell apart** 區別 及

用法
- tell sth apart / tell apart sth
  辨別某事物
- tell sb apart / tell apart sb
  辨別某人
→ As babies, the twins were so alike that I just couldn't **tell** them **apart**. 這對雙胞胎嬰兒長得好像，我無法**分辨**出他們。

同 distinguish from

💡 **tell apart** 前面通常會與 **can** 或 **be able to** 搭配使用，表示「能夠辨別」。

- The teacher had a hard time **telling** the twins **apart**. 老師不太能夠**辨別**雙胞胎。
- Can you **tell** these two kittens **apart**? 你可以**分辨**出這兩隻小貓嗎？

6

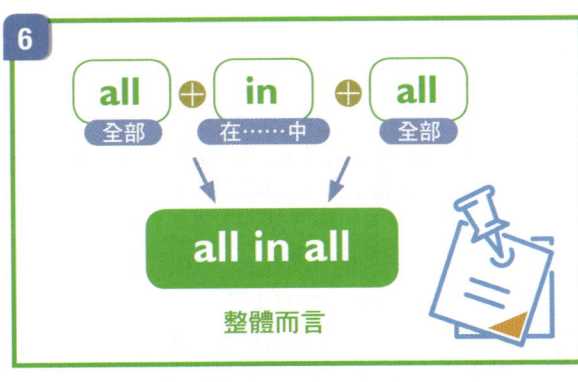

all(全部) + **in**(在……中) + **all**(全部) → **all in all** 整體而言

💡 **all in all** 可置於句首、句中和句尾。置於句首和句中時，後需使用逗號。

同
❶ on the whole
❷ by and large
❸ in general
❹ in the main
❺ at large

副詞片語

- Despite the fact that the car broke down, **all in all** it was a fun day.
  儘管車子壞了，**整體而言**，今天依然是愉快的一天。
- **All in all**, this is a very interesting class. 大致說來，這堂課非常有趣。

7

be in(在……中) + **(the/one's) way**(某人的去路) → **be in (the/one's) way** 阻礙；造成不便

用法 ◆ be in the way of sth 阻礙某事

同
❶ get in the way
❷ stand in the way

- You know I won't **stand in your way** if you want to apply for a job abroad.
  如果你想要申請海外的工作，你知道我不會**阻止**你的。

反 讓路 get out of the way

慣用片語

- The only annoying thing about having a puppy is that he **is** always **in the way**.
  養狗最擾人的就是**不方便**。
- You'**re in the way**; please give me some space!
  你**妨礙**到我了，請給我一些空間！

8

bite(咬) + **off**(斷掉) → **bite off** 咬斷 及

用法 ◆ bite off sth 咬斷某物

片語動詞

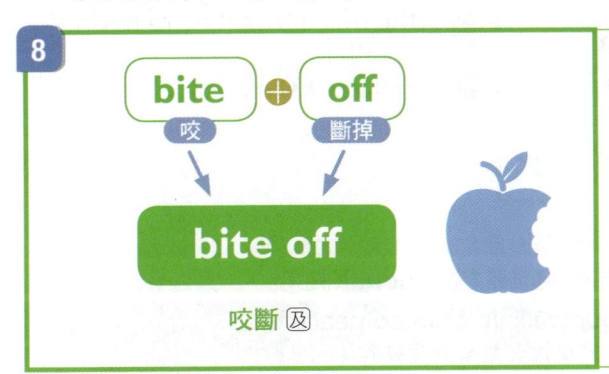

- Your dog **bit off** a piece of my Christmas decoration. 你的狗咬掉了我的耶誕裝飾。
- Felix **bit off** a piece of the chocolate bar and threw the rest away because it tasted terrible. 因為巧克力棒很難吃，菲力斯咬了一塊後便把剩下的都丟掉。

🔊 083

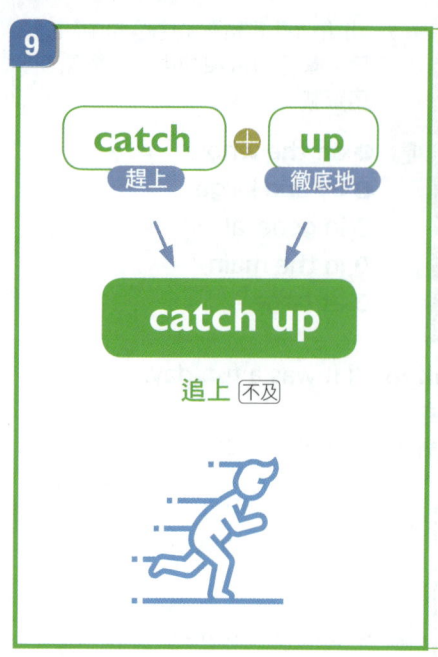

9 片語動詞

catch（趕上）＋ **up**（徹底地）
↓
catch up
追上 [不及]

比較
- **catch up with sth** 趕上某事物的進度
  → After Peter missed a month of school because of the flu, it took him several weeks to **catch up with** his schoolwork.
  彼得因感冒而一個月沒去上課，他花了好幾個星期才**趕上**學校課業。

- **catch up with sb** 趕上某人
  → Although Amy ran as fast as she could, she never **caught up with** her friend, who was a faster runner.
  艾咪就算使盡全力地跑，也不可能**追上**她那位跑得飛快的朋友。

- **catch up on** 趕完；補上
  → I have to **catch up on** my reading.
  我得**趕上**我的閱讀進度。

反 落後 fall behind

- He was out of school for a while and is finding it hard to **catch up**.
  他一陣子沒去學校上課，所以很難**趕上進度**。

10 片語動詞

go（移動）＋ **around**（到處；繞一圈）
↓
go around
❶ 四處走動 [及] ❷ 流傳 [及]
❸ 足夠分配 [不及]

用法
- **go around sw** 在某處四處走動
  → For a few weeks in the summer, visitors are able to **go around** Buckingham Palace.
  在夏天的幾個星期中，遊客可以到白金漢宮**四處走走看看**。

- **sth go around sw** 某事在某地流傳
  → There's a rumor **going around** the office that they're having an affair.
  辦公室裡**流傳**著他們有一腿的緋聞。

💡 go around 表示「四處走動」時，有時可後接名詞；表示「散播」時，是指「疾病或消息」四處散播；表示「分配」時，主詞為物，通常會搭配 **enough** 使用。

❶ Let's **go around** the lake on our walk; it looks so peaceful.
我們今天就在這座湖的**四周逛逛吧**，這裡看起來一片祥和。

❸ At the picnic, there were hardly enough sandwiches to **go around**.
三明治根本不夠**分給**野餐的每個人。

11

put 施加 + **on** 在……上
→ **put on**
增加（如體重）及

用法
◆ put sth on / put on sth 增加體重
→ He's **put on** 20 pounds in the last month.
他上個月增重了20磅。

比較
◆ put on 穿戴
→ Susan **put on** her jacket. 蘇珊穿上了夾克。

同 gain weight
反 減重 lose weight

- When Clarence returned from visiting his family for the summer, he had **put on** a few pounds. 克萊倫斯自從夏天探望家人回來後，他的體重便增加了好幾磅。

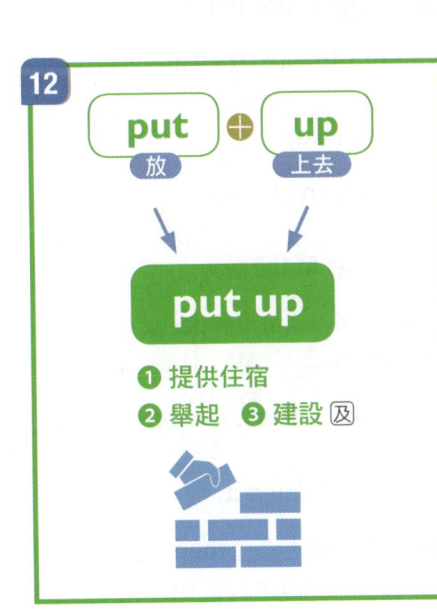

12

片語動詞　可分開　受詞為代名詞時定要分開

put 放 + **up** 上去
→ **put up**
❶ 提供住宿　❷ 舉起　❸ 建設 及

用法
◆ put sb up / put up sb 提供某人住宿
→ Molly is **putting** me **up** for the weekend. 莫莉週末留我下來過夜。

◆ put up sth / put sth up 舉起某事物
→ I **put** my hand **up** to ask the teacher a question. 我舉手問了老師一個問題。

◆ put up sth / put sth up 建造某事物
→ We're going to **put up** a new fence around our garden.
我們要在花園四周蓋新的籬笆。

同 建造 set up
反 拆毀 pull down

💡 表示「舉起」時，通常後接 hand 等名詞；表示「建造」時，可用於被動語態。

❶ When Carl visited Chicago, I **put** him **up** in my apartment.
卡爾來芝加哥玩時，我安排他住在我的公寓。

❷ Vicky **put** the painting **up** above the fireplace. 薇琪把畫舉起來，掛在火爐上方。

❸ Did you know that they're **putting up** a new cafe next to the supermarket?
你知道他們要在超市旁邊蓋一家咖啡廳嗎？

Unit 19 Test Yourself!

A 選擇題

1. Melvin _____ part of the apple and threw the rest away.
   Ⓐ bit off   Ⓑ caught up   Ⓒ passed out   Ⓓ put up

2. If you come to visit, I can _____ you _____ in my place.
   Ⓐ pass . . . out   Ⓑ bite . . . off   Ⓒ put . . . up   Ⓓ tell . . . apart

3. Fortunately, there was enough candy to _____, so all the students got a piece.
   Ⓐ be in the way   Ⓑ put on   Ⓒ bite off   Ⓓ go around

4. Although Rob is not the best student, _____, he is a very smart guy.
   Ⓐ in vain   Ⓑ all in all   Ⓒ day in and day out   Ⓓ over and under

5. Erin has a very annoying bird that is always making noise; I'm not sure how she _____ it.
   Ⓐ bites off   Ⓑ puts up with   Ⓒ passes out   Ⓓ goes around

6. If you don't walk faster, we'll never _____ with our friends; they are way ahead of us.
   Ⓐ catch up   Ⓑ pass out   Ⓒ bite off   Ⓓ be in the way

7. Although it was my turn to speak to the bank teller, an old man _____ and I couldn't get up to the counter.
   Ⓐ went around   Ⓑ passed out   Ⓒ put up   Ⓓ was in the way

8. Eve _____ a copy of the photo to everyone who arrived at the party.
   Ⓐ bit off   Ⓑ told apart   Ⓒ passed out   Ⓓ put up

9. Cindy's efforts to write the perfect application letter to Harvard were _____; she was not accepted there.
   Ⓐ in the way   Ⓑ in vain   Ⓒ all in all   Ⓓ day in and day out

10. Because Joel and I have the same car, we can't easily _____ them _____.
    Ⓐ bite . . . off   Ⓑ tell . . . apart   Ⓒ catch . . . up   Ⓓ pass . . . out

B 閱讀文章，從字表中選擇詞彙填入，並依人稱時態等做適當的變化

put up with	in vain	pass out
all in all	go around	put on
tell apart	day in and day out	catch up

Unit 19 Applying to a University 申請大學

On James' first day at college, he awoke early and got dressed. Before he left the house, he looked at himself in the mirror. He knew that he had ❶ _____ some weight over the summer, but he thought that by walking to the university every day, he would get back in shape. He walked fast and arrived early at his class.

Actually, he was the first student there. The professor asked him to ❷ _____ some handouts to his classmates. However, there weren't enough copies to ❸ _____. When the professor gave him some new copies, he was confused because he wasn't sure which students had a handout and which ones didn't. He had trouble ❹ _____ them _____. Just as he was finishing giving out the papers, he saw someone familiar in the classroom. It was his mother! She was out of breath from running to ❺ _____ with him and give him his lunch, which he had left at home. All of his classmates laughed at him. Even the professor was laughing.

❻ _____, it was an embarrassing first day. It was hard to ❼ _____ his mother sometimes, but as long as he lived at home, he would have to get used to her doing things like this all the time, ❽ _____. At times like this, James thought that all his attempts to be independent were ❾ _____. The thought of renting an apartment was becoming more attractive every day.

C 引導式翻譯，並依人稱時態等做適當的變化

1. 整體而言，我認為你做得很好。
   _____ _____ _____, I think you've done very well.

2. 大衛為了趕報告，在辦公室熬夜加班。
   David is staying late at the office to _____ _____ _____ his workload.

3. 他們計劃在原為博物館的地方蓋一家飯店。
   They're planning to _____ _____ a hotel where the museum used to be.

4. 原子筆足夠分配給每個人嗎？
   Are there enough pens to _____ _____?

5. 我喝多了，昏了過去。
   I drank too much and _____ _____.

6. 我可以忍受房子凌亂不堪，但我討厭不乾淨的房子。
   I can _____ _____ _____ the house being untidy, but I hate it when it's not clean.

167

Unit 20

🔊 084

Finding a Lost Cat
尋貓啟示

Ivy and Andy talk about a funny incident with a cat.
艾薇和安迪在討論一個有關貓咪的有趣意外。

Ivy: What's **the matter**[1]? You look exhausted.

怎麼了？你看起來累壞了。

Andy: I took the cat in for his first visit to the vet, and he just couldn't **hold still**[2]. It was annoying!

我第一次帶我的貓去看獸醫，可是他就是不能**不動**。很討厭！

Ivy: What happened? Did he run away?

發生了什麼事情？他跑走了嗎？

Andy: Yes, he did! The vet said this was the craziest cat he's ever seen, **by far**[3].

沒錯，他跑了！獸醫說他**顯然**是他所看過最難馴服的貓。

Ivy: Well, **no wonder**[4]! It sounds like your dear cat was pretty mad! I hope he hasn't **gotten lost**[5].

嗯，也**難怪**了！聽起來你的貓不太聽話！希望他別**迷路**才好。

Andy: Don't worry, I'll find him; I **know** him **by sight**[6].

別擔心，我會找到他的，我**認得**他。

Ivy: Get going! I'll **see** you **off**[7] right now. And remember to look everywhere; don't **rule out**[8] any possible hiding places.

快點開始找吧！我現在就**送**你**離開**。記得每個地方都要找，別**漏掉**任何地方。

hold still 不動

run away
離家出走；逃跑

168

Unit 20　Finding a Lost Cat 尋貓啟示

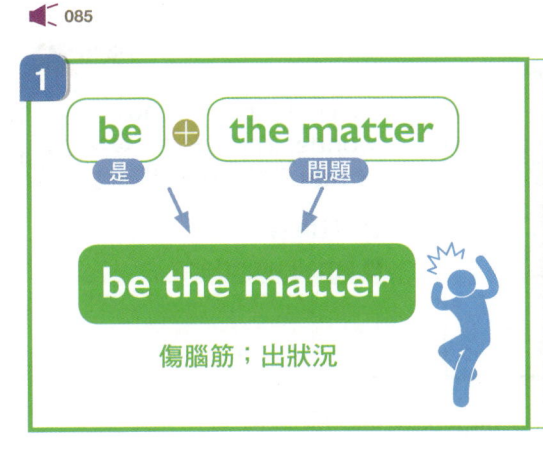

1　慣用片語

be (是) + **the matter** (問題) → **be the matter** 傷腦筋；出狀況

用法
- **be the matter with sth** 某事物出問題
→ What's **the matter with** your hand? It's bleeding.
你的手怎麼了嗎？一直在流血。

- **be the matter with sb** 某人出問題
→ You are acting strange; what's **the matter with** you?
你怪怪的，怎麼了嗎？

- Are you okay, or **is** something **the matter**?　你沒事吧？還是哪裡**不舒服**嗎？

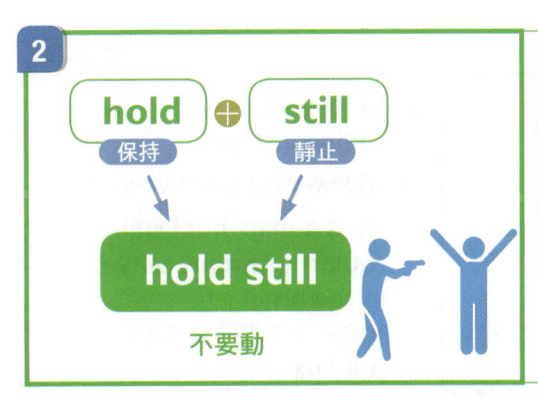

2　慣用片語

hold (保持) + **still** (靜止) → **hold still** 不要動

比較
- **stand still** 站著不動
- **sit still** 坐著不動
→ Children find it difficult to **sit still** for very long.
孩子們很難長時間**坐著不動**。

同
① remain still
② keep still
③ stay still

- Amy is only three years old, so it is hard for her to **hold still** when she visits the dentist.　艾咪才三歲，所以看牙醫時很難要她**不要動**。
- **Hold still**; this won't hurt.　不要亂動，不會痛的。

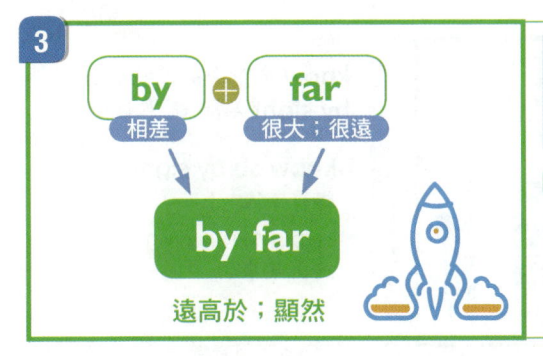

3　副詞片語

by (相差) + **far** (很大；很遠) → **by far** 遠高於；顯然

比較
- **so far** 到目前為止
→ **So far,** we've made one hundred dollars.　我們**到目前為止**賺了一百塊。

同　非常 very much

💡 **by far** 為程度副詞，表示「非常地」，可與形容詞**比較級**或**最高級**搭配使用。

- This weekend in Venice was one of the best weekends of my life, **by far**.
這次在威尼斯度週末**顯然**是我這輩子最棒的週末之一。
- This lesson is, **by far**, one of the most boring I've ever seen.
這堂課**顯然**是我上過最無聊的課之一。

169

4. no + wonder

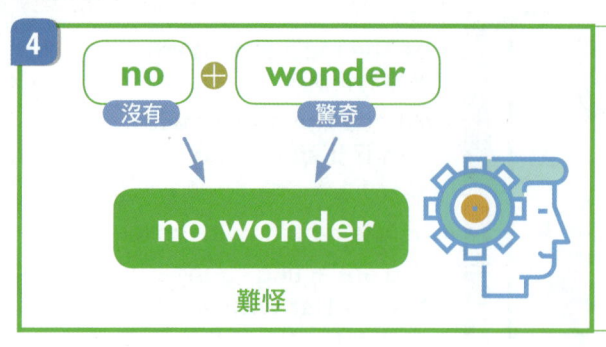

no 沒有 + **wonder** 驚奇 → **no wonder** 難怪

> **no wonder** 為 **it is no wonder** 的省略形式，後常接 **that** 子句，**that** 可省略。

同 ① little wonder
② small wonder

- **No wonder** you're tired; you were up till 3 a.m. last night!
  難怪你累了，你昨晚熬夜到凌晨三點！
- **No wonder** I couldn't find my keys! They were in the car all along.
  難怪我找不到鑰匙！原來一直都在車上。

5. get + lost

get 達到某種狀態 + **lost** 遺失的 → **get lost** 迷路

同 ① lose one's way
② become lost

反 找到路 **find one's way**

- I had a map, but I still couldn't **find my way** back to the hotel.
  我有一份地圖，但還是找不到回飯店的路。

> **get lost** 可表示「失去方向；迷路」，亦可表示叫某人「滾開」。

- It was Dan's first time visiting San Francisco, so it's no surprise that he **got lost**. 這是丹第一次到舊金山，所以他會迷路一點也不令人意外。

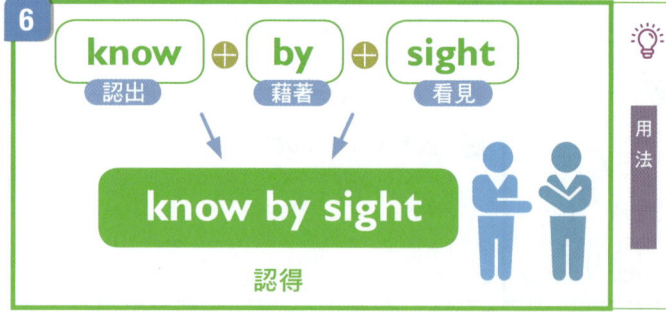

6. know + by + sight

know 認出 + **by** 藉著 + **sight** 看見 → **know by sight** 認得

> **know** 通常後接人或事物，**by sight** 為副詞，作修飾語。

用法
- **know sb by sight** 認得某人
- **know sth by sight** 認出某事物

- I'm not sure of Gina's address, but I **know** the house **by sight**.
  我不確定吉娜家的地址，但我認得她的房子。
- Although Carla has never spoken with Will, she **knows** him **by sight**.
  雖然卡拉從未和威爾說過話，但她認得他。

170

7

see (看著) + **off** (離開) → **see off** （幫某人）送行 [及]

片語動詞 | 可分開 | 受詞為代名詞時定要分開

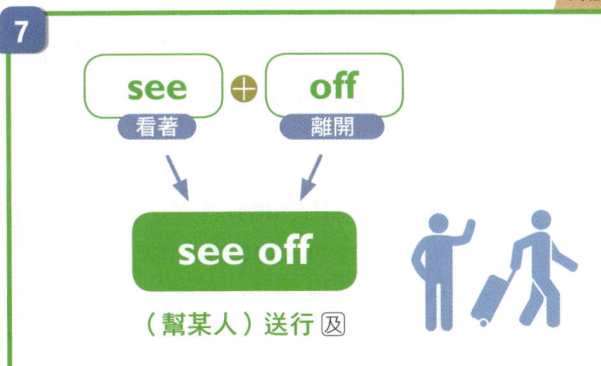

用法 ◆ **see sb off / see off sb** 送某人離開

💡 **see off** 可表示「送某人到機場、車站等」，亦可表示「被警衛送走」。

- When my uncle Chip was leaving, the whole family went with him to the airport to **see** him **off**.　我叔叔奇普要離開時，我們全家人陪他到機場**為**他**送行**。
- I'd like to go to lunch with you tomorrow, but I have to **see off** my friend who is traveling to Bermuda.
  我明天想和你吃中餐，但我必須**為**要去百慕達的朋友**送行**。
- My parents **saw** me **off** at the airport.　我父母到機場為我送行。
- Families gathered at the dock to **see** the sailors **off** to war.
  家人聚集在碼頭邊為征戰的船員們**送行**。

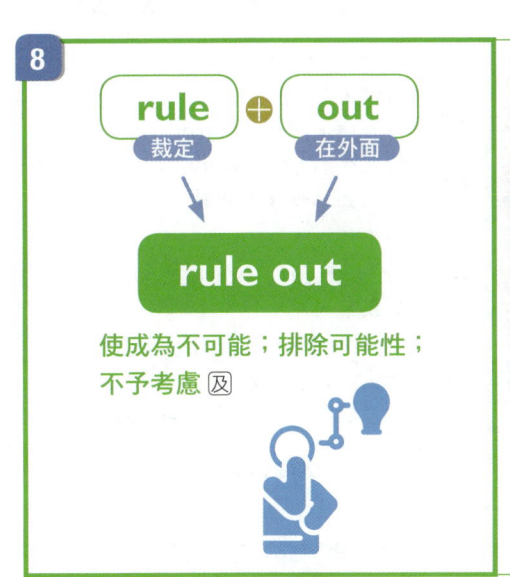

8

rule (裁定) + **out** (在外面) → **rule out** 使成為不可能；排除可能性；不予考慮 [及]

片語動詞 | 可分開 | 受詞為代名詞時定要分開

用法
- ◆ **rule sb out / rule out sb** 排除某人
  → The police have not **ruled** him **out** as a suspect.
  警方尚未**排除**他涉案的嫌疑。
- ◆ **rule sth out / rule out sth** 排除某事
  → The steady rain **ruled out** any chance of a tennis game.
  雨下不停，網球比賽**不可能**舉行了。
- ◆ **rule sb out of sth**
  取消某人參加某事的資格

同 排除 ❶ exclude　❷ eliminate
反 使成為可能 rule in

- The constant rain **ruled out** Sophia's plans to go sunbathing.
  外頭一直下雨，蘇菲亞做日光浴的計畫**泡湯**了。
- Because mom **ruled out** my plans to get a pet snake, I decided to ask her for a pet spider.　既然媽媽**不考慮**讓我養寵物蛇，我決定要求她讓我養寵物蜘蛛。

171

9

🔊 087

see(看著) + **out**(出去) → **see out**

❶ 送某人到門口　❷ 持續到結束 及

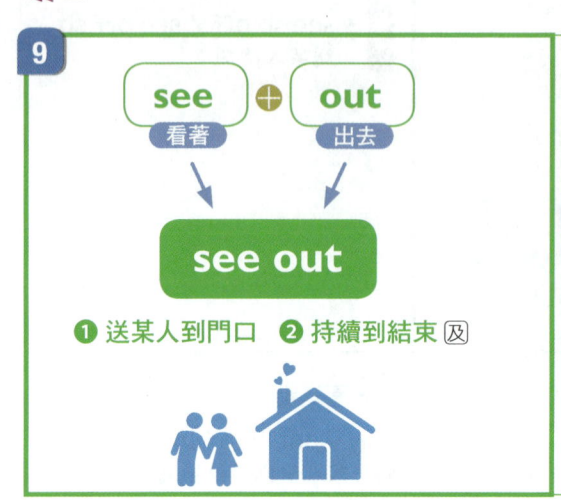

| 片語動詞 | 可分開 | 受詞為代名詞時定要分開 |

用法
- ◆ **see sb out** 送某人到門口
  → My secretary will **see** you **out**.
  我的秘書會送你**到門口**。
- ◆ **see sth out** 持續到某事物結束
  → They will **see out** the storm by staying in a shelter.
  他們待在一處安全的避難所中**直到**暴風雨**結束**。

同 坐到……結束 sit through

💡 see out 中間為人時，表示「送某人到門口」；中間為 match、play 等時，表示「看完比賽或表演」；中間為 winter 等季節，表示「持續到……結束」。

❶ After dinner, we **saw** Ben **out** the front door. 晚餐後，我們送班**到**前門口。

❶ It is polite to **see** your guests **out** after they visit.
送來訪的客人**到門口**是一種禮貌。

10

hold(抑制) + **up**(徹底) → **hold up**

❶ 拖延　❷ 搶劫 及

| 片語動詞 | 可分開 | 受詞為代名詞時定要分開 |

用法
- ◆ **hold sth up / hold up sth**
  搶劫某物
  → They **held** the same bank **up** twice in one week.
  他們在一個星期內**搶**了同一家銀行兩次。
- ◆ **hold sb up / hold up sb**
  耽誤某人
  → Sorry to **hold** you **up**, but my train was late.
  抱歉**耽誤**到你，我的火車延誤了。

同 持槍搶劫 stick up

💡 hold up 後接 bank、store 等名詞表示「搶劫」，可使用被動語態；表示「耽誤」時，亦可用於被動語態。

❶ Because my mother was stuck in traffic, the family meeting was **held up**.
我媽媽遇上塞車，因此家庭聚會**延後了**。

❶ Derek's delayed flight **held** the workshop **up**.
由於戴瑞克的班機延誤，所以研討會**延後了**。

172

Unit 20 Finding a Lost Cat 尋貓啟示

片語動詞

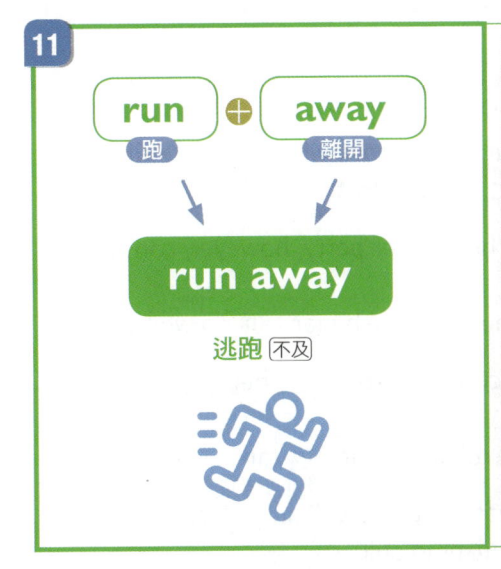

11 run 跑 + away 離開 → **run away** 逃跑 [不及]

用法
- run away from sb 逃離某人
- run away from sw 從某處逃走
- run away from danger 脫離危險
- run away from school 逃學
- run away from sth 逃離某事

→ You can't **run away from** your problems by watching videos all day. 你不能夠藉由整天看影片來逃避問題。

- run away from home 逃家

→ Jack **ran away from home** when he was only 15. 傑克只有15歲的時候逃家。

同 逃走 ❶ run off ❷ escape

- Last week my dog **ran away**, and I haven't seen him since. 自從上星期我的狗跑掉後，我就沒再見過他。
- When the children heard the loud bang of the fireworks, they got scared and **ran away**. 小朋友聽到巨大的煙火聲後，都被嚇跑了。

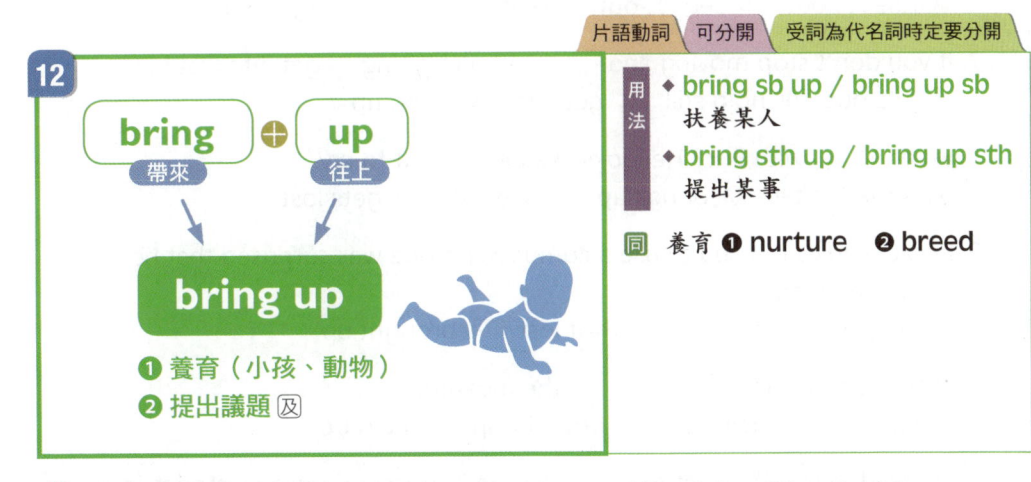

片語動詞 | 可分開 | 受詞為代名詞時定要分開

12 bring 帶來 + up 往上 → **bring up** ❶ 養育（小孩、動物）❷ 提出議題 [及]

用法
- bring sb up / bring up sb 扶養某人
- bring sth up / bring up sth 提出某事

同 養育 ❶ nurture ❷ breed

💡 **bring up** 除了「扶養」外，亦可表示「提出……」，後接 **advice**、**idea** 等名詞。

❶ Gary **brought up** his five children by himself. 蓋瑞獨自扶養五個小孩。
❶ They **brought** him **up** as a Christian. 他們將他養育成為基督教徒。
❷ Some of the students **brought** questions **up** with the teacher after class. 下課後，有些學生向老師提出問題。

173

Unit 20 Test Yourself!

🅐 選擇題

1. When I was a kid, I _____ for a day, but I came back when I got hungry.
   Ⓐ saw out   Ⓑ ran away   Ⓒ ruled out   d) got lost

2. Melissa was surprised no one came to her dinner party; however, considering that she is a terrible cook, it's really _____.
   Ⓐ holding something up   Ⓑ seeing her out   Ⓒ by far   Ⓓ no wonder

3. When Mr. Gussman fired Claire, the security guard _____ her _____ to make sure she really left the office.
   Ⓐ brought . . . up   Ⓑ saw . . . out   Ⓒ ruled . . . out   Ⓓ ran . . . away

4. We should not _____ the possibility that the plane will arrive late.
   Ⓐ rule out   Ⓑ see off   Ⓒ run away   Ⓓ hold still

5. Prof. Tubman is _____ the best professor at the college.
   Ⓐ ruled out   Ⓑ no wonder   Ⓒ by far   Ⓓ seen out as

6. Will anyone _____ you _____ at the train station tomorrow?
   Ⓐ rule . . . out   Ⓑ see . . . out   Ⓒ see . . . off   Ⓓ bring . . . up

7. If you don't stop moving and _____, you're going to get into trouble.
   Ⓐ rule out   Ⓑ hold still   Ⓒ get lost   Ⓓ bring up

8. What _____ with Eric? He looks like he is about to cry.
   Ⓐ is the matter   Ⓑ brings up   Ⓒ sees off   Ⓓ gets lost

9. Because Jules refused to use a compass, no one was surprised that he _____ on his camping trip.
   Ⓐ got off   Ⓑ ruled out   Ⓒ got lost   Ⓓ brought up

10. Ms. Stefford's late arrival _____ the meeting.
    Ⓐ got off   Ⓑ held still   Ⓒ brought up   Ⓓ held up

11. I asked my mother not to _____ any embarrassing personal stories in front of my girlfriend.
    Ⓐ get lost   Ⓑ bring up   Ⓒ hold up   Ⓓ see off

B 閱讀文章，從字表中選擇詞彙填入，並依人稱時態等做適當的變化

rule out	by far	see off
no wonder	run away	get lost
bring up	be the matter	

　　Last night, when Trish and Kyle went on their third date, Trish noticed something was wrong almost right away. Trish asked Kyle what ❶ _____, but he just said he was tired and stressed out. They went for dinner and then took a walk in the park, where they ❷ _____. They spent an hour looking for the way out.

　　Trish could still see something was wrong, but she had no idea what it could be. She didn't want to ❸ _____ anything, even the possibility that she had done something to upset him. Although her father had ❹ _____ her _____ to be kind to everyone, Kyle was acting so unusual that she couldn't help but feel a bit angry at him. She even thought about ❺ _____ and going home early. This was ❻ _____ the worst date she had ever been on. Finally, when Kyle ❼ _____ her _____, he told her that he wanted to break up. It was a surprise, but it was a relief, too. ❽ _____ he had been acting strangely!

C 引導式翻譯，並依人稱時態等做適當的變化

1. 你不**坐好**的話，我就無法幫你梳頭了。
   I can't brush your hair if you don't _____ _____.

2. 蘇和山姆**顯然**是全班最優秀的學生。
   Sue and Sam are _____ _____ the best students in the class.

3. 南西是由她的祖母**一手帶大**的。
   Nancy was _____ _____ by her grandmother.

4. 單獨健行時要小心，別**迷路**了！
   Be careful if you go hiking alone. Don't _____ _____!

5. 這場意外造成了交通**延誤**了好幾個鐘頭。
   Traffic was _____ _____ for several hours by the accident.

6. 我從未和裘蒂說過話，但我**認得**她。
   I've never spoken to Judy, but I _____ her _____ _____.

Unit 21

Handing in a Paper
交報告

🔊 088

Francine and Albert talk about the deadline for their papers.
法蘭欣和艾伯特在談論有關報告的截止日期。

Francine: Did you finish your research paper? You know you have to **hand** it **in**[1] today.

你的研究報告寫完了嗎？你知道今天一定要**交**吧。

Albert: I was up all night checking it over **in case**[2] I made some mistakes. I don't want to be **taken by surprise**[3] with a bad grade.

以**防**錯誤，我昨晚整夜沒睡仔細檢查了一遍。我可不想看到成績時**嚇一跳**。

Francine: Good job! I'm nearly done too. However, as soon as class starts, I'm going to **go up to**[4] the professor and ask him a few questions.

做得好！我也快要寫完了，只要一開始上課，我就要**過去**問教授一些問題。

Albert: It may be a bit late for that. You'd better try to finish now. Trust me, you'll **be better off**[5] that way.

那可能有點太遲了吧。妳最好現在就完成。相信我，我覺得那樣會**比較好**。

Francine: You know, Albert, that's a good idea. You're smart! I bet you're **named after**[6] Albert Einstein!

艾伯特，這主意不錯。你真聰明！我想你的名字是以艾柏特‧愛因斯坦來**命名**的吧！

176

Unit 21 Handing in a Paper 交報告

1 片語動詞 可分開 受詞為代名詞時定要分開

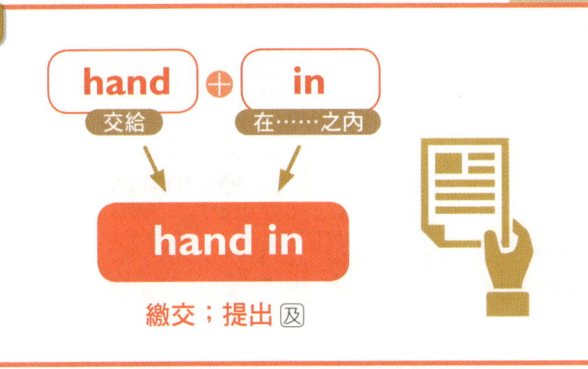

hand（交給）＋ **in**（在……之內）
→ **hand in** 繳交；提出 [及]

用法
- **hand sth in** 繳交某事物
- **hand in sth** 繳交某事物

同
❶ send in
❷ submit

💡 **hand in** 通常用來表示「將文件、資料或作業等交給老師或主管」。

- Ms. Applebee told us we had to **hand in** our reports by next week.
  艾波比女士說我們下星期前一定要交報告。
- Did you **hand** your essay **in** yet? 你交論文了嗎？
- I've decided to **hand in** my resignation. 我已經決定要遞出辭職信了。
- The teacher told the children to **hand in** their exercise books.
  老師要孩子們繳交練習簿。

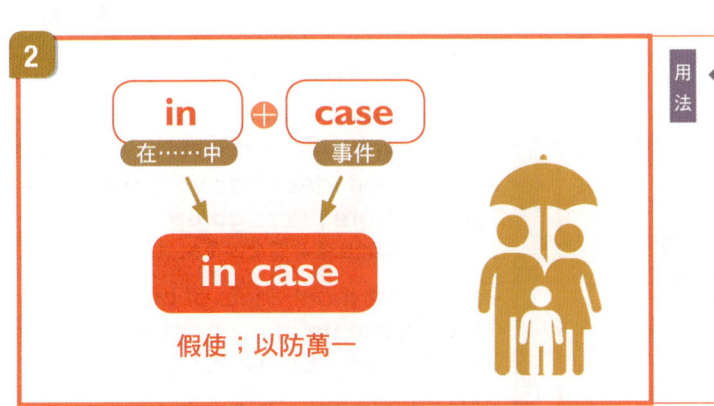

2 副詞片語

in（在……中）＋ **case**（事件）
→ **in case** 假使；以防萬一

用法
- **in case of sth** 遇到某種狀況時

💡 **in case** 可作連接詞，後接子句表示「以防萬一；如果……的話」；**in case** 前面亦可加上 **just**，作修飾語，置於**句尾**。

- You should take your umbrella to work today **in case** it rains.
  你今天最好帶把傘去上班，以防下雨。
- **In case** of emergency, remember that you can always call my cell phone.
  如果有任何緊急狀況，記得你都可以打手機給我。
- I don't think I'll need any money, but I'll bring some just **in case**.
  我不認為我會需要用到錢，但我會帶著以防萬一。
- Bring a map **in case** you get lost. 把地圖帶著，免得你迷路了。

3

take (帶領) + **by** (由) + **surprise** (驚訝)
→ **take by surprise** 感到意外

用法 ◆ take sb by surprise
令某人感到意外

同 ❶ happen by surprise
❷ catch by surprise

- Mohammed's new haircut really **took** me **by surprise**; I hardly recognized him!
  穆罕默德的新髮型讓我很意外，我幾乎認不出他來了！
- I was **taken by surprise** with your mobile's new ringtone—it is very original!
  我對你的手機鈴聲感到很意外，真有創意！
- Lisa's resignation **took** us completely **by surprise**.
  莉莎的辭呈令所有人感到相當地意外。

4

go (走) + **up** (上) + **to** (去)
→ **go up to** 接近

用法 ◆ go up to sth 接近某事物

比較 ◆ go up 上升；建立（建築物）
→ It's a good idea to do your shopping now, before prices **go up**.
趁物價還沒上漲前買東西是個很好的主意。
→ Since last month, lots of buildings have **gone up** in my neighborhood.
從上個月開始，我家附近蓋了許多棟大樓。
→ New buildings are **going up** everywhere. 到處都在蓋新的大樓。

- Bill told his little sister never to **go up to** strangers.
  比爾告訴妹妹不要接近陌生人。
- Irene **went up to** the next person she passed on the street and asked for directions. 艾琳走向街上迎面而來的路人問路。
- Let's **go up to** the second floor of the restaurant to eat because there are more tables there. 我們上這家餐廳的二樓吃東西吧，樓上的座位比較多。

5

be better (較好的) + **off** (在……情況中) → **be better off** 比較好的狀況

比較
- ◆ **be well-off** 生活富裕
- → Michel's mother is a lawyer and his father is an engineer, so you can say the family **is** pretty **well-off**. 米歇爾的母親是律師，父親是工程師，所以他們**生活富裕**。
- → After buying the new house, the Goldman family **was** less **well-off**. 高曼一家人在買了新房子後，就比較沒那麼**富裕**了。

同 情況變好 **be in a better situation**
反 情況變糟 **be worse off**

💡 **be better off** 可用來表示「情況好轉」，亦可表示「更有錢」。

- After a few months in driving school, Victoria **was better off** on the roads.
  維多莉亞到駕訓班上了幾個月的課後，她的開車技術**好多了**。
- We **were better off** once we got off the plane and got some fresh air.
  我們在下了飛機、呼吸到新鮮的空氣後，便**感覺好多了**。
- He'd **be better off** working for a bigger company.
  他在大公司工作的話大概會**比較有錢**。

片語動詞 | 可分開

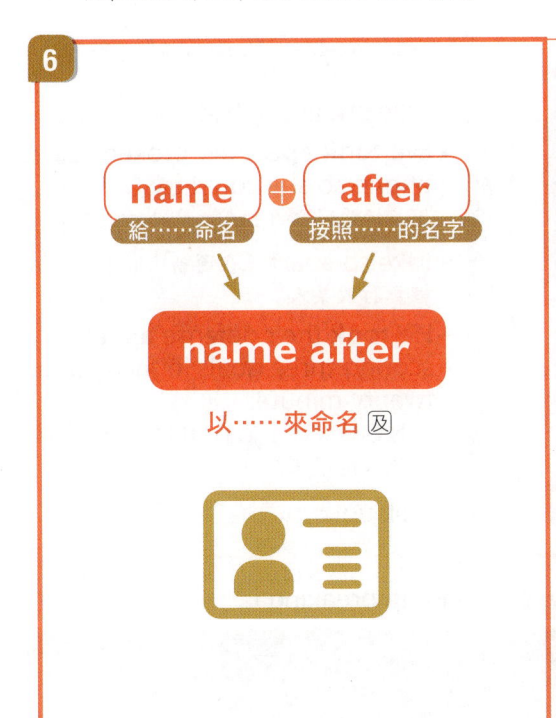

6

name (給……命名) + **after** (按照……的名字) → **name after** 以……來命名 及

用法
- ◆ **name A after B** 以B的名字為A命名
- → Lucas **named** his first son **after** his older brother. 盧卡斯以哥哥的名字為大兒子命名。

- ◆ **A is named after B** A是由B的名字來命名
- → Paul **was named after** his grandfather. 保羅是以其祖父的名字來命名。

- ◆ **name sb/sth for sb/sth** 以某人或事來為某人或事命名
- → Helen told us about her brother, Apollo, who was born in 1969 and **was named for** the U.S. astronauts' mission to the moon. 海倫告訴我們說，她弟弟出生於1969年，名叫阿波羅，是**以**美國太空人登陸月球的任務**而命名**的。

- Harriet is **named after** her grandmother. 哈莉特是**以**其祖母的**名字來命名**。

7

hold（抓住）＋ **on**（繼續） → **hold on**

❶ 稍等　❷ 抓緊　❸ 堅持下去 [不及]

比較
◆ hold onto sth 抓緊某事物
→ **Hold onto** the rope, and don't let go. 抓緊繩子，別放手。

同 緊抓 hang on
反 掛斷電話 ❶ ring off ❷ hang up

❶ **Hold on**, I'll be with you in a minute. 請您**稍等**一下，我馬上就回來。

❶ The receptionist asked us to **hold on** for a while because there were many visitors in the office.
由於辦公室有許多訪客，所以接待員請我們**稍等**一下。

❷ **Hold on** to your hat when the wind is blowing, or it will blow away!
起風時要**抓緊**你的帽子，否則會被吹走！

❸ If you can **hold on**, I'll go and get some help.
如果你能夠**撐**下去，我會去找人幫忙的。

8

片語動詞　可分開　受詞為代名詞時定要分開

take（拿走）＋ **apart**（分開） → **take apart**

拆開 [及]

用法
◆ take sth apart 拆開某事物
→ Eve **took apart** her broken cell phone so she could try to fix it.
伊芙**拆開**壞掉的手機，試圖把它修好。

◆ take sb apart（在運動比賽中）輕鬆打敗某人
→ He **took** their defense **apart**, scoring three goals in the first twenty minutes.
他輕鬆地突破了他們的防守，前20分鐘就取得了三分。

同 break up

● If you **take** the computer **apart**, you may end up breaking it.
如果你把電腦**拆開**，最後可能會把它弄壞。

9

pull 拉 + **together** 在……一起 → **pull together** 同心協力 [不及]

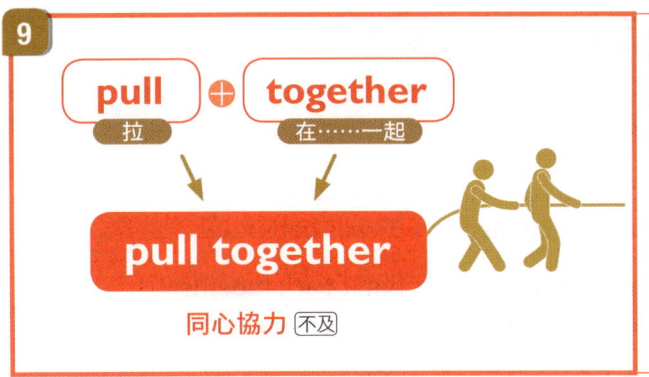

用法 ◆ **pull (oneself) together** 振作起來

同 cooperate

💡 **pull together** 表示同心協力做某事，主詞通常為人。

- Everyone in the office **pulled together** to finish the project.
  這份企畫案是由公司上上下下每個人**共同合力**完成的。
- If we want to meet the deadline, everyone has to **pull together** and work all night. 如果我們想要趕上截止日期，就必須**同心協力**，熬夜趕工。
- Everyone on our street really **pulled together** after the fire.
  火災發生後，街上的人全都**團結在一起**。

10

keep 拿走 + **in touch with** 與……有聯繫 → **keep in touch with** 和某人保持聯絡

用法 ◆ **keep in touch with sb** 與某人保持聯絡
→ His family has **kept in touch with** me since his death.
他的家人在他過世後就一直和我保持聯繫。

同 ❶ communicate with
❷ stay in touch with
❸ be in touch with

- **Are** you still **in touch with** any of your old school friends?
  你還有和老同學聯絡嗎？

反 ❶ lose touch with
❷ lose contact with

- Please don't **lose touch with** me after you move away.
  你搬走後千萬不要和我**斷了**聯絡。

- Although Rachel moved away from home, she **keeps in touch with** her family by calling every week. 雖然瑞秋離家了，但她依然每個禮拜打電話和家人**保持聯絡**。
- Karin bought a new cell phone so she could **keep in touch with** her friends more easily. 卡琳買了一支新手機，好更方便她和朋友**保持聯絡**。

181

Unit 21 Test Yourself!

A 選擇題

1. Timmy _____ after his doctor gave him some medicine.
   Ⓐ took apart   Ⓑ went up   Ⓒ handed in   Ⓓ was better off

2. Wayne _____ his keyboard, but he couldn't put it back together.
   Ⓐ went up   Ⓑ took apart   Ⓒ handed in   Ⓓ was named after

3. Cheryl's math grade _____ after she got an "A" on the final exam.
   Ⓐ went up   Ⓑ pulled together   Ⓒ handed in   Ⓓ took apart

4. I'm coming; just _____ while I tie my shoe.
   Ⓐ hand in   Ⓑ hold on   Ⓒ take apart   Ⓓ pull together

5. New technologies such as email, SMS, and chat programs help people _____ their friends and family.
   Ⓐ take apart   Ⓑ keep in touch with   Ⓒ take by surprise   Ⓓ put together

6. Tony was _____ when the phone rang at 3 a.m., waking him up.
   Ⓐ better off   Ⓑ pulled together   Ⓒ handed in   Ⓓ taken by surprise

7. Although the kids in my study group didn't know much about European history, when we _____, we wrote a great paper.
   Ⓐ turned over   Ⓑ dropped off   Ⓒ pulled together   Ⓓ made up

8. Lucy _____ her goldfish _____ her favorite actress.
   Ⓐ pulled . . . together for   Ⓑ named . . . after
   Ⓒ handed . . . in to   Ⓓ took . . . apart for

9. My dream is to win the lottery and _____.
   Ⓐ go up   Ⓑ pull together   Ⓒ hand in   Ⓓ be well-off

10. Faye _____ the boy and asked him to turn the music down.
    Ⓐ took apart   Ⓑ handed in   Ⓒ went up to   Ⓓ pulled together

11. Let's get to work; I just found out that we must _____ our reports tomorrow!
    Ⓐ name after   Ⓑ go up to   Ⓒ pull together   Ⓓ hand in

12. We don't have much time, but if we all _____, we should get the job done.
    Ⓐ hold on   Ⓑ take apart   Ⓒ pull together   Ⓓ hand in

B 閱讀文章，從字表中選擇詞彙填入，並依人稱時態等做適當的變化

name after	go up to	be well-off
in case	take by surprise	keep in touch with
hold on		

On my first day back to work, I was putting together a computer for a new customer when I realized that she looked familiar. " ① _____," I thought to myself. "Who is that?" So I ② _____ her and introduced myself. I was ③ _____ when she recognized me, too. She reminded me that we were classmates in high school. Then I remembered her name: Meredith. She was ④ _____ her mother.

I hadn't ⑤ _____ her since we graduated nearly a decade ago. She was dressed in expensive-looking clothes and looked like she ⑥ _____. After we talked for a while, we decided to meet again; so I gave her my phone number just ⑦ _____ she couldn't find it in the phone book. I'm sure we'll have a good time when we see each other again.

C 引導式翻譯，並依人稱時態等做適當的變化

1. 告訴他們**等一下**，我會馬上過去。
   Tell them to _____ _____; I'll be there in a minute.

2. 健康就是**財富**。
   If you have your health, you _____ _____.

3. 我預料不會塞車，但**為了避免**塞車，我想我們應該要早點出發。
   I don't expect much traffic, but _____ _____ there is some, I think we should leave early.

4. 你**交了**歷史論文了嗎？
   Have you _____ _____ your history essay yet?

5. 我們**拆開**引擎，看看問題出在哪裡。
   We _____ the engine _____ to see what the problem was.

6. 我認為你買一台新車**會比較好**，別再修理舊車了。
   I think you'd _____ _____ _____ if you bought a new car rather than trying to repair your old one.

Unit 22

The New Teacher
新老師

🔊 092

Molly and Philip have a chat about their new teacher.
茉莉和菲利普在聊他們新來的老師。

Molly:	How do you like our new history teacher?	你喜歡新來的歷史老師嗎？
Philip:	Well, after hearing that he studied at Harvard, I really **look up to**[1] him; but the fact is, he seems to **look down on**[2] his students.	唔，自從知道他是哈佛畢業的，我就很**尊敬**他。但事實上，他似乎有點**瞧不起**學生。
Molly:	Yeah, he may be a smart guy, but he's not so friendly. Yesterday I **came across**[3] him in a café, and though I **took pains**[4] to be nice, he was pretty cold.	是啊，他博學多聞，但不是很友善。我昨天在咖啡店**巧遇**他，雖然我**努力**釋出善意，但他看來很冷漠。
Philip:	I know what you mean. I **stopped by**[5] his office a little while ago with some questions, and he wasn't very helpful.	我懂你的意思。我前一陣子**到**辦公室請教他一些問題，但他不是很樂意幫忙。
Molly:	Nope. The last teacher was better; he even told us to **drop** him **a line**[6] by email if we had any questions about the assignments.	沒錯，之前的老師比較好。他甚至說如果我們有課業方面的問題，隨時可以用電郵**寫信**給他。
Philip:	Exactly. Plus, this class seems harder— I don't think I **stand a chance**[7] of getting an "A."	是啊，加上課程越來越難了，我不認為我**有希望**得到「A」。

184

Unit 22 The New Teacher 新老師

1

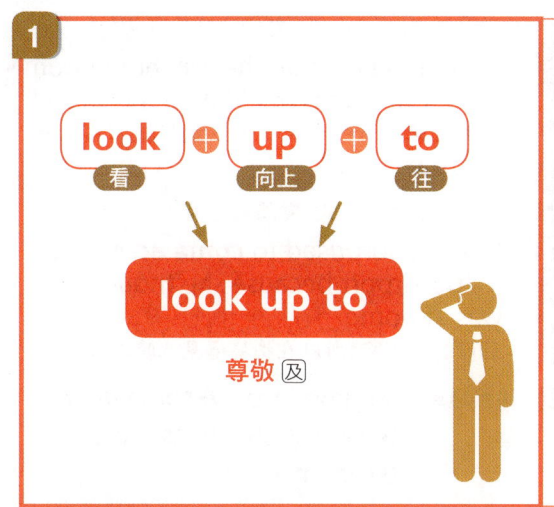

look（看）＋ up（向上）＋ to（往）

→ **look up to** 尊敬 及

用法 ◆ **look up to sb** 尊敬某人
→ He'd always **looked up to** his father. 他一直都很尊敬他父親。

比較 ◆ **look up** 查詢
→ If you don't know what the word means, **look** it **up** in a dictionary. 如果你不知道這個字的意思，就去查一下字典。

同 admire
反 ❶ look down on
　　❷ look down upon

- Ariel **looks up to** her older sister. 艾芮兒很尊敬她姐姐。
- Whom do you **look up to** most? 你最尊敬的人是誰？
- Judy was older and more experienced, and I **looked up to** her.
  裘蒂年紀較長，經驗較豐富，我很尊敬她。

2

look（看）＋ down（向上）＋ on（在……上）

→ **look down on** 瞧不起 及

用法 ◆ **look down on sb** 輕視某人

同 ❶ look down upon
　　❷ look down one's nose at

- I always thought he **looked down his nose at** me because I spoke with a strong accent. 我總覺得他因為我的口音很重而瞧不起我。

反 look up to

- A good boss doesn't **look down on** his employees. 好老闆不會看不起員工。
- Sometimes I feel as if my professor is **looking down on** me because I got a "D-" on the exam. 自從考試得到「D-」後，我有時覺得教授看不起我。

3

come (來) + **across** (穿越)

↓

come across

❶ 被認為是 [不及]
❷ 突然遇見或發現 [及]

用法
- **come across sth** 突然發現某事物
  → It's a great day; on the way home from class, I **came across** $50 on the street!
  今天真是美好的一天。我在放學回家路上發現50塊錢！

- **come across sb** 突然遇見某人
  → Fay was surprised to **come across** Lou in the airport because she thought he was at home.
  菲以為盧在家，所以在機場遇見他時很驚訝。

同 偶然遇到　❶ bump into　❷ come upon
　　　　　　　❸ meet with　❹ run across
　　　　　　　❺ run into

- ❶ Mariah **comes across** really well on television. 瑪莉亞在銀光幕前的形象很好。
- ❶ Although Melinda is a nice girl, she can **come across** as a bit mean sometimes.
  記住，就算瑪琳達是個好女孩，她有時也是很難相處的。

慣用片語

4

take (承擔) + **pains** (辛苦)

↓

take pains

不辭辛勞；費盡苦心

用法
- **take pains to do sth**
  不辭辛勞地做某事
  → They **took** great **pains to** ensure that no one felt left out.
  他們費盡苦心以確保沒有人覺得被忽略。

同 ❶ be at pains
　　　❷ go out of one's way
　　　❸ go to great pains

💡 take pains 的 pains 需使用**複數形**，除了指「疼痛」外，還有「辛苦」的意思，pains 前可加上 **great** 表示「極為盡心盡力」。

- Adriana **took pains** to walk quietly so as not to awaken the baby.
  艾卓恩娜**努力**走路不發出聲音，以免吵醒小寶寶。
- Dan **took** great **pains** to eat right so he would lose weight.
  丹為了減輕體重，很**努力**養成正確的飲食習慣。

5

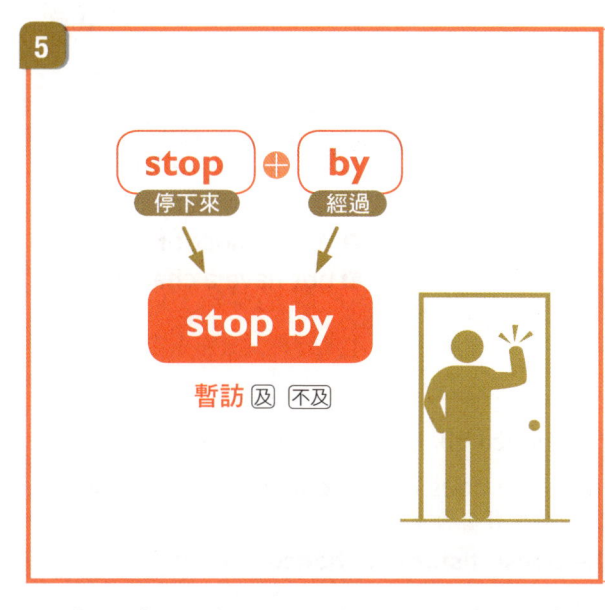

stop (停下來) + **by** (經過)
↓
stop by
暫訪 及 不及

用法
- **stop by sw** 暫訪某處
→ On the way to school, we **stopped by** a café and got some coffee.
上學途中，我們在一家咖啡店**停下來**買咖啡。

同
1. come around
2. come over
3. drop by
4. stop over
5. stop off
6. stop in

- I **stopped in** at work on the way home to check my mail.
我回家的時候順便到公司看有無我的信件。

- If you have time tomorrow, **stop by** in the afternoon.
明天如果有空，就下午**過來**吧。
- **Stop by** on your way home, and I'll give you that DVD.
回家路上**順便到**我這裡來一下，我要拿那片 DVD 給你。

6

drop (丟) + **a line** (一行字)
↓
drop (someone) a line
寫信給某人（通常是短信）

用法
- **drop a line to sb / drop sb a line**
寫一封短信給某人
→ Just **drop** me **a line** when you've decided on a date.
你決定日期後再**寫封短信**給我。

- This weekend, I'll **drop** my friend Jerry **a line** if I have time.
如果有時間，我這週末會**寫信**給我的朋友傑瑞。
- I would have **dropped** you **a line** earlier, but I lost your address.
我之前本來要**寫信給你**，但我弄丟了你的地址。
- I really do like hearing from you, so **drop** me **a line** and let me know how you are. 我真的很想知道你的消息，**寫封信給我**，讓我知道你的近況。

Unit 22 The New Teacher 新老師

187

7

stand (擁有) + **a chance** (一個機會) → **stand a chance** 有機會；有希望

用法	◆ stand a good/fair chance 很有機會
比較	◆ take a chance 冒險
反	❶ not a ghost of a chance ❷ not have a chance

💡 **stand** 在此片語中表示「擁有；占有」；**chance** 則是指 chance of success。

- Matilda isn't a very good swimmer; she doesn't **stand a chance** of winning the gold medal. 瑪蒂蓮達游得不快，她沒什麼**希望**贏得金牌。
- Rory's mom is mad at her, so she doesn't **stand a chance** of going to the movies with us this weekend.
  蘿芮的媽媽在生蘿芮的氣，所以她這週末不**可能**會和我們去看電影了。

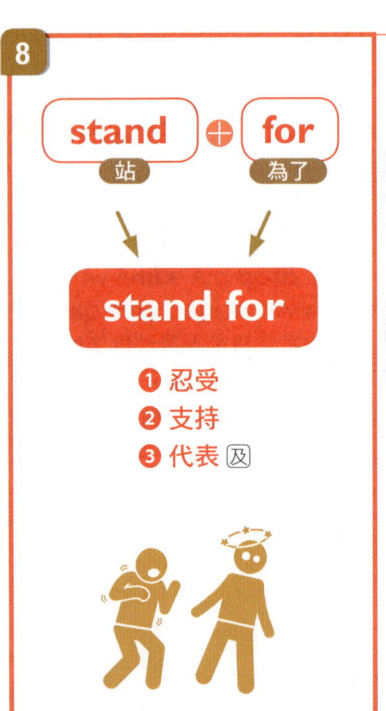

不可分開 | 片語動詞

8

stand (站) + **for** (為了) → **stand for**
❶ 忍受
❷ 支持
❸ 代表 及

用法	◆ stand for sth 忍受某事物 → I wouldn't **stand for** that kind of behavior from her, if I were you. 如果我是你，我無法忍受她那種行為。 ◆ stand for sth 支持某事物 → This party **stands for** low taxes and individual freedom. 這個政黨擁護低稅制和個人自由。 ◆ stand for sth 代表某事物 → "GMT" **stands for** Greenwich mean time. 「GMT」表示格林威治標準時間。
比較	◆ stand by 待命
同	忍受 ❶ put up with ❷ tolerate 支持 back up 代表 ❶ represent ❷ act for
反	反對 object to

❶ Don't use foul language with me; I won't **stand for** that kind of talk.
和我講話別用粗話，我無法忍受那種說話方式。

❸ The stars on the U.S. flag **stand for** states. 美國國旗上的星星**代表**各州。

9

take 拿 ➕ off 離開

⬇ ⬇

take off
❶ （飛機）起飛 [不及]
❷ 突然受到歡迎 [不及]
❸ 脫掉 [及]

用法 ◆ take off sth / take sth off
脫掉某物

反 穿上 put on

- ❶ **take off** 表示「（飛機）起飛」時，為不及物動詞。
- ❷ 可用來表示「（觀念、產品）突然大受歡迎」時，同為不及物動詞。
- ❸ 表示「脫掉」時，則為及物動詞，可參考第 4 頁。

❶ Because of the snowstorm, no planes **were taking off** or landing at the airport.
由於暴風雪的因素，機場所有的飛機都無法起降。

❷ Her singing career had just begun to **take off**.
她的歌唱事業才剛爆紅。

10

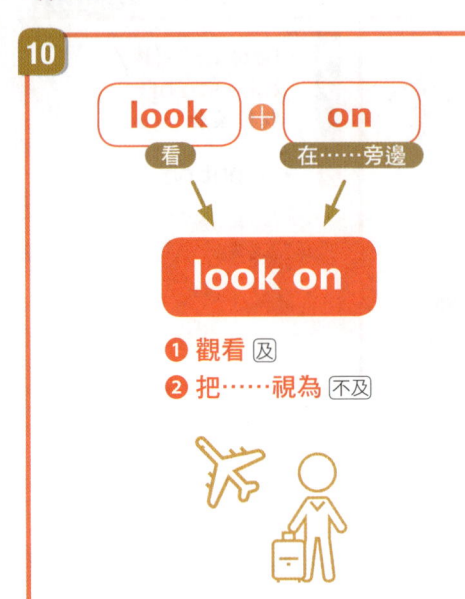

look (看) + **on** (在……旁邊) → **look on**

❶ 觀看 [及]
❷ 把……視為 [不及]

片語動詞 | 可分開 | 受詞為代名詞時定要分開

用法
- **look on sb as sth** 把某人視為某事
→ We **looked on** him **as** a son.
  我們把他當作兒子來看待。

- **look on sth as sth** 把某事視為某事
→ I've lived there so long I **look on** the town **as** my home.
  我已經住在那裡很久了，所以我把那個城市當作我的家鄉

同 旁觀 ❶ **stand by** ❷ **watch**
- I can't just **stand by** and **watch** you waste all our money.
  我無法眼睜睜地看著你花光所有的錢。

💡 **look on** 表示「觀看」時，為不及物動詞；表示「考慮」時，為及物動詞，後可接 **plan** 等名詞。

❶ Because Toby arrived at the airport late, he could only **look on** as the plane left without him. 陶比太晚到機場，所以他別無選擇只能**眼看**著飛機離開。

❶ Janet had a broken leg, so she could only **look on** as the other students played soccer. 珍娜自從腿骨折後，就只能**看**著其他學生踢足球。

慣用片語

11

keep (遵守) + **time** (時間) → **keep time**

❶（鐘錶的時間）精準 ❷ 計時

用法
◆ **keep good time**
（鐘錶）走得很準

反 走得不準 **keep bad time**

❶ This old clock doesn't **keep** good **time**. 這個老舊的時鐘不準。
❶ Does your cell phone **keep time**? 你手機的時鐘準嗎？
❷ When I go running, I like to **keep time** on my watch.
  慢跑時，我喜歡用手錶來**計時**。

12 pull + off
拉開　完

→ **pull off**
❶ 拉掉
❷ 成功辦到 [及]

片語動詞 | 可分開 | 受詞為代名詞時定要分開

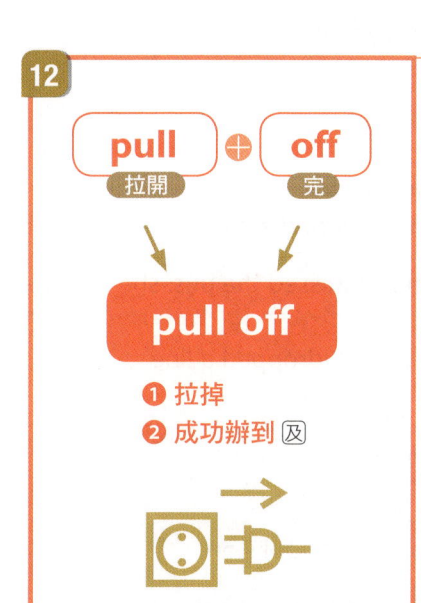

Unit 22 The New Teacher 新老師

用法
- **pull sth off** 成功辦到某事
- **pull off sth** 成功辦到某事
→ The central bank has **pulled off** one of the biggest financial rescues in recent years.
中央銀行**成功**地解決了近年來最大的金融危機。

同 脫掉 **take off**
- She **took off** her clothes and got into the bathtub.
她**脫掉**衣服後進入浴缸。

反 穿上 **pull on**
- I **pulled on** my jeans and ran downstairs.
我**穿上**牛仔褲後跑下樓。

❶ I **pulled off** my wet clothes as soon as I got home.
我一到家就趕緊**脫掉**濕衣服。

❷ It was a hard exam, but in the end I **pulled** it **off** and got an "A."
考試很難，但我還是**成功**地得到「A」。

❷ Although no one thought he could do it, Corey **pulled off** the best business deal in company history.
雖然沒有人認為柯瑞能夠成功，但他**談成了**公司有史以來最好的一筆交易。

Unit 22 Test Yourself!

A 選擇題

1. Amy _____ as her boyfriend danced with a pretty girl.
   Ⓐ pulled off   Ⓑ came across   Ⓒ looked on   Ⓓ stood a chance

2. Melissa _____ to get to school on time; when she missed the bus, she hailed a cab.
   Ⓐ took pains   Ⓑ came across   Ⓒ stopped by   Ⓓ dropped a line

3. What sort of politics do you _____?
   Ⓐ stand for   Ⓑ pull off   Ⓒ keep time   Ⓓ look on

4. Carol's plane _____ five minutes after yours.
   Ⓐ keeps time   Ⓑ takes off   Ⓒ stands a chance   Ⓓ looks on

5. Whom do you _____ more, your mother or your grandmother?
   Ⓐ pull off   Ⓑ look up to   Ⓒ stop by   Ⓓ take off

6. Jackson is talented and _____ winning the art competition.
   Ⓐ looks down on   Ⓑ stands a chance of   Ⓒ takes off   Ⓓ looks up to

7. How did you _____ that perfect score on the exam without even studying?
   Ⓐ look down on   Ⓑ come across   Ⓒ pull off   Ⓓ take off

8. When are you planning on _____ for a little visit?
   Ⓐ pulling it off   Ⓑ stopping by   Ⓒ taking off   Ⓓ coming across

9. On the way home, I _____ my cousin sitting on the side of the road.
   Ⓐ took off   Ⓑ stopped by   Ⓒ looked on   Ⓓ came across

10. I've been waiting for your email all day; when will you _____ me _____?
    Ⓐ drop . . . a line   Ⓑ pull . . . off
    Ⓒ read . . . through   Ⓓ take . . . off

11. Greg's watch _____ perfectly.
    Ⓐ drops a line   Ⓑ takes off   Ⓒ comes across   Ⓓ keeps time

12. No matter how educated you are, you should never _____ anyone.
    Ⓐ take off   Ⓑ look down on   Ⓒ come across   Ⓓ take pains to

B 閱讀文章，從字表中選擇詞彙填入，並依人稱時態等做適當的變化

look on	come across	take pains
look up to	stop by	drop a line
pull off	stand a chance	look down on

When I ❶ _____ my boss at the supermarket last Monday, I was surprised when he suggested I ❷ _____ his apartment later that day. I thought that he just wanted to make small talk and have some coffee, so I was surprised to learn that he was thinking about promoting me to a position that I really wanted. I have always ❸ _____ great _____ to impress my boss, but I didn't think I ❹ _____ at getting this position! I thought my boss didn't like me and ❺ _____ me.

I believed that I would have to ❻ _____ as one of my coworkers got the job.

Although my boss told me he was still unsure about the promotion, the next day, he ❼ _____ me _____ to tell me that I could start the new job next week. I had ❽ _____ it _____!

I really ❾ _____ my boss now because I know he makes great decisions!

C 引導式翻譯，並依人稱時態等做適當的變化

1. 我剛好經過你家，所以想說**過來**和你閒聊一下。
   I was passing your house, so I thought I'd _____ _____ for a chat.
2. 假如傑克努力用功，他便**很有機會**通過考試。
   Jack _____ _____ _____ _____ of passing his exam if he studies hard.
3. 克萊兒認為他們因為她沒有唸大學而**輕視**她。
   Claire thinks they _____ _____ _____ her because she never went to college.
4. 我的班機會在午夜過後**起飛**前往紐約。
   My flight to New York _____ _____ at a little past midnight.

Unit 22　The New Teacher　新老師

193

Unit 23

🔊 097

The Weekend Party
週末派對

Zack and Ursula talk about Ursula's party.
查克和娥蘇拉在討論娥蘇拉的派對。

Zack: How did your party go last weekend?

上週末的派對辦得如何？

Ursula: Bad. I worked so hard to make it nice. I **cleaned out**[1] all the shelves and cabinets and washed all the dishes; I really did my best to **make do**[2] with my small apartment.

糟透了。我非常努力想讓一切看起來都很棒，我把床鋪下面都**清理乾淨**了，也把所有的盤子都洗乾淨了。我真的**盡力**把公寓整理乾淨了。

Zack: Did your roommates **go in for**[3] the idea of a party?

妳的室友們**喜歡**辦派對這點子嗎？

Ursula: At first, my roommates **got on my nerves**[4] when they **put down**[5] the idea of a party. However, when I told them that their friends could come too, they almost **took over**[6] the party planning.

他們剛開始**批評**這個想法時**讓**我**很緊張**，但我說他們的朋友也可以來參加後，他們幾乎**接手**計畫了整個派對。

Zack: So what went wrong? It sounds good so far.

那是哪裡出了錯？到目前為止聽起來都很好啊。

Ursula: I **stayed up**[7] the entire night before to make sure all the details were right. The next day, I **stayed in**[8] waiting for the guests. I didn't go to work; I didn't study. I just waited.

我為了確認所有細節都沒錯，前一天晚上**熬夜**沒睡。隔天我**在家**等候客人的光臨，沒去上班，也沒唸書，我只是等待。

Zack: And?

然後呢？

Ursula: No one **showed up**[9]!

都沒有人**來**！

Unit 23 The Weekend Party 週末派對

1

clean (清理) + **out** (徹底) → **clean out** 清理乾淨 及

片語動詞 | 可分開 | 受詞為代名詞時定要分開

用法
- **clean sth out / clean out sth**
  清出某事物
  → I found these letters while I was **cleaning out** my cupboards.
  我在整理廚櫃的時候發現了這些信。

比較
- **clean up** 打掃；梳洗
  （將某個地方整理乾淨；排整齊）
  → We'll go out as soon as I've **cleaned up** the kitchen.
  等我一打掃完廚房，我們就出門。
  → I need to **clean up** before we go out. 我出門前得梳洗一番。

同 clean up

💡 **out** 在此雖表示「徹底」，但亦有「向外」的含義，故 **clean out** 是指「將不要的東西清掃出去」。

- The fridge smelled terrible, so Damian **cleaned out** all the old food.
  冰箱的味道很臭，所以戴明恩把過期食物都清理乾淨。
- Someone better **clean out** the garage soon; it is filling up with junk.
  車庫堆滿了垃圾，最好盡快把它清理乾淨。

慣用片語

2

make (使) + **do** (做) → **make do** 將就

用法
- **make do with sth/sb**
  湊合著用某事物或人
  → Because I work and you go to school, we really need two cars—I don't think we can **make do with** only one.
  因為我要上班，而你要上課，所以我們需要兩台車，我不認為一台車就夠了。

- **make do without sth/sb**
  在沒有某事物或人的情況下完成某事
  → Tina isn't here, so we'll have to **make do without** her.
  緹娜不在這裡，所以我們必須在沒有她的情況下設法解決。

💡 **make do** 表示「在資源不足的情況下，設法完成某事」，常搭配 **with** 後接名詞。

- After Mindy quit her job, she had to **make do** with less.
  敏蒂辭職後，必須依存較少的物資得過且過。

195

3

go in + **for**
進入　　為了

↓

go in for

❶ 參加比賽
❷ 喜歡
❸ 把……當作興趣 及

用法
◆ **go in for sth** 參加某事物；喜愛某事物
→ Richie really **goes in for** pop music.
瑞奇完全沉迷於流行音樂。
→ Are you planning to **go in for** the 200-meter race?
你打算**參加**200公尺賽跑嗎？

比較
◆ **go for** 特別喜歡；努力爭取
→ I don't **go for** war movies much.
我不太**喜歡**戰爭電影。
→ John has been practicing for this volleyball competition for weeks now; he's **going for** the gold.
約翰為排球比賽已經練習了好幾個星期，他想要**贏得**金牌。

同 參加 **take part in**

💡 **go in for** 可用來表示「從事某職業、活動；參加某項比賽；喜好某種事物」，通常為**及物動詞**，不可用於被動語態。

❶ All Scott's coworkers **went in for** the idea of having a surprise party for his retirement. 史考特所有的同事都**參與**了為他舉辦退休驚喜派對的計畫。

❷ Abe doesn't **go in for** baseball, but he sometimes watches his friends play.
艾比不**喜歡**棒球，但他有時會去看朋友打球。

4

get + **on** + **one's nerves**
抓住　在……之上　某人的神經

↓

get on one's nerves
令人心煩或討厭

比較
◆ **make sb nervous**
令某人緊張

💡 **nerves** 在此需使用**複數形**，表示「焦躁不安」的意思。

• My neighbor's dog really **gets on my nerves** when he barks all night.
鄰居的狗叫了整晚，**令我心浮氣躁**。

• After spending so much time together on the cruise, Jan and Gary **got on each other's nerves**. 珍和蓋瑞自從一起參加郵輪之旅後便很**討厭**對方。

Unit 23 The Weekend Party 週末派對

5

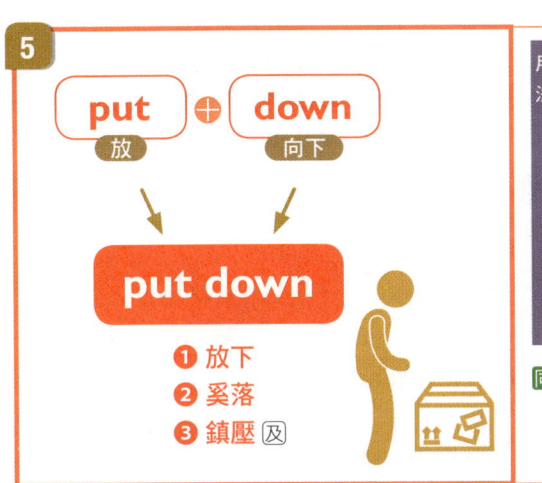

片語動詞 | 可分開 | 受詞為代名詞時定要分開

put 放 ＋ **down** 向下 → **put down**
❶ 放下
❷ 奚落
❸ 鎮壓 及

用法
◆ put sth down 放下某事物
→ I **put** my bags **down** while we spoke. 我們在說話的時候，我把袋子放了下來。

◆ put sb down 奚落某人
→ Why did you **put** me **down** in front of everybody like that? 你為何要在所有人面前奚落我？

同 放下 ❶ lay down ❷ let down ❸ set down ❹ take down

❷ It was very embarrassing when my brother **put** me **down** in front of all my friends. 我的哥哥在所有朋友面前奚落我，令我很難堪。

❸ The dictator used the army to **put down** the democratic rebellion. 獨裁者用武力鎮壓民主反抗團體。

6

片語動詞 | 可分開 | 受詞為代名詞時定要分開

take 拿 ＋ **over** 越過 → **take over**
❶ 接管
❷ 帶至某處 及

用法
◆ take sth over / take over sth 接管某事物
◆ take sth over from sb 從某人手中接管某事

反 移交 hand over

❶ When the CEO was in the hospital, his assistant **took over** the company for a few weeks. 執行長住院時，他的助理接管了公司好幾個星期。

❶ After the rebellion, a new leader **took** the country **over**. 叛亂結束後，新的領導者接管了整個國家。

❶ Richard has **taken over** responsibility for this project. 理查已經接手負責整個企劃。

❷ The delivery boy **took** the package **over** to my aunt. 送貨員把包裹交給我阿姨。

197

7

stay (保持) + **up** (起來) → **stay up**

熬夜 [不及]

同
① sit up
② burn the midnight oil
③ pull an all-nighter

反 去睡覺 go to sleep

- The children get to **stay up** all night on New Year's Eve.
  孩子們除夕夜可以整晚**不睡覺**。
- How late did you **stay up** last night? You look very tired.
  你昨晚**熬夜**到幾點？你看起來很累。

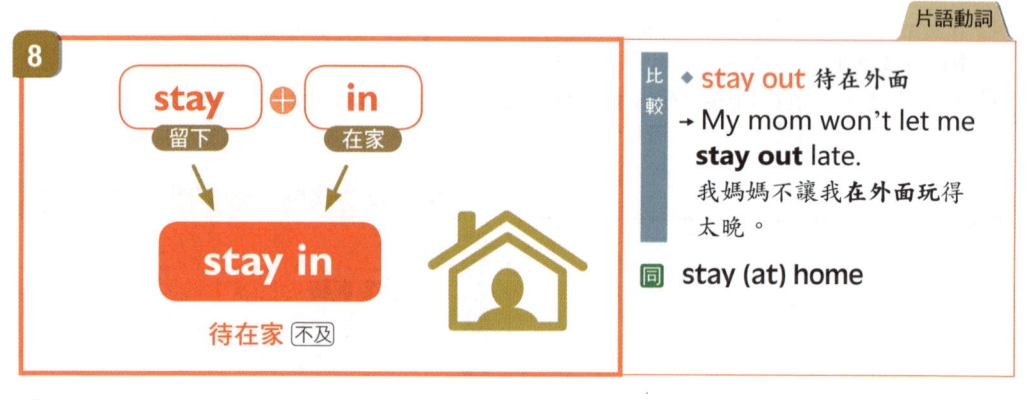

8

stay (留下) + **in** (在家) → **stay in**

待在家 [不及]

比較
◆ stay out 待在外面
→ My mom won't let me **stay out** late.
我媽媽不讓我**在外面**玩得太晚。

同 stay (at) home

💡 in 在此片語中作副詞，後不需接受詞。

- Although Ralph planned to go to a club, he ended up **staying in** and watching a movie on TV. 瑞夫雖然計劃要去俱樂部，但他最後**待在家裡**看電影。
- Instead of going to a restaurant, let's **stay in** and make dinner here.
  我們**待在家裡**自己做晚餐，別上館子了。

9

show (顯示) + **up** (上來) → **show up**

到達；出現 [不及]

比較
◆ show sb up
使某人難堪

同 出現 turn up

- Unfortunately, we **showed up** at the movie a few minutes late, so we missed the beginning. 可惜我們電影開演了幾分鐘才**進場**，所以錯過了開頭。
- I invited her for eight o'clock, but she didn't **show up** until eight-thirty. 我約她八點見面，但她一直到八點半才**出現**。

10 名詞片語

close (接近的) + call (判決) → **close call** 千鈞一髮；倖免於難

💡 **close call** 原指「做出判決的瞬間」，現在引申為「千鈞一髮；倖免於難」。

同 **close shave**
- I had a **close shave** this morning—someone almost knocked me off my bike. 我今天早上**差點發生意外**，有人差點把我從腳踏車上撞倒。

- I almost didn't get into the university; my test scores were barely high enough, so it was a **close call**. 我差一點就上不了大學，我的考試成績勉強夠高，真是**千鈞一髮**。
- I really had a **close call** today on the way home from school—I almost drove off the icy road! 我今天放學回家真的**差點就發生意外**，我的車子在結冰的路上打滑，差點就駛出車道。

11 慣用片語

give (給) + birth (誕生) + to (動作的對象) → **give birth to** 生（孩子）

用法
- **give birth to sb** 生下某人
  → Lydia **gave birth to** a beautiful baby boy early this morning. 莉蒂亞今天早上**生**了一個很漂亮的小男嬰。
- **give birth to sth** 某事物誕生
  → This extraordinary experience **gave birth to** her latest novel. 這項奇特的經歷**孕育**出了她的最新小說。

比較
- **give rise to sth** 引起某事物
  → His experiences have **given rise to** the passion he expresses in his poetry. 他的經歷**造就**了他在詩中表達出的滿腔熱情。

- Our rabbit **gave birth to** seven baby bunnies last weekend! 我們養的兔子上週末**生**了七隻小兔子！

Unit 23 Test Yourself!

A 選擇題

1. Ignatius was mad when his coworker _____ him _____ in front of his boss.
   Ⓐ cleaned . . . out   Ⓑ put . . . down   Ⓒ kept . . . up   Ⓓ took . . . in

2. How late did you _____ last night?
   Ⓐ stay up   Ⓑ clean out   Ⓒ go for   Ⓓ put down

3. Someone better _____ the trash can; it's really disgusting!
   Ⓐ stay up   Ⓑ go in for   Ⓒ clean out   Ⓓ give birth to

4. The students don't have money for furniture, so they _____ without.
   Ⓐ clean out   Ⓑ stay up   Ⓒ give birth   Ⓓ make do

5. Please turn the TV down; the noise _____.
   Ⓐ is giving birth   Ⓑ is getting on my nerves   Ⓒ is going in   Ⓓ is cleaning out

6. Vanessa will probably _____ twins in the next two weeks.
   Ⓐ go in for   Ⓑ stay up with   Ⓒ clean out   Ⓓ give birth to

7. Bill and Diane do not _____ action movies; they are more interested in comedies and science fiction.
   Ⓐ go in for   Ⓑ stay up   Ⓒ clean out   Ⓓ give birth to

8. Iain arrived one minute before the bus left, so it was really _____.
   Ⓐ cleaned out   Ⓑ stayed up   Ⓒ a close call   Ⓓ went in for

9. I could sure _____ some Italian food for lunch.
   Ⓐ go for   Ⓑ stay up   Ⓒ show up   Ⓓ clean out

10. Kathy was planning on _____ at 5, but her car broke down.
    Ⓐ going for   Ⓑ showing up   Ⓒ cleaning out   Ⓓ staying up

B 閱讀文章，從字表中選擇詞彙填入，並依人稱時態等做適當的變化

give birth to	close call	make do	go in for
stay up	show up	clean out	go for

　　Last weekend, Betty ① _____ at the club where she likes to dance, but the music was terrible. At first, she tried to ② _____, but she wasn't enjoying herself. Aside from the bad music, she was tired because she ③ _____ the entire night before at the hospital while her sister was ④ _____ her new nephew. After that, her brothers took her to a restaurant, but she doesn't usually ⑤ _____ eating breakfast. The smell of eggs and coffee upset her stomach, and she almost threw up. It was definitely a ⑥ _____!

　　So Betty left the club, ⑦ _____ a snack, and then took a taxi home. At her apartment, she ⑧ _____ her closets. It wasn't as much fun as dancing, but it was calming, and it felt nice to get organized.

C 引導式翻譯，並依人稱時態等做適當的變化

1. 請不要再發出怪聲了！那聲音**搞得我很煩**。
   Please stop making that noise! It really _____ _____ _____ _____.

2. 傑森在和他父親學開車的時候，好幾次都**差點發生意外**。
   Jason had several _____ _____ while he was learning to drive with his dad.

3. 我們等了他一整天，但他從頭到尾都沒**出現**過。
   We waited all day for him, but he never _____ _____.

4. 我一直不太**喜歡**古典音樂，但我愛死了爵士樂。
   I've never really _____ _____ _____ classical music, but I love jazz.

5. 我沒有廚櫃，所以只好用箱子**將就一下**。
   I didn't have cupboards, so I _____ _____ with boxes.

6. 我們全家上星期五到附近的餐廳**去吃披薩**。
   Last Friday, my family _____ _____ pizza at the neighborhood restaurant.

7. 傑瑞兩個星期前**接下**了經理一職。
   Jerry _____ _____ as manager two weeks ago.

Unit 23　The Weekend Party　週末派對

Unit 24

Schoolwork Problems
課業問題

Walt is telling Debby about some problems in his class.
華特告訴黛比他上課遇到的一些問題。

Debby: Is everything ok? You look like you need to **cheer up**[1].

一切還好嗎？看來你需要**振作**一下。

Walt: Well, I **ran into**[2] some problems with my schoolwork in philosophy.

唉，我在寫哲學作業時**遇到**一些問題。

Debby: What happened? Are you having trouble doing what you **set out to**[3] do in that class?

怎麼了？你在**準備**做那堂課的作業時遇到困難了嗎？

Walt: Bingo. I just can't finish this report. I'm even thinking about **dropping out of**[4] this philosophy class.

沒錯。這份報告我就是寫不完。我甚至考慮**退掉**這門哲學課。

Debby: That's so extreme that it doesn't even really **make sense**[5]. If I were you, I'd **draw up**[6] a list of goals you need to **carry out**[7] and then complete them one by one.

太誇張了，那樣做一點**意義**也沒有。如果我是你，我會**擬訂**一張要**達成**目標的清單，然後一項一項去完成。

Walt: But I set out to finish this report by next week!

但我打算下星期前要完成這份報告耶！

Debby: Relax, I **believe in**[8] you. Just don't give up, and everything will be okay, I'm sure.

放輕鬆，我**相信**你。只要別放棄，我確定一切都會很順利的。

Unit 24 Schoolwork Problems 課業問題

1

片語動詞 | **可分開** | **受詞為代名詞時定要分開**

cheer（高興） + up（起來） → **cheer up**

❶ 使高興　❷ 使生動　及 / 不及

用法
- **cheer sb up** 使某人高興
- **cheer sth up** 使某事物引人注目

比較
- **cheer sb on** 鼓勵某人
  → As the runners went by, we **cheered** them **on**.
  跑者經過時，我們向他們歡呼。

反 使心煩意亂 shake up

❶ When Gary was sick in bed for a month, his friend visited him dressed in a funny costume to try and **cheer** him **up**.
蓋瑞在病床上躺了一個月，為了讓他開心，朋友去探望他時穿了很滑稽的服裝。

❷ A coat of paint and new curtains would really **cheer** the kitchen **up**.
油漆和新的窗簾讓廚房完全明亮了起來。

2

片語動詞

run（跑） + into（進入） → **run into**

❶ 偶遇　❷ 撞上 及

用法
- **run into sb** 遇到某人
- **run (sth) into sth** 撞上某事物
  → I couldn't believe it when that car **ran into** our mailbox and knocked it over.
  我實在不敢相信我看到一輛車撞倒了我家的信箱。
- **run (sth) into sb** 撞上某人
  → I had to brake suddenly, and the car behind me **ran into** me.
  我突然非得緊急煞車，於是後面的車子撞上了我。

同 遇到
❶ bump into　❷ come across
❸ come upon　❹ meet with
❺ run across

💡 **run into** 可用來表示「偶然遇到」解時，通常後接人；若作「撞上」時，是指**交通工具**的碰撞。

❶ We **ran into** a lot of traffic on the way to the airport.
我們在前往機場的路上遇上塞車。

❶ Jack **ran into** Betty at the supermarket; it was the first time he had seen her in years. 傑克在超市偶遇貝蒂，這是他多年來第一次看到她。

3

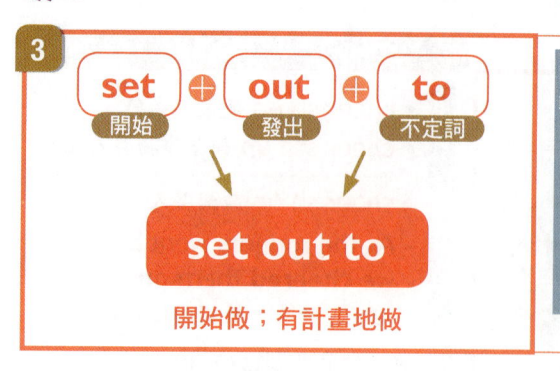

set（開始）＋ **out**（發出）＋ **to**（不定詞）

→ **set out to**
開始做；有計畫地做

比較
- **set out** 出發；離開；計劃做……
→ At what time do you plan to **set out** on your trip to Canada?
你計劃何時前往加拿大旅遊？
- **set out for** 出發前往
→ Tomorrow we **set out for** Japan. 我們明天要出發前往日本。

💡 set out 指「出發」，而 set out to 則表示「開始進行某事」。

- Although we **set out to** buy some milk and eggs, we ended up buying a new laptop. 雖然我們計劃要買一些牛奶和雞蛋，但最後我們卻買了一台新的筆記型電腦。
- What will you **set out to** do after graduation? 你大學畢業後計劃做什麼？
- Ryan **set out to** write the perfect college application letter.
雷恩打算寫一份最理想的大學推薦信。

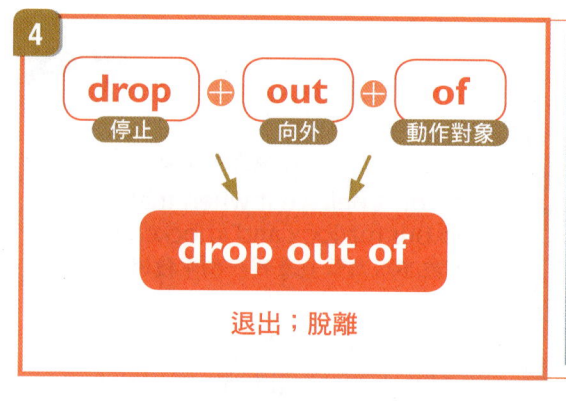

4

drop（停止）＋ **out**（向外）＋ **of**（動作對象）

→ **drop out of**
退出；脫離

比較
- **drop out** 退出
→ Paul **dropped out** the night before the race, saying he had an injury. 保羅在比賽的前一個晚上因傷而退出比賽。
- **drop in** 拜訪
→ I **dropped in** on George on my way home from school.
我在放學回家路上到喬治家拜訪。

- After breaking his leg, Will **dropped out of** the race. 威爾腿骨折後便退出了比賽。
- When the judges discovered that Tracy had copied her artwork from another painting, they made her **drop out of** the competition.
當評審發現崔西的作品是模仿別幅畫時，便要她退出比賽。

5

make（使得）＋ **sense**（有道理）

→ **make sense**
有邏輯；合乎道理

用法
- **make sense of**
了解……的意義

💡 sense 表示「感覺；道理」，為不可數名詞，故不可加 **a** 或作複數形，但前面可加入 **a lot of**、**any** 等作修飾。

- If you didn't do the homework, the teacher's lecture will not **make sense**.
  你如果不做功課，會聽不懂老師教的。
- This assignment is hard; I don't think it **makes** any **sense**.
  這份作業很困難，我不認為這是**合理**的。

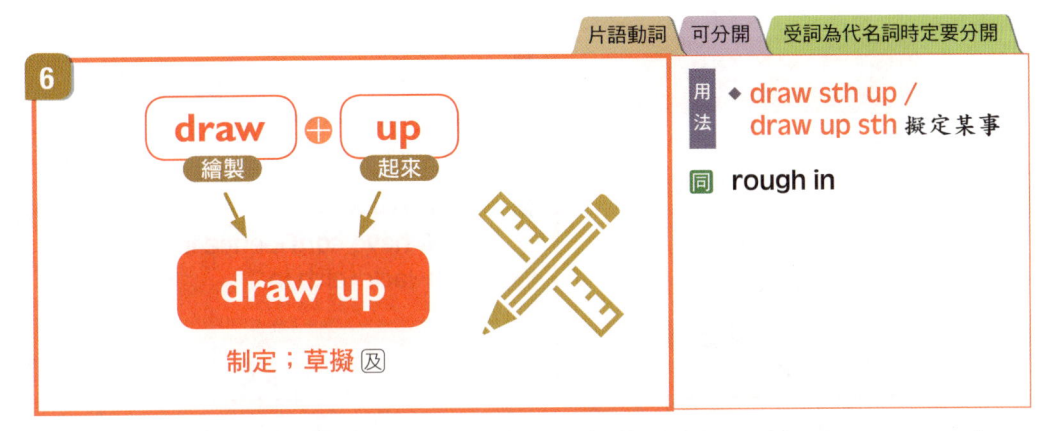

6

draw 繪製 + up 起來 → **draw up** 制定；草擬 及

| 片語動詞 | 可分開 | 受詞為代名詞時定要分開 |

用法 ◆ draw sth up / draw up sth 擬定某事

同 rough in

- The lawyer **drew up** a document putting Calvin in charge of his elderly mother's affairs. 律師**擬定**了一份文件，指定凱文負責照顧年邁母親的生活起居。
- Felix **drew** a list **up** so that he could plan his week better.
  菲力斯**擬定**了一張週計畫表以便做規畫。

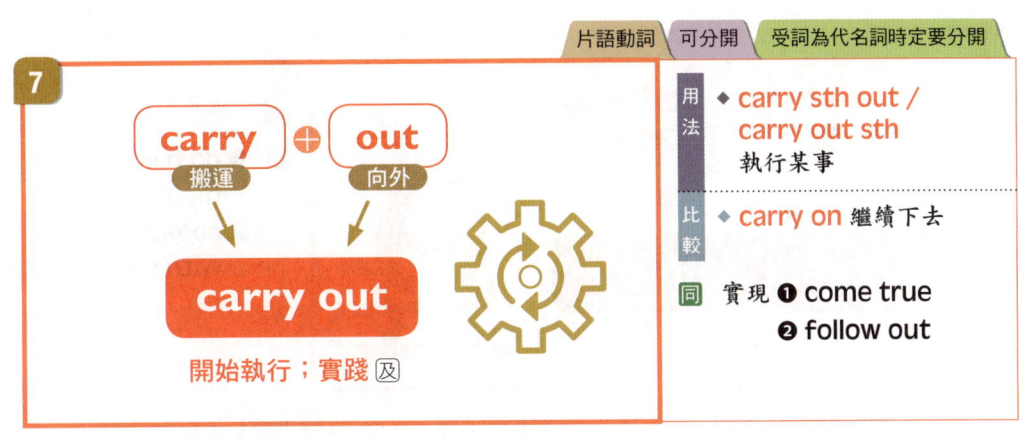

7

carry 搬運 + out 向外 → **carry out** 開始執行；實踐 及

| 片語動詞 | 可分開 | 受詞為代名詞時定要分開 |

用法 ◆ carry sth out / carry out sth 執行某事

比較 ◆ carry on 繼續下去

同 實現 ❶ come true ❷ follow out

💡 此片語原指「搬出某事物」，常引申表示「實行計畫、任務」或「實現夢想」。

- The students were told to **carry out** every task their teacher expected of them.
  老師期望學生能**完成**所有的任務。
- I know you have a plan, but I hope you have time this weekend to **carry** it **out**.
  我知道你有計畫，但我希望你有時間在這週末**開始執行**。

8

believe (相信) + **in** (在……之內) → **believe in**

❶ 相信　❷ 相信……的存在（通常指幽靈或宗教信仰）及

用法
- ◆ **believe in sb** 深信某人；對某人有信心
  → Since her divorce, Linda is gradually beginning to **believe in** herself again.
  從琳達離婚後，她開始慢慢找回自信心。
- ◆ **believe in sth** 相信某事物
  → I don't **believe in** living together before marriage.
  我不認同婚前同居。

同 相信 ❶ trust in
　　　　❷ have confidence in
反 不信任 lack faith in

💡 表示「信仰」時，通常是指**宗教**或**思想**，後接 **theory**、**ghosts** 等；亦可用來表示**信任某人**。

❶ Although Rachel failed a few classes this semester, I **believe in** her; I think she'll be successful.
雖然瑞秋這學期有幾門課被當掉，但我還是**相信**她。我認為她會成功的。

❷ Patty doesn't **believe in** ghosts. 派蒂不**相信**幽靈的存在。

9

meet (遇到) + **halfway** (中途) → **meet halfway**

妥協

用法
- ◆ **meet sb halfway** 與某人妥協

同 ❶ go halfway to meet sb
　　　❷ compromise with sb

💡 此片語透過「在半路遇到某人」來比喻「各自退讓一步」，意指「與某人妥協」。

- Diane wanted to be paid $500 for her translation, and I wanted to pay her only $250. In the end, we **met** each other **halfway** and agreed on $375.
黛安想要我付她 500 元的翻譯費用，而我只想付她 250 元，我們最後以 375 元**妥協**。

- Just when it seemed that the negotiations would never end, Jane found a way to **meet halfway** and lowered the price of the minivan.
眼見協商沒完沒了，珍發現降低小卡車的售價是一種**妥協**的方法。

10

give (給) + **and** (和) + **take** (拿)
↓
give-and-take
相互退讓

> 💡 **give and take**，字面意思是「有給也有拿」，引伸為「有商有量，互相遷就，妥協折衷」。多用在商務用語中。

名詞片語

Unit 24 Schoolwork Problems 課業問題

- Good business practices require a level of **give-and-take**.
  想要完成一筆愉快的交易，包括一定程度的**相互妥協**。
- Happy family relations require **give-and-take**, I think.
  我認為家庭的和諧需要**相互讓步**。
- They reached an agreement after many hours of bargaining and **give-and-take**.
  經過了好幾個小時的協商和**退讓**後，他們終於達成了協議。
- In every friendship, there has to be some **give-and-take**.
  每一段友情中都會需要**相互退讓**。

11

片語動詞 | 可分開 | 受詞為代名詞時定要分開

knock (擊) + **out** (昏迷)
↓
knock out

❶ 使昏迷
❷ 使筋疲力盡
❸ 擊倒；摧毀 及

用法
◆ **knock sb out** 使某人昏迷不醒
→ Vera fell down and hit her head, **knocking** herself **out**.
薇拉跌倒撞到頭，**昏**了過去。

◆ **knock sth out** 摧毀某事物
→ Enemy aircraft have **knocked out** 25 tanks. 敵機**摧毀**了25架坦克車。

同 使昏迷 **knock cold**

❶ Phil fell off his bike and **knocked** himself **out**. 菲爾從腳踏車上摔下來後**昏倒**了。
❶ The sleeping tablets **knocked** me **out** for 18 hours. 安眠藥讓我**昏睡**了18個小時。
❷ The doctor warned me that this painkiller might **knock** me **out**.
醫生警告我，服用這種止痛藥可能會**感到疲倦**。

207

Unit 24 Test Yourself!

B 選擇題

1. That movie is weird and confusing. I don't think it _____.
   Ⓐ makes sense   Ⓑ draws up   Ⓒ runs into   Ⓓ carries out

2. Don't focus on bad news. _____ and enjoy life!
   Ⓐ Draw up   Ⓑ Set out   Ⓒ Cheer up   Ⓓ Make sense

3. You should _____ yourself more. You're a great person!
   Ⓐ set out   Ⓑ draw up   Ⓒ drop out of   Ⓓ believe in

4. Despite her excellent grades, Harriet _____ college.
   Ⓐ drew up   Ⓑ dropped out of   Ⓒ believed in   Ⓓ ran into

5. Every good marriage requires at least some _____.
   Ⓐ drawing up   Ⓑ cheering up   Ⓒ give-and-take   Ⓓ knocking out

6. After Emma was hired, her new boss _____ an employment contract.
   Ⓐ drew up   Ⓑ believed in   Ⓒ cheered up   Ⓓ ran into

7. Ten years ago, Mary _____ write a great book, but so far she has written only two chapters.
   Ⓐ set out to   Ⓑ carried out to   Ⓒ drew up to   Ⓓ knocked out to

8. We'll _____ tonight at 6.
   Ⓐ cheer up   Ⓑ knock ourselves out   Ⓒ run into   Ⓓ set out

9. Rich won the boxing match when he _____ his opponent.
   Ⓐ drew up   Ⓑ knocked out   Ⓒ ran into   Ⓓ carried out

10. Susana _____ a friend of her father's at the gas station.
    Ⓐ ran into   Ⓑ set out to   Ⓒ carried out   Ⓓ drew up

11. Lola is _____ a research project on the history of the Roman Empire.
    Ⓐ running into   Ⓑ carrying out   Ⓒ knocking out   Ⓓ cheering up

B 閱讀文章，從字表中選擇詞彙填入，並依人稱時態等做適當的變化

set out to	knock out	drop out of
carry out	run into	believe in
cheer up	draw up	make sense

　　Last Tuesday was one of the craziest days in Doug's life. Doug is an artist, and he had ❶ _____ work on a new painting. The first step was to ❷ _____ some designs. Although his idea for the painting was very unusual, he really ❸ _____ it. In the first week or two, he started over several times on the painting, which was very frustrating. As he ❹ _____ his work, however, he began to feel better about it and to ❺ _____. When the first part of the painting was complete, he called over a colleague whom he had ❻ _____ earlier at the bus station. Doug thought she might be interested in buying the painting.

　　He was right. When the woman told him how much she was willing to pay for the artwork, Doug was so shocked that he fell down and nearly ❼ _____ himself _____. This did not ❽ _____; it wasn't even his best painting! The woman told Doug that she wanted to buy five more just like it so she could hang one in every meeting room of her company. Soon, Doug would be a very rich man and maybe even a famous artist-even though he had ❾ _____ art school!

C 引導式翻譯，並依人稱時態等做適當的變化

1. 我已經**寫下**想要進行面談的應徵者名單了。
   I've _____ _____ a list of candidates whom I'd like to interview.
2. 我已經把信看了兩遍，但我還是**看不懂**。
   I've read the letter twice, but I can't _____ _____ of it.
3. 赫伯特在姐姐打電話來前心情一直不好，後來他**打起精神**了。
   Herbert was in a bad mood until his sister called; then he _____ _____.
4. 莉莎在頭撞到天花板後便**昏迷不醒**。
   Lisa hit her head when she fell on the hard floor and _____ herself _____.
5. 我昨天在第七大道**遇見**傑森。
   I _____ _____ Jason on Seventh Avenue yesterday.

209

Unit 25

Cheating on a Test
考試作弊

Diane and Pete have a chat about a recent test.
黛安和彼得在聊最近的考試。

Diane: I can't believe you **got away with**[1] cheating on the test.

我不敢相信你考試作弊竟然還能**逃過一劫**。

Pete: Well, it was tough. I think the girl next to me knew what I was doing, but she didn't **let on**[2]. If she did, I'm sure things would have **gone wrong**[3].

是啊,這件事實在很棘手。我想隔壁的女生知道我在做什麼,但她沒有**洩漏**出去。如果她說了,我想事情一定**會變得很嚴重**。

Diane: Lucky for you that you don't **stand out**[4] as the kind of person who would cheat.

幸好你不像那些會作弊的人那麼**引人注目**。

Pete: Right. It's a good thing that the teacher never **checked up on**[5] me too carefully.

是啊,老師從來不會仔細**檢查**我,真好。

Diane: Well, if you ask me, getting caught would **serve** you **right**[6].

唔,我認為啊,你**活該**被抓。

Pete: Hey! How else can I **keep up with**[7] this class?

嘿!不這麼做,我怎麼**趕上**班上的程度呢?

Diane: Try studying like the rest of us!

就和我們其他人一樣讀書啊!

Unit 25 Cheating on a Test 考試作弊

1

get（獲得） + away（遠離） + with（與……）
→ **get away with** 成功地逃過懲罰 [及]

用法
- **get away with sth** 逃過懲罰
  → Mark cheated on the test and thought he could **get away with** it. 馬克考試作弊，還以為他可以**不受到懲罰**。

比較
- **get away** 逃離
  → When Tammy started her vacation in California, she said it felt great to **get away** from the stress of work. 泰咪在加州度假時，覺得**遠離**工作壓力的感覺很棒。
  → When Henry turned 18, he decided he needed to **get away** from his parents, so he moved to L.A. 18歲時，亨利決定**遠離**父母搬到洛杉磯。

💡 常用來描述做壞事、錯事而未被發覺或受到懲罰。

- Mindy **got away with** stealing strawberries from her neighbor's garden; nobody ever caught her.
  敏蒂在鄰居家的院子裡偷摘草莓卻**逃過一劫**，至今還沒有人抓到她。
- Nobody **gets away with** cheating in this class.
  這個班上從來沒有人能夠作弊而**不受到懲罰**。

2

let（讓） + on（放開的）
→ **let on** 洩漏（秘密）[不及]

用法
- **let on that/who/how/why . . .** 透露……
  → Joel **let on that** he once dated my girlfriend.
  喬爾**透露**他曾和我的女朋友約過會。
- **let on about sth** 透露某事
  → Don't **let on about** the party to Chris. It is a surprise party for him.
  別**告訴**克里斯有關派對的事情，那是要給他的驚喜派對。

💡 **let on** 後常接由 **that** 等所引導的子句，來表示「透露某消息、秘密」。

- I suspect Sally knows more about this than she's **letting on**.
  我懷疑莎莉知道的比她所**透露**的還要多。
- I tried not to **let on** that I knew the answer. 我試著不**透露**其實我已經知道答案。

211

3

go（做） + **wrong**（錯誤地） → **go wrong** 情況不順利；弄錯

慣用片語

💡 **go wrong** 為固定用法，wrong 在此雖作副詞用，但不可以 **wrongly** 來代替。

- Every detail about the trip to the seaside had been carefully planned, so we believed nothing could **go wrong**. And then it poured.
  海邊之旅的所有細節都經過詳細的規畫，因此我們相信事情是不會**出錯**的，不過後來卻下了傾盆大雨。
- After studying for a week, Amanda was confident about the test; she was sure nothing would **go wrong**.
  亞曼達唸了一整個星期的書，所以對考試很有信心，她確信一切不會**有問題**的。
- I thought I had done this correctly; I can't understand where I **went wrong**.
  我以為這件事情我做對了，我不知道究竟是哪裡**出了錯**。

4

stand（站著） + **out**（突出地） → **stand out** 引人注目；優秀傑出 [不及]

片語動詞

💡 表示比某人或事物較突出或優秀時，其後常會加上 **from**、**above** 或 **among**，再接受詞。

📗 **stand out in a crowd**

- Donald never dressed conservatively like his colleagues, and the bright colors he wore really made him **stand out** in a crowd.
  唐諾的穿著從不像同事那麼保守，因此穿著鮮豔的他在人群中非常**引人注目**。
- It **stands out** as an excellent school among many very good schools.
  在許多好學校中，它顯然是一所聲譽極佳的學校。
- We had lots of good applicants for the job, but one **stood out** from the rest.
  這個職位有許多條件不錯的人選，但其中一位應徵者在所有人當中**脫穎而出**。
- His bright red hair helps him **stand out** at comedy clubs.
  他那亮紅色的頭髮是他在喜劇俱樂部**引人注目**的原因。

5

check（檢查） + up（做強調用） + on（針對）

↓

check up on

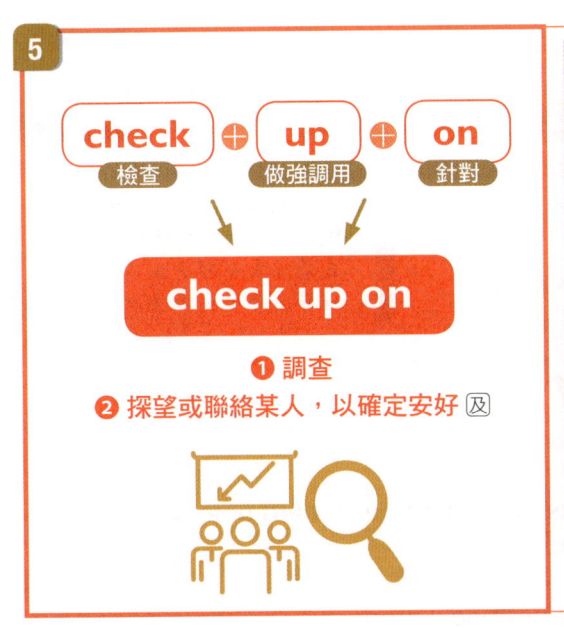

❶ 調查
❷ 探望或聯絡某人，以確定安好 [及]

用法
- **check up on sth** 檢查某事物
  → The detective is **checking up on** Gareth's work schedule to make sure he was out of town on the night of the murder.
  刑警正在**檢查**葛瑞的工作行程，以確定他在兇案當晚不在城裡。

- **check up on sb** 調查某人
  → I think she stops by my office to **check up on** me, to make sure I'm actually working.
  我認為她是到辦公室來**檢查**我是否真的有在工作。

比較
- **check on** 檢查；調查
- **check over** 檢查；調查

💡 常用來表示「調查某人的背景、行為」或「某事是否屬實」。

❷ Derek's mother called him at summer camp to **check up on** him.
戴瑞克的母親打電話到夏令營找戴瑞克，**以確定他安然無恙**。

6

serve（對待） + right（正確）

↓

serve (someone) right

某人應得的懲罰

比較
- **sb deserve sth** 某人值得……
  （可表示獎勵或懲罰）
  → Holly **deserves** our special thanks for all her efforts.
  荷莉的付出**值得**我們特別感謝她。

- **sb be worth it** 某人值得……
  （可表示獎勵或懲罰）
  → Forget her—she's just not **worth it**.
  忘了她吧，她不**值得**你的付出。

- Because Lucas delayed the flight by coming late, everyone onboard thought that losing his first-class seat **served** him **right**.
  由於盧卡斯遲到使得班機延誤，機上所有人都認為他**活該**喪失頭等艙的位子。

- It **serves** Marla **right** that she got an "F" in class because she never studied.
  因為瑪拉從不唸書，所以她**本該**得到「F」。

7

keep (保持) + **up** (徹底) + **with** (與……一起)

→ **keep up with**

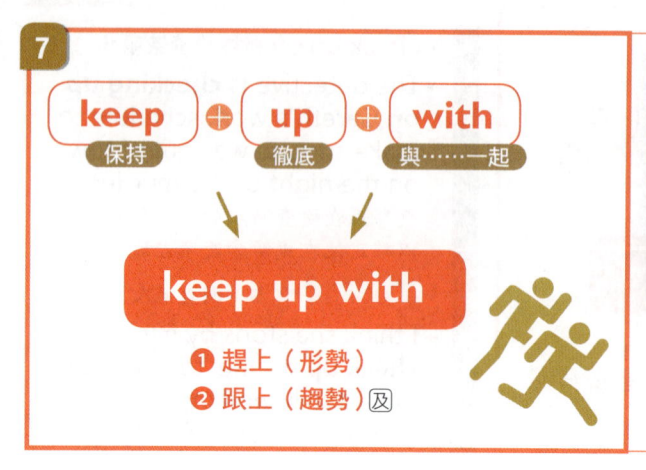

❶ 趕上（形勢）
❷ 跟上（趨勢）及

用法
- **keep up with sb** 趕上某人
- **keep up with sth** 跟上某事
→ I read the online news to **keep up with** what's happening in the world.
我看線上新聞是為了掌握外面世界所發生的事情。

❶ Because Alfred missed a few weeks of class, he had a hard time **keeping up with** his classmates.
亞佛烈德好幾個星期沒去上課，他為了趕上同學的進度所以很辛苦。

❷ My grandmother doesn't **keep up with** new product.
我外婆不太能跟上流行產品。

8

片語動詞 | 可分開 | 受詞為代名詞時一定要分開

keep (保持) + **up** (完全)

→ **keep up**

❶ 持續（某種情況）
❷ 使保持清醒 及

用法
- **keep sth up / keep up sth**
維持某種情況
→ I have a great relationship with my boyfriend now, and I'm doing my best to **keep** that **up**. 我和男朋友目前進展地很順利，我會盡力繼續維持下去。
→ **Keep up** the good work! 繼續努力！

- **keep sb up / keep up sb**
使某人保持清醒
→ You're making so much noise! You're going to **keep up** the whole neighborhood! 你太大聲了，你會把附近鄰居都吵醒的。
→ I hope I'm not **keeping** you **up**.
希望我沒有吵醒你。

❶ If you **keep up** the good work, there's no question that you'll get an "A" in this class. 你如果繼續努力，這堂課肯定能得到「A」。

❶ Wow, you're doing great work; be sure to **keep** it **up**!
哇，你做得很好，一定要繼續保持！

9

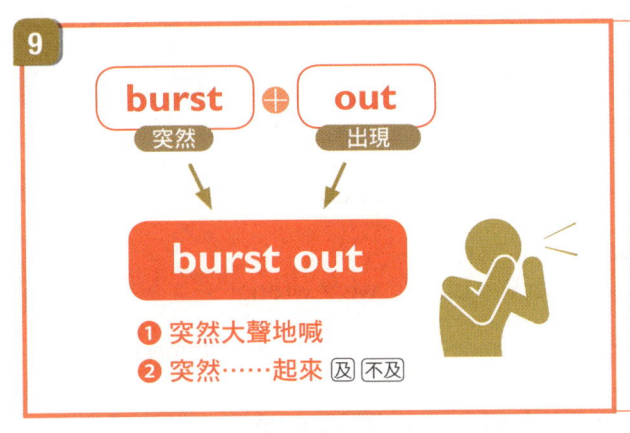

burst (突然) + **out** (出現)
→ **burst out**

❶ 突然大聲地喊
❷ 突然……起來 [及] [不及]

用法
- burst out crying / burst into tears 放聲大哭
- burst out laughing / burst into laughter 大笑
→ Bill **burst out laughing** at the funny parts of the film.
比爾看到有趣的電影片段時，**大聲笑了出來**。

❶ "Come back!" Marc **burst out** as his girlfriend walked away.
馬克的女朋友離去時，他**大聲地喊**：「回來！」

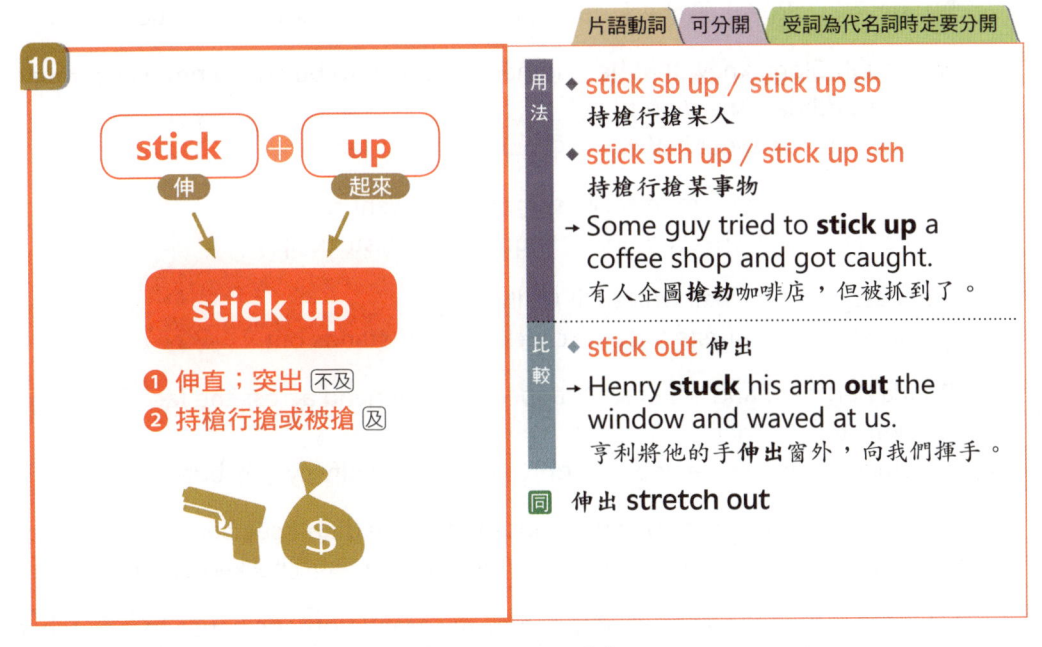

10

片語動詞 | 可分開 | 受詞為代名詞時定要分開

stick (伸) + **up** (起來)
→ **stick up**

❶ 伸直；突出 [不及]
❷ 持槍行搶或被搶 [及]

用法
- stick sb up / stick up sb 持槍行搶某人
- stick sth up / stick up sth 持槍行搶某事物
→ Some guy tried to **stick up** a coffee shop and got caught.
有人企圖**搶劫**咖啡店，但被抓到了。

比較
- stick out 伸出
→ Henry **stuck** his arm **out** the window and waved at us.
亨利將他的手**伸出**窗外，向我們揮手。

同 伸出 stretch out

❶ Some large rocks were **sticking up** out of the water.
有一些巨大的石頭**伸出**在水面上。

❶ When Betsy wakes up in the morning, her hair is always **sticking up**.
貝西早上起床時，頭髮總是**翹起來**。

❷ The robbers **stuck up** the bank and stole all the money.
搶匪**持槍搶劫**銀行，並且拿走了所有的現金。

215

Unit 25 Test Yourself!

A 選擇題

1. If you _____ that bad behavior, you won't be able to go out this weekend.
   Ⓐ stick up   Ⓑ burst out   Ⓒ get away   Ⓓ keep up

2. Without any warning, the baby _____ crying.
   Ⓐ stuck up   Ⓑ burst out   Ⓒ checked up   Ⓓ went wrong

3. The clothing store seemed to be making money; when it closed, customers were left wondering what _____.
   Ⓐ stuck up   Ⓑ went wrong   Ⓒ checked up   Ⓓ kept up

4. Jane found a way to _____ Arnie _____, so she accepted the terms and signed the contract.
   Ⓐ serve . . . right   Ⓑ check up . . . on   Ⓒ meet . . . halfway   Ⓓ stick . . . up

5. Although Gloria knew that her mother was going to buy her a new cell phone for her birthday, she didn't _____.
   Ⓐ stick up   Ⓑ meet halfway   Ⓒ burst out   Ⓓ let on

6. Natasha _____ for a month last summer and went to Italy.
   Ⓐ got away   Ⓑ checked up   Ⓒ burst out   Ⓓ stuck up

7. Your essay is very well written; it really _____.
   Ⓐ sticks up   Ⓑ bursts out   Ⓒ checks up   Ⓓ stands out

8. Maria hurt her hand when she slapped her boyfriend across the face for no reason; it _____ her _____.
   Ⓐ stuck . . . up   Ⓑ served . . . right   Ⓒ met . . . halfway   Ⓓ burst . . . out

9. Ursula _____ driving so badly because the police didn't see her.
   Ⓐ got away with   Ⓑ burst out   Ⓒ stood out for   Ⓓ checked up on

10. On the way to the zoo, we stopped by my grandmother's house to _____ her.
    Ⓐ stick up   Ⓑ burst out   Ⓒ check up on   Ⓓ stand out

B 閱讀文章，從字表中選擇詞彙填入，並依人稱時態等做適當的變化

keep up with	stand out	get away with
get away	serve (someone) right	keep up
go wrong	let on	burst out

　　There's no doubt that Ed **①**_____ as the best basketball player in class. He's a great athlete, and no one can **②**_____ him. As soon as someone looks like they're going to steal the ball, Ed manages to **③**_____. Once, one of the players on the other team tripped Ed. It looked like that guy would **④**_____ it. However, my friends and I all **⑤**_____ yelling, and the referee threw him off the court. We thought it **⑥**_____ him _____. The coach **⑦**_____ that he thinks Ed could be a professional player one day, if he **⑧**_____ playing this well. It looks like nothing can **⑨**_____ as far as Ed's basketball career.

C 引導式翻譯，並依人稱時態等做適當的變化

1. 我們試著找出失敗的科學試驗究竟是哪裡**出了問題**。
   We tried to find out what _____ _____ with the failed science experiment.

2. 我媽媽每個晚上幾乎都會**檢查**我是否寫完作業了。
   My mom _____ _____ _____ me most evenings to see if I've done my homework.

3. 你們每個人都做得非常好，**繼續保持**！
   You're doing very well, everybody. _____ it _____!

4. 我一走進去，每個人全都**爆笑**了起來。
   I walked in and everyone _____ _____ laughing.

5. 你聽說了昨天有人**持槍搶劫**郵局嗎？
   Did you hear that someone _____ _____ the post office yesterday?

6. 迪托從未**洩漏**蓋楚已婚的秘密。
   Tito never _____ _____ that he knew Gertrude was married.

217

Unit 26

The New Coworker
新同事

Amy tells Carl about a new coworker.
艾咪把新同事的事情告訴卡爾。

Amy: The new employee we hired is really **living up to**[1] my expectations.

新來的員工真的很**符合**我的期望。

Carl: Is that so? I'm glad to hear it, but I thought you didn't want to hire anyone new at your company.

真的嗎？真替妳高興，但我以為你們公司不想聘人。

Amy: Well, this one guy does the work of four people; so, in a way, hiring him has helped us **cut corners**[2].

嗯，這個人做了四人份的工作，所以就一定的程度來說，僱用他能幫公司**節省**成本。

Carl: You think he'll help **bring about**[3] some positive change, too?

你認為他還會**帶來**一些正面的改變嗎？

Amy: Definitely. His former boss really **built up**[4] his reputation when we spoke on the phone, and I can see that he deserves it.

當然，我和他之前的老闆通過電話，他可是對他讚譽**有加**，我看得出來他說的沒錯。

Carl: How so?

怎麼說？

Amy: For example, when he starts a project, he **sticks to**[5] it until he is totally done. He also knows how to **stand up for**[6] his ideas, even if the boss disagrees.

舉例來說，當他開始進行一項企畫後，便會**堅持**到完成。就算與老闆意見不合，他也知道要如何**支持**自己的想法。

Carl: Wow! He sounds like the perfect coworker.

哇！聽起來他是一位很理想的工作伙伴。

1

live(生活) + **up to**(達到) → **live up to**
實踐；達成 及

片語動詞

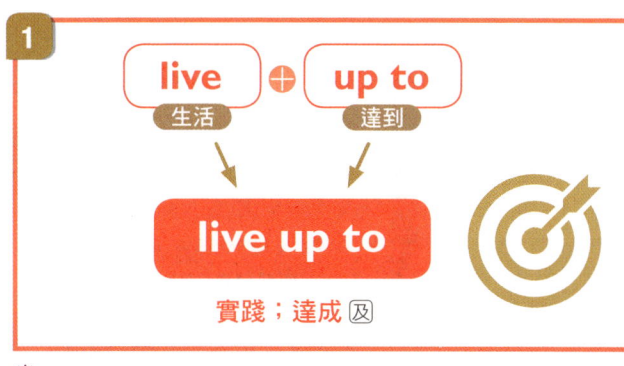

用法 ◆ live up to sth
遵守某事物；達成期望

同 come up to

反 未達……的期望
❶ fall short of
❷ let . . . down

💡 **live up to** 表示「達到某標準、水平或期望」等，常與 **one's expectation** 等連用。

- Linda's parents were both world-famous surgeons, so she had a hard time **living up to** their expectations.
  由於琳達的雙親是世界有名的外科醫生，所以她很努力地想要**達成**父母的期望。

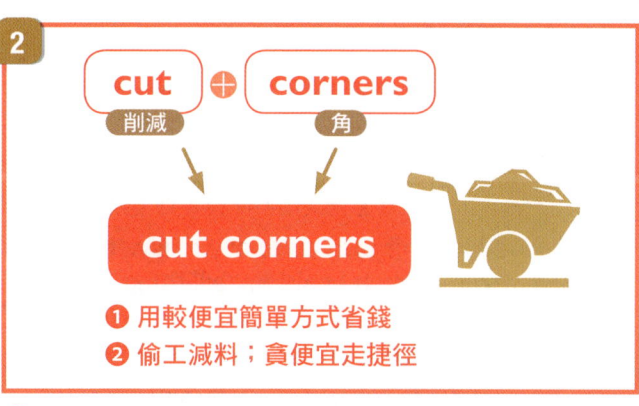

2

cut(削減) + **corners**(角) → **cut corners**
❶ 用較便宜簡單方式省錢
❷ 偷工減料；貪便宜走捷徑

慣用片語

💡 **cut corners** 字面上是切掉角，走路時抄捷徑走最短的距離較省時，它的含義是「為了省時間或錢貪便宜、走捷徑；偷工減料」，這個說法帶有貶義，使用時需要注意。

❶ The trick to saving money is knowing when to **cut corners**.
存錢的竅門就是要知道何時該**節省開銷**。

❶ If we **cut corners** this year, maybe we can afford to go on vacation next summer.
如果我們今年省一點，也許明年夏天就有足夠的錢能夠去度假。

3

bring(產生) + **about**(對於) → **bring about**
引起；造成 及

片語動詞

同 ❶ give rise to
❷ lead to
❸ result in
❹ bring on
❺ cause

- Mike **brought about** his company's collapse with his reckless spending.
  麥可無盡的揮霍是**造成**公司倒閉的原因。

- Eleanor is the kind of woman who can **bring about** results; that's why my company hired her. 伊莉諾是個能**帶來**成效的女人，這就是我們公司僱用她的原因。

219

4

build (建立) + **up** (起來) → **build up**

❶ 建立　❷ 增強　❸ 加深印象 [及]

片語動詞 / 可分開 / 受詞為代名詞時定要分開

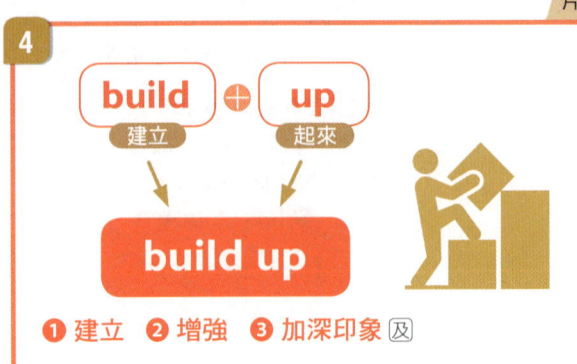

用法
- **build up sb / build sb up**
  鼓勵某人
- **build up sth / build sth up**
  增強某事物
→ It took Lindsay ten years to **build up** her publishing business.
  琳西花了10年才**建立**起她的出版事業。

❶ Aaron is a great visionary; he **built up** a new business from nothing.
亞倫是個極有遠見的人，他白手起家，**開創**了新的事業。

❸ Natalie **built** her Spanish vocabulary **up** in preparation for her trip to Mexico.
娜塔莉**學**了許多西班牙文單字，為墨西哥之旅作準備。

5

片語動詞

stick (堅持) + **to** (動作對象) → **stick to**

❶ 堅持（通常指困境）
❷ 遵守 [及]

用法
- **stick to sth** 遵守某事

比較
- **stick it to** 惡意或不公平地對待某人
→ My credit card company really **stuck it to** me when I paid my bill three months late. 我晚了三個月付帳單，那時信用卡公司真的**催我催得很緊**。
→ If you come late to class one more time, the teacher will really **stick it to** you and give you a detention.
  如果你上課再遲到，我敢肯定老師一定會**嚴厲地要你留校查看**。

同 堅持 ❶ adhere to　❷ cling to
　　　　❸ hold on to　❹ keep to
反 違反 ❶ depart from　❷ deviate from

❶ I understand that you're having a hard time in this class, but just **stick to** the schedule and do the best you can.
我知道這堂課你上得很辛苦，但你只要**堅持**下去、全力以赴就行了。

❶ It is hard to understand the class because the teacher never **sticks to** his point—he always changes the topic and never finishes any ideas.
這門課很難理解，因為老師從不**堅守**立場。他總是任意變換主題，而不下結論。

❷ It won't be easy to **stick to** my academic schedule because I have classes every morning at 8:30. 我每天早上8點30分都有課，所以要我**遵守**課表很難。

Unit 26　The New Coworker 新同事　片語動詞

6

stand (站) + **up** (起來) + **for** (為了)
↓
stand up for
維護權利；支持 [及]

用法
- **stand up for sb** 支持某人
- **stand up for sth** 支持某事
→ Sometimes you have to **stand up for** your rights. 你有時候必須要**維護**自己的權利。

比較
- **stick up for** 維護
→ His friends **stuck up for** him when other people said he was guilty. 當其他人都說他有罪時，他的朋友**挺身支持**他。

- **stand up** 站起來；經得起；爽約
→ I don't know if I've been **stood up** or if she's just late—I'll wait another half hour. 我不知道我是被**放鴿子**了或是她遲到，我會再等半個小時看看。

- **stand up to** 對抗；勇於面對
→ Jason wasn't afraid to **stand up to** bullies. 傑森並不害怕挺身對抗惡棍。

- Martin Luther King, Jr., **stood up for** the rights of his fellow African Americans. 馬丁路德金恩**捍衛**了非裔美國人的權利。

- I **stood up for** my math teacher when all my friends were complaining about him. 當我所有的朋友都在抱怨數學老師時，我卻為他**挺身而出**。

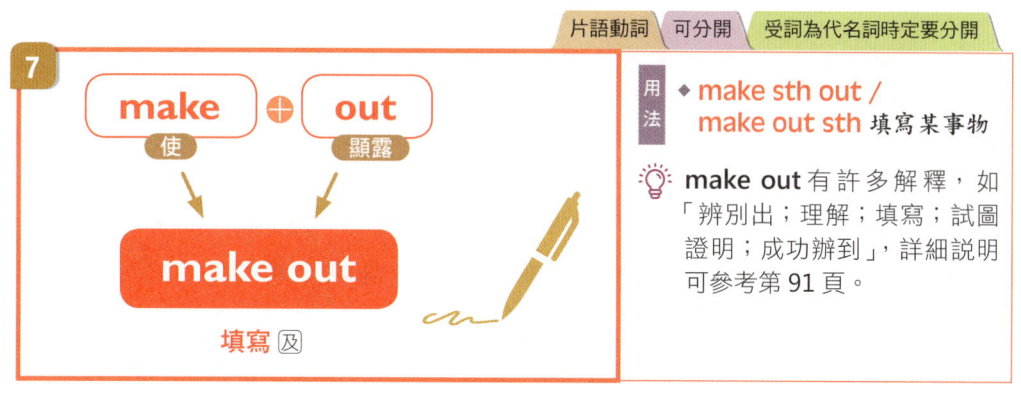

7

片語動詞　可分開　受詞為代名詞時定要分開

make (使) + **out** (顯露)
↓
make out
填寫 [及]

用法
- **make sth out** / **make out sth** 填寫某事物

💡 **make out** 有許多解釋，如「辨別出；理解；填寫；試圖證明；成功辦到」，詳細說明可參考第 91 頁。

- Elaine **made out** a legal will that leaves everything to her daughter. 伊蓮在遺囑上**註明**會將所有財產留給她女兒。

- Jared **made** a check **out** for $50 to cover the expenses. 傑瑞德**開**了一張 50 元的支票把費用付清。

8

come (出現) + **about** (對於) → **come about** 發生 [不及]

同 ❶ occur
❷ happen
❸ take place

- The concert **takes place** next Friday. 演唱會於下星期五舉行。

- How did this terrible situation **come about**? 怎麼會發生這麼嚴重的事情？
- Do you know how the tradition of decorating a Christmas tree **came about**?
  你知道裝飾聖誕樹的傳統是如何出現的嗎？
- How did the problem **come about** in the first place? 問題是怎麼發生的呢？

9

die (消失) + **down** (向下) → **die down** 變少；減弱 [不及]

同 die away

- The sound of her footsteps gradually **died away**.
  她的腳步聲逐漸消失。

💡 **die down** 表示「熄滅；減弱」，用來強調「逐漸減弱的過程」，通常指聲音、情緒或氣氛等。

- As the party was ending, the noise level began to **die down**.
  喧鬧聲在派對結束後逐漸消失。
- Pam's anger over her son's decision to leave school took a few weeks to **die down**. 潘很生氣兒子決定休學，她花了好幾個星期才逐漸氣消。
- By morning, the storm had **died down**. 暴風雨在早晨的時候逐漸平息下來。
- It was several minutes before the applause **died down**.
  掌聲持續了好幾分鐘才減弱下來。

10

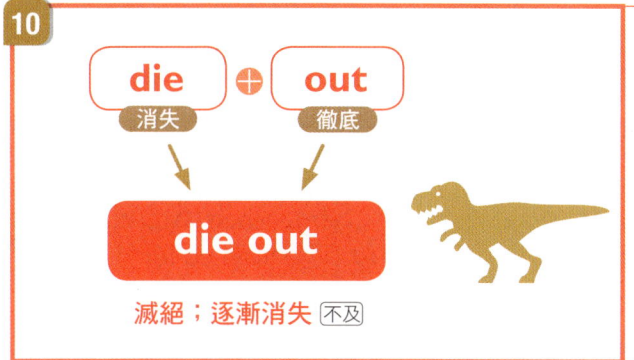

die (消失) + out (徹底) → **die out**
滅絕；逐漸消失 [不及]

用法
- **die off** 相繼死去
  → He was ninety-one, and all his friends had **died off**.
  他91歲了，他的朋友們都**相繼走了**。

💡 die out 表示「滅絕；消失」，通常用來指**生物**、**種族**、**習俗**、**觀念**等。

- No one knows for sure why the dinosaurs **died out**. 沒人知道恐龍為何會**滅絕**。
- The traditional customs of the native people **died out** after a few years.
  幾年後，原住民的傳統習俗**漸漸消失**。
- It's a custom that is beginning to **die out**. 這項習俗正在**慢慢消失**。

11

fade (凋謝) + away (離開) → **fade away**
（影像、想法）慢慢消失；死亡 [不及]

同 fade out

- As the harbor filled with fog, the boats **faded away**.
  船隻因為濃霧籠罩著港口而**漸漸消失**。
- As time went by, my childhood memories began to **fade away**.
  我的童年記憶隨著時間過去而**逐漸消失**。
- As the years passed, the memories **faded away**.
  記憶隨著時間的過去而**逐漸消失**。

223

Unit 26 Test Yourself!

Ⓐ 選擇題

1. Avery is very rich, so he never has to _____; he always buys whatever he wants.
   Ⓐ cut corners　Ⓑ come about　Ⓒ make out　Ⓓ build up

2. Sydney was a perfect student who always _____ her teachers' expectations.
   Ⓐ lived up to　Ⓑ brought about　Ⓒ stuck it to　Ⓓ stood up for

3. The repairman really _____ Jasmine, leaving her with a huge bill for the electrical repairs.
   Ⓐ stood up for　Ⓑ stuck it to　Ⓒ came about　Ⓓ lived up to

4. No one knew how the problem _____; it was a real mystery.
   Ⓐ cut corners　Ⓑ came about　Ⓒ made out　Ⓓ built up

5. Kevin _____ some pretty big changes in the company after he became the CEO.
   Ⓐ made out　Ⓑ brought about　Ⓒ died out　Ⓓ stuck it to

6. As soon as I woke up, my dream _____.
   Ⓐ made out　Ⓑ cut corners　Ⓒ faded away　Ⓓ died out

7. If you don't _____ yourself, people at your company may use you.
   Ⓐ make out　Ⓑ come about　Ⓒ stick it to　Ⓓ stand up for

8. In the beginning, Ian wasn't a very talented photographer, but he _____ the training program and, in the end, he became famous.
   Ⓐ stuck to　Ⓑ brought about　Ⓒ built up　Ⓓ made up

9. The anger about the political scandal _____ after a few months.
   Ⓐ made out　Ⓑ cut corners　Ⓒ stuck to it　Ⓓ died down

10. If whale hunting continues, some types of whales may _____.
    Ⓐ make up　Ⓑ come about　Ⓒ die out　Ⓓ cut corners

11. Over the years Logan _____ his stamp collection, which is now huge; he may even sell it to a museum.
    Ⓐ built up　Ⓑ came about　Ⓒ stood up for　Ⓓ died out

B 閱讀文章，從字表中選擇詞彙填入，並依人稱時態等做適當的變化

live up to	cut corners	die down
build up	come about	fade away
stick it to	make out	stick to

The worst class I have this semester is astronomy. I never even wanted to take this course. However, as I was ❶ _____ my class schedule, my older brother really ❷ _____ the reputation of this class and made it sound very interesting.

He told me that a class this good doesn't ❸ _____ very often. The fact is, the class doesn't ❹ _____ its reputation as an excellent introduction to the topic, and sometimes I don't know if I should ❺ _____ it or give it up. Moreover, astronomy is very difficult, and my classmates are so noisy that I often can't hear what Prof. Jones is saying. Even after the noise ❻ _____, Prof. Jones' voice is so weak that it ❼ _____ each time someone's cell phone rings or there is any interruption.

Worse still, in an effort to ❽ _____, the university makes the students pay for their own handouts. Sometimes it seems like the professor is trying to ❾ _____ us because there are many, many handouts!

C 引導式翻譯，並依人稱時態等做適當的變化

1. 如果給了別人承諾，你就應該要**遵守**。
   If you make a promise, you should _____ _____ it.

2. 恐龍好幾百萬年前就已經**滅絕**了。
   Dinosaurs _____ _____ millions of years ago.

3. 我以為能看到自己最喜愛的搖滾樂團演出是一件很棒的事情，但表演卻不太**符合我的期望**。
   I thought it would be cool to see my favorite rock band play at the arena, but the show didn't _____ _____ _____ my expectations.

4. 艾文會把票投給承諾會**帶來**轉變的總統候選人。
   Ivan will vote for the candidate who promises to _____ _____ change.

5. 我們必須**節省**一點，才能以極少的預算製作一部電影。
   We've had to _____ _____ to make the film on such a small budget.

Unit 27

Falling Behind in Class
課業落後

Ricardo is telling Pauline about some troubles at school.
里卡多把在學校遇到的困難告訴寶琳。

Ricardo:	Sometimes I think Ms. Conway really **has it in for**[1] me.	有時候我覺得康威女士常常**和**我**過不去**。
Pauline:	Why do you say that?	怎麼說？
Ricardo:	For one thing, she seems mad at me for **falling behind**[2] in class.	首先，我**跟不上**學習進度，她似乎很生氣。
Pauline:	I didn't know you were behind. I guess your plans to catch up last weekend **fell through**[3].	我都不曉得你跟不上進度。我想你上週末準備趕進度的計畫**泡湯了**。
Ricardo:	Unfortunately, they did. And now both my parents and Ms. Conway want to **have it out with**[4] me.	是不幸取消了，而現在我父母和康威女士都想要**找**我**算帳**。
Pauline:	Did you at least prepare for tomorrow's test? Ms. Conway **gave out**[5] a handout to help us review.	至少你會準備明天的考試吧？康威女士**發**了一張幫助我們複習的講義。
Ricardo:	Actually, I'm going to **hold off**[6] on studying; I'm spending all my free time trying to beat this new video game I got.	事實上，我的讀書計畫要**延後**了。我現在一有空，就在玩新買的電動玩具。
Pauline:	Well, if you ask me, you should either forget about the game or **give in**[7] and accept an "F" in the class . . .	唔，我認為你應該忘掉電動，或是**默默接受**得到「F」的事實……。
Ricardo:	No way! I can pass this test without studying.	不可能！我不用唸書就可以考及格了。
Pauline:	Really? I doubt it. It seems like you **took on**[8] more classes than you can handle.	是嗎？我很懷疑。看來你**修**的課數超出你的負荷。

226

Unit 27 Falling Behind in Class 課業落後

1 慣用片語

have it (有不愉快的) + in (在……上) + for (針對)
→ **have it in for**
① 與……過不去
② 對……伺機報復

用法 ◆ have it in for sb 與某人過不去

❶ Sometimes I think my tutor really **has it in for** me; no matter how hard I work, she always complains.
有時我覺得助教常常**和**我**過不去**。無論我多用功，她老是有話要說。

❶ My boss must really **have it in for** me; that was the third lecture this week!
我的老闆一定是在**和**我**過不去**，那已經是這星期第三次訓話了！

2 片語動詞

fall (落) + behind (在後)
→ **fall behind**
① 落後；跟不上　② 延遲 及 不及

用法 ◆ fall behind with sth 在某方面落後
→ He was ill for four weeks and **fell behind with** his schoolwork.
他請了四個星期的病假，所以課業進度落後了。

同 落後 ❶ lag behind　❷ drop behind　❸ get behind

- Will **lagged** far **behind** his classmates in reading and math skills.
威爾的閱讀和數學能力遠遠**落後**班上的同學。

反 迎頭趕上 catch up with

- I had to run to **catch up with** the others. 我必須要用跑的才能夠**趕上**其他人。

❶ After three weeks' vacationing in the United Kingdom, Nick realized he was **falling behind** on his research project.
尼克在英國度假三個禮拜後，才發現他的研究報告**進度落後**了。

❶ Frank **fell behind** on his schoolwork and couldn't graduate with his friends.
法蘭克**跟不上**課業，所以無法和同學一起畢業。

❷ You're **falling behind** with the rent. 你**遲交**房租了。

3

fall (落下) + **through** (穿過) → **fall through** 無法實現 [不及]

同 go wrong
反 come true

💡 常以計畫或夢想作主詞，不以人為主詞。

- Corey's plan to buy a car **fell through** when he lost his job.
  柯瑞買車的計畫在工作丟了後便**告吹**了。
- Wade's plan to be the coolest kid in school **fell through** when he got an embarrassing haircut. 偉德的頭髮剪壞了，他**無法**成為全校最酷的小孩了。
- We found a buyer for our house, but then the sale **fell through**.
  我們找到了房子的買主，但這場交易後來**告吹**了。

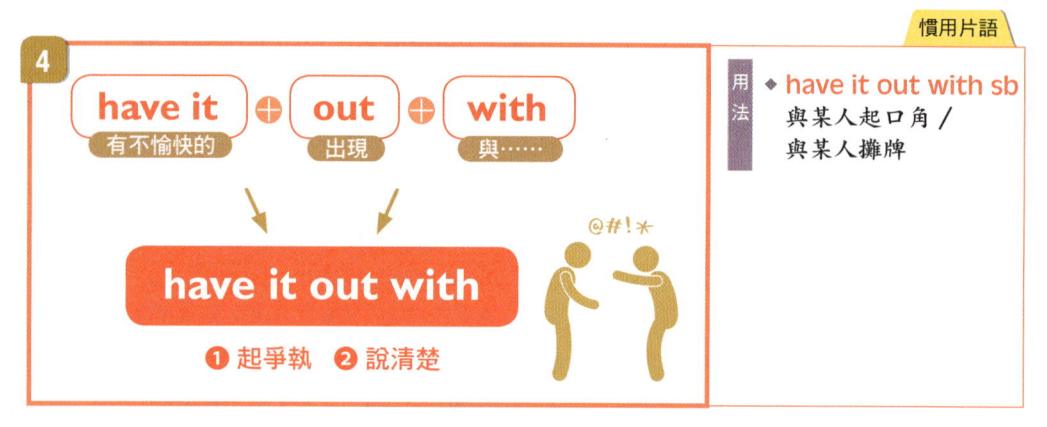

4 慣用片語

have it (有不愉快的) + **out** (出現) + **with** (與……) → **have it out with** ❶ 起爭執 ❷ 說清楚

用法 ◆ have it out with sb
與某人起口角／
與某人攤牌

❶ I really **had it out with** Archie when I found out he was the one who stole my bike.
當我發現就是阿奇偷了我的腳踏車後，便和他**起了口角**。

❶ Taylor and Lydia disagree about how best to do the project; I think they'll **have it out with** each other soon.
泰勒和莉蒂雅對執行這項企畫的最佳方式意見不一，我認為他們很快就會**吵起來**。

❷ Judy was late for work every morning this week, and I thought I'd better **have it out with** her. 裘蒂這星期每天早上上班都遲到，我認為我最好和她**說清楚**。

5

give 給 + **out** 向外 → **give out**

❶ 分發 〔及〕 ❷ 用盡 〔不及〕

片語動詞 | 可分開 | 受詞為代名詞時定要分開

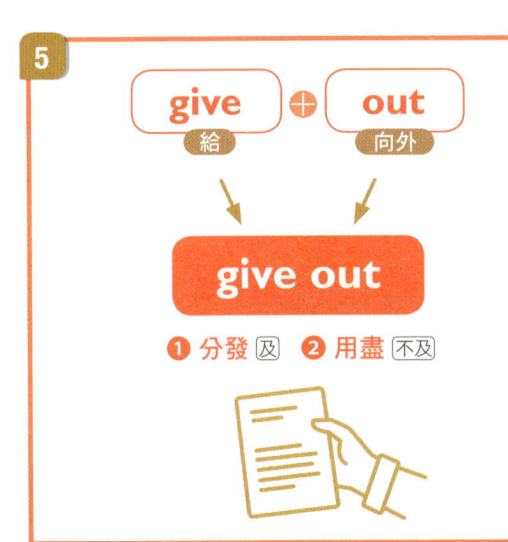

比較
◆ **give off** 散發出（味道等）
→ The rotten meat was **giving off** a terrible odor. 壞掉的肉散發出一股很可怕的味道。
→ This perfume **gives off** the smell of flowers. 這瓶香水散發出一股花香。

同 分發 ❶ pass out ❷ hand out
用盡 run out

❶ To promote its new flavor of gum, the company hired some people to **give out** samples to passersby.
公司為了宣傳新口味的口香糖，請了一些人把試吃包發給路人。

❶ The teacher **gave** a study guide **out** to everyone who asked for one.
老師把學習導引手冊發給需要的人。

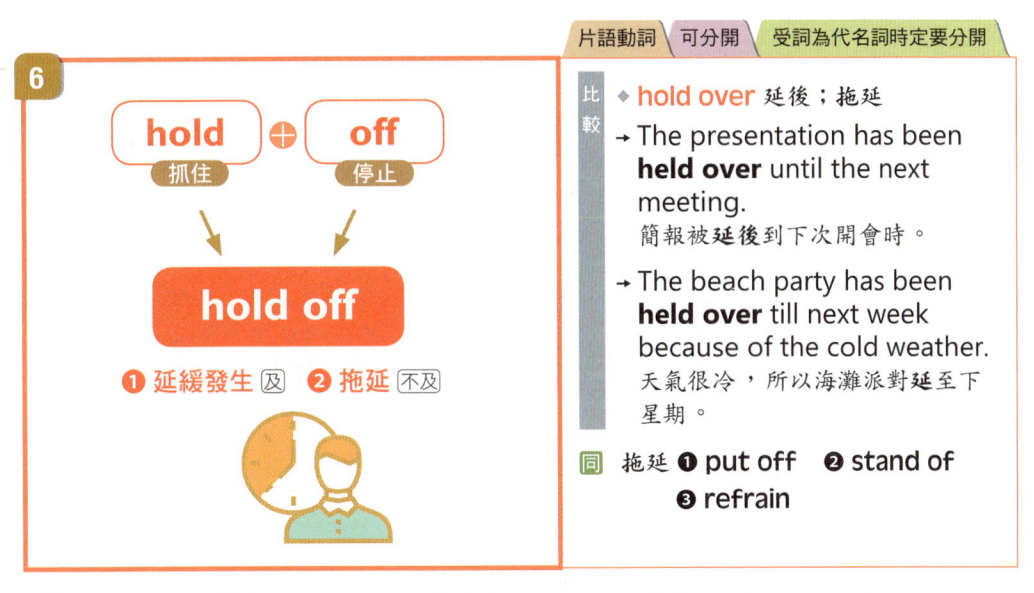

6

hold 抓住 + **off** 停止 → **hold off**

❶ 延緩發生 〔及〕 ❷ 拖延 〔不及〕

片語動詞 | 可分開 | 受詞為代名詞時定要分開

比較
◆ **hold over** 延後；拖延
→ The presentation has been **held over** until the next meeting. 簡報被延後到下次開會時。
→ The beach party has been **held over** till next week because of the cold weather. 天氣很冷，所以海灘派對延至下星期。

同 拖延 ❶ put off ❷ stand of ❸ refrain

❶ They **held off** buying a new digital camera until the price went down.
他們一直拖到數位相機降價才買了一台新的。

❶ I think we should **hold off** going downtown until we find the bus schedule.
找出公車時間表前，我們應該暫緩去市中心的計畫。

❷ **Hold off** on calling a taxi; maybe my aunt can give us a ride.
先別叫計程車，也許我阿姨可以載我們一程。

Unit 27 Falling Behind in Class 課業落後

7

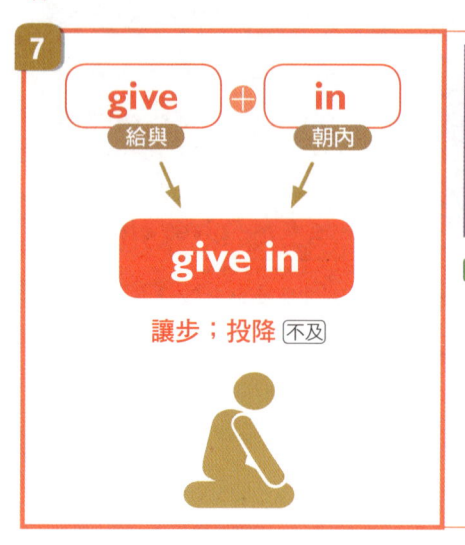

give（給與） + **in**（朝內） → **give in** 讓步；投降 [不及]

用法
- give in to sb 向某人屈服
- give in to sth 向某事屈服
→ The government cannot be seen as **giving in to** terrorist' demands.
政府不可以對恐怖份子所提出的要求**讓步**。

同
1. give in to
2. give way
3. give way to
4. make concessions to
5. submit to
6. yield to

- I know you're not the best football player, but you shouldn't **give in** and quit the team without trying a little harder.
我知道你並非最棒的足球員，但你不應該沒再多試幾個星期，就**輕易放棄**和退出球隊。

- After a few months of trying to live without a TV, I finally **gave in** and bought one.
過了幾個月沒有電視的日子後，我終於**放棄**且買了一台新的。

- I finally **gave in** and let him stay up to watch TV. 我終於**讓步**，讓他熬夜看電視。

8

片語動詞　可分開　受詞為代名詞時定要分開

take（掌握） + **on**（在……上） → **take on** ❶ 承擔 ❷ 聘僱 [及]

用法
- take sth on / take on sth 承擔某事
→ My sister **took on** the responsibility of caring for our elderly mother.
我的姐姐**扛下**了照顧年邁母親的責任。

- take sb on / take on sb 聘請某人
→ Lucy was **taken on** as a laboratory assistant. 露西被**聘僱**為實驗室助理。

比較
- take off 脫掉；起飛
- take up 開始做

同 解僱 lay off

1. I'm not sure if I can **take on** any more classes; my schedule is already full.
我不確定我是否能應付多修幾門課，我的課表很滿了。

2. My company **took on** three new employees last week.
我們公司上星期**聘用**了三位新員工。

9 take + down

take 拿 + **down** 下來 → **take down**

❶ 取下　❷ 寫下 [及]

| 片語動詞 | 可分開 | 受詞為代名詞時定要分開 |

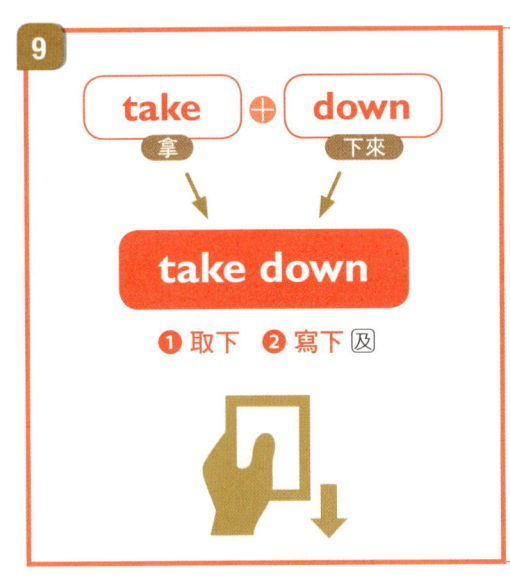

用法
- **take sth down / take down sth** 寫下某事
  → Tom **took down** my address and phone number and said he'd call back. 湯姆抄下了我的地址和電話，說他會回電給我。
- **take sth down / take down sth** 取下某物
  → I've **taken** the pictures **down**. 我已經把照片取了下來。

同 ❶ write down　❷ put down　❸ set down

❶ After Florence's art exhibit, the workers **took down** all of the paintings that hadn't sold. 佛羅倫斯的藝術展覽結束後，工作人員把所有沒賣出的畫拿了下來。

❶ Jim's mom made him **take** the rock 'n' roll posters **down** from his wall. 吉姆的媽媽要他把牆上的搖滾樂團海報拿下來。

❷ Did you **take down** any notes during physics class? 你有抄物理課的筆記嗎？

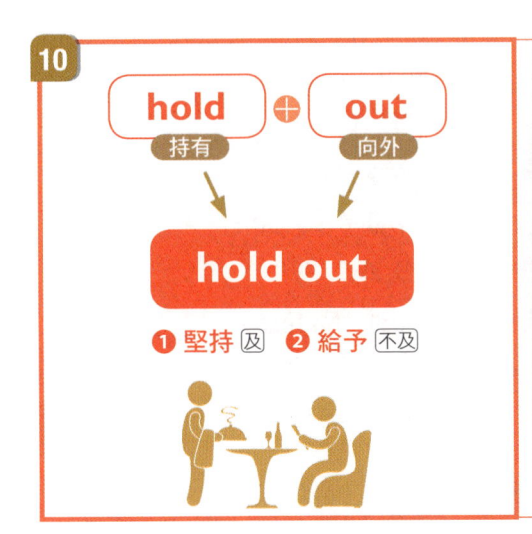

---

10 hold + out

hold 持有 + **out** 向外 → **hold out**

❶ 堅持 [及]　❷ 給予 [不及]

| 片語動詞 | 可分開 | 受詞為代名詞時定要分開 |

用法
- **hold out against sth** 為某事堅持到底
  → The city won't be able to **hold out** much longer **against** the bombing attacks. 這座城市已經沒有辦法再繼續抵抗炸彈攻擊了。
- **hold sth out / hold out sth** 給予希望
  → We don't **hold out** much hope of finding more survivors. 我們對於找到生還者不抱有太大的希望。

比較
- **hold up** 阻礙
- **hold back** 抑制

💡 表示「給予」時，通常是指幫助、承諾或希望。

❶ Don't buy the first car you find; **hold out** until you see the perfect model. 別買你第一輛看到的車，要堅持到你看到最理想的車款才下手。

❷ The waiter **held out** a tray of drinks and offered them to everyone at the party. 服務生把飲料放在托盤上，給所有參加派對的人喝。

Unit 27 Test Yourself!

A 選擇題

1. Ely didn't sell his computer to the first person who wanted to buy it; he _____ to see if someone would pay more.
   Ⓐ took on　Ⓑ held over　Ⓒ held out　Ⓓ gave off

2. Dad really _____ me for taking the car without asking him.
   Ⓐ held over　Ⓑ had it out with　Ⓒ gave out　Ⓓ took down

3. The professor was forced to _____ more students than she could handle.
   Ⓐ give out　Ⓑ take on　Ⓒ hold out　Ⓓ have it in for

4. After Cindy's birthday party was over, her parents _____ all the decorations.
   Ⓐ took down　Ⓑ had it in for　Ⓒ gave in　Ⓓ held off

5. University classes are tough, but if you remain confident and don't _____, you can graduate.
   Ⓐ take on　Ⓑ give out　Ⓒ give in　Ⓓ hold off

6. Something in the fridge was _____ a disgusting smell.
   Ⓐ taking on　Ⓑ holding off　Ⓒ giving off　Ⓓ giving out

7. Bernie's acceptance to Yale _____ when he failed his senior year of high school.
   Ⓐ gave off　Ⓑ took on　Ⓒ held over　Ⓓ fell through

8. Rachel volunteers for a group that _____ food to the needy.
   Ⓐ takes on　Ⓑ holds over　Ⓒ takes down　Ⓓ gives out

9. The class discussion has been _____ for tomorrow's lesson.
   Ⓐ held over　Ⓑ taken down　Ⓒ taken on　Ⓓ given out

10. After Clementine got her friend George in trouble, he really _____ her.
    Ⓐ had it in for　Ⓑ took down　Ⓒ gave off　Ⓓ held over

11. Despite running as fast as she could in the race, it wasn't long before Tanya _____ the others.
    Ⓐ had it in for　Ⓑ fell behind　Ⓒ gave out　Ⓓ held over

12. Let's _____ going on a hike until the weather gets better.
    Ⓐ hold off　Ⓑ have it in for　Ⓒ give out　Ⓓ hold on

B 閱讀文章，從字表中選擇詞彙填入，並依人稱時態等做適當的變化

| take on | give in | give out | have it in for |
| hold off | fall through | give off | fall behind |

　　The restaurant called Raul's Taco Buffet is probably the worst place to eat in the city. However, if you end up going there for some reason, you won't need this review as proof; the smell this place ❶ _____ should be enough to make you want to ❷ _____ eating, no matter how hungry you might be.

　　If you are one of those people who avoid ❸ _____ to better judgment or who like to ❹ _____ deadly challenges, any plans you may have the next day are likely to ❺ _____ as you wait to recover from the terrible food. Don't worry if you get sick, though; it isn't that the cook ❻ _____ you; it's just that he has no skills. Maybe he ❼ _____ in his cooking class, or more likely, he never even went to cooking class. The fact is, the food at Raul's Taco Buffet is so bad that they couldn't ❽ _____ it _____ for free.

C 引導式翻譯，並依人稱時態等做適當的變化

1. 米蘭達**擔**了太多專案，因而把自己累垮了。
   Miranda _____ too many projects _____ and made herself ill.

2. 他們星期天健行的計畫因下雨而**泡湯**。
   Their plans to go hiking on Sunday _____ _____ because it rained.

3. 在得到完整的道歉前，我是不會**讓步**的。
   I wouldn't _____ _____ until I received a full apology.

4. 少有人還對能找出更多生還者**抱持**希望。
   Few people _____ _____ any hope of finding more survivors.

5. 我希望雨在我們到家前都**先別下**。
   I hope the rain _____ _____ until we get home.

Unit 27　Falling Behind in Class　課業落後

Unit 28

Breaking Up[1]
分手

Gavin calls Judy on the phone.
蓋文打電話給裘蒂。

Gavin: Hello, Judy! It's me, Gavin.

哈囉，裘蒂！我是蓋文。

Judy: Gavin? Please **leave** me **alone**[2]! I told you never to call me again!

蓋文？請不要**煩**我！我說過別再打電話給我！

Gavin: Judy, please don't **break off**[3] our relationship. I know that things have been very **touch and go**[4] between us lately, but I miss you! I must see you again.

裘蒂，拜託不要**結束**我們的關係。我知道最近我們的關係變得**岌岌可危**，但我很想念妳！我一定要見妳。

Judy: I don't think so. Your attitude really **wears** me **down**[5]. You can drop by one more time, but only so you can **bring back**[6] those CDs I lent you.

我不覺得。你的態度真的令我很**累**。唔，我們再見一面吧，只有這樣你才可以把我借給你的 CD **還給**我。

Gavin: And that's it? After that, I must **let** you **alone**[7]?

就這樣？之後我便**不再打擾妳**？

Judy: Yes. Although we had some good times, **on the whole**[8] our romance was pretty boring. I'm sorry, but it's over!

是的。雖然我們在一起很快樂，但這段感情**大致來說**非常無趣。很抱歉，我們之間結束了！

Unit 28 Breaking Up 分手

1

break(打破) + **up**(徹底地) → **break up**
❶ 打碎　❷ 分手 及

片語動詞　可分開　受詞為代名詞時定要分開

用法
- **break up sth / break sth up**
  弄碎某事物
  → **Break up** the chocolate bars so they will melt more quickly in the microwave.
  把巧克力棒**弄碎**，這樣它們才能在微波爐裡更快融化。

同　使成碎片　❶ break up into　❷ go to pieces

❶ The company has been **broken up** and sold off. 這家公司已經**解散**，並且廉價售出了。
❷ I've just **broken up** with my boyfriend. 我才剛和男朋友**分手**。

2

慣用片語

leave(留下) + **alone**(單獨地) → **leave (sb or sth) alone**
讓某人獨處；別打擾

用法
- **leave sth alone**
  別觸碰某物；別涉入某事
- **leave sb alone** 別打擾某人

• **Leave** Rick **alone**. He's making a very important phone call.
別打擾瑞克，他在講一通很重要的電話。

3

片語動詞　可分開　受詞為代名詞時定要分開

break(折斷) + **off**(切斷) → **break off**
❶ 分離　❷ 中斷 及

💡 **break off** 常用來表示「斷絕關係」、「終止契約」或「結束婚約」等。

用法
- **break sth off / break off sth**
  中斷某事物

❶ Corey **broke off** a piece of the cookie and gave it to his younger brother.
柯瑞把餅乾**分成**一小塊給弟弟。
❶ Can you **break** me **off** a piece of that chocolate? 可以**分**一塊巧克力給我嗎？
❷ When the phone rang, Mrs. Williams **broke off** the conversation and ran to answer it. 電話聲響起時，威廉斯太太**停止**了談話，然後跑向電話。

235

形容詞片語

4 touch ＋ and ＋ go
接觸　而　前行

→ **touch and go**
❶ 情況危急的　❷（形勢）不確定的

💡 **touch and go** 來源不可考，有一說是來自「船在觸到河床後仍前行」，表示相當危險。現在用來指「事態無法預料，不知結果如何、步步危險」的情況，近似中文「一觸即發」，也可來表示飛機觸地重飛的情況。

❶ The dental work was going well at first, but then it was **touch and go** for a while.
牙醫的工作剛開始很正常，但後來有一段時間**不是很順利**。

❷ Marc wasn't sure if he had passed his exams; it was really **touch and go**.
馬克不確定他考試是否及格，**不到最後關頭真的無法論定**。

片語動詞　受詞為代名詞時定要分開

5 wear ＋ down
使疲乏　向下

→ **wear down**
使疲累 及

用法　◆ **wear sb down**
使某人疲累

同　**exhaust**

• This boring class really **wears** me **down**; I'm always nearly asleep before it's even half over!　這堂無聊的課**把我累壞了**，通常課還不到一半我就快要睡著！

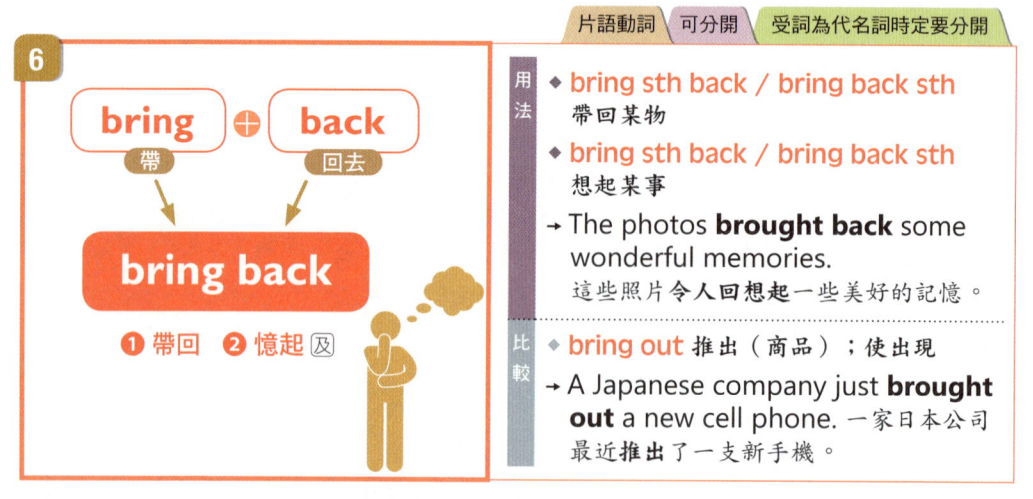

片語動詞　可分開　受詞為代名詞時定要分開

6 bring ＋ back
帶　回去

→ **bring back**
❶ 帶回　❷ 憶起 及

用法　◆ **bring sth back / bring back sth**
帶回某物

◆ **bring sth back / bring back sth**
想起某事
→ The photos **brought back** some wonderful memories.
這些照片令人回想起一些美好的記憶。

比較　◆ **bring out** 推出（商品）；使出現
→ A Japanese company just **brought out** a new cell phone. 一家日本公司最近推出了一支新手機。

❶ If you go to the store, can you **bring back** some ice cream?
如果你要去商店，可以帶些冰淇淋**回來**嗎？

7

let (讓) + **alone** (單獨地) → **let (sb) alone**

不打擾某人做某事（※少用）

慣用片語

比較
- ◆ **let alone** 更不必說〔連接詞〕
  → I barely know how to play the happy birthday song on the piano, **let alone** Beethoven.
  我連怎麼彈生日快樂歌都不知道，**更不用說**彈貝多芬了。
  → Abe's leg hurt so much he could barely walk, **let alone** run.
  艾比的腳痛到不能走路，**更不用說**是跑步了。

同 leave sb alone

💡 **let someone alone** 表示「讓某人獨處」；**let alone** 則表示「某事根本不可能發生，沒有必要說起」。

- **Let** Seth **alone**. He's trying to finish his report. 別煩塞斯，他正試著要完成報告。
- I wish she would **let** me **alone** so I could get some sleep.
  我希望她**不要來打擾我**，這樣我才可以睡點覺。

8

on (在……之上) + **the whole** (單獨地) → **on the whole**

概括；就整體而言

副詞片語

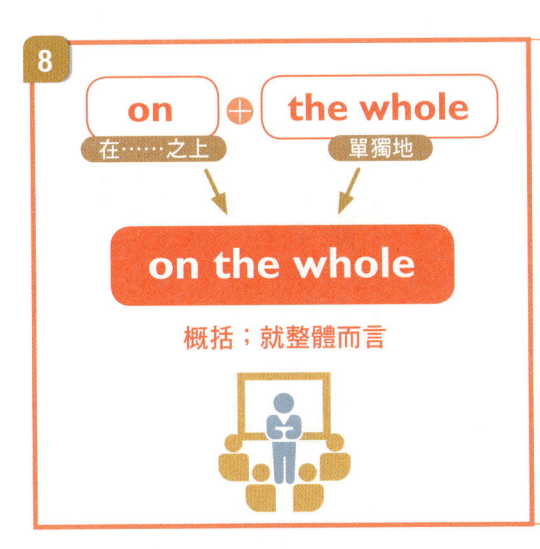

比較
- ◆ **as a whole** 整體看來
  → Unemployment here is much higher than for the country **as a whole**.
  整體看來，這個地方的失業率比全國還要高出許多。

同
❶ all in all
❷ by and large
❸ generally speaking
❹ in the main
❺ for the most part

- **On the whole**, my vacation was excellent, though there were a few problems.
  雖然遇到了一些困難，但**整體而言**，我的假期還是很棒的。
- It was a fun party **on the whole**, but I wish the music had been better.
  整體而言，這個派對很好玩，但我希望音樂能有所改善。
- **On the whole**, I think my dinner party was a success.
  整體而言，我認為這次的晚餐聚會辦得很成功。
- We have had some bad times, but **on the whole** we're fairly happy.
  我們遇到了一些不開心的事情，但**整體來說**還是過得很快樂。

237

9

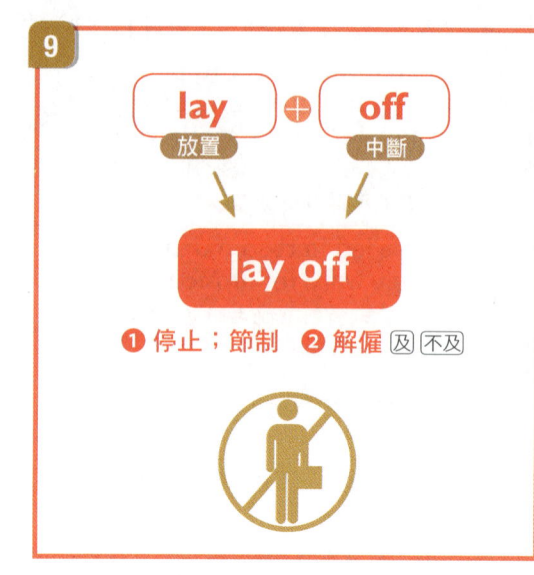

lay 放置 + **off** 中斷 → **lay off**

❶ 停止；節制　❷ 解僱 [及] [不及]

片語動詞 | 可分開 | 受詞為代名詞時定要分開

用法
- ◆ **lay off sb / lay sb off** 解僱某人
  → After our company lost a lot of business, my manager **laid off** many workers to save money.
  自從我們公司失去了多筆生意後，經理為了降低成本資遣了許多員工。
- ◆ **lay off sth** 節制某事物
  → Now that school has begun, you should **lay off** the partying for a while.
  開學了，你應該停止狂歡一段時間。

比較
- ◆ **get the sack** 被解僱

❶ My coworkers didn't **lay off** our boss for the entire dinner; they were very critical of her. 用餐時，我的同事毫不客氣地批評老闆，他們對她非常不滿。

❶ I usually run several miles every day but **lay off** in the hot weather. 我每天通常會跑好幾英里，但在大熱天就不跑了。

❷ He was **laid off** along with many others when the company moved to New York City. 公司搬遷至紐約市時，他和許多員工都被解僱了。

10

wear 磨出 + **off** 消除 → **wear off**

逐漸消失 [不及]

片語動詞

同 ❶ diminish
　　❷ wear away

💡 常用來表示**疼痛**、**藥效**或**喜怒哀樂**等抽象狀態逐漸消失。

- As soon as the coffee began to **wear off**, Jill felt tired.
  隨著咖啡的效用逐漸消失，吉爾感覺很累。
- When the aspirin **wore off**, Lou's headache returned.
  當阿斯匹靈逐漸失去效用時，盧的頭又痛了起來。
- The effect of the injection will gradually **wear off**. 打針後的藥效會逐漸消失。

11

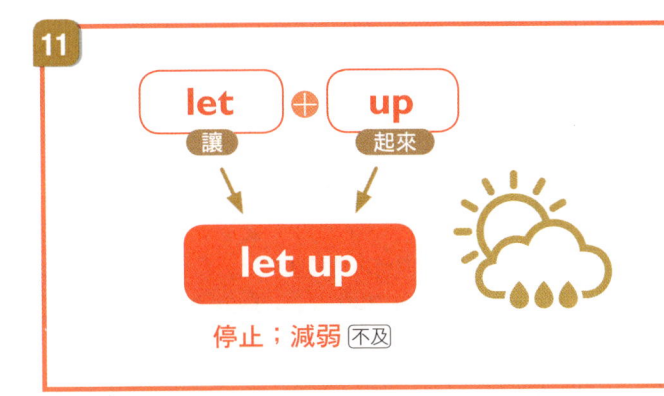

let (讓) + **up** (起來) → **let up**

停止；減弱 [不及]

同 ❶ ease up
❷ ease off
❸ diminish

💡 此片與通常用來表示**疼痛**、**刮風下雨**或**下雪**等情況停止或減弱。

- If the snow ever **lets up**, we'll drive to the store.
  如果**停止**下雪，我們就會開車去商店。
- When the rain **lets up,** we'll go for a walk.　我們雨**停**後就去散步。
- The rain shows no sign of **letting up**.　雨一點也沒有要**停**的樣子。

12　慣用片語

wait (等待) + **up** (起來) + **for** (為了) → **wait up for**

❶ 為了等某人而不睡覺
❷ 停下來等某人

❶ Mom was **waiting up for** me when I walked in the door, and she was not happy!
當我回到家時，媽媽**還沒睡在等**我，而且不太高興！

❶ If you're planning on returning home before midnight, I'll try to **wait up for** you.
如果你打算在午夜前回家，我會**等**你的。

❶ I'll probably be out very late tonight, so don't **wait up for** me.
我今天晚上會很晚才回來，所以不要**為**我**等門**了。

❶ Let's **wait up for** Sherry to see how her date went.
我們**等**雪莉回來吧，了解一下她的約會是否進展順利。

❷ We're so far ahead of our friends; let's **wait up for** them here.
我們超前了朋友許多，我們**停**在這裡**等**他們吧。

Unit 28 Test Yourself!

A 選擇題

1. Frank will be at the party until very late, so don't _____ him.
   Ⓐ wait up for   Ⓑ bring back   Ⓒ let alone   Ⓓ wear off

2. After an hour, the lousy music at the club was beginning to _____ Theo ____.
   Ⓐ let . . . up   Ⓑ wear . . . down   Ⓒ bring . . . about   Ⓓ let . . . alone

3. The rain didn't _____ the entire weekend.
   Ⓐ wait up for   Ⓑ bring back   Ⓒ let up   Ⓓ wear off

4. The admissions office told me it was _____ whether I'd be accepted at the university.
   Ⓐ brought out   Ⓑ touch and go   Ⓒ let alone   Ⓓ broken off

5. I wonder if they will ever _____ a camera that can play MP3s.
   Ⓐ bring out   Ⓑ wear off   Ⓒ let alone   Ⓓ wait up for

6. _____ Harry _____ when he's driving.
   Ⓐ Lay . . . off   Ⓑ Leave . . . alone   Ⓒ Break . . . off   Ⓓ Let . . . up

7. After the terrible argument, Mary-Anne _____ relations with her neighbors.
   Ⓐ broke off   Ⓑ let up   Ⓒ brought out   Ⓓ let alone

8. Mr. North is a good teacher _____, but of course he isn't perfect.
   Ⓐ touch and go   Ⓑ left alone   Ⓒ on the whole   Ⓓ broken off

9. If you go to Hawaii, can you please _____ a T-shirt for me?
   Ⓐ lay off   Ⓑ let alone   Ⓒ wear off   Ⓓ bring back

10. Because Jared is on a diet, he has to _____ the snacks.
    Ⓐ lay off   Ⓑ let alone   Ⓒ wear off   Ⓓ break off

11. Nate couldn't get to sleep until the effects of the espresso _____.
    Ⓐ let alone   Ⓑ wore off   Ⓒ broke off   Ⓓ wore down

B 閱讀文章，從字表中選擇詞彙填入，並依人稱時態等做適當的變化

> lay off　　　bring back　　　touch and go　　　wear off
> wear down　　let up　　　　 on the whole　　　break off
> leave (someone or something) alone

　　The librarian really won't ❶ _____ me _____; he's called my cell phone twice today to tell me that I must ❷ _____ the books I borrowed as soon as possible. The problem is that I'm very tired, and as soon as this cappuccino ❸ _____, I'll need to sleep. Also, the wind hasn't ❹ _____ all day, and I have no jacket.

　　I really don't want to go to the library! However, if I don't return those books soon, the library may ❺ _____ relations with me and ban me from borrowing any more books.

　　The reason I'm so lazy is that all this studying really ❻ _____ me _____. I'm so tired of working. I can't stop, though, because my academic situation is still very ❼ _____. Although I've done well in some classes, ❽ _____, I'm doing pretty poorly.

　　I've promised myself that after this semester, I'm going to ❾ _____ playing video games and spend more time doing my homework so I can improve my grades.

C 引導式翻譯，並依人稱時態等做適當的變化

1. 他們何時會**推出**便宜一點的筆記型電腦呢？
   When will they _____ a cheaper laptop _____?

2. 大部分的病人都認為，打針過後麻木的感覺會在一個小時候**逐漸消失**。
   Most patients find that the numbness from the injection _____ _____ after about an hour.

3. 我半夜才會回家，所以別**為我等門**了。
   I'll be home after midnight, so don't _____ _____ _____ me.

4. 你最好一陣子**不要喝酒**。
   You'd better _____ _____ alcohol for a while.

5. 醫生說要**到最後才能夠知道**傑瑞是否可以康復。
   The doctor says that it's _____ _____ _____ whether Jerry will be okay.

Unit 29

Being a Designer
成為設計師

Amanda has some excellent news to share with Joy.
亞曼達有天大的好消息要和喬伊分享。

Amanda:	I've got great news! You know that I **have my heart set on**[1] becoming a designer and have worked a lot lately on making my own clothes.	好消息！因為我**已經下定決心**要成為一名設計師，所以我最近都在設計衣服。
Joy:	So what's the news? Did your style **catch on**[2]?	所以妳要告訴我的消息是什麼？是妳設計的衣服**廣受歡迎**嗎？
Amanda:	It sure did! It seems I'**m** really **cut out for**[3] fashion design.	沒錯！看來我真的很**適合**成為一位服裝設計師。
Joy:	Why? What happened, exactly?	怎麼說？究竟怎麼回事？
Amanda:	Well, I was showing a few samples to a local store, and they loved the style so much that they **bought up**[4] everything. The next day, they called to tell me that everything had already **sold out**[5].	嗯，我拿了一些樣本到這附近的一家店，他們非常喜歡我的設計，而且全數**買下**。隔天，他們還打電話跟我說衣服全**賣完**了。
Joy:	Fantastic! Did you make a lot of money?	真了不起！妳賺了不少吧？
Amanda:	Yup! It **works out**[6] to about a 200% profit for me.	是啊！我**一共**約賺了兩倍的利潤。
Joy:	Congratulations!	恭喜妳！

Unit 29 Being a Designer 成為設計師

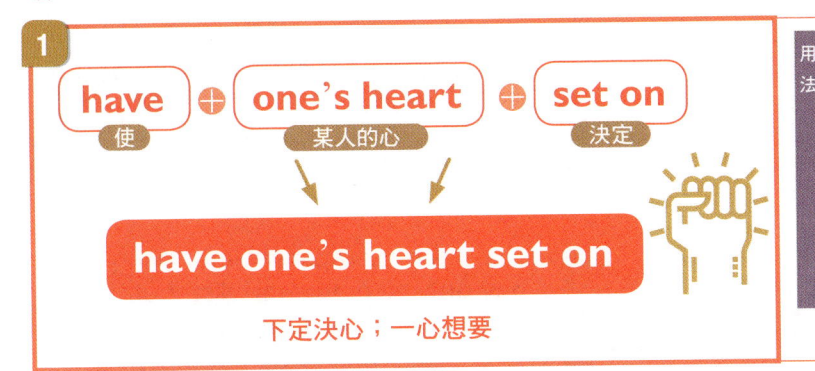

1 慣用片語

have (使) + **one's heart** (某人的心) + **set on** (決定)
→ **have one's heart set on**
下定決心；一心想要

用法
- have one's heart set on sth 一心想要某事
- have one's heart set on doing sth 下定決心做某事

- I **had my heart set on** becoming a doctor. 我已經**下定決心**要成為一名醫生了。
- Sarah **has her heart set on** going to Bermuda next year.
  莎拉**下定決心**明年要去百慕達。

2 片語動詞

catch (聽清楚) + **on** (集中在……上)
→ **catch on**
❶ 受到歡迎　❷ 聽懂（意思或玩笑）[不及]

同 使理解 get through

❶ The new clothing brand has really **caught on** among college students.
   這個新牌子的衣服很**受到**大學生的**歡迎**。
❷ Raul didn't **catch on** that we were making fun of him.
   勞爾**聽不懂**我們在開他玩笑。

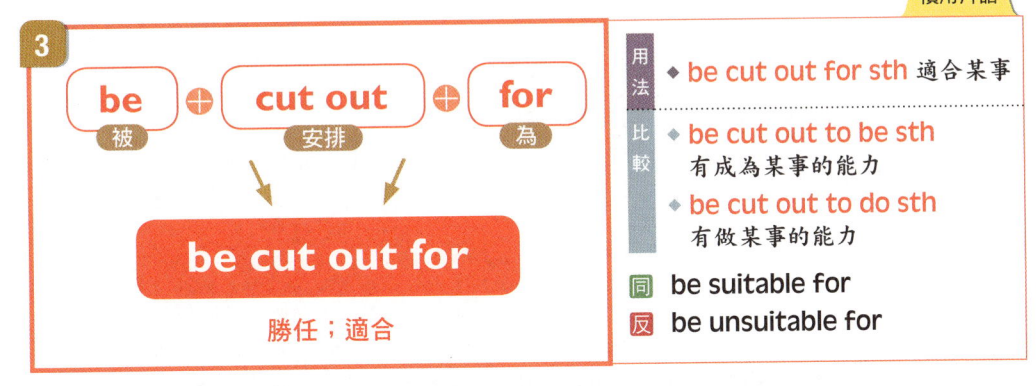

3 慣用片語

be (被) + **cut out** (安排) + **for** (為)
→ **be cut out for**
勝任；適合

用法
- be cut out for sth 適合某事

比較
- be cut out to be sth 有成為某事的能力
- be cut out to do sth 有做某事的能力

同 be suitable for
反 be unsuitable for

💡 **be cut out for** 用來描述「某人很適合某項工作、行業」等，通常使用**被動語態**。

- Darren **is** not **cut out for** a job in a big company. 戴倫不**適合**在大公司工作。
- Francesca **is cut out for** environmental work with her master's degree in natural science. 法蘭契斯卡擁有自然科學碩士學位，她很**適合**環保工作。

243

🔊 123

4

buy 買 + **up** 徹底

→ **buy up**
全部買下 [及]

| 片語動詞 | 可分開 | 受詞為代名詞時定要分開 |

用法 ◆ **buy sth up** / **buy up sth** 買下某物

比較 ◆ **buy out** 收購（企業、股份）
→ The energy company keeps trying to **buy out** the petroleum distributor. 該電力公司不斷試圖**收購**石油供應商。
→ Ariel hoped that some big company would **buy out** her little company and make her rich. 艾芮兒希望有大公司能**收購**她那間小公司，然後讓她成為有錢人。

- Tabitha **bought** all the chocolate **up** because she was crazy for it.
  由於泰貝莎超愛吃巧克力，所以她買下了所有的巧克力。
- Flynn **bought up** all the batteries in the store because he needed them for his stereo. 佛林為了音響而買下了這家店所有的電池。
- Chris **bought up** all the land in the surrounding area.
  克里斯買下了附近所有的土地。

5

sell 賣 + **out** 徹底地

→ **sell out**
銷售一空；出清 [不及]

SOLD OUT

| 片語動詞 |

用法 ◆ **sell out of sth**
某事物銷售一空
→ They **sold out of** the T-shirts in the first couple of hours.
T恤在他們開賣的幾個小時內便**銷售一空**了。

💡 名詞為 **sellout**。

- The new edition of his book **sold out** in just a few hours!
  他的書出了新版本，幾個小時內便**銷售一空**了！
- The store **sells out** of ice cream whenever it is hot.
  每當天氣很熱時，店裡的冰淇淋便會**銷售一空**。

片語動詞　可分開　受詞為代名詞時定要分開

Unit 29　Being a Designer 成為設計師

6

work（努力）＋ out（顯露）
→ **work out**

❶ 健身 [不及]
❷ 擬定（計畫）[及]
❸ 想出 [及]
❹ 總共 [不及]
❺ 得到……的結果 [不及]

用法
◆ **work sth out / work out sth**
鏨清某事
→ There will be another meeting tomorrow to **work out** the details of the plan.
明天會舉辦會議鏨清這個計畫的細節。

◆ **work sb out** 理解某人（英式用法）
→ Why does she behave like that? —I can't **work** her **out** at all.
她為何要那樣做呢？我一點也不了解她。

同 想出 ❶ figure out
　　　　❷ straighten out

💡 work out 指「得到……的結果」時，後可加 **well** 或 **all right**，表示「得到好結果」；加上 **badly** 或 **terrible** 則表示「得到不好的結果」。work out 亦指「健身、訓練」，名詞為 workout。

❶ Emmy wants to be healthier, so she **works out** three times a week.
艾咪想要健康的身體，所以每星期會做三次運動。

❸ Byron **worked out** a way to save a lot of money over the summer.
拜倫想出了一個夏天的省錢大計。

❹ The total cost **worked out** to around $400. 一共約 400 元。

7

片語動詞

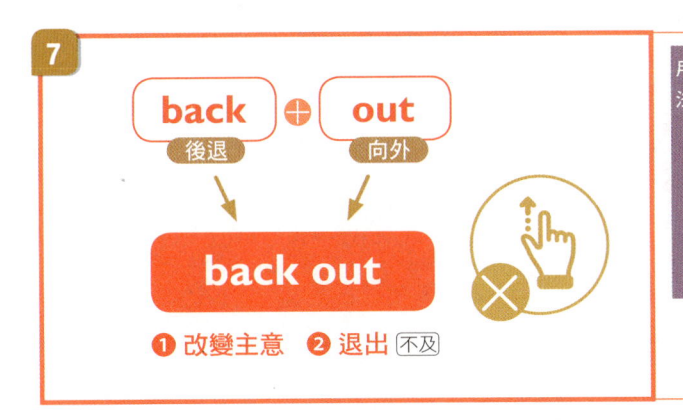

back（後退）＋ out（向外）
→ **back out**

❶ 改變主意　❷ 退出 [不及]

用法
◆ **back out of sth** 退出某事
→ We **backed out of** the deal the day before we were due to sign the contract.
我們在簽約的前一天退出了這項交易。

❶ Although Bryan had agreed to buy Tracy an espresso machine, he **backed out** and gave her a new purse instead.
雖然布萊恩答應買一台咖啡機給崔西，但他改變主意買了一個新皮包給她。

❷ Laura **backed out** of her work contract and quit.
蘿拉中止工作合約後便辭職了。

245

8

back (在背後支撐著) + **up** (起來) → **back up**

❶ 聲援 [及]
❷ 倒車 [不及]

片語動詞 | 可分開 | 受詞為代名詞時定要分開

用法
- **back sb up / back up sb** 支持某人
  → My family **backed** me **up** throughout the court case.
  我的家人在整個打官司的過程中都**支持**著我。
- **back sth up / back up sth** 支持某事
  → My claims are **backed up** by recent research.
  我透過最近的研究來**支持**我的論點。

💡 名詞為 **backup**。

❶ The central idea of your research paper is very interesting, but you need to **back** it **up** with some evidence.
你的研究報告的論點非常吸引人，不過你需要一些證據來**支持**這個論點。

❶ A good theory is **backed up** with observations and data.
完整的學說會以觀測資料**作為支援**。

❷ The taxi driver passed by my apartment, so he had to **back up**.
計程車司機駛過了我家公寓，所以他必須**倒車**。

9

throw (丟) + **out** (向外) → **throw out**

❶ 丟棄　❷ 驅逐
❸ 提出　❹ 駁回（意見、計畫等）[及]

片語動詞 | 可分開 | 受詞為代名詞時定要分開

用法
- **throw sb out** 驅逐某人
- **throw sth out** 駁回某事

比較
- **throw away** 丟棄

❶ Those shoes are really old; it's time to **throw** them **out**.
這些鞋子真的很舊了；該**丟**了。

❷ Tim got **thrown out** of the club because he tried to start a fight with some people. 提姆因為險些釀成打群架而被**趕出**俱樂部。

❸ Let me **throw** this concept **out** to you and see if you like it.
請讓我**提出**我的想法，再看看你是否喜歡。

❹ The lawsuit was **thrown out** of court because there wasn't enough evidence.
這件訴訟案因證據不足而被法院**駁回**了。

246

10

throw(拋) + **up**(向上) → **throw up**

❶ 嘔吐
❷ 產生新想法或問題
❸ 提起 [及][不及]

用法

◆ throw up sth / throw sth up
吐出某物
→ I **threw up** my breakfast all over the back seat of the car.
我把早餐吐得車子後座都是。

◆ throw up sth / throw sth up
提出想法（英式用法）
→ The meeting **threw up** some interesting ideas.
會議中出現了一些很有趣的想法。

同 嘔吐 vomit

❶ Diane had a stomachache and **threw up** on the school bus.
黛安胃痛，於是在校車上吐了。

❷ The discussion group **threw up** some great ideas.
這個討論小組想出了一些很棒的方法。（英式用法）

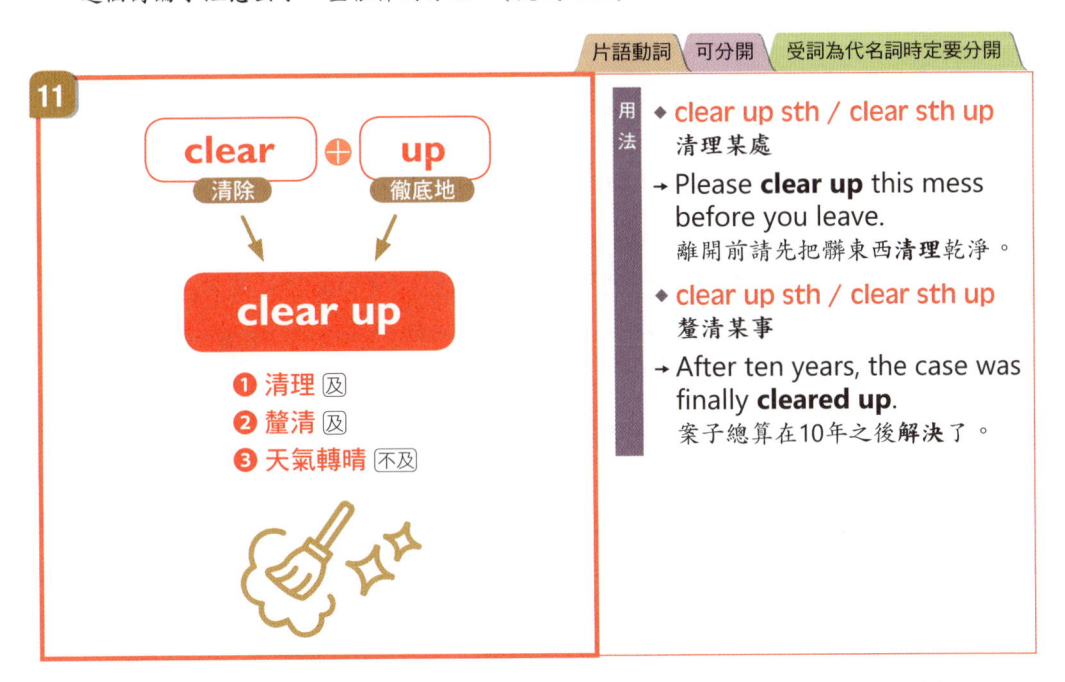

11

clear(清除) + **up**(徹底地) → **clear up**

❶ 清理 [及]
❷ 釐清 [及]
❸ 天氣轉晴 [不及]

用法

◆ clear up sth / clear sth up
清理某處
→ Please **clear up** this mess before you leave.
離開前請先把髒東西清理乾淨。

◆ clear up sth / clear sth up
釐清某事
→ After ten years, the case was finally **cleared up**.
案子總算在10年之後解決了。

❷ Joanne's doctor **cleared up** any questions about her worsening health.
瓊安的醫生釐清了她健康每況愈下的因素。

❷ Wade asked his tutor to help **clear up** his confusion about the English homework. 偉德請家庭老師幫忙釐清他做英文作業時遇到的難題。

❸ The sky began to **clear up** in the afternoon, so football practice wasn't canceled after all. 下午天空開始放晴，所以足球練習並沒有取消。

Unit 29 Test Yourself!

A 選擇題

1. My best friend's software company was _____ by a bigger company last month.
   Ⓐ worked out   Ⓑ caught on   Ⓒ backed up   Ⓓ bought out

2. The total weight of his luggage _____ to be just under thirty pounds.
   Ⓐ caught on   Ⓑ worked out   Ⓒ bought up   Ⓓ threw out

3. Joel _____ all the socks in the shop because they were on sale.
   Ⓐ bought up   Ⓑ caught on   Ⓒ threw out   Ⓓ worked out

4. Please _____ those old books; they're taking up too much space.
   Ⓐ work out   Ⓑ throw out   Ⓒ catch on   Ⓓ back up

5. No scientist will _____ what Dr. Beacon says because his ideas are too hard to prove.
   Ⓐ work out   Ⓑ throw out   Ⓒ back up   Ⓓ catch on

6. Sometimes I'm not sure if you _____ a job with computers; you don't seem to know much about programming.
   Ⓐ buy out   Ⓑ are cut out for   Ⓒ sell out   Ⓓ back up

7. Seymour always makes plans and then _____ of them; you can't rely on him.
   Ⓐ backs out   Ⓑ sells out   Ⓒ clears up   Ⓓ backs up

8. Alice _____ getting a new car, so she is working as much as possible.
   Ⓐ sells out   Ⓑ is cut out for   Ⓒ catches on   Ⓓ has her heart set on

9. The family hired a private detective to help _____ the case of the missing painting.
   Ⓐ sell out   Ⓑ have their heart set on   Ⓒ clear up   Ⓓ back up

10. If we don't buy those movie tickets soon, I'm sure they'll _____.
    Ⓐ sell out   Ⓑ back up   Ⓒ buy out   Ⓓ catch on

11. The CEO of the company hopes that the new running shoes will _____ with athletes around the world.
    Ⓐ catch on   Ⓑ buy out   Ⓒ back up   Ⓓ sell out

B 閱讀文章，從字表中選擇詞彙填入，並依人稱時態等做適當的變化

back out	buy up	be cut out for
work out	have one's heart set on	back up
sell out	clear up	catch on

Yesterday, I found out that my neighbor Tim is selling his baseball card collection. I've ❶ _____ getting those cards, so as soon as I heard that he wanted to ❷ _____ his collection, I told him that I'd ❸ _____ every last one. Tim told me that I should do it soon because interest in these cards was ❹ _____ among his friends. I realized then that I had no money to pay for the cards; however, I knew I shouldn't ❺ _____ of my offer to buy them all. So I sat down and ❻ _____ the numbers: If I sold my car and video games, I'd have enough cash.

Well, that ❼ _____ one problem—I'd have enough money to buy those cards. But it created another problem: I need a car to get to work. I wondered about taking the bus instead. The bus wouldn't get me to work on time, however. I would have to promise to work harder to make up for the lost time. My boss would probably make me ❽ _____ that claim by doing more paperwork, though. Maybe he'd even end up firing me. That would be okay, because I never felt that I ❾ _____ that job. Anyway, at least I would have a great baseball card collection!

C 引導式翻譯，並依人稱時態等做適當的變化

1. 海倫試著唸過幾次大學，但她最後決定她並不**適合**接受高等教育。
   Helen tried college a couple times, but she finally decided she wasn't _____ _____ _____ higher education.

2. 藍尼**下定決心**要娶克莉絲汀，不過我覺得不可能。
   Lenny _____ _____ _____ _____ marrying Christina, though I don't think it'll happen.

3. 這本雜誌的第一刷兩天前便**賣光**了。
   The first issue of the magazine _____ _____ two days ago.

4. 我在想這個遊戲是否會受到年輕人的**歡迎**？
   I wonder if the game will ever _____ _____ with young people?

5. 這件訴訟案因證據不足而被法院**駁回**了。
   The case was _____ _____ by the courts because of lack of evidence.

Unit 30

The Ruined Cake
毀掉的蛋糕

Suzie and Emory are chatting about a ruined cake.
蘇西和艾墨利在聊一個毀掉的蛋糕。

Suzie: I'm so upset! The cake I made last night is ruined! Oh boy, I worked so hard on it . . .

我好生氣！我昨晚做的蛋糕全毀了！天啊，我可是費盡心力耶……。

Emory: Don't **beat around the bush**[1]! Just tell me what happened.

講話別**兜圈子**了！快告訴我怎麼回事。

Suzie: Someone left it uncovered in the fridge, and it **dried out**[2]. It looks like someone took a bite out of it as well! It looks terrible.

有人沒把蛋糕蓋上盒蓋就放入冰箱，整個蛋糕都**乾掉**了，好像還有人偷吃了一口！真糟糕。

Emory: I bet your roommate was just **fooling around**[3]. He probably did it as a joke.

我賭是妳室友**搞的鬼**。他可能只是開個玩笑。

Suzie: No, I think he did it to **get even with**[4] me. He's trying to **stir up**[5] a fight!

不，我認為他是在**報復**我。他只是想要**激怒**我，和我吵一架！

Emory: **Slow down**[6]! You're talking too fast. Do you really think he **is up to something**[7]?

說**慢一點**，妳講太快了。妳真的認為他在**盤算**些什麼嗎？

Suzie: There's no question. He's still mad at me for **putting an end to**[8] his dream of becoming a famous architect by accidentally spilling coffee all over his designs.

沒錯。他還在氣我不小心把咖啡灑在他的設計圖上，害他**結束**了成為名建築師的夢想。

Emory: Aha! Well, that explains things . . .

啊哈！喏，這不就解釋了一切……。

250

Unit 30 The Ruined Cake 毀掉的蛋糕

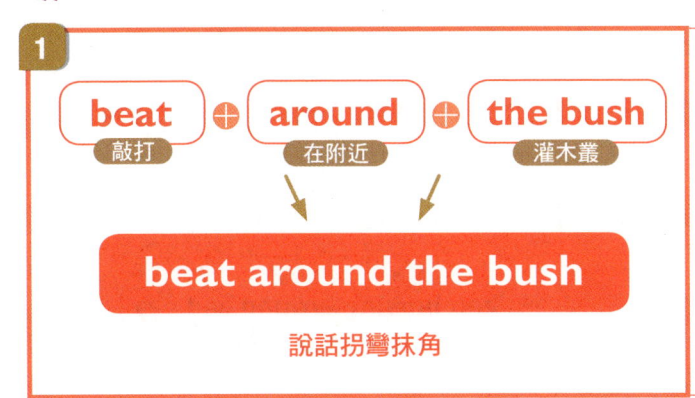

1 慣用片語

beat (敲打) + **around** (在附近) + **the bush** (灌木叢)
→ **beat around the bush**
說話拐彎抹角

同 beat about the bush
反 有話直說
  ❶ get to the point
  ❷ come to the point

💡 原指「打獵時，繞著灌木叢四周拍打，尋找獵物」，後引申為「旁敲側擊；拐彎抹角」。

- Kyle was embarrassed to tell his boss that he was quitting, so he **beat around the bush** for a while. 凱爾不好意思告訴老闆他要辭職，所以他講話一直兜圈子。
- Lyle **beat around the bush** before he asked Jenna to the prom.
  萊爾在邀請珍娜參加舞會前，講話一直**拐彎抹角**。
- Quit **beating around the bush** and tell me what you really think about my idea.
  別**拐彎抹角**了，告訴我你覺得我的意見如何。
- Don't **beat around the bush**—get to the point! 別**拐彎抹角**了，有話就直說吧！

2 片語動詞

dry (變乾) + **out** (徹底)
→ **dry out**
使變乾 及 不及

比較 ◆ **dry up** 枯竭
→ Every fall, the stream behind my house **dries up**.
  我家後面的小溪每年秋天都會**枯竭**。
→ The puddles left by the rainstorm during the night **dried up** in the morning sun.
  晚上下了一場大雨，早晨的太陽照得地上的積水都**乾**了。

同 dry off

💡 **dry out** 表示「變乾」，用來強調「逐漸失去水分而變乾的過程」。

- The potatoes I left in the sun **dried out** and became hard.
  我放在太陽底下**曬乾**的馬鈴薯變硬了。
- In the countryside, people sometimes hang meat in the sun so it **dries out**.
  鄉下人有時會把肉掛在太陽底下**曬乾**。

251

3

fool (愚弄) + **around** (到處) → **fool around**

開玩笑；遊手好閒 [不及]

同 鬼混
① fool about
② goof around
③ idle away
④ mess about（英式用法）
⑤ horse around
⑥ mess around

- Stop **horsing around** and pay attention to your father!
  別鬧了，注意聽你父親所說的話！
- The kids were just **messing around** at the mall.
  孩子們只是在購物中心**打發時間**。

💡 fool around 表示「閒混度日；無所事事；虛擲光陰」，意指「鬼混」，後使用 with 再接人則可表示「與某人鬼混」。

- Ed **fooled around** all weekend and didn't do any work.
  艾迪週末都在**鬼混**沒寫作業。
- Don't **fool around** in class, or the teacher will call your parents!
  上課別**打混**，否則老師會打電話給你的父母！
- Jimmy is always getting in trouble for **fooling around** in class.
  吉米老是因為上課**打混**而惹上麻煩。

4

get (使) + **even** (相等) + **with** (與……) → **get even with**

報復

用法
- get even with sb
  向某人報復
- get even with sb for sth
  為某事向某人報復

同
① be even with
② take revenge on

- Jackie decided to **get even with** Mohammed for teasing her in front of her friends. 穆罕默德在賈姬朋友的面前取笑她，所以賈姬決定**報復**他。
- How do you plan to **get even with** Juliana for ruining your party?
  茱莉安娜破壞了你的派對，你要如何**報復**她？
- I want to **get even with** the guy who hit me with the ball. 我想**報復**用球打我的人。

5

stir（鼓勵）＋ **up**（起來）→ **stir up**

激起；引起問題 [及]

| 片語動詞 | 可分開 | 受詞為代名詞時定要分開 |

用法
- **stir up sb / stir sb up**
  鼓勵某人行動
- **stir up sth / stir sth up**
  惹上麻煩；產生不開心的情緒
→ The teacher told me to stop **stirring up** trouble.
  老師要我不要再惹上麻煩了。

[同] get under one's skin

- Looking at her high school yearbook **stirred up** some sad memories for poor Tina.　可憐的緹娜在看高中畢業紀念冊時，激起了許多不愉快的回憶。
- The fight between the two boys **stirred** the problem **up** even more.
  這兩個男孩之間的爭吵引起了更嚴重的紛爭。

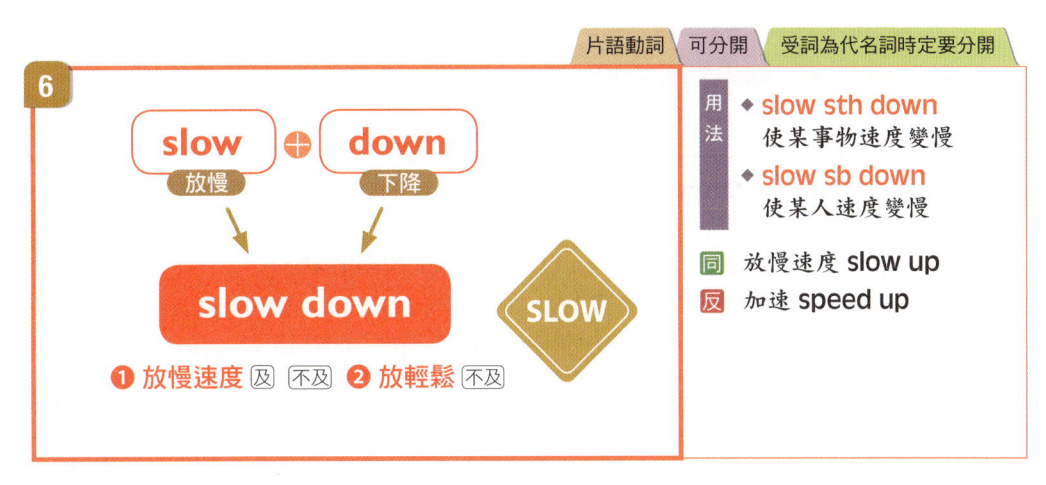

6

slow（放慢）＋ **down**（下降）→ **slow down**

❶ 放慢速度 [及][不及]　❷ 放輕鬆 [不及]

| 片語動詞 | 可分開 | 受詞為代名詞時定要分開 |

用法
- **slow sth down**
  使某事物速度變慢
- **slow sb down**
  使某人速度變慢

[同] 放慢速度 slow up
[反] 加速 speed up

💡 **slow down** 的意思與 **slow up** 相同，但 **slow down** 的用法較為常見。

❶ You're driving close to a school; please **slow down**.
  你開到學校附近了，請開慢一點。

❶ I wish the driver would **slow** the bus **down**; he's driving dangerously fast!
  我希望有人能讓公車司機開慢一點，開這麼快很危險！

❷ The doctor told him to **slow down** or he'll have a heart attack.
  醫生要他放輕鬆，否則會得心臟病。

7

be up to (忙於) ⊕ **something** (某事)
↓
be up to something
策劃；盤算

用法 ◆ be up to something bad / be up to no good
圖謀不軌

💡 此片語通常用來表示「策劃不好的事情」。

- Eli is acting pretty strange; I think he **is up to something**.
  依萊最近舉止怪異，我想他在**暗中盤算些什麼**。

- It seems as if Carl **is up to something**—he's probably planning a surprise party.
  卡爾看來在**策劃些什麼**，他可能打算辦一場驚喜派對。

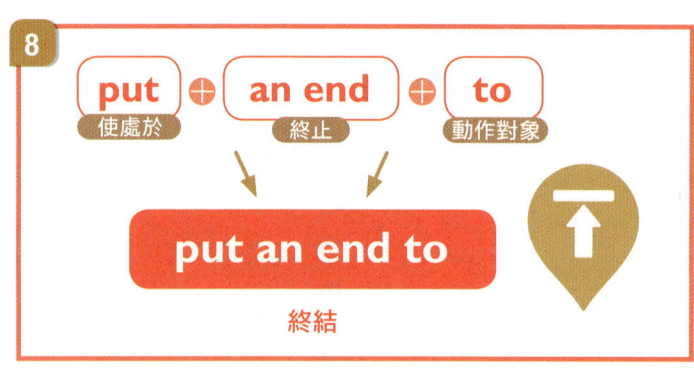

8

put (使處於) ⊕ **an end** (終止) ⊕ **to** (動作對象)
↓
put an end to
終結

同 bring sth to an end

💡 此片語的意思與 come to an end 相同，但用法不同。此片語的**主詞可以為人或事物**，表示「某人或某事物終止了某事」。

- The ringing phone **put an end to** our private conversation.
  我們的私下談話因為電話聲響起而**結束**。

- A terrible rainstorm **put an end to** our day at the beach.
  一場暴風雨來襲，**結束**了我們在海邊的行程。

9

come to (達到) ⊕ **an end** (終止)
↓
come to an end
終結

💡 此片語義同 put an end to 相同，但用法不同。此片語的主詞為**物**，表示「某事結束了」。

同 come to a close

- There is an English idiom that says "All good things must **come to an end**."
「天下無不散的筵席」是一句英文諺語。
- When my boss asked for our opinions, I thought the meeting would never **come to an end**. 當老闆問起我們的意見，我感覺這個會議永遠不會**結束**。

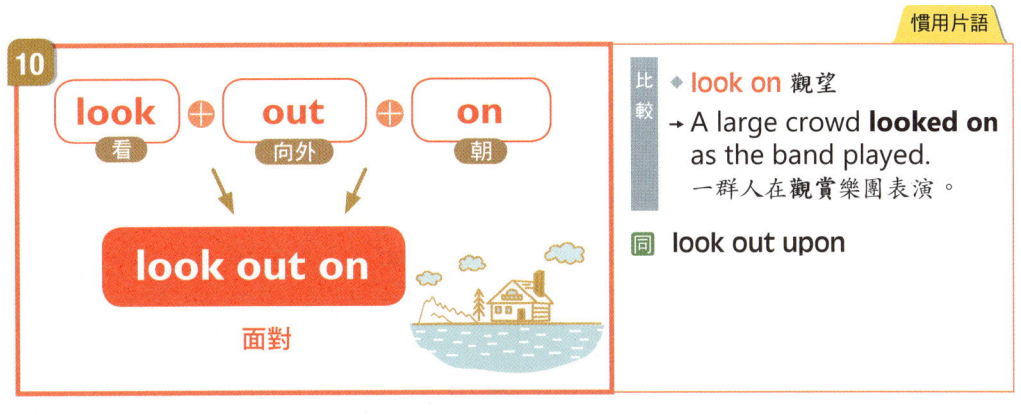

10 慣用片語

look（看）＋ **out**（向外）＋ **on**（朝）
→ **look out on** 面對

比較
- **look on** 觀望
  → A large crowd **looked on** as the band played.
  一群人在**觀賞**樂團表演。
- 同 **look out upon**

💡 **look out on** 表示「某地面向某地方」，主詞和受詞皆為表示地方的名詞。

- Sam's new apartment **looks out on** the Brooklyn Bridge.
山姆的新公寓**正對著**布魯克林大橋。
- The five-star hotel **looks out on** the ocean. 這間五星級飯店**面對著**大海。

11 片語動詞　可分開　受詞為代名詞時定要分開

take（接受）＋ **in**（在裡面）
→ **take in**
❶ 學習；理解　❷ 欺騙
❸ 拜訪　❹（衣服）改小 及

用法
- **take sth in / take in sth**
  理解某事
- **take sb in / take in sb**
  欺騙某人
- **take sth in / take in sth**
  改小某物

同
理解 **catch on**
欺騙某人 **take sb for a ride**
放大尺寸 **let out**

❶ Gwen was very interested in the class, so she **took in** everything the professor said. 關對這門課非常有興趣，所以她把所有教授說的話都**記住**了。

❷ The old lady was **taken in** by the used car salesman, who convinced her to buy a car she didn't want.
這位老太太被賣二手車的推銷員**騙**了，他說服她買了一台她不想要的車。

❸ During their first night in Paris, the happy couple walked around and **took in** the sights.　在抵達巴黎的第一個夜晚，這對幸福的夫妻四處**拜訪**了許多名勝。

❹ I'll have to **take** this dress **in** at the waist. It's too big.
我必須把這件洋裝的腰圍**改小**，它太大了。

Unit 30 Test Yourself!

A 選擇題

1. The crying baby _____ a good night's sleep.
   Ⓐ dried out   Ⓑ got even with   Ⓒ put an end to   Ⓓ fooled around

2. The lake where I used to go fishing has _____.
   Ⓐ dried up   Ⓑ slowed down   Ⓒ fooled around   Ⓓ beat around the bush

3. Mrs. Stein talked and talked, but because Miranda was tired, she didn't _____ anything _____.
   Ⓐ dry . . . out   Ⓑ take . . . in   Ⓒ slow . . . down   Ⓓ stir . . . up

4. Ursula ripped Francis' favorite sweater to _____ for losing her earrings.
   Ⓐ fool around   Ⓑ get even with her   Ⓒ be up to something   Ⓓ take in

5. I could tell by the way Pat answered the phone that he was _____.
   Ⓐ dried up   Ⓑ coming to an end   Ⓒ up to something   Ⓓ slowing down

6. Please _____. You're walking so fast I can't keep up.
   Ⓐ slow down   Ⓑ come to an end   Ⓒ dry out   Ⓓ beat around the bush

7. Although Barry should have been working this afternoon, he spent his time _____ instead.
   Ⓐ drying out   Ⓑ slowing down   Ⓒ fooling around   Ⓓ stirring up

8. This has been a really stressful semester; I can't wait for it to _____.
   Ⓐ beat around the bush   Ⓑ fool around   Ⓒ dry out   Ⓓ come to an end

9. The hotel room _____ the pool.
   Ⓐ puts an end to   Ⓑ stirs up   Ⓒ looks out on   Ⓓ slows down

10. Ms. Han told Dolores to stop _____ trouble and get to work.
    Ⓐ stirring up   Ⓑ drying out   Ⓒ slowing down   Ⓓ looking out on

11. Brian wasted a few minutes _____ before he proposed to his fiancée.
    Ⓐ beating around the bush   Ⓑ drying up
    Ⓒ slowing down   Ⓓ coming to an end

12. Before I went to work, I left these apples in the sun so they would _____.
    Ⓐ slow down   Ⓑ dry out   Ⓒ come to an end   Ⓓ fool around

B 閱讀文章，從字表中選擇詞彙填入，並依人稱時態等做適當的變化

beat around the bush	get even with	slow down
be up to something	come to an end	put an end to
take in	stir up	fool around

　　I'm not going to ① _____. Let me get straight to the point. As the last semester of high school is finally ② _____, many students are acting crazy. Some have started to ③ _____ trouble; even students who are usually well behaved ④ _____. Some students have tried to ⑤ _____ teachers they dislike by playing jokes on them. I don't think any of my classmates are ⑥ _____ anything the teachers are saying. I suppose the students are excited to begin their life in college—they just want to ⑦ _____ their time in high school. But they have to stop running around. If you ask me, they should ⑧ _____, relax, and stop ⑨ _____ so much.

C 引導式翻譯，並依人稱時態等做適當的變化

1. 每個人都希望戰爭能快點**結束**。
   Everyone wishes the war would _____ _____ _____ _____ soon.

2. 水泥要一段時間過後才會**乾**。
   It will take a while for the plaster to _____ _____.

3. 這堂課很無聊，根本無法**學**到任何東西。
   This lecture is so boring that it is hard to _____ anything _____.

4. 我們要如何才能夠**停止**鬥爭呢？
   How can we _____ _____ _____ _____ the fighting?

Unit 31

Moving Away From Home 離家

🔊 129

Emma asks Marcus what his family thinks of his plan to move to Nebraska.
艾瑪詢問馬克斯關於他的家人對他計劃搬到內布拉斯加州的看法。

Emma:	How did your dad take the news that you've decided to move to Nebraska?	你爸對於你要搬到內布拉斯加州的看法如何？
Marcus:	Actually, he really **kept his head**[1]. At first, he thought I was **putting** him **on**[2].	事實上，他還挺**冷靜**的。他起初以為我在**騙**他。
Emma:	And when he found out you were serious?	那他發現你是認真後的反應是？
Marcus:	Well, **it goes without saying**[3] that he'd prefer me to stay at home, but I guess he isn't as narrow-minded as I thought.	唔，**那還用說**，他當然希望我待在家裡，但他不像我想像中的不開明。
Emma:	And how about your mom? Did she **lose her head**[4]?	那你媽覺得如何呢？她有**慌了手腳**嗎？
Marcus:	Yeah, my mom's different. As soon as I began to tell her the news, she **cut** me **short**[5] and told me I was **wasting my breath**[6].	是啊，我媽的反應就不同了。我才一提起這件事情，她便**打斷**了我的話，還說我在**白費唇舌**。
Emma:	Boy! You must really be **on edge**[7] now!	天啊，那你現在一定**坐立難安**！

258

Unit 31 Moving Away From Home 離家

1

keep (保持) + **one's** (某人的) + **head** (理智)
→ **keep one's head**
保持冷靜；沉著

慣用片語

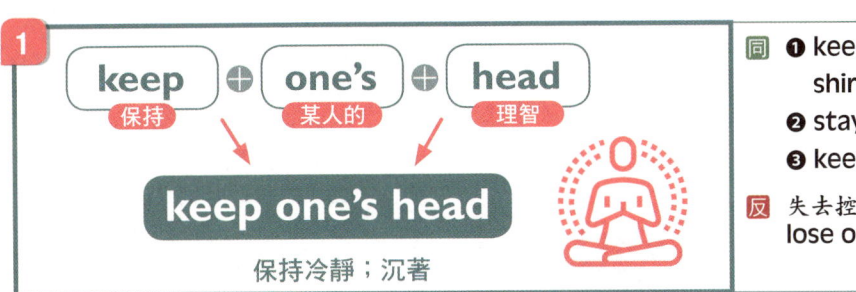

同
❶ keep one's shirt on
❷ stay calm
❸ keep calm

反 失去控制
lose one's head

💡 one 若改為複數時，則 head 也需變成複數形。

- One of Juliet's best qualities is her ability to **keep her head** when things seem totally crazy. 即便事情失控，茱麗葉也能夠**保持冷靜**，這就是她的個人特質之一。
- Calm down and **keep your head**; there's no reason to get stressed out.
  冷靜下來，**保持鎮定**，沒必要那麼緊張。

2

put (使處於) + **sb** (某人) + **on** (在上面)
→ **put (sb) on**
（以開玩笑的方式）欺騙他人

慣用片語

同 joke with sb

- You told me that you were going to study, and now I see you at the movies; it looks like you were **putting me on**.
  你說要去唸書，但我現在發現你在看電影，看來你是在**騙我**。
- I didn't really win a sailboat; I was just **putting you on**.
  我並沒有贏得一艘帆船，我只是**騙你的**。

3

it (它) + **goes** (處於……) + **without** (不用) + **saying** (說)
→ **(it) goes without saying**
不用說

慣用片語

同 needless to say

- **It goes without saying** that in today's world, time is money.
  在現今的社會，**不用說**，時間就是金錢。

259

🔊 131

慣用片語

4

lose 失去 ＋ **one's** 某人的 ＋ **head** 理智

→ **lose one's head** 失去理智

同 **lose one's mind**
- You just spent all that money on a pair of shoes? Have you completely **lost your mind**?
  你把所有的錢都花在一雙鞋子上？你瘋了嗎？

反 保持冷靜 **keep one's head**

- I was so frightened that I **lost my head** completely. 我很害怕到完全**失去理智**了。
- Although Tim is usually calm in class, for some reason he really **lost his head** today. 提姆上課通常都很安靜，但他今天為了一些因素而**失控**了。
- Erin **lost her head** in the meeting this afternoon, and our boss fired her.
  艾琳今天下午開會時**情緒失控**，所以老闆把她解僱了。
- I usually stay quite calm in meetings, but this time I just **lost my head**.
  我開會時通常都很冷靜，但這次我真的**失去理智**了。

慣用片語

5

cut 削減 ＋ **short** 短的

→ **cut short**
❶ 打斷談話
❷ 中斷

用法
- **cut sb short** 打斷某人的話
- **cut sth short** / **cut short sth** 中斷某事

💡 表示「打斷」時，可在 **cut** 與 **short** 之間加人。

❶ While Wanda was telling Chris a boring story about her day at work, he **cut** her **short** and turned on the TV.
當汪達在告訴克里斯辦公室發生的無趣瑣事時，他**打斷**了她，並把電視打開。

❶ Just as Alfredo was getting to the funny part of the joke, his cell phone rang and **cut** him **short**. 當阿爾弗雷多正要進入笑話最精采的部分時，手機鈴聲**打斷**了他。

❶ I started to explain, but she **cut** me **short**, saying she had to catch a bus.
我開始解釋時，她**打斷**了我的話，說她必須去趕公車了。

❷ James **cut** his workday **short** to go home early. 詹姆斯**結束**工作，提早回家。

260

6

waste (浪費) + **one's** (某人的) + **breath** (一口氣)

waste one's breath 白費唇舌

慣用片語

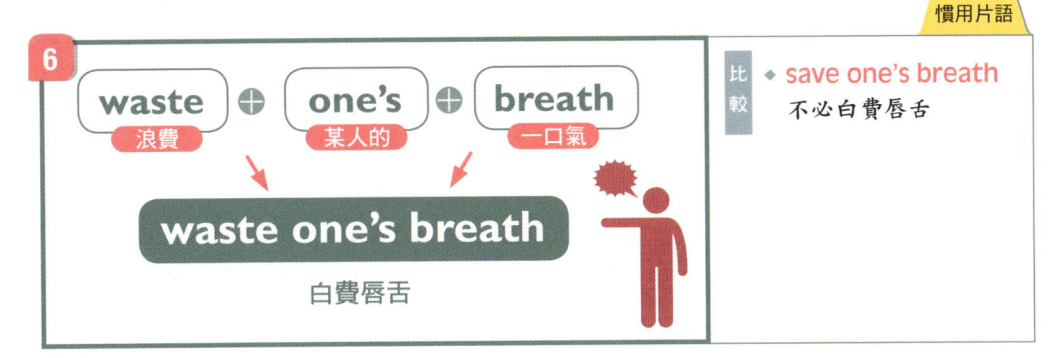

比較 ◆ **save one's breath** 不必白費唇舌

- Don't **waste your breath**—I've already asked him to help, and he said no.
  別**白費唇舌**了，我已經請他幫忙了，但他不願意。
- Phillip is so stubborn; don't **waste your breath** making suggestions.
  菲力普很固執，別**浪費唇舌**提供他意見。
- Eddy lectured his sister on how dangerous it is to go out alone in the city at night. However, he was just **wasting his breath** because she wasn't listening.
  艾迪告訴妹妹晚上獨自到市區很危險，但他只是在**白費唇舌**而已，她根本沒在聽。
- Honestly, you're **wasting your breath**—she doesn't want to hear what anyone else has to say. 老實說你在**白費唇舌**，她並不想要聽其他人的看法。

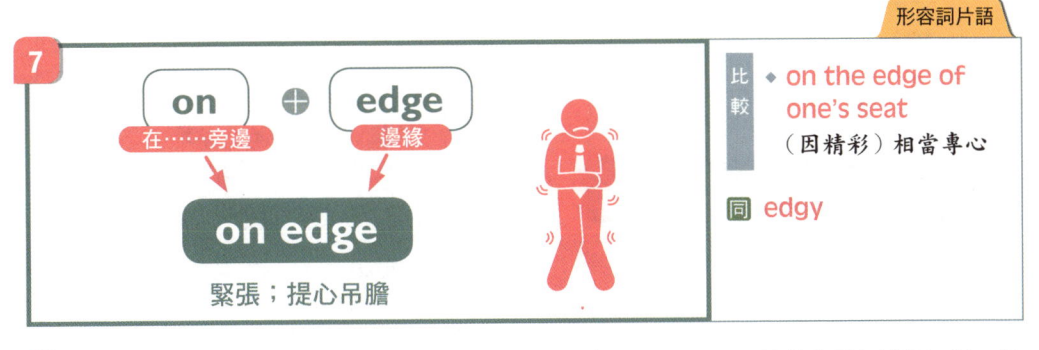

7

on (在……旁邊) + **edge** (邊緣)

on edge 緊張；提心吊膽

形容詞片語

比較 ◆ **on the edge of one's seat** （因精彩）相當專心

同 **edgy**

💡 **on edge** 可置於 **be 動詞**後作主詞補語，亦可置於 **keep**、**stand** 等後作受詞補語。指一個人如果站在懸崖或高樓的邊緣，若一不小心就會喪命，心裡充滿了緊張不安的恐懼，時刻提心吊膽。

- My sisters and I were **on edge** while we waited to hear whether our flight was delayed. 在等待飛機是否會延誤的消息時，我姊妹和我很**緊張**。
- It was the night before her first day of college, and Mel was **on edge**.
  梅兒上大學的前一個晚上非常**緊張**。
- Is something wrong? You seem a bit **on edge** this morning.
  怎麼了嗎？你今天早上看起來有點**不安**。
- You're always **on edge** waiting for an important call because you don't know when the phone will ring.
  你在等重要電話的時候總是很**不安**，因為你無法得知電話何時會響。

🔊 132

8

get 獲得 ＋ **the better of** 比……好

→ **get the better of** 打敗；戰勝

慣用片語

用法
- **get the better of sb** 打敗某人
- **get the better of sth** 戰勝某事物

同
❶ get the best of
❷ have the best of

- Although my teammates and I played our best, the other team **got the better of** us. 雖然我們球隊打得很好，但我們還是被別支球隊**打敗**了。
- My brother **got the better of** his asthma and rarely gets sick anymore. 自從我哥哥的氣喘病**治癒**了後，他便很少生病了。
- Her curiosity **got the better of** her, and she opened the letter. 她在好奇心的驅使下，打開了信。

9

go 走 ＋ **through** 經過

→ **go through** ❶ 找出 ❷ 經歷 ❸ 大量使用 及

片語動詞

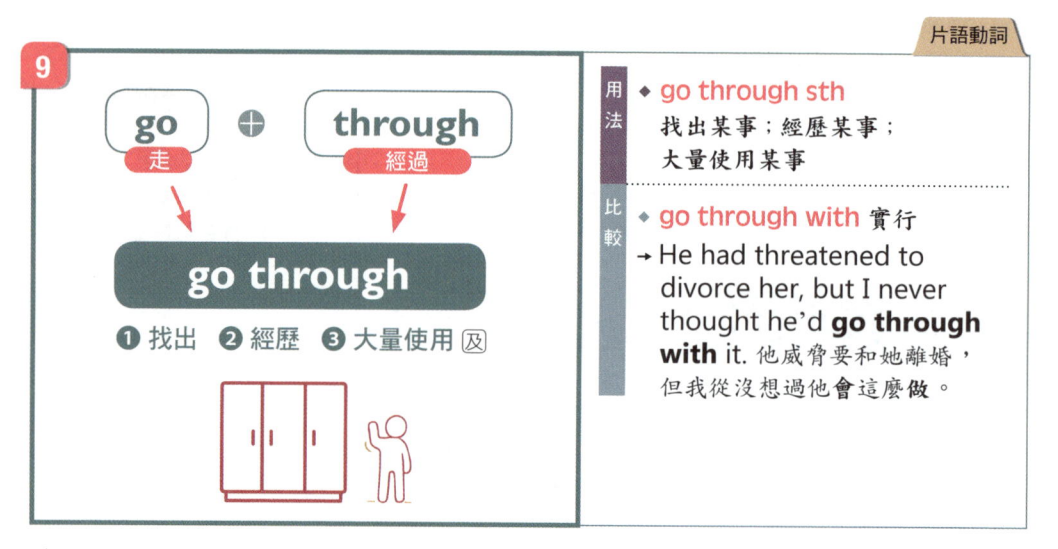

用法
- **go through sth** 找出某事；經歷某事；大量使用某事

比較
- **go through with** 實行
  → He had threatened to divorce her, but I never thought he'd **go through with** it. 他威脅要和她離婚，但我從沒想過他會這麼**做**。

💡 表示「經歷」時，通常是指「不好的事情」。

❶ Olivia is **going through** her closet to find some clothes to donate to charity.
奧立薇亞**翻遍**了衣櫃，找出一些衣服捐給慈善機構。

❷ We'd better let Seth relax; he **went through** a terrible situation at school today.
我們最好讓塞斯休息一下，他今天在學校**經歷**了很不愉快的事情。

❸ My Italian friend **goes through** so much pasta because she eats it for lunch and dinner every day.
我的義大利朋友**吃**了很多義大利麵，她每天中餐和晚餐都會吃。

262

10

break (弄壞) + **loose** (未束縛的) → **break loose**
❶ 掙脫 ❷ 逃跑

慣用片語

比較 ◆ **all hell breaks loose** 亂成一團

❶ We saw a movie where the hero is tied to a chair but he manages to **break loose**. 我們看了一部電影，劇中的男主角被綁在椅子上，但他後來設法**掙脫**了。

❷ During the thunderstorm, all three horses **broke loose** from the barn and ran into the forest because they were scared.
暴風雨來襲時，這三匹馬因害怕而從馬廄**逃**了出來，跑進了森林裡面。

❷ People worry that they will be unsafe if that tiger ever **breaks loose**.
人們很擔心那隻老虎要是**逃跑**了，他們會有危險。

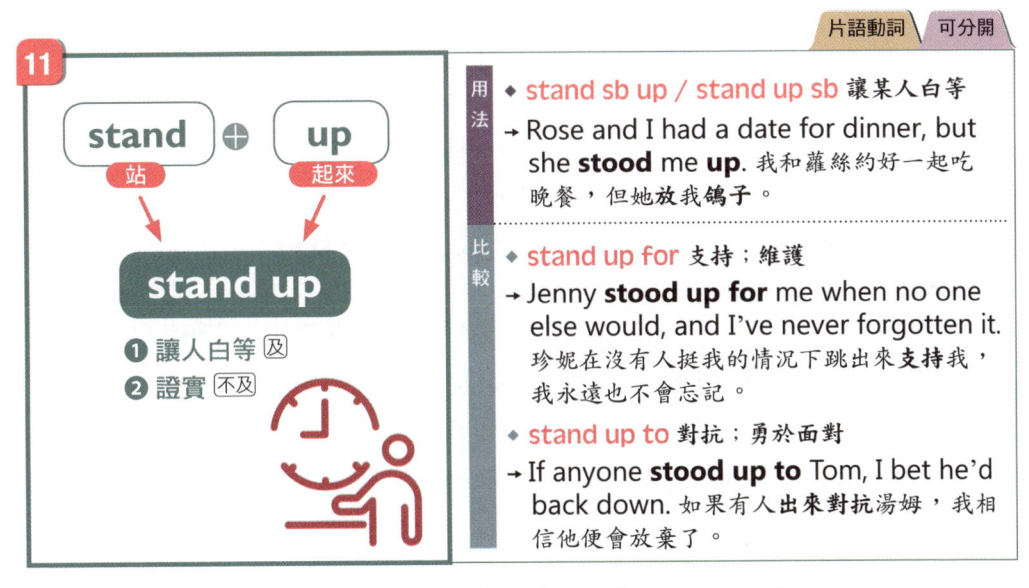

11

片語動詞 / 可分開

stand (站) + **up** (起來) → **stand up**
❶ 讓人白等 及
❷ 證實 不及

用法 ◆ **stand sb up / stand up sb** 讓某人白等
→ Rose and I had a date for dinner, but she **stood** me **up**. 我和蘿絲約好一起吃晚餐，但她**放我鴿子**。

比較 ◆ **stand up for** 支持；維護
→ Jenny **stood up for** me when no one else would, and I've never forgotten it.
珍妮在沒有人挺我的情況下跳出來**支持我**，我永遠也不會忘記。

◆ **stand up to** 對抗；勇於面對
→ If anyone **stood up to** Tom, I bet he'd back down. 如果有人**出來對抗湯姆**，我相信他便會放棄了。

❶ I had planned to take Martin out for dinner, but he **stood** me **up** and never showed up. 我原本打算帶馬汀出去吃晚餐，但他**放我鴿子**，沒有出現。

❷ The information Joel used in his report will never **stand up** to critical review.
喬爾報告中的資料無法**證實**這篇評論。

❷ Their evidence will never **stand up** in court.
他們的證據在法庭上永遠無法**證實**。

263

Unit 31 Test Yourself!

🅐 選擇題

1. When Darryl found out that he didn't get the promotion, he really _____.
   Ⓐ went through Ⓑ put you on Ⓒ stood up Ⓓ lost his head

2. Adrian is _____ trying to convince Florence to study more because she'll never do it.
   Ⓐ breaking loose Ⓑ on edge Ⓒ wasting his breath Ⓓ standing her up

3. I know Travis told you that he bought a ticket to Bermuda, but I think he is _____.
   Ⓐ standing you up   Ⓑ breaking you loose
   Ⓒ putting you on   Ⓓ losing your head

4. Please _____ these documents to find my calendar.
   Ⓐ cut short Ⓑ go through Ⓒ stand up Ⓓ break loose

5. The bell _____ the university lecture, and all the students left.
   Ⓐ stood up Ⓑ lost its head Ⓒ cut short Ⓓ broke loose

6. Don't let the other runners _____; you must go as fast as you can.
   Ⓐ waste your breath   Ⓑ get the better of you
   Ⓒ keep your head   Ⓓ put you on

7. When Ryan crashed his car, I was surprised to see that he _____ and stayed calm.
   Ⓐ kept his head Ⓑ stood you up Ⓒ wasted his breath Ⓓ lost his head

8. On the Sunday before his first day of work, Jay was really _____.
   Ⓐ standing up Ⓑ on edge Ⓒ breaking loose Ⓓ cutting short

9. How did the criminal _____ from the handcuffs?
   Ⓐ break loose Ⓑ cut short Ⓒ stand up Ⓓ waste his breath

10. Please _____ these documents and throw out anything that is more than five years old.
    Ⓐ cut short Ⓑ stand up Ⓒ go through Ⓓ break loose

11. If you ask me, it _____ that you have to work hard to get ahead.
    Ⓐ goes without saying   Ⓑ keeps your head
    Ⓒ stands up   Ⓓ breaks loose

264

B 閱讀文章，從字表中選擇詞彙填入，並依人稱時態等做適當的變化

get the better of	go through	cut short
keep one's head	on edge	it goes without saying
waste one's breath	put on	lose one's head

　　Trust me when I say that I'm not ①_____ you _____ with what I'm about to tell you. I really mean it. ②_____ that Cynthia is one of the most stubborn coworkers in the world. You shouldn't ③_____ _____ trying to help her; just let her do what she wants. Last week, for example, she was having trouble ④_____ her files, so I gave her some advice on how to do it more quickly. Instead of being happy and thanking me, she ⑤_____ and got very mad.

　　She was upset and offended that I even made the suggestion. As she was yelling at me, I ⑥_____ her _____ by leaving the office. I didn't want to hear it anymore! I'm usually a calm person, and I ⑦_____ _____ even though the situation really put me ⑧_____. The point is that no matter how frustrating Cynthia can be, don't let her ⑨_____ you.

C 引導式翻譯，並依人稱時態等做適當的變化

1. 在戒菸之前，我一天要**抽** 30 根香菸。
   Before I gave up smoking, I was _____ _____ 30 cigarettes a day.

2. 試著保持冷靜，別讓憤怒**控制**了你。
   Try to remain calm—don't let your anger _____ _____ _____ _____ you.

3. **不用說**，多練習你的技巧就會進步。
   _____ _____ _____ _____ that you will improve your skills with practice.

4. 這件意外讓我們**緊張不安**了好幾天。
   The accident put us _____ _____ for several days.

5. 你一定是在**騙**我！
   You must be _____ me _____!

Unit 32

Being Kicked Out of School 被退學

Amy tells Arthur about getting kicked out of the university.
愛咪告訴亞瑟有關她被退學的事情。

Arthur: What did your mom say when you told her that you were kicked out of the university?

妳媽知道妳被學校退學後有說什麼嗎？

Amy: She really **went off the deep end**[1].

她**大發雷霆**。

Arthur: Well, I suppose that's understandable. After all, you did copy some texts in your report; you really did **goof up**[2].

嗯，我想那是可以理解的。畢竟，妳真的抄襲了別人的文章。妳真的是**大錯特錯**。

Amy: But it's not fair! I didn't know doing this would be such a big problem! I never knew that copying texts would **screw up**[3] my life so much. And nothing I do helps. I've been **kissing up to**[4] the teacher of that class, but she doesn't care.

可是太不公平了！我不知道這樣做會引起這麼大的麻煩！我又不曉得抄襲他人的文章會**搞砸**我的人生。我後來想要補救，但是都沒有用。我一直想去**討好**該科老師，但她都不理我。

Arthur: Kissing up isn't the best way to deal with this problem. You've really **lost your touch**[5], Amy. You used to be a model student, **more or less**[6]. Now you have to **step down**[7] from your position on the debate team and from your role in the honor society.

討好老師不是處理這個問題的最佳方式。愛咪，妳真是太**沒有經驗**了。**好歹**妳以前也是模範生。現在妳得**退出**辯論社和榮譽學會了。

Amy: What a disaster!

真是糟透了！

Unit 32 Being Kicked Out of School 被退學

1 慣用片語

go off (爆炸) + **the deep end** (極盡頭)
→ **go off the deep end**
勃然大怒

- Alan was a great guy until he **went off the deep end** and started gambling all the time. 艾倫在**脾氣變差**、開始賭博前，一直是個好好先生。
- When Daphne told her father that she had crashed his car, he was so mad that he **went off the deep end**. 當達芙妮告訴父親她把他的車撞壞時，他**勃然大怒**。

2 片語動詞

goof (弄糟) + **up** (程度增加)
→ **goof up**
犯錯 〔不及〕

比較 ◆ goof around 鬼混

- Valerie **goofed up** and showed up at the university on Saturday.
  薇樂麗**搞錯**日子了，她星期六還跑去學校。
- If I go near a skateboard, I'm sure I will **goof up** and fall off.
  我若是站在滑板上，肯定會**玩不好**摔下來。

3 片語動詞 可分開 受詞為代名詞時定要分開

screw (用螺絲拴) + **up** (完全)
→ **screw up**
❶ 搞砸 ❷ 使混淆 ❸ 傷害 〔及〕

用法 ◆ screw sth up / screw up sth
搞砸某事

💡 原指「用螺絲拴緊」，但這裡是表示「搞砸」。

❷ The waiter **screwed** Mira's order **up** and brought her mashed potatoes instead of French fries. 服務生**弄錯**了米拉的餐點，他應該要送薯條過來，而不是馬鈴薯泥。

❸ Nicole really **screwed** Sam **up** when she left him.
妮可離開山姆時真的**把他傷得很重**。

267

4 慣用片語

kiss (吻；輕撫) + **up** (靠近) + **to** (動作對象)
→ **kiss up to** (someone) 討好

- Amanda always **kisses up to** her boss when she wants to take a day off.
  每當亞曼達想休假時，她都會**討好**老闆。
- Kyle **kisses up to** our soccer coach because he thinks it will help him get promoted to team captain.
  凱爾老是在**討好**足球隊教練，因為他認為這樣做就能成為隊長。

5 慣用片語

lose (失去) + **one's** (某人的) + **touch** (觸感)
→ **lose one's touch** 變生疏

💡 此片語原本表示「音樂家失去彈奏樂器時的觸感」，後來引申指「對事物、工作等變生疏」。

- Although Gene's first book was a bestseller, it seems he **lost his touch**—his second book is not so good. 雖然金的第一本書非常暢銷，但他顯然**退步**不少。他的第二本書就沒賣那麼好了。
- When I watched my favorite actress in her newest movie, I saw that she still hasn't **lost her touch**. 我最愛的演員在最新的電影中，演技可是一點都沒**退步**。
- The goalkeeper's performance in the game shows he is not **losing his touch**.
  守門員在這場競賽的表現一點也沒有**變生疏**。

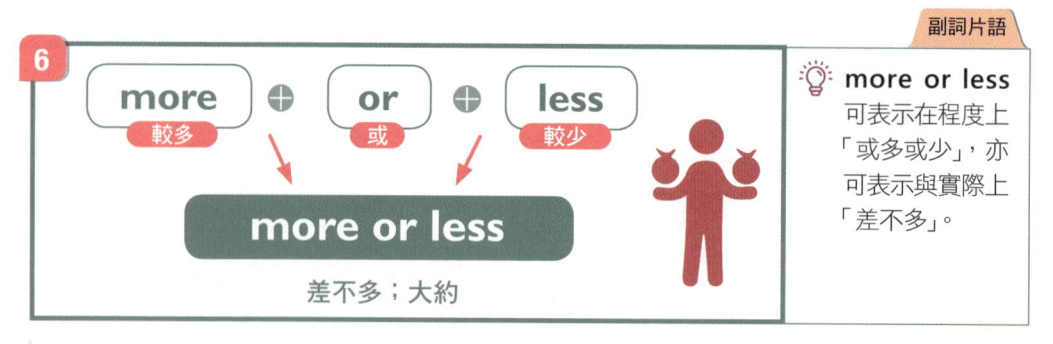

6 副詞片語

more (較多) + **or** (或) + **less** (較少)
→ **more or less** 差不多；大約

💡 **more or less**
可表示在程度上「或多或少」，亦可表示與實際上「差不多」。

- Going on vacation was **more or less** worthwhile; the only problem was that it rained the entire time. 這假期**大致上來說**都很好，唯一的問題是一直在下雨。
- This bag weighs 20 pounds, **more or less**. 這袋東西**大約**重 20 磅。
- The project was **more or less** a success. 這項企畫**大致上來說**是成功的。

片語動詞

7

step 站 + down 起來

→ **step down**

❶ 下來 [不及]
❷ 退休 [不及]
❸ 辭職 [不及]
❹ 減少 [及]

用法

- **step down as sth** 從某職位退休
- → Henry has decided to **step down as** captain of the team.
  亨利決定**辭去**球隊隊長**一職**。
- **step sth down** / **step down sth**
  減少某事物
- → The doctor has said that I can start **stepping down** my medication in a few days. 醫生說我再過幾天便可以開始**減少**藥物量了。

比較

- **step aside** 讓位
- → Amanda is unwilling to **step aside** in favor of a younger person.
  亞曼達不願意**把工作讓給**年輕人。

同 辭職 resign
下降 go down
- Gina **went down** on her knees and begged for forgiveness.
  吉娜跪**下來**請求原諒。

反 上升 go up
留住 stay on
- They asked Ivan to **stay on** as youth leader for another year.
  他們請求艾文**繼續擔任**青年領袖一職。

💡 此片語表示「辭職」時，有「被迫辭職」的意思。

❶ Biff **stepped down** from the ladder and shook Hank's hand.
比夫從梯子**上下來**與漢克握手。

❷ We need to hire a new manager at our company because the last one just **stepped down**. 我們公司需要聘請一位新的經理，上任經理才剛**退休**。

❸ After Ronny got in trouble for taking too long of a vacation, his boss asked him to **step down**. 朗尼因休假太長而造成困擾，老闆要求他自動**請辭**。

8

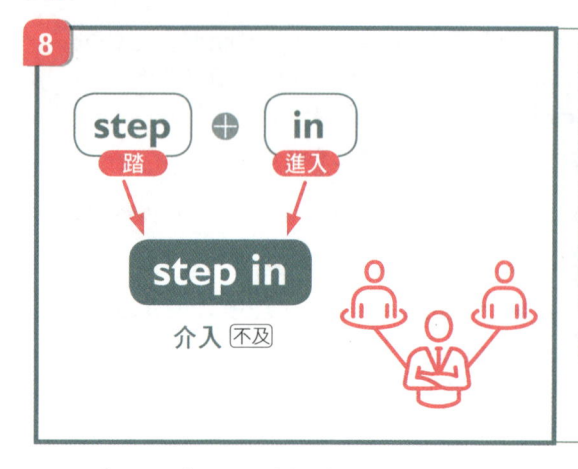

step (踏) + **in** (進入) → **step in**
介入 [不及]

比較
- **step into** 輕鬆找到某工作
  → Ethan **stepped** straight **into** a job as soon as he left college.
  伊森大學一畢業就找到了工作。
- **step on it** 趕快
  → Can you **step on it**? I'm late.
  你可以快一點嗎？我已經遲到了。

同
❶ tamper with
❷ stick one's nose into
❸ poke one's nose into

- When Luke saw his sisters arguing, he **stepped in** and helped them reach an agreement. 路克介入了他兩位姊姊的爭吵之中，幫助他們達成協議。
- I know you haven't asked for my advice, but please let me **step in**.
  我知道你沒有問我的意見，但請容我插句話。
- When Isabelle couldn't teach the class, her sister **stepped in** and gave the lesson.
  伊莎貝爾無法授課，她的姊姊到學校代她上課。
- After the leading actress broke her leg, Jane **stepped in** and played the role.
  女主角摔斷了腿後，珍加入並且接下了這個角色。

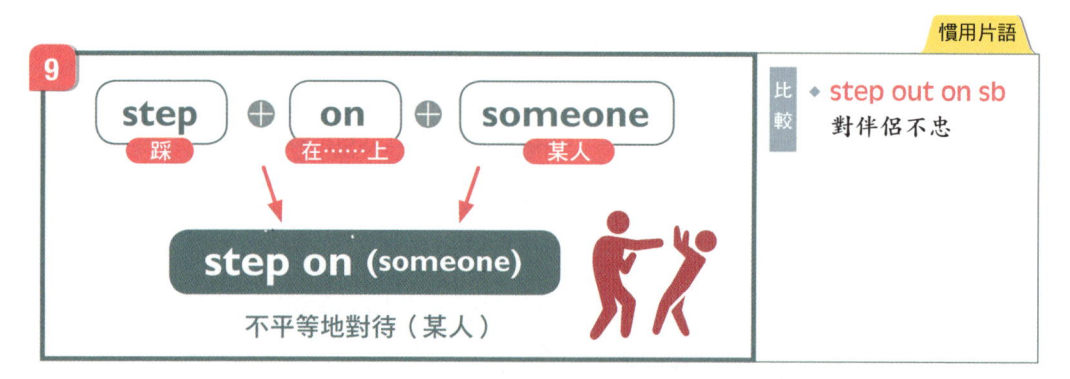

9

step (踩) + **on** (在……上) + **someone** (某人) → **step on** (someone)
不平等地對待（某人）

比較
- **step out on sb**
  對伴侶不忠

- Sometimes the nicest people get **stepped on** the most.
  心地善良的人有時是最會受欺負的。
- You should be more confident and stop letting people **step on** you.
  你應該對自己要有點信心，別再被其他人欺負了。

10

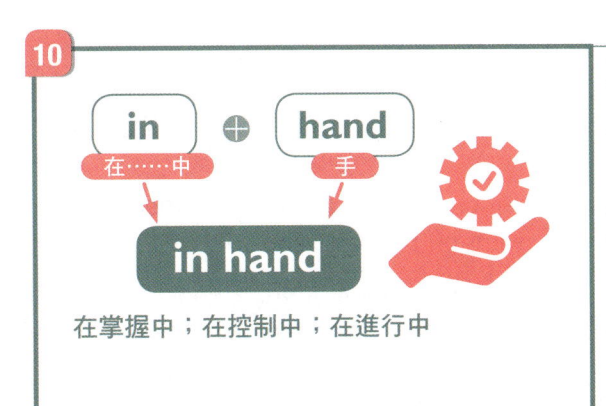

in (在……中) + **hand** (手) → **in hand**

在掌握中；在控制中；在進行中

比較
- **in safe hands** 得到妥善照顧
  → Dr. Grey is doing the operation, so your husband is **in safe hands**.
  格蕾醫生正在動手術，你的先生一定會得到妥善的照顧。

同 under control
反 ❶ out of control
　 ❷ out of hand

💡 **in hand** 表示「在手中」，可用來引申指「事情在掌握之中」。

- Regarding the matter **in hand**, I suggest we cancel the next meeting.
  就目前這件事情而論，我認為應該取消下次會議。
- Because Elaine's birthday is next week, the preparations for the party should be well **in hand** by now. 伊蓮的生日就在下星期，派對現在應該都準備好了。

11

on (在……旁邊) + **hand** (手) → **on hand**

❶ 在手邊；在附近　❷ 待執行

同 在附近
　 ❶ around the corner
　 ❷ at hand

❶ If you don't have a calculator **on hand**, please ask to use your partner's.
如果你手邊沒有計算機，請向組員借。

❶ I need to make a phone call; do you have your cell phone **on hand**?
我需要打通電話，你身上有手機嗎？

12

a (一件) + **steal** (贓物) → **a steal**

真划算

💡 此片語用來誇飾東西就像是偷來的一樣便宜、不用錢。

同 a bargain

- I can't believe you found a computer for only $100—what **a steal**!
  我不敢相信你買了一台才 100 塊錢的電腦，真是太超值了！
- I bought this used cell phone at a good price; it was **a** real **steal**!
  我用很便宜的價格買下了這支中古手機，真是賺到了！

271

Unit 32 Test Yourself!

A 選擇題

1. The two children were fighting until their uncle _____ and calmed them down.
   Ⓐ stepped in   Ⓑ played up to   Ⓒ went off the deep end   Ⓓ goofed up

2. Vince's MP3 player was _____ because he bought it during a huge sale.
   Ⓐ goofed up   Ⓑ a steal   Ⓒ losing his touch   Ⓓ more or less

3. I don't know how much you owe me, maybe $50, _____.
   Ⓐ in hand   Ⓑ more or less   Ⓒ a steal   Ⓓ stepped in

4. Do you have an extra pen _____?
   Ⓐ stepping in   Ⓑ losing its touch   Ⓒ on hand   Ⓓ played up

5. It's no use _____ Ms. Robertson—she will give you the same grade whether she likes you or not.
   Ⓐ goofing up   Ⓑ kissing up to   Ⓒ stepping on   Ⓓ stepping in

6. I know you're trying to be a good guy, but just be careful that your colleagues don't _____ you.
   Ⓐ step off   Ⓑ step in   Ⓒ step down   Ⓓ step on

7. Lyle _____ and locked his keys in the car.
   Ⓐ goofed up   Ⓑ stepped down   Ⓒ kissed up   Ⓓ lost his touch

8. The house painters really _____: They painted the house pink instead of white.
   Ⓐ kissed up   Ⓑ stepped down   Ⓒ screwed up   Ⓓ stepped in

9. I'm thinking of _____ from my position and looking for a new job.
   Ⓐ losing touch   Ⓑ kissing up   Ⓒ losing my touch   Ⓓ stepping down

10. After Jon's girlfriend broke up with him, he really _____ and started acting crazy.
    Ⓐ goofed up   Ⓑ went off the deep end
    Ⓒ played up to himself   Ⓓ lost his touch

B 閱讀文章，從字表中選擇詞彙填入，並依人稱時態等做適當的變化

step down	lose one's touch	step on
go off the deep end	kiss up to	a steal
step in	more or less	

272

June was once a great singer, but for some reason, she has ❶_____ over the last few months. No one knows why; maybe her voice is changing, or maybe she hasn't been practicing enough. A few weeks ago, she tried singing a difficult song; when she couldn't do it, she got really frustrated and ❷_____. A few days later, she ❸_____ from her position as lead singer of the band. June felt she didn't deserve the honor.

A few days later, her mother heard her complaining about this to her friend. June's mother ❹_____ and suggested that June give up singing and instead try to get a job managing another singer. June didn't like that idea; she was afraid that she'd have to ❺_____ that person regardless of whether she liked him or her. She was also afraid that she'd feel ❻_____ and disrespected.

June is not the kind of person to give up easily. She decided that if she couldn't sing, she would do the next best thing: play the guitar. June started looking online, and before long, she found a cool guitar that was so cheap it was ❼_____. So far, she's pretty good at it, ❽_____. However, to be honest, she still has a long way to go before she'll be an expert.

❸ 引導式翻譯，並依人稱時態等做適當的變化

1. 羅伊從摩托車上摔下來時傷到了腿，他現在行動不便。
   Roy really _____ _____ his legs when he fell off his motorbike; now he has trouble walking.

2. 這個箱子約重 50 磅。
   The box weighs 50 pounds, _____ _____ _____.

3. 在伯奈特的新書中，他創造有趣故事主角的**技巧**似乎已經**生疏**了。
   In his latest book, Burnett seems to have _____ _____ _____ for creating interesting characters.

4. 一位外面的買家**介入**，把公司從破產邊緣中救了起來。
   An outside buyer has _____ _____ to save the company from going out of business.

5. 如果派特再不還他欠的錢，吉米就會**大發雷霆**。
   Jimmy will _____ _____ _____ _____ _____ if Pat can't pay him the money he owes.

6. 我們有許多時間可以準備，所以一切的安排都在**掌握**中。
   We've had plenty of time to prepare, so the arrangements should be well _____ _____.

7. 史密斯先生等一下會**在旁邊**回答有關於這部電影的問題。
   Mr. Smith will be _____ _____ later to answer questions about the film.

Unit 33

Kicking the Habit
戒掉惡習

Ronald tells Wendy about his new plan.
羅納德把新計畫告訴溫蒂。

Wendy: Why are you smiling? Something must be **looking up**[1] for you.

你為何笑得這麼開心呢？一定是有什麼**好事**。

Ronald: You got it! I'm in a good mood because I've been **kicking around**[2] an interesting idea.

沒錯！我的心情很好，因為我一直在**思考**一項有趣的計畫。

Wendy: What's the idea? Tell me!

什麼計畫？快告訴我！

Ronald: Well, I noticed yesterday that I had gained five more pounds, and that's the **last straw**[3]. I watch too much TV, and I'm too fat. It's time for me to **kick the habit**[4] of eating junk food and being lazy.

唔，我昨天發現體重增加了五磅，我**不能再這樣下去**了。我看太多電視，吃太多東西了。我該**戒掉**吃垃圾食物和懶惰的**壞習慣**了。

Wendy: Sounds like you're really **on the ball**[5] with this idea. But what are you going to do?

看來你已經很**清楚**你的想法了，但你要怎麼做呢？

Ronald: A group of friends and I will **put together**[6] a basketball team, and we'll practice three times a week. This way, we'll all have a good time. I can lose some weight, and when my girlfriend sees how good I look, maybe she'll want to **make up with**[7] me. So, you want to join us?

我會和一群朋友**組成**一支籃球隊，每個星期練三次球。這樣一來我們可以玩得很愉快，而我的體重也會減輕。等我女朋友看到我帥氣的模樣時，她也許會想和我**重修舊好**。所以，妳想不想加入我們呢？

Wendy: No thanks. I'm going home to watch a movie and eat some pizza—but have fun!

不，謝了。我想回家看電影，吃披薩，反正你開心就好！

1

look (朝) + **up** (上面) → **look up** 變好 [不及]

比較 ◆ **look up to sb** 敬仰某人

💡 **look up** 在此表示「變好；上漲」，作不及物動詞，另有「查詢；拜訪」的意思，可參考第 29 頁。

- Ever since Jasmine got a raise at work, things have been **looking up**.
  潔絲敏加薪後，一切都變得很美好。
- Things are really **looking up** this semester, and I'm getting excellent grades.
  這學期一切都變得很順利，而我的成績也很優異。
- I hope things will start to **look up** in the new year.
  我希望在新的一年事情會變得很順利。

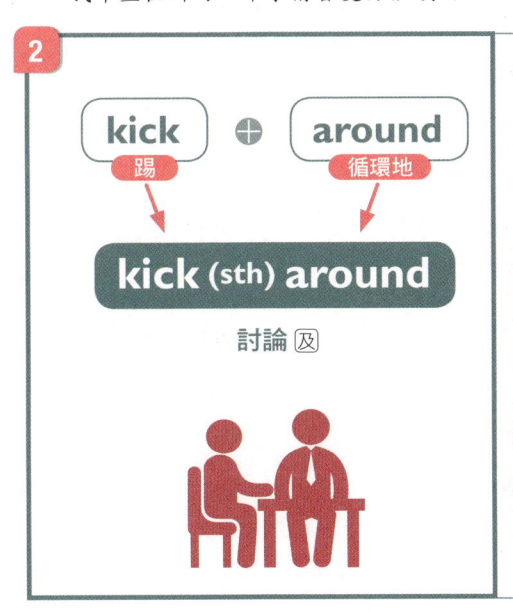

2

kick (踢) + **around** (循環地) → **kick (sth) around** 討論 [及]

片語動詞 | 可分開 | 受詞為代名詞時定要分開

用法 ◆ **kick around sth / kick sth around**
討論某事

比較 ◆ **kick sb around / kick around sb**
仗勢欺人
→ When her boss didn't promote her, she felt as if she'd been **kicked around** long enough, and she finally quit. 老闆不升她官，她覺得自己長期被壓榨，於是最後便辭職了。

◆ **kick around** 存在
→ Jack is one of the most creative people **kicking around** advertising today.
傑克是目前**在**廣告界最具有創意的人物之一。

💡 **kick around** 是指「對某議題進行非正式的討論」。

- We **kicked around** the plan of going on vacation in Spain, but in the end we never went. 我們一直在**討論**西班牙之旅的計畫，但我們最後並沒有去成。
- Agatha **kicked around** the idea of studying psychology, but in the end, she decided not to. 雅嘉薩**考慮**過是否要修心理學這門課，但她最後還是決定放棄。
- I need to get everyone together so we can **kick** a few ideas **around**.
  我必須把所有人聚集在一起，**討論**一些想法。

3

last(最後的) + **straw**(稻草) → **last straw**
造成崩潰的最後一件事

名詞片語

同 ❶ final straw
　 ❷ be fed up with

💡 此片語源自諺語 **the straw that broke the camel's back**（壓垮駱駝的最後一根稻草）。駱駝以其堅忍耐勞的負重特性聞名，但就算是再能負重的動物，也是有極限的，就像人一樣，即便只是一件輕如稻草般的小事情，也足以讓人無法承受而倒地不起。因此，**last straw** 現在常用來表示「忍無可忍；忍耐到了極限」。

- There's a well-known English proverb that says it's "the **last straw** that breaks the camel's back." 「壓垮駱駝的**最後一根稻草**」是一句著名的英文諺語。
- Saul's car breaking down on the way to work was pretty bad, but when it broke down again on the way home, that was the **last straw**.
  索爾的車在上班途中壞掉已經很不幸了，然而車子又在回家路上拋錨，真是衰到了極點。
- Paula has always been rude to me, but it was the **last straw** when she started insulting my mother.
  寶拉對我一直很沒有禮貌，但令人忍無可忍的是她開始羞辱我的母親。

4

慣用片語

kick(戒絕) + **the habit**(壞習慣) → **kick the habit**
戒掉（壞）習慣

同 ❶ break the habit
　 ❷ drop the habit

- Steven used to be a heavy smoker, but he **kicked the habit** last year.
  史帝芬曾經是個老菸槍，但他去年戒菸了。
- Ike finally **kicked his bad habit** of biting his fingernails.
  艾克最後終於**戒掉**咬手指頭的**壞習慣**了。
- Researchers said smokers who **kick the habit** have less chance of developing cancer. 研究人員表示，已戒菸的人罹患癌症的機率會較低。

5

be on (在……上) + **the ball** (球) → **be on the ball** 快速理解；反應靈敏

> 慣用片語
>
> 💡 此片語原指棒球中，打擊者需專注在投手所投出來的球。現在則引申表示「反應靈敏；機警」。

- After his third cup of coffee, Harry **was** really **on the ball**.
  哈利在喝了三杯咖啡之後，終於**清醒**了。
- After getting little sleep the night before, Corey **was** not **on the ball**.
  柯瑞昨晚沒什麼睡，所以**頭腦不清楚**。

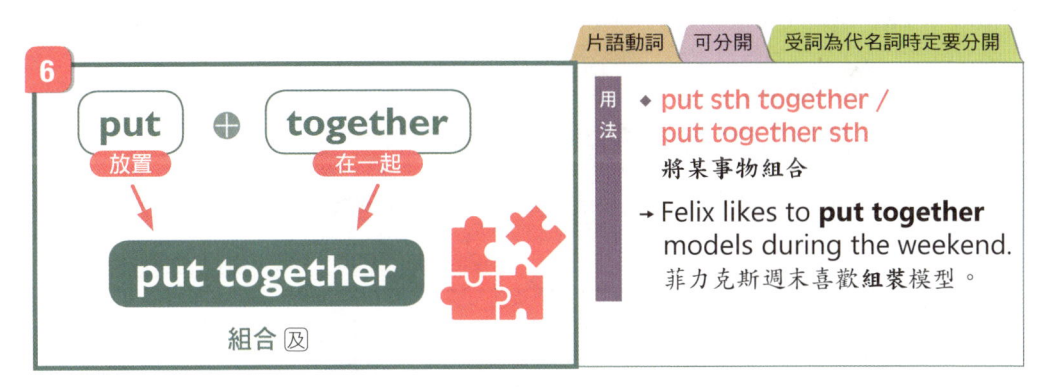

6

put (放置) + **together** (在一起) → **put together** 組合 及

> 片語動詞 | 可分開 | 受詞為代名詞時定要分開
>
> 用法
> ◆ put sth together /
> put together sth
> 將某事物組合
> → Felix likes to **put together** models during the weekend.
> 菲力克斯週末喜歡**組裝**模型。

- Taylor really knows a lot about motorcycles. If you give him all the parts, he can **put** one **together**! 泰勒真的很懂摩托車。只要給他所有的零件，他就可以**組裝**好！
- Model airplanes come in pieces that have to be **put together**.
  模型飛機是一片片的，必須**組裝**起來。

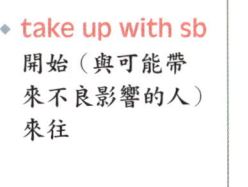

7

make up (補足) + **with** (與……) → **make up with (sb)** 與某人重修舊好

> 慣用片語
>
> 比較
> ◆ take up with sb
> 開始（與可能帶來不良影響的人）來往

- After the argument, Taylor **made up with** Rachel by giving her some flowers.
  爭吵過後，泰勒送花給瑞秋，和她**重修舊好**。
- Joel and Alice had a big fight, and I'm not sure if they'll ever **make up with** one another. 喬爾和艾莉絲大吵了一架，我不確定他們是否還會**合好如初**。

277

8

make (製作) + **up** (完成) → **make up**

❶ 捏造 [及]　❷ 組成 [及]
❸ 化妝 [及][不及]　❹ 和解 [不及]

| 片語動詞 | 可分開 | 受詞為代名詞時定要分開 |

用法
- **make up sth / make sth up**
  虛構某事物
- **make up sth** 組成某事物
- **make (sb/sth) up /
  make up sth** 化妝

❶ Because Ron didn't want to go to the party, he **made** an excuse **up** about having to write a report. 因為朗不想參加派對，所以他用寫報告作為藉口。

❶ Kate **made up** a great story about a princess, which she told her daughter at bedtime. 凱特在女兒睡前念了一個她編的公主故事。

❷ Two halves **make up** a whole. 把兩個二分之一合起來就變成了一整個。

❸ The fashion model was all **made up** for the photo shoot.
時尚模特兒已完妝準備照片拍攝的工作。

❹ They kissed and **made up**, as usual. 他們親吻對方，然後合好，一如往常。

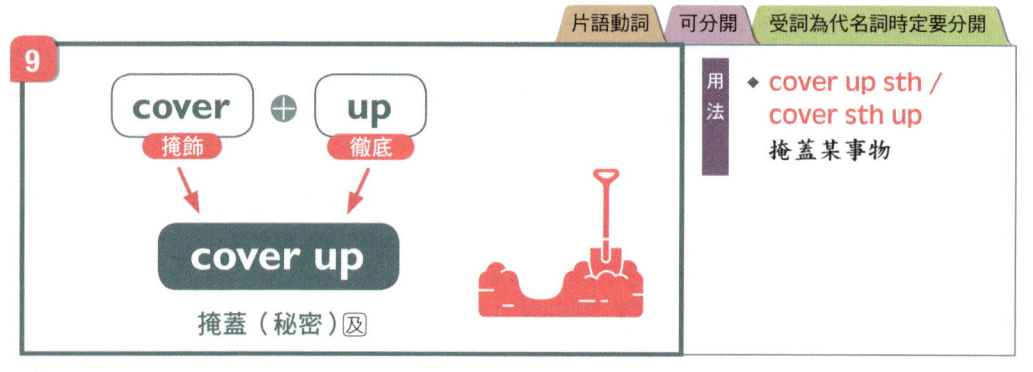

9

cover (掩飾) + **up** (徹底) → **cover up**

掩蓋（秘密）[及]

| 片語動詞 | 可分開 | 受詞為代名詞時定要分開 |

用法
- **cover up sth /
  cover sth up**
  掩蓋某事物

💡 名詞為 **cover-up**。

- Will tried to **cover up** the fact that he was caught cheating, but everyone found out about it. 威爾企圖掩飾他考試作弊被抓的事實，但大家都發現了。

- If you are caught doing something illegal, it may not be a good idea to **cover** it **up**. 做違法的事情如果被抓到，最好不要企圖隱瞞。

- The company tried to **cover up** its employment of illegal immigrants.
公司企圖掩蓋僱用非法移民的事實。

- I was amazed that the building contractors we hired tried to **cover up** the problems they had.
我很意外我們所聘用的建築承包商，竟然企圖掩飾他們所遇到的問題。

10 drop + off

drop (下車) + off (離開) → **drop off**

❶ 留下來 [及]　❷ 在途中下車 [及]　❸ 減少 [不及]

片語動詞｜可分開｜受詞為代名詞時定要分開

用法
- **drop off sb / drop sb off**
  讓某人下車
- **drop off sth / drop sth off**
  留下某事物

💡 表示「載某人到某地後，讓某人下車」時，需點出下車的地點。

❶ Melissa **dropped off** her passport at the hotel and then went off to explore Paris. 瑪莉莎將護照**留在**飯店後，便開始在巴黎觀光。

❷ Jordan **dropped off** her sister at the park and then went to the movies.
喬登讓妹妹在公園**下車**後，便去看電影。

❸ The price of plane tickets to California always **drops off** after the summer.
夏天過後，飛往加州的機票總是會**降價**。

❸ The demand for mobile phones shows no signs of **dropping off**.
人們對於手機的需求一點也沒有**減少**的現象。

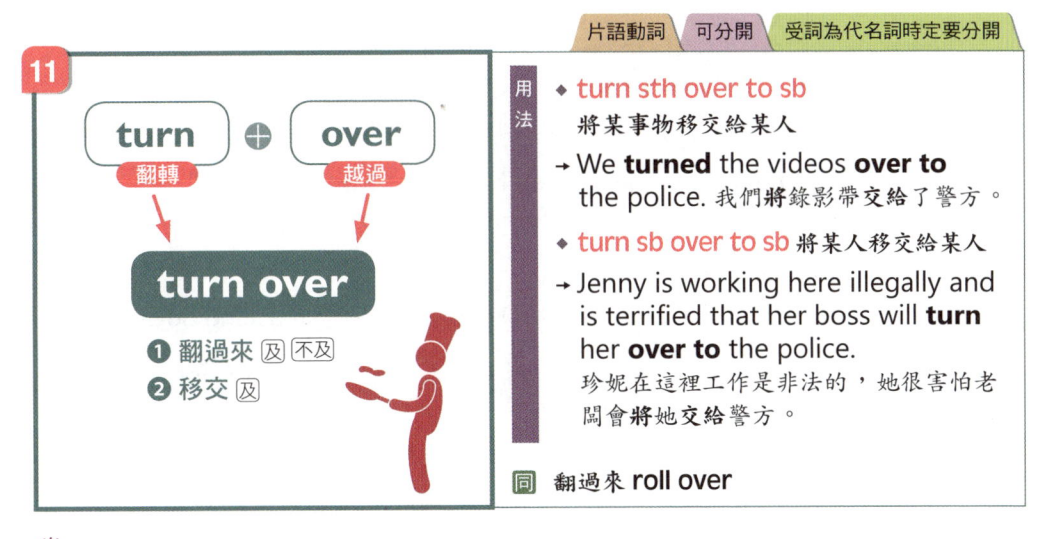

11 turn + over

turn (翻轉) + over (越過) → **turn over**

❶ 翻過來 [及][不及]
❷ 移交 [及]

片語動詞｜可分開｜受詞為代名詞時定要分開

用法
- **turn sth over to sb** 將某事物移交給某人
  → We **turned** the videos **over to** the police. 我們**將**錄影帶**交給**了警方。
- **turn sb over to sb** 將某人移交給某人
  → Jenny is working here illegally and is terrified that her boss will **turn** her **over to** the police.
  珍妮在這裡工作是非法的，她很害怕老闆會**將她交給**警方。

同 翻過來 **roll over**

💡 表示「翻過來」時，可作及物或不及物動詞。

❶ In the middle of the night, Nancy **turned over** and slept on her back.
南西在半夜**翻了個身**，變成仰躺。

❷ Before leaving her job, Dolores **turned over** her tasks to a coworker.
辭職前，桃樂絲把工作**交付**給同事。

Unit 33 Test Yourself!

A 選擇題

1. Mike _____ an excuse after arriving late to school.
   Ⓐ was looking up   Ⓑ dropped off   Ⓒ made up   Ⓓ turned over

2. After we _____ Miriam at the restaurant, we were finally alone.
   Ⓐ kicked around   Ⓑ made up with   Ⓒ dropped off   Ⓓ turned over

3. Gary used to chew a lot of gum, but after talking with his dentist last week, he decided to _____.
   Ⓐ kick the habit   Ⓑ cover up   Ⓒ drop off   Ⓓ turn over

4. Can you help me _____ this puzzle, which I accidentally knocked off the table?
   Ⓐ go up to   Ⓑ put together   Ⓒ take by surprise   Ⓓ hand in

5. Jack got an "A" on his algebra test, asked a girl out on a date, and even won a game of basketball; yes, things definitely _____ for him.
   Ⓐ are looking up   Ⓑ make up with   Ⓒ cover up   Ⓓ drop off

6. The boss got the workers together to _____ a few ideas _____.
   Ⓐ kick . . . around   Ⓑ make . . . up   Ⓒ cover . . . up   Ⓓ drop . . . off

7. I have always found Linda to be rather impolite. However, when she made some ugly comments about my sister, that was the _____.
   Ⓐ last straw   Ⓑ looking up   Ⓒ cover up   Ⓓ big news

8. Jamal _____ the meat in the oven so both sides would cook well.
   Ⓐ made up   Ⓑ dropped off   Ⓒ turned over   Ⓓ put together

9. Sammy is really smart—she is always _____.
   Ⓐ on the ball   Ⓑ kicking around   Ⓒ making up   Ⓓ reaching down

10. After ignoring Frank for several years, Caroline gave him a CD for his birthday as a way to _____ him.
    Ⓐ turn over   Ⓑ make up with   Ⓒ look up to   Ⓓ cover up

11. When the teacher asked Martin if he had copied his article from a newspaper, he tried to _____ it _____.
    Ⓐ cover . . . up   Ⓑ make . . . up   Ⓒ kick . . . around   Ⓓ reach . . . over

B 閱讀文章，從字表中選擇詞彙填入，並依人稱時態等做適當的變化

last straw	cover up	make up
kick the habit	on the ball	drop off
look up	make up with	

Janet and Lou have been a couple for a few years, but last month Janet got really mad at Lou because he forgot her birthday. Of course, at first he tried to ❶_____ his mistake by ❷_____ a story that he and his friends had pulled together a surprise party; but this wasn't true. He was always forgetting things and was never ❸_____. Just a few weeks ago he had forgotten their anniversary, too. Janet felt that forgetting her birthday was the ❹_____, and she broke up with him.

The first days after the breakup were a bit difficult for her, though. She was used to talking to Lou every day, so it was hard to ❺_____ of calling him after work. After a few days, however, things were ❻_____. Janet had changed her life a bit, too. For example, because she usually saw Lou on the bus on the way to work in the morning, Janet arranged to have a taxi ❼_____ her _____ at her company.

After a couple of weeks Lou called Janet. He wanted to ❽_____ her, but as soon as she heard his voice, she hung up. Janet was happy to be alone.

C 引導式翻譯，並依人稱時態等做適當的變化

1. 他昨天清晨五點才醉醺醺的回家，真令人忍無可忍。
   Yesterday, he came home drunk at 5 o'clock in the morning, and that was the _____ _____.

2. 我們將行李留在飯店後便開始觀光。
   We _____ our luggage _____ at the hotel and went sightseeing.

3. 卡門曾經是個老菸槍，但她後來終於戒菸了。
   Carmen used to smoke a lot, but she finally _____ _____ _____.

4. 我們的財務狀況終於開始變好了。
   Our financial situation is _____ _____ at last.

281

Unit 34

Getting Married
結婚

Cleo tells Felix about her uncertainty about marriage.
克莉歐將她對婚姻的遲疑告訴了菲力斯。

Felix: So are you really getting married tomorrow?

看來妳明天真的要結婚了?

Cleo: Actually, I think I'm **getting cold feet**[1], but I could never tell that to my fiancé **face-to-face**[2].

事實上,我有點**害怕**,但我不會把這件事情**當面**告訴我的未婚夫。

Felix: Are you serious? What's happening? Come on, you have to **fill** me **in**[3]!

妳是說真的嗎?怎麼了?說吧,**告訴**我吧!

Cleo: Well, there's no question that I've really **fallen for**[4] him, but I'm just not sure that I want to **be with him**[5] forever.

嗯,我真的非常**愛**他,但我不確定我是否想要和他**共度**一生。

Felix: I think that's perfectly normal. However, you're right—once you get married, it isn't as if you can **trade in**[6] one husband for another! **It figures**[7] that you would be nervous. I guess you really should think carefully about what you want.

我想這很正常,不過妳說的沒錯,一旦結了婚,老公就不能**換**人了!妳會緊張是**理所當然**的。我想妳應該好好想想自己想要什麼。

1

get (處於……狀態) + **cold feet** (雙腳冰冷)

get cold feet 緊張；害怕

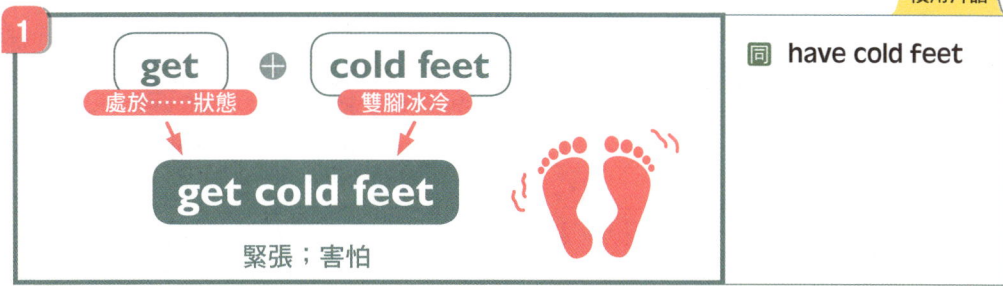

同 have cold feet

💡 用來表示對已決定的事感到懷疑及猶豫緊張。

- Ten minutes before the wedding, Francis **got cold feet** and ran off.
  婚禮前 10 分鐘，法蘭西斯**太緊張**所以臨陣脫逃了。
- You have always wanted to go bungee jumping, so don't **get cold feet** now!
  我知道你一直都想要嘗試高空彈跳，所以別**緊張**嘛！

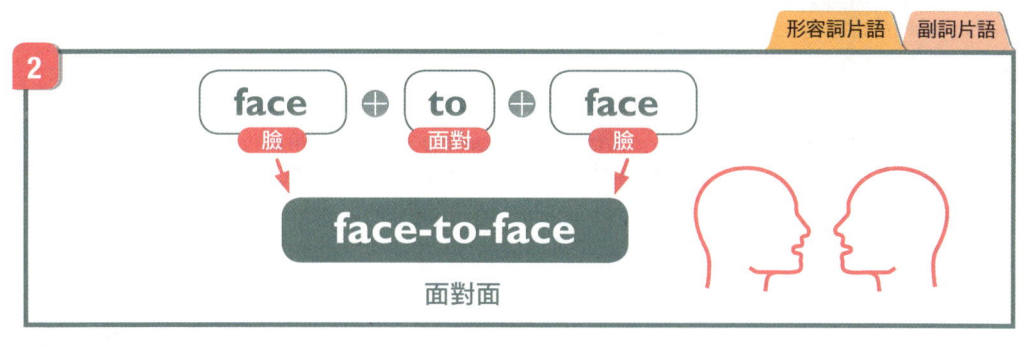

2

形容詞片語　副詞片語

face (臉) + **to** (面對) + **face** (臉)

face-to-face 面對面

💡 可作形容詞或副詞。

- Nate had spoken with Jeb a few times on the phone, but they had never met **face-to-face**. 奈特和傑伯通過幾次電話，但他們從未見過**面**。
- She has refused a **face-to-face** interview, but she has agreed to answer my questions in a letter. 她拒絕**面對面**會談，但同意在信中回覆我提到的問題。

3

片語動詞　可分開　受詞為代名詞時定要分開

fill (滿足) + **someone** (某人) + **in** (在……方面)

fill (someone) in 告訴

用法 ◆ **fill sb in on sth** 告訴某人某事

- Anne **filled** the class **in** on her trip to Canada. 安把加拿大之旅的事情**告訴**全班。
- After Clarence was **filled in** by Tyrone, the two guys got to work.
  泰倫**告訴**克萊倫斯該怎麼做後，兩人便開始行動。

4

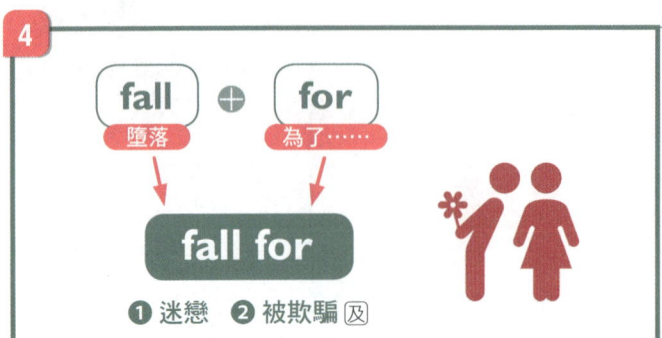

fall + **for**
墜落 + 為了……

→ **fall for**

❶ 迷戀 ❷ 被欺騙 [及]

用法
- **fall for sb** 迷戀某人
- **fall for sth** 因某事物而被騙

❶ Poor Kim! She **fell for** a married man. 可憐的金！她愛上了有婦之夫。
❶ Barry married the first woman he **fell for**. 拜瑞和初戀女友結婚了。
❶ I always **fall for** unsuitable men. 我總是愛上了不該愛的男人。
❶ They met at a friend's party and **fell for** each other immediately.
他們在朋友的派對上相遇，迅速地陷入熱戀。
❷ I stupidly **fell for** her story until someone told me she was already married.
在別人告訴我她已婚之前，我一直傻傻相信她說的話。
❷ Our teacher **fell for** Dylan's story about being sick yesterday; actually, he was at the beach. 狄倫騙老師說他昨天生病，其實他昨天去了海邊。
❷ He told me he owned a castle in Spain, and I **fell for** it.
他說他在西班牙擁有一座城堡，而我真的相信了。

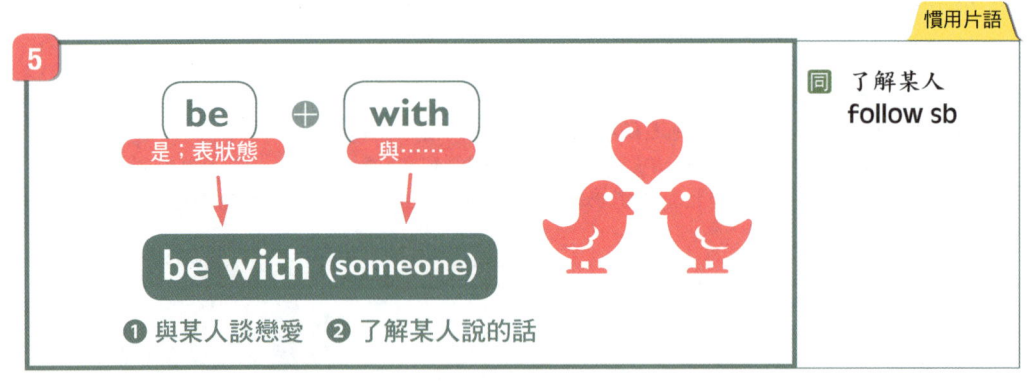

5

be + **with**
是；表狀態 + 與……

→ **be with (someone)**

❶ 與某人談戀愛 ❷ 了解某人說的話

同 了解某人
follow sb

❶ **Are** you **with** Patty, or are you still single?
你和派蒂在交往嗎？還是你依然單身呢？
❷ You look puzzled—**are** you **with** me? 你看起來很困惑，你了解我說的話嗎？

6

trade + **in**
交易 + 以……

trade in
（非金錢的）折抵；
以物換物；以舊換新 及

片語動詞 / 可分開 / 受詞為代名詞時定要分開

名詞為 **trade-in**。

用法
- **trade sth in / trade in sth**
以某事物折抵

- Erin got the price of the new car down when she offered to **trade in** her old SUV.
艾琳新買的車子不貴，因為她用舊的 SUV **折抵**。
- If I **trade in** this TV, will you lower the price of the new one?
如果我用這台電視來**折抵**，你願意算我便宜一點嗎？

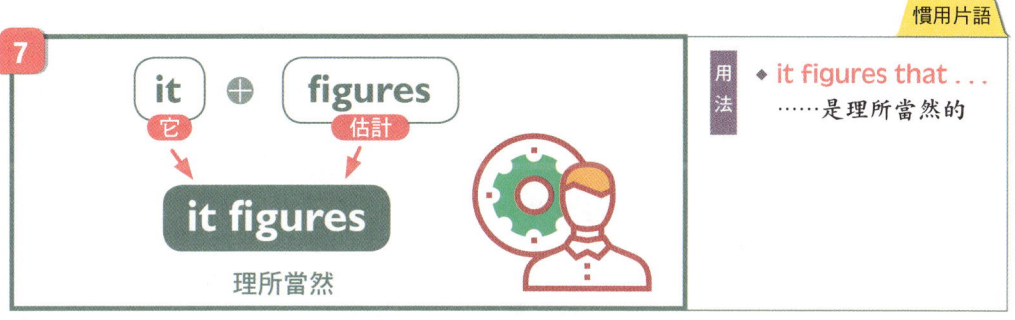

7

慣用片語

it + **figures**
它 + 估計

it figures
理所當然

用法
- **it figures that ...**
……是理所當然的

此片語原表示「計算出來」，後來則引申指「理所當然；果不其然」。

- **It figures** that it rained on my only day off of work this week.
在我這星期唯一不用上班的這天，**果然**下雨了。
- **It figures** that you woke up late since you were at that party till 3 a.m.
你狂歡到半夜三點，今天**當然**會很晚起床。

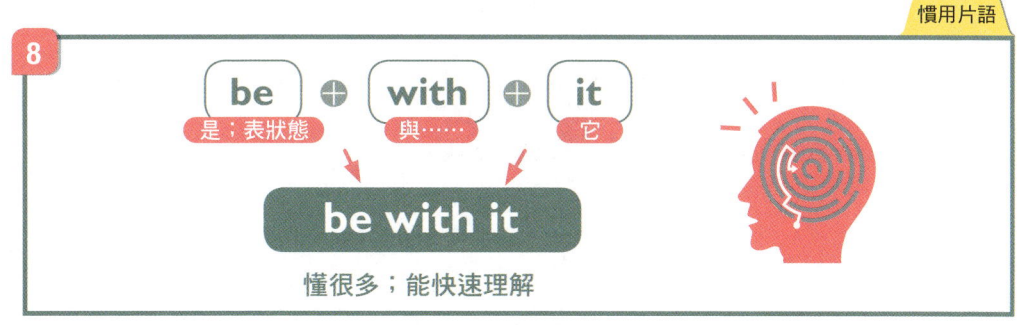

8

慣用片語

be + **with** + **it**
是；表狀態 + 與…… + 它

be with it
懂很多；能快速理解

- Although my parents are not young people, they're really **with it**.
雖然我的父母年紀不小，但他們**理解力**真的**很強**。
- If you want to **be with it**, you'd better start paying more attention.
如果你真的想要**把它搞懂**，最好專心一點。
- After a long night out, Jenna **wasn't** really **with it** at work the next day.
珍娜昨晚在外面瘋了一整夜，隔天上班效率很差。

285

9 make + someone + tick

make 讓 + **someone** 某人 + **tick** 有動作

make (someone) tick
使做出某行為；賦予動機

慣用片語

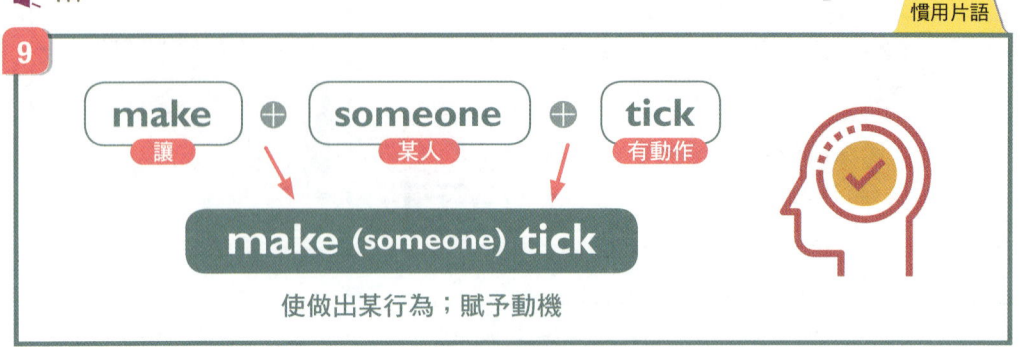

- Lance is a strange guy; I really don't know what **makes** him **tick**.
  藍斯是個怪人，真不知道他為何要**做出**這些事情。
- I always wondered what **makes** the president **tick**.
  我一直在想是什麼**讓**總裁**行動**了。

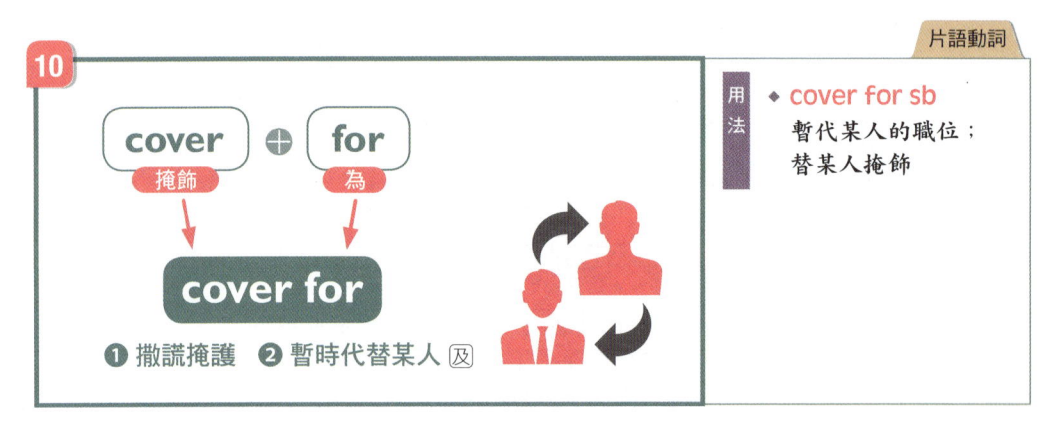

10 cover + for

cover 掩飾 + **for** 為

cover for
❶ 撒謊掩護　❷ 暫時代替某人 及

片語動詞

用法　◆ **cover for sb**
暫代某人的職位；
替某人掩飾

💡 **cover for** 可表示「某人因病或出差，而請同事暫時代替其職務」，亦可表示「替某人撒謊掩飾，以避免某人受到懲罰」。

❶ Although he knew his brother had eaten all the cookies, Dale **covered for** him.
戴爾雖然知道弟弟吃了所有的餅乾，但還是**幫他隱瞞**。

❷ Please **cover for** Donna; she's sick this week.
唐娜這星期請病假，請**暫代她的職位**。

11

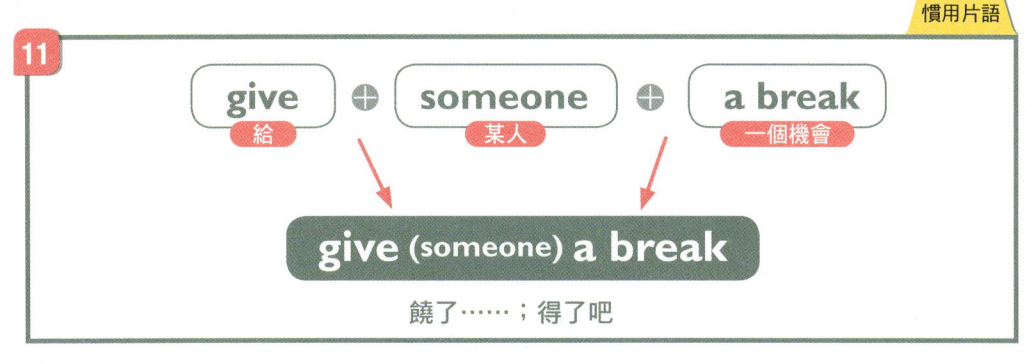

give（給）＋ someone（某人）＋ a break（一個機會）

→ **give (someone) a break**

饒了……；得了吧

💡 此片語常用來表示「給某人一個機會；別再為難某人；饒了某人」。

- I know that Ruth is not doing her job well, but **give** her **a break**—it's her first day here! 我知道茹絲的工作表現不理想，但**饒了她吧**，她才第一天上班！
- I know you're disappointed about your low test score, but **give** yourself **a break**. It was a very hard test, and no one did well!
我知道你因為考試成績不好很失望，但**放過自己吧**，這次的考試很難，大家都考不好！

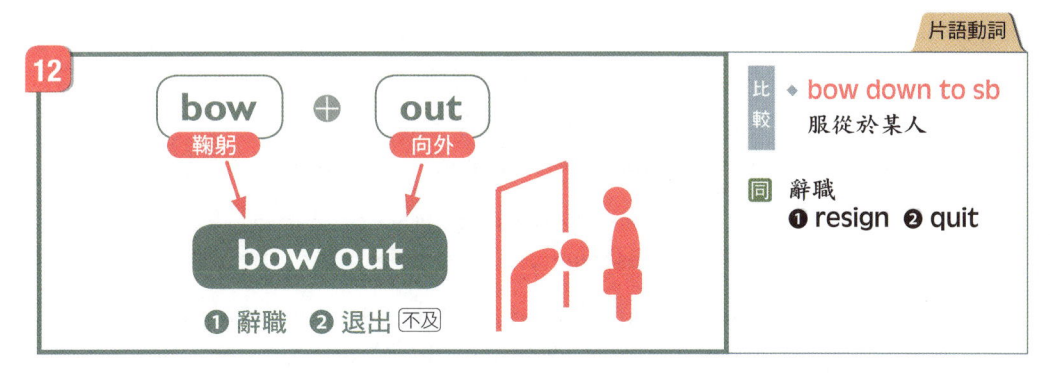

12

bow（鞠躬）＋ out（向外）

→ **bow out**

❶ 辭職　❷ 退出 〔不及〕

比較：◆ bow down to sb 服從於某人

同：辭職
❶ resign　❷ quit

❶ Mark plans to **bow out** in six weeks, after having spent 20 years with the company. 馬克在公司服務了 20 年之後，打算在六個星期後**退休**。

❶ After working as a senator for just a few months, Ms. Luther **bowed out** to accept a different job.
在當了幾個月的參議員後，路瑟女士決定**卸任**，接受別份工作。

❷ An accident forced Jennifer to **bow out** of the show just before the first performance. 一場意外讓珍妮佛在首演之前被迫**退出**。

Unit 34 Test Yourself!

A 選擇題

1. After chatting on the Internet for a few weeks, Clark and Adriana agreed to _____.
   Ⓐ cover for themselves   Ⓑ be with it
   Ⓒ meet face-to-face   Ⓓ get cold feet

2. Derek was sure that he loved Alice and that he wouldn't _____ on his wedding day.
   Ⓐ get cold feet   Ⓑ make her tick   Ⓒ fall for her   Ⓓ be with it

3. Diane _____ of her position as president of the chess team after she was elected to the student council.
   Ⓐ gave a break   Ⓑ bowed out   Ⓒ filled herself in   Ⓓ got cold feet

4. At that record store you can _____ your old CDs.
   Ⓐ trade in   Ⓑ be with   Ⓒ cover for   Ⓓ bow out

5. Will you please _____ me _____ on what's going on here?
   Ⓐ trade . . . in   Ⓑ give . . . a break   Ⓒ make . . . tick   Ⓓ fill . . . in

6. Who will _____ Suzie when she is on vacation?
   Ⓐ bow out   Ⓑ give a break to   Ⓒ trade in   Ⓓ cover for

7. It looks like Rich _____ Ariel—he just sent her a dozen roses.
   Ⓐ has given a break   Ⓑ has fallen for   Ⓒ bowed out   Ⓓ traded in

8. Jake really _____. He is going to be president of the company one day.
   Ⓐ is with it   Ⓑ is with her   Ⓒ fills himself in   Ⓓ bows out

9. _____ your brother _____ and stop annoying him!
   Ⓐ Give . . . a break   Ⓑ Make . . . tick   Ⓒ Trade . . . in   Ⓓ Fill . . . in

10. _____ that Jim lost his job, since he's always coming to work late.
    Ⓐ Trade in   Ⓑ Give a break   Ⓒ It figures   Ⓓ Who knew

11. I want to know you better. Tell me what _____ you _____.
    Ⓐ fills . . . in   Ⓑ makes . . . tick   Ⓒ gives . . . a break   Ⓓ trades . . . in

B 閱讀文章，從字表中選擇詞彙填入，並依人稱時態等做適當的變化

```
face-to-face        get cold feet       be with
be with it          cover for           give (someone) a break
fill (someone) in   fall for            it figures
```

Isaac's manager was in love with Isaac's friend, Kyle. Who knows why she had ① _____ him? Nevertheless, they seemed happy to ② _____ each other and decided to go on a trip together. So Isaac's manager asked him to ③ _____ her for a few days. Although Isaac ④ _____ because he had never worked as a manager before, he agreed to do it. He looked his manager in the eye and promised her ⑤ _____ that he would do his best. Then, he shook her hand.

Because the position was so different from his usual job, ⑥ _____ that Isaac had a hard time. No one had really ⑦ _____ him _____ on what to do. It was a hard first day. Although the CEO told Isaac that he wasn't doing everything exactly right, she ⑧ _____ him _____ because it was his first day and he seemed to be trying really hard. Although it was a new job, Isaac understood what was happening and ⑨ _____ by the end of the week.

C 引導式翻譯，並依人稱時態等做適當的變化

1. 我昨天用吉普車**折抵**買了一台紅色的賓士車。
   Yesterday, I _____ _____ my Jeep for a red Mercedes.

2. 好的業務會知道顧客消費的**動機**。
   A good salesperson knows what _____ a customer _____.

3. 我已經請馬汀**告訴**行銷團隊秋季相關計畫了。
   I've asked Martin to _____ _____ the marketing team about plans for the fall.

4. 我明天要去看牙醫，你可以**幫**我**代**班嗎？
   I'm going to the dentist tomorrow, so do you think you can _____ my shift _____ me?

5. **饒**了他吧，他只是個孩子，他不是故意的。
   _____ him _____ _____—he's only a child, and he didn't mean any harm.

Unit 35

The Missing Phone
失竊的手機

Gina and Mick talk about Dilbert.
吉娜和米克在談論狄伯特。

Mick: Do you know where Dilbert is?

你知道狄伯特在哪嗎？

Gina: **Search me**[1]! I haven't seen him for a few days.

不知道！我好幾天沒看到他了。

Mick: Are you trying to **get a rise out of**[2] me? I just saw you speaking with him a few hours ago.

妳想**惹火**我嗎？我幾個小時前才看到妳和他在聊天。

Gina: Okay, okay. Let me **get something off my chest**[3]. I'll be honest with you. I have seen Dilbert, but he doesn't want to talk to you.

好吧，那我就**實話實說**了。老實說，我是有看到狄伯特，但他不想和你說話。

Mick: But I have to talk to him. He's trying to **pin** the blame **on**[4] me for stealing his phone—but I didn't do it.

可是我有事情要告訴他。他想要把手機被偷的事情**怪罪**到我身上來，但又不是我做的。

Gina: I see. Fine, **stick around**[5] here, and I'll go get Dilbert. **By the way**[6], I don't think he'll **let** this **slide**[7] until he finds his phone or someone pays for a new one.

我知道了。好吧，在這裡**耐心等一下**，我去找狄伯特過來。噢，**對了**，在他找回手機，或有人買新的給他之前，我想他不會對這件事情**充耳不聞**的。

Mick: I don't blame him, but there's no way I'll **pick up the tab**[8] for a new one. I didn't take it!

我不怪他，但我不會**付錢**買新的給他。又不是我偷的！

1

search（搜索） + **me**（我）
→ **search me** 我不知道

≡ I don't know.

💡 此片語透過「就算搜遍全身也找不到」來形容「我不知道」。

- **Search me**! I have no idea where Fourth Avenue is.
  不知道！我完全不知道第四大道在哪裡。

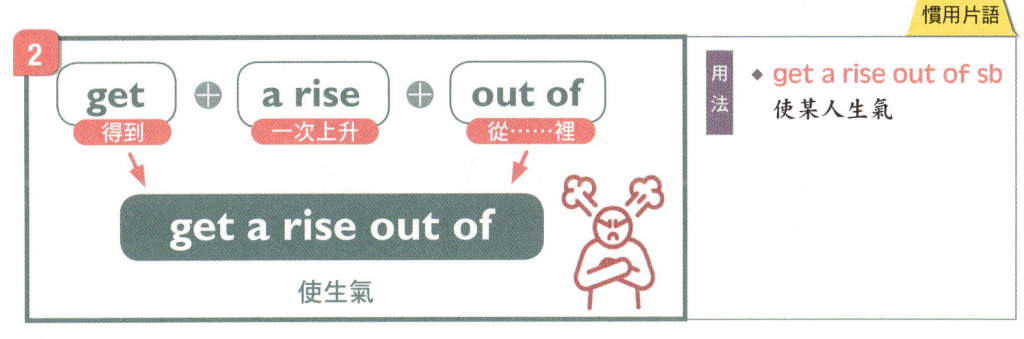

2

get（得到） + **a rise**（一次上升） + **out of**（從……裡）
→ **get a rise out of** 使生氣

用法 • **get a rise out of sb** 使某人生氣

💡 英式英語的用法為 **take a rise out of**。

- Arnold **got a rise out of** Gerald with his insulting comments.
  阿諾無禮的批評令傑拉爾德很**生氣**。

- Donny's teasing always **gets a rise out of** Mildred.
  唐尼的揶揄總是令米卓瑞德非常**生氣**。

3

get off（離開） + **one's chest**（某人的胸膛）
→ **get (something) off one's chest** 把……傾吐出來；表明

- After Justin told Hailey his secret, he said it felt good to **get it off his chest**.
  賈斯汀把秘密告訴荷莉之後，他覺得**說出來**心情變好了許多。

- We listened as Brooke **got** her worries **off her chest**. 我們在聽布洛克**說**她的困擾。

- I had spent six months worrying about it, and I was glad to **get it off my chest**.
  我已經為這件事情煩惱了六個月，很高興終於能夠把它**說**出來了。

4 pin + on

pin 釘 + **on** 在……上面 → **pin on** 怪罪 [及]

片語動詞
用法
- **pin sth on sb** 將某事怪罪於某人

- The police tried to **pin** the blame **on** Vanessa even though she wasn't there. 雖然凡妮莎當時不在場，但警察還是企圖讓她背黑鍋。
- Gustavo **pinned** the crime **on** his neighbor. 葛斯塔佛怪罪到鄰居身上。

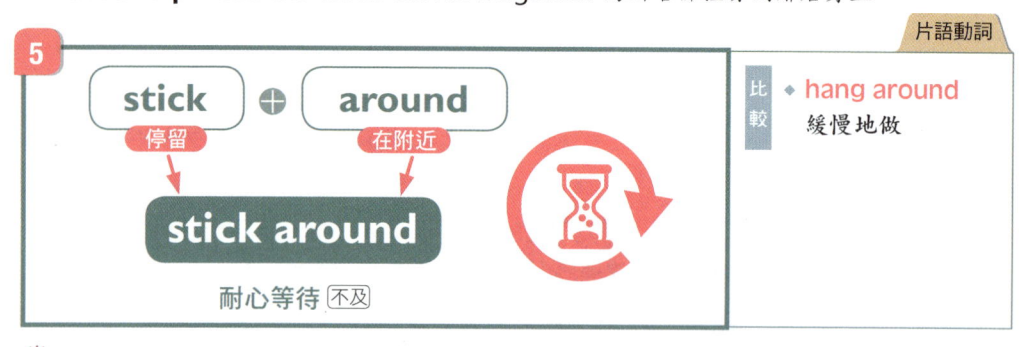

5 stick + around

stick 停留 + **around** 在附近 → **stick around** 耐心等待 [不及]

片語動詞
比較
- **hang around** 緩慢地做

💡 **stick around** 常用來比喻「某事情的時間比預料中還要久，故需耐心等待」。

- Please don't **stick around** here anymore; go home. 請不要在這裡等了，回家去吧。
- Although they didn't have any money to spend, the teenagers **stuck around** the mall all day. 這些年輕人即使沒有錢可花，但還是在購物中心待了一整天。

6 by + the way

by 藉由 + **the way** 此方法 → **by the way** 附帶一提

慣用片語
用法
- **BTW** 順帶一提（用在簡訊或非正式文體中）

💡 表示「對了；附帶一提」，通常置於句首，用來表示說話說到一半，突然想到某事或突然改變話題。

- It's nice meeting you; **by the way**, I'm Rick. 很高興認識你，對了，我叫瑞克。
- It sure has been a busy day at the office! **By the way**, what are you doing this weekend? 今天上班真的很忙，對了！你週末有什麼計畫嗎？
- I think we've discussed everything we need to. **By the way**, what time is it? 我想所有需要討論的事情我們已經談完了。對了，現在幾點了？

7

let 讓 + **slide** 悄悄地走 → **let slide** 丟下不管；忽視眼前的情況 及

片語動詞 | 可分開 | 受詞為代名詞時定要分開

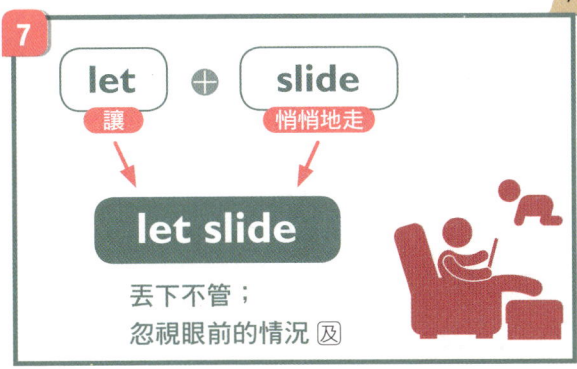

用法
- **let sth slide** 忽視某事情
- **let sb slide** 丟下某人不管

💡 比喻「任由某事情從眼前經過、從手滑落」，意指「丟下不管」。

- It's important to not **let** your responsibilities **slide**. 千萬別忽視了你應負的責任。
- Alexis **let** her research paper **slide** and, in the end, never finished it.
  艾莉克絲忽略了她的研究報告，所以她最終沒有完成。
- I was doing really well with my diet, but I'm afraid I've **let** it **slide** recently.
  我的節食計畫原本進展得很順利，但恐怕我最近有點疏忽了。
- It's easy to **let** exercise **slide** when you feel bad, but that's when you need it the most. 身體不舒服時最需要運動，但人們常會忽略這點。

8

pick up 拿起 + **the tab** 帳單 → **pick up the tab** 付帳

慣用片語

用法
- **pick up the tab (for sth)** 付……的錢
  → We shouldn't have to **pick up the tab** for the new road if only one family will be using it.
  若只有一戶人家需要使用這條道路，我們就不應該花錢開通這條新的道路。

同 ❶ pay the bill ❷ pick up the bill

- Taxpayers will have to **pick up the bill** for political campaigns.
  納稅人將為競選活動的經費買單。

💡 美式英語中，**tab** 指「在餐廳等消費的帳單」，為口語用法。

- Don't worry if you don't have any money. Andrea will **pick up the tab**.
  沒帶錢沒關係。安德麗雅會付錢的。
- Because I was the only one with a credit card, my friends asked me to **pick up the tab**. As usual, they didn't have enough money.
  朋友身上的錢一如往常地不夠，由於我是唯一擁有信用卡的人，所以朋友要我先付帳。

293

🔊 148

慣用片語

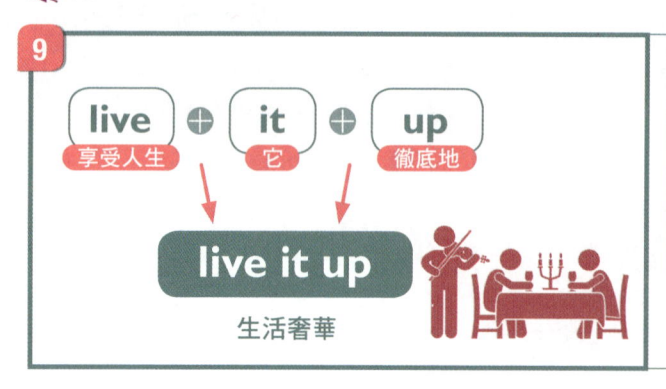

9

live （享受人生） ＋ it （它） ＋ up （徹底地）

→ **live it up** 生活奢華

比較
- **live up to (sth)** 達成期望
  → The performance was brilliant—it **lived up to** my expectations.
  這場演出太精采了，符合我的期望。

💡 此片語含有「放縱；揮霍」的意思。

- Ella and Connor **lived it up** for a weekend in Las Vegas.
  艾拉和康諾在拉斯維加斯度過了一個**奢華**的週末。
- The couple **lived it up** during their honeymoon in Hawaii.
  這對夫妻到夏威夷度過了一個非常**奢華**的蜜月。
- She's alive and well and **living it up** in the Bahamas.
  她在巴哈馬的生活過得很好也很**奢華**。

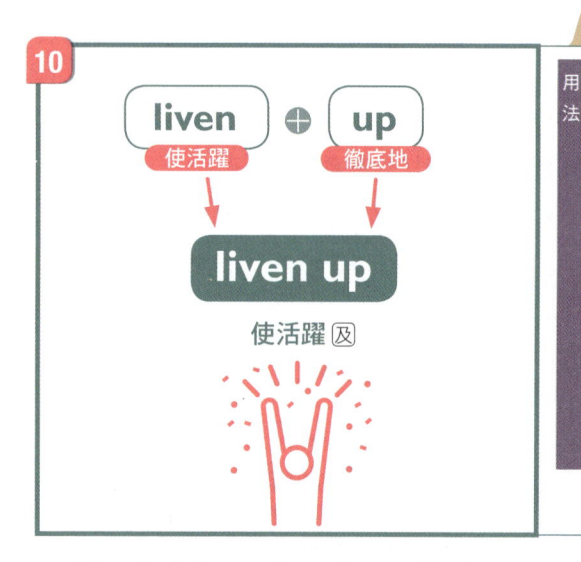

片語動詞　可分開　受詞為代名詞時定要分開

10

liven （使活躍） ＋ up （徹底地）

→ **liven up** 使活躍 及

用法
- **liven (sb) up** 使某人有活力
  → Tina was a bit shy to start with, but after a while she **livened up**.
  緹娜剛開始的時候有點害羞，但一陣子後她便**開朗**了起來。
- **liven (sth) up** 使某事物活躍起來
  → There was a live band at the party, and that really **livened** things **up**.
  有樂團在派對現場表演，使整個氣氛都**活躍**了起來。

- The chef **livened up** the vanilla ice cream with fresh fruit and chocolate sauce.
  在主廚用新鮮水果和巧克力醬的裝飾下，香草冰淇淋變得非常可口動人。
- The meeting **livened up** when the CEO started telling some funny jokes.
  在執行長說了一些笑話後，這個會議**變得活潑許多**。
- A colored shirt can certainly **liven up** an outfit.
  色彩鮮明的襯衫絕對能夠**讓**穿搭**活**起來。

11

go to (前往) + **town** (市中心)
→ **go to town**
❶ 花錢無節制 ❷ 全心投入

用法 ◆ **go to town on sth**
全心投入地做某事

💡 此片語通常用來描述「全心投入某件需支付大筆金錢的活動」。

❶ You can go out to eat anywhere you like, but don't **go to town** and spend all your money on one meal.
你可以到任何你喜歡的餐廳吃飯，但別**太過頭**而把所有的錢都花在一頓飯上面。

❷ Tom and Nicole have really **gone to town** on their wedding.
湯姆和妮可**全心全意地投入**籌備婚禮。

12

have (擁有) + **a voice** (發言權) + **in** (在……方面)
→ **have a voice in**
擁有發言權

用法 ◆ **have a voice in sth**
對某事物有發言的權利

• In a true democracy, everyone **has a voice in** what the government does.
在真正的民主國家中，人民都**擁有發言權**。

• Whenever my company has an open position, the boss lets everyone **have a voice in** choosing the new employee.
每當我們公司要聘請新員工時，老闆讓所有人**都擁有選擇新同事的權利**。

Unit 35 Test Yourself!

Ⓐ 選擇題

1. After dinner, the friends argued about who would _____ because everyone wanted to pay.
   Ⓐ stick around   Ⓑ go to town   Ⓒ pick up the tab   Ⓓ live it up

2. Don't _____ this opportunity _____!
   Ⓐ let . . . slide   Ⓑ live . . . up   Ⓒ pin . . . on   Ⓓ stick . . . around

3. After getting her new job, Kayla started _____ with her brother every summer in Paris.
   Ⓐ letting it slide   Ⓑ pinning it on   Ⓒ living it up   Ⓓ picking up the tab

4. I need to _____, so please listen while I tell you some personal things.
   Ⓐ stick around   Ⓑ live it up
   Ⓒ get something off my chest   Ⓓ go to town

5. Hannah _____ her dorm room with posters of her favorite bands.
   Ⓐ let slide   Ⓑ livened up   Ⓒ stuck around   Ⓓ pinned up

6. Don't _____ the blame _____ me; I'm innocent!
   Ⓐ pin . . . on   Ⓑ let . . . slide   Ⓒ live . . . up   Ⓓ move . . . on

7. I think I'll _____ this weekend and help out with the housework.
   Ⓐ go to town   Ⓑ stick around   Ⓒ pick up the tab   Ⓓ live it up

8. Let's go out dancing tonight—_____, how old are you?
   Ⓐ by the way   Ⓑ sticking around   Ⓒ picked up the tab   Ⓓ livened up

9. On the school council, students _____ deciding how things go.
   Ⓐ live it up   Ⓑ pick up the tab   Ⓒ have a voice in   Ⓓ stick around

10. Members of the Stone family _____ on their new entertainment center; they bought a huge TV with great speakers.
    Ⓐ lived it up   Ⓑ stuck around   Ⓒ let it slide   Ⓓ went to town

11. Delia kept telling her brother to mow the lawn until she _____.
    Ⓐ stuck around with him   Ⓑ got a rise out of him
    Ⓒ let him slide   Ⓓ got something off her chest

B 閱讀文章，從字表中選擇詞彙填入，並依人稱時態等做適當的變化

pick up the tab	let slide	live it up
get something off one's chest	liven up	get a rise out of
have a voice in	go to town	stick around

Gloria spent yesterday looking for Max. She really wanted to ❶_____ _____ by letting him know that she was mad at him. Last weekend, the two friends were celebrating their graduation, and they decided to ❷_____ with a fun night out. However, when it came time to pay, Gloria was the one who kept ❸_____.

It just wasn't fair. It happened first at the restaurant. Max let her pay for the entire meal. Then, they decided to ❹_____ the evening by going to a club—and she ended up paying for both of them to get in. Lastly, she paid for the taxi home. When they got back to her dorm, Max ❺_____ for a while because he needed to use her phone. He called his family in Alaska, and they talked for a long time. The fact was, Max really ❻_____ and Gloria paid for it. She deserved to ❼_____ how her own money was spent. At first, she thought about ❽_____ it _____, but she couldn't. The fact was, Max had really ❾_____ her, and she couldn't forget it.

C 引導式翻譯，並依人稱時態等做適當的變化

1. 你不可以**把事情怪罪到**我頭上來，意外發生的時候我並不在場啊。
   You can't _____ the blame _____ me—I wasn't even there when the accident happened.
2. 你先走吧，我要在這裡**等**瑞克**出現**。
   You go ahead. I'll _____ _____ until Rick shows up.
3. 大衛充滿歧視的玩笑總有辦法**把我惹火**。
   David always manages to _____ _____ _____ _____ me with his racist jokes.
4. 貝絲的父母**費盡心力**為她準備生日派對，我想他們花了一萬多塊。
   Beth's parents really _____ _____ _____ on her birthday party. I think they spent more than $10,000.
5. 我們在加勒比海度了六個星期**奢華**的假期。
   We took a six-week holiday and _____ _____ _____ in the Caribbean.

Unit 36

Checking In
辦理住宿登記

149

Joanne checks into a hotel.
瓊安在飯店登記住宿。

Clerk:	Good evening, ma'am. Would you like to **check in**[1]?	晚安，女士。您要**辦理住宿登記**了嗎？
Joanne:	Yes, I would. Are there still nonsmoking rooms available?	是的。請問一下，禁菸樓層還有空房間嗎？
Clerk:	Don't worry. You haven't **missed the boat**[2]. There are plenty.	別擔心，您並沒有**錯過**。我們還有許多空房間呢。
Joanne:	That's good news; if there were no nonsmoking rooms here, I'm afraid I'd **lose my cool**[3]. My husband and I have been looking for a hotel all day! How much is one night here?	太好了；若是沒有禁菸房間的話，我可能會**不知所措**。我和我先生整天都在找飯店投宿！請問住宿一晚的費用是多少錢？
Clerk:	A double room is $95 a night. I'll just need to see some ID.	雙人房每晚是 95 元。我需要查看您的身分證。
Joanne:	That's a great price. Oh, no! I think I left my ID with my husband. Can I show it to you later?	價錢很合理。噢，不會吧！我想我的身分證在我先生那裡。我能夠等一下再給你看嗎？
Clerk:	No problem. I'll **take you at your word**[4] for now—but please remember to stop by with it later.	沒關係，我**相信**您，但稍後請務必拿過來。
Joanne:	Of course. I won't **cop out**[5].	放心，我不會**逃避責任**的。
Clerk:	Here's your key. Remember you must **check out**[6] by 10:30 tomorrow morning.	這是您的鑰匙。請您記得明天早上 10 點 30 分前要**辦理退房**。
Joanne:	Is it possible to **leave open**[7] tomorrow night, too? We may stay two nights if this hotel **serves our purpose**[8].	我們可以明天晚上**才決定**嗎？如果這裡**符合**我們的需求，我們可能會待兩個晚上。
Clerk:	That's fine.	好的。

Unit 36 Checking In 辦理住宿登記

1. check + in

- check 核對
- in 向內
- → **check in** 住房登記 [不及]

比較
- ◆ **check sth in**
  托運；記錄某人已歸還某物；點收貨運或訂單
- ◆ **check in with sb**
  問候某人平安，聯繫某人以確認安好

反 退房 **check out**

💡 check in 可指「在飯店辦理住房登記」或「在機場辦理報到手續」等，名詞為 **check-in**。

- Before you can stay at this hotel, it is necessary to **check in** at the front desk.
  入住飯店前，要先到櫃檯**辦理住宿登記**。
- Is it possible to **check in** at the hotel after midnight? 我可以在半夜**登記住宿**嗎？

2. miss + the boat

- miss 錯過
- the boat 船
- → **miss the boat** 錯過機會

同 miss the chance

💡 就字面上來看是指「錯過了上船的時間」，在此表示「錯過機會」。

- We could have bought cheap tickets to L.A. yesterday, but we **missed the boat** by thinking about it too much, and now they're all gone.
  我們昨天本來可以買到飛往洛杉磯的便宜機票，但我們因為考慮了太多而**錯失機會**，票現在都賣完了。
- This is your last chance to accept this job; if you are still unsure, I'm afraid you'll have **missed the boat**.
  這是你最後接受這份工作的機會，如果你還是無法決定，恐怕會**錯過機會**。

3. lose + one's + cool

- lose 失去
- one's 某人的
- cool 冷靜
- → **lose one's cool** 失去冷靜；情緒激動；沉不住氣

反 keep one's cool

- When Aaron heard that he had failed the class, he **lost his cool** and started crying like a child. 亞倫知道他這科的成績不及格後，**情緒很激動**，接著哭得像個孩子。

4 慣用片語

take (接受) + **one** (某人) + **at** (由於) + **one's word** (某人的話)

→ **take one at one's word**
相信某人說的話

同 take one's word for it

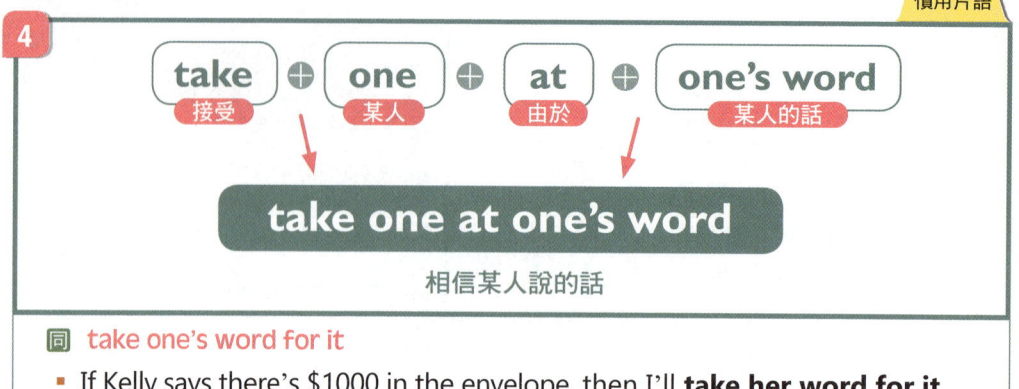

- If Kelly says there's $1000 in the envelope, then I'll **take her word for it**.
  假如凱莉說信封裡有一千元，那我便**相信她說的話**。

- Although Aiden didn't have a written agreement, he **took his boss at his word** and started working the next day.
  雖然艾登沒有接到書面通知，但他**相信老闆說的話**，並且隔天就開始上班。

- Joel is an honest guy. You can definitely **take him at his word**.
  喬爾絕對是個老實人，你可以完全**相信他說的話**。

5 片語動詞

cop (抓到) + **out** (向外)

→ **cop out**
逃避（責任）[不及]

用法：◆ cop out of sth 逃避某事

- Go talk to that pretty girl; don't **cop out** now!
  去和那個漂亮女孩說話吧，別再**逃避**了！

- Just as the group was about to go mountain climbing, Diane **copped out** and said she was too nervous.
  就在登山隊準備出發時，黛安因為太緊張，所以**放棄**了。

- Martin **copped out** of the parachute jump at the last minute with some feeble excuse. 馬汀在最後一刻因為一些牽強的理由而**放棄**了跳傘。

6

片語動詞 | 可分開 | 受詞為代名詞時定要分開

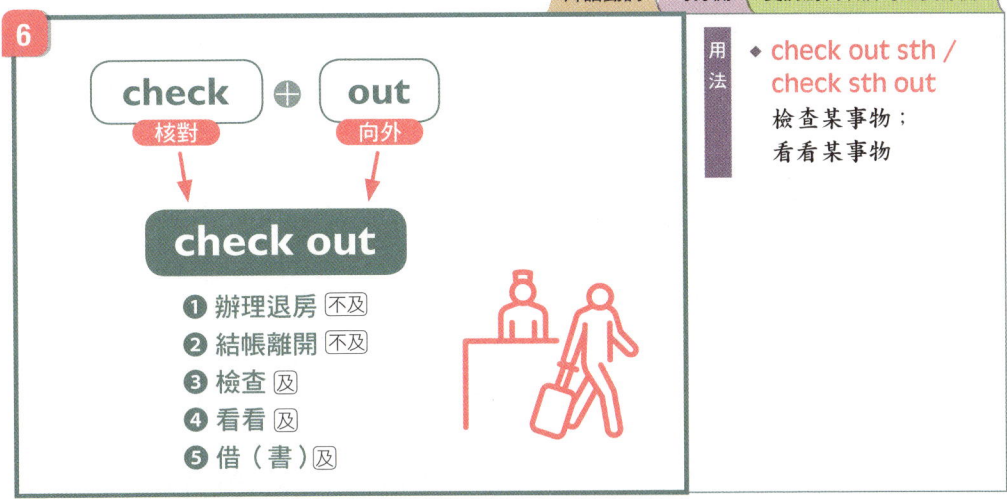

```
check (核對) + out (向外)
    ↓           ↓
       check out
```

❶ 辦理退房 [不及]
❷ 結帳離開 [不及]
❸ 檢查 [及]
❹ 看看 [及]
❺ 借（書）[及]

用法 ◆ check out sth / check sth out
檢查某事物；看看某事物

💡 **check out** 除了表示「在飯店辦理退房登記」、「在超市的櫃檯結帳」和「在圖書館辦理借閱登記」外，還有「檢查」的意思。

❶ Be sure to **check out** before noon tomorrow. 明天中午前一定要**辦理退房**。
❸ If you have time today, could you please **check out** the weather forecast for this week? 你今天有時間的話，可以請你**查**一下這週的天氣預報嗎？
❹ I'm going to **check out** that new club. 我要去**看看**那家新開的俱樂部。
❺ I **checked** three books **out** of the library this afternoon.
我今天下午向圖書館**借**了三本書。

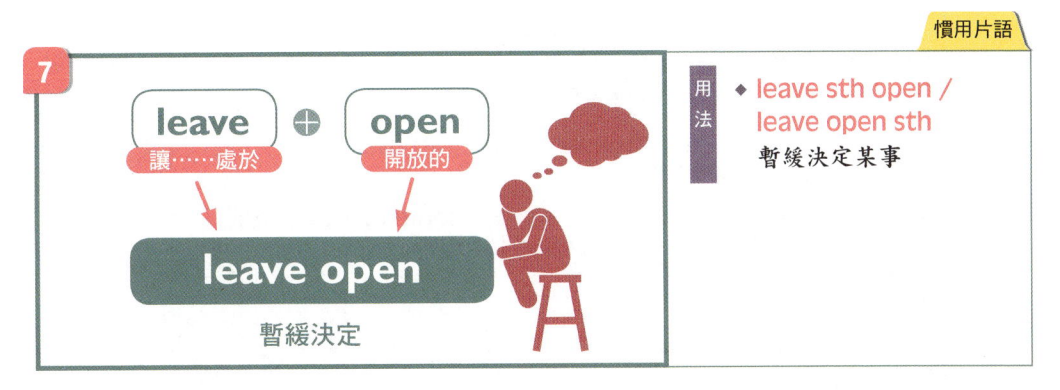

7

慣用片語

```
leave (讓……處於) + open (開放的)
    ↓                 ↓
       leave open
       暫緩決定
```

用法 ◆ leave sth open / leave open sth
暫緩決定某事

💡 **leave open** 原表示「讓……開著」，但也可引申為「暫緩決定，讓某事有更多選擇的空間」。

- Danielle **left open** the possibility that she could drive me to school, but she said she wasn't sure yet. 丹妮葉拉**暫時還沒決定**是否要載我去學校，她還不確定。
- Brenda **left** the weekend **open** just in case her boyfriend invited her to the party.
布蘭達**先把週末空下來**，免得男朋友邀請她參加派對。

8

serve (適合) + **one's** (某人的) + **purpose** (目標)
→ **serve (the/one's) purpose**
符合需求

慣用片語

同 ❶ satisfy one's needs
❷ meet one's needs

- Before you spend a lot of money on those programs, you should be sure they will **serve your purpose**.
  你在投入資金前，應該要先確定這些案子是否**符合你的需求**。
- This new laptop will surely **serve the purpose**.
  這台新的筆記型電腦肯定能**符合需求**。

9

line (成一排) + **up** (靠近)
→ **line up**
❶ 排隊 及 不及
❷ 安排 及

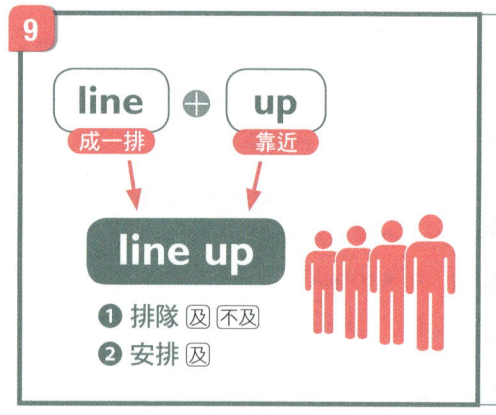

片語動詞　可分開　受詞為代名詞時定要分開

用法
- **line sb up / line up sb** 使排隊
  → The soldiers **lined** us **up** against a wall, and I thought they were going to shoot us.
  士兵**把**我們靠牆**排成一列**，我以為他們要朝我們開槍。
- **line sth up / line up sth** 安排某事情
  → Have you got anything interesting **lined up** for the weekend?
  你這週末有**安排**什麼有趣的計畫嗎？

💡 表示「排成一線」，英式用法為 **queue up**。

❶ The security guards made us **line up** to get into the club.
  安全人員要我們**排隊**進入俱樂部。
❶ The little boy **lined up** all his toy cars so he could see each one.
  小男孩把所有的玩具車都**排成一列**，以便他看到每台車。

10

turn (轉動) + **on** (對著)
→ **turn on**
❶ 由……決定　❷ 持敵對的態度　❸ 使高興 及

片語動詞　可分開

用法
- **turn on sth**
  由某事物決定
- **turn on sb**
  與某人敵對
- **turn sb on**
  引起某人的興趣

💡 **turn on** 除表「打開」（參考第 4 頁）外，亦可表「取決於……；與……敵對；引起……的」。

❶ Your grade in this class **turns on** how well you do on the final paper.
你的期末報告**決定**了你在班上的成績。

❷ The dog **turned on** Lola and tried to bite her.
那隻狗**對**蘿娜**產生敵意**，而且還企圖咬她。

❷ Suddenly, Vicky just **turned on** me and accused me of undermining her.
維琪突然**對**我**產生敵意**並且指責我暗中說她壞話。

❸ What **turns** kids **on** these days? 現在的孩子**喜歡**些什麼？

11

副詞片語

in (在) + **the worst** (最壞的) + **way** (方面)

→ **in the worst way**

渴望地；緊急地；非常地

- Jasmine wants to live in Texas **in the worst way**. 潔絲敏**非常**想要住在德州。
- Phil wanted to buy that video game **in the worst way**, but he didn't have enough cash. 菲爾**非常**想要買那台電動玩具，但他的錢不夠。
- After a day in the hot sun, I needed a shower **in the worst way**.
在大太陽底下待了一天，我**非常地**想要沖澡。

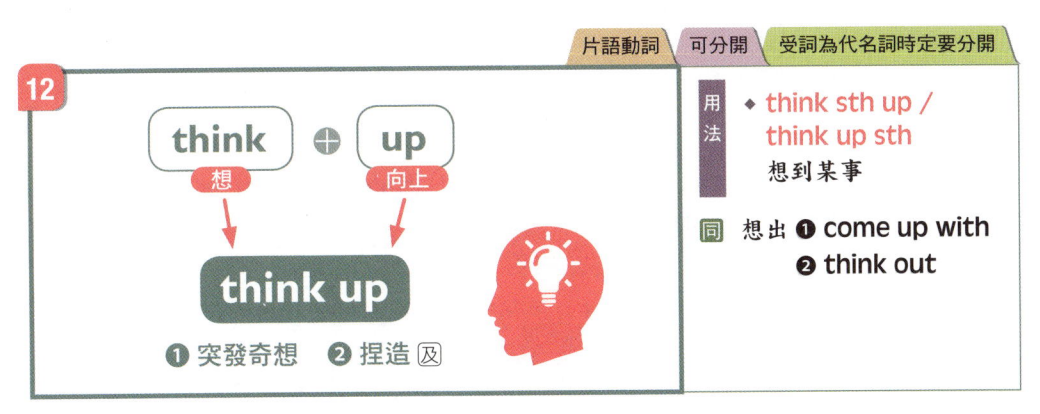

12

片語動詞 | 可分開 | 受詞為代名詞時定要分開

think (想) + **up** (向上)

→ **think up**

❶ 突發奇想　❷ 捏造 [及]

用法 ◆ **think sth up / think up sth**
想到某事

同 想出 ❶ come up with
　　　❷ think out

❶ Harriet **thought up** a great topic for her thesis.
哈莉葉**突然想到**一個很棒的論文主題。

❶ Paul **thought up** his own chicken soup recipe. 保羅**想出**了獨家的雞湯食譜。

❷ I don't want to go tonight, but I can't **think up** a good excuse.
我今晚不想去，但我**想不到**好的理由拒絕。

303

Unit 36 Test Yourself!

A 選擇題

1. Kyle isn't sure when he wants to meet, but he asked that you _____ Monday and Tuesday evenings.
   Ⓐ think up   Ⓑ cop out   Ⓒ leave open   Ⓓ turn on

2. The teacher made the students _____ in order of height.
   Ⓐ think up   Ⓑ cop out   Ⓒ line up   Ⓓ lose their cool

3. I'm sorry, but without a passport it is impossible to _____ at this hotel.
   Ⓐ check in   Ⓑ line up   Ⓒ cop out   Ⓓ turn on

4. Jim desperately wants that MP3 player. He wants it _____.
   Ⓐ checked in   Ⓑ losing its cool
   Ⓒ serving his purpose   Ⓓ in the worst way

5. Whether you get this job _____ how well you do in the interview with my boss.
   Ⓐ turns on   Ⓑ cops out   Ⓒ thinks up   Ⓓ checks in

6. Try to _____ something interesting that we can do this weekend.
   Ⓐ cop out   Ⓑ think up   Ⓒ check in   Ⓓ turn on

7. Jane decided to _____ of her agreement to come to work on Sunday because she was too tired.
   Ⓐ line up   Ⓑ miss the boat   Ⓒ cop out   Ⓓ lose her cool

8. This phone really _____ because it is also an organizer, a camera, and an MP3 player.
   Ⓐ loses my cool   Ⓑ serves my purpose   Ⓒ cops out   Ⓓ lines up

9. I can't prove to you that I will be studying at Harvard; you'll just have to _____.
   Ⓐ take me at my word   Ⓑ check me out
   Ⓒ serve my purpose   Ⓓ lose my cool

10. Leonardo had a chance to invest in IBM 15 years ago, but he _____ and didn't do it.
    Ⓐ checked out   Ⓑ served his purpose   Ⓒ missed the boat   Ⓓ turned on

11. I know it is scary, but you must stay calm and do everything you can to avoid _____.
    Ⓐ leaving open   Ⓑ turning on   Ⓒ losing your cool   Ⓓ missing the boat

12. The hotel was so bad that after 15 minutes, the couple decided to _____ and look for a better place.
   Ⓐ turn on   Ⓑ check out   Ⓒ miss the boat   Ⓓ lose their cool

Ⓑ 閱讀文章，從字表中選擇詞彙填入，並依人稱時態等做適當的變化

> serve the purpose   in the worst way   think up   line up
> turn on   lose one's cool   take one at one's word
> check in   check out   miss the boat

　While Stephen was ❶_____ at the new hotel on his first night in the United States, he realized that he had lost his passport somewhere. He asked the clerk if she would ❷_____, but the clerk said that staying the night at this hotel ❸_____ having a passport. Stephen asked if his French driver's license would ❹_____, but the clerk said that a passport was totally necessary.

　Stephen tried to ❺_____ some way around the problem, but his only option seemed to be to look again for his passport. So he emptied out his backpack right on the hotel counter and ❻_____ all his documents. He wanted to find that passport ❼_____. Stephen stayed calm; although he was concerned, he never ❽_____, even for a second. Then, at the bottom of his bag he found his passport. What a relief!

　He showed the passport to the clerk, but the clerk told him that he had ❾_____. Someone else had taken the room he wanted on the top floor. Stephen didn't care anymore. He decided to take any room and see about switching when that other person ❿_____ tomorrow.

Ⓒ 引導式翻譯，並依人稱時態等做適當的變化

1. 保羅突然**對我產生敵意**，指責我沒有在他需要的時候支持他。
   Paul suddenly _____ _____ me and accused me of not supporting him when he needed me.

2. 我在最後一刻才寄出大學申請函，差一點就**錯過了機會**。
   I sent off my university application at the last minute and nearly _____ _____.

3. 西德在**辦理退房**時，才發現他的錢不夠付住宿費。
   Sid realized that he didn't have enough money to pay the hotel bill when he was trying to _____ _____.

Unit 37

Showing Off
炫燿賣弄

Bob shows Angie his new mobile phone.
鮑伯把新手機拿給安姬看。

Bob: Take a look at my new cell phone! It is also a camera and an MP3 player, and it can even go online. It can also do a lot of other cool stuff, but I'm still **learning the ropes**[1].

妳看我的新手機！它也是相機、MP3 播放器，還可以上網。我想它還有許多很新的功能，但我還在**摸索**當中。

Angie: Hmm . . . that's interesting. When someone calls you, does it have a special ring?

嗯，聽起來不錯。那有人打電話給你時，有什麼特別的鈴聲嗎？

Bob: That's the best part! Whenever I get a call, it makes the sound of a cow. That's sure to **make waves**[2].

這就是這支手機最棒的地方！只要有人打電話給我，手機就會發出牛叫聲。許多人肯定會**非常驚訝**。

Angie: I'm sure. You know, it is a cool phone, but you shouldn't **show off**[3] so much. Where did you buy it, anyway?

我也覺得。這支手機很棒，但你不應該到處**炫燿**。總之，你在哪裡買的呢？

Bob: This phone **was up for grabs**[4] in a hot dog-eating competition, and I won! Those competitions are a great way to win prizes. There's another one next month, and the winner gets a flat screen TV. You want to compete, too?

每位參加吃熱狗大賽的人**都有機會贏得**這支手機，所以手機是我贏來的！參加比賽是贏得獎品很好的方式。下個月還有一場比賽，贏的人可以得到液晶電視。妳也想參加比賽嗎？

Angie: No way, man. **Not on your life**[5]!

才沒有。**想都別想**！

Bob: Okay. Well, **keep your fingers crossed**[6] for me.

好吧。那就為我**祈禱**吧。

Unit 37 Showing Off 炫耀賣弄

1 慣用片語

learn (學習) + **the ropes** (繩索) → **learn the ropes** 摸索

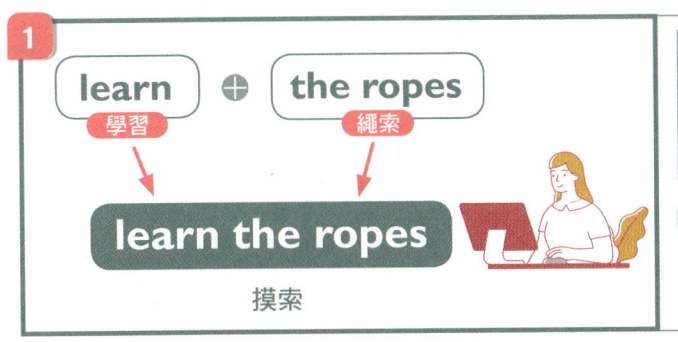

比較：
- ◆ **teach sb the ropes** 教某人訣竅
- ◆ **show sb the ropes** 教某人訣竅

同：**know the ropes**

原表示水手需花費許多時間和精力摸索船上的器具和繩索等，現常用來引申指「摸索工作內容；學會訣竅」。

- It's my first day working here, so I still need to **learn the ropes**.
  今天是我第一天上班，所以我還在**摸索**當中。
- No one will expect you to do much around the office until you are trained and have **learned the ropes**. 在你完成培訓並**抓到要領**前，公司是不會派給你太多任務的。
- It'll take time for the new receptionist to **learn the ropes**.
  新來的接待員要花一些時間來**摸索工作內容**。

2 慣用片語

make (製造出) + **waves** (波浪) → **make waves** 引起眾人議論；引起抱怨

同：興風作浪
1. make trouble
2. rock the boat

反：不惹事生非
keep your nose clean

就字面上來看，「興風作浪」可引申指「引起眾人議論紛紛」，其中的 **waves** 需使用複數，常以 **not make waves** 的形式出現，表示「要求某人不要興風作浪」。

- Pam got fired from her job because she was always **making waves** during important meetings. 潘老是在重要會議中**挑起事端**，所以她被解僱了。
- The key to working well with a team is to not **make** too many **waves**.
  團隊合作的關鍵就是不要**興風作浪**。
- Our culture encourages us to fit the norm and avoid **making waves**.
  我們的文化鼓勵我們行為舉止要合乎規範，不要**興風作浪**。

3 show + off

- show 展現
- off 完全地

show off 炫耀 及/不及

片語動詞 | **可分開** | **受詞為代名詞時定要分開**

用法
- **show off sth / show sth off**
  炫耀某事物
- **show off sb / show sb off**
  炫耀某人

💡 名詞為 **show-off**。

- Don can be really annoying. Whenever there are pretty girls around, he always tries to **show off** his physical strength.
  唐有時很討人厭，只要有漂亮女生在旁邊，他總會想要**炫耀**他那壯碩的身材。
- I think Melissa could be a good basketball player if she stopped **showing off** and was more of a team player.
  只要梅麗莎別再**炫耀**，多點團隊精神，我認為她會成為一名優秀的籃球員。

4 be up + for + grabs

慣用片語

- be up 向上
- for 給……
- grabs 奪得

be up for grabs 人人都有機會可以爭取

- The new car **is up for grabs** in the marathon!
  贏得馬拉松比賽的人可以**得到**這台新車！
- The math teacher's job **is up for grabs** because he's quitting.
  他要辭職了，所以數學老師一職**空了出來**。

5 not + on + your life

慣用片語

- not 不會
- on 在……的時候
- your life 你的一生

not on your life 別妄想

同 除非我死（表強烈反對）
over my dead body

- You think I'll let you go to New York by yourself? **Not on your life**!
  你以為我會讓你獨自去紐約嗎？**想都別想**！

6

keep 維持 + one's fingers 某人的手指 + crossed 交叉

→ **keep one's fingers crossed** 祈求

同 祈求好運
① have one's fingers crossed
② cross one's fingers

- I'm just going to **cross my fingers** and hope it works.
  我**祈禱**這麼做會有用。

💡 有些人相信將食指和中指交叉的手勢（猶如十字架）能夠用來「祈求好運的降臨；為某人祈福」。**keep one's fingers crossed** 亦含有「**撒謊**」的意思，但若是在背後比出食指和中指交叉的手勢時，則就不算說謊。

- Your little sister has a big test today, so **keep your fingers crossed** for her.
  你妹妹今天有重要考試，所以為她**祈禱**吧。
- **Keep your fingers crossed**! I have a job interview this afternoon.
  我今天下午有工作面談，替我**祈禱**吧！

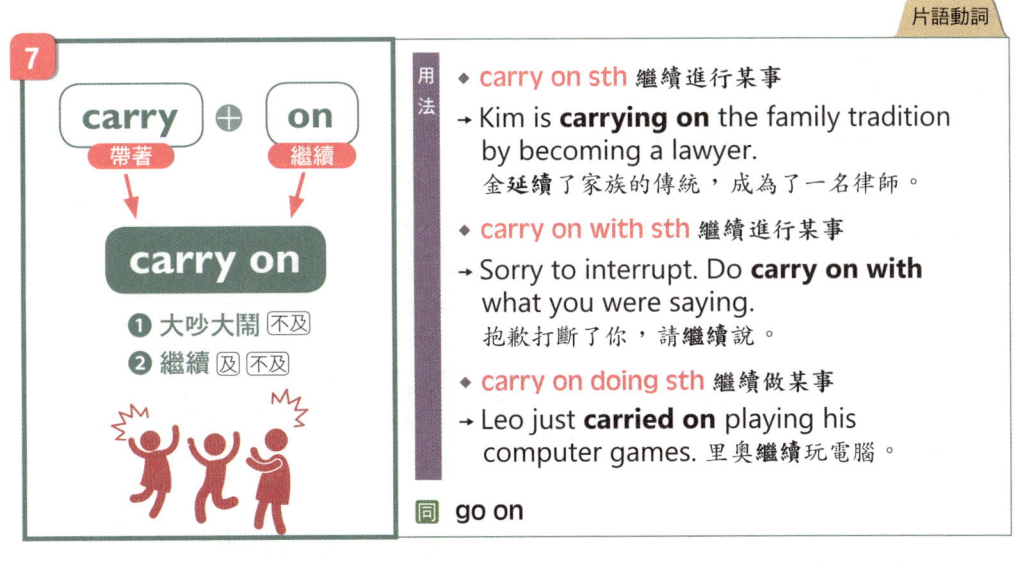

7

carry 帶著 + on 繼續

→ **carry on**
① 大吵大鬧 [不及]
② 繼續 [及][不及]

用法
- **carry on sth** 繼續進行某事
→ Kim is **carrying on** the family tradition by becoming a lawyer.
  金延續了家族的傳統，成為了一名律師。

- **carry on with sth** 繼續進行某事
→ Sorry to interrupt. Do **carry on with** what you were saying.
  抱歉打斷了你，請繼續說。

- **carry on doing sth** 繼續做某事
→ Leo just **carried on** playing his computer games. 里奧繼續玩電腦。

同 go on

❶ The little kids **carried on** all night because they had eaten too much candy.
孩子們整個晚上**吵個不停**，因為他們吃了太多的糖果了。

❷ As soon as the movie was over, Caroline **carried on** with her homework.
電影一演完，卡若琳便**繼續做功課**。

309

8

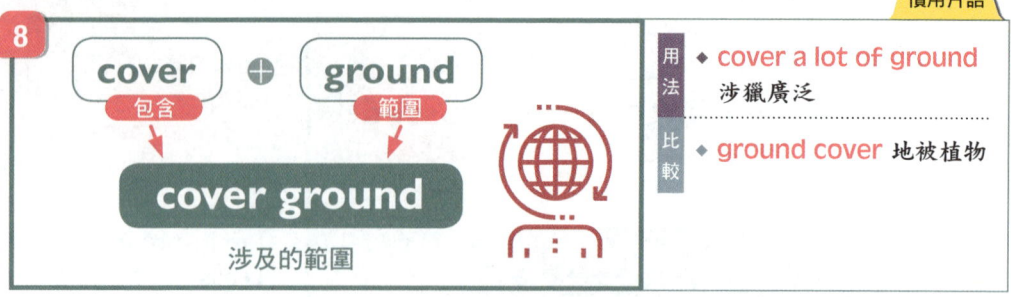

cover (包含) + **ground** (範圍) → **cover ground** 涉及的範圍

用法	◆ **cover a lot of ground** 涉獵廣泛
比較	◆ **ground cover** 地被植物

- The big research project is due soon, so we tried to **cover** a lot of **ground** before Monday.
  這份報告再不久就要送出，我們必須趕在星期一之前**完成**所有的**細節**。
- The students **covered ground** on all the issues during their discussion.
  學生的討論**涉及**了所有的議題。

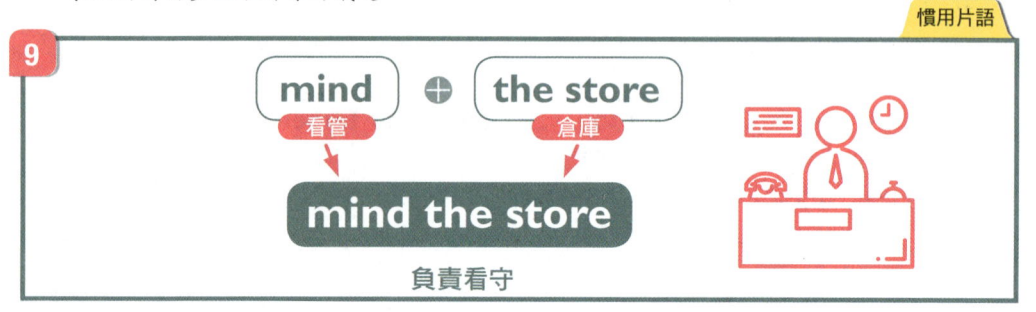

9

mind (看管) + **the store** (倉庫) → **mind the store** 負責看守

- While Mr. Richardson was away from the office, Jack **minded the store**.
  理查森先生不在辦公室時，是由傑克暫時**打理一切**。
- Who's going to be **minding the store** while your manager's away?
  經理不在時，是由誰**負責管理**的？

10

throw (扔) + **the book** (書) + **at** (動作對象) → **throw the book at (someone)** 嚴厲懲罰

- When Julia was first caught by the police officers, they didn't punish her too much; the second time, however, they **threw the book at** her.
  警察第一次抓到茱莉亞時，並沒有很嚴厲地懲罰她。然而他們第二次抓到她時，便對她**施以嚴懲**。
- After several arrests for drunken driving, the judge finally **threw the book at** Jack. 傑克好幾次被抓到酒醉駕車，法官終於對他**做出嚴厲的判決**。

11 慣用片語

throw（扔）＋ someone（某人）＋ a curve（一個曲球）

throw (someone) a curve
提出（某人）意想不到的事情（常表負面）

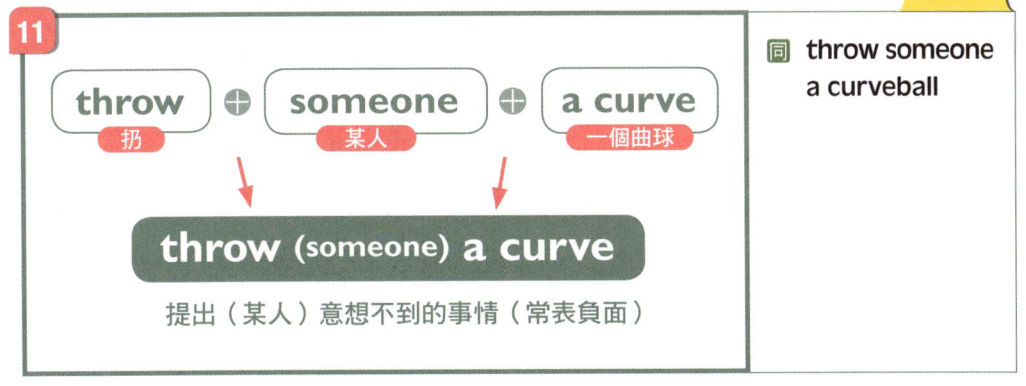

同 throw someone a curveball

💡 原指棒球中投手對打擊者擲出曲球，後引申表示「提出某人意想不到的話題」。

- Victoria's dad really **threw** her **a curve** when he said she couldn't do anything special for her birthday—the fact was, he had planned a surprise party.
  維多莉亞的爸爸**騙**她沒有準備特別的生日計畫。事實上，他策劃了一場驚喜派對。
- Lisa **threw** me **a curve** by asking me to go to the theater instead of the mall.
  莉莎**意想不到地**約我去看電影，而不是去逛街。
- Jerry really **threw** me **a curve** when he asked me a personal question at work.
  傑瑞上班時**問**了一個令我意想不到的私人問題。

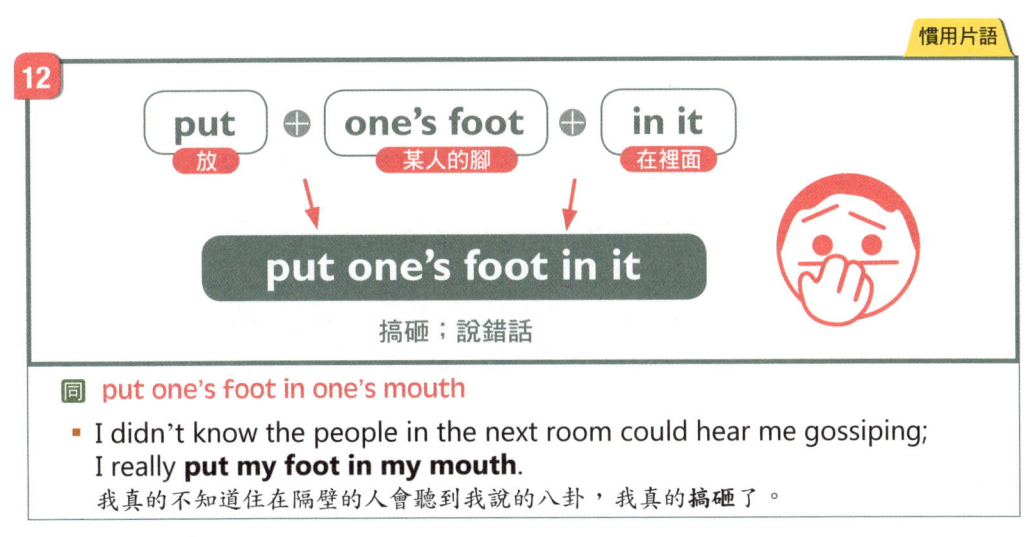

12 慣用片語

put（放）＋ one's foot（某人的腳）＋ in it（在裡面）

put one's foot in it
搞砸；說錯話

同 put one's foot in one's mouth

- I didn't know the people in the next room could hear me gossiping; I really **put my foot in my mouth**.
  我真的不知道住在隔壁的人會聽到我說的八卦，我真的**搞砸**了。

💡 亦可寫成 put one's foot into it。

- I really **put my foot in it** yesterday when the boss overheard me making fun of her. 老闆昨天無意中聽到我在開她玩笑，我想我真的**搞砸**了。
- I really **put my foot in it** with Diane. I didn't realize she was a vegetarian.
  我真的**搞砸**了與黛安之間**的關係**。我並不知道她吃素。

311

Unit 37 Test Yourself!

A 選擇題

1. Please stop _____ and acting so childishly with all your crying!
   Ⓐ carrying on   Ⓑ learning the ropes
   Ⓒ showing off   Ⓓ keeping your fingers crossed

2. Let's _____ for a sunny weekend so we can go scuba diving!
   Ⓐ cover ground   Ⓑ make waves   Ⓒ keep our fingers crossed   Ⓓ learn the ropes

3. When meeting with his English tutor, Arnie tried to _____ on everything having to do with next week's test.
   Ⓐ cover ground   Ⓑ make waves   Ⓒ carry on   Ⓓ show off

4. Jess _____ when she accidentally told her brother about the surprise party.
   Ⓐ carried on   Ⓑ showed off   Ⓒ covered ground   Ⓓ put her foot in it

5. Linda always mentions how big her house is because she wants to _____ her wealth.
   Ⓐ keep her fingers crossed   Ⓑ show off   Ⓒ carry on   Ⓓ cover ground

6. A lot of prizes are _____ in the lottery.
   Ⓐ up for grabs   Ⓑ showing off   Ⓒ throwing the book at you   Ⓓ coving ground

7. Karin really _____ when she told me she would be in Chicago tomorrow; I never guessed that she was planning a surprise party for me!
   Ⓐ made waves   Ⓑ showed off   Ⓒ threw me a curve   Ⓓ covered ground

8. It took me a few weeks to _____ here, so don't feel bad if you don't understand everything right away.
   Ⓐ keep my fingers crossed   Ⓑ throw you a curve
   Ⓒ mind the store   Ⓓ learn the ropes

9. Claire isn't a very good manager; they should hire someone else to _____.
   Ⓐ throw the book at me   Ⓑ make waves   Ⓒ mind the store   Ⓓ put her foot in it

10. When I asked dad if I could borrow $50, he said "_____!"
    Ⓐ Put your foot in it   Ⓑ Keep your fingers crossed
    Ⓒ Not on your life   Ⓓ Make waves

11. The judge _____ at the criminal and sentenced her to life in prison.
    Ⓐ threw the book   Ⓑ made waves   Ⓒ kept his fingers crossed   Ⓓ covered ground

12. You should follow the teacher's rules in this class; she doesn't like students who _____.
    Ⓐ cover ground   Ⓑ make waves   Ⓒ mind the store   Ⓓ keep their fingers crossed

B 閱讀文章，從字表中選擇詞彙填入，並依人稱時態等做適當的變化

not on your life	keep one's fingers crossed	show off
put one's foot in it	throw the book at	make waves
throw (someone) a curve	learn the ropes	be up for grabs

My boss really ❶_____ me for taking so many days off. It's my fault that I got in trouble, though; I ❷_____ when I accidentally told my coworker that I had a lot of fun on vacation, scuba diving in Brazil. The trouble was, I had told my boss that I was sick. It was a stupid mistake to ❸_____ to my coworker like that, but I was so proud of having learned to scuba dive. I never knew that telling my coworker would ❹_____ with my boss.

I don't normally lie, especially to my boss; however, when I asked for the time off, he told me "❺_____!" I knew he meant it. That's why I tried to ❻_____ with this story about being sick. Well, when people started hearing about my vacation, it wasn't long before my boss heard about it, too.

I'm not sure how I'll be punished. My boss says he has to think about it. A colleague told me that he heard that my job ❼_____, but that can't be true. I'm ❽_____ that this is only a rumor. It's hard work ❾_____ for this job, so I think it'll be hard for my boss to find someone else who can do what I do here.

C 引導式翻譯，並依人稱時態等做適當的變化

1. 尼克買那台跑車只是為了**炫耀**他買得起。
   Nick only bought that sports car to _____ _____ and prove he could afford one.

2. 我們**希望**能一直有好天氣。
   We are _____ _____ _____ _____ that the weather stays nice.

3. 今天的籃球練習仍照常舉行，可是巴特卻**意外**地告訴我練習取消了。
   Bart _____ _____ _____ _____ when he told me that basketball practice was canceled today even though it wasn't.

4. 教授開除作弊的學生，以示**嚴懲**。
   The professor _____ _____ _____ _____ the cheating students by expelling them from the university.

Unit 38

The First Week at College
大學生活的第一個星期

Samantha talks to Al about her first week at college.
莎曼莎跟艾爾說起她第一個星期的大學生活。

Al:	How was your first week at college?	妳在大學的第一個星期過得如何呢？
Samantha:	Well, it was hard! In the beginning, I felt like I **was over my head**[1].	唉，很難熬！我一開學就**忙得一個頭兩個大**。
Al:	Why do you say that?	怎麼說？
Samantha:	I needed help all the time. Luckily, I had the best tutor a student could **ask for**[2], but I knew things weren't supposed to be that tough.	我總是需要別人的幫助。幸好我有一位可以**求助**的好助教，可是我覺得事情應該沒那麼困難才對。
Al:	So what happened?	發生了什麼事情嗎？
Samantha:	I had to **take the bull by the horns**[3] and really study harder. College **is a far cry from**[4] high school, and although my professors are happy to **give me a hand**[5] sometimes, I had to learn how to be a better student.	我得**不畏艱難**，並且更用功唸書；大學**和**高中**不同**，雖然有時教授很樂意**幫助**我，但我必須要學會如何成為好學生。
Al:	So now you can deal with what your professors **dish out**[6]?	所以妳現在能夠應付教授**指派**的作業了嗎？
Samantha:	**By all means**[7]! There's no doubt.	**那當然**！別懷疑。
Al:	It sure sounds like you **landed on your feet**[8] after those early difficulties. Congratulations!	看來妳已經從之前所遇到的困難中，**重新振作起來**了。恭喜妳！

慣用片語

1

be over (超過) + one's head (某人的才智)

→ **be over one's head** 太難以致無法理解

同 go over one's head

- I tried to take in what he was saying about nuclear fusion, but most of it **went over my head**.
  我試著了解他說的關於核融合的事情，但大部分都**超出了我所能理解的範圍**。

- Jonny is pretty young, so a lot of the jokes that the older boys were telling **were over his head**.
  強尼年紀很輕，那些較年長的男孩所開的玩笑，**超出了他所能理解的範圍**。

- Everything Aiden heard in the class was really interesting, but a lot of it **was over his head**. 艾登在課堂上所學到的東西都很有趣，但有些**超出他所能理解的範圍**。

- The math homework was really tough. It **was** way **over my head**.
  數學作業真的很難，這已經遠**超出我所能理解的範圍**了。

片語動詞

2

ask (要求) + for (為了)

→ **ask for**
  ① 自討苦吃
  ② 要求 及

用法
- ask for sth 要求某事物
- ask for sb 要求見某人

比較
- ask for it 自找麻煩
  → Picking a fight with those hooligans was really **asking for it**.
  挑釁那些流氓簡直就是在**自找麻煩**。

- ask for trouble 自找麻煩
  → If you come home late again, you're **asking for trouble**.
  你如果再晚歸，就是在**自找麻煩**。

❶ You are **asking for** it if you don't clean up your room like mom ordered.
  如果你不照媽媽要求打掃房間，就是**自討苦吃**了。

❷ Dr. O'Maley is the best dentist anyone could **ask for**; he's professional, friendly, and kind.
  歐邁利醫生是最優秀的牙醫，每個人都**想給他看診**。他很專業、友善和親切。

315

3

take 取得 ⊕ **the bull** 公牛 ⊕ **by** 藉由 ⊕ **the horns** 角

take the bull by the horns
不畏艱難

💡 此片語藉由「抓住公牛的雙角勇往直前」來表示「不畏艱難、勇敢地去做某事」。

- Roland didn't want Alison at his party, but he was too shy to **take the bull by the horns** and tell her to leave.
  羅蘭不想要艾莉森參加他的派對，但他太膽小而**不敢**開口要她離開。

- If you are unhappy with your life, it may be time to **take the bull by the horns** and try something new. 如果你對生活不滿意，應該要**不畏艱難**去嘗試新事物。

4

be a 是一個 ⊕ **far** 遠的 ⊕ **cry** 喊叫 ⊕ **from** 從

be a far cry from
與……相差甚遠

用法 ◆ **be a far cry from sth** 與……有很大的差異

- New York **is** really **a far cry from** the little village where I was born.
  紐約和我所出生的小村落真的**有很大的差異**。

- This little stream **is a far cry from** the Mississippi River.
  這條小溪和密西西比河相比，簡直就是**天壤之別**。

5

give 給 ⊕ **someone** 某人 ⊕ **a hand** 幫助

give (someone) a hand
幫助

比較 ◆ **give (sb) a big hand** 鼓掌
→ The host asked us to **give a big hand** to the actors after the performance.
表演結束後，主持人要我們給予演員熱烈的掌聲。

比較 → The parents **gave** their children **a big hand** after the school play.
學校話劇表演結束後，家長為孩子們**鼓掌**。

- Will someone please **give** me **a hand** moving these boxes?
  有人可以**幫**我搬這些箱子嗎？
- Ivan **gave** Muriel **a hand** with her work because she needed help.
  穆芮需要幫忙，艾文便**幫**她做功課。

6

dish 盛於盤子中 + **out** 向外 → **dish out**
❶ 脫口而出 ❷ 分發 [及]

片語動詞 | 可分開 | 受詞為代名詞時定要分開

用法
- **dish sth out / dish out sth**
  脫口而出某事
- **dish sth out / dish out sth**
  分發某事

比較
- **dish the dirt** 責罵
→ Some journalists enjoy **dishing the dirt**.
  有些記者喜歡揭人瘡疤。

同 上菜 **dish up**

💡 此片語是由「盛裝食物給人享用」所引申出來的，但現在並不限用於食物上。

❶ Mira was in a great mood, and she **dished out** compliments to everyone she saw. 米拉心情很好，她**不假思索地**稱讚每個她見到的人。

❷ The waiter **dished out** soup to everyone at our table.
服務生**送**湯給在座的每個人。

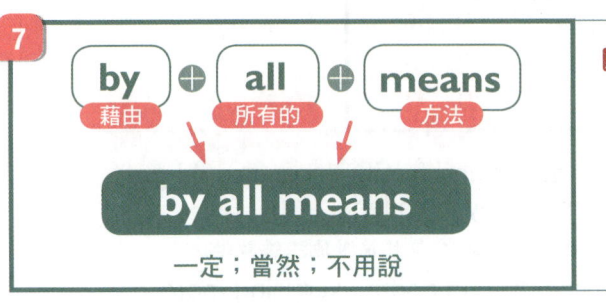

7

by 藉由 + **all** 所有的 + **means** 方法 → **by all means**
一定；當然；不用說

副詞片語

反 ❶ **not by any means**
　 ❷ **by no means**

- It is **by no means** certain that we'll finish the project by next Friday. 我們**絕不可能**在下星期五前完成這份企畫的。

💡 表示「就算不惜一切代價，也一定要達成某事」，亦可用來表示「答應別人的請求」。

- **By all means**, feel free to use my apartment when I'm on vacation.
  我去度假時，你**當然可以**隨意使用我的公寓。
- Well, there's still an extra seat available in the car, so come along with us, **by all means**. 嗯，車子還有空位，你**當然可以**和我們坐同台車。
- "May I borrow this pen?" "**By all means**."「可以借我這支原子筆嗎？」「**當然**。」

317

8

land 降落 + **on** 以……的方式 + **one's feet** 某人的雙腳

→ **land on one's feet**
安然脫險；重新振作起來

慣用片語

同 **fall on one's feet**
- Mei has really **fallen on her feet** with that new job.
梅真的靠那份新工作重新振作起來了。

- No matter what crazy things happen to Tiffany, she always **lands on her feet**; she's a very smart woman.
無論蒂芬妮遇到什麼事情，她總是能夠**安然脫險**；她是一個很聰明的女人。

- Bobby really **landed on his feet** with that raise at work.
巴比靠著工作加薪而**重新振作**起來。

- It may take a few months to get a job, but I'm sure you'll **land on your feet**.
找工作可能會花上好幾個月，但我相信你一定會**重新振作**起來的。

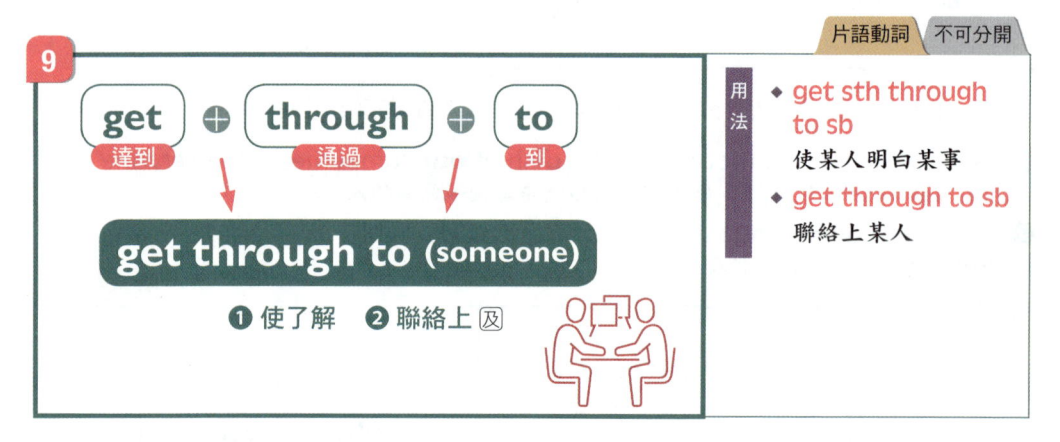

9

片語動詞 / 不可分開

get 達到 + **through** 通過 + **to** 到

→ **get through to (someone)**
❶ 使了解 ❷ 聯絡上 及

用法
- **get sth through to sb**
使某人明白某事
- **get through to sb**
聯絡上某人

❶ Despite the best efforts of Jeff's friends and family, no one could **get through to** him and convince him to stay in college.
除了傑夫的朋友和家人，沒有人能夠與傑夫**溝通**，並且說服他繼續就學。

❶ Barney finally **got through to** his girlfriend about exercising more.
巴尼終於讓女朋友**了解**到她必須多運動了。

❶ We can't **get through to** the government just how serious the problem is!
我們無法讓政府**理解**問題的嚴重性！

❶ Pictures can sometimes help you **get through to** people more effectively than writing can. 圖片有時候比文字更容易幫助人們**理解**。

❷ I **got through to** the wrong department. 我**聯絡錯**部門了。

10

get out (擺脫) + **from** (從) + **under** (處於……的情況下)

→ **get out from under**
解決債務；擺脫負擔

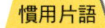

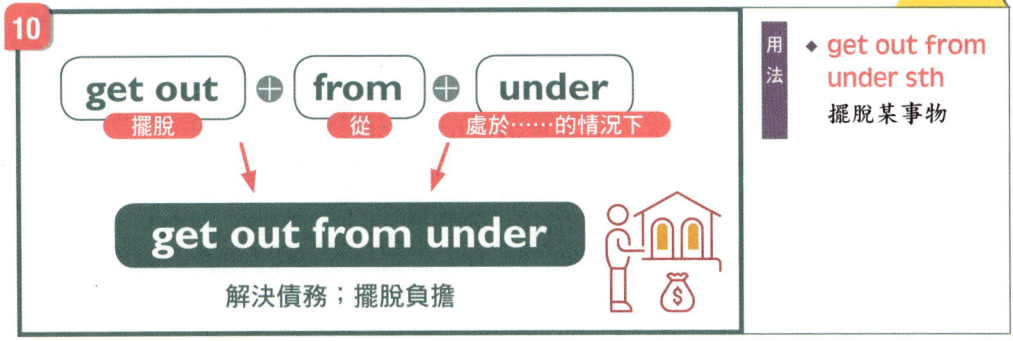

用法
- ◆ get out from under sth
  擺脫某事物

💡 此片語常用來表示「擺脫負擔」或「解決債務」，可後接「所處的情況」或「所承受的負擔」，亦可單獨使用。

- Ron wasn't sure how to **get out from under** his credit card debt, so he started looking for a second job.
  朗不知道要如何**解決**卡債，所以他開始找兼職工作。

11

keep (擺脫) + **one's word** (從)

→ **keep one's word**
遵守約定；值得信任

同 keep one's promise
反 ❶ break one's promise
　 ❷ break one's word

- Paul has **broken his word** so many times that no one can believe him any more.
  保羅不斷**違背他的承諾**，所以沒有人會再相信他了。

- You can really count on Dan—he's the kind of guy who **keeps his word**.
  你可以相信丹──他是個**說話算話**的人。

- I hope I can trust you to **keep your word**.
  我希望你能夠**遵守約定**。

- I said I'd visit him, and I shall **keep my word**.
  我說過會去拜訪他，而我應該**遵守約定**。

- Jeff is someone who **keeps his word**—you can rely on that.
  傑夫是個**說話算話**的人，很可靠。

Unit 38 Test Yourself!

A 選擇題

1. If Jean says she'll come at 9, she will—she always _____.
   Ⓐ keeps her word　　　　Ⓑ is over her head
   Ⓒ gets through to herself　Ⓓ lands on her feet

2. I know things seem a little scary since your father lost his job, but don't worry. I'm sure that when this is all over, we'll all _____, and things will be okay.
   Ⓐ give ourselves a hand　Ⓑ be over our head
   Ⓒ land on our feet　　　Ⓓ keep our word

3. This astronomy class sure sounds interesting, but I bet it _____.
   Ⓐ keeps its word　　　Ⓑ is over my head
   Ⓒ lands on its feet　　Ⓓ gets through

4. The audience _____ to the musicians.
   Ⓐ gave a big hand　Ⓑ got through　Ⓒ dished out　Ⓓ kept their word

5. When Lula asked if she could borrow Dave's laptop, he said, "_____."
   Ⓐ Give her a big hand　Ⓑ By all means
   Ⓒ Get out from under　Ⓓ Keep her word

6. No one could explain to Wayne that quitting his job was a bad idea. He's so stubborn that it's very hard to _____.
   Ⓐ keep his word　　　　Ⓑ land on his feet
   Ⓒ give himself a hand　Ⓓ get through to him

7. The old car _____ my brand-new Mercedes.
   Ⓐ asks for　Ⓑ dishes out　Ⓒ gets out from　Ⓓ is a far cry from

8. The boys _____ their mother _____ with the farm work.
   Ⓐ gave . . . a hand　　Ⓑ got . . . through
   Ⓒ gave . . . a big hand　Ⓓ dished . . . out

9. By not studying, Tuck is basically _____ an "F" in this class.
   Ⓐ asking for　Ⓑ getting through　Ⓒ dishing out　Ⓓ reading about

10. I can see that you don't like your job, but it's up to you to _____ and get what you want out of life.
    Ⓐ get through　　　　　　　Ⓑ dish out
    Ⓒ take the bull by the horns　Ⓓ keep your word

11. I hope you can deal with everything your teachers _____.
    Ⓐ dish out　Ⓑ land on your feet　Ⓒ get through　Ⓓ keep your word

320

B 閱讀文章，從字表中選擇詞彙填入，並依人稱時態等做適當的變化

give (someone) a hand	be over one's head	land on one's feet
be a far cry from	ask for	take the bull by the horns
get through to	keep one's word	get out from under

When Uncle Saul promised that he'd take me sailing soon, I never expected that we'd really do it. He ❶_____, though, and told me on Saturday we would be taking the boat out later that afternoon. Although I had fished from a canoe in a lake once or twice, that ❷_____ being on a sailboat in the ocean! When Uncle Saul told me that I would be steering the boat, I was pretty scared. I felt like I ❸_____. Still, in these situations, the best thing to do is be brave and ❹_____. It took some time, but I eventually ❺_____ my uncle that I didn't feel comfortable steering a boat this big yet.

Before we could set sail, Uncle Saul needed help preparing the boat, and I ❻_____. Actually, being on the sailboat while we were still on land helped me to calm down. I felt like I was beginning to ❼_____ _____ my fear. I was sure that as long as I was with an experienced sailor like my Uncle Saul, I'd ❽_____, even if something went wrong. Yes, there is no question about it—Uncle Saul is the best uncle a kid could ever ❾_____.

C 引導式翻譯，並依人稱時態等做適當的變化

1. 這間公寓和我們以前住的房子**相差甚遠**。
   This apartment is _____ _____ _____ _____ the house we had before.
2. 如果這台舊電腦對你來說有用的話，**儘管留著吧**。
   If you can find a use for this old computer, _____ _____ _____ keep it.
3. 我最近似乎都無法**聯絡**上賴瑞。
   I am not able to _____ _____ _____ Larry these days.
4. 傑森，可以請你**裝**一些紅蘿蔔給我嗎？
   Jason, could you _____ the carrots _____ for me, please?
5. 如果你有功課方面的問題，我會很樂意**幫助**你的。
   If you have any trouble with your homework, I'll be glad to _____ you _____ _____.

Unit 39

Getting Home Late
晚回家

Ernie calls his mom to tell her he got in trouble at school and will be home late. 爾尼打電話告訴媽媽他在學校惹上麻煩，所以會晚點回家。

Ernie:	Hi, Mom? I won't **be in**[1] until late today. I have to stay after school.	嗨，老媽？我今天會晚點**回家**。我放學後必須留下來。
Mom:	Why? What did you do?	為什麼？你做了什麼好事？
Ernie:	It was all Ms. Butterworth's fault. She's the one who is making me stay late.	都是巴特沃斯老師的錯，是她要我留那麼晚的。
Mom:	Were you **goofing off**[2]?	你又**偷懶**了嗎？
Ernie:	Well, yeah, a little. Also, when Ms. Butterworth asked where my report was, I **talked back to**[3] her.	嗯，算是吧。還有，巴特沃斯女士問我報告交了沒時，我和她**頂嘴**。
Mom:	Why did you do that?	你為何要那麼做？
Ernie:	She was **keeping after**[4] me to finish my report . . . I was in a bad mood.	她一直**嘮嘮叨叨**，要我寫完報告……而我當時心情不太好。
Mom:	I guess that's where she **drew the line**[5]. Anyway, if I **were in her shoes**[6], I'd probably do the same thing. You were really **getting out of line**[7].	我想這就是她**無法接受**的原因了。總之，如果我**是她**的話，我可能也會這麼做。你真是太**沒規矩**了。
Ernie:	Can I still go to the dance this weekend?	那我這星期還可以去參加舞會嗎？
Mom:	Hmm, I'm not sure. Let's **play it by ear**[8].	嗯，我還不確定。**要看你的表現**囉。
Ernie:	Oh, Mom!	噢，老媽！

Unit 39 Getting Home Late 晚回家

1 慣用片語

be (是；在) + **in** (裡面) → **be in**
❶ 在家　❷ 在公司　❸ 流行

比較
- **be out** 不在家；不在公司；落伍
- If you call after 6, most of my coworkers will **be out**.
  如果你六點過後打電話過來，就會發現大部分的同事都**下班**了。
- Randy **is out** for lunch, so please come back later.
  藍迪**外出**用餐，請晚點再過來。
- If you ask me, blue jeans will never **be out**; they're the sort of pants that will always be cool.
  我認為藍色牛仔褲永遠不會**退流行**；牛仔褲一直都很酷。

同 流行 **in fashion**
反 過時 **out of fashion**

💡 **in** 在此作形容詞，而非介系詞。

❶ What time will you **be in** tomorrow? 你明天幾點會**在家**？
❷ I'm sorry, but the doctor **is** not **in** today. 很抱歉，醫生今天休診。
❸ I heard that colorful sandals **are in** this summer.
  我聽說今年**流行**顏色鮮豔的涼鞋。

2 片語動詞

goof (摸魚) + **off** (離開) → **goof off**
摸魚；偷懶 [不及]

比較
- **goof around** 混日子
- **fool around** 鬼混

💡 此片語原指士兵「混日子；偷懶」，現在則引申表示「上班摸魚；整天無所事事」。

- Jan **goofed off** last weekend and went camping when she should have been painting the house. 珍上週末本來應該要油漆房子，但她**偷懶**跑去露營。
- The reason you're getting a bad grade in this class is because you **goofed off** when you should have been doing your homework.
  該做功課時，你卻在**摸魚**，這就是你在班上成績不好的原因。

323

3 片語動詞

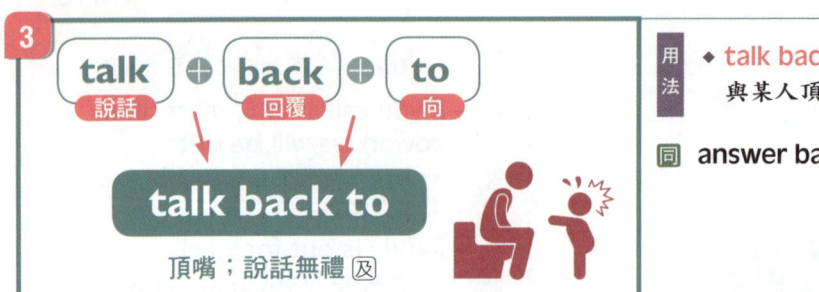

talk（說話） + **back**（回覆） + **to**（向）
→ **talk back to**
頂嘴；說話無禮 及

用法
- **talk back to sb**
  與某人頂嘴

同 answer back to

💡 **talk back** 表示「頂嘴」，**talk back to** 則需後接人，表示「向某人頂嘴」。

- Grandpa was mad when my little sister **talked back to** him.
  爺爺對我妹妹和他**頂嘴**感到很生氣。
- Don't you ever **talk back to** me again! 你還敢**頂嘴**！

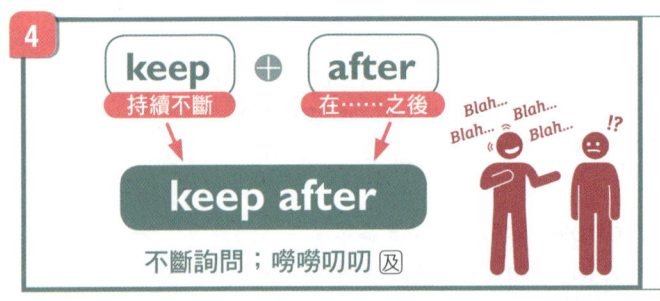

4 慣用片語

keep（持續不斷） + **after**（在……之後）
→ **keep after**
不斷詢問；嘮嘮叨叨 及

用法
- **keep after sth**
  不斷詢問某事
- **keep after sb**
  不斷詢問某人

- The teacher **kept after** Art until he finished his report.
  老師**一直嘮嘮叨叨**直到亞特寫完報告。
- I **kept after** Lucas to let me borrow his car for the weekend, and in the end, he agreed. 我**一直問**盧卡斯週末是否可以把車借給我，他最後終於同意了。

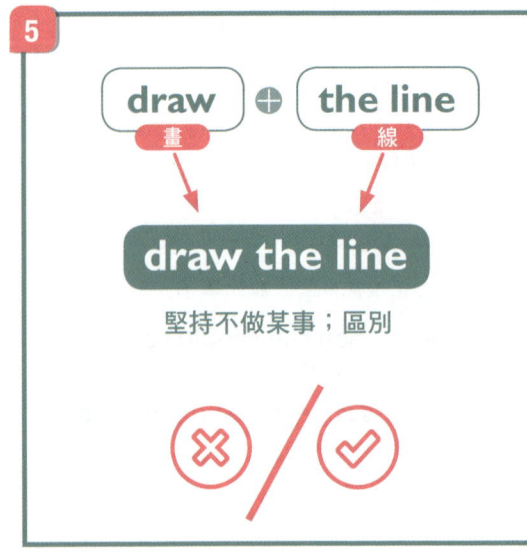

5 慣用片語

draw（畫） + **the line**（線）
→ **draw the line**
堅持不做某事；區別

- **draw the line between sth**
  使……有差異
  → It all depends on your concept of fiction and where you **draw the line between** fact and fiction.
  這就要看你如何定義虛構，還有事實與虛構之間的差異。

- **draw the line at sth**
  拒絕某事物
  → I swear quite a bit, but even I **draw the line at** saying certain words.
  我時常講髒話，但我**堅持不說**某些特定的字。

- Although Phil sometimes has a piece of chocolate or two, he **draws the line** at cake because he is trying to lose weight.
  雖然菲爾有時會吃一、兩塊巧克力，但他為了減肥**拒**吃蛋糕。
- My parents told me I have to be home by midnight; although they don't mind if I'm a little late, they **draw the line** at 12:30.
  我父母要我在午夜前回家，雖然我覺得晚點到家無所謂，但他們**堅持不**超過 12 點 30 分。

6

慣用片語

be in + someone's + shoes
穿著　　某人的　　鞋子

→ be in (someone's) shoes
站在某人的立場

同 be in (sb's) place

💡 **shoes** 在此用來表示「立場」。

- Oh, boy! I wouldn't like to **be in** your **shoes** when you tell your dad that you locked the keys in the car!
  噢，天啊！**如果我是你**，就不會把你是如何把鑰匙留在車內的事情告訴你爸！
- What would you do if you **were in** my **shoes**? 如果你是我的話，會怎麼做呢？

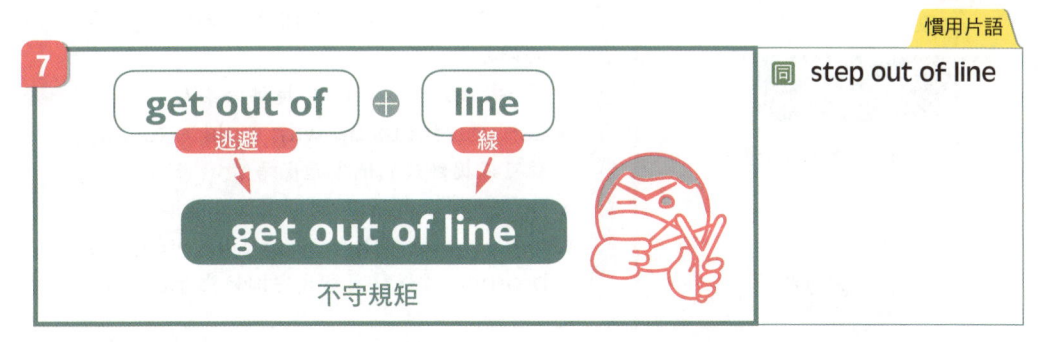

7

慣用片語

get out of + line
逃避　　　　線

→ get out of line
不守規矩

同 step out of line

- Please behave when we visit my aunt and don't **get out of line**.
  到我阿姨家拜訪時，要注意你的行為舉止，不可以**不守規矩**。
- The teacher told Amanda that if she **gets out of line** one more time, he'll have to kick her out of class.
  老師告訴亞曼達要是再**不守規矩**，他就只好把她趕出教室了。

8

play (演奏) + **something** (某事物) + **by** (藉由) + **ear** (耳朵)

→ **play (something) by ear**
① 憑印象演奏　② 隨機應變；見機行事

💡 此片語原指「憑印象演奏，不看樂譜」，現在則引申表示「隨機應變；見機行事」。有時亦可搭配其他動詞使用，如 **write by ear**。

❶ Maggie can **play** anything on the piano **by ear**.
瑪姬只要聽過一遍旋律，便可以用鋼琴彈奏出來。

❷ For now, John is a math major in college. He has decided to **play** it **by ear** as to whether he'll get a degree in physics instead.
約翰目前在大學主修數學，但他決定要**見機行事**，看能否轉為主修物理。

❷ I'm not sure if we'll go to the park this weekend; let's **play** it **by ear**.
我不確定這週末是否要去公園；**看情況吧**。

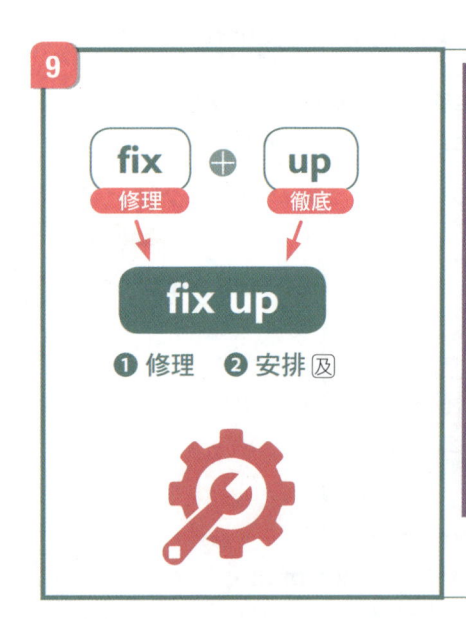

9

fix (修理) + **up** (徹底)

→ **fix up**
① 修理　② 安排 及

片語動詞 | 可分開 | 受詞為代名詞時定要分開

用法
- fix sth up / fix up sth　修理某事物
- fix sth up / fix up sth　安排某事物
  → I'd like to **fix up** a meeting with Mr. Whiteman next week sometime.
  我希望能在下星期的某個時間和懷德曼先生**安排見面**。
- fix sb up / fix up sb　提供給某人
  → Can you **fix** us **up** with a place to stay?
  你可以**提供**我們地方過夜嗎？
- fix sb up / fix up sb　替某人安排相親
  → Peter tried to **fix** me **up** with his older brother. 彼得試圖為我**安排**和他哥哥相親。

❶ The teenagers spent the weekend **fixing up** the old truck. By Sunday night, it was working like new!
一群年輕人利用週末**修理**卡車，他們在星期日傍晚前就讓卡車變得像新的一樣！

10

dry(乾的) + **run**(溪流) → **dry run** 排練；預演

同 dummy run

- We'd better have a couple of **dummy runs** before we do the real thing.
我們最好在正式演出前先做幾次**預演**。

💡 就字面上來看，**dry run** 表示暴風雨來臨之前「乾涸的溪流」，就好比正式演出之前的「演練」。現在，**dry run** 亦可用來表示「非實彈軍事演習」或各種事物的「排練」。

- Although Sandra thought she had practiced playing the flute enough, she made some mistakes during the **dry run** and realized that she needed to practice a lot more before the performance.
雖然珊卓拉認為她的長笛已經吹得非常熟練，但她在**排練**時犯了一些錯，她覺得在表演前需要再多練習一下。

- In the weeks before he went onstage with his monologue, Brian did a **dry run** every night. 在演出的好幾個星期前，布萊恩每天晚上都在為獨角戲**排練**。

- They decided to do a **dry run** at the church the day before the wedding.
他們決定婚禮前在教堂做一次**預演**。

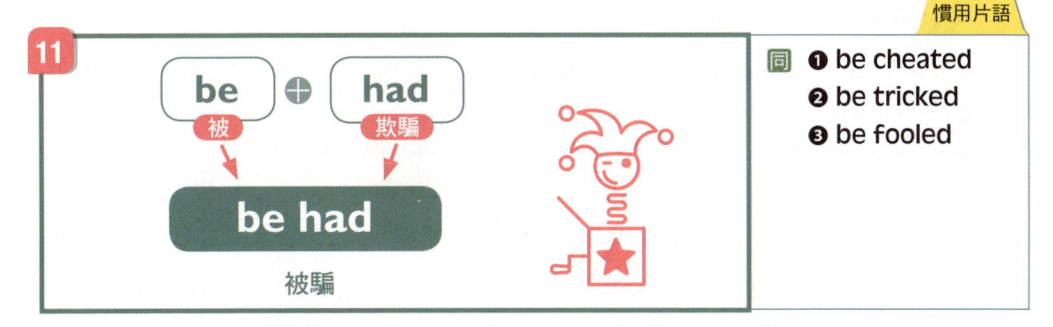

11

be(被) + **had**(欺騙) → **be had** 被騙

同
❶ be cheated
❷ be tricked
❸ be fooled

- When you go shopping for a new computer, it's a good idea to bring along an expert so you don't end up **being had**.
買新電腦時，最好找一位內行人陪你去，才不會**被騙**。

- I'm sorry to tell you this, but if you just spent $1,200 on this stereo, you **were had**.
很遺憾地告訴你，如果你花了 1,200 元買了這個音響，你肯定**被騙了**。

- If you paid much for this car, you've **been had**!
如果這台車花了你很多錢，那你肯定是**被騙了**！

Unit 39 Test Yourself!

A 選擇題

1. I wouldn't like to _____ when the boss hears what he's done!
   Ⓐ keep after John　　　Ⓑ be in John's shoes
   Ⓒ fix John up　　　　　Ⓓ play John by ear

2. When the used car he bought just two days ago broke down, Gary realized that he'd _____.
   Ⓐ played it by ear　Ⓑ fixed it up　Ⓒ been had　Ⓓ kept after

3. The children _____ when their parents left them with a babysitter; they acted like monsters!
   Ⓐ got out of line　Ⓑ were had　Ⓒ fixed up　Ⓓ played it by ear

4. Zoe _____ me until I paid her back the money I had borrowed.
   Ⓐ was had　Ⓑ got out of line with　Ⓒ kept after　Ⓓ fixed up

5. After Adrian _____ his mother, she told him he could not go out with his friends for the entire weekend.
   Ⓐ fixed up　Ⓑ was out　Ⓒ talked back to　Ⓓ was had

6. When Rick called Erin, she _____, so he called her cell phone.
   Ⓐ talked back　Ⓑ fixed up　Ⓒ played it by ear　Ⓓ was out

7. I know you want to go somewhere nice for dinner tonight, but I don't know if I'll have enough time; so let's _____.
   Ⓐ play it by ear　Ⓑ be in my shoes　Ⓒ fix up　Ⓓ be had

8. Sorry, but my supervisor won't _____ this weekend.
   Ⓐ fix up　Ⓑ be in　Ⓒ play it by ear　Ⓓ be had

9. Two days before opening night, the students did a _____ of the performance.
   Ⓐ dry run　Ⓑ quick discussion　Ⓒ talk over　Ⓓ goof off

10. Irma _____ over the holiday and didn't write a single page of her report.
    Ⓐ goofed off　Ⓑ fixed up　Ⓒ kept after　Ⓓ played it by ear

11. Jeff really enjoys _____ old computers and other electronics.
    Ⓐ being in　Ⓑ fixing up　Ⓒ keeping after　Ⓓ being had by

12. Sometimes Tammy swears, but she _____ at saying words that are too tasteless.
    Ⓐ is out　Ⓑ fixes up　Ⓒ keeps after　Ⓓ draws the line

B 閱讀文章，從字表中選擇詞彙填入，並依人稱時態等做適當的變化

draw the line	talk back to	be in	be had
keep after	be out	goof off	dry run
in (someone's) shoes		play (something) by ear	

Eric is a professional pianist. It was Sunday, so he was ①_____ at home doing nothing, as usual. Then, his boss Linda called and told him that he needed to ②_____ to work at 7 a.m. the next day to do a ③_____ of the music show. It would be a busy day, she told him. He would have to ④_____ of the studio by 3 p.m. in order to pick up the sheet music at the printers. After he hung up, he remembered that Monday was supposed to be his day off! He decided to call Linda back, but first he tried to put himself ⑤_____. He knew she was probably stressed out, so he didn't want to act rude or ⑥_____ her. He didn't want to get fired!

When he called back, Linda asked him to come in that very day—Sunday! That's where Eric ⑦_____. He said that every good pianist also needs time to rest, and he wasn't sure if he would come in tomorrow either. He told Linda he would see how things go and ⑧_____.

Linda was unhappy, but she asked Eric to at least ⑨_____ the printer to make sure everyone had a copy of the new music. The fact was, Eric was beginning to feel as though he had ⑩_____ by his boss. He was, after all, a pianist, not her personal assistant!

C 引導式翻譯，並依人稱時態等做適當的變化

1. 如果我是你，我會和那女孩的父母談一談。
   If I _____ _____ your _____, I'd speak to the girl's parents.

2. 我不確定是否能去滑雪，**看情況吧**。
   I'm not sure if I can go skiing after all. I'll just have to _____ it _____ _____.

3. 這棟房子看起來不錯，但可以請人稍微**整修**一下。
   This old house is interesting, but someone needs to _____ it _____ a bit.

Index

A

a bargain（划算） 271
a few（不多） 80
A goes with B（A與B相配） 87
a good few（相當多） 80
a good many（相當多） 80
a great many（相當多） 80
a great number（相當多） 80
A is named after B（A是由B的名字來命名） 179
a large number（相當多） 80
a small number（不多） 80
a steal（買到便宜貨） 271
above all things（尤其是） 147
above all（特別；尤其） 147
accidentally on purpose（假裝不小心但其實故意地） 25
according to（根據；據……所記載） 153
act for（代表） 189
adhere to（堅持） 220
again and again（一再） 67
agree to（同意；接受） 86, 145
agree with（一致） 137
all along the line（到處；在每一個階段、環節或時刻） 17
all along（從一開始就；自始至終；一直） 17
all at once（突然） 50
all by oneself（靠某人自己） 22
all day long（一整天） 22
all hell breaks loose（亂成一團） 263
all in all（整體而言；總括來說） 163, 237
all month long（一整個月） 22
all night long（一整晚） 22
all night（一整晚） 22
all of a sudden（突然；毫無預警）50
all right（沒問題；好吧；好的） 17
all the time（自始至終） 17
all the while（自始至終） 17
all week long（一整個星期） 22
all year long（一整年） 22
allow for（加以考慮） 114
answer back to（頂嘴） 324
around the corner（在附近） 271
as a matter of fact（事實上） 123
as a rule（一如往常） 15
as a whole（整體看來） 237
as always（一如往常） 15
as far as . . . be concerned（關於） 105
as for sb（關於某人） 105
as for sth（關於某事） 105
as for（關於） 105
As it turns out . . .（結果原來是……） 114
as regards（關於） 105
as respects（關於） 105
as soon as possible（儘快） 76
as soon as（立即；一……就……） 76
as to（關於） 105
as usual（一如往常；照常） 15
ask for it（自找麻煩） 315
ask for sb（要求見某人） 315
ask for sth（要求某事物） 315
ask for trouble（自找麻煩） 315
ask for（應得；要求） 115, 315
at all（絲毫；根本） 31
at any rate（至少） 31
at first（起初；原來；剛開始） 8
at hand（在附近） 271
at heart（實際上；內心是） 155
at its heart（本質上） 155
at large（一般而言） 163
at last（最後；終於） 8
at least（至少） 31
at most（至多） 31
at no time（從不；絕不） 77
at once（馬上；立即） 6, 77
at the beginning（某階段的開始）8
at the least（至少） 31
at the most（至多） 31
at times（有時候） 86
attend to（照顧） 121

B

back and forth（來來回回） 80
back out of sth（退出某事） 245
back out（反悔；食言；退出） 245
back sb up / back up sb（支持某人） 246
back sth up / back up sth（支持某事） 246
back up（支持；聲援；倒車） 189, 246
bank on（依賴） 50
be a far cry from sth（與……有很大的差異） 316
be a far cry from（與……相差甚遠） 316
be about to do sth（正要做某事) 68
be about to（正好；準備要；正要去做；準備去） 68, 154
be accustomed to（習慣於） 79, 81
be at pains（費盡苦心） 186
be better off（比較好的狀況） 179
be bound to〔可能（肯定）會發生〕153
be carried away（開心到忘我的境界） 96
be certain to（一定會） 153
be cut out for sth（適合某事） 243
be cut out for（勝任；適合） 243
be cut out to be sth（有成為某事的能力） 243
be cut out to do sth（有做某事的能力） 243
be cheated（被欺騙） 243
be even with（報復） 252
be fed up with（忍無可忍） 276
be fooled（被騙） 243
be had（被騙） 327
be in (someone's) place（站在某人的立場） 325
be in (someone's) shoes（站在某人的立場） 325
be in (the/one's) way（阻礙；造成不便） 163
be in a better situation（情況變好） 179
be in charge of（管理……；負責） 76
be in love with（愛上） 71
be in the charge of（由……管理） 76
be in touch with（與……聯絡） 181
be in（在家；在公司；流行） 323
be just going to（即將要；正要做） 68, 154
be no question of (doing) sth（不可能做某事情） 67
be on the ball（快速理解；反應靈敏） 277
be on the point of（即將要；正要做） 68, 154
be out of the question（某事不可能發生） 67
be out of touch（失去聯絡） 75
be out（不在家；不在公司；落伍） 323
be over one's head（太難以致無法理解） 315
be over（結束） 58
be responsible for（負責） 76
be rid of（擺脫；廢除） 86
be seated（坐下） 23
be sorry for（同情） 108
be stuck on（愛上） 71
be suitable for（適合） 243
be sure to（一定會） 153
be the matter with sb（某人出問題） 169
be the matter with sth（某事物出問題） 169
be the matter（傷腦筋；出狀況） 169
be tricked（被欺騙） 243
be to do with（與……有關） 69
be unaccustomed to（不習慣於……） 81
be under the weather（生病） 47

330

be unsuitable for（不適合） 243
be up for grabs（讓他人也能得到或贏得） 308
be up to no good（圖謀不軌） 254
be up to sb（由某人決定） 95
be up to something bad（圖謀不軌） 254
be up to something（策劃） 95, 254
be up to〔正在做某事；由……決定；做壞事（違法的事情）〕 95
be up〔醒來；（時間）到了〕 57
be used to sb（與某人熟悉） 81
be used to sth（已經習慣某事） 81
be used to（已經習慣於……；熟悉；習慣於） 79, 81
be well-off（生活富裕） 179
be with (someone)（與某人談戀愛；了解某人說的話） 284
be with it（得到訊息；快速理解） 285
be worse off（情況變糟） 179
be/get mixed up in sth（被捲入、牽扯某事物） 90
be/get mixed up with sb（與某人廝混） 90
be/get mixed up（被弄亂；被搞糊塗） 90
bear in mind（記住） 138
beat about the bush（拐彎抹角） 251
beat around the bush（說話拐彎抹角） 251
become better（變好） 61
become lost（迷路） 170
become of sb（某人發生何事） 148
become of sth（某事結果如何） 148
become of（發生） 148
become used to（逐漸適應；習慣於） 78
believe in sb（深信某人；對某人有信心） 206
believe in sth（相信某事物） 206
believe in〔相信；相信……的存在（通常指幽靈或宗教信仰）〕 206
bit by bit（逐漸地；逐步地） 15
bite off sth（咬斷某物） 163
bite off（咬斷） 163
blow out（吹熄（蠟燭）；（輪胎）爆裂） 147
blow up（使爆炸；使勃然大怒；使（氣球、輪胎）膨脹；使（照片）放大） 107
bow out（引退；退出） 287
bow down to sb（服從於某人） 287
break down sth（使某事物衰退、腐敗） 117
break down〔（機器）故障；崩潰；衰退；腐敗〕 117
break in（闖入；打斷談話；使用後逐漸適合） 146

break into（闖入） 146
break loose（掙脫；逃跑） 263
break off（分離；中斷） 235
break one's promise（違反承諾） 319
break one's word（違反承諾） 319
break out in (a) sweat（突然冒冷汗） 108
break out in a rash（突然起疹子） 108
break out in spots（突然起斑點） 108
break out〔突然發生（爭執、戰爭）；爆發（傳染病）；逃跑〕 108
break sb down（使某人情緒崩潰） 117
break sth in / break in sth（使用後逐漸適合某物） 146
break sth off / break off sth（中斷某事物） 235
break the habit（戒掉習慣） 276
break up into（使成碎片） 235
break up sth / break sth up（弄碎某事物） 235
break up（分開；打碎；分手） 180, 235
bring . . . to an end（終止） 254
bring about（引起；造成） 219
bring back（歸還；憶起） 236
bring on（造成） 219
bring out（推出（商品）；使出現） 236
bring sb up / bring up sb（扶養某人） 173
bring sth back / bring back sth（帶回某物；想起某事） 236
bring sth up / bring up sth（提出某事） 173
bring up（養育（小孩、動物）；提出議題） 173
brush up on sth（複習某事物） 65
brush up on（複習） 65
brush up（溫習） 65
build up sb / build sb up（鼓勵某人） 220
build up sth / build sth up（增強某事物） 220
build up（增強；增強；加深印象） 220
bump into（偶然遇到；遇到） 186, 203
burn (sth) to the ground（燒掉） 104
burn down（燒毀；燒成灰燼） 104, 107
burn off（燒掉） 106
burn oneself out（把自己給累壞） 107
burn out〔使筋疲力盡；（機器）燒壞；燒盡〕 106, 107

burn sb up（使某人發怒） 106
burn sth down（燒毀某物） 104
burn the midnight oil（熬夜） 198
burn up sth / burn up sth（燒光某物） 106
burn up with sth（因某事而發怒） 106
burn up（燒光；使發怒；發燒） 106, 107
burst into laughter（大笑） 215
burst into tears（放聲大哭） 215
burst out crying（放聲大哭） 215
burst out laughing（大笑） 215
burst out（突然大笑、大哭；大聲地喊） 215
buy out（收購（企業、股份）） 244
buy sth up / buy up sth（買下某物） 244
buy up（全部買下） 244
by all means（一定；當然；不用說） 317
by and large（一般而言；總括來說） 163, 237
by far（遠高於；顯然） 169
by heart〔記住（詩、歌、故事）〕 88
by no means（絕不） 317
by oneself（獨自；某人自己；單獨地） 22
by the way（附帶一提） 292
by turns（交替；輪流） 65

C

call for（需要；要求；接某人） 115
call it a day（結束當天的工作；到此為止） 61
call it a night（結束當晚的工作） 61
call off〔取消（會議、事件）；叫走〕 42
call on sb to do sth（請某人做某事） 16
call on sb（拜訪某人） 16
call on（課堂上點名回答問題；請求；號召；呼籲；拜訪） 16, 29
call sb/sth off（喊走某人或狗） 42
call sth off（終止某事） 42
call up sb（打電話給某人；徵召某人入伍） 3
call up sth（回想起某事） 3
call up（打電話給某人） 3
can/could do without sth（某事物造成困擾） 157
care for（照顧） 121
carry on doing sth（繼續做某事） 309
carry on sth（繼續進行某事） 309
carry on with sth（繼續進行某事） 309

331

carry on（繼續；繼續下去；驚慌失措） 48, 205, 309
carry out（實現；開始執行；實踐） 125, 205
carry sth out / carry out sth（執行某事） 205
catch (a) cold（感冒（喉嚨痛、輕微咳嗽、流鼻涕）） 40
catch a bad/heavy/severe cold（重感冒） 40
catch a slight cold（輕微感冒） 40
catch by surprise（感到意外） 178
catch fire（著火） 104
catch hold of（抓住） 99
catch on〔受到歡迎、聽懂（意思或玩笑）；理解〕 243, 255
catch sth from sb（被某人傳染某疾病） 40
catch up on（趕完；補上） 164
catch up with sb（趕上某人） 164
catch up with sth（趕上某事物的進度） 164
catch up with（迎頭趕上） 149, 227
catch up（追上） 164
change one's mind about doing sth（改變做某事的決定） 41
change one's mind（改變主意） 41
check in（住房登記） 299
check in with sb（問候某人平安） 299
check on（檢查；調查） 213
check out sth / check sth out（檢查某事物；看看某事物） 301
check out（辦理退房；結帳離開；檢查；看看） 301
check over（檢查；調查） 213
check up on sb（調查某人） 213
check up on sth（檢查某事物） 213
check up on（調查；探望某人或聯絡某人以確定某人安好） 213
check up（檢查） 156
check sth in（托運） 299
cheer sb on（鼓勵某人） 203
cheer sb up（使某人高興） 203
cheer sth up（使某事物引人注目） 203
cheer up（使高興；使生動） 203
clean down（徹底清洗） 195
clean out（清理乾淨） 195
clean sth out / clean out sth（清出某事物） 195
clean up（打掃；梳洗；清理） 195
clear up sth / clear sth up（清理某處；釐清某事） 247
clear up（清理；釐清；天氣轉晴） 247
cling to（堅持） 220
close call（千鈞一髮；倖免於難） 199

close shave（僥倖脫險） 199
come about（發生） 222
come across sb（突然遇見某人） 186
come across sth（突然發現某事物） 186
come across（被認為是；突然遇見或發現；遇到） 186, 203
come around（順便來訪） 187
come back（回來） 40
come from sth（來自於某事物；由……引起） 89
come from sw（來自某地） 89
come from（出生於；來自；從……取得結論；由……引起） 89
come of（來自） 89
come over（順便來訪） 187
come to a close（結束） 254
come to an end（結束） 254
come to life（醒過來） 116
come to one's senses（醒過來） 116
come to oneself（醒過來） 116
come to sb（突然想起） 116
come to sth（合計） 116
come to the point（有話直說） 251
come to（恢復意識；合計） 116
come true（實現；成真） 125, 205, 228
come up to（達到標準） 219
come up with（想出；提出辦法） 149, 303
come upon（偶然遇到；遇到） 186, 203
communicate with（與……聯絡） 75, 181
compromise with sb（妥協） 206
cop out（逃避責任） 300
count on sb（依靠某人） 50
count on sth（預期某事發生） 50
count on（依靠；指望；相信） 50, 122
cover a lot of ground（涉獵廣泛） 310
cover for（撒謊掩護；暫時代替某人） 286
cover ground（涉及的範圍） 310
cover up sth / cover sth up（掩蓋某事物） 278
cover up（掩蓋（秘密）） 278
cross off（刪除） 117
cross one's fingers（祈求好運） 309
cross out sth / cross sth out（刪除某事物） 117
cross out（畫線刪除） 117
cut-and-dried（可預期的；明確的） 123
cut back（減少） 79

cut corners（節約；偷工減料） 219
cut down on sth（減少某事物的量） 79
cut down on（削減；減少） 79
cut down（削減；縮短） 79
cut it out（停止） 140
cut off〔切斷；剪短；中斷（電話、有線電視、網路）〕 139
cut out（剪下；停止） 140
cut sb down to size（使某人有自知之名） 79
cut sb off / cut off sb（打斷某人；中斷某人的通訊；孤立某人） 139
cut sb short（打斷某人的話） 261
cut short（打斷談話；中斷） 260
cut sth off / cut off sth（切斷某事物；隔離某事物） 139
cut sth out / cut out sth（剪下某事物；戒除某事物） 140
cut sth short / cut short sth（中斷某事） 261

D

day after day（日復一日） 162
day in and day out（每天） 162
depart from（違反） 220
depend on/upon（依賴） 50
derive from（來自） 89
deviate from（違反） 220
die away（逐漸消失） 222
die down（變少；減弱） 222
die off（相繼死去） 223
die out（滅絕；逐漸消失） 223
dine out（外出用餐） 121
dish out（脫口而出；分發） 317
dish sth out / dish out sth（分發某事；脫口而出某事） 317
dish the dirt（責罵） 317
dish up（上菜） 317
distinguish from（區別） 162
do away with（擺脫；廢除） 86
do over（重做） 95
do sth over / do over sth（重做某事） 96
do without (sth)（沒有某事物也可以） 157
do without（沒有……而將就；過著沒有……的日子） 157
drag on（拖延） 39
draw sth up / draw up sth（擬定某事） 205
draw the line at sth（拒絕某事物） 325
draw the line between sth（使……有差異） 325
draw the line（堅持不做某事；區別） 324

draw up（制定；草擬）205
dress sth up（裝飾；粉刷）13
dress up（特殊打扮；為正式場合盛裝打扮）13
dress down Fridays（便服日；上班時不用穿制服的日子）13
dress-down（非正休的休閒穿著）13
drop (someone) a line（打電話給某人；寫便條給某人）187
drop a line to sb（寫一封短信給某人）187
drop behind（落後）227
drop by（順便來訪）187
drop in（拜訪）204
drop off sb / drop sb off（讓某人下車）279
drop off sth / drop sth off（留下某事物）279
drop off（在途中下車；減少）279
drop out of（退出；脫離）204
drop out（退出）204
drop the habit（戒掉習慣）276
dry off（變乾）251
dry out（使變乾）251
dry run（排練；預演）327
dry up（枯竭）251
dummy run（預演）327

E

ease up（停止；減弱）239
ease off（停止；減弱）239
eat at a restaurant（外出用餐）121
eat in（在家用餐）121
eat out（在餐廳用餐）121
edgy（緊張）261
escape from（擺脫；廢除）86
every now and then（有時候）86
every other (one)（每隔……）89
every other sth（所有其他的；每隔……）89
every so often（有時候）86

F

face-to-face（面對面）283
fade away〔（影像、想法）慢慢消失；死亡〕223
fade out（慢慢消失）223
fall behind with sth（在某方面落後）227
fall behind（落後；跟不上；延遲）164, 227
fall for sb（愛上某人；迷戀某人）71, 284
fall for sth（因某事物而被騙）284
fall for（迷戀；被欺騙）284

fall in love with sb at first sight（與某人一見鍾情）71
fall in love with sb（愛上某人）71
fall in love（墜入情網）71
fall on one's feet（重新振作）318
fall out（吵架；結果）71, 114
fall short of（未達到……的期望）219
fall through（無法實現；落空）125, 228
feel like (doing) sth〔想要（做）某事〕124
feel like（想要做某事）124
feel sick（作嘔；想吐）58
feel sorry for（深表同情）108
feel under the weather（感覺不舒服）47
few and far between（稀有；獨特）51
figure out（想出；找出答案；解決問題）57, 245
figure sb out / figure out sb（理解某人）57
figure sth out / figure out sth（理解某事）57
fill (someone) in（告訴）129, 283
fill (sb) in on sth（告訴某人某事）283
fill in（填寫；代替）129, 130
fill out（填寫；增胖）129, 130
fill sth in / fill in sth（填寫某事物）129
final straw（忍無可忍）276
find fault with sb（挑某人的毛病）95
find fault with sth（挑事物的毛病）95
find fault with（挑毛病；找碴）95
find one's tongue（開口說話）146
find one's way（找到路）170
find out that或wh-引導的名詞子句（發現某事）15
find out who引導的名詞子句（發現某人做了壞事）15
find out（發現；找出）15
find sb out（發現某人做了壞事）15
find sth out（發現某事）15
fix sb up / fix up sb（提供給某人；替某人安排相親）326
fix sth up / fix up sth（修理某事物；安排某事物）326
fix up（修理；安排）326
follow out（實現）205
fool about（鬼混）252
fool around（開玩笑；遊手好閒；鬼混）252, 323
for certain（確定）155
forever（永遠的）43
for good（永遠；永久）41, 43

for now（目前）41
for once（僅這一次）137
for sure（肯定；確定地）155
for the moment（目前）41
for the most part（總括來說）237
for the present（目前）41
for the time being（現在；目前）41
forever and ever（永遠的）43
from day to day（日復一日）162
from now on（從今以後）97
from time to time（有時候）86

G

gain weight（增重）130
generally speaking（總括來說）237
get (a) cold（感冒）40
get (sb) through sth（渡過難關）97
get (something) off one's chest（把……傾吐出來；表明）291
get a rise out of sb（使生氣；使某人生氣）291
get accustomed to（習慣於……）79, 81
get across（通過）97
get along (with)（和睦相處；進展）23
get along with sb（與某人相處融洽；與某人相處）23, 140
get along with sth（某事有所進展）23, 140
get along（有進展；處理；生存）140
get away with sth（逃過懲罰）211
get away with（成功地逃過懲罰）211
get away（逃離；離開）40, 211
get back from sw（從某地方回來）40
get back to sb（回覆某人）40
get back to sth（回到某事物上）40
get back（取回；回來）40
get behind（落後）227
get better（使情況好轉）61
get busy（忙碌）58
get carried away（興奮不已）96
get cold feet（緊張；害怕）283
get even with sb for sth（為某事向某人報復）252
get even with sb（向某人報復）252
get even with（報復）252
get hold of（抓住）99
get in touch with sb（與某人取得聯絡）75
get in touch with（與……聯絡）75

333

get in touch（與……取得聯絡） 75
get in 交通工具（上某種小型而密閉的交通工具） 7
get in〔上車（汽車、計程車等小型車）；到達〕 7, 99
get lost（迷路） 170
get mad（生氣） 59
get off（下車,用於大型的交通工具） 7
get on one's nerves（令人心煩或討厭） 196
get on〔上車（大型交通工具：巴士、火車、飛機、船等；相處融洽）〕 7, 140
get one's way（隨心所欲） 123
get oneself up（打扮自己，尤指較為特別的裝扮） 3
get out from under sth（擺脫某事物） 319
get out from under（解決債務；擺脫負擔） 319
get out of bed（起床） 3
get out of line（不守規矩） 325
get out of the way（讓路） 163
get out of（下車,用於小型的交通工具） 7
get over it（將……忘卻；別再傷心難過） 39
get over sb（忘卻某人） 39
get over sth（從生病或悲傷中恢復過來） 39
get over〔（從生病、悲傷中）復原；恢復〕 39
get rid of sb（擺脫某人） 86
get rid of sth（丟棄某物；脫手某事物） 86
get rid of（去除；丟棄） 85
get sb back / get back at sb（向某人報復） 40
get sb up（叫醒某人） 3
get shot of（擺脫；廢除） 86
get sick（生病） 58
get sth back（取回某物） 40
get sth in / get in sth（購買生活用品） 3
get the best of（勝過） 262
get the better of sb（打敗某人） 262
get the better of sth（戰勝某事物） 262
get the better of（打敗；戰勝） 262
get the sack（被解雇） 238
get through sth（完成某事；通過某事） 97
get through to (someone)（使了解；聯絡上） 318
get through（使理解；完成；通過；聯絡上） 97, 243

get tired（累了） 58
get to sb（使某人惱怒；影響某人） 49
get to the point（有話直說） 251
get to（可以做（某事）；到達；感到困擾） 49
get under one's skin（惹惱某人；刺激某人） 253
get up sth / get sth up（籌備某事） 3
get up（叫醒某人；起床） 3, 57
get used to something（逐漸習慣於某事） 79
get used to（逐漸適應；習慣於……） 78, 81
get well（好了） 58
get wet（濕了） 58
get worse（變糟） 61
give (someone) a big hand（鼓掌） 317
give (someone) a break（饒了……；得了吧） 287
give (someone) a hand（幫助） 316
give-and-take（相互退讓） 207
give birth to sb（生下某人） 199
give birth to sth（某事物誕生） 199
give birth to（生孩子） 199
give in to sb（向某人屈服） 230
give in to sth（向某事屈服） 230
give in to（容許；屈服） 230
give in（讓步；投降） 230
give off〔散發出（味道等）〕 229
give out（分發；用盡；分配） 161, 229
give rise to sth（引起某事物） 199
give rise to（造成） 219
give sb a call（打電話給某人） 3
give sb a ring（打電話給某人） 3
give sb time off（准某人休假） 53
give way to（容許；屈服） 230
give way（容許；屈服） 230
go around sth（在某處四處走動） 164
go around（四處走動；流傳；足夠分配） 164
go down（下降） 269
go for（特別喜歡；努力爭取） 196
go halfway to meet sb（妥協） 206
go in for sth（參加某事物；喜愛某事物） 196
go in for〔共同分攤（禮或餐廳的）錢；參加比賽；喜歡；把……當作興趣〕 196
go into（調查） 98
go off the deep end（勃然大怒） 267
go off（機器停止；離開；警報響起；爆炸；發生；變糟；食物壞掉） 139

go on doing sth（繼續做某件正在做的事情） 49
go on to do sth（完成某事後，繼續做另一件事情） 49
go on with sth（繼續做某事情） 48
go on（發生；繼續下去） 48, 309
go out doing sth（外出做某事） 66
go out for sth（為某事而外出） 66
go out of one's way（費盡苦心） 186
go out to eat（外出用餐） 121
go out with sb（與某人約會、交往） 66
go out〔離開（家、學校、辦公室）外出；熄滅〕 66
go over one's head（難以理解） 315
go over sth（仔細檢視某事物；複習某事物） 156
go over（查看；被接納；仔細檢視；複習） 51, 156
go round（散播；足夠分配） 164
go through sth（找出某事；經歷某事；大量使用某事） 262
go through with（實行） 262
go through（找出；經歷；大量使用） 262
go to bed（上床） 3, 57
go to great pains（費盡苦心） 186
go to pieces（使成碎片） 235
go to sleep（上床） 3, 198
go to town（全心投入） 295
go up to sth（接近某事物） 178
go up to（接近） 178
go up〔上升；建立（建築物）〕 178, 269
go well with（與……很相配） 87
go with sb（與某人交往） 87
go with sth（與某事物看法相同） 87
go with〔與……搭配（通常指衣服、食物）；與……交往；與……看法相同〕 86
go wrong（情況不順利；弄錯） 212, 228
(it) goes without saying（不用說） 259
goof around（混日子；鬼混） 252, 267,323
goof off（摸魚；偷懶） 323
goof up（犯錯） 267
ground cover（地被植物） 310
grow into sb（長大成為某人） 141
grow into sth（長大而穿得下某衣物） 141
grow out of sth（產生於某事；長大而戒某事） 141
grow out of〔因長大而不適合（衣服、鞋子）；產生於；因長大而戒除〕 141

334

H

had better（應該；最好） 61
had rather（寧願） 59
hand in sth（繳交某事物） 177
hand in（繳交；提出） 177
hand out（分發；分配） 161, 229
hand over（移交） 197
hand sth in（繳交某事物） 177
hang around（緩慢地做） 292
hang on（不掛斷電話；緊抓） 48, 180
hang sth up（懸掛某物） 48
hang up on sb（掛某人電話） 48
hang up〔懸掛（衣服）；掛斷電話〕 48, 180
happen on（碰巧遇見） 178
hard of hearing（重聽的） 138
have (a) cold（感冒） 40
have (time) off（休假） 53
have a bad time（過得不愉快） 77
have a good time（玩得愉快） 77
have a hard time（過得不愉快） 77
have a look at（看） 14
have a lot of fun（玩得開心） 77
have a voice in sth（對某事物有發言的權利） 295
have a voice in（擁有發言權） 295
have confidence in（相信） 206
have cold feet（害怕） 283
have fun（玩得開心） 77
have got sth（擁有某事物） 148
have got to（必須） 148
have got（擁有；持有） 148
have in mind（想到；打算） 138
have it in for sb（與某人過不去） 227
have it in for（與……過不去；對……伺機報復） 227
have it out with sb（與某人攤牌） 228
have it out with（與某人起爭執） 228
have much to do with（與……有很大關係） 69
have nothing to do with（與……沒有關係） 69
have on〔穿戴（衣服、首飾、鞋子）〕 117
have one's fingers crossed（祈求好運） 309
have one's heart set on doing sth（下定決心做某事） 243
have one's heart set on sth（一心想要某事） 243
have one's heart set on（下定決心；一心想要） 243
have one's way（照某人的意思去做；為所欲為） 123
have pity on（同情） 108

have poor eyesight（視力不良） 138
have poor sight（視力不良） 138
have poor vision（視力不良） 138
have something to do with（與……有些關係） 68
have sth on（穿戴某事物） 117
have the best of（勝過） 262
have to do with sb（與某人有關） 69
have to do with sth（與某事有關） 69
have to do with〔與……有關；在不同的情況（困境）中生存〕 68
hear about（得知；聽到） 122
hear from sb（從某人那聽到） 122, 124
hear from（接到某人的消息） 124
hear of sb（聽說過某人） 122
hear of sth（聽說某事） 122
hear of（聽說；得知；考慮） 122
hold back（抑制） 231
hold off（延緩發生；拖延） 39, 229
hold on to（堅持） 220
hold on（不掛斷電話；稍等；抓緊；堅持下去） 48, 180
hold one's peace（保持沉默） 146
hold onto sth（抓緊某事物） 180
hold out against sth（為某事堅持到底） 231
hold out（堅持；給予） 231
hold over（延後；拖延） 229
hold pace with（跟上） 148
hold sb up / hold up sb（耽誤某人） 172
hold sth out / hold out sth（給予希望） 231
hold sth up / hold up sth（搶劫某物） 172
hold still（不要動） 169
hold up（拖延；搶劫；阻礙） 172, 231
horse around（鬼混） 252

I

I don't know（我不知道） 291
idle away（鬼混） 252
ill at ease（緊張；不安） 99
in a bad way（狀況不佳） 47
in a hurry（匆忙；緊急） 21
in accordance with（依照） 153
in and out（內外顛倒） 129
in case of sth（遇到某種狀況時） 177
in case（假使；以防萬一） 177
in connection with（關於） 105
in contact（有聯繫） 130
in effect（事實上） 123

in fact（事實上） 123
in fashion（流行；流行的） 103, 323
in general（一般而言） 163
in hand（在掌握中；在控制中；在進行中） 271
in next to no time（立即） 77
in no time（馬上；很快地；立刻；立即） 6, 77
in nothing flat（立即） 77
in order（情況良好） 52
in reality（事實上） 123
in regard to（關於） 105
in relation to（關於） 105
in respect of（關於） 105
in safe hands（得到妥善照顧） 271
in style（流行的） 103
in the long run（從長遠來看；一段時間後） 132
in the long term（長遠來看） 132
in the main（一般而言；總括來說） 163, 237
in the short run（短時間內） 132
in the short term（短時間內） 132
in the worst way（渴望地；緊急地；非常） 303
in time for sth（及時趕上某事） 60
in time to do sth（及時去做某事） 60
in time（及時） 58, 60
in touch with sb（和某人有聯繫） 130
in touch with sth（知道某事） 130
in touch〔透過電話、信件、電子郵件或其他方式和某人聯絡〕 130
in truth（事實上） 123
in turn（按順序） 65
in vain（白費） 162
in vogue（流行的） 103
inquire into（調查） 98
inside and out（內外顛倒） 129
inside out（內外反過來；徹底地） 129
It doesn't matter.（沒關係！不要緊！） 14
it figures that . . .（……是理所當然的） 285
it figures（理所當然） 285
It turns out that . . .（結果證明是……） 114

J

join in（參與某活動） 30
joke with sb（欺騙某人） 259
just for once（僅此一次） 137
just now（剛才） 68, 154
just this once（僅此一次） 137

335

K

keep after sb（不斷詢問某人） 324
keep after sth（不斷詢問某事） 324
keep after（不斷詢問；嘮嘮叨叨） 324
keep away (from)（遠離；不許靠近） 98
keep away from sb（遠離某人） 98
keep away from sth（遠離某事物） 98
keep bad time（走得不準） 190
keep calm（保持冷靜） 259
keep company with（與……在一起） 86
keep good time（走得準） 190
keep in mind（記得；將某事放在心上） 88, 138
keep in touch with sb（與某人保持聯絡） 181
keep in touch with（與……保持聯繫） 97, 181
keep in touch（與……保持聯絡） 75
keep off（遠離） 98
keep on（繼續） 48
keep one's cool（保持冷靜） 299
keep one's fingers crossed（祈求） 309
keep one's head（保持冷靜；沉著） 259, 260
keep one's promise（遵守承諾） 319
keep one's shirt on（保持冷靜） 259
keep one's word（遵守約定；值得信任） 319
keep out（遠離；不許進入；避免捲入某種情況） 98, 99
keep pace with（跟上） 148
keep sb away from sth（使某人遠離某事） 98
keep sb away（不讓某人接近） 98
keep sb out of sth（避免某人捲入某事） 99
keep sb out（禁止某人進入） 99
keep sb up / keep up sb（使某人保持清醒） 214
keep sth away（不接近某事物） 98
keep sth in mind（記住某事） 138
keep sth out of sth（避免某事扯上某事） 99
keep sth out（禁止某事物進入） 99
keep sth up / keep up sth（維持某種情況） 214
keep time〔（鐘錶的時間）精準；計時〕 190
keep to（堅持） 220

keep track of sb（追蹤某人的行蹤） 96
keep track of sth（追蹤某事） 96
keep track of（追蹤；密切注意） 96
keep up with sb（趕上某人） 149, 214
keep up with sth（跟上某事） 149, 214
keep up with（不落後於；跟上；與……保持聯繫；趕上） 149, 214
keep up〔持續（某種情況）；使保持清醒〕 214
keep your nose clean（不惹事生非） 307
kick (sth) around（討論） 275
kick around sth / kick sth around（討論某事） 275
kick around（存在） 275
kick sb around / kick around sb（仗勢欺人） 275
kick the habit（戒掉壞習慣） 276
kiss up to (someone)（討好） 268
knock cold（使昏迷） 207
knock out（擊倒；使昏迷；使筋疲力盡；摧毀） 161, 207
knock sb out（使某人昏迷不醒） 207
knock sth out（摧毀某事物） 207
know by sight（認得） 170
know sb by sight（認得某人） 170
know sth by heart（熟記某事物） 88
know sth by sight（認出某事物） 170
know the ropes（懂得訣竅） 307

L

lack faith in（不信任） 206
lag behind（落後） 227
land on one's feet（安然脫險；重新振作起來） 318
last straw（已達極限） 276
laugh at（嘲笑） 125
lay down（放下） 197
lay off sb / lay sb off（解雇某人） 238
lay off sth（節制某事物） 238
lay off（停止；節制；解僱） 230, 238
lead to（造成） 219
lean on/upon（依賴） 50
learn sth by heart（熟記某事物） 88
learn the ropes（摸索） 307
leave (sb or sth) alone（讓某人獨處；別打擾） 235
leave open（暫緩決定） 301
leave out（刪掉） 140

leave sb alone（別打擾某人） 235
leave sth alone（別觸碰某事物；別涉入某事） 235
leave sth open / leave open sth（暫緩決定某事） 301
let (sb) alone（不打擾某人做某事） 237
let . . . down（未達到……的期望） 219
let alone（更不必說） 237
let down（放下） 197
let go（放開） 99, 146
let on about sth（透露某事） 211
let on that/who/how/why . . .（透露……） 211
let on〔洩漏（秘密）〕 211
let out（放大尺寸） 255
let sb slide / let slide sb（丟下某人不管） 293
let slide（丟下不管；忽視眼前的情況） 293
let sth slide / let slide sth（忽視某事情） 293
let up（停止；減弱；天氣轉晴） 239
lie down on the job（工作偷懶打混） 24
lie down（躺下） 24
lie low（不出聲；隱藏） 24
lie up（藏匿） 24
line sb up / line up sb（使排隊） 302
line sth up / line up sth（安排某事情） 302
line up（排隊；安排） 302
little by little（逐漸地） 15
little wonder（不足為奇） 170
live it up（生活奢華） 294
live up to (sth)（遵守某事物；達成期望） 219, 294
live up to（實踐；達成） 219
liven (sb) up（使某人有活力） 294
liven (sth) up（使某事物活躍起來） 294
liven up（使活躍） 294
look after sb（照顧某人） 121
look after sth（照顧某事） 121
look after（照顧） 121
look at（注視；看） 14
look back（回顧） 122
look down on sb（輕視某人） 185
look down on（瞧不起；輕視） 185
look down one's nose at（輕視） 185
look down upon（輕視） 185
look for（尋找） 13
look forward to（期待；盼望） 122
look into sth（調查某事） 98
look into（調查；研究） 98

look on . . . as（誤認為） 156
look on sb as sth（把某人視為某事） 190
look on sth as sth（把某事視為某事） 190
look on（觀看；把……視為；觀望） 190, 255
look out for sb（留意某人） 43
look out for sth（留意某事） 43
look out on（面對） 255
look out upon（面對） 255
look out（小心；注意） 43
look over sb / look sb over（快速檢視某人） 51
look over sth / look sth over（快速檢查某事） 51
look over（檢查；查看） 51
look sb up（拜訪某人） 29
look sth up（查詢某事） 29
look up to sb（欽佩某人；尊敬某人） 29, 185, 275
look up to（尊敬） 185
look up〔查詢（字典等）；仰視；轉好；拜訪；變好〕 29, 185, 275
lose contact with（與……失去聯繫） 181
lose one's cool（失去冷靜；情緒激動；沉不住氣） 299
lose one's head（失去控制；失去理智） 259, 260
lose one's mind（失去理智） 260
lose one's touch（變生疏） 268
lose one's way（迷路） 170
lose touch with（失去聯絡；與……失去聯繫） 75, 181
lose track of（失去……的聯繫） 97
lose weight（減重） 6, 130
lost cause（敗局已定；毫無希望） 145

M

make (sb/sth) up / make up sth（化妝） 278
make (someone) tick（賦予動機） 286
make a big difference（造成很大的差別） 23
make a difference to sth/sb（對某事或某人造成差別） 23
make a difference（造成差別；對……產生影響） 22
make a world of difference（造成很大的改善） 23
make all the difference（讓一切變得很不同） 23
make certain（確認） 85
make clear sth / make sth clear（使某事清楚明白） 116
make clear（使清楚明白） 116
make concessions to（容許；屈服） 230
make do with sth/sb（湊合著用某事物或人） 195
make do without sth/sb（在沒有某事物或人的情況下完成某事） 195
make do（將就） 195
make friends with sb（與某人交朋友） 47
make friends（交朋友） 47
make fun of sb（取笑某人） 125
make fun of sth（取笑某事物） 125
make fun of（嘲笑） 125
make game of（嘲笑） 125
make good someone's something（成功地完成某件難事） 109
make good time（很快地結束旅行；做事快速） 88
make good use of（利用） 132
make good（成功；實現承諾） 109
make head or tail of（理解） 116
make it clear that . . .（將某事解釋清楚） 116
make it（成功） 109
make no difference（沒有造成差別） 23
make nothing of（不理解） 91
make out（辨別出；理解；填寫；試圖證明；成功辦到） 91, 221
make sb nervous（令某人緊張） 196
make sb out（理解某人） 91
make sense of（理解） 91
make sense（有邏輯；合乎道理的） 204
make sport of（嘲笑） 125
make sth out / make out sth（填寫；寫出；理解某事） 91, 221
make sure of sth（確認某事） 85
make sure that（確定……） 85
make sure to do sth（確定要去做某事） 85
make sure whether（確定是否） 85
make sure（確定；確認） 85
make the best of sth（充分利用某事物） 137
make the best of（充分利用） 137
make the most of（充分利用） 137
make trouble（興風作浪） 307
make up one's mind / make one's mind up（使某人下定決心） 42
make up sth / make sth up（虛構某事物） 278
make up sth（組成某事物） 278
make up with (sb)（與某人重修舊好） 277
make up（捏造；組成；化妝；和解） 278

make waves（引起眾人議論；引起抱怨） 307
manage without（沒有……也可以） 157
meet (someone) halfway（與人妥協） 206
meet one's needs（符合某人的需求） 302
meet with（偶然遇到；遇到） 186, 203
mess about（鬼混） 252
mess around（鬼混） 252
mind the store（負責看守） 310
miss the boat（錯過機會） 299
miss the boat（錯過機會） 299
mistake for（誤認為） 156
mix sb up / mix up sb（把某人搞混） 90
mix sth up / mix up sth（弄亂某物；把某事搞亂） 90
mix up（使混亂；搞混） 90
more or less（差不多；大約） 268

N

(every) now and again（有時候） 86
name A after B（以B的名字為A命名） 179
name after（以……來命名） 179
name sb/sth for sb/sth（以某人或事來為某人或事命名） 179
needless to say（不必說） 260
never mind（別在意；不要緊） 14
no matter（無論；縱使） 133
no wonder（難怪） 170
not a ghost of a chance（沒有希望） 188
not at all（不客氣；一點也不） 31
not by any means（絕不） 317
not have a chance（沒有希望） 188
not make any difference（沒有造成任何差別） 23
not make the slightest difference（沒有造成任何差別） 23
not on your life（別妄想） 308
now and then（有時候；偶爾） 86

O

object to（反對） 137, 189
of no use（徒勞地） 162
on edge（緊張；提心吊膽） 261
on hand（在手邊；在附近；待執行） 271
on occasion（有時候） 86
on one's own（靠某人自己） 22
on one's toes（機警的） 141

337

on purpose（刻意；有目的地） 25
on schedule（準時） 58
on the edge of one's sear（因精彩而相當專心） 261
on the one hand（從一方面） 149
on the other hand（另一方面；相對地） 149
on the whole（一般而言；概括；就整體而言） 163, 237
on time（準時；依照時間） 58
once again（一再） 67
once and away（僅此一次） 124
once and for all（永遠地；一勞永逸地） 43, 124
once for all（僅此一次） 124
once in a blue moon（很少；不常） 113
once in a while（有時候） 86
originate from（來自） 89
out of commission（故障） 52
out of control（失去控制） 271
out-of-date（過時的） 103
out of fashion（過時；過時的） 103, 323
out of hand（失去控制） 271
out of order（故障） 52
out of question（無疑地） 67
out of sorts（身體不適） 47
out of the question（不可能發生） 67
out of touch（失去聯絡；對事情毫無概念） 131
over and over (again)（一再；再三） 67
over my dead body（除非我死了） 308

P

park yourself（坐下） 23
part with（放棄） 115
participate in（參與某活動） 30
pass away（去世） 161
pass out cold（昏倒） 161
pass out（分配；昏厥） 161, 229
pass sth out / pass out sth（分配某事物） 161
pass through（通過） 97
pay a visit to（拜訪） 29
pay attention (to)（注意；專心） 66
pay attention to sth（留意某事） 66
pay the bill（付帳） 293
pick (sth) up（被打斷之後再繼續） 7
pick holes in（挑毛病） 95

pick out（挑選；辨認出） 25
pick sth up（用便宜的價錢買到某物；自學或藉由練習而學會某種技術或語言） 6
pick up the bill（付帳） 293
pick up the tab (for sth)（付……的錢） 293
pick up the tab（付帳） 293
pick up（拾起；用汽車搭載某人或接某人；增加；起色；感染上某種病） 6
pin on（怪罪……） 292
pin sth on sb（將某事怪罪於某人） 292
play (something) by ear（隨機應變；見機行事） 326
play a joke on（嘲笑） 125
play a trick on（嘲笑） 125
play on（利用） 132
play upon（利用） 132
point out（指出；提醒） 60
point sb out / point out sb（指出某人） 60
point sth out / point out sth（指出某事；提醒某事） 60
poke fun at（嘲笑） 125
poke one's nose into（干涉） 270
prefer to（寧願） 59
proceed with（繼續） 48
pull an all-nighter（熬夜） 198
pull down（拆毀） 155
pull off sth（成功辦到某事） 191
pull off（拉掉；成功辦到） 191
pull on（穿上） 191
pull sth off（成功辦到某事） 191
pull together（同心協力） 181
put (sb) on（〔以開玩笑的方式〕欺騙他人〕 259
put an end to（終結） 254
put away（收拾；收起來；儲存；大吃特吃） 34
put down（放下；奚落；鎮壓） 197, 231
put off（脫掉；拖延；延期） 4, 39, 229
put on lipstick（抹口紅） 5
put on makeup（上妝） 5
put on perfume（搽香水） 5
put on weight（體重增加） 5
put on〔打開；穿上；穿戴（衣服或配件）；塗抹；愚弄；增加（如體重）；穿戴〕 4, 6, 165, 189
put one's finger on（指出） 60
put one's foot in it（搞砸；說錯話） 311
put one's foot in one's mouth（說錯話） 311
put out sb / put sb out（對某人帶來不便） 52

put out sth / put sth out（使某物停止燃燒；推出；生產） 53
put out（拿出去；關閉；熄滅；打擾；推出） 52, 147
put sb down（奚落某人） 197
put sb in charge of（讓某人負責……） 76
put sb off（推遲與某人的約會） 39
put sb up / put up sb（提供某人住宿） 165
put sth away（收拾某東西） 34
put sth down（放下某事物） 197
put sth off（拖延某事） 39
put sth together / put together sth（將某事物組合） 277
put together（組合） 277
put up sth / put up sth（建造某物；舉起某事物） 165
put up with sb（忍受某人） 161
put up with sth（忍受某事） 161
put up with（忍耐；忍受） 161, 189
put up（建造；提供住宿；舉起；建設） 155, 165
put 金錢 away（存錢） 34
put 食物 away（吃了很大量的某食物） 34

Q

quite a few〔許多；相當多（介於 a few 和 a lot 之間）〕 80

R

read over（全部讀過） 156
recover from（恢復） 39
refer to（查詢） 29
rely on（依賴） 50
rest on/upon（依賴） 50
result in（造成） 219
right along（自始至終） 17
right away（馬上；立刻；立即） 6, 77
right now（馬上） 6
right off（立即） 77
ring off〔掛斷電話（英式用法）〕 48, 180
ring up（打電話給某人） 3
rip up（撕碎；毀壞） 154
rock the boat（興風作浪） 307
roll out of bed（起床） 3
roll over（轉過來） 279
rough in（草擬） 205
rule in（使成為可能） 171
rule out（使成為不可能；排除可能性；不予考慮） 171
rule sb out / rule out sb（排除某人） 171

338

rule sb out of sth（取消某人參加某事的資格） 171
rule sth out / rule out sth（排除某事） 171
run (sth) into sb（撞上某人） 203
run (sth) into sth（撞上某事物） 203
run across（偶然遇到；遇到） 186, 203
run away from danger（脫離危險） 173
run away from home（逃家） 173
run away from sb（逃離某人） 173
run away from school（逃學） 173
run away from sth（逃離某事） 173
run away from sw（從某處逃走） 173
run away（離家出走；逃跑） 173
run into sb（遇到某人） 203
run into（偶然遇到；偶遇；撞上） 186, 203
run off（逃走） 173
run out of（用完；用盡某事物） 153
run out（用盡；過期） 153, 229

S

satisfy one's needs（符合某人的需求） 302
save one's breath（不白費唇舌） 261
sb be tired out（表示某人非常疲倦的狀態） 16
sb be worth it（某人值得……） 213
sb deserves sth（某人值得……） 213
screw sth up / screw up sth（搞砸某事） 267
screw up（搞砸；使混淆；傷害） 267
search after（尋找） 13
search for（尋找） 13
search me（我不知道） 291
see about sb（注意某人） 87
see about sth（留意某事物；考慮某事） 87
see about（留意；安排；關照；考慮） 87
see eye to eye on sth（對某事看法一致） 137
see eye to eye with sb（和某人看法一致） 137
see eye to eye（看法一致） 137
see into（調查） 98
see off〔（幫某人）送行〕 171
see out（送某人到門口；持續到結束） 172
see sb off / see off sb（送某人離開） 171

see to（照料） 87
seek after（尋找） 13
seek for（尋找） 13
sell out of sth（某事物銷售一空） 244
sell out（銷售一空；出清） 244
send in（遞交） 177
serve (someone) right（某人應得的懲罰） 213
serve (the/one's) purpose（符合需求） 302
serve a purpose（有用處） 25
set back（拖延） 39
set down（放下） 197, 231
set out for（出發前往） 204
set out to（開始做；有計畫地做） 204
set out（出發；離開；計畫做……） 204
set sth off / set off sth（爆炸；燃放） 139
set up（建造） 155
shake hands with sb（與某人握手） 43
shake hands（握手） 43
shake sb by the hand（與某人握手） 43
shake sb's hand（與某人握手） 43
shake up（使心煩意亂） 203
show off sb / show sb off（炫耀某人） 308
show off sth / show sth off（炫耀某事物） 308
show off（炫燿） 308
show someone the ropes（教某人訣竅） 307
show sb up（使某人難堪） 198
show up（到達；出現） 198
shut (sb) up（使（某人）安靜） 146
shut (sth) up（使（某物）關閉） 146
shut down（關閉） 146
shut off（關掉） 5, 114
shut sb/sth up（把某人或動物關起來） 146
shut up（關閉；閉嘴（不禮貌的用法）） 146
sit by（旁觀） 189
sit down（坐下） 23
sit still（坐著不動） 169
sit through（坐到……結束） 172
sit up（熬夜） 198
slow down（放慢速度；放輕鬆） 253
slow sb down（使某人速度變慢） 253
slow sth down（使事物速度變慢） 253
slow up（放慢速度） 253

small wonder（不足為奇） 170
so far as . . . be concerned（關於） 105
so far（到目前為止） 35, 169
some day or other（遲早有一天） 5
sooner or later（遲早；總有一天） 5
speed up（加速） 253
stage by stage（逐漸地；逐步地） 15
stamp out（撲滅） 53
stand a chance（有機會；有希望） 188
stand by（待命；旁觀） 189, 190
stand for sth（忍受某事物；支持某事物；代表某事物） 188
stand for（忍受；支持；代表） 188
stand in the way（阻撓） 163
stand off（拖延） 229
stand out in a crowd（出眾） 212
stand out（引人注目；優秀傑出） 212
stand sb up / stand up sb（讓某人白等） 263
stand still（站著不動） 169
stand to reason（合理的；自然） 105
stand up for sb（支持某人） 221
stand up for sth（捍衛或堅持某事；支持某事） 24, 221
stand up for（維護權利；支持） 221, 263
stand up to sth（經得住某物） 24
stand up to（對抗；勇於面對） 221, 263
stand up（站起來；經得住；站得住腳；爽約；經得起；讓人白等；證實） 24, 221, 263
starting (from) now（從現在起） 97
stay (at) home（待在家） 198
stay calm（保持冷靜） 259
stay in touch with（與……聯絡） 181
stay in（待在家） 198
stay on（留任） 269
stay out（待在外面） 198
stay up（熬夜） 198
step aside（讓位） 269
step by step（逐漸地；逐步地） 15
step down as sth（從某職位退休） 269
step down（下來；退休；辭職；減少） 269
step in（介入） 270
step into（輕鬆找到某工作） 270
step on (someone)（受到不平等的待遇） 270
step on it（趕快） 270
step on sb's toes（冒犯某人） 141
step sth down / step down sth（減少某事物） 269

step out on sb（對伴侶不忠） 270
step out of line（不守規矩） 325
stick around（耐心等待） 292
stick it to（對某人很嚴厲） 220
stick one's nose into（干涉） 270
stick out（伸出） 215
stick sb up / stick up sb（持槍行搶某人） 215
stick sth up / stick up sth（持槍行搶某事物） 215
stick to sth（遵守某事） 220
stick to〔堅持（通常指困境）；遵守〕 220
stick up for（維護） 221
stick up（伸直；突出；持槍行搶或被搶） 172, 215
stir up sb / stir sb up（鼓勵某人行動） 253
stir up sth / stir sth up（惹上麻煩；產生不開心的情緒） 253
stir up（激起；引起問題） 253
stop by sw（暫訪某處） 187
stop by（暫訪） 187
stop in（順便來訪） 187
stop off（順便來訪） 187
stop over（順便來訪） 187
straighten out（想出） 245
stretch out（伸出） 215
strike off（取消） 42
submit to（容許；屈服） 230
switch off（關掉） 4, 114
switch on（打開） 4

T

tag together（拼湊） 180
take (a) cold（感冒） 40
take a chance（冒險） 188
take A for B（把A誤認為B） 156
take a seat（坐下） 23
take a stroll（散步） 33
take a trip down memory lane（回憶往日的美好時光） 34
take a trip（遠行；旅行） 34
take a walk down memory lane（回憶往日的美好時光） 33
take a walk（散步；閒逛） 33
take account of（加以考慮） 114
take advantage of sb（欺騙某人；捉弄某人；利用某人） 132
take advantage of sth（善用某事；利用某事） 132
take advantage of（善用；乘人之危） 131
take after sb（和某人長得像） 133
take after〔長得很像（通常指親戚）〕 132

take apart（拆開） 180
take by surprise（感到意外；撞見） 178
take care of（照料；照顧） 87, 121
take charge of（負責） 76
take down（放下；取下；寫下） 197, 215
take fire（著火） 104
take for granted（將……視為理所當然；不重視；想當然） 113
take for（誤以為） 156
take hold of sb（抓住某人） 99
take hold of sth（抓住某事物） 99
take hold of（抓住） 99
take in〔學習；理解；欺騙；拜訪；（衣服）改小〕 255
take into account（加以考慮） 114
take into consideration（加以考慮） 114
take it for granted that . . .（想當然……） 113
take it in turns（輪流做） 65
take no account of（不予考慮） 114
take note of（注意） 66
take off sth / take sth off（脫掉某物） 189
take off〔脫掉（衣鞋、首飾）；（飛機）起飛；突然受到歡迎〕 4, 189, 191, 230
take on（承擔；聘僱） 230
take one at one's word（相信某人說的話） 300
take one's time over sth（不慌不忙地做某事） 21
take one's time（慢慢來；別急） 21
take one's turn（輪流做） 65
take one's word for it（相信某人說的話） 300
take out sth/sb（把某樣東西拿出來，或是找某人出去約會） 25
take out（拿出來；和某人約會） 25
take over（接管；帶至某處） 197
take pains to do sth（不辭辛勞地做某事） 186
take pains（不辭辛勞；費盡苦心） 186
take part in（參加；參與） 30, 196
take pity on（同情） 108
take place（舉行；發生） 29, 222
take revenge on（報復） 252
take sb apart（在運動比賽中輕鬆打敗某人） 180
take sb by surprise（令某人感到意外） 178
take sb for granted（不重視某人） 113
take sb in / take in sb（欺騙某人） 255
take sb into account（將某人列入考慮） 114

take sb on/take on sb（聘請某人） 230
take sb out of themselves（改變某人的心情，讓他們不要一直陷在憂鬱的情緒中） 25
take someone for a ride（欺騙某人） 255
take sth apart（拆開某事物） 180
take sth down / take down sth（取下某物；寫下某事） 231
take sth for granted（把某事視為理所當然） 113
take sth in / take in sth（改小某物；理解某事） 255
take sth into account（將某事列入考慮） 114
take sth off（……休假） 53
take sth on / take on sth（承擔某事） 230
take sth out on sb（拿某人出氣） 25
take sth over / take over sth（接管某事物） 197
take sth over from sb（從某人手中接管某事） 197
take sth up with sb（對某人提出某事） 131
take the bull by the horns（不畏艱難） 316
take the place of sb/sth（代替某人或某物） 29
take the time（力圖） 21
take (time) off（（一段時間）不工作；休假） 53
take time out（暫時停止某種活動） 21
take time（需要花比較久的時間，主詞通常用物） 21
take turns doing sth（輪流做某事） 65
take turns to do sth（輪流做某事） 65
take turns（輪流） 65
take up with sb（和某人交往） 131, 277
take up with（與某人商量某事） 131
take up〔開始（某興趣）；佔據（時間）〕 131
talk back to sb（與某人頂嘴） 324
talk back to（頂嘴；說話無禮） 324
talk over with sb（和某人商量某事） 21
talk over（商量；討論） 21
talk sb over（說服某人改變主意或看法） 21
talk sth over（詳細討論某事） 21
tamper with（干涉） 270
teach someone the ropes（教某人訣竅） 307
tear down（拆除；拆毀） 154, 155
tear off（脫掉；撕掉） 154
tear sth up / tear up sth（撕毀某物；毀約） 154

340

tear up（撕毀） 154
tell apart（區別） 162
tell sb apart / tell apart sb（辨別某人） 162
tell sth apart / tell apart sth（辨別某事物） 162
the moment (that)（一……就……） 76
the whole night（一整晚） 22
think about（考慮） 59
think of sth/sb（對某事或某人的看法；猜想某人或某事；想到某事） 59
think of（想到；對某人產生評價） 59
think out（想出） 303
think over（仔細考慮；深思熟慮） 32, 156
think sth out（考慮很周詳） 32
think sth over（仔細考慮某事） 32
think sth through（仔細考慮清楚某事直至得出結論） 32
think sth up / think up sth（想到某事） 303
think sth up（想出新的點子） 32
think twice（再三考慮） 87
think up（突發奇想；捏造） 303
throw (someone) a curve（提出意想不到的事情） 311
throw away（丟棄） 246
throw away（扔掉；浪費（才能或機會）） 70
throw in（插入） 70
throw off（扔掉；擺脫） 70
throw one's money around（亂花錢） 70
throw out〔丟棄；驅逐；駁回（意見、計畫等）；提出〕 246
throw over（拋棄；斷絕關係） 70
throw sb out（驅逐某人） 246
throw someone a curveball（提出意想不到的事情） 311
throw sth away（扔掉某事物） 70
throw sth out（駁回某事） 246
throw the book at (someone)（嚴厲懲罰） 310
throw up sth / throw sth up（吐出某物；提出） 247
throw up（嘔吐；產生新想法或問題；提起） 247
thus far（到目前為止） 35
till now（到目前為止） 35
time and again（一再） 67
tire out（使筋疲力竭；耗盡） 16, 69
tire sb out（使某人疲憊） 16
to and fro（來來回回） 80
touch and go（情況危急；不到最後無法定論） 236
trade in〔（非金錢的）折抵；以物換物；以舊換新〕 285

trade sth in / trade in sth（以某事物折抵） 285
tread on one's toes（冒犯某人） 141
trust in（相信） 206
try on（試穿） 33
try out for sth（參加選拔） 157
try out（試用） 157
try sth on（試穿；試戴） 33
try sth out / try out sth（試用某事物；試驗；試用） 33, 157
turn around（轉向；使……轉向；使情勢徹底改觀） 70
turn down sb / turn sb down（拒絕某人） 145
turn down sth / turn sth down（拒絕某事） 145
turn down〔拒絕；降低（電視、收音機的）音量、亮度〕 145
turn off（關掉） 4, 114
turn on sb / turn upon sb（突然攻擊某人；抨擊某人） 5, 303
turn on sth（由某事物決定） 303
turn on〔打開（電器或設備）；突然攻擊某人；由……決定；持敵對的態度；使高興〕 4, 114, 302
turn out to be . . .（結果是……） 114
turn out〔結果是；出席；生產（產品）；關掉〕 114
turn over（翻過來；移交） 279
turn sb on (to sth) / turn sb on (to sb)（使某人對某事或某人感興趣） 4
turn sb on（引起某人的興趣） 303
turn sb over to sb（將某人移交給某人） 279
turn sth around（改善某事物的情況） 71
turn sth on / turn on sth（打開電器或設備） 4
turn sth over to sb（將某事物移交給某人） 279
turn up（增加音量；出現） 145, 199

U

under control（掌控中） 271
under the weather（身體不舒服；生病） 47
up-to-date（擁有最新資訊；現代的；流行的） 103
up to now（到目前為止） 35
upside down（上下顛倒） 129
use up（用盡） 153
used to do something（過去經常做某事；過去習慣做某事） 78
used to（過去經常；過去習慣） 78

V

very much（非常） 169

W

wait at table(s)（上菜，英式） 30
wait on table(s)（上菜，美式） 30
wait on〔（服務生或店員的）服務；接待〕 30
wait up for（為了等某人而不睡覺；停下來等某人） 239
wake sb up（叫醒某人；使某人覺醒） 75
wake up to sth（開始警覺到某事） 75
wake up（醒來；使覺） 75
waste one's breath（白費唇舌） 261
watch out（小心） 43
watch over（照顧） 121
wear away（逐漸消失） 238
wear down（使疲累） 236
wear lipstick（抹口紅） 6
wear makeup（上妝） 6
wear off（逐漸消失） 238
wear out（使筋疲力竭；穿舊；使壞；耗盡） 16, 69
wear perfume（擦香水） 6
wear sb down（使某人疲累） 236
wear sb out（耗盡某人的精力） 69
wear sth out / wear out sth（用壞某事物） 69
with reference to（關於） 105
with regard to（關於） 105
with relation to（關於） 105
with respect to（關於） 105
without effect（徒勞地） 162
work out〔總共；健身；擬定（計畫）；解決；想出；得到……的結果〕 57, 245
work sb out（理解某人） 245
work sth out / work out sth（釐清某事） 245
would rather . . . than . . .（寧可……也不……） 59
would rather（寧願） 59
write down（寫下） 231

Y

yield to（容許；屈服） 230

Answer Key

Unit 1 — p. 10-11

A

1	A	2	D	3	C	4	B	5	B	6	B
7	A	8	C	9	D	10	C				

B

1	got on	2	take off	3	turned on
4	got up	5	turned off	6	got off
7	At first	8	call up	9	picked up
10	sooner or later				

C

1	pick up	2	got off	3	Sooner or later
4	At first	5	turned on		

Unit 2 — p. 18-19

A

1	A	2	B	3	D	4	C	5	A	6	D
7	A	8	A	9	D	10	C				

B

1	As usual	2	find out	3	all along
4	little by little	5	dress up	6	looked at
7	look for	8	all right	9	tired out

C

1	all along	2	calling on	3	dress up
4	Never mind	5	find out	6	looking for

Unit 3 — p. 26-27

A

1	C	2	D	3	A	4	B	5	D	6	A
7	B	8	D	9	C	10	C	11	B	12	D

B

1	picked out	2	took her time	3	talk . . . over
4	lay down	5	on purpose	6	made a difference
7	took out	8	all day long	9	got along with
10	by herself				

C

1	makes a . . . difference	2	pick out	3	stood up
4	get along with	5	by yourself	6	lying down

Unit 4 — p. 36-37

A

1	A	2	B	3	C	4	D	5	A	6	B
7	A	8	B	9	B	10	D				

B

1	took a trip	2	looked up	3	take a walk
4	tried on	5	at all	6	think . . . over
7	waiting on	8	take place	9	put away
10	so far	11	at least		

C

1	take place	2	put away	3	looking up
4	tried out				

Answer Key

Unit 5 (p. 44-45)

A

1	D	2	C	3	C	4	A	5	B	6	C
7	B	8	A	9	D	10	B	11	A		

B

1	made up his mind	2	caught a cold	3	putting off
4	call off	5	for good	6	shook hands
7	gotten back	8	for the time being	9	changes her mind

C

1	look out	2	for good	3	called off
4	get over	5	put off		

Unit 6 (p. 54-55)

A

1	B	2	B	3	C	4	A	5	B	6	A
7	C	8	B	9	C	10	A	11	C		

B

1	under the weather	2	making friends	3	count on
4	few and far between	5	all of a sudden	6	had . . . off
7	looked . . . over	8	hanging up	9	out of order

C

1	put . . . out	2	hang up	3	went on
4	getting to	5	All of a sudden		

Unit 7 (p. 62-63)

A

1	A	2	C	3	D	4	A	5	A	6	A
7	B	8	C	9	B	10	A	11	D	12	B

B

1	on time	2	pointed . . . out	3	got better
4	had better	5	was up	6	figured out
7	thought of	8	was over	9	would rather
10	in time				

C

1	think of	2	call it a day	3	figure out
4	on time				

Unit 8 (p. 72-73)

A

1	B	2	A	3	B	4	B	5	A	6	B
7	B	8	D	9	B	10	B	11	B	12	C

B

1	over and over again	2	worn out	3	go out
4	was about to	5	brush up on	6	turned around
7	out of the question	8	falling in love	9	pay attention to

C

1	fell in love	2	wore . . . out	3	is about to
4	throw . . . away				

Unit 9 (p. 82-83)

A

1	A	2	B	3	A	4	C	5	B	6	A
7	D	8	A	9	C	10	C	11	A		

B

1	woke up	2	as soon as	3	was in charge of
4	get in touch with	5	used to	6	back and forth
7	have a good time	8	Quite a few	9	was used to

C

1	getting used to	2	is used to	3	be in charge of
4	in no time	5	back and forth		

343

Unit 10 (p. 92-93)

A
1	B	2	C	3	B	4	A	5	C	6	C
7	C	8	D	9	A	10	D	11	C		

B
1	Now and then	2	make sure	3	by heart
4	mixed up	5	make out	6	get rid of
7	went with	8	coming from	9	see about

C
1	come from	2	mix up	3	go with
4	see about	5	make out		

Unit 11 (p. 100-101)

A
1	B	2	B	3	A	4	C	5	D	6	B
7	B	8	B	9	A	10	C	11	A		

B
1	ill at ease	2	find fault with	3	be up to
4	do over	5	look into	6	be carried away
7	keep away	8	took hold of	9	from now on

C
1	ill at ease	2	do . . . over	3	been up to
4	finding fault with	5	get through		

Unit 12 (p. 110-111)

A
1	C	2	A	3	B	4	D	5	B	6	C
7	A	8	D	9	B	10	A	11	C	12	D

B
1	out-of-date	2	caught fire	3	blew up
4	burning up	5	As for	6	made good
7	stands to reason	8	burn down	9	feel sorry for
10	up-to-date				

C
1	caught fire	2	blow up	3	stands to reason
4	make good				

Unit 13 (p. 118-119)

A
1	B	2	B	3	D	4	B	5	B	6	A
7	D	8	A	9	B	10	A	11	B		

B
1	calls for	2	make clear	3	taken into account
4	come to	5	turns out	6	broke down
7	give up	8	once in a blue moon		

C
1	takes into account	2	broke down	3	turn out
4	had on	5	calls for	6	give . . . up

Unit 14 (p. 126-127)

A
1	B	2	B	3	B	4	C	5	D	6	B
7	C	8	D	9	B	10	A				

B
1	came true	2	heard from	3	heard of
4	eat out	5	looking forward to	6	have my way
7	look after	8	as a matter of fact	9	once and for all

C
1	look after	2	come true	3	cut-and-dried
4	making fun of	5	heard of	6	looking forward to

Unit 15 (p. 134-135)

A
1	A	2	B	3	A	4	C	5	A	6	C
7	B	8	A	9	C	10	D				

B
1	take advantage of	2	taking up	3	in touch
4	in the long run	5	filling out	6	no matter
7	take . . . up with	8	inside out	9	takes after

C
1	take up	2	took advantage of	3	filling in
4	in touch	5	in the long run	6	out of touch

Unit 16 (p. 142-143)

A
1	C	2	A	3	D	4	A	5	C	6	B
7	B	8	A	9	C	10	A				

B
1	on my toes	2	see eye to eye	3	get along
4	grows out of	5	cuts off	6	For once
7	keep in mind	8	went off	9	made the best of

C
1	For once	2	on my toes	3	gone off（英式用法）
4	cut off	5	get along with	6	see eye to eye

Unit 17 (p. 150-151)

A
1	C	2	A	3	C	4	A	5	B	6	B
7	C	8	A	9	B	10	D	11	A		

B
1	broken in	2	shut . . . up	3	Above all
4	become of	5	a lost cause	6	turned down
7	has got to	8	keeps up with		

C
1	turned down	2	blow out	3	have . . . got to
4	broke in	5	has . . . got	6	broken . . . in

Unit 18 (p. 158-159)

A
1	C	2	B	3	A	4	B	5	B	6	A
7	B	8	B	9	C	10	D				

B
1	was bound to	2	According to	3	gone over
4	was about to	5	tearing . . . up	6	for sure
7	ran out of	8	do without		

C
1	tear down	2	at heart	3	do without
4	are bound to	5	was about to	6	ran out of
7	for sure				

Unit 19 (p. 166-167)

A
1	A	2	C	3	D	4	B	5	B	6	A
7	D	8	C	9	B	10	B				

B
1	put on	2	pass out	3	go around
4	telling . . . apart	5	catch up	6	All in all
7	put up with	8	day in and day out	9	in vain

C
1	All in all	2	catch up with	3	put up
4	go around	5	passed out	6	put up with

345

Unit 20 (p. 174-175)

A
1	B	2	D	3	B	4	A	5	C	6	C
7	B	8	A	9	C	10	D	11	B		

B
1	was the matter	2	got lost	3	rule out
4	brought ... up	5	running away	6	by far
7	saw ... off	8	No wonder		

C
1	hold still	2	by far	3	brought up
4	get lost	5	held up	6	know ... by sight

Unit 21 (p. 182-183)

A
1	D	2	B	3	A	4	B	5	B	6	D
7	C	8	B	9	D	10	C	11	D	12	C

B
1	Hold on	2	went up to	3	taken by surprise
4	named after	5	kept in touch with	6	was well-off
7	in case				

C
1	hold on	2	are well-off	3	in case
4	handed in	5	took ... apart	6	be better off

Unit 22 (p. 192-193)

A
1	C	2	A	3	A	4	B	5	B	6	B
7	C	8	B	9	D	10	A	11	D	12	B

B
1	came across	2	stop by	3	taken ... pains
4	stood a chance	5	looked down on	6	look on
7	dropped ... a line	8	pulled ... off	9	look up to

C
1	stop by	2	stands a good chance		
3	look down on	4	takes off		

Unit 23 (p. 200-201)

A
1	B	2	A	3	C	4	D	5	B	6	D
7	A	8	C	9	A	10	B				

B
1	showed up	2	make do	3	stayed up
4	giving birth to	5	go in for	6	close call
7	went for	8	cleaned out		

C
1	gets on my nerves	2	close calls	3	showed up
4	gone in for	5	made do	6	went for
7	took over				

Unit 24 (p. 208-209)

A
1	A	2	C	3	D	4	B	5	C	6	A
7	A	8	D	9	B	10	A	11	B		

B
1	set out to	2	draw up	3	believed in
4	carried out	5	cheer up	6	run into
7	knocked ... out	8	make sense	9	dropped out of

C
1	drawn up	2	make sense	3	cheered up
4	knocked ... out	5	ran into		

Unit 25 (p. 216-217)

A
| 1 | D | 2 | B | 3 | B | 4 | C | 5 | D | 6 | A |
| 7 | D | 8 | B | 9 | A | 10 | C | | | | |

B
1	stands out	2	keep up with	3	get away
4	get away with	5	burst out	6	served . . . right
7	let on	8	keeps up	9	go wrong

C
| 1 | went wrong | 2 | checks up on | 3 | Keep . . . up |
| 4 | burst out | 5 | stuck up | 6 | let on |

Unit 26 (p. 224-225)

A
| 1 | A | 2 | A | 3 | B | 4 | B | 5 | B | 6 | C |
| 7 | D | 8 | A | 9 | D | 10 | C | 11 | A | | |

B
1	making out	2	built up	3	come about
4	live up to	5	stick to	6	dies down
7	fades away	8	cut corners	9	stick it to

C
| 1 | stick to | 2 | died out | 3 | live up to |
| 4 | bring about | 5 | cut corners | | |

Unit 27 (p. 232-233)

A
| 1 | C | 2 | B | 3 | B | 4 | A | 5 | C | 6 | C |
| 7 | D | 8 | D | 9 | A | 10 | A | 11 | B | 12 | A |

B
1	gives off	2	hold off	3	giving in
4	take on	5	fall through	6	has it in for
7	fell behind	8	give . . . out		

C
| 1 | took . . . on | 2 | fell through | 3 | give in |
| 4 | hold out | 5 | holds off | | |

Unit 28 (p. 240-241)

A
| 1 | A | 2 | B | 3 | C | 4 | B | 5 | A | 6 | B |
| 7 | A | 8 | C | 9 | D | 10 | A | 11 | B | | |

B
1	leave . . . alone	2	bring back	3	wears off
4	let up	5	break off	6	wears . . . down
7	touch and go	8	on the whole	9	lay off

C
| 1 | bring . . . out | 2 | wears off | 3 | wait up for |
| 4 | lay off | 5 | touch and go | | |

Unit 29 (p. 248-249)

A
| 1 | D | 2 | B | 3 | A | 4 | B | 5 | C | 6 | B |
| 7 | A | 8 | A | 9 | C | 10 | A | 11 | A | | |

B
1	had my heart set on	2	sell out	3	buy up
4	catching on	5	back out	6	worked out
7	cleared up	8	back up	9	was cut out for

C
| 1 | cut out for | 2 | has his heart set on | 3 | sold out |
| 4 | catch on | 5 | thrown out | | |

Answer Key

347

Unit 30
p. 256-257

A
1	C	2	A	3	B	4	B	5	C	6	A
7	C	8	D	9	C	10	A	11	A	12	B

B
1	beat around the bush	2	coming to an end	3	stir up
4	are up to something	5	get even with	6	taking in
7	put an end to	8	slow down	9	fooling around

C
1	come to an end	2	dry out	3	take . . . in
4	put an end to				

Unit 31
p. 264-265

A
1	D	2	C	3	C	4	B	5	C	6	B
7	A	8	B	9	A	10	C	11	A		

B
1	putting . . . on	2	It goes without saying		
3	waste your breath	4	going through	5	lost her head
6	cut . . . short	7	kept my head	8	on edge
9	get the better of				

C
1	going through	2	get the better of
3	It goes without saying	4	on edge
5	putting . . . on		

Unit 32
p. 272-273

A
1	A	2	B	3	B	4	C	5	B	6	D
7	A	8	C	9	D	10	B				

B
1	lost her touch	2	went off the deep end		
3	stepped down	4	stepped in	5	kiss up to
6	stepped on	7	a steal	8	more or less

C
1	screwed up	2	more or less	3	lost his touch
4	stepped in	5	go off the deep end		
6	in hand	7	on hand		

Unit 33
p. 280-281

A
1	C	2	C	3	A	4	B	5	A	6	A
7	A	8	C	9	A	10	B	11	A		

B
1	cover up	2	making up	3	on the ball
4	last straw	5	kick the habit	6	looking up
7	drop . . . off	8	make up with		

C
1	last straw	2	dropped . . . off	3	kicked the habit
4	looking up				

Unit 34
p. 288-289

A
1	C	2	A	3	B	4	A	5	D	6	D
7	B	8	A	9	A	10	C	11	B		

B
1	fallen for	2	be with	3	cover for
4	got cold feet	5	face-to-face	6	it figures
7	filled . . . in	8	gave . . . a break	9	was with it

C
1	traded in	2	makes . . . tick	3	fill in
4	cover . . . for	5	Give . . . a break		

Unit 35 (p. 296-297)

A
| 1 | C | 2 | A | 3 | C | 4 | C | 5 | B | 6 | A |
| 7 | B | 8 | A | 9 | C | 10 | D | 11 | B | | |

B
1	get something off her chest	2	live it up
3	picking up the tab	4	liven up	5	stuck around
6	went to town	7	have a voice in	8	letting . . . slide
9	gotten a rise out of				

C
| 1 | pin . . . on | 2 | stick around | 3 | get a rise out of |
| 4 | went to town | 5 | lived it up | | |

Unit 36 (p. 304-305)

A
| 1 | C | 2 | C | 3 | A | 4 | D | 5 | A | 6 | B |
| 7 | C | 8 | B | 9 | A | 10 | C | 11 | C | 12 | B |

B
1	checking in	2	take him at his word
3	turns on	4	serve the purpose	5	think up
6	lined up	7	in the worst way	8	lost his cool
9	missed the boat	10	checked out		

C
| 1 | turned on | 2 | missed the boat | 3 | check out |

Unit 37 (p. 312-313)

A
| 1 | A | 2 | C | 3 | A | 4 | D | 5 | B | 6 | A |
| 7 | C | 8 | D | 9 | C | 10 | C | 11 | A | 12 | B |

B
1	threw the book at	2	put my foot in it	3	show off
4	make waves	5	Not on your life	6	throw him a curve
7	is up for grabs	8	keeping my fingers crossed		
9	learning the ropes				

C
| 1 | show off | 2 | keeping our fingers crossed |
| 3 | threw me a curve | 4 | threw the book at |

Unit 38 (p. 320-321)

A
| 1 | A | 2 | C | 3 | B | 4 | A | 5 | B | 6 | D |
| 7 | D | 8 | A | 9 | A | 10 | C | 11 | A | | |

B
1	kept his word	2	was a far cry from
3	was over my head	4	take the bull by the horns
5	got through to	6	gave him a hand	7	get out from under
8	land on my feet	9	ask for		

C
| 1 | a far cry from | 2 | by all means | 3 | get through to |
| 4 | dish . . . out | 5 | give . . . a hand | | |

Unit 39 (p. 328-329)

A
| 1 | B | 2 | C | 3 | A | 4 | C | 5 | C | 6 | D |
| 7 | A | 8 | B | 9 | A | 10 | A | 11 | B | 12 | D |

B
1	goofing off	2	be in	3	dry run
4	be out	5	in her shoes	6	talk back to
7	drew the line	8	play it by ear	9	keep after
10	been had				

C
| 1 | were in . . . shoes | 2 | play . . . by ear | 3 | fix . . . up |

349

Step by Step! 圖解
狄克生片語
一本學會470個關鍵日常英文片語

作者	Matt Coler	發行人	黃朝萍
審訂	Judy M. Majewsky	出版者	寂天文化事業股份有限公司
翻譯	李盈瑩	電話	02-2365-9739
編輯	王采翎／丁宥暄	傳真	02-2365-9835
主編	丁宥暄	網址	www.icosmos.com.tw
內文排版	劉秋筑／林書玉	讀者服務	onlineservice@icosmos.com.tw
封面設計	林書玉	出版日期	2025 年 6 月 初版三刷
圖片	Shutterstock		（寂天雲Mebook單字學習APP版）
製程管理	洪巧玲		

Copyright © 2025 by Cosmos Culture Ltd.
版權所有 請勿翻印
郵撥帳號 1998620-0 寂天文化事業股份有限公司

● 訂書金額未滿1000元，請外加運費100元。
【若有破損，請寄回更換，謝謝。】

國家圖書館出版品預行編目(CIP)資料

Step by step圖解狄克生片語：一本學會470個關鍵日常英文片語(寂天雲Mebook單字學習APP版)/ Matt Coler著. -- 初版. -- 臺北市：寂天文化事業股份有限公司, 2025.06印刷
　　面；　公分
ISBN 978-626-300-313-2(20K平裝)

1.CST: 英語 2.CST: 慣用語
805.123　　　　　　　　　114006488

DIXON'S
IDIOMS